D0465471

$3 OFF

any ONE title by best-selling author

Randy Alcorn

Valid through Sept. 30, 2007.

Coupon must be presented at time of purchase.

Limit one coupon per customer.

Limited to stock on hand.

Coupon not valid in combination with any other offer.

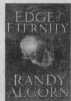

Retailer return these coupons for credit to your account no later than Dec. 30, 2007.

Mail to:
Foundation Distributing, Inc.
P.O. Box 98
Orono, Ontario
L0B 1M0
Canada

Phone: 905-983-1188

DEADLINE

A NOVEL

RANDY ALCORN

Multnomah Books

This book is a work of fiction. With the exception of recognized historical figures, the characters in this novel are fictional. Any resemblance to actual persons, living or dead, is purely coincidental.

DEADLINE
© 1994 by Eternal Perspective Ministries

published by Multnomah Books

A division of Random House, Inc.

Cover design by The DesignWorksGroup, Inc.

International Standard Book Number: 978-1-60142-065-7

Printed in the United States of America.

ALL RIGHTS RESERVED
No part of this publication may be reproduced, stored in a retrieval system, or transmitted in any form or by any means—electronic, mechanical, photocopying, recording, or otherwise—without prior written permission.

For information:
MULTNOMAH BOOKS
12265 Oracle Boulevard, Suite 200
Colorado Springs, Colorado 80921

Library of Congress Cataloging-in-Publication Data
Alcorn, Randy C.
    Deadline/by Randy Alcorn.
         p. cm.
    ISBN 0-88070-826-3
    ISBN 1-59052-592-2
    1. Journalists—Oregon—Fiction.   I. Title
PS3551.L292D43   1994   94-20108
813'.54—dc20   CIP

07 08 09 10 — 30 29 28 27 26

TO STEVE KEELS
loyal and treasured friend,
with whom I've enjoyed great fun and rich
brotherhood in the faith.
Even if you never write a book, old buddy,
at least now you can say one was
dedicated to you.

ACKNOWLEDGMENTS

Special thanks for their valuable time and assistance to all of these people, who were a personal and professional help to me in this novel:

Columnist Steve Duin, reporter Sura Rubenstein, and editor David Reinhard of the *Oregonian;* Charlie and Lori Nye and Russell Pulliam of the *Indianapolis News;* Don Feder, syndicated columnist at the *Boston Herald.* Thanks also to Marvin Olasky, journalism professor at the University of Texas at Austin, for his helpful writings.

Detectives Tom Nelson and Neil Crannell of the Portland Police Bureau, and Officer Jim Carl of the Gresham Police Department, for their generous assistance and helpful insights. Randy Martin, M.D., and Rainy Takalo, R.N., for their time and medical expertise. Dr. Gordon Canzler and his wife Christy, for passing on their medical journals, with relevant articles highlighted. Master mechanic Dyrk Van Zanten, firearms and forestry consultant Jay Rau, and old friend and Green Beret Captain Stu Weber, for their invaluable input and suggestions.

Rod Morris of Multnomah Books, my editor and friend, for his encouragement and wise and discerning eye. Al Janssen for his early input on the manuscript. Frank Peretti for his thoughtful and valued advice in the later stages. Ron Norquist for reading and dialoguing with me on the manuscript and for working side by side with me in ministry. Diane Meyer, special sister, who enthusiastically waited for the book, and whose life is a great encouragement to me.

Thanks to A. W. Tozer, C. S. Lewis, Francis Schaeffer, Charles Colson, and Peter Kreeft, among others, for the constant stimulation of their timeless and challenging writings.

My heartfelt thanks in this and all things go to my wonderful wife Nanci and delightful daughters Karina and Angela, God's greatest gifts to me besides himself. And highest praise to him, my best of all friends, the Audience of One, Lord of the long tomorrow. For all you are and have graciously prepared for us, I can hardly wait!

DEADLINE

CHAPTER ONE

T he canary yellow three-by-five card fell to the floor, face down. Retrieving the card and turning it face up, he stared at it curiously. It was a single sentence, consisting of only four words in all-caps pica type. A waitress wiped the table next to him and happened to glance over just as a look of startled unbelief overtook him. She watched his eyes widen and hands shake, and wondered what could possibly be on that card to trigger such a reaction.

Chilled to the bone, he was forced to begin a radical reinterpretation of the flurried trauma of his past eight days. He slowly mouthed the four words, as if doing so would make them less menacing and bizarre.

Three pairs of eyes focused together on the twenty-seven-inch screen. Kansas City's placekicker planted his left foot and swung his right into the football. His teammates' focused energy seemed to lift it that extra six inches above the bar. The fifty-four-yard field goal was good, the first half over.

"All right!" Doc and Finney reached across Jake, slapping their hands over him in symbolic victory.

"No way. Gimme a break." Jake's buddies' celebration added insult to injury. His Seahawks headed for the locker room ten points down.

The three childhood friends—now doctor, businessman, and journalist—slouched back on the recliner-couch. Doc occupied the recliner on one end, Finney the other. As usual, Jake Woods sat between them, feet propped up on a stool and pillow. All three wore blue jeans, Finney a navy blue Microsoft Windows sweatshirt, Doc a snazzy maroon polo shirt, and Jake a torn and faded gray sweatshirt with an indecipherable message.

It began for the three men like almost every Sunday afternoon the last twenty years. None of them had a clue this one would end so differently.

"Okay guys," Finney announced, "it's pizza time—let's flip." The routine was automatic, a no-brainer. They'd done it since childhood times, to decide who got to bat first or who had to buy popcorn at the matinee. In the adult version, at half time they staged two coin flips and a tie-breaker, if necessary. Loser drove, loser bought the pizza. No home deliveries. While the winners gloated and kicked back, the loser raced to and from Gino's in an attempt to miss as little of the third quarter as possible.

Shoulders squared and back straight, Doc looked like a career military officer, though he hadn't been in uniform for twenty-five years. "Tell you what, Finn," he jabbed. "Let's just send Woody now and flip later."

Jake Woods, having lost the flip three weeks in a row, flashed a "shut up and flip the coin" glare. His sturdy jaw jutted out in mock insult, as if to say an award-winning syndicated columnist shouldn't have to endure this kind of abuse. Despite his tough no-holds-barred reputation in this city, it was difficult to imagine fit but frumpy Jake being able to intimidate the dapper and ever-confident Doc. Standing there in his misshapen fur-lined sheepskin slippers, with disheveled hair, stray eyebrows veering out, and a two-day beard, Jake was in weekend gear.

"Hang on," Jake said, pulling a quarter from his pocket. "This time I'll flip. I think you guys have been rigging this. Let's see how you do against an honest two bits. Okay, this is between you two—I'll take on the loser. Call it, Finn."

Finney's face screwed up in feigned tension as if he'd been called on to kick a fifty-four yarder. "I can't take the pressure."

"Shut up and call it," Doc said. "I'm hungry. You can pray about it later."

As the coin reached the top of its flight, Finney called "Tails." It landed on the coffee table, which from a distance appeared smooth and shiny, but up close showed countless tiny dents from years of half time coin tosses. The quarter hit on its edge and rolled around like a rim shot, seemingly taking forever to settle.

"Son of a..." Doc said under his breath, staring at the coffee table. The quarter had stopped rolling around the middle of the coffee table. But it hadn't fallen flat. Balancing precariously, it stayed right on its edge. No heads, no tails.

"What are the chances of that happening?"

"Girls, look at this."

The "girls," each in their upper forties, were fast friends. It came with the package. Married to the three musketeers—or the three stooges, as they sometimes called them—the girls were destined to spend a lot of time together. They might as well like it, and they did. Janet wasn't around as often now, since her divorce from Jake three years ago. But the relationship was amiable—it was a good modern divorce—and Sue and Betsy often persuaded Janet to keep them company during the Sunday afternoon ritual.

Sue, Finney's wife, marched into the living room first, followed by Janet and Betsy. "Oh, did we miss the coin toss? Too bad—it's always so exciting." Noting the look on Jake's face she added, "Lose again, Jake? Hope the *Tribune* pays you well. We appreciate you keeping us fed."

"I didn't lose. No one lost. Look."

Sue followed Jake's gaze to the coin on the coffee table. "You're kidding. Don't anyone breathe or it'll fall."

"So what are you going to do, boys? Toss again?"

"Nah," Doc replied. "Let's leave it right there. No one wins, no one loses." He looked at Jake and Finney. "Let's just all go together."

"Together." A familiar thought. Forty years ago the three had played army, hunted lions, dug up treasures and discovered aliens together in the fields and hillsides and forests of Benton County. Together they'd exasperated their mothers, annoyed their brothers, harassed their sisters, confounded their teachers and principals, though not nearly as much as they remembered. Together they'd spiffed up and swaggered into Kathy Bates's eighth-grade party, and trembled wide-eyed later that night when the police showed up. In high school they each earned letters in three sports, fought side by side in the state championship football game, and took their dates to the prom together. They'd gone off to college, joined ROTC, and graduated together. They'd entered the Army, traveled off to three different parts of the world, then shipped out to Vietnam as greenhorn lieutenants within three months of each other. In the almost quarter century since the war, they'd been best man in each other's weddings, and seen their children grow up together. And together they'd gone off on more hunting and camping trips than they could count, the kind where it was miserably cold and you hunched in close to the fire and the smoke stung your eyes and permeated your coats and flannel shirts, and you never got off a good shot at anything but an empty chili can, and you told stories you'd told a hundred times and laughed harder than you ever remembered laughing before. This was just Sunday pizza, but "together" sounded good.

"I'll drive," Doc said. Finney saluted good naturedly. Jake kicked off his slippers, which he brought to Finney's every Sunday, and slipped into his Nikes, not bothering to lace them. The guys all grabbed their coats.

"We've got twenty minutes till the third quarter." Doc was half way out the door when he turned. "You made the call, Betsy?"

"Have I ever fumbled the ball, Doc? Of course I made the call. One giant Hula Lula and a deep dish heart-attack-on-a-crust." This was the girls' nickname for the Meat Eater's special, full of the cholesterol their used-to-be-jock husbands' arteries didn't need but especially craved during football season.

"And, guys, don't slam the—" The loud crash toppled a photograph from the mantle. "Door," Sue added weakly, as Janet and Betsy giggled. Nobody noticed the coin fall on its side.

"Bulls in a china shop," Sue said, with more fondness than exasperation.

"Yeah, and there's no china left," Betsy added. "Not in my house. But the bull's still charging!" All three flashed a what-can-you-do expression, laughing together.

As the three bulls made the brisk walk to the car, Jake glanced up at the swirling gray of the Oregon sky. It looked as if it had been rubbed hard with a dirty eraser. No rain yet, but the sky felt heavy, and to someone born and raised here, even the air's smell and taste signaled the threat of long heavy rain. *A storm's coming*, Jake felt certain.

"With you in a sec, Jake." Doc and Finney were taking care of something by Finney's car, while Jake waited by Doc's. He didn't mind. He breathed in that air, that rich fresh Oregon air. There was no place like this one. Jake, along with Doc and Finney, had grown up in a small town in this same Willamette Valley, less than a hundred miles south of where they lived now. Anyone raised in the Pacific Northwest always wants to come home, and after college and the army Jake's internal homing device reeled him back, along with his friends. He loved the rugged mountains forty minutes to the east, and the jagged Oregon coastline ninety minutes to the west. He loved the endless towering Douglas firs, so thick you could pull over to the side of the road, walk half a mile and be a world apart from everyone else on earth, inhaling the aroma those car air fresheners tried in vain to imitate. He loved something green growing everywhere you turned, and the four distinct seasons, each with its singular beauty, precisely ticking off the cycle of each year. Most of all he loved sharing this huge state with far fewer people than inhabited single cities in the east, midwest, south, or down the coast in California. In Oregon you could drive some roads and see more deer than cars.

Oregon was paradise for the hunter, fisherman, boater, hiker, backpacker, outdoorsman and wilderness lover. There was some of most of those in Jake. But he loved something else about this place, at least this northern Willamette Valley that had always been home. He loved the independent spirit, the rugged individualism, the free thinking initiative of people who weren't slaves to tradition or convention. People who didn't like being told what was right and wrong, who decided for themselves what they should and shouldn't do. A progressive state, Oregon had become home to nuclear protesters, animal rights protesters, environmentalist protesters, homosexual protesters, "legalize marijuana" protesters, "right to die" protesters, and representatives of any and every challenge to the status quo. Why, Jake wasn't sure. Maybe they'd inherited genes of individualism and autonomy from their forebears who braved the Oregon trail, who kept leaving behind the established order of American civilization, going west until the land ran into the Pacific Ocean, stopping only then, so far from the political power brokers of the east or the midwest conservatives or the southern Bible Belters that they could live their own lives as they saw fit. Church attendance was lower here than anywhere in the nation. People had better things to do on weekends than sit in stuffy old buildings, bored and feeling guilty. Oregon was free spirited, a great place to live, Jake's kind of place. He'd been all across his country and a dozen others, but wouldn't trade this place for any other.

Of all times, Sunday afternoons with his friends left Jake feeling free and content. But today an uneasiness gnawed at him. The coin and the clouds and the time of his life conspired to fill him with uncertainty and dread.

"Okay, let's go. Time's wastin'!" Doc took charge again, and they piled into his cherry-red Suburban, a fully loaded four-wheel-drive with a 454 engine. Doc hopped in the driver's seat, Jake scooted to the middle, Finney squeezed against Jake to close the passenger side door. It was a snug fit in the bench seat, but no one thought of hopping in back. It was only a ten minute drive, seven minutes for Doc, half of it on open highway.

Jake always marveled at Doc's cars, thinking they'd be more at home sitting in a shopping mall. This one was a year and a half old, but meticulously clean, with gleaming windows. The smell of the rich gray upholstery was so strong Jake could taste it. *How can Doc keep this thing smelling like he bought it yesterday?*

"A man's vehicle," Doc started in immediately, before he'd even shifted from reverse to first. "Three men, one of them a real hunk, shoulder to shoulder in the front seat. Must have been a thrill to drive it this week, huh Finn? Made you feel like a man, didn't it?" Doc eyed Finney, who'd borrowed the Suburban two days earlier to move some office equipment. "Not one of those wimpy cars guys low in testosterone drive."

Just as he pulled out, Doc flashed concern at some faint vibration only he would notice. Jake shook his head in wonder. *He takes this car into the mechanic faster than some mothers take their kid to the doctor.*

Finney noticed Doc's concern too, and traded a knowing smile with Jake. "Hey, it was working perfectly when I had it, Doc! Of course, I had to pull in for gas every other stop light. My wimpy car could make it to Tokyo on the gas this monster burns on the way to Gino's."

"Yeah, well it's still wimpy. You are what you drive. And you always were a wuss, Finney."

"Doc, old buddy," Finney began with a sigh, as if he'd been coerced into dredging up an ancient story. Doc knew exactly what was coming but forced himself to look like he didn't.

Leaning forward and turning to look past Jake, Finney asked Doc, "Remember the dorm wrestling championship? You actually made it to the finals. You were almost in shape back then." Doc sucked in his waist and flexed his arms against the steering wheel to prove he still was.

Finney resumed the familiar folklore. "But somebody beat you, Doc, he beat you real bad. And despite the brain damage you suffered that day—and Lord knows you couldn't afford any more brain damage—I'll bet if you think real hard you can remember who that somebody was."

Doc closed one eye and squinted the other, as if trying to remember.

"And if that somebody is a wuss, Mr. Macho Chief of Surgery, would you explain what that makes you?"

"Hey, I had a wrenched shoulder and torn cartilage in my knee." Doc began rustling through his duffel bag of favorite excuses that grew with the years. "And I'd just had the flu."

"Yeah, and as I recall you'd donated blood that afternoon," Finney added.

"No, that was in the morning. In the afternoon I was having a heart transplant." Both men laughed heartily, the way you laugh with your oldest and best friends. At the same moment, both realized Jake wasn't laughing. His face was scrunched and his expression distant and uncharacteristically troubled.

"Jake," Finney said. "You're awfully quiet. Doc could bore a guy to death, I know, but that's nothing new. Something wrong?"

Jake, right index finger aimlessly stroking his graying temple, made a slow dissolve from the inner world to the outer. "Wasn't that thing with the quarter sort of...eerie?"

Doc flashed him his familiar screwed-up face that called people "weird" without a spoken word. "You still thinking about that? What's the big deal?"

Jake, his reputation as Mister In-Control and Unflappable on the line, tried to downplay his response. "I don't know," he finally answered. "For some reason, it's almost like...like it means something."

Doc flashed a spacy look and hummed the theme from *The Twilight Zone*. "Don't get spooky on me, ol' buddy. Things don't mean something. They mean nothing. Zilch. They just happen. Unless you buy into Finney's way of thinking, that is, which someday you may if you get Alzheimer's. One kook's enough for this threesome. Right, Finn?"

Finney knew how to roll with Doc's punches and counter with his own. But right now his energies focused on Jake, who appeared to need more than a light-hearted slough-off. "Well, I don't know if the quarter means anything. But I know life does. Things have meaning and purpose. Maybe even a coin toss. Who knows?"

"Sure, Finney, whatever you say." Doc rolled his eyes back so far all Jake could see was white. "But I've always found that meaning in life is no substitute for a cold beer with your pizza. Know what I mean, Woody?" Slapping Jake on the thigh, Doc turned suddenly into the 7-Eleven, his tires bouncing off the curb.

As Doc hopped out, Jake seized the opportunity. "It's weird, Finney. Why is that quarter bugging me? It's like it's...a sign or something."

"Maybe it is a sign, Jake. I don't know. Maybe Somebody's trying to get through to you again."

Jake sighed and asked Finney, as if reading from a script, "Is this the part where you tell me life is a brief window of opportunity, and today could be my last day here, and I should prepare for eternity, or one day I'll stand before God and wish I'd done something different?"

Finney broke into his patented dimple-to-dimple grin that took fifteen years off his already too-young face. "Well said. Sounds like you don't need to be told. The question is, what will it take to convince you it's true? What you said is right on target. Life is short. And you don't have forever to decide what it's about. None of us do."

"I'll say one thing for you, Finn." Jake wavered between irritation and admiration. "You're as dependable as Big Ben and Oregon rain. You always sing the same tune."

"It's a tune I've come to love," Finney said sincerely, his confident deep blue eyes peering into Jake's cynical but uncertain chocolate browns. "I'm just looking forward to the day I hear it sung in one of your columns."

"Don't hold your breath," Jake retorted. "I'm not a Bible waver. I work for the *Tribune*."

"Isn't there room for both? I read the Bible and the *Tribune* every day." Finney grinned. "Guess I just like to know what both sides are up to."

Jake winced. Finney made no secret he thought Jake's newspaper was biased and unfair, especially concerning matters of religion and morality. His friend, Jake reminded himself again, just didn't understand the role of the newspaper, that it was neither adversary nor advocate. It simply told the truth, no matter whose toes it stepped on. Finney would never get it, Jake knew. Not until hell froze over which, in Finney's theology, it never would.

Suddenly the driver's side door opened and Doc's megaphone voice boomed,

"Okay, six pack of Coors for me, three Buds for Jake, and a Shirley Temple for the Preacher." He handed Finney a Diet 7-Up. Holding up a Coors he announced, "This may send me to hell, but it sure washes down the pizza!"

"Come on, Doc," Finney replied. "You know I've never cared about that. Where you spend eternity isn't about what you drink. It's about who you know."

"Sure, sure," Doc said. "Well, I do know the young lady behind the counter at Gino's...and I'd love to get to know her in the biblical sense, if you get my drift."

Jake got it and smiled. Finney got it and didn't. As surely as if he had a verbatim transcript in front of him, Jake knew what both his friends were thinking. Doc didn't let his marriage to Betsy get in the way of his sexual liberties. That fact created endless conflict between the friends. Or, rather, Jake corrected himself, it was Finney who created the conflict because he was so intolerant, refusing to just mind his own business and keep his mouth shut when Doc's eyes wandered and he crossed the fence to other pastures.

The remaining three minutes of the drive seemed destined for wordless discomfort. Jake's mind traveled back to an incident a year earlier when the three amigos headed for an overnight duck hunt. Doc flirted with a woman at a truck stop. Just when she was writing down her phone number for him, Finney said, "You're wearing a wedding ring, Doc." Suddenly the embarrassed woman covered her own wedding ring. In a flash, she and her phone number disappeared. An outraged Doc turned on Finney with every foul word he could draw from his sizable repertoire. Finney was almost as angry as Doc. Jake couldn't remember everything, but he'd never forget Finney telling Doc, "Stop trying to prove you're a man and start acting like one." It had taken all Jake's wits and even some physical restraint to prevent a rematch of the dorm wrestling championship. Jake had often shuddered as he'd wondered, *What if Doc's shotgun had been in his hands, instead of in the truck?*

Later, around the campfire, Finney apologized for getting angry. But, in vintage Finney style, he made it clear he wasn't sorry for reminding Doc of his obligation to remain faithful to his wife. Again, Finney's words stuck in Jake's mind—"I stood next to you when you said your vows, Doc. Friends help you stick to your vows. They don't look the other way when you're tempted to violate them."

This comment still rankled Jake, perhaps because he was Doc's other best man at the wedding, and he'd said nothing to stop Doc on that occasion or dozens like it. *Does this mean you think you're a better friend to Doc than I am? Who appointed you judge of the universe? What right do you have to tell Doc what to do?* It still infuriated Jake, but he knew that wasn't the whole story. What right did Doc have to cheat on his wife? *Yes, and what right did I have to cheat on Janet?* The questions couldn't be separated. It all hit too close to home. A cloud hung over the rest of the hunting trip and, for one of the first times in his life, Jake looked forward to getting away from his buddies. Even now, as the feelings filling the Suburban dredged up the memories, it caused Jake to physically cringe. He desperately hoped this all-too-familiar tension wouldn't culminate in another explosion today.

The Suburban pulled into Gino's. As the rig gave its final lurch from the sudden stop in the ten minute pick-up space, Doc bounded out like a man on a mission.

Finney and Jake walked quietly behind him, both dreading the next few moments.

"Hey, sweetheart, I hoped you'd be here."

Doc aimed his syrupy voice at the slim hazel-eyed eighteen-year-old in the emerald green dress. Reaching across the counter like an old pro, Doc touched her arm, his fingers lingering. She didn't withdraw, obviously taken with the handsome, well-built head of surgery from Lifeline Medical Center.

"Your hair sure looks pretty today, Sheila." Doc read her name tag, but said "Sheila" as if he'd remembered her name. She smiled shyly, soaking in the attention. Doc played her like a fiddle, enjoying every moment. Jake hung back, desperately hoping either Doc would back off or Finney would keep still.

Suddenly Finney strode toward Doc and slapped him on the back, bursting the bubble of the private space he'd established with the girl. *Here it comes,* Jake thought, bracing himself.

"She really looks like Molly, doesn't she, Doc?" Addressing the confused and suddenly self-conscious girl Finney explained, "Molly's his teenage daughter—about your age. Yeah, Doc and his wife Betsy have two lovely children. Doc and I, and Jake here, we all fought in Vietnam. You've probably read about that war in your history class—it was over before you were born. Hard to believe, but we must be about your dad's age. Maybe older."

"Yeah?" the girl mumbled, more to the counter top than to Finney. "Whatever." The spell broke.

"That'll be $28.50."

Doc plopped down his VISA, waving off Finney and Jake as they reached for their wallets. No one said anything more until the pizzas were in hand and they headed out the door.

"We must be about your dad's age," Doc mouthed sarcastically as they stepped out in the parking lot, now pelted by sheets of rain. Jake laughed, partially from relief. If Doc was joking about it, things would probably be okay. As he ran to the car, arms crossed in a vain attempt to keep his sweatshirt from getting soaked, Jake thought, *Maybe we've avoided another duck hunting disaster—at least for now.*

After the three jumped in the Suburban, Doc jammed the key into the ignition, but didn't turn it. The tension started building again, as the men sat shoulder to shoulder, each looking straight ahead, as if the parking lot dumpsters in front of them were as interesting as sunset at the Grand Canyon. Jake stared at the beads of water on the windshield, watching them join into little waterfalls. The heavy smell of wet fabric pressed itself on Jake. After an interminable ten seconds, Doc abruptly leaned over toward Finney, giving Jake a close up view of his right ear. His baritone voice dripping with sarcasm, Doc asked, "Oh, what would I do without you, Preacher Finney, Mother Theresa of my life? Thank you, thank you, for being my conscience."

"It's a tough job, but someone has to do it." After a moment's pause Finney added, "You should try it yourself. It might keep you out of trouble."

"I don't want to keep out of trouble. What you call trouble is what I call life. What you call life, well..." Doc chortled, "thanks, but no thanks!"

"I've had my share of the kind of trouble that comes from making wrong choices. Enough to avoid it when I can."

"Well," Doc sounded distinctly unconvinced, "how about you watch out for your life, and I watch out for mine? Sound like a plan?"

"And how about I watch out for Sue and my kids, and you watch out for Betsy and yours? Sound like a plan?"

The irresistible force and the immovable object. Finney was as adamant as Doc, two ocean rocks stubbornly refusing to be beaten down.

Doc shook his head in disgust. "Finney, you're hopeless. I don't know why we put up with you and your stone-age morality. You're a fossil, a throwback to the Puritans. You were born in the wrong century. You'd have fit right in during the Dark Ages. But not here, not now. We're tired of your holier-than-thou attitude."

Jake and Finney both noticed the "we." Doc was ushering support, and looked to Jake for a nod of agreement. Jake turned and gave Doc a sympathetic look that Finney couldn't see, but refrained from an overt nod. *I'm staying out of this one.*

"Have I ever told you what a major pain in the rear you can be, Finney? Yes, I see that I have. Sometimes," his tone turned icy, "I think you're the biggest fool I've ever met." Just as suddenly, Doc's voice returned to normal. "But, call me sentimental, you're still my friend." Hesitating just a moment he added, "Don't push it, though, because big as my heart is, even it has limits."

Jake turned enough to see Finney's quiet nod of resignation. For the moment the two bombs sitting on each side of him had been defused. He saw in Finney's eyes what he'd seen before. The confrontation stung him, and he hated the conflict. *So why do you make it happen?* Finney could be so inexplicable, judgmental and...obnoxious. It irritated Jake, and frustrated him. Sure, Doc wasn't a saint, and not always the easiest guy to get along with, but he had a good heart and was fiercely loyal to his closest friends. Jake couldn't ask for more. Why didn't that ever seem to be enough for Finney?

As Doc finally started the engine, Jake drew within himself again. The bantering between his two friends was as familiar as his worn-out bedroom slippers. To the casual observer it seemed impossible these men could be friends. Anyone hearing this exchange would be certain any past friendship was over. But Jake knew otherwise. Now, as always, these men were the two defining personalities of his life. Their polarized beliefs and philosophies seemed like matter and antimatter—two contradictory world views inevitably hostile, explosively hostile, to each other. Yet they were embodied in men who all their lives had been thrown together. No matter how great the explosion and how far it threw them from each other, something always brought them back together. And always Jake was there, right in the middle.

Jake fancied himself a livable compromise between many of their extreme views. But in moments of honesty he had to admit his own beliefs were, as he'd confessed to his journal no more than two weeks ago, "a formless bowl of mush." They were an almost random combination of the views of college professors, media colleagues, and his own interpretations of his life experiences. Despite his rep as a no-nonsense cut-to-the-chase journalist, Jake was an iron filing pulled between these two powerful magnets he called friends. He identified much more with Doc's beliefs, politics, and self-determined lifestyle. But he was drawn more to Finney's character and quality of family life. He admired Doc's sense of power and Finney's sense of peace.

Jake admitted to his journal what he told no one else. *I feel like a moral chameleon, a* Star Trek *shape-shifter—I can blend in with Doc when we're at a bar, or Finney, when I'm having dinner with his family. I'm at home with both, yet ultimately not at home with either.*

Doc and Finney both exuded confidence in their own beliefs. Both passionately and consistently acted on those beliefs. Doc the dedicated atheist and humanist, Finney the devout Christian. Doc the relativist, Finney the absolutist. Doc trusting in himself, Finney trusting in a Christ he called God. Jake wavered between these worlds, much closer to Doc's, but never fully at home in either. Neither world was his.

Since turning fifty a few months ago, Jake had paused to think more about the big questions of life. But he didn't really know how to phrase the questions, much less where to go for answers.

He'd written, *Half a century old now, and I don't have time to think—only to record thoughts. I live under the tyranny of 800 words.* He referred to the columns due on his editor's desk by noon every Monday, Wednesday, and Friday. Finished or not, facts checked out or not, he spoke through those columns to a half million loyal readers three times a week, and many more in the two that went out under syndication. As together as he appeared on the outside, on the inside Jake Woods knew his world was a muddled mess of uncertainty and confusion. He felt like...almost like a coin tossed in the air, a coin that was supposed to land on one side or the other, but hadn't.

Suddenly Doc's roaring voice yanked Jake back to reality. He was yelling at someone on the highway, someone Jake couldn't see through the driving sheets of rain.

"Watch where you're going, you idiot!" Doc's shoulder jammed into Jake as he threw the Suburban into a sharp swerve to the right. When, in an instant, Jake heard Doc's loud voice turn from anger to panic, his blood froze. Suddenly a disorienting blur of images overwhelmed him.

"I can't stop! I can't stop!" he heard Doc bellow.

The Suburban embarked on a wild ride, carving its own path, as if declaring independence, celebrating its free will. A towering telephone pole and billboard appeared out of nowhere. The Suburban cut through them as if they were Jell-O, then careened into a ten-foot-high embankment. Jake watched in slow motion the pizza flying up against the windshield, just before the bone crushing impact. The car bounced off the embankment back onto the highway. Like a raging wild beast shot in the chest, the out of control Suburban kicked and thrashed away its last moments of life, determined to take down with it anything and anyone it could.

Somewhere between the sound of Doc's last cry and the cold sickening crunch of bent metal from the car's first roll, Jake lost consciousness. His last sensation was being pressed hard from both sides by two men whose bodies lunged against their harnesses like wild stallions against a corral.

In the unearthly silence that followed the chaos, his upside-down frame sagged limply, held aloft only by his seat belt. Jake's body hung between two friends; his soul between two worlds.

CHAPTER TWO

The roaring blast of wild heat knocked Jake Woods back into the Huey hovering over Bien Hoa. It felt like being snapped in the face with a hot wet towel. In training he'd been taught to always strap himself in, but no one did that in Vietnam airspace. This was a different world, with different rules. The dents and nicks on the M-60s mounted on the Huey reminded him how different. When they touched down on the tarmac he felt like an astronaut taking his first step onto the moon.

The private who grabbed the gear as he got off the chopper told the twenty-four-year-old Jake, "Welcome to the Hilton, Sir." He was no doubt thinking, *One more green officer in charge of guys who know twice as much as he does.*

Jake Woods had heard that ageless private speak these words of greeting in a hundred dreams. Now, twenty-six years later, he heard him speak them again as he lay unconscious in a hospital bed the morning after the accident.

It was one of those dreams where you know you're dreaming, but it still seems absolutely real. In this case it *was* real, because it had all happened to Jake before, in a penetrating reality that had forever shaped his life. He watched the dream of that year of his life as one watches a play. The stark reality of it all kept drawing him back in, provoking high pitches of vivid sensation.

It was night, first night in camp, second in country. Night two of 365. The commercial 707, stripped of all amenities and crammed to capacity, had brought him to this country yesterday, and here he was, a stone's throw from the mouth of hell. Jake Woods racked out in the bunk but didn't sleep a wink in the stagnant inferno that was his hooch. *Who can sleep in a steam bath?* he wondered. *Who can sleep with the stench of warm garbage and raw sewage?*

When you're twenty-four and know you're about to die you hold on to whatever life is left, even the half life of lying in that pathetic tent. It was three days before Jake really slept, and then from pure exhaustion.

The siren blasted, as it so often did. Jake saw guys running at the perimeter, jumping into bunkers. He watched himself duck down in his tent, tucking his head low to the ground. Mrs. Green would be proud, he thought. It was she, his high school teacher—not a boot camp instructor—who taught him and Doc and Finney and their peers the fine art of head-tucking, in the air raid drills back in the days of Khrushchev and the Bay of Pigs and the bomb shelter Dad built. He always wondered what difference it would all make when the end finally came.

Rockets and tracers blistered the sky, and Jake watched air burn as he never knew it could. The mortar barrage curled his toes so bad it cramped his legs, and despite his fit youthful body, he felt like a crippled old man. After he thought it was all over and lifted his head, a piece of shrapnel flew in one side of the tent and out the other, as if to remind him of his mortality. As if Death were saying to him, "Tonight you live—but one day I'll be back, and nothing will save you from me." Jake saw that shrapnel in perfect slow motion. The loop had run through his mind hundreds of times. It did again, flawlessly, with its own macabre beauty, as if set to music.

His first week in Nam a supply clerk pointed him to a crate of ammo. Jake saw him clearly now, his untucked fatigues, glasses, and Southern accent. Most of these guys hailed from places like Sebastopol, Mississippi and Arnoldsville, Georgia. He heard the clerk say the strangest words about the ammo—"Take as much as you want." The rules really were different here. No meticulous counting of each round. Hand grenades piled on each other like ingredients in a tossed salad. Nothing like the neatly stacked rows at noncombat bases. War seemed neat and tidy until you were in one.

Looking at the crate filled with grenades, Jake shot the clerk a questioning look. "Yeah, grenades too. Just take whatever you want." *You just take stuff till it runs out?* Jake took six grenades. He felt greedy, like he'd taken too large a slice of pie. But coming up one grenade short could cost him his life, or his buddy's. Now he saw himself toting a Claymore mine as well, its seven hundred steel balls sandwiched between layers of plastic explosives, unbelievably decimating to anyone within range. It was the most effective weapon in Nam.

The new guys always looked new. They could be older, bigger, wear identical uniforms but they stuck out, walked different, talked different. The veterans walked with steely purpose, alert but not jumpy. The new guys looked at them as if they were gods. Beneath all their mystique and machismo was a nearly impenetrable aura of mutual trust and brotherhood. The perennial greeting "What's up, bro?" and the familiar backslapping sprung from something deep within. The uninitiated longed to enter into that camaraderie forged only in life and death struggle. But newcomers were on the outside. To get on the inside, they had to prove their mettle. They had to show they were men. On such terms, friendship was won, and once won never lost.

Young men, if not from Texas or Louisiana, then equally foreign places such as Iowa and Nebraska, with rifles slung over their shoulders, marched across the theater screen of Jake's mind. Helicopters in Dolby sound served as the audio background. Armies of mosquitoes did perfect little helicopter imitations, using sun-baked soldier flesh as their LZ. Phalanx of black ants and whole battalions of big red fire ants fanned out on the ground. Jake imagined them fighting their own war. In his mind's eye he saw them hoisting their sand bags, stringing out thimble-sized ribbons of barbed wire, carrying mortars and ammo for their buddies, maybe wearing little ant ear plugs when they fired their artillery. The black ants were friendlies, the red ants hostiles. Or was it the other way around? He got down on his knees to take a closer look.

"We're like those ants," the young man wrote in his journal that quarter of a century ago. "Except we stand on our back legs and trudge clear across this insane jungle of oversized philodendrons and razor sharp elephant grass, pretending to be brave and sometimes convincing ourselves we really are."

After a few weeks Jake's heart descended from constant dread to periodic dread, from red alert to yellow alert. He often wondered, *Am I getting braver, or just getting accustomed to being terrified?* There was always somebody new coming in, somebody you liked spending time with, because you knew he was more scared than you were, which by comparison made you brave.

There's Harvey, from Zionsville, Indiana. "Harvey," Jake chided. "You look like you shaved blindfolded!" This was what a sergeant said to him the first day he had a run in with a thorn bush. He hadn't thought it funny then, but got a good laugh out of saying it now. Between mosquitoes and thorns and elephant grass you could be a mass of welts for days. Fortunately, you had things like diarrhea and bleeding feet to take your mind off how impossibly sore your face was. Yet, underneath all the unappealing aspects of this place ran a current of dignity, a nobility. Something every man needed, whether he knew it or not. A reason, a purpose for living, a mission. A cause.

Jake came here to fight for Dad and Mom and his brother Bryce, and his extended family and friends back home, and the children and grandchildren he'd probably never have precisely because he was here. Now, though, his world shrunk to the thirty men in his platoon. It was reduced to the guy on his right and the guy on his left, guys who reminded him of Doc and Finney. His loftiest dream was no longer a career in journalism, or winning the Pulitzer Prize. It was to keep his buddies and himself alive, survive that day, and to put a year of those twenty-four-hour survivals back to back, to be done and to go home.

"Twenty-four is a ripe old age here," Jake wrote Janet, his college sweetheart, whose life was on hold while she waited for her man to come home standing, not in a box, to start a life and a family. The average age of the combat soldier was nineteen. Though as a lieutenant he outranked them, all those nineteen-year-olds had seemed seasoned veterans when Jake first got off the chopper. Once he had a couple of months under his belt, Jake was the veteran, and he exuded a veteran's confidence, partly because he knew he was supposed to.

Jake watched himself now in his dream, playing poker by moonlight. That dripping blast furnace wound down at midnight just enough to give a hint of relief, only to begin its swing into the fires of hell known as tomorrow. The stench of dead fish and rotting vegetation seemed to ease when the oven turned down. The night sky lit up like fireworks, a surreal Disneyland extravaganza minus Tinker Bell. What would have absorbed your full attention any other place became mundane here. The luminous trail of tracer bullets and explosions in the darkness far outshone the brilliant Northern Lights Jake once saw in Canada. And then it would be morning again, too soon. You were never ready.

Snakes and insects Jake and Doc and Finney would have used to terrorize every young female in Benton County, here they routinely brushed aside. At first Jake whistled and commented on them, now he just flicked them off and moved on. There was Bilbo, the tree monkey his company adopted. He was the closest thing to Champ, his golden retriever he missed more than he wanted to admit. Bilbo would crawl up Jake's back, dance on his shoulders, reach out and steal rations from his hand just as they came within inches of his mouth.

Jake shunned the tempting shortcuts through the vegetation, where VC booby traps killed two men in his platoon, Jim from Oak Ridge and Warren from Port Angeles. The uncertainty of it all plagued him. He saw himself poised, as he had been dozens of times, to shoot the man in the bushes over there, only to discover that moving body was one that slept by him at night.

He cursed the NVA for not having the decency to stand row by row in bright colorful uniforms, marching in perfect lines to the beat of a drummer, like the British in the Revolutionary War. If only the VC got their training from the Redcoats. It would have been fun, Jake thought, to pick them off one by one as if in target practice. To leisurely call in a 105mm howitzer, give a signal for the war to start, and for once to actually see what you were shooting at. But it would never happen here. Victor Charlie wasn't civilized like the British of old. He was wily and crafty and unpredictable. Knowing that made the most routine patrol about as relaxing as walking along the six-inch window ledge of a ten-story building. But knowing that was what kept you alive.

You could scan the horizon with binoculars and never see Charlie, only to look down and watch a bayonet come out your chest, flicking your dog tags up to your mouth to give you one final metallic taste of life in this world. Only once had Jake looked into the eyes of the enemy. There he was now, right in front of him, as real as he'd been so long ago. He could see deep in his eyes, those dark brown eyes frozen forever in his memory. Charlie looked young and dedicated and brave and scared, just like Jake. One would have to kill the other.

Charlie carried the Russian AK-47, three pounds heavier than Jake's M-16. The smaller man carrying the larger weapon. Jake always thought that mismatch saved his life, allowing him to move his weapon a fraction of a second faster, hitting Charlie in the chest while his round flew four inches above Jake's left ear. As he stared at Charlie, watched his life leave him, he wondered about things young men usually leave to philosophers and priests. *Where did he go? Where will I go? And when? Does friendship die forever with the friend? Do either survive death? Is there a reason for all this? Will I ever understand?*

There was the captain he'd talked with once at the officer's club. "On this side of life," the captain said, "there's the Old Man, the commander, reviewing the troops. You do your best to please him, don't you?" Yes, Jake did. Everybody did. "Then there's the Supreme Commander," he said. "He'll review the troops on the other side. Our mission here is to please him, our highest goal to one day be reviewed favorably by him."

By now he'd eaten dirt in a couple of firefights. Knowing he could die any day made Jake think about such words. As the captain said, "There are no atheists in fox holes." But in the years since, these words had lost their interest and urgency. They managed to scale the wall of life's busyness only when his guard was down, here in his dreams.

Jake now sat around the campfire, smirking at C-ration labels that sounded like gourmet feasts but always tasted like cardboard casseroles. He could still taste Ham & Lima Beans, half salt, the other half fat, with just enough hidden food particles to make finding them an adventure. He tore the top off a basket, creating a makeshift basketball hoop, then listened to Gordy, Baton Rouge Gordy, play his twelve string Martin. Gordy sang Simon and Garfunkel songs, straining on Garfunkel's high notes, trying to reach them before getting hit with the usual barrage of catcalls and dirt clods. "A Bridge over Troubled Water." He could hear it now, as clearly as the first morning song blaring out of a radio alarm clock.

Bravo Company. It sounded so macho. Sometimes it was. Sometimes Jake felt like a man should feel, like he only feels when he's spent himself, when he's dug deep and discovered that when he's sure he can't possibly trudge another step, he can go ten more miles. When he's taken risks and accomplished great feats and come home from the hunt carrying game in his hand and scars on his back, ready to celebrate the conquest. *There's no celebration like the one you've earned,* Jake thought.

Jake celebrated in the city, with his buddies, and with the dark-skinned nameless women trafficking and profiteering their only marketable features. Their faces and bodies provided momentary breaks from the ugliness of war. Like his buddies, Jake ignored all the warnings about venereal diseases, even the dreaded "Black Syph," thinking he'd be grateful living with a disease, if only it meant he would live. It wasn't that drunkenness and casual sex were so great, it was just that they offered temporary relief from the boredom and the terror. That's what war seemed sometimes—periods of boredom interrupted by periods of terror.

Jake heard babies crying. That was the worst. Going through a village and feeling a man's best instincts, wanting to comfort a crying child. Then realizing you're carrying an M-16, wearing an ammo belt, and the poor kid is afraid. Looking at old grandmothers and women and children holding their ears and running scared, other times reaching out their arms like they wanted you to pick them up. And you wanted to open your heart and arms to them, but knew they could be VC, that they could kill you, hand you a basket with a live grenade.

Children. They were here to save these children from the ravages of totalitarianism descending from the north. The war could deliver them, Jake thought, if only they were allowed to win the war. But someone had fixed the rules so they couldn't win. Meanwhile, children died. Nothing was more tragic than the death of a child. Jake had cause to think about that before the war, and he thought it again there. The death of a child. One could only endure the thought by steeling himself against it, by pretending it hadn't happened.

There was Hyuk, Jake's closest friend among the Montagnards, the original inhabitants of the central highlands, called 2 Corps by U.S. forces. Hyuk was a brave and loyal Yard, strong in ways his slight build never suggested, kind and lighthearted, a lover of life and a lover of his little family. He was the sort that convinced you these people were worth fighting for, even if the reports from back home convinced you American college students weren't. Hyuk would smile broadly whenever he'd see Jake, and ask him, "Wha's sup, bro?"

Hyuk's son, wife, and mother lived with him in a tiny little hut, reinforced with metal scraps, cardboard, and wood pallets. Mamasan and her young slender daughter-in-law favored Jake with their delicacies, including that rotten fish sauce, the name of which he couldn't remember. They were warm and generous, good women, loyal to Hyuk and his infant son. One day, ten months into Jake's tour of duty, the unthinkable happened. While Hyuk was out on patrol, a VC, known locally, fragged Hyuk's hut, wasting his wife, mother, and son. Then, like a cockroach, he scampered back into the darkness.

Hyuk returned to discover the madness two days later. He fell to his knees and wept and screamed, and afterward was never the same. He became reckless, took foolish risks, maybe because there was nothing left to live for. Jake never saw a hint of meanness in Hyuk before, but he got darker and harder, and his big smile became scarce and twisted. One day he disappeared into the jungle by himself, armed to the hilt, and Jake knew why. He was going to find the man, the traitor, who had taken from him the mother who gave him life, the son to whom he gave life, and the wife who was his life. And finding him, Jake had no doubt what he would do to him.

When Hyuk broke off, Jake knew he would never see him again. He didn't. He never said good-bye. Hyuk often appeared in Jake's dreams. He wondered if his Yard friend had managed to take the family-killer with him when he left this world. Jake understood the visceral drive that compelled a man to protect mother and wife and child and to sacrifice anything to extract vengeance on those who ravaged them. This was not mere macho craziness. In the face of such a thing, this was merely SOP—standard operating procedure. It came from deep inside a man and transcended race and culture.

Jake watched this movie as if for the hundredth time. Except each time was slightly different, a buried memory newly unearthed by one little variation, one slight association not made before, taking him a new direction. He experienced again the magic of mail drop, the chopper coming in a couple times a week with troop replacements and mail bag, the latter even more welcome than the former. The sacred letters, each spread out carefully, some bringing words of joy and hope, others words of grief and broken commitments. Whether flowering love sonnets or "Dear John" letters or just newsy hometown updates and clippings, the letters distracted them from a time and place that cried out for distractions. Jake consumed his letters along with sips of too strong coffee from a tarnished aluminum cup, dinged from jostling in his pack on patrol. He savored every word from home as if each were a drop of dew collected by a man dying of thirst.

The letters reminded him how much he missed Oregon air, clean and exhilarating, and Oregon water, flowing and refreshing and blue, not stagnant brownish green. He longed for the gentle rain from gray clouds rather than the monsoons from black clouds that could turn dry dusty ground to muddy mush in ten minutes. But even more than the place, he missed the people. The letters offered much needed proof that other world was real, still there, waiting for his return. On

Thanksgiving and Christmas, when he got hot meals he swore never to take for granted again, he'd take out those letters and pictures again, and share his meal with all they represented.

After basking in the warmth of their letters, Jake would write his own back to Janet and Mom. He'd propped up both their pictures by his bunk. There was no picture of Dad. Somehow it seemed appropriate. Dad had never been there when Jake needed him. So it seemed, anyway.

Sometimes one of the guys would toss his porn mag near the picture of Janet. More than once Jake turned her face away as he thumbed through the pages. He felt ashamed, but also lonely, so very lonely. Porn was like pot, an anesthetic that dulled the pain of loneliness, yet somehow with its counterfeit love seemed only to deepen the void inside him. It wasn't just the round bodies of the women in the pictures, it was their round eyes, eyes like the girls he went to school with, eyes that reminded him of home. Home. What was happening at home? Would he ever see it again? If so, would it ever seem the same?

Visions of his first leave marched onto the center stage of Jake's fevered mind. There he was, sitting in Bangkok, reading an American newspaper, his insides boiling with shock and anger. Who were these nitwit reporters who couldn't even get the basic facts right, much less interpret their meaning? They talked as if Lieutenant Calley and the My Lai massacre were typical behavior for U.S. military. Even the communist atrocities, their vicious massacres of the innocent, were laid at the feet of U.S soldiers. If only we'd stop bombing these nice North Vietnamese, they wouldn't hurt anybody. *Yeah, right. Who started this war against innocent people? It wasn't us!* If Jane Fonda had her way U.S. school children would get the day off on Ho Chi Minh's birthday instead of George Washington's. Jake blamed her, but not as much as he blamed the journalists who promoted the shallow uninformed ideas of people like her. She was just ignorant and stupid and self-centered like the rest of Hollywood. But they, the journalists, should have known better.

What made these reporters think they were a cut above the farm boys dying in the jungle to keep their "free press" free? Who were they, pontificating on what was right and wrong, what was or was not a "just war" ten thousand miles away? What did they know of those who fought on the front lines for a freedom they were quick to spend, but which cost them nothing? Cost them nothing because other men, brave men, had paid for it with their lives? Distortion was SOP for these parasites building careers off other men's sweat. They were like those blood-sucking slugs he had to peel off after crossing the rivers. Had these journalists walked the Ho Chi Minh trail, holed up at Khe Sanh or stood tall during the Tet Offensive they were so quick to herald, falsely, as an NVA victory? These bozos couldn't lift a backpack or load a rifle or zip up their pants without an instruction manual. They wouldn't know a Claymore mine if it blew up in their rear ends, and Jake found himself wishing it would. They didn't know beans, the arrogant jerks. He resented them big time—"boo koo resentment," he thought, commandeering the old Vietnamese expression from the French *beaucoup*.

The memories suddenly turned sweet as the movie rolled on, because on that same leave he linked up with Finney and Doc. Though they'd gone through training at Fort Benning the same time, there was no guarantee their years in Nam would overlap each other. But they did. Even then, as three lieutenants in different companies they could easily have gone the year without seeing each other. But as fate would have it—as fate seemed always to have it with them—they'd ended up in the same battalion, over seven hundred strong. Though they wouldn't trudge through the jungles side by side, they would always know their buddies were out there, somewhere in 2 Corps, less than a thirty-minute chopper ride away, which compared to the rest of the world was like sleeping in the same bunk. And if they stopped Charlie today, they might be stopping him from killing their best friends three weeks from now. In Vietnam you clung to thoughts like that, to any thought that made the job a little easier, that gave it a little more meaning.

It was Doc who managed to get them together for that precious week of R & R. They all applied for the same week, requesting Bangkok, but knew it was unlikely all three of them would get it. But Doc, the consummate poker player, Doc who could bluff the devil himself, had won enough money to convince a clerk at HQ they should have their reunion. When the three friends met in Bangkok, it was no small triumph.

Finney was the first to reach their appointed meeting place. Jake snuck up on him from behind, grabbed him and cried, "What's up, bro?" They slapped each other on the back and poked each other in the stomach, and wrestled, the way men hug each other without hugging. Doc joined them within the hour. They bragged of their exploits, told of close calls. They sang a few rounds of "A comin' home soldier." There was nothing so rousing, nothing so exhilarating as to anticipate coming home at last after having served faithfully. All three were on the homeward slide of their tours, Jake only three months from the end. They vowed to survive, to serve their remaining year in safer places and go on with their lives together back home. Jake watched in his dream as Doc raised his Budweiser in an elegant toast. "Gentlemen, it may not be much of a war, but it's the only war we've got!"

They all got drunk that night—Finney too (it was back before the change)—and for one glorious evening, or so it seemed, they pretended to be home. Jake wrote in his journal when he got back to his post, "Drunkenness knows no geography. It makes where you are seem beside the point, which is probably why it's the most popular way to spend your leaves here." He had signed off 86, or some such number—the number of days he had to survive before hopping the chopper that would take him to the 707 that would fly him home. One day closer to Janet and his dog Champ and Corvettes and Dea's hamburgers and flush toilets and real seasons, seasons with a wider venue than "boiling" and "insufferable."

Jake reviewed the troops he'd known, seeing visions of gentleness and meanness. Some who fought beside him were the kindest, finest men he'd ever know. Moving in and out of his dream were three little boys in Benton County, playing war in the wheat fields, back when losing meant you had to buy the other guys a bottle of pop at Miller's store, rather than be sent home to your family in a pine box.

Wasn't that Slider, the grunt from Pensacola with the dense accent and the big smile? No, it was happening again. Slider, don't go over there. Get back! The VC mine, not nearly as potent as a Claymore but deadly nonetheless, blew off Slider's leg and splattered Jake with his blood. Someone cried out in pain. It wasn't Slider. He was too far gone. It was Jake himself. Exploding with anger and anguish, he held his right ear, which felt like it had been punctured and still plagued him periodically twenty-six years later. Instead of rushing to Slider he turned away, later ashamed that in his own pain he'd let someone else reach his buddy first. Commotion and panic trailed off into silence, the silence of surrender that always followed death. Then the vacancy. The loss of a familiar voice, and smile, a familiar snore. Slider, a guy who choked on cigarettes but smoked anyway, a guy with a lousy poker face that would never play poker again. A guy who always carried his girl friend's picture, who would never see his girl again.

Death. That was the enemy, wasn't it? The only real enemy. The one enemy of all the young men in that jungle. The one enemy Jake had in common with the NVA he fought.

Jake writhed on his back, drenching the hospital bed with sweat from a jungle heat twenty-six years old. He saw disturbing images now he hadn't seen until coming home, some of them worse than war itself, moving pictures of protests and debates and politicians' lies. They'd made a promise to those good people, Hyuk's people, and they hadn't kept it. Men died, some of them his friends, to keep that promise, and the nation broke it. Then they turned and looked at those they'd sent as if they were bastard children, reminders of an ugly episode they just wanted to forget. Jake trembled with anger even now, and the anger gave him energy, pulling him back from the dreams and memories that consumed him, pulling him closer to the present time and place.

Jake saw light and heard noises. Were these incoming mortar rounds? He couldn't hear the dreaded "whump" sound that warned of the coming blast like lightning warns of thunder. He had a splitting headache. He reached to his pocket for the aspirin he chewed like candy, but couldn't seem to find it. There wasn't even a pocket there. What was he wearing? Why couldn't he get his bearings? Funny, it didn't seem as hot as it should be. And the noises weren't the right noises.

He heard voices, hoping they were English. Yes, English. Something besides a rock or blanket was under his head. Wait. Was this a hospital? He must be at Cam Ranh Bay. He frantically wiggled both sets of toes. Yes, he still had his legs, both of them.

He was so tired. Vietnam was a year without real sleep, only catnaps and dozes. *I can't fall asleep. My buddies' lives are in my hands. I can't fall asleep.* His body obeyed. It would not fall back asleep. He would not let it. Jake opened his eyes again and held them open, stung by the light. Good. The pain would wake him up.

In the white and blue swirls above him Jake saw fleeting images of busy figures hovering about. One of them was mumbling and another nodded her head. Was this still a dream? No, he could feel the tension of the sheets against his toes. He also felt localized discomfort he couldn't identify, from an IV and catheter.

"Where am I," Jake tried to ask, but it came out garbled. The woman in white looked surprised.

"Mr. Woods. Glad you could join us."

"Where...?" Jake sensed the word coming out his mouth wasn't the one he was getting at. He hoped someone would fill in the blanks.

"You're in Lifeline Medical Center," said white dress. "It's Monday morning, about ten o'clock."

Jake considered this a few moments. Lifeline? That was where Doc worked, wasn't it? "Car...hit," he stammered. Yes, that was it. A car wreck. He and Finney and Doc were coming back with the pizza, Doc was screaming, he swerved and...

"Yes, Mr. Woods." The nurse's lips tightened. "There was a car wreck."

"What...How...?"

Jake didn't like the expression on her face. It was the look of a competent in-control professional faced with the prospect of bearing bad news.

"I think I should get the doctor to answer your questions, Mr. Woods. I'll be back in a moment." She walked out quickly, as if to outrun the sound of his voice in case it tried to follow her.

CHAPTER THREE

The moment seemed an hour. It was really four minutes. White dress was now accompanied by blue coat, a tall and commanding presence. There was someone else, someone smaller, who was almost hidden behind him. It was Sue, Finney's wife. Jake moved his head to the side, glad it obeyed his brain's command, and caught Sue's eye. Sue smiled at him, but the smile washed up out of a sea of pain, and the implicit message frightened Jake.

Blue coat cleared his throat as if everyone was waiting for gems of insight to fall off his lips, which hid beneath his thick brown mustache. He seemed slightly perturbed that Jake's eyes were on Sue rather than himself.

"Mr. Woods...Jake," blue coat said as if he wasn't reading it off the chart in front of him, which he was. *Are you going to tell me my blood type and impress me some more?* Jake had a way of sizing up people quickly, and for some reason he didn't like this doctor.

"I am Dr. Bradley." Jake sensed he was supposed to be impressed. He wasn't.

"You, Mr. Woods, have a renal contusion."

Jake waited for the explanation. It didn't come, suggesting anyone with a three digit IQ was supposed to get it.

"What does that mean?"

"It means you have a bruised kidney. You've still got blood in your urine, but it's subsiding. You also have some soft tissue injury, including neck and lumbar strain." Though Jake could figure this one out, Dr. Bradley was quick to add, "an injury to your lower back caused by the whiplash." He added with just a hint of a scold, "You also have a mild concussion that we're watching. Your injuries are considerable, but we think they'll heal without complications. Considering the condition of the vehicle, so I'm told, you're fortunate to be alive."

"Doctor...what about my friends?"

The doctor paused a moment too long. "Dr. Lowell has a fractured larynx. We intubated him...put a tube into his throat, to allow breathing, which is otherwise prevented by the swelling. We're administering steroids to reduce the swelling until he can breathe on his own. He's been given penathol. He's still unconscious." The doctor paused again, as if working up to something. "He also has some injury to his spinal chord. We're not sure how extensive. We won't run the necessary tests until we get his breathing under control." The dull pain in Jake's side got worse.

"The other individual," the doctor turned to hear the voice behind him, then turned back, "Yes, Mr. Finney." Another pause. "Yes, Mr. Finney *Keels* has a subdural hematoma."

"A what?"

The doctor looked up in the air as if searching for alternative expressions, straining to put the cookies on the lower shelf.

"There's a blood clot pressing on his brain. It's between his brain and skull, restricting proper blood flow."

Jake hesitated, then asked the question as if he were suddenly diving off a fifty foot cliff. "Will they live?" It was more than a question. It was a plea.

"Both are in critical condition. It's too early to say whether they will live. There are too many variables to take into account. In medicine you cannot just…"

Jake's dull ache spread within him to every corner of his body, drowning out the rest of the doctor's words, which meant nothing to him. His friends could die. For a moment he was three hundred miles away and thirty-five years younger, standing with Doc and Finney down by Benton Stream, pocketknife in hand, performing that silly blood brother ceremony they'd laughed about so often over the years, but cherished nonetheless. They'd survived so much, even Nam. And now…a stupid car accident?

Jake's focus abruptly returned to the room in the form of a threatening glare. He thought of vowing to write a column on physician incompetence, naming names, if either of his friends died. He realized this was irrational. The doctors would do everything they could to save Doc and Finney. Yet the adversarial feelings welled up inside. In desperate times, Jake was still a warrior, and warriors needed enemies to do battle with. If they couldn't find enemies, they made them. It gave them an obstacle to overcome, a reason to push on.

"Make sure they live, Doctor."

"Well, of course, the ICU staff is doing everything possible, but you have to understand…"

"You understand—they have to live." Jake said it in such a way that everyone knew the conversation was over. The high-control doctor, caught in a low-control situation, mumbled he had other patients to attend to and slunk out of the room.

Now Jake's view of Sue was unobstructed. She moved right in where the doctor had been. Even in her weakness, Sue emanated strength. Jake had seen it numbers of times, especially ten years ago when Sue and Finn's little Jenny had died at the hands of that drunk driver. Sue grieved deeply, but her trust was unshakable. She was a rock.

"Jake, you're just as ornery as ever." Sue's eyes sparkled. She loved to tease him, and the chance to do so was a welcome relief from the weight of her last eighteen hours. "After all these years working as a nurse, let me give you just a little piece of advice—threatening the doctors is generally not the way to endear yourself to the hospital staff."

"I just want them to take good care of my buddies."

"I know, Jake. Me too." Now her tears flowed freely. A few dropped on Jake's forearm, above his right hand which Sue now held tightly with both hers. Her tears were warm. The rock was soft and vulnerable.

Jake felt helpless. He'd never been good in the hard moments of life. He ran from people in pain, unless there was a story. But there was nowhere to run now.

The thought of a loved one's death paralyzed him. When his dad died, he never said anything to his mother. What was there to say? In Vietnam two men—no, boys—in his platoon had died, and as a young lieutenant he tried to write letters to their mothers and girlfriends, but never sent them. In the middle of these thoughts, Jake caught himself. *Finney and Doc aren't going to die. They can't die!*

Sue rested her head on her limply folded arms. Jake grew self-conscious about his own silence. If only Janet were here. She'd know what to say.

As if reading Jake's mind, Sue said, "I called Janet when you started waking up. She spent the night here, but had to go back this morning to take Carly to school. She's at work, but she's getting off early to come see you."

"Janet...spent the night here?"

"Sure she did, you big lug. She still loves you, you know."

There was no response. Jake couldn't begin to respond to that one. Three years they'd been divorced. He felt guilty life was easier without his wife and daughter. It was also much emptier, and perhaps that penance helped ease the guilt.

The nurse reappeared. "I'm sorry, Mrs. Keels. Mr. Woods needs his rest."

"Sure. Thanks for letting me see him." She glanced at Jake, and gave his hand a last squeeze. With an apologetic tone she pointed to Jake and said to the nurse, "He can be cranky, but after twenty years or so he kind of grows on you." Sue smiled back at him. Jake forced a grin. Both were in terrible pain.

Jake awoke again three hours later. He told the doctor he felt like eating and wanted to get up. He asked to have the IV and catheter removed. To his surprise, the doctor agreed. Thirty minutes later Jake tried to get up, but felt woozy, falling back on the bed. He tried again after a few minutes, and this time walked around the room until he could do it without buckling or grabbing the bed rail. He was practicing his best "I'm really okay" walk. He had a reason.

Once he sat and rested a few minutes, Jake rang for the nurse. He waited for what seemed like too long, then rang again. Twenty seconds later a busy but cheerful figure came sweeping into the room.

"Yes?" It was white dress, still on duty. "Did you have a good nap, Jake?"

This time he read her name badge, determined to prove his mental faculties. "Natalie," he said in his strongest voice. "I'm feeling really great now, and I'm getting claustrophobic in here. The doctor said it would be good to take a little walk in the hallway when I feel up to it. With your permission, that is."

The nurse looked at him skeptically. She checked the chart. "Well, your contusion doesn't appear to be severe. No sign the concussion's getting worse. You must be awfully sore. The doctor said it was okay to take a walk?"

Jake lied with a nod, and she shrugged her shoulders. "Sure you can handle it?"

Jake put forth his best effort, slid out of bed and stood there convincingly, posing as if he had just run the 100 meters in world record time, winded but fit, so how could anyone even think he might not be able to handle it?

"No problem, Nurse Natalie. I won't go far. Scout's honor." Jake the charmer.

A page out of Doc's book.

"No, you won't go far. Just around this nurses station here," she pointed outside. "A lap around that main desk is a hundred feet or so. Don't go any further. If you get tired, there's plenty of chairs. Just sit down. I've got other patients. Be back in ten minutes. Walk very slowly, okay?"

"Sure, Nurse Natalie. Take twenty minutes. In fact, I'll give you the rest of the day off." Natalie gave Jake an uncertain look, not sure yet how to read him. Just as she was reconsidering, a gray-haired nurse stuck her head in the room.

"I need your help with Mr. Sonfeld."

"Coming." With one last look at Jake, she said, "Behave yourself. Don't go far."

"Aye aye, Colonel," Jake said, saluting, but with no intention of obeying. Once out in the hall he looked for a floor plan. There it was, a cut-out in several colors. On the left side was an alphabetical list—Administration, Ambulatory Care, Anesthesiology. Jake skipped down the list. In-Patient Admissions, Infectious Diseases, Inhalation Therapy. *Ah, now we're cookin'*. Intensive Care Units. Third floor, east side of the building. Perfect. He was in 2294, east side. Only an elevator ride and a few hallways. Piece of cake.

Jake walked to and from the elevator with all the aplomb of a man who must have had a perfectly good reason for walking around at will wearing a hospital gown. He strolled cautiously yet naturally, or so he supposed, into Intensive Care's family waiting room. He expected to see Sue and Betsy. Neither was there. They'd probably stepped out for lunch. What remained in the waiting room were just a half dozen worn-out people with lots of lines on their faces, pretending to read magazines, while they hoped for miracles and waited for bad news.

Jake sat down and eyed his target, the door that said "Intensive Care Units." *Garamond*. Beneath were imposing block letters. AUTHORIZED PERSONNEL ONLY. *Helvetica Bold*, Jake thought, and chuckled at himself. Who but a newspaper man would ponder the typeface of a sign he was about to disobey?

Jake pretended to read a *Modern Maturity* magazine, while running reconnaissance on the room and door and figuring out his entry strategy. A doctor came in, pushed the red button on the panel next to the door, heard a voice over an intercom, identified himself, and entered. Just before the doctor opened the door, Jake stepped over to get another magazine. The doctor swung the door open wide enough that Jake could see the hallway leading to a hub of activity at the far end. The door shut quietly behind him and locked itself with a soft click. The doctor never looked back. Jake wished he'd followed right then, but knew it was better to survey the situation and figure out his tactics in advance. So he took his seat and bided his time.

Suddenly a doctor came out the locked door and went over to one of the mascara-smeared magazine readers, then in hushed tones explained her loved one's condition. Jake buried himself in the magazine, looking perfectly natural, other than being in bare feet and wearing a thin sissy dress that blew around every time a door shut or the furnace turned on. As the doctor headed back to the door, he flashed a suspicious look at Jake, followed by an atoning "have a nice day" smile when Jake looked him straight in the eyes. Jake's air of confidence won the moment.

As the doctor walked through the door, Jake covered the eight feet between them and grabbed the handle just before it clicked. He paused a few moments, peeked in, and saw only the doctor's back, receding down the hallway. Then he walked through. As he did, one man in the waiting room stared curiously, but Jake smiled and gave him a reassuring look. A background in investigative journalism paid off, especially when it came to sheer audacity and a penchant for faking it.

Jake walked near the right side of the wall. Cardiac Intensive Care Unit, Chest Surgery Intensive Care Unit, Dialysis Acute Care Unit, Respiratory ICU, Neonatal ICU. *Good grief, whatever happened to plain old ICU?* Jake eliminated dialysis and neonatal, and decided to start with the general sounding "Medical Intensive Care Unit," mostly because he could enter it without first parading by the nurses station at the hub. If it came to that he could try crawling under their line of sight, but the difference between combat fatigues and his flimsy gown made him hope that wouldn't be necessary.

He did wish he could have a quick look at the nurses station to find out his friends' room numbers, but any attempt to do so would guarantee a quick ticket out. He started room by room down Medical ICU. After six rooms with unfamiliar names and faces, Jake hit the jackpot. The name on the chart, plain vanilla Courier 12 pitch generated by a dot matrix printer, was "Gregory Victor Lowell." Otherwise known as Doc. Jake's heart raced as he stepped inside.

He expected to see Doc's familiar face, a face that always looked straight off the cover of *Gentleman's Quarterly*—sculptured, poised, tanned, confident. But what Jake saw was a pale plastic looking face, a mannequin with tubes coming out of it, a practice dummy for medical students. Obviously this was the wrong room. If this was a human being, it certainly wasn't Doc. And yet...

It *was* Doc. Head of the neighborhood, head of the class, head of the team, head of his squad, head of surgery. The head of everything, now shrunken and hollow. As helpless as a newborn child, as frail and dependent as an unborn. The tube coming out of his neck was his umbilical cord to life, attesting to his lack of viability. His life was utterly dependent on the will and expertise of others. Jake drew closer, looking at the pale skin with blue penciled veins. The thought that the spinal column injury could be permanent seemed more believable now. It hit Jake like a freight train. That would be worse than death for Doc. He'd be so embarrassed to see himself like this.

The chair near Doc surprised Jake. Doctors and nurses didn't sit, he thought, and visitors weren't allowed. He sat down gratefully, needing the rest. His hospital gown embarrassingly displayed some of his white parts. He pulled and tucked it, barely enough to avoid arrest for indecent exposure. Tentatively, with slight embarrassment, he reached out his hand to Doc's. Slap Doc on the back, kick him in the rear, punch him in the stomach, grab his hand to get up from the basketball court, yes. But Jake didn't ever remember holding Doc's hand, not like this. It felt cold and clammy, drained of life. None of Doc's strength was in this hand. It frightened Jake.

The face in front of him slowly resolved into Doc's face. Gazing at him took Jake back forty years to a younger, more pudgy face, with all the cuts and bruises of careless little boys. Jake eagerly recalled Doc's youthful escapades, knowing he deserved to be thought of in ways different than this.

Doc had been a Type A personality before anyone knew what that was, goal oriented and highly motivated. If Ulysses S. Grant High School had voted "Most Likely to Succeed" (it didn't), Doc would have won. Finney might come away with the silver, Jake maybe the bronze. But the gold medals always belonged to Doc.

One memory led to the next, like beads on a chain. Jake grunted out loud as he thought of Doc's homework. It had always been neat as a pin, rows lined up as if designed in drafting class rather than scrawled out early that morning. A left hander with an impossible wrist-breaking upside down writing posture, Doc produced manuscripts worthy of framing. Mr. Fieldstein, their seventh grade English teacher, joked that Doc's homework should be put in clay jars and set aside in a cave so future civilizations would be as impressed with mid-twentieth century America as scholars are with the Dead Sea Scroll community at Qumran. The kids didn't know anything about Qumran, but they were impressed. Everyone was always impressed with Doc. His handwriting remained meticulous, surviving the ultimate challenge—twenty years as a doctor. Doc was one of a kind.

Jake looked again at the chart hanging next to the bed. "Gregory Victor Lowell." The few who called him Doc were those who knew him long before he was a doctor. Jake remembered the day in eighth grade when Mr. Bailey asked everyone in the class to write down three possible future vocations in order of preference. Jake wrote down professional basketball player, ambassador to Australia, and writer. Beautiful blonde Joanie Miller, Jake's first girlfriend, wrote gymnast, teacher, and dress designer. The rest of the class spouted similar combinations of wishful and unlikely professions. But Gregory Victor Lowell simply wrote "Doctor." When Mr. Bailey pointed out he must write three vocations, Gregory promptly wrote "Doctor" two more times. Old man Bailey acted indignant, but Jake saw the corners of his mouth turn up in a suppressed smile. Teachers always seemed pleased with Doc. He always knew exactly what he wanted to be, and no more doubted whether he'd be a doctor than the rest of the class doubted whether they'd ride the school bus home that afternoon.

From that day forward Jake and Finney called their best friend "Doc." Students who wouldn't remember what they wrote down that day would never forget what Doc wrote. By taking home every academic award, as well as the "all around" awards because he was a great athlete, Doc reminded himself and everyone else he was the best. Jake and Finney collected a few awards themselves, but Jake always thought this was only because those in charge felt they couldn't give everything to Doc.

Jake straightened the top sheet on the hanging clipboard. Doc would want his little room here to look just right. He was meticulous not only in his homework, but—and this was most shocking to anyone who knew adolescent boys—his room was always immaculate. Every sock was matched in his drawers, and not because his mother did it. In fact, he had told her not to do it because so often she got it wrong. (At least, Doc recited two occasions when she had.) Jake and Finney always ribbed Doc that he didn't do a lick of work around the rest of the house, inside or outside, but poured all his efforts into his own room. Doc unapologetically said, "I don't care about the rest of the house. I care about my room." Once when Finney and Jake trashed his room as a joke, they found out the hard way how much he meant it.

Jake's own room had been such a pigsty it now left only a general nondescript image in his mind. He remembered what happened there, but it was all in the form of snapshots with no depth of field, where he didn't recall the details of the room's appearance. But Doc's room was so clean, the angles so sharp, everything so perfectly in place, it was forever etched in Jake's mind as a still picture, an ageless Ansel Adams photograph.

Jake remembered Doc walking tall, back straight, years before the military. He was always trying to stretch his 6'1" to 6'2". That posture made every step he took look purposeful. There was a measured and almost mechanical sense to his stride. Doc was a man of discipline and purpose. He was also a man who knew how to party. Doc once told Jake, "Put that on my tombstone, ol' buddy—'He knew how to party.'" *No, Doc. You'll make it. Hang in there—you've got to make it.*

The three musketeers went together to Bosworth College. Small college, high standards, great pride. You could play two sports. You had to be good, but not great. It was the Vietnam era, and something drew Jake and Finney to join ROTC. It wasn't just the rightness of the cause, though as America's brightest and best they cherished freedom and hated communism. They were competitors, fighters eager to stand for something, to test their mettle. Doc was in pre-med and figured to go straight to medical school from college, continuing his student deferment status. Their junior year Doc saw Jake and Finney's attentions move more and more to an exciting four years of proving their manhood in the military. Doc quietly weighed the fact that even with scholarships he'd have to work his way through med school, and face the distractions. He secretly talked to a recruiter. When he found out the GI Bill would help with medical school, he surprised and delighted his friends by joining them in ROTC, preparing to enter the army as an officer.

Initially they were stationed places far apart, one in the U.S., one in Germany, and one in Korea. They stayed in touch, any two of them intersecting on their leaves whenever they could. And then came the year in Vietnam. All three had gone in as second lieutenants, received the customary one-year promotion to first lieutenant, and were given their platoons of some thirty men. All three had excelled, each making captain by the time they left the army.

Jake's thoughts hovered a moment, then landed squarely on Finney. He always looked like a farm boy, strong and disciplined, built like a fire plug, but quick and agile. His 5'10" frame carried 190 pounds like it was 150. He knew how to drink, how to fight, and he knew all about loyalty. In Nam you had to trust guys with your life. Jake often wished he could pull Finney into his own company, and Doc too. Yet coming together to share their stories and out drink each other a few times at Division headquarters—and above all that glorious week in Bangkok—was somehow even better. It was a way of proving themselves, each as leaders in their own right, as equals understanding the responsibilities and privileges of command.

Finney and Doc. Doc and Finney. *Finney!* Suddenly Jake realized he'd been daydreaming, forgetting part two of his mission. He had to find Finney. He felt like the plate spinner at the circus, hoping that if he could go back and forth between his friends perhaps he could keep either from dying.

Jake squeezed Doc's hand. He could almost hear him say, "Don't get weird on me now, Buddy," or, "Save your affection for the ladies, will ya?" Jake smiled the numb smile of crisis, and quickly left the room to find Finney. His head spinning, side aching, and feeling nausea at his sudden movement, Jake turned into the hall-way from Doc's room and ran straight into a man in surgical blues, nearly knocking both of them to the floor.

"What's going on? Who are you? What were you doing in there?"

"Sorry, doctor." Jake didn't feel repentant, but overtures of repentance seemed the best strategy to accomplish his goal. "Doc, I mean Greg Lowell, is one of my best friends. I just had to see him."

The doctor studied Jake's face. Then the light turned on.

"You're Jake Woods, aren't you? Greg introduced me to you at Halley's Bar and Grill a few years ago, remember? Barry Simpson. We had some drinks together. I read your column."

Jake didn't remember, but then, Doc had introduced him to lots of people in lots of bars over lots of drinks, and bar memories were usually the most vague. "Sure, I remember you, Dr. Simpson." Maybe Jake could trade that one night of bar bonding for a ticket to see Finney.

"I heard you were in the accident with Greg, you and another guy."

"Yeah, that's Finney. He's in here too. He and Doc and I have always been thick, since we were kids. Played ball together. Same college. Same battalion in Nam."

"Listen, I won't say anything about you coming in here unauthorized, but you've really got to get out. You don't look that great yourself. I'll have you taken back to your room in a wheelchair."

"Doctor, look, I know I've overstepped the boundaries, but I've got to ask a favor. Could you let me go see Finney just for a few minutes? Then I promise I'll go right back to my room."

"No way. I can't let you in there."

Jake tried to look pathetic enough to change the man's mind, but he was already making plans to sneak back in if he had to. He'd borrow some surgical blues and come in undercover, if that's what it took.

"Please, doctor. Only for a minute. It's killing me not to see him."

The doctor's face softened. "Well, Greg was a colleague—I mean, is a col-league. And I suppose he'd bend the rules to let you see your friend." Simpson said it as if Doc's rule bending was legendary. "I guess I can do it, but let's be quick about it. I think your friend's in the next hall. Let's go."

Dr. Simpson started to escort Jake from the room, just as a nurse came around a corner to check in on Doc. Simpson stopped suddenly in front of the nurse, whose badge said "Robin."

"Dr. Lowell's fine, nurse. I just checked him. This guy was in his room. I want you to get on top of security in this whole unit! If he could just walk in, anybody could come in off the street!"

Nurse Robin gave a wide-eyed, "Yes, doctor" and marched to the nurses station to pass on his lecture on ICU security.

As they walked to Finney's room, Jake now remembered Simpson. He'd come into the bar after Jake and Doc's second or third beer. The three had swapped stories, impressed each other and complained about women. Especially about complaining women. And about how a lot of women seemed madder at men now than back in the seventies before men started trying so hard to please them. It went from what was it women wanted, anyway, to who gives a rip, to let's have a few more beers. A typical happy hour with three modern professional males, as Jake recalled.

When they entered the room, both Jake and the doctor were surprised to see the petite brown-haired woman holding Finney's hand. Sue turned to the men, raised her eyebrows admiringly at Jake, and said to Dr. Simpson, "I'm Sue Keels, Finney's wife. I'm also an emergency room nurse. Dr. Milhall let me in. I'm not in the way, Doctor."

"Yes, no doubt." Dr. Simpson didn't sound convinced. "Mr. Keels has persistent friends and family, I'll say that for him. We can't seem to keep them away regardless of the rules."

"If you knew him, you'd understand why." Sue looked at the bedraggled, scantily clad journalist, trying to keep from laughing. "Jake, good to see you. How are you?"

Before Jake could answer, Dr. Simpson said, "I caught him sneaking around ICU. He needs to get back to his room. We're on our way."

"Let him sit here with me, Doctor. I can take care of both of them. I've got eighteen years as a nurse, including a few in ICU."

"I can see you're as stubborn as Mr. Woods here." Jake welcomed Simpson's air of resignation.

"Yes, Doctor. Maybe more so." Sue smiled, but she wasn't kidding.

"All right, I've got surgery. No more time for this nonsense. I'll tell the nurses to give you fifteen minutes, Mr. Woods. That's all. Then they wheel you back to your own room. You try this again and we'll strap you down. Deal?"

"Deal. Thanks."

The doctor grabbed another chair from the corner of the room and set it down, not so gently, for Jake. "Don't mention it. That's what we're here for, right? Who cares about rules and policies? Excuse me while I go try to be a doctor instead of a hall monitor!" He was gone.

Sue pursed her lips and raised her eyebrows at Jake. "I have this way with people," he explained. Both chuckled, like people who needed to.

Jake eyed Sue's big leather Bible in her hands. It always looked out of proportion, Sue so small and the book so big. She stood up and moved her chair so Jake could pull alongside her, closer to Finney. The two sat quietly, saying nothing and focusing their thoughts and hopes on Finney.

Finnegan Douglas Keels. Friendly to a fault. Open heart and open hand. A vagrant prospecting for a handout would always approach him first. Broad shoulders, the look of an athlete. No longer the washboard stomach he once had, but as fit as any fifty-year-old had the right to be. His hair hadn't changed since high school, except the graying temples. Short, wavy, the straight cut of the ex-athlete, ex-soldier.

You're an institution, Finn. The Berlin Wall could come down, the Yankees could finish last, but Finney would always be there. Like the rising sun, like the stars, something you could set your watch by. A beacon. A lighthouse. And sometimes a major pain in the rear.

Finney's laugh. That's what was so conspicuously absent from this tomb-like room. Finney's great, powerful, heartfelt laugh. A laugh that was always spontaneous, never self-conscious. He didn't notice and didn't seem to care if people turned and looked, as if a laugh was never something to apologize for. It was the laugh of someone who enjoyed life. But here he was, teetering on life's edge, threatening to fall over the other side. Jake could sense it. Finney was further gone than Doc.

Finney's thick shoulders seemed so out of place in a sick bed. Those shoulders had been there for a lot of people. For the Cambodian family the Keels had adopted. For the pregnant girls they'd opened their home to. For hungry people overseas who were fed from an established percentage of the profits from Finney's business. Finney was the kind of guy people instinctively trusted and opened up to. Jake remembered that store clerk who poured out her heart to Finney after he saw something in her eyes and asked if he could help. Finney was at his best with people who were serving, those who were used to being under-appreciated and pushed around and told what to do. They could tell Finney respected and appreciated them. He always said "thank you." He always left a generous tip but never expected them to trade their dignity or sincerity to get it. He always said the thing that set them at ease, that made them feel equals rather than subordinates.

Like that waitress at Corey's who spilled coffee on him. Finney assured her everything was fine, as if he'd often been scalded by his waitress. Jake was surprised it hadn't done more damage, that fresh steaming cup of coffee straight on his lap. Later Janet talked to Sue and learned the skin on his thigh had been badly burned, and he was in pain for days afterward. But he didn't let the girl see that, didn't even tell Jake or Doc. Jake watched carefully as they were leaving. Finney put down a five dollar bill. The lunch had come to maybe nineteen dollars and he'd left a five-dollar tip. It was his way of saying, "Everything's okay, don't worry about it. Sorry you had to go through the embarrassment."

Jake realized, as he looked at Finney's weak body, that he'd spent his life watching him, studying him. And Doc too. Part of Jake's success as a journalist came from his ability to observe, to capture the essence of a man in details and incidents others didn't notice or thought inconsequential. He could write a book on these two guys.

Then there was the other side of Finney, the troubling, infuriating side. His self-assured manner about his beliefs. His clearly defined concept of right and wrong that sent such a judgmental message. Some were offended when they learned 10 percent of profits from his software business went back into the four crisis pregnancy centers in the area. Planned Parenthood and National Organization of Women cooperated in boycotting his business. But Finney wouldn't back down. Some people admired him for it. Doc thought he was a fool. Jake argued he was just being stubborn. "Why not just back down gracefully and cut your losses, so you'll have more to give to any cause you want?" But Finney wouldn't listen.

During that flap Ryan Dennard, Jake's columnist colleague at the *Tribune,* labeled Finney "a right-wing fundamentalist preacher in a business suit." It was one thing to have your beliefs at church, it was another to bring them into your business and community. That was forcing your religion on others.

Jake once told Finney, "I know you're sincere, but you've got to think of image and perceptions. If you want to sell people on your values, you've got to tone it down! Otherwise you'll be painted with the same brush as David Koresh or any other religious nut. And you'll have no one to blame but yourself."

Still, Jake knew that while most people covered up and explained away their shortcomings, and blamed them on others, Finney admitted his and worked hard to change them. You could disagree with Finney—and half the time Jake did—but if you knew him, you couldn't dismiss him.

Finnegan Douglas Keels. No one called him Finnegan but his mom. He was born to be Finney. And he would die Finney. *O God, please don't let him die.*

This man lying there was and yet somehow was not the same Finney Jake grew up with, the Finney he knew in Nam. It had been four years after the war that the new Finney had emerged. After the army Finney went to his grandparents' home in Indiana, where his mom had moved. Two years later he married Sue. He and Sue and baby daughter Jenny moved back to Oregon to be near his buddies and start a business. Doc was half way through medical school, Jake was getting his master's degree and working part-time at a newspaper. Finney saved up his money and opened his office products store, a forerunner to the computer software business he'd turned into a gold mine. The three old friends worked hard and played hard. The familiar chemistry hadn't lost its magic. Their wives became almost as close as the men, their young children played and grew together.

Then came the change—Finney's conversion. Doc wanted nothing to do with this zealous and dogmatic new Finney, and at times Jake shared the sentiment. But Finney wouldn't let go of his friendships. Jake discovered the new Finney had all the qualities that made the old Finney so special. He had the same wit, the same humor and something else. A kindness and sensitivity. The big heart that was even bigger. A confidence. A sense of faith and trust. A peace. And a purpose.

When Jake's dad died, it was Finney who was there for him. Then Finney and Sue had their third child, after Jenny and Angela. They'd been warned something was wrong. The baby had Down's Syndrome. Their doctor recommended an abortion. Rather than give up on the baby, they gave up on the doctor. And when he was born, the most amazing thing happened, something Jake never got over. They named him Finney, Jr.

Only a few years later Jenny had died. It still made Jake sick to think about it. Little Jenny, taken out by a stupid drunk. Thoughts of death seemed to keep coming at Jake, and he tried in vain to push those thoughts away. He dared not allow death to take hold in this room.

Jake's inner world was interrupted suddenly by a distinct and familiar voice, spoken with a thick tongue that couldn't quite pronounce the words.

"Hi dere, Unca Jake!" Jake was so absorbed in his thoughts he hadn't notice Sue slip out of the room. Now she'd returned with Little Finn.

"Hi there, Little Finn." For Little Finn it was never just "hi." It was "hi there," with his inimitable accent. Jake was always glad to see him.

"Daddy had uh accident."

"Yeah, he did, Little Finn."

"And you were wid him, weren't you, Unca Jake?"

"Yeah, I was."

"What was it like?"

"The accident? It's hard to remember. It happened so fast."

"Unca Jake...do you dink my daddy is gonna die?"

"No, no, he'll be okay, Little Finn."

"Well, da doctors say he could probly die."

"Well, I think the doctors are wrong."

"I hope he doesn't die. But if he does, he'll be in heaven, ya know."

Simple Little Finn. The faith of a child. If only it were so simple.

"Don't talk like that, Little Finn. He'll make it. I promise he'll make it." Finn gave Jake a curious look, as if wondering how he could make such a promise.

"Know what I told Dada dis morning? I told him if he dies to be sure and give my sister Jenny a big hug, and tell her it's from me." Little Finn looked very proud for having the foresight to think of this. "Mama says he probly heard me, cause people in hospital beds always hear more dan we dink. Right, Mama?"

"Right, Finn." For a moment Sue looked weak, like a withering flower. "Finn, I need to read to your Dad now, so you listen, okay?" Sue situated her big Bible just right, so the back touched against Finney's chest. "This is from the last two chapters of Revelation."

"Revelation is da last book of da whole Bible," Finn whispered loudly to Jake, his head bobbing and his eyes big, emphasizing just how important this information was. Jake nodded soberly, and Sue smiled as she often did at the interactions between the two.

Jake faded in and out, catching snatches of what Sue was reading. "Then I saw a new heaven and a new earth, for the first heaven and the first earth had passed away....And I heard a loud voice from the throne saying, 'Now the dwelling of God is with men, and he will live with them. They will be his people and God himself will be with them and be their God. He will wipe every tear from their eyes. There will be no more death or mourning or crying or pain, for the old order of things has passed away.'"

Sue paused to look at Finney's face, seeing a large tear that had formed in his right eye. As if on cue to the verse she'd just read, Sue reached over with her tissue and wiped away Finney's tear. Then she kissed him softly on the corner of his mouth, whispering "I love you, Finney."

She continued reading, while Jake wandered in and out of grade school, Benton Stream, high school, summer jobs, college, Vietnam, and Sunday's coin flip. Sue's voice seemed to build, to take on a strength not its own, as if energized by the big book. Jake looked up to see her finger pointing at a verse within a few paragraphs of the Bible's last words. Little Finn leaned forward, listening breathlessly. Jake decided to listen a bit more closely himself.

Sue read, "Behold, I am coming soon! My reward is with me, and I will give to everyone according to what he has done. I am the Alpha and the Omega, the First and the Last, the Beginning and the End. Blessed are those who wash their robes, that they may have the right to the tree of life and may go through the gates into the city. Outside are the dogs, those who practice magic arts, the sexually immoral, the murderers, the idolaters and everyone who loves and practices falsehood."

Jake cringed. This book seemed so full of hope for some, so condemning of others.

"Whoever is thirsty, let him come; and whoever wishes, let him take the free gift of the water of life."

Suddenly a loud gasp filled the air. Startled, Sue and Jake looked at each other, each thinking the gasp came from the other. They turned to Little Finn, on the other side of the bed, leaning over his father. There was Finney, his head lifted six inches off the pillow, eyes wide open, looking intently at something beyond the room, beyond the moment. Finney gasped again, his lips suddenly turned up in that patented grin, and for a moment he was full of life. Just as quickly his head fell back to the pillow.

Jake felt something like a brush of wind. His spine tingled with the eerie sensation someone had just left the room.

Finney was gone.

CHAPTER FOUR

H e stood immersed in the passageway's twilight, unable to decide which direction to go. At one end, the closest, was a murky shadowy light, at the far end the brightest light he'd ever seen, yet not a light that hurt his eyes, but drew them. He sensed excitement and activity from beings at both ends, one excitement surrounded by uncertainty and longing, the other by certainty and fulfillment. He remembered what lay beyond the passageway's near end, the murky one from which he'd come. But he wasn't sure what awaited him at the other. The explorer in him tingled with anticipation as he considered the mystery end—be it exit or entrance—from which a magnetic pull beckoned him to come join the radiance.

Finney felt his energy being siphoned off, his body growing weaker. He sensed efforts being made, whirring machines and tubes of fluids desperately trying to keep him from leaving his old world. Strangely, though, he felt energized, as if the dynamism siphoned off his body was draining back into a vast energy supply somewhere else, from which it had come. He felt less and less connected to his body. He was a fighter, a survivor, a soldier who would never easily let go of life. But that was just the thing—what awaited him at the other end of the passageway was not lack of life, but Life itself. Not an end, but a beginning. He could feel it. Its power and lure were palpable, almost overwhelming. He was a ship on a stormy sea, caught between two ports, unsure which he could reach. But the storm itself seemed to be making the decision for him. That was all right because, strangely, he trusted the storm. His course was now out of his hands.

Though his eyes were closed, Finney could periodically, just for a moment, sense the light through his eyelids. He'd heard voices from time to time, ever since he'd been here. At first they were all unfamiliar voices—concerned, professional, muffled. When he heard that first familiar voice, that beautiful voice, it infused him with strength, so much so that for a moment he thought it enough to bring him back. He couldn't hear every word, but he caught many phrases, including "I love you, Finney."

He wanted to say "I love you, Sue," but his mind couldn't make his lips move any more than it could lift his eyelids. He was trapped within a mutinous body that no longer took his orders. So he just listened, unable to give to Susan, able only to receive from her. He received, thankfully.

Beautiful Sue. He could see her clearly in his mind's museum of film clips, exactly as he first saw her when he was a high school sophomore and she an eighth grader, at Brady's Roller Rink in that little town, hidden from the rest of the world in the Willamette Valley. He relived the sights and sounds and silliness and youthful exuberance of the "All Skate," the smell of cotton candy blended with buttered popcorn and the inimitable flavor of the "graveyard" mix of cola and orange and 7-Up. Now came the feelings of dread at the "Couples Only" where he finally asked Sue to skate with him, and his excitement when she said "yes." They didn't marry till his last year in the army, the year after Vietnam. Sue. He basked in her quiet presence next to him.

Soon there came another voice, like Sue's but higher, with fewer years and fewer life experiences behind it, but with her mother's incisive mind and wit. A voice full of wonder, and full of fear.

"Daddy, it's me, Angela. I hope you can hear me. I love you." Her voice broke. "I've been praying for you. Everybody's praying for you."

Angela. In love with life, twenty-one years old, married less than a year, but still and forever Finney's little girl. They'd always been close, but since Jenny died when Angie was eleven, they'd been inseparable. There was a pause and some sobs, and words of comfort from Sue to Angela that Finney couldn't quite make out.

"Please get better. You're the best Daddy in the world. When you get out of the hospital, I'll make you your favorite beef stew. Just the way you like it. You know how you always say I make it better than anybody? And I'll make those cornbread muffins, too. And we'll play tennis, and I'll let you beat me. Oh, Daddy."

Finney felt Angela's head fall gently on his chest. She abruptly lifted it, perhaps thinking it could impair his breathing. *No, honey, keep your head right there. I want to feel you against me.* Finney was disappointed not to hear his own voice, because he knew it meant Angela couldn't hear him either.

After a few minutes of silence, Sue said, "Finney, I'm taking out Angie and then I'm coming back with Little Finn. They won't let all three of us in here at once. Angie will come back later."

"Bye, Daddy. I'll see you soon." That voice so precious to Finney carried two loads—one hope, the other anguish.

Good-bye, Angela. I will see you soon...one way or the other.

Silence prevailed, releasing him to drift from that end of the passageway toward the other. Angela's words renewed his resolve to try to stay in the old world, not for his sake but for hers and his family's. The other world reached out to him, gripping him with growing strength. If the choice were his, and nothing but his own welfare was at stake, it would be no more difficult than the choice between a bright sunny ocean beach and the dark shadows of a crime-infested slum. But he knew the prerogative over life and death wasn't his. The choice belonged to Another. He was glad, because this was the only way he could be sure the choice was right.

Soon another voice drew Finney back to the entry point, a voice beautiful in a different way than Sue's and Angela's. This voice belonged to a boy, still high pitched but bubbling with youthful masculinity. For a moment Finney hesitated, looking over to the far end of the passageway, thinking he'd been mistaken, that this special voice came from there, from the world beyond. It had an unearthly quality. But no, it couldn't be. In his mind's eye, Finney turned again to the entry end, the world he'd come from, and listened attentively to the voice.

"Hi dere, Dada. Mama says maybe you can hear me and maybe you can't, so I should just talk like I dink you can. Is dat okay wid you?"

Finney smiled, wondering if the smile made its way to his lips. *It's more than okay with me, bud.* The words stayed at the level of thought. Finney finally resigned himself to the fact that the road between his thought and speech had been washed out.

"I was at Martin's house when Mama called me from da hospital right after the football game an said dere was uh accident. Martin's Mom, Mrs. Janic, she drove me to da hospital. She didn't know if she should park in da mergency place or by da big doorway. She said she didn't want to get in trouble or park in a doctor's space or get towed or nothin'. Finally she said 'Shucks, I don't give a darn, I'm just going to park it here.' Really, Dada, she didn't say dat exac'ly. She swore, but Mama told me I shouldn't repeat da swear words. She's a nice lady and I never heard her swear before, but Mama said she was just scared or somethin'. I've heard Martin swear a few times, but not too bad. Mama says you didn't get to see da second half cause of da accident. So I'll just tell ya all about it since ya didn't see it or nothin', okay?"

Yes, Little Finn, tell me all about it. Finney didn't care about the game. He cared very much about hearing this precious voice, as inviting as a stream of cold water to a hot and thirsty hiker. It didn't matter where it flowed, only that it did. Little Finn talked on and on, holding Finney as close as he could get to that end of the passageway.

Finally he heard a kind and only vaguely familiar voice. "He needs to rest. You can see him later."

Let them stay. They're the only rest I need. Finney said it, but no one heard.

How much time passed Finney didn't know, because he was between a world with time and a world without it. This was an odd feeling, but not unpleasant. His sense of anticipation deepened as he heard music, singing, conversations, and laughter at the other end. Remarkable laughter. Not like the response to a joke's punch line, where there's a moment of delight before returning to a world of burdens, but the spontaneous laughter of sheer joy that shows no signs of stopping, uninhibited by the dark cloud of stark reality. People always remarked about Finney's hearty laugh. But this laughter was something more, something enchanting, alluring, enticing. It made him want to run full speed to the other end and leap unreservedly into it, losing himself in the wonder beyond.

Finney was torn between two worlds. He longed for the anchor to the old world to be pulled up, freeing his ship to sail to the new shore, to step forth as Columbus or Magellan on new land, and above all to meet the inhabitants of that land. He longed for the labor pains to end, for the birth to take place, for the umbilical cord to the old world to be cut at last.

Finney lost himself in thought, wondering if the memories of this time would fade if he went back out to live the rest of his life on earth. Would the sensations and distractions of that world cause him to lose touch with the experiences and insights here in the passageway? He earnestly hoped not.

Suddenly Finney embarked on a strange adventure. He was now viewing what seemed to be a motion picture of his entire life on earth. He thought it must have been edited for it to pass so swiftly before him, yet it seemed complete, every life incident intact. Somehow he was able to comprehend it. He saw it with the objectivity of an outsider. He very much liked some things he saw, and disliked terribly other things. The life portrait began in a dark and warm place, a secure enclave, where at first he could see only a subdued opaque sort of light, and could only hear muffled sounds and a steady reassuring pounding noise nearby. His mind raced through the cinema at a torrid pace, like a fallen leaf down powerful rapids. He felt he should be dizzy, yet Finney was able to thoughtfully view it as if it were a course summary at the end of the term.

"I'm Sue Keels, Finney's wife. I'm also an emergency room nurse. Dr. Milhall's been letting me stay here with him. I'm not in the way, Doctor."

"Yes, no doubt," came the unfamiliar voice. "Mr. Keels has persistent friends and family, I'll say that for him. We can't seem to keep them away regardless of the rules."

"If you knew him, you'd understand why," Sue said.

That's Sue, Finney thought. *So loving and loyal. More than I ever deserved. Thank you, Lord.*

"Jake, good to see you. How are you?"

Jake! In here? Then you're okay, old buddy!

The unfamiliar voice said, "I caught him sneaking around ICU. He needs to get back to his room. We're on our way."

The thought of Jake sneaking up and down corridors like a commando tickled Finney. His clarity of thought surprised him. Weak as his body was, he was hearing everything, as if the dramatic presentation of his life that ended not long ago had sharpened his touch with his former world. If only he could open his eyes and see as clearly as he was hearing. But Sue's and Jake's faces were so clearly etched in his mind's eye he didn't need to see them.

Silence reigned again. Finney could sense Sue's presence very close to him, as she held his hand and stroked his cheek. He breathed in her perfume. Its scent was inseparable from her. He could sense her silent prayers, almost hearing the words forming in her mind. At one point Sue let go of his hand and a larger tougher hand awkwardly took its place. It was Jake. Finney knew this must be hard on him. He prayed, *Father, help Jake through this. Show yourself to him. Give him the grace to turn to you.*

Finney didn't know how he could be alert enough to understand all this, yet so weak he couldn't make Sue and Jake know he was there. The thought occurred to him that he was separating from his body, and every inch his body was losing, his soul was gaining. He felt as if he were an egg timer turned upside down, leaving only a short time until the last grain of sand that was his life would move from one receptacle to another. Suddenly another voice jerked him back to the room.

"Hi dere, Unca Jake."

Little Finn!

"I hope he doesn't die. But if he does, he'll be in heaven, ya know." Affection and pride warmed Finney.

"Don't talk like that, Little Finn. I promise he'll make it."

The decision isn't yours, Jake.

"Know what I told Dad dis morning? I told him if he dies to be sure and give my sister Jenny a big hug, and tell her it's from me. I told him not to forget. Mama says he probly heard me, because people in hospistal beds always hear more than we dink. Right, Mama?"

"Right, Finn."

Right, Finn. I'm hearing everything, at least for now. I don't remember hearing you say to hug Jenny, but somehow I knew you'd said it. I won't forget, Little Finn. I won't forget.

"Finn, I need to read to your Dad now, so you listen, okay?" Finney felt the gentle comforting weight of Sue's Bible leaning up against him. He could smell the old worn pages mixed with her perfume, creating the most beautiful hybrid fragrance.

"This is from the last two chapters of Revelation."

"Revelation is da last book of da whole Bible." Finney smiled, though his lips didn't move. He guessed Sue was smiling too. Yes, she was smiling. But how could he see her when his eyes were closed? He listened intently as Sue read of a new heaven and new earth, and the promise that God would forever be with his people. He knew who awaited him on the other side, and the very thought moved him to tears, good tears, right at the moment Sue read, "He will wipe every tear from their eyes."

Suddenly Sue stopped reading. Finney longed for her to continue. He faintly felt something, perhaps a tissue, on his face, miles away from him. Was he crying? Yes, now he could see his own face, as if above it, looking down. He saw the back of her hand as Sue wiped away his tear.

The words of God penetrated him, electrified him. Finney understood them better in his present state than when his body was functioning normally. Perhaps part of it was there was nothing to distract him. Thoughts of business and travel and yard work were gone. Distractions of television and radio and the morning paper, of telephone and computers had no place here. There was nothing to focus on now but what was worthy of his focus—the very words of God.

Sue continued to read, "Behold, I am coming soon! My reward is with me, and I will give to everyone according to what he has done."

Finney's crystal clear perspective on the room below startled him. This was not imaginary. The images grew more vivid by the moment, his vision improving rather than fading. He could see Little Finn's cowlick, and Jake's slight bald spot, and the pages of Sue's Bible which were facing away from his body lying on the bed, but toward him as he hovered invisibly above. Like a dry sponge he soaked up every word Sue read, all the while feeling as if a powerful winch cable was tightening, ready at a moment's notice to pull him beyond the reach of earth's gravity.

Abruptly he realized that in moving away from the hospital room, he was moving toward the other end of the passageway. And he was not alone. Someone was escorting him. Not coming to get him, but leaving earth with him. It was a huge and powerful being, looking like a man but somehow different, with placid but purposeful face, striding like a nobleman warrior. He looked battle-worn. Finney sensed he should know this being. But thoughts of the one beside him faded as the voices and images at the other end became more vivid and alluring. What had been background noises and movements now shifted to the foreground. The sound of Sue reading in the room was still clear and captivating, but the volume diminished to a whisper while he hung on every word.

"Whoever is thirsty, let him come; and whoever wishes, let him take the free gift of the water of life."

Finney's head jerked forward and let out a gasp of wonder. This time it bridged the gap between thought and action, erupting into the room. In his peripheral vision he saw a startled Sue, Jake and Little Finn, but his eyes looked not at the old world but at a new one. Suddenly the tent stakes had been pulled, the ropes to the boat landing untied. Finney was cut loose.

He moved beyond and above the room, seeing Angela in the waiting room with her husband, her head bowed. Though her prayers for him were silent, he could clearly hear them, every word. He wanted to go to her, to hold her hand for the last time before his exodus, but he could not. He said "good-bye" to his loved ones, though he knew they could not hear him. At the same time he realized this was not the end of relationship, but only an interruption. Today's inadequate good-bye in this place would be followed by a wondrous hello in another. And though he did not know what the place he was going would look like, everything in him was eager to go find out.

Finney could now see many excited images at the far edge, some reaching in toward him. The other, his mysterious companion, now marched ahead of him. The giant slipped out the passageway's end artfully, as if he'd done this before, and moved immediately to the side. Another great being greeted the giant with what appeared to be a salute. Finney moved more slowly, more tentatively, like his first time on water skis. This was the first time he'd ever died.

The crowd visible beyond the passageway grew with each step he took. Some faces he did not recognize, many he did. He took the last step—or was it the first—and entered the new world. As he came out the end—or was it the beginning—over the threshold, he gasped his first breath of heaven's air. The gasp was a gasp of wonder at the beauty of this place, and the magnificence of its inhabitants. His only earthly experience he could compare to it was the first time he'd been snorkeling, in the Red Sea, when he went beneath the surface and saw the incredible multicolored beauty of the ocean and its wondrous inhabitants. He remembered that loud startling sound very near him, then the realization it was the sound of his own gasp in his snorkel. This was such a gasp, but as much greater than that on earth as the place he was now seeing was greater than that marvelous underwater world.

Many hands grabbed Finney's, which he stretched out toward them, as if to confirm they were real. He must have some sort of body, since he could feel their touch. This struck a chord of familiarity. It had happened before. Or something very much like it. Yes, of course, when he was born into the other world. The passageway had been the birth canal between earth and heaven. And these were the midwives of heaven, supervising his birth, pulling him into the world, fussing over him and proudly presenting him to his new family. This was the real world, which he'd been no more capable of imagining before than an unborn child can imagine the infinite wonders that lie beyond the womb.

There to greet him was a beaming female face he was sure he knew, yet how could he, for it was so bright and beautiful, more majestic than any face he'd seen until that moment. This must be someone holding a place of great honor here. Finney was accustomed to recognizing body first and character second. But here it was the character, somehow coming out, that made him then recognize the body. At that very moment he heard his name on her lips—"Finnegan!"

"Mom!" The others cheered and laughed and nodded.

"Welcome, Finnegan." His mother's flowing tears surprised him, but apparently tears of joy had a place here. She threw her arms around him, and he embraced her tightly. He'd missed her so much. He remembered with joy the role he'd played in sharing the good news with her, as she had shared her life with him. She was there to give birth to him and embrace him after his entrance on earth. And here she was now, the first to embrace him in heaven.

Part of him, the part still fresh from earth's air of skepticism, could not believe anything so wonderful could be true. Being new to this place, he didn't yet understand that things which are true are by their nature wonderful, and things that are truly wonderful are inevitably true. He kept hugging his mother and wanted to talk with her, but with all the others surrounding him, he had to content himself to talk only briefly for the moment. It was much as the bride and groom cannot have lengthy conversations with each other in the reception line after the wedding, but know there will be time ahead for that. The rest of heaven's welcoming committee, hundreds of people hand picked for the new arrival, swarmed around him like bees around the queen.

Finney looked at his welcoming party and wondered if they were wearing special attire or if this was simply the standard dress of heaven. Yet actually he wasn't sure this was clothing at all. It seemed at first like white robes, dazzlingly bright yet not hurtful to his eyes. But each person's appearance was distinctly different from the other. The similarity spoke of their shared purity and common Lord, and the differences of their unique personalities and gifts and histories. But the clothing, if that's what it was, seemed more an organic growth from the body than separate apparel. Rather than concealing, it seemed designed to reveal something which on earth would have been hidden within. When he looked at an individual, as he did dozens and dozens of them now, one after the other, he seemed to see so much more than he'd ever seen before. On earth the outward appearance could deceive and often did. But here the outward appearance seemed to reflect and draw attention to the inner person, to his or her character. And somehow Finney caught hints and impressions of the person's unique background and history.

A chorus of welcomes sang out, some in languages he didn't know, but all of which he instinctively understood. Each bid him come in, make himself at home. He felt like a miner rescued from a collapsed cavern and emerging to excited well-wishers in the land of the living. Except this was his first time here, and he wasn't sure how things worked. But he knew he was going to have the time of his life finding out.

At the fringes of the crowd stood a group of a dozen beings who seemed to be of the same race as the towering figure who left the hospital room with him. At the back of the crowd stood one being glowing with a soft light that did not blind, but attracted and captivated the eyes. He smiled at Finney, who trembled with joy at the immediate realization of who it was. To this moment he'd stood quietly, absorbing all this, delighting in it, smiling knowingly as if he were the one who'd arranged it. And, indeed, Finney knew he had done just that.

This was the ageless one, the Ancient of Days, who is eternally young. He stepped forward, and at his first move the crowd quickly and reverently made way for him, as flimsy shacks make way for a hurricane. This was a good hurricane, but no one mistook goodness for weakness here. He who had spun the galaxies into being with a single snap of his finger, he who could uncreate all that existed with no more than a thought, extended his hand to Finney, as if the hand he extended was that of a plain ordinary carpenter. Everyone knew he was anything but ordinary. His riveting eyes commanded their full attention. All eyes were fixed on those eyes. For the moment, it was impossible to look elsewhere, and no one in his right mind would have wanted to.

"Welcome, my son! Enter the kingdom prepared for you, by virtue of a work done by another, a work you could not do. Here you shall receive reward for those works you did in my name, works you were created to do."

And then, with a smile that communicated more than any smile Finney had ever seen, the Great One looked into his eyes and said with obvious pride, "Well done my good and faithful servant. Enter into the joy of your Lord!"

As the crowd broke out in cheers, Finney felt overwhelmed, and dropped to his knees, then flat on the ground, face down, as if the knees were still too lofty a position before the Lord of Heaven. Out of the corner of his eye he saw everyone else follow his lead and fall flat. Mostly this was out of respect for the one before whom they bowed, but Finney also sensed the emulation of his form of worship was out of respect for him, perhaps as the new arrival, the party's guest of honor.

"Rise, my son. You bowed your knee to me in the other world, where it was much harder to do so. I know your devotion, and I treasure it. Stand now before me. You have made your exodus from mortality to life. This is a new world, which I've made for you to enjoy." Finney rose up and the welcoming committee rose too, a half step behind him.

Finney gazed into those eyes that could have killed him with a look, but which instead conveyed unmistakable approval. But he could also sense something more in those great eyes, something different than he would have expected. And then Finney's gaze moved to those carpenter's hands that had been placed on his shoulders. On them he saw deep and ugly scars. Flinching at the sight, he looked down at the feet. They too were torn in a ghastly disfigurement. How could this be? All was to be perfect here, was it not? The first of many surprises.

In a flash of insight, Finney knew what every child understands about heaven, that every body there would be perfect, unblemished, and unscarred. But now he saw that the scars of earth were not pretend or imaginary, but very real, and could only be gone here because someone else had chosen to take them on himself. The carpenter's scars would remain forever. The only one who would appear less than perfect in eternity would be the eternally perfect one himself.

Finney looked into the eyes again, knowing they saw every thought within him. The perfect and scarred one said simply, "For you, my son, for you."

Finney swallowed hard, and loved him more than he could ever have imagined loving anyone.

They stood and looked at each other for a time, then Finney listened attentively as his Master spoke to him again.

"Like a newborn child, your eyes will take time to adjust to the brightness of your new world. You must learn to walk here before you can run or fly. You have much to learn, and you will have the finest teachers. You and I have much to discuss. I will walk with you often. Later I will give to you the name I have chosen for you. A name that only you and I will know. And one day, when the time is right, I will give you a place of service, a place you earned by serving me in the dark world."

A hush of silent wonder followed these words. The bright one stepped back, smiling warmly, as if to defer to the others, to encourage them to resume their eager welcomes to the new arrival.

But Finney could not take his mind off the carpenter. He was the center of gravity, the force that held this place together, that gave it meaning and purpose. Finney thought back to his last moments on earth. He felt as if he'd been a loyal dog, scratching at the door of heaven, not knowing what was behind the door except only that his beloved Master was there. That was all he needed to know then, and that was all he needed to know now. Wherever this One was, it was by definition heaven.

Finney scanned the crowd, seeing the smiling faces of old friends and teachers and customers, and an old war buddy. And there were Garland and Emma, and Daniel and Laura. He'd known them as elderly, but now they were so strong and well, so much more alive than the most vibrant young athlete or actress in the other world. And there were his old friends Jerry and Greg and Leona and so many others who'd invested in his life, then gone home before him.

But now he searched for one face only, and much as he wanted to renew his acquaintance with all the others, he would not allow himself to talk to anyone until finding that face. They all seemed to know this, standing back and beaming as he scanned them. There, finally, at the far end, grinning ear to ear in just the way of her father, was the one he sought. She had deliberately held back rushing to him, so she could treasure the intensity of his search and the moment of his recognition.

"Jenny!" Finney shouted her name and by the time the great echo reverberated, she landed in his arms, arms that had ached to hold her for ten long years.

"Daddy! I've been waiting for you."

"Oh, Jenny, my Jenny."

Finney hugged her and wept, in the wonderful way you weep at reunions long overdue. He swung her around, and danced with her and laughed. Though she seemed in a sense older here than when she had died, she was just as young in spirit, and he knew in this moment that the childlike qualities he treasured would always be hers. Tears gushed from both of them, uninhibited and unrestrained. As they gazed in each others' eyes, they laughed at one another's tears, and all the welcoming committee laughed with them.

Finney said to his daughter, "Here's a kiss from your mother, and another from Angela. They both miss you so, Jen. And here's..."

"A hug from Little Finn!" Jenny interrupted, wearing the same impish grin she used to when her Dad presented her with birthday presents she already knew about. "I heard him ask you to give me a hug," Jenny explained. "But I wasn't sure you could hear him!"

As he whirled her around again in glorious celebration, he caught glimpses of everyone there at the welcome party, including the One before whom they all had bowed. He seemed to be enjoying the celebration more than anyone. And no wonder, since he was the creator of celebration, the inventor of joy, and he who planted within his creatures his own capacity for joy. As Finney had always taken special delight in his children enjoying each other's company, so this one who was the Creator of all family and friendship took the highest delight in the exuberant expressions of family and friendship that filled this place now.

Then Finney's eyes returned to a very tall and muscular being, looking for all the world like a decathlon champion, only three feet taller, standing at the edge of the crowd. His face seemed expressionless but his eyes were alive with interest and a keen sense of participation in the party, as if he had vested interests in Finney's homecoming. Around him were still crowding those dozen of his kind, who seemed to Finney like comrades in arms, welcoming a buddy home from a special mission, exchanging stories and celebrating a long awaited return in the unique way soldiers do. Finney recognized him as the one who'd come through the passageway with him.

Finney contemplated the mystery. *Who exactly is this, and why did we leave the other world together?*

CHAPTER FIVE

Sue sobbed quietly, head in hands. Jake barely heard her whisper, "Goodbye, best friend."

Jake sat in dazed silence. Only once in Vietnam had he been there at the moment of death. Moments before and moments after, often. He'd seen vibrant, pulsing, youthful soldiers, then an hour later helped carry off their lifeless bodies on a stretcher. He'd seen the badly injured, but when they died it was in a medical compound, not with him. When death seemed near, he'd never lingered. He'd always managed to put distance between him and it. Except that one time, and here again now.

Having given herself but a moment, Sue turned to Little Finn. He seemed strangely reconciled to what had just happened, almost excited, as if he understood it somehow. *Must be denial,* Jake thought. Little Finn hugged his mom, giving more strength than he received.

As the two shared their intimate grief, Jake stared wide eyed at Finney. *Or is it Finney?* The body so familiar to him, once his friend's house, now seemed no more alive than the furniture or light fixtures. It wasn't frightening, like dead bodies were supposed to be. Who could be scared of a piece of furniture?

Finney's gone. But gone where? Gone into oblivion? Or merely relocated outside the range of Jake's senses? The house had been vacated. Was there a forwarding address?

Suddenly the room teemed with medical staff. A nurse, as though acting under specific instructions, pushed a wheel chair up to Jake. He didn't resist. He could do nothing for Finney now. The nurse said nothing as she wheeled Jake to the elevator, then toward his room. He was grateful for the small favor of her silence.

As they rounded the corner near Jake's room, Nurse Natalie appeared, hands on her hips. The ICU nurse noticed her stern and frustrated glare. She stopped, walked ahead between Natalie and Jake, took her aside, and whispered briefly. Natalie nodded, her features softened, and she quietly helped Jake out of the chair and back in his bed.

"Please rest now, Jake. I'm sorry about your friend."

Jake didn't respond. He was exhausted, drained, depleted. There no longer seemed any reason to stay awake. He welcomed the escape of sleep. It was the waking up again he did not look forward to.

Three hours later he woke. For a moment he hovered in that netherworld of uncertainty, when in the very core of your being you fervently wish your vivid memories of an event are either reality and not a dream, or a dream and not reality. Jake's gut ached as his growing consciousness convinced him Finney's death was not a dream.

He pushed the button, calling for a nurse. He was glad it wasn't Natalie, for both their sakes. She was young, blonde, and competent. He didn't have the energy to be charming.

"Can you tell me about my friend, Doctor Lowell?"

"Let me call ICU and get an update."

Unexpectedly, she picked up Jake's phone and dialed an outside line. The phone cradled between her left shoulder and cheek, she said to Jake, "It's much easier for me to call than to send out a search party to find you." She smiled sweetly to say she was just teasing, but made clear she'd been warned about him. Jake groaned, managing a slight smile himself.

"Hello, Rainy. This is Sharon from second floor. Would you do me a favor and give me an update on Dr. Lowell? It would be a big help to a patient of mine...yeah, that's the one." She smiled again at Jake. "Yes, right, we're keeping a close eye on him."

Jake looked out the window and pretended he was interested in three twelve-year-old boys on bicycles, weaving through the hospital parking lot in the clear cool of late October, wearing their winter coats, dreaming already of holidays and escapades in the snow. Jake remembered playing hide and go seek on countless snowy days with Doc and Finney. It was all a matter of following footprints in the snow. You'd try to hide your tracks by climbing trees or crawling on fences or walking on wood piles or luring the seeker down some trail where you could lose him. Sometimes Jake would see both of his friends footprints in the snow, diverging from one another, going their different paths to make them harder to find. Then he'd have to choose between them. Would he follow Doc's path or follow Finney's?

Life had been so simple, so innocent once, Jake told himself, as he looked at the boys on bikes. So little behind, so much ahead. Childhood and the friends of childhood. It would never be again.

The nurse kept nodding and saying "Uh huh" to what Jake assumed was a technical explanation of Doc's condition. "And the prognosis? Best guess? Okay, that's what I needed. Thanks, Rainy. Yes, I'll tell him," she laughed.

"Rainy wanted me to tell you two things. First, she loves your column."

"And?"

"They've posted killer Dobermans outside ICU and given them a scrap of your hospital gown to expose them to your scent."

"Very funny. How's Doc? I mean, Dr. Lowell?"

"Still critical, but vital signs are steady. He's stabilized enough they'll probably upgrade him to 'serious' in the morning."

"That means he'll live?"

"Probably. No guarantees, but they won't move him to serious unless he's out of immediate danger."

"Thanks." Jake didn't want to ask more. He just wanted to hear Doc would make it.

"No problem. Dinner's in another hour and a half. Get some rest."

For an hour he laid back, closing his eyes whenever a nurse peeked in his room, which was often, no doubt because he'd been labeled an escapee. Just as sleep was about to overtake him again, in came a short, dark, long-haired man, with a huge beard that moved across his chest as he stepped. He bore the distinctive curling ear-locks of a Hasidic Jew. Jake had seen one years ago on a New York street. The few parts of his face actually visible outside the wild beard seemed chiseled from stone, the sockets deep and the eyebrows thick. His eyes were dark, with pinpoints of white light playing in them as if they were black stones in the sun.

With a thick Brooklyn accent, and with no hint of uncertainty or apology, he said, "I am looking for Jacob."

Jake paused a moment, studying the enthralling face. "No Jacob here."

"I was sent here to him."

"I'm Jake. That's close. But no Jacob. Sorry, must be another room."

"I see." The strange old man made no move to leave.

I see? The man stood by the door, gazing at Jake. The silence was uncomfort-able, but for some reason Jake didn't mind his presence. He wasn't one to share his feelings, and rarely struck up conversations in even the best of times, and these were not them. He surprised himself by doing so now.

"May I ask you something, old man?" Jake would normally consider "old man" offensive, but he sensed this one would receive it as a compliment.

"Certainly, my son."

"One of my best friends died this morning. I was with him."

"That is a great privilege. You are very fortunate."

"I don't feel very fortunate right now."

"Nonetheless, you are. Death is life's defining moment. It is the point where the final touch is put on each person's life's portrait. The masterpiece is signed and the paint dries, never to be changed again. It is finished."

Jake stared at the man. *He must be a rabbi or something.* "I guess what I've been thinking about is this strange sensation I had right when he died. It was as if he...just left the room."

"He did."

"Well, I mean, I could almost feel it happening. It seemed like one moment he was there, but then suddenly his body was, well, just a body, nothing more."

The man nodded politely and waited, as if Jake had merely stated the obvious, and must now be leading up to some worthy observation. When none came, finally the bearded one said, "I understand. I have been present at many deaths."

"You've had the same sensation, then? Can you explain it to me?"

The man paused a moment, as if looking for just the right word. Finally, he seemed to find it.

"Ichabod."

Jake waited, but no explanation followed. Other than a character in Irving's *The Legend of Sleepy Hollow*, he'd never heard of Ichabod.

"Ichabod?"

"Yes. Do you remember Ezekiel?"

Jake nodded, faking it, since he had no idea whether Ezekiel was a king, an angel, or an apostle. Ask Jake who sang "Do Wah Diddy" and he could tell you the man and the year. But as a Jeopardy contestant, "BIBLE" would be his category of last resort.

"The shekinah glory of God dwelt in the temple. Ezekiel watched it depart. When it was gone, the temple was called 'Ichabod.' In the holy language it means, 'the glory has departed.' Once the Spirit of God left, the temple was empty, an abandoned shell. Your friend's body is empty, abandoned. And so shall it remain until one day it is raised again to serve your friend and his master much better than before. The body that remains is not your friend. *Ichabod*—the glory has departed."

"I can't believe he's dead. He was...too young."

"Too young? No one is too young to die. A time is appointed for all of you."

All of you?

"May I tell you an ancient story, Jacob?"

Jake decided not to correct the confusion about his name. It didn't matter.

"Sure. Tell me a story, old man."

"A slave and his master come to Baghdad. Early one morning, in the market-place, the slave sees Death in human form. Death gives him a threatening look, and the slave is terrified, convinced that Death intends to take his life that very day. The slave runs to his master and says 'Master, help me. I have seen Death and his threatening look tells me he intends to take my life today. I must escape him. Please let me leave now and flee on my camel so that by tonight I can reach Samara, where death cannot find me.'

"His master agrees, and the terrified servant is off to ride like the wind for the fifteen hour journey to Samara. A few hours later the master sees Death milling among the crowds in Baghdad. He boldly comes up to Death and asks him, 'Why did you give my servant a threatening look today in the marketplace?'

"'That was not a threatening look,' Death replies. 'That was a look of surprise. You see, I was amazed to see your servant today in Baghdad, for I have an appointment with him tonight in Samara.'"

The old man riveted his eyes to Jake's.

"Death will come at its appointed time, my son. There is nothing you can do to escape it. The only question when it comes will be this—are you prepared for what awaits you on the other side?"

With a great deal of effort, Jake broke away from the old man's gaze. He looked down, simultaneously fascinated and repulsed by the man and his story. Finally, he looked back up. The old man was gone. Dismayed, Jake realized he must have been looking down longer than he thought. The man must have stepped out in the hall-way, perhaps to find the real Jacob.

Jake rang his bell. Sharon showed up in fifteen seconds.

"Hi, Sharon. Sorry to bug you again." Jake knew it was a bad sign Sharon didn't say, "You're not bugging me."

"I'm looking for a little guy, an old man with a beard. Jewish, looks like a rabbi or something. You can't miss him. He must be out in the hall?"

"I saw him ten minutes ago. Asked him if he was looking for someone. He gave me a name, but nobody's name on this floor. I told him to check back with admitting to get the right room number. Then I saw him again just a minute ago. I asked him if he'd found who he was looking for. He said 'yes' and walked away."

That evening, still the day after the accident, Janet Woods walked tentatively into Jake's hospital room.

"Hello, Jake."

"Hello, Janet....So, what's new?" Jake smiled, with his lips but not his eyes.

"Nothing much new with me, Jake. But a lot's happened to you."

"Nah. Typical day in the life of a journalist. I'm under cover. Doing a piece on hospitals that overcharge. We had to stage the accident just to make it look good."

It was Jake all right. Uncomfortable with her presence and his vulnerability, and having to cover it with bravado and a joke. He couldn't fool Janet for a moment. He could never fool her. He wondered why he tried.

Suddenly Janet sobbed. "O Jake. I'm so sorry about Finney."

Jake stiffly reached his hand toward her shoulder, then, when it refused to land, drew it back again.

"Me too." The pause was uncomfortable. "How's Sue?"

"She's hurting. But you know Sue. She's doing a lot better than I am. Or Betsy."

"What are they telling Betsy about Doc?"

"Same as before. He's stable. They think he's going to make it. They won't speculate on the damage to his spine, though. Betsy thinks it's a bad sign. She's scared he might wind up in a wheelchair or something. She could handle it, but ..."

She didn't continue. *But Doc couldn't,* Jake filled in. He told himself not to sell Doc short. Jake had seen athletic looking men in wheelchairs, guys with bulging biceps and virility accentuated by the contrast of the chair. Doc could be one of those guys. Jake pictured him starring in a wheelchair basketball league or at the starting line in a marathon, wheeling his way up hills and around corners. No, even if the worst came true, Doc would cope. Jake would help him.

Janet stared at Jake, as you do at someone you used to know. She wanted to stay, but being alone together dredged up such painful memories for both of them. It was a terrible feeling to know you'd be more comfortable with a stranger than with the person you'd vowed to love and cherish until death.

"I think I should let you rest," Janet said finally. Jake offered no argument, confirming she should leave. She squeezed his hand lightly.

As she got to the door, Janet hesitated, then turned and said, "Carly wanted to come, but she's got a volleyball game, and the team counts on her." She regretted it the moment she said it. It sounded so hollow. It *was* hollow. A daughter should be there at the hospital with her dad at a time like this. Volleyball didn't matter. But then, Jake figured Janet was thinking, if her dad had bothered to be at her volleyball games the other times, she would have been here with him today. If it hadn't been the game, it would have been something else. They both knew it.

"Good-bye, Jake."
"Good-bye, Janet."

The fitful evening of remote control hopping between pointless sitcoms and sensational news shows slid into a fitful night of hot and cold sweats, coupled with vague and illusive dreams. Jake woke up several times as nurses checked his vital signs and gave him shots or pills, or whatever, he couldn't exactly remember. *They tell you to rest, then they keep waking you up.* Jake wasn't wired for life in a hospital. He wanted out.

He picked at his breakfast, begrudgingly admitting to himself some of it was pretty good, a level higher on the evolutionary scale than airplane food. Winston, his editor, called and said to just get better, don't worry about work, and Thursday's trip to Cleveland had been canceled for him. *At least there's one bright side to all this.*

At 9:40, an unusually somber and subdued Dr. Bradley came in, dressed in a suit. Obviously he wasn't on duty. So why was he here? It had to be about Doc. Was he going to end up in a wheelchair?

"Hello, Jake." Dr. Bradley sounded tender, which put Jake on red alert.

"Doctor?"

"You've been through a lot the last few days."

"And?"

"And...I'm afraid there's more bad news. It's about Dr. Lowell...Greg." Jake braced himself, ready to hear Doc would never walk again.

The doctor looked both deflated and puzzled. "Apparently early this morning he woke up—"

"Woke up?!"

"Yes, but...somehow...he managed to extubate himself."

"What?"

"He...pulled out the tube from his larynx."

Jake stared numbly, wanting to know, but not wanting to ask.

"I'm sorry, Mr. Woods." Dr. Bradley gestured helplessly. "He's dead."

Jake's head throbbed as he sat behind the wheel of his lapis blue '94 Mustang, pulling in to Fairlawn Funeral Chapel. Immaculately landscaped, with multicolored flowers and trees erupting everywhere, it seemed designed to make the visitor think of anything but what the whole place was about. Jake had dreaded this day since getting out of the hospital two days earlier. It was Friday, five days after the accident. The day of Doc's funeral.

Finney had already been buried, without a funeral. Instead, a memorial service was scheduled for Sunday, still two days away. Jake knew this would be the worst weekend of his life.

He felt ashamed he'd seen Betsy only once, when she came to his room the day Doc died. Poor Betsy. She couldn't understand how the accident had happened. "Doc was such a good driver." Jake nodded. But it *did* happen, and there was no going back. And then they'd just as much told Betsy Doc was going to live. It was still a mystery. The doctors said he must have woken up delirious and somehow just pulled out the air tube. *How could they let him do that?*

No one had said out loud the other possibility, but it haunted Jake. Maybe Doc *wasn't* delirious. Maybe he woke up, assessed the situation, found out how bad he was, and deliberately pulled out the tube. Jake shuddered at the thought, but couldn't shake it.

It seemed so senseless. Sitting by his hospital bed, Betsy had asked Jake, "How could Doc die? How could this happen?" How should *he* know? He was just a journalist, just a reporter of facts, a dispenser of opinions, not a custodian of ultimate truth. Death was out of his league. Maybe that strange rabbi would have an answer. *If so, I'd like to hear it.*

The anticipation of Doc's recovery gave his death the effect of standing in a secure elevator, then hearing the cable snap and suddenly dropping ten floors. If Jake didn't know better, he'd think Doc was behind it, pulling the strings in an elaborate practical joke. Like when they were boys, and they'd lie on the kitchen floor with butcher knives held between their arms and chests and strawberry jam spilled over their T-shirts, trying to horrify their mothers, and occasionally succeeding. Doc loved to fake people out. For a fleeting moment Jake entertained the notion Doc had pulled a Huck Finn, pretending to die, then attending his own funeral to see what they'd say about him. If only it were true.

Betsy said Doc left no instructions about funeral or burial arrangements. She told Jake, "We never even discussed his preferences about disposing of the body."

Disposing of the body? Obviously she'd been talking to a funeral director who could no more conceive of people failing to have an enchanting luncheon conversation about "disposing of the body" than a lawyer could imagine why people didn't make out wills. *Of course they don't. If you contemplate death and plan for it, it's liable to come sooner.*

Betsy chose the coffin. It looked to Jake like a Corvette without the wheels. Sleek blue fiberglass exterior, and luxurious white upholstered interior. Yet no one had been in it to enjoy the plush comfort. Only the shell Doc left behind. The irony gnawed at Jake. They would all go to Doc's grave after the funeral. Everyone, that is, but Doc. Betsy told him on the phone Doc's brother Del suggested the body be cremated and the ashes spread out near a hunting cabin, because "Doc loved the woods." *How about a grave site with a view? Maybe we could find a spot near a river, stick a pole in his grave, bait it up and cast the line so he could get in some fly fishing?* Jake's bitter sarcasm surprised him.

He stood near the back of the funeral parlor, scanning the hundred or so people attending. Here came the funeral director, or one of his minions. Whoever it was, he looked to Jake like a walking corpse in his mausoleum suit, appropriately pale and solemn, as if he was only allowed a few days of sunshine a year. Welcome to *Dawn of the Living Dead.*

Pale N. Solemn, as Jake dubbed his host, led him out of the main seating area, around the corner into the "family room." Jake had never been in one of these, where the family could see guests, but guests couldn't see them. But then, he'd been to as few funerals as possible, coming late and walking out the back rather than taking the parade route past the deceased.

Mr. Solemn led him into the family room, made hand signals like a deaf-mute to his coworker, whom Jake dubbed "The Count," then nodded and sat him down in the second row of family, not far behind Betsy. On Betsy's left, between her and son Franklin, sat a young woman Jake didn't recognize. *That can't be Molly?* It was Molly, Doc and Betsy's daughter, no longer a little girl. *Carly's age,* Jake thought. Seventeen. He and Doc had become proud fathers within two months of each other, and Carly and Molly had been best friends as little girls.

On Betsy's right, directly in front of Jake, sat Sue. Next to her was Janet. Jake looked around nervously for Carly. He longed to see her, but dreaded the discomfort of not knowing what to do or say. He felt disappointed and relieved when it became obvious she wasn't there.

Jake reached forward and numbly laid his hand on Betsy's shoulder. The obligatory gesture of affection. Not that Jake didn't care about her. It's just that others had much more to offer her. This wasn't his thing. Betsy, Sue, and Janet all turned to face him in unison, like synchronized swimmers. All six eyes shed tears at the sight of Jake. *Great. Just great.*

Suddenly Jake felt a presence up against him.

"Hi dere, Unca Jake."

"Hi there, Little Finn." Jake always felt comfortable with this little guy. Even at a funeral, Little Finn was guaranteed entertainment.

The organ played something classical, solemn and dignified. *Doc hated organs. The only thing worse would be an accordion.*

The "officiate" stood up. Jake noticed the flyer didn't call him a "minister," which was good, because Doc had no time for ministers. In his book, they were all charlatans and hypocrites. Before the officiate talked twenty seconds, Jake pegged him as out of touch. *Did you ever even meet the guy?* Had he spent nights with him in tree houses, the dorm, an Asian jungle, or the back of campers on hunting trips?

"His oldest and dearest friends called him 'Doc,' as did his dear wife Betsy. She has asked that I call him 'Doc' as well." Then with a knowing look he added, "Pardon me if I slip up and call him Gregory." He smiled with self-satisfaction, apparently thinking this amusing. It wasn't.

The man droned on and on, saying things about Doc that weren't blatantly wrong, just slightly inaccurate, off target or pointless. He'd obviously pieced together input and impressions from here and there, but he was shooting in the dark. Sometimes the results were painful. "Doc was a faithful husband . . ." Jake hung his head, wanting him to move on. "A loving father . . ." Jake knew Doc loved Betsy and the kids. He wasn't sure they always knew it.

"Gregory—Doc—loved life. He was an example for all of us. He didn't let life pass him by. He grabbed for all the gusto. Permit me to read from Dylan Thomas:

Do not go gentle into that good night,
Old age should burn and rave at close of day;
Rage, rage against the dying of the light.

"Doc cheated death by making the most of life." The man looked as if he wanted to say something comforting and profound, but lacked the resources. Finally he reached the crowning point of his message, substituting a new name for the old ones crossed out in his notes. "Gregory lives on in all of us. As long as we remember him, he will always go on living."

What does that mean? He's either alive or he's not. Memories have nothing to do with it. Jake felt guilty for being so cynical. But the syrupy sing-song voice and patronizing manner of the officiate grated on him like fingernails on a blackboard.

"Gregory told his brother Del if there was any song sung at his funeral, he'd want it to be 'I Did it My Way.'" Chuckles surfaced throughout the crowd, and this obviously pleased the speaker. "He was not content to walk in the paths that others walked. He would not let himself be squeezed into the mold of others' expectations. He was a man of independent courage, with a solid self-esteem and inner confidence that helped him rise to meet the challenges of life. He realized his greatest contribution to others was to be true to himself. When he latched on to a goal he achieved it. Whether that was being the best athlete, the best student, the best military officer, or the best doctor. He did it his way, and it was a fine way indeed. Listen now to the song he requested."

He was joking. Don't play the dumb song, you bozo! But the song was playing, Sinatra was crooning, and people were smiling. "I did it my way..."

Something about the bizarre irreverence of it all seemed to put people at ease. It was like Doc to violate taboos, even in death. Was he winking from beyond the grave?

After the song ended—it seemed forever—someone from the hospital got up and read a letter from one of Doc's patients, thanking him for saving his life. A representative from the National Organization of Women rose and called Doc "A Champion of Women." Commendations followed from several other civic groups.

The service ended awkwardly and abruptly. Mr. Solemn was now back up front, looking pleasantly morose and nodding to people to get up and walk down the aisle. Jake had a good view, and with his never-forget-a face but often-forget-a-name memory, he recognized at least half the people. He saw probably a dozen physicians, Drs. Bradley and Simpson among them, a few teary eyed nurses, including a weeping Nurse Robin who Simpson had lectured about ICU security outside Doc's room. Doc's secretary Mary Ann, a few hospital administrators, some guys from the health club. *Who's that guy? Oh yeah, the owner of the sporting goods store. He's lost his best customer.*

Two men in dark suits were among those Jake didn't recognize. They seemed out of place. One was fiftyish and stocky, with combed back red hair that looked like it spent the morning under a sprinkler. His companion was ten years younger, dark haired, hard bodied, with the face of a boxer, rugged and worn beyond its years. They each took an expressionless look at Doc's body, then filed out, leaving Jake with the curious impression they had no personal connection to Doc.

Those in the family room came out last. In the second row, Jake and Little Finn filed out before Janet, Sue, Betsy, and Doc's kids. Jake walked slowly toward Doc's body, so slowly that Little Finn passed him on the right, oblivious to funeral protocol. Little Finn stopped and stared into the casket, reaching his hand out and pointing a finger. For one horrified moment Jake thought he was going to touch Doc's body. Little Finn had set up a screen, forcing Jake to abandon his plan of the swift bypass around the body. Despite his inclinations, he too now gazed in the casket.

The mannequin didn't look like Doc, but like a very good sculpture of him, made out of the same stuff as fake fruit. But the suit, perfectly tailored, was really something, and it took some kind of suit to win Jake's admiration. He'd seen Doc wear it once, at the hospital banquet last spring, when he received the "Physician of the Year" award. Jake looked at the face. That pale face, faded and pasty. Doc was always bronze—twenty minutes in the sun and he was a perfect brown.

The body still cut an impressive image. Years of weight training, running, and cross country skiing had done their job. His heart had been strong. A "masterpiece" Doc had called it, and having done a few dozen heart transplants himself, he should know. This body was a real specimen, thanks to Doc's good genes and self-discipline. *Doesn't do him much good now.*

Jake reached forward to nudge Little Finn, who was taking entirely too long. Finn seemed to be exuding some sense of troubled insight, as if he was profoundly sorry Doc didn't have another chance at life.

Following the nudge, Jake took one last side glance at Doc, then stood agog, nearly choking on a sudden intake of air. As he walked out hurriedly, passing Little Finn, the image cemented itself in his mind. For a fleeting but unmistakable moment he'd seen another face in the casket. His own.

After sitting in his Mustang for ten minutes in a very full parking lot, Jake entered Good Shepherd Community Church. It was 2:55 Sunday afternoon, seven days almost to the minute since the accident. He wanted Sue to see him there early, but not so early it forced him to talk with people. Something still tore at his innards from Doc's funeral two days ago, and Jake wasn't ready for an encore.

Pictures and displays and Finney-related memorabilia decorated the place. The crowd was huge. Probably seven hundred chairs were packed in the multipurpose auditorium, and people were already standing. A vaguely familiar tall blonde guy about Jake's age walked up and shook his hand.

"Hi, Jake. Alan Weber. You probably don't remember me. A few years ago I rounded out a foursome with you and Finney and Doc, over at Edgewood."

"Hi. Yeah, I remember." Jake recalled him as friendly, likable, and a decent golfer. Finney had mentioned Alan often. Jake knew they were close. Still, there was something creepy about ministers. So many of them seemed like phonies.

"Sue's expecting you up front." Self-consciously, Jake walked up the center aisle beside the pastor. He'd never walked up a church aisle since his own wedding. He had no intention of making it a habit.

Little Finn, perched in the second seat from the aisle in the front row, beamed when he saw Jake. "Hi dere, Unca Jake!" Jake was sure everyone in the back row, not to mention the seven hundred in between, heard Finn's exuberant greeting. This only fueled his self-conscious discomfort at being in a church. Next to Finn sat Sue, then Angela and her husband. Sue's parents were next, then Betsy and Janet. For a second Jake didn't recognize the striking young lady by Janet. Suddenly, startled, he realized it was Carly. His own daughter.

She'd changed so much in the months since he'd seen her, as much as Doc's Molly. It hadn't been *that* long. Had it? Carly was looking the other way, at nothing, but Jake had the distinct impression she'd seen him.

"Welcome, Jake. We've got a box seat for you." Sue pointed at the aisle seat, next to Little Finn.

"Thanks." He looked straight ahead to the cross-shaped pulpit, only two steps up and a few feet away. He fidgeted uncomfortably at his closeness to that cross. Little Finn chattered on, explaining everything to Jake, including where they put the overhead projector on Sunday mornings, where the choir sang, and countless other details that would fascinate only him. Finn pointed with pride to the basketball hoops, on the sides, raised up so they were hardly noticeable on solemn occasions. Finney invited Jake to church several times, but he never pushed it, sensing his discomfort. He'd invited him to play basketball here many times, but Jake always had an excuse even for that.

He found himself wishing he could go one on one with Finney under those hoops right now. *Sorry I never came here to play ball with you, old buddy. If I had another chance, I would.*

An older man led some songs, including several he said were Finney's favorites. One of the few Jake recognized was "Amazing Grace." Two men and women stood up, accompanied by a synthesizer, and sang an upbeat song with the words "This I know, my God is for me, this I know," and another, "You're my Anchor beyond the veil."

The room darkened abruptly and projected images, accompanied by energetic music, appeared on the huge screen. Jake watched the black and white images of Finney as a young child. Memories of Finney's mom and that old house surged through him. There was Finney on what looked like the first day of school, smiling that inimitable ear-to-ear smile. Everyone burst out laughing, Jake along with them.

Now three little boys took over the screen, hair mussed, T-shirts stained, looking like a band of ragamuffins. Trouble waiting to happen. They stood by playground monkey bars, posing and pretending they weren't. Jake remembered the exact day. It was his eleventh birthday. His stained T-shirt was from the strawberry shortcake his mom made at his request. After gobbling it down, they'd climbed over the cyclone fence onto the old school playground just a block from Jake's house.

His mother followed the long way around and took this picture.

His mother—Jake realized he hadn't talked to his mother since the accident. Hadn't told her about Doc and Finney. She'd probably read about it, or heard the story circulating in the retirement home. Maybe Janet had called her. He felt ashamed.

Jake refocused on the slides, seeing Finney at his grade school graduation, he and Doc seeming to creep into every picture, often clowning around. There they were in a dozen other pictures, then with the high school football team, state champs. Their proudest moment. Now Finney donned a uniform, standing proudly beside two other young and virile soldiers. Jake looked at himself, the young man sandwiched between Finney and Doc. It was so long ago, yet only yesterday. There he was again, standing beside Finney and Sue at their wedding. And there was Jenny as a little girl. Little Jenny. Jake felt the lump in his throat. He glanced at Sue and saw the strange blend of joy and pain in her eyes.

Now there was little Angela on the screen beside Jenny, then Little Finn in both girl's arms. The family of five in slide after slide, until suddenly, abruptly, it was only the four of them. Jenny wouldn't appear in any more pictures, a silent testimony to the tragedy.

There was the family of four on vacations, at sporting events, on the back lawn, everywhere. And there...Finney and Jake and Doc on a hunting trip, standing together. Another hunter had taken it. The three of them again after playing football in the mud, just a few years ago. Finney with one of the young pregnant girls they'd taken in. Finney holding a baby. Finney playing ball with minority kids in the inner city. And finally, a slide of text only, New Century Schoolbook font, Jake and no one else noticed. It said, "Well done my good and faithful servant. Enter into the joy of your Lord."

The slide projector shut off, the lights slowly came up, and the audience erupted into applause, spontaneous thunderous applause. Jake joined it, knowing the applause wasn't for whoever put together the presentation. The applause was for Finney. For a man who'd lived well. A man who'd kept his promises to his family. A man who'd been there for those who needed him. Impossibly, Jake felt warmed and chilled in the same moment.

Alan Weber got up behind the pulpit, eyes red and puffy. He paused, gaining composure, voice slightly cracking. "Finney was a good friend. I'm going to say some things on Finney's behalf, what I think he'd say if he could step back and join us here today."

Jake braced himself, wishing he could be just about any place else.

"In his final illness, D. L. Moody said, 'Soon you will read in the newspaper that I am dead. Don't believe it for a moment. I will be more alive than ever before.' Well, folks, you read in the newspaper this week that Finney Keels is dead. Don't believe it for a moment. Finney is more alive than ever before." Affirming murmurs rose from all over the auditorium.

If only I could believe that.

"You and I have a hard time imagining life after death, don't we? Picture two twins in their mother's womb, debating about what's outside. The one says, 'There's a whole world out there—grassy meadows and mountains and streams, horses and dogs and cats and giraffes, and huge blue-green oceans with whales and dolphins and fish of every color. And there's people like us, only much bigger, and they can walk, run, and jump, and play games like football and baseball. There's skyscrapers and stadiums and freeways. And soon we're going to leave here and join them in that world.' His twin brother scrunches up his face, looks at him and says, 'Are you crazy? Get real. There's no life after birth!'" Laughter rippled through the audience.

"The point is, reality isn't determined by the limits of our ability to believe or understand, is it? Life after birth is real, even if unborn children can't imagine it. Life after death is real even if we can't imagine it."

But how do you know it's real? How do you know we're not just zeroes, coming from nowhere and going nowhere? How do you know we're not just annihilated or reincarnated or absorbed into the cosmos, or whatever? How can you possibly know?

"I want to make four brief statements about death." Jake looked at his watch and fidgeted. "First, life's greatest certainty is death. The statistics never change. Of those who are born, 100 percent die."

Now there's an encouraging thought.

"Second, death will come whether or not you're prepared for it. Talking about death won't hasten it. Denying death won't delay it. Psalm 39 says, 'Each man's life is but a breath.' The only question is whether or not you and I are ready when death comes."

Okay, okay, we get the point!

"Third, death is not an end. It's a transition. Death dissolves the bond between spirit and body. Ecclesiastes 12:7 says, 'The dust returns to the ground it came from, and the spirit returns to God who gave it.' Death is simply a doorway to another world.

"If I were to suddenly walk out this door," Alan pointed to a door on the left side of the auditorium, "you'd no longer be able to see me, but would you conclude I no longer existed? Of course not. I would simply have moved out of your sight. Finney has walked out the door, moved out of our sight. That's all."

You can't know that. Is death a door? Maybe it's just a hole.

"My final point is this—death will bring us face to face with our Creator. There is a God, and all of us will stand before him. Hebrews 9:27 says, 'Man is destined to die once, and after that to face judgment.' The fundamental issue for each of us will be whether our name is written in the Lamb's book of life. This will determine whether we spend eternity in heaven or hell."

Jake cringed at the word. *Can't you guys preach just one sermon without talking about hell?*

"In the front of his Bible Finney wrote these words spoken by Jim Elliot, a missionary killed taking the gospel to a tribe in Ecuador: 'He is no fool who gives what he cannot keep to gain what he cannot lose.'"

Alan paused, looking across the auditorium. Suddenly Jake thought he was looking right at him. "Make no mistake, friends. Finney was no fool."

Jake felt pulled two directions, as if two forces greater than himself waged war within him.

"The Bible says one day 'each of us will give an account of himself to God.' Finney was ready for that day. He lived his life in light of eternity. So should we all."

Alan paused, fighting a wave of emotion that threatened to take his voice for a ride. "I already miss Finney. We had lunch together every Tuesday. I look forward to seeing him again on the other side." Alan's voice finally broke. "The certainty of that reunion is what makes the parting bearable."

Certainty? How can you say that? You don't know. No one can know.

"Let me end with a true story. Alfred Nobel was a Swedish chemist who made his fortune inventing dynamite and other powerful explosives, bought by governments to produce weapons. When Nobel's brother died, one newspaper accidentally printed Alfred's obituary instead. It described him as a man who got rich helping people kill each other in unprecedented quantities. Shaken from this assessment of his life, Nobel resolved to use his fortune to reward accomplishments that benefited humanity, including what we now know as the Nobel Peace Prize.

"Nobel had a rare opportunity—to look at the assessment of his life at its end, but to still be alive and have opportunity to change that assessment. Let's put ourselves in Nobel's place. Let's read our own obituary, not as written in the newspaper by uninformed or biased men, but as an onlooking angel might write it, from heaven's point of view. Let's examine it carefully. Then, remembering Finney's example, let's use the rest of our lives here to edit that obituary into what we really want it to say."

Jake watched Weber sit down, unsure how to assess the man. Then a tall young man with an incredible voice got up and sang, "May all who come behind us find us faithful." This song especially touched Sue.

Finally, they stood and sang a song Jake hadn't heard before, but which made him think of marching into battle, fighting for some great cause. "A Mighty Fortress Is Our God." Again, someone said it was one of Finney's favorites. Jake felt strange to be unfamiliar with "favorites" of one of the two closest friends he'd ever had. He knew Finney tried often to bring him into this part of his life, but he'd always resisted. This religious stuff just wasn't Jake, and never would be.

Almost an hour after the service, to his surprise Jake found himself still at the church. Person after person introduced himself and expressed his sympathy. Little Finn wouldn't let go of Jake. He introduced him to everyone and gave him the grand tour that included his Sunday school class, where his dad taught the high school group, where his mom went to women's Bible study, and on and on. When they reemerged from the quiet recesses of the church building, people still lingered. Many were chatting and laughing and still wiping away tears.

Sue and Angela were next to Alan Weber, still talking to everyone who wanted to talk, and clearly a lot of people did. Jake found himself drawn to the pictures and memorabilia on the tables. He quietly fingered various objects of importance to Finney, including an old baseball glove from his childhood, now Little Finn's. Jake looked closely at a certain place in the lower part of the webbing. There it was. His faded signature, and Doc's. Each had signed the other's glove when they played together in Little League.

It's the end of an era. No more Sunday afternoon football. No more hunting trips. No more excursions in Doc's latest spotless macho vehicle. No more howling games of Wolfenstein 3-D on Finney's computer. No more Doc. No more Finney. He needed a drink. Or a long nap. Maybe both.

Come tomorrow, I'll get some distance from all this. Jake had no way of knowing how wrong he was.

Those still remaining in the church were reluctant to leave. *You'd think they'd want to get as far away from death as possible.*

But there was something compelling about this day, this place, this service, and especially this life—Finney's life—that made people *want* to linger, to contemplate, to evaluate, to anticipate. For the first time Jake could ever remember, *he* wanted to stay in a place like this, if only for the moment. He felt simultaneously repulsed and drawn by what he'd experienced here. Part of him resented the smug aura of certainty about the inherently uncertain realm of death. Yet another part was drawn to the inexplicable faith held on to so resolutely by Finney and his friends.

Yes, he'd stay here a few minutes more. If for no other reason, he knew the world awaiting him outside was harsher and a good deal less hopeful than this one. And he also knew this unexpected "ring of truth" feeling that had descended on him the last two hours would abruptly disappear when tomorrow, Monday, he reentered what was for him the real world.

CHAPTER SIX

J ake Woods pulled up to his favorite row of parking meters on Morrison, two blocks from the front door of the *Tribune*. He hadn't been here since a week ago Friday. It was now the eighth day since the accident.

He popped in six quarters, buying himself three hours. He could pay for all day parking at one of the drive in structures, but enjoyed this mandatory break from his desk every three hours. The fresh air and sights and sounds invigorated him, rewarding him with fresh perspective. Sometimes he moved the car a space or two, but if no space was available he'd leave it where it was. The parking patrol knew his car and rarely enforced the "new space" rule as long as he kept the meter fed.

Jake walked pensively to the old brownish marble archway defining the front door of the *Tribune*, stepping gingerly because of his sore back, neck, and midsection. Much as he wanted to bury himself in his work once again, he dreaded this day. He hated special attention, and above all he hated pity. He prepared himself for sympathetic looks and understanding nods.

Jake took a deep breath and walked in the door. The first eyes to meet him were Joe's. Loud mouthed, cocky Joe, the security guard, who was also friendly Joe, proud to work at the *Tribune*, proud to call Jake by his first name.

"Hello, Mr. Woods," Joe said in a kind and respectful voice, totally unlike his real one.

Here we go. "Hi, Joe. What's up?"

Jake didn't want an answer, and Joe didn't offer one. He pulled his security pass out of his front right pants pocket and clipped it to his shirt pocket. Only visitors had to wear passes until three years ago, but after a series of threatening incidents everyone had to now, still another concession to the social deterioration of a city once considered safe and honest. The face on the pass was three years younger and a lot less worn than the face Jake wore today.

Elaine, the receptionist, caught his eye and said, "Good to have you back, Jake." She hesitated, then added, "I'm so sorry about your friends."

"Yeah, me too," Jake said, with a bitter edge that cut the air like a scalpel. Elaine bit her lip, wishing she'd said the right thing. She didn't realize there was no right thing to say to Jake Woods this moment.

Jake walked the thirty feet to the elevator, people stepping out of his way as if he were a leper. *It's like the parting of the Red Sea in that Cecil B. DeMille movie.* It bothered him when people spoke to him and it bothered him when they didn't.

Two other reporters waited outside the elevator. Doug Jarmer from sports, the other guy a business reporter. Jake couldn't remember his name and didn't care to try. Back in the old days, before the *Tribune* bought out the *Herald*, he knew everybody. But when the *Herald* reporters got assimilated, Jake gave up. He knew most of the faces, and from reading bylines, a lot of the names. He just didn't bother trying to match them up any more. The larger newspaper permitted a selective anonymity that suited Jake.

Mr. Business was the first to talk. "Jake. How are your friends' families?"

"They're fine," Jake said, lying. He knew how stupid it sounded, so he added, "Obviously it's tough on them. But they'll make it."

"How 'bout you? I guess you got beat up pretty bad, huh?"

"Just some cuts and bruises. I'm fine."

Why should I be fine, when Doc and Finney are dead? It made him think of Vietnam.

The elevator ride, usually quick, was interminable.

When they reached the third floor, the others stepped out quickly. Jake emerged slowly, scanning and soaking in the closest thing to home he'd had the last few years. The newsroom.

The excited buzz of this place at once comforted and exhilarated him. It burst with activity and motion, some serious and urgent, some casual and playful, all weaving together into an unequaled rhythm. Paper dominated the landscape and scented the air. Not just newspaper, but notepads, fax paper, copy paper, magazines, letters, brown wrapping paper, manila envelopes, small paper packages. Pieces of paper thumbtacked to corkboard, taped to computers, hung on walls. Blue, green, red, and gold paper desperately trying to get attention by their contrast to the ubiquitous white. Yellow phone books, Rosetta Stones unlocking the outside world, punctuated the horizon. It was a world of words and ideas and contacts and deadlines and production and influence and impact. It was Jake's world. He was glad to be back. He had only to get through this day, he thought, and things would be normal again.

Well over a hundred low-partitioned cubicles were linked together, cookie cutter workspaces that took on individualized looks by various knickknacks, photos and degrees of disorder. Over three hundred reporters shared the newsroom, many occupying the same desk on different shifts or different days. Some, like Jake, commanded sole ownership of their work spaces. To the uninitiated the newsroom was a hopeless maze. You had to take careful bearings to make it back to where you started. To Jake it was as familiar as the home he grew up in.

He walked past the hallway leading to the main editorial offices, which provided the only real privacy on the floor. Most reporters were surrounded with people sitting less than six feet to their right and left, four feet directly across from them, and seven feet behind them, across the aisle. As he walked through the maze to his own desk, he passed Seth Harper, a columnist holed up in what was called a private cubicle. "Private" was relative. It wasn't a separate office like some of the editors had, just a self-contained space enclosed on three sides, with partitions rising three feet above the desktop, rather than eighteen inches, and adjacent to but not buried in the main partition maze. People could see Harper's back side, but he could pretend it was private, and it was easier to ignore the hum of the office. Jake smiled as he noted the green foam ear plugs hanging out Seth's ears, reminiscent of the neck plugs in Frankenstein's monster, a desperate tactic Jake rarely used. Deadline loomed, and Harper was trying to shut out the world. It was a pressure Jake knew well.

The *Trib* awarded Jake his own cubicle five years ago, but after six weeks he gave it up and asked to go back to the ordered chaos of the central newsroom. He found he played off the stimulation around him, drawing energy from it. He craved the action, the forward motion creating the wake that pulled him along when he needed it. Sitting out there in the center of breaking stories, Jake always knew what was hot, what was happening, what would be the lead stories in the evening *Tribune* and on the evening news. It gave him an edge over the more reclusive and elite columnists, including Harper, who could easily lose touch.

He paused a moment, bracing himself to make the left turn into the aisle leading to his desk. It was so familiar to him, perfectly etched in his mind's eye. Facing him from the other side of the partition would be Jerry, the human thesaurus, who always knew just the right word Jake groped for. To Jake's right would be Sandy, her terminal within arm's reach, inviting him to fool with the adjustments on the back, just to freak her out and make her think she'd lost data. Sandy was a gem, a perpetual source of helpful information. One of his thickest files was labeled, "Column Ideas from Sandy."

He stepped out around the corner. Jerry saw him first, his eyes immediately connecting with Sandy's, whose back was to Jake. She turned around tentatively. Jake knew they'd been talking about him, waiting for him, and he hated it. He decided to set the tone before he lost control to a wave of sentimentality.

"Okay, reporters number 183 and 197, columnist number 3 is back, and there'll be no more goofing off." Jerry stood and leaned over the partition, which came to his waist, and reached out his hand to Jake.

Sandy rose, hesitated, then hugged him. "Welcome back, Jake. We really missed you."

"Yeah, well it's good to be back. I was afraid they were going to get desperate and ask Jerry to write my columns for me."

"At least they'd be spelled right," Jerry came back, relieved Jake was his old self, which is exactly what Jake wanted them to think. Sandy knew better, in the way women do.

"Guess I better dive in. Don't let me distract you guys." Jake looked at Sandy out of the corner of his eye and saw her teary eyes. He turned away.

Jake surveyed his desk. His in-box overflowed. He leafed through dozens of handwritten personal notes mixed in with the standard fare of memos and photocopies and smelly faxes. The rest of his desktop had been cleaned and organized. He'd left it an archaeological dig, with older artifacts buried deep and younger near the top layers. The order was Sandy's work, he knew. She did this for him every once in a while, knowing to stay clear of the vital area closest to his terminal, where he knew just which note on what color and size paper buried ten inches down the pile was what he needed, unless someone ruined the arrangement by cleaning it up.

Jake gazed at the monitor, already turned on, the green cursor blinking at him, welcoming him home. He typed in his six-letter handle, JHWOOD, and immediately got the "Messages Pending:" notation, followed by a short delay and the number 64. Jake groaned. Usually he'd have six or seven of these E-mail interoffice memos that had become so popular between reporters and editors the last few years. And why not? They couldn't be lost, copied incorrectly, or picked up by the wrong person, as paper messages left on a desk invariably were. Jake vividly recounted that infamous pre-E-mail message to call the governor's office immediately if he wanted a hot story, a message he bumped into five days after someone had left it on his desk, somewhere down in the bronze age layer. E-mail had another benefit reporters loved—it was easier to send your editor a message without having to wait for him to get off the phone, or having to look him in the eye. Especially if you were asking for some time off.

Six desks over and one aisle across perched Hector, with his three radio scanners, eavesdropping for breaking news. His goal was to get a reporter to the scene of the crime before the police got there, and sometimes he succeeded. The scanners squawked incessantly, and to an outsider it seemed impossible that anyone within fifty feet of Hector could get anything done. But in the newsroom you learned to filter the noise and pick out the sounds that could help you. While reporters occasionally barked at Hector to turn down the volume, once or twice a day they'd crowd around him to hear a breaking story, and he always reminded them if he hadn't been tuned in, the whole newsroom would be in the dark.

A row beyond Hector, still in Jake's standard landscape, sat two of his favorite studies in contrast—Art, the classical music critic, and Kurt, the rock and pop music critic. Each had a music lover's dream job, going to concerts for free and getting paid for it, meeting the artists back stage. Every day they unwrapped an assortment of the latest releases from studios, then plugged in their headphones and listened, sometimes for hours. Art sported one of the classiest suits in the newsroom, and still wore a tie every day without failure, as did a third of the reporters and most of the editors, even though as of five years ago the *Trib* dress code no longer required it. (Jake regarded that decree on the level of the Emancipation Proclamation and hadn't worn a tie since except on big-name-in-their-office interview days.) Art's workspace was neat and tidy and ordered, creatively enhanced, like a Beethoven concerto. Kurt, his long hair held together in a pony tail reaching half way down his back, wore worn Adidas, faded jeans, and T-shirts plugging old rock band tours. Jake smiled as he watched Art the connoisseur swaying melodically to his music, while Kurt drummed his hands on the desk, mouthing out words and gyrating to the beat.

"Woods!" The familiar voice boomed from the corner office fifty feet away. "Get in here!"

Winston. He'd seen him once in the hospital, but that didn't count because it wasn't Winston to be hanging about in a hospital. Some body-snatching alien posed as Winston, Jake told himself. *This* was Winston, perpetually gruff, bellowing, harried and hurried, a walking ulcer. In short, an editor. It felt good to be treated normally. *I should have known I could count on Winston.*

As he walked what they called the "gauntlet" between his desk and Winston's office, he passed by a half dozen reporters on both sides, catching a number of nods, smiles, pensive looks, and a few tears. There were some "Good to see you's" and "Welcome back, Jake's."

Good people. They mean well. He felt himself losing his edge of defensiveness.

Jake opened the door to see Winston holding a big box that originally contained ten reams of paper. "Woods, this is yours. I want it out of my office."

Jake didn't get it, even when Winston shoved the box at him.

"It's your fan mail. Don't let it go to your head. It's not going to get you a raise either. And read it on your own time."

"Thanks, Winston. Jealous because you don't get any mail?"

Winston looked at him sternly, waving him off as if to say "I don't have time for this. I'm an editor; I've got dozens of reporters whose messes I have to clean up."

As Jake, box in hand, turned around to walk out Winston said, "Look, this is just a catch up day for you. Don't work too hard. Maybe you should just read your mail."

"I know what you meant, Winston. And I was going to read my mail anyway."

Winston moved his hand as if swatting a pesky fly. "Get out."

Jake walked out to the sea of eyes. You were always on display when you emerged from Winston's office. Several smiled, knowing what was in the box. Jake announced, "Look, if anybody sent cookies, I'll share them, okay?" There was a ripple of laughter, too much laughter, Jake thought.

Back at his desk he opened the Fed-X and overnight mail and UPS shipments first, some of them now over a week old. Back when he was an investigative reporter, if he was out of the office more than a day his editor would open all these, because you never knew when something story-breaking could come in. But the columnist's life was different. Some of the overnight mail was books, even though he didn't do book reviews, and cassette tapes of radio programs or lectures or magazines. He could never understand why they were sending them in the first place, much less paying so much to get it to him a few days sooner.

Opening a large envelope, he shook his head in wonder as he surveyed someone's college alumni newsletter with a "great little letter from the president" Jake should turn into a column, the note told him, and also enclosed was a school catalogue in case he wanted to know more about it, and an assurance they'd be glad to give him a memorable tour of the campus. *Right.*

About two dozen big manila envelopes contained special reports on something he'd written on, or should write on, from people who'd be glad to help him anyway they could. It was like panning for gold. There was little he could ever use, but you had to wade through the mud and rocks to find the nuggets. Some columnists dumped their "helpful" mail without reading it. Jake had learned to skim it and hang on to the five per cent he might use.

He arranged the rest of the mail into stacks, by a combination of size and postmark, tossing unopened everything that wasn't first class. He opened those in business envelopes first. Most of the personal letters were responses to columns. As usual, he shook his head because the writers were talking on and on about his October 18 column, or his October 16 column, and he never remembered columns by dates, just by subjects. If they didn't make some clear reference to the subject matter, and many didn't, he had to play Sherlock Holmes to deduce which column they were raving or complaining about.

One letter from a college professor gushed, "You said just what I was thinking, but you said it so much better than I could. Thanks." One of his favorite compliments, and he got it a lot.

People liked that personal touch with the columnist. Even when they didn't always like what he said. In his early years, when criticism bothered him more, his old mentor Leonard reminded him, "I used to watch Monday Night Football just so I could take shots at Howard Cosell. They don't have to like your column, as long as they read it."

A brief note about Jake's accident and his friends' deaths had been put in place of his column last week, explaining why the great bulk of the mail was personal notes of sympathy and encouragement. Included were notes from the mayor, a few congressmen, several athletes, and other luminaries. The ones he appreciated most were from the people who had nothing to gain by his favor. People whose careers or reputations he couldn't further or derail. These people could have only one motive for writing. They cared.

One note came from a boy whose dog had been run over. Another, a girl whose best friend died of cancer. He read letter after letter, oblivious to the newsroom other than an occasional raised voice, a burst of static from Hector's command center, or a "Hi, Jake" from the aisle behind him or across the cubicle on Jerry's side.

Suddenly his wristwatch alarm went off. Only ten minutes left on his meter. Had it really been almost three hours? The huge pile of opened letters and cards said it had. He decided to take an early lunch. He grabbed a bunch of unopened mail and crammed it in his briefcase. Often he ate lunch alone. Today his mail would keep him company.

Walking out the front door past Elaine and Joe, Jake headed to his favorite nearby hangout, the Main Street Deli, up the street and two blocks down. He smiled at Toni, who was talking to a vagrant right across the street. She was a year out of Columbia's School of Journalism, a talented g.a.—general assignment reporter. She had the hungry, semi-desperate look of a journalist trolling for stories. Jake knew it well. Sometimes you could beat your head on your desk for a story, when all you had to do was take a walk and meet some people on the street, and the stories would materialize.

Jake came up with innumerable columns just taking the walk to feed the meter. The adventures of bicycle messengers; kids who should be in school but spend their days skateboarding in City Square; hotel doormen and the secrets they know; the daily life of a hot-dog and kraut vendor. Profiles, feature stories, columns, all these had come from walking within a few blocks of the *Trib*. Twenty years ago, when Jake was a g.a., he'd hustle around like Toni, reminding himself of Leonard's five rules of a good story—conflict, impact, timeliness, novelty, and reader interest. Leonard hadn't invented them, but he'd honed them to an art form.

Jake settled down at the deli, sipping his cappuccino, waiting for his turkey on whole wheat. He read letter after letter. One, whose handwriting and return address ("Vista Manor") was most familiar, covered with embossed daisies, he opened slowly and laboriously, as if his hands were arthritic. It was from his mother, he knew. The handwriting had deteriorated, the notes were always brief now. She sent them to the *Tribune*, because his home address had changed several times in the last few years, and she knew the Trib was his real home anyway. Her hearing was so bad she didn't call him anymore, because it frustrated both of them.

> Dear Jake, I was so sorry to hear about your accident. Janet called me, and then I read about it. Everyone was talking about it here at Vista Manor. I was so worried. And I was sick about Finney and Greg. I wish I could have gone to Greg's funeral. I hoped you would come and pick me up, but I guess you were in no condition to do that. Maybe you were still in the hospital? I get confused now, I can't remember what Janet told me. I read that Finney's service is on Sunday. Could you come over and pick me up? I'd like to be there, to see Finney's family again and let them know I care. Please call me or come see me. I miss you. Love, Mother.

The handwriting degenerated as the letter went on, and only the M in Mother was legible. Jake felt the same thing he always felt at any contact from his mother—guilt. But instead of motivating him to action, the guilt paralyzed him. The more time that went by without contacting her, at that retirement home only eighteen miles away, the more uncomfortable when he finally saw her.

He hated such places, even the nice ones, where people's lives faded to an inglorious end. He hated the wheelchairs and the walkers and the painfully slow shuffling steps of men whose lives were behind them, and fragile bluish gray-haired women looking for someone to talk to and latching on to each new face in hopes it was one that would finally stop to listen. To wait for death seemed so degrading and pathetic. Hospitals were bad enough, but at least lots of people got better and left. No one in those homes got better and left. An occasional call to his mother, once a month Jake thought (though in fact they were several months apart), assuaged the guilt just enough that it didn't interfere with his life.

He put away the letter from his mother, thinking he needed to give her a call sometime soon, and assuring himself he would, as soon as his schedule allowed. He reminded himself that every month he wrote out a check to the Vista Manor, paying half her rent, supplementing her Social Security check. Feeling better, he dove into other letters, each putting a little more welcome distance from the one with the daisies on it.

Forty minutes later he felt the urge to get back to the office. He told himself he had time to read one more of the two dozen or so unopened letters. He scanned return addresses, looking for something promising. One stood out just because it had no return address. It was a plain white envelope, typed by what appeared to be an old style typewriter, pica in all caps. Crank mail, Jake guessed. That's usually what no return address meant.

He opened the envelope, and a canary yellow three-by-five card fell to the floor, face down. He gingerly made the awkward motion to pick up the card, reminding himself exactly where he still hurt from the accident. On the card was a single sentence, consisting of only four words, in that same all-caps pica type. A waitress wiped the table six feet from Jake, and happened to glance over just as the look of startled unbelief overtook his face. She watched his eyes widen and his hands shake, and wondered what could possibly be on that card to trigger such a reaction.

"It wasn't an accident."

Finney's engorged senses kept putting him on overload. This place was incredibly beautiful, not just in general, but in specific detail after detail. He had to close his eyes and shut out the spectrum of marvelous sights to choose and isolate which one he would now contemplate and enjoy. Then he'd cover his ears, to focus on one particular sound, freshly recorded in his memory, without being distracted by a thousand others, equally wondrous.

Like a starving man offered an endless smorgasbord of delicious foods, Finney felt overwhelmed by heaven. It was a disorienting experience, but nonetheless joyous and exhilarating. The perspective here had dimensions unknown in the other world. Circles there were spheres here. Squares there were cubes here. Triangles there were pyramids here. And as much as his understanding had increased already, he sensed it was only the beginning; there were other dimensions yet to learn that would amplify the cube as much as the cube amplified the square.

Finney opened his eyes and scanned the horizon for one particular face. It was time to interact again, to gain further reference points that could help him make more sense of this fabulous world bombarding him on every level. It was time to sit and talk again with Zyor. He who had stood at his side on earth by day, and stood by him sleeplessly, thousands and thousands of nights. Zyor, who had left the hospital room with Finney and escorted him through the passageway to heaven's birthing room. Because his mission on earth centered on Finney, when Finney's time on earth ended, so did the warrior's mission, and he was free to return home. He couldn't get over his initial delight of discovering that the mysterious stranger he'd first seen in the passageway had in fact been with him day and night for many years.

He'd already asked Zyor innumerable questions. Finney's mind was a sponge, with a capacity to absorb new information beyond anything he'd ever imagined. He resisted the notion he had to get every answer now. It was as if he feared this was a wonderful dream that could end any moment, and any question not asked here and now would forever go unanswered. He assured himself otherwise, but couldn't escape the feeling this really was too good to be true. But there was no conflict between goodness and truth here, he was realizing. The supply of both was unlimited.

Finney's eyes caught Zyor, sitting with his massive legs crossed, quietly singing some ancient saga of adventure and conquest. The angel watched him cautiously approach, but the look on Zyor's face sent Finney a clear message of welcome.

Finney took a breath, then plunged into the bubbling sea of impressions that filled his inner being. "I feel like an orphan who's grown up in the crime infested garbage heaps of a poverty stricken slum. Someone has come and rescued me, and taken me to a breathtaking palace with a view of the endless ocean and majestic mountains. Neither my mind nor body can diminish the experience, because for the first time in my life, both are as they should be. Do you understand these feelings, Zyor?"

Zyor gave a thoughtful look, and replied, "Not entirely. But the link forged between us in the dark world still exists. I sense these things in you, these feelings you describe, in a way I cannot sense in others of Adam's race. To a degree, I can experience them through you. Only in faint echoes, perhaps, but they are real nonetheless. I am grateful for what I can learn from you."

Finney smiled at Zyor's words. It seemed so ludicrous to think of this magnificent being, so superior in mind and body to the greatest super heroes of Greek myths or comic lore, learning from him. He probed Zyor with more and more questions, his mind ravenously devouring every answer. Yet every answer produced a dozen more questions.

He asked, "Why do I have a body now when the resurrection is yet to come?" Zyor explained this was a temporary body designed for this intermediate period before the plan of God on earth was culminated. He compared it to an Artist's preliminary sketch of a later masterpiece, assuring him it would pale in comparison to the body that would one day be his. That was impossible to comprehend given its incalculable superiority to his old body. Finney asked, "Did I die early?" Zyor replied, "You did not die early, any more than if you had died at twenty-five or ninety-five. Whoever walks with God is immortal until his work on earth is done. For such a one, there are no accidents."

Zyor qualified as the most fascinating and insightful being Finney had ever encountered, except of course for Elyon's Son. Neither Finney nor Zyor tired from their weighty discussions. The dialogue energized them both, as if intellectual exercise were rest rather than labor. Though he wasn't fatigued, he began to feel like a python swallowing a meal much larger than itself—as though his mind was so full he needed to crawl off to a corner of heaven and lie still to digest it all.

"May I ask you one more question, Zyor?" Finney smiled ear to ear, that same patented grin, realizing Zyor knew as well as he did "one more question" invariably meant many more.

"I was made to serve Elyon and to serve you. It pleases me to answer any question I can."

"I've learned a great deal since coming here to Elyon's realm," Finney said. "I understand things so much more clearly than when I was in the other world. But there's still so much I don't yet know, so much I fail to understand."

Zyor looked puzzled. "That surprises you?"

"Well, yes. It does. I always thought when we got to heaven we'd understand everything."

The angel made no attempt to hide his surprise at this statement. Finney wasn't sure Zyor was capable of hiding anything. He was what he was, and thought what he thought, with no duplicity or hidden agenda. What you saw was what you got. This was one of the things about him and his kind Finney found so refreshing. It reminded him of Little Finn and his Down's Syndrome friends. The sheer innocence, transparency, and lack of pretension was delightful. He and Sue had spoken often of Little Finn's angelic qualities, never realizing until now how literally accurate the assessment was.

"Do you mean," Zyor measured his next words, "that you thought you would be God?"

"Well, no. Of course not."

"Who but Elyon understands everything? To expect to understand everything is to expect to be God."

On earth, Zyor's piercing logic would have seemed incriminating, laying guilt on the questioner. Here it served to enlighten Finney without accusing him.

"But," Finney explained, "Elyon's Word tells us that while on earth we saw in a mirror dimly, in heaven we would see face to face. That we used to know in part, but in heaven we would know fully. Isn't this heaven? Then why is my understanding still so...partial?"

"You see much more clearly, my master, because the obstacles that blurred your vision are now removed. Your mind is sharper and able to focus. But you do not see all there is to see. Did you not also read in Elyon's Book his promise that in the coming ages he will continuously reveal to us the incomparable riches of his grace? How then could you expect to know everything there is to know? Or to know immediately everything you will one day know? This would defy the way of process and discovery designed by Elyon for his creatures."

The angel's voice trembled with excitement, suggesting to Finney he was but skimming a vast reservoir of truth. Even as Zyor spoke, Finney sensed him reveling in doing that for which he was created—making known to men the ways of God.

"Elyon is the Creator, we are the creatures, and always shall be. Heaven does not make you inhuman. It allows you to become all it means to be human. The Creator knows all, and knows all at once. The creature's knowledge is and always will be both partial and gradual. It will grow continuously throughout eternity. Every day we will understand better the greatness of our King, and the multifaceted wonders of his character. In this way we will worship him with a keener awareness and vitality. With a freshness that comes not only from considering what we already know about him, but anticipating what we do not yet know. And while our knowledge will one day be many times what it is now, even then we will be no closer to exhausting the riches of his person. He is as worthy now as he will be then, but we will worship him anew because we will have learned more of his worthiness than we ever knew before."

Pulled in the wake of the angel's excitement, Finney responded, "Of course. It makes sense when I hear you say it. For some reason I thought process and growth were part of the other world, and it would be different here—that everything we'd ever experience in heaven would be ours immediately."

"And then what?" Zyor asked.

"Well, then we'd just keep enjoying it forever, I suppose."

"Without the joy of discovery? With no meditation and study? No interaction with Elyon or one's fellow creatures? No process of revelation and learning? No exploration of Elyon's realm that rewards us with enlightenment and renews our thirst for further adventure? With no effort?" The thought was obviously as impoverishing to the angel as it was incomprehensible.

Though Finney knew Zyor meant nothing personal, for a moment he felt as close as he had, in the new world, to having asked a stupid question.

"Well, yes, Zyor, I have to admit I did think that."

The great wise warrior seemed genuinely perplexed. "I do not understand why. And I certainly cannot imagine anyone would want such a thing. Learning requires curiosity, exploration, evaluation, and dialogue. To be granted the product of knowledge without this process would violate what it means to be a creature. It would circumvent the process of growth in the grace and knowledge of our Lord...may his name be ever praised.

"If we knew all," Zyor continued, "for us there could be no growth. Mystery is the food of the creature's mind. Your people love to read their mysteries, but most of them do not devote their attention to the grand mysteries of the universe, the mysteries rooted in the Creator himself. If we understood all the mysteries of Elyon, our wonder would be focused on a knowledge that had a past but no future. Each moment of discovery, each event of disclosure and understanding is a point of worship, a point of wondrous arrival for the moment. But that point of arrival is not the ultimate destination. It is but one more step on the stairway, one more rock on which we tread in crossing the water..." Finney thought he noticed a gleam in Zyor's eye as he added, "just as when you were a child, and stepped on one rock after another to cross Benton Stream."

Benton Stream! What a flood of memories it brought back. Finney's spine tingled as he was reminded again this magnificent being had been there by his side even as a child, when he was growing up in the other world.

"Elyon said in his Book you must enter heaven as a little child. Despite your continuous growth here, in relation to the Father you shall always be a child. And while on earth a child may long to grow old, and an adult may long to be a child again, here you are able to mature without ever losing the wonder of being a child. Indeed, in maturing you become more child-like. For the child's joy here is in the discovery of each step, and knowing that while we have for the moment completed our quest, the larger quest will go on and on. Each cave we enter to explore opens into new passageways, which enter into others, and others. Our delight is not only in being at the place we are, but in knowing the Adventure will never end, and therefore the Joy will never end. Indeed, both the Adventure and the Joy are just now beginning. And," Zyor paused for a moment and looked toward Elyon's throne, "when the great nebula of Orion grows dim with age, when the star systems of Andromeda collapse upon themselves and breathe no more, the Adventure will still be young."

Set free by each new revelation of truth, Finney's mind probed the subtle implications of all this in a way his old mind couldn't have begun to. The angel continued to instruct, and Finney sat at his feet as an eager pupil, wildly inscribing notes on the clean slate of his new mind.

"Even among the creatures of heaven," Zyor said, "knowledge is not equal. Michael and Gabriel know things I cannot now imagine. But someday I will grow to their present understanding. Meanwhile they will grow to an understanding of which they now can only dream. Yet the Seraphim know things they do not, or so I have been told. Just as I can know things you cannot. And, indeed, as you know things I cannot."

This last statement astonished Finney. Zyor had been created ages before him and had been with Finney from conception to death, in all of his conversations and experiences and classrooms. What could he possibly know that this great and wise being did not? But Zyor was going on, so Finney had to file this with all the other questions that were adding up faster than the answers, which were coming at a torrid pace. Finney could only praise Elyon for his improved mind, which seemed as far advanced beyond the old as a computer beyond an abacus.

"I am old in my knowledge, so old that in comparison you are but a newborn child," Zyor said, with no hint of arrogance or condescension. "Yet when my knowledge is compared to Elyon's, it is no different than yours, no different than if I had been born this very moment. The difference between us is a difference in degree. The difference between us and him is a difference in kind. Only he is Creator. All others are creatures. We are the worshippers. He alone, the Ancient of Days, is the one to be worshipped."

Zyor's voice took on a hushed awe, as if what he was about to say was more important than anything, and must be said and heard with only the greatest care.

"He bridged the gulf of a broken relationship between himself and you—may the Lamb of God be forever praised—but the gulf between his capacities and ours shall always be infinite. We can never know but the tiniest fraction of what he knows. The fraction would seem to increase with the knowledge, but a fraction of an infinite amount will always be infinitely small in relation to the whole. We will increase in knowledge throughout eternity, always learning as he reveals himself and his wonders to us. But we will never begin to catch up with his knowledge. The most educated, insightful creature is still only a creature. The most he can know is but a drop of water in Elyon's infinite ocean of truth."

"So, we'll always be learning and exploring," Finney said. "Doesn't sound like we'll be bored."

Zyor gazed at Finney, as puzzled as his placid face could look.

"Boredom? Here? It is...unthinkable. Heaven is the very opposite of boredom. It puts one in the presence of the Beloved himself, and of multitudes of beloved ones. Lovers are never bored, for their delight is in each other. Even if no other diversions are available, the study of each other is enough. He who loves Elyon could never be bored in his presence. You shall not merely stare at Elyon here, as one might stare at a picture of his beloved in the dark world. You shall investigate Elyon's very being, and the delights of doing so are beyond comprehension. If that was all heaven is, it would be infinitely more than enough.

"Yet because our Beloved takes delight in always designing and creating new things to display his wonders, this realm is an endless repository of wealth, a continuous succession of adventures to benefit and delight his children. Boredom? There is only boredom where man would be sovereign instead of God, gutting the world of wonder and leaving no riches to treasure and no realms to explore. On earth there is boredom. In eternity there shall be no boredom, except in hell."

Zyor reached down and put his arm around Finney's shoulder. Finney sensed somehow it was not a natural gesture for the angel, but an expression of affection he'd learned from humans in his many years on earth.

"It is time to travel and explore the wonders of this place. On earth you needed exercise and diversion and fresh air to allow your insights to assimilate. Something similar is true here. Your capacity to understand has grown hundreds of times, but it is only the beginning."

Zyor smiled in the almost-human way of one privileged to initiate someone to an experience of joy and delight.

"I have much to show you about what is happening on earth, where Elyon's plan is at work. About how your own death, and the circumstances surrounding it, is affecting the life of someone you have prayed for many years. But first, come with me. I will introduce you to an undiscovered country that awaits your exploration. You will be the child, and I will show you wonders beyond your wildest dreams."

t wasn't an accident."

Jake pondered the message in bewildered disbelief. Was this someone's idea of a joke? Bad taste, sure, but bad taste was nothing new, not in his mail anyway. What else could "it" be besides the accident that killed his friends? He checked the postmark. Two days after the accident. If that's what it really was.

Who sent this, and why? Someone he'd offended with a column? Maybe a right-wing fanatic? They were capable of this sort of thing. Or maybe politics had nothing to do with it. Just a disturbed person wanting to intimidate a public figure but without the guts to accost him on the street. Or maybe it was someone sincere but mistaken. Or maybe it was true.

If it was true, how did this person know? Who was it? The postmark was the same downtown zip as the *Trib*, which meant nothing. Anyone could have mailed it here. Why didn't the writer identify himself? Was he at risk? Someone who accidentally witnessed something? Or overheard something? Or was it someone on the inside? If so, the inside of what?

Jake reprimanded himself for being suckered into this. It was a prank, and the perpetrator had succeeded. But he had to check it out.

Where do I begin? Two words came to mind. *Ollie Chandler.*

Jake befriended Chandler, a cop, five years ago when he was up on a police brutality charge. Several reporters at the *Trib* had hung Ollie out to dry, convicted him before the jury ever heard any evidence. It bugged Jake. He did some investigating on his own and got a very different picture of Chandler. He was a Vietnam vet, and Jake felt an immediate loyalty to him. The other reporters made an issue of his being ex-military—they'd said he came from a "background of violence" and was "accustomed" to it. Perhaps "life was cheaper" to him. Jake stood by Ollie as he would a buddy in the trenches. He even suggested in a column that perhaps life was cheaper to those who had never had to lay theirs down for others. This hadn't won him points at the *Trib*.

The jury finally acquitted Chandler and he was reinstated to the force. Some credited Jake's investigation and sympathetic portrayal for preventing him from being made a scapegoat. Taken off a street beat, Ollie made the switch from uniformed officer to detective, homicide detective, something he'd always wanted to do anyway. He and Jake shared information. Every journalist needed one detective he could trust. Every detective needed one journalist he could trust. Jake and Ollie had found each other.

Jake tossed a dollar by his plate and stuffed the letters in his briefcase, slipping the yellow note card back in its envelope and putting it in the upper fold of his briefcase.

The police station was only six blocks away. Jake meandered in the front door, unconsciously squaring his shoulders as if reporting for duty. *Safest place in the city,* he thought. He didn't share the cynicism about police officers that permeated some circles at the *Trib.* Maybe because he'd been a soldier doing the dirty work of protecting his country, and he could only respect people who put their lives on the line daily. Of course, he knew there were dirty cops, just like there were dirty soldiers. But he always began by assuming they were clean, and that made all the difference. He was one of the few reporters whose face was a welcome sight at the bureau.

Some days any visitor had direct access to the central precinct elevators. It always amazed Jake when he could go straight up the elevator and walk unimpeded right into the office of the chief of police. Other times, like today, they'd roped off the lobby, and you had to check in at the main desk before getting through to the elevators.

A thirtyish woman in blue uniform put down the front desk phone and asked, "May I help you?" A flash of recognition. "Oh, Jake Woods. Hi! I love your column—usually, anyway." She grinned. "Got an interview with the Chief or somebody?"

"Not an interview. Not even an appointment. Something important just came up. I need to see Ollie Chandler."

"Just saw him come back from lunch, hot dog in hand. Let me check his office." She pressed a button and spoke into the headset microphone. "Detective Chandler? Jake Woods is here to see you. By himself. He says he doesn't have an appointment, but was hoping...Yeah, sure. I'll tell him."

She pushed the button and gave Jake the nod. "Detective Chandler says"— suddenly her voice was deep and raspy—"Jake Woods doesn't need an appointment. Send him up, but tell him the hot dog is mine—he can stop at the vending machines if he's hungry."

"Nice impersonation," Jake acknowledged. He always kidded Ollie about his habit of eating out of the fourteenth floor vending machines with their "Steak sub with pizza sauce" delicacies that looked like they'd been created just before the pyramids.

"Fourteenth floor. I guess you know that. Any elevator but the first one."

"Thanks." Jake walked to the elevators on his right, getting nods of recognition from a few uniformed officers standing around chatting. He noticed a veteran telling a young cop who he was. It felt good. He stepped in the elevator, which gave him only five options despite the building's sixteen floors. Floors two and three were courtrooms, four to eleven were jail space, both accessible only from the other side of the building. Twelfth floor, his first option, was ID, Intelligence, Juvenile, and Narcotics. Thirteenth floor (yes there was one) housed Internal Investigations, the D.A.'s office and a hodgepodge of smaller departments. Fourteenth, the button he pushed, was the detective floor. Above it was the Chief of Police's office, the media room, and the police museum.

Jake hadn't seen Ollie on his turf for six months. The display photos, the first thing he saw when the elevator door opened, had changed. They featured six bright shiny photos of detectives at work. One was Ollie, who looked decidedly uncomfortable posing for this "natural" shot. Jake chuckled.

Almost everyone was plain clothes on this floor, so Jake didn't stand out. Unlike every other floor, which allowed free access to hallways, detective division had only one place the general public could go, the reception desk, with a thick bullet-proof window but no accessible door. You didn't just go in. Someone had to come out for you.

Jake gave his name to the receptionist, who picked up the phone and motioned him to sit and wait. Two minutes later Ollie came through the lone door on the far end of the floor and motioned to him.

"Jake! Come on in. Want a bite of my dog?" Ollie asked the question just as he popped the last remaining inch in his mouth, followed by a "that was delicious" expression and a big swig of Coke from the giant-sized red cup. Jake smiled because Ollie's raspy basement voice had been so perfectly captured by the girl at the front desk.

"No thanks, Ollie. Just had a sandwich down at the deli."

"Still hang out there, huh? I've looked for you a few times. By the time you're ready to enjoy your afternoon, I'm back keeping the city safe so civilians like you can walk the streets."

"Eternal vigilance is the price of liberty."

Ollie wrinkled his nose thoughtfully and retorted, "A rolling stone gathers no moss."

"A stitch in time saves nine."

"Hell knows no fury like a woman scorned." Both laughed.

They walked through or by all the major detective divisions—Robbery, Sex Crimes, Child Abuse, Fraud, Burglary, Auto, Pawn Shop Detail, all the way to the far end, where Ollie worked in Homicide. This place always fascinated the investigator in Jake, the tireless researcher who loved to solve problems and find answers. Sometimes he envied Ollie's career.

They wandered through a maze of desks back to Ollie's, as far away from the front desk as it could possibly be. He had a great view of the city, but to Ollie it was "just a bunch of buildings." Chandler excavated a spiral notebook from his desk, buried under piles of papers and notebooks.

"Like my new desk?"

"Don't know, Ollie. Can't see it. Come to think of it, never saw the old one either." Actually, it looked remarkably like half the desks at the *Trib*, including his own.

"Well, if I take the time to clean it off I figure that's a few more hours for one of the slime balls I'm chasing to blow away somebody else."

"So your messy desk is saving lives, is that what you're telling me?"

"You got it. Hey, the lieutenant's office is empty all day. It'll give us more privacy." Ollie waved him to follow.

They walked past the open door of an unused interview room where suspects were brought in from the custody elevator. That elevator, which could be opened only with a special key, went to and from this floor and the jail. Jake glanced at the stark room, with nothing on the wall, where Ollie had shaken down hundreds of suspects over the years, often playing good cop/bad cop with his partner Steve. While most guys seemed made for one role or the other, Ollie prided himself in his skills both as "bad cop," intimidating and threatening the suspect, or "good cop," becoming the suspect's advocate, getting Steve to calm down or back off, and becoming the listening ear when the guy was willing to talk. Even with all the play this had been given in the movies, Ollie once told Jake, crooks still fell for it all the time.

The lieutenant's office, eight feet deep, ten feet wide, was the alter ego to Ollie's workspace—neat as a pin, uncluttered, a single painting on the entire left wall, two posters on the right one, nothing behind the desk, and the front consisting of a big window overlooking the homicide department. No candy wrappers or donut boxes. No signs of life.

Ollie took the lieutenant's chair, and waved Jake to one of the two chairs across the desk. He eyed Jake and cleared his throat. Jake braced himself for what he knew was coming.

"Listen, Jake, I'm...I'm really sorry about your buddies, Finney and the other guy, the surgeon. Doc? Yeah, Doc. I know how close you were."

"Yeah, thanks."

"There's no friend like an old friend. They were good men."

"They were. I...miss them," Jake choked. For some reason he could talk about it to Ollie. He wasn't sure why, but he knew it had something to do with the fact they shared in common an Asian jungle on the other side of the world, a jungle that had no place in the lives of Elaine and Joe and Jerry and Sandy and most of the other people he knew.

"What's up, bro? I don't ever remember you dropping in without calling. Not that I mind. What can I do for you?"

Jake opened his briefcase and handed him the envelope, without comment. Ollie handled it by its edges only, turned it carefully, front and back, eyed the postmark, then puffed open the envelope enough to let the yellow card slide out to two fingers of his other hand, which firmly but oh-so-carefully pressed on the cards edges. He showed the skill and care of a surgeon or a jewelry cutter, neither of which fit Ollie's rough and tumble image. He read the card under his breath.

"It wasn't an accident." He looked confused for a moment, then flashed his eyes at Jake. "The car accident? Your friends?"

"I don't know what else," Jake said. "It could be a tasteless joke. Wouldn't be the first time."

"What's your gut-level feeling?"

"I'm not sure. What's yours?"

"Well, we've got to check it out. Immediately, while there's still something to look at. The first seventy-two hours are critical, and we're way past that now."

Ollie pulled a clear plastic evidence bag out of a drawer and gingerly placed the envelope and card in it. Then he scribbled something illegible with a black marker.

"Where's the car? A wrecking yard, I assume."

"I don't even know."

"Yeah, it'd be in a yard unless anything was suspect at the time, or there was a death. Then it would have been taken to the police garage. But this is the first sign of foul play, right?"

"Right, as far as I know." It unnerved Jake for Ollie to take this so seriously. "Two people died though."

"But not at the scene. See, if somebody dies at the scene, or even if they're DOA at the hospital, they always call for a fatal traffic investigator. He examines the car to see if there's any problems, anything suspicious. Your friends didn't die till, when?"

"A couple days later."

"Right. So nobody looked at the car. The policy's not retroactive. If somebody dies later, nobody goes back to the car. Unless there's a specific reason to check it, case closed."

Ollie picked up the phone and pressed a few buttons. "I'm calling Records." He drummed his fingers impatiently on the desk. "Jean? Ollie here. I need to see an accident report. Happened over on the Northwood highway. Date was, week ago Sunday?" Jake nodded. "Vehicle owned by a Doctor . . ." Ollie looked at Jake. "Lowell. Gregory Lowell. Yeah, as soon as you can get it. I'll be right down. Make two copies, would you? You're a doll."

Jake cringed at the word *doll*. Ollie's cozy little nicknames for female coworkers, ranging from sweetheart to babe, would have him up on sexual harassment charges at the *Trib*.

Ollie marched out the front of his office and headed to the elevator, Jake close on his heels. They arrived down at records within a minute, to see the receptionist putting two pieces of paper into a clean manila file folder.

"Perfect timing," she said to Ollie.

"You're the best, Jean. She's a sweetheart, eh Jake?"

"Um, yes, right, sure is."

"That's my job, boys. Just give me the credit when you crack the case, Ollie."

"Count on it, hon."

As quickly as that they were back waiting for the elevator, Ollie looking over the report, Jake wondering why Ollie bothered with the elevator for one lousy floor when the stairs would be faster.

"Yep, they handled it like we thought—routine. No reason to suspect anything. Okay, here it is." Ollie pointed to the bottom of the report as he walked in the elevator. "It's actually legible. I've got to put in this officer for a commendation. Car was taken by Brownlee Towing."

They were back in the lieutenant's office and Ollie was pulling a phone book out of the lower left drawer of the desk. Within fifteen seconds he circled a number and dialed.

"Yeah, this is Detective Chandler, calling from city police. We need to locate and possibly impound a vehicle towed to your yard week ago Sunday, from an accident on the Northwood Highway. Yeah, I'm sure that's the one. Hang on. Red Suburban?" Jake nodded. "Yeah, that's it, the Suburban. Anything been done to it since it came in? No? Good. Don't touch it. That's official—I don't want anyone near it, okay? I'll be there in half an hour."

Ollie listened. "Yeah, I hear you. Yep, one survivor. In fact, I think he'll be coming with me. Okay thanks." Pause. "No kiddin'? See ya soon.

"Guy's a real talker once you get him goin'. Ready?" Jake nodded, knowing Ollie must be dropping a dozen important things to help him.

"He says when we see the car we'll think it's a miracle you're still alive." Ollie swung around the front desk to sign out and get some car keys, without breaking stride. Jake could barely keep up as Ollie charged in the elevator, and again as he marched out into underground parking. His acceleration from zero to maximum walking speed was remarkable, Jake thought, especially for a guy so...round. They hopped in a plain brown, two-door sedan that looked civilian on the outside and cop on the inside, complete with police radio and a few high-tech gadgets Jake didn't recognize.

The drive to the wrecking yard seemed twice as long as it was. Neither man spoke much. When they pulled in, Jake immediately noticed a familiar cherry red hue on a crumpled wad of metal off to the left. It looked even less like Doc's car than Doc looked like himself in the hospital. But in the middle of the wad Jake saw a curled but legible personalized license plate that said, "Gusto." Doc's. This looked like a car that didn't just roll, but fell from the sky. Jake felt queasy.

Ollie followed Jake's gaze and hopped out, heading straight to the mangled car corpse. Out of the "main office," a shack with a sign, emerged a chubby, grease smeared bearded man wearing a blue striped shirt with a white patch that said "Ed Maxwell" in red script letters. He rubbed his hand on a towel. "You the cops?" He sounded skeptical, eyeing Ollie's non-uniformed attire.

"Yeah," Ollie flashed his badge as second naturely as a teenage boy runs a comb through his hair. "Let me take a look under the hood."

Ed reached in the driver's side window, now half its original height, with no glass left at all. He pulled the lever, which didn't pop.

" 'Fraid of that. Gonna need a crowbar."

Ed marched over next to the office to a huge metal rack and examined three crow bars, selecting just the right one, like a dentist choosing the perfect instrument for the job at hand. Ed carried the chosen crow bar like it was an extension of his big right arm, placed the end between hood and body, and pushed downward, to the sound of rippling metal. He did this in three places before it released and they could get a good look at the engine.

Ollie worked his right hand into a skin tight plastic glove, then ran it over the engine, distributor, fuel line, wiring, everything. After a few minutes he said, "Everything seems okay up here. If there's a problem, we'll find it underneath."

He got down on both knees trying to get a look under the car, but it was smashed down too low to the ground.

"Ed. Any chance you could raise this thing up for me?"

"Sure. We could jack it up. Or I can just pull over the crane."

"Whatever you think's best."

"Crane."

Ed was already on his way, enjoying every minute of this and thinking about the story he'd have over tomorrow's breakfast for the guys at the truck stop diner.

Ed pulled over the mini-crane, swung the huge hook in where the front windshield used to be, then hopped back up on the seat and pulled a lever. The taut cable raised the car inch by inch, so it looked like a dog moving up on its back haunches in slow motion. He locked a lever and hopped off again, walking right up to the underside with no visible fear. The huge misshapen vehicle hung at a forty-five degree angle, looking like a trap, eager to drop on anyone dumb enough to get under it.

Jake looked at Ed skeptically.

"It's okay. It'll hold fine."

Famous last words. Ollie was already standing underneath.

"I could use your advice here, Ed. Bottom line, was this driver error or a problem with the vehicle?"

"A year-old Suburban? This was a solid vehicle. I'll tell you right now it wasn't the car's fault."

"Maybe. Take a look with me anyway, will you?"

Ed went over everything, grabbing this and pulling on that. The search seemed routine and predictable when all of a sudden he said, "What the...?"

"Yeah?" Ollie was right there.

"A broken tie-rod. Broke right here on the thread, next to the adjusting sleeve."

Ollie took a closer look, then quickly went over to the tie-rod on the other side. "Look at this." Ed was already beside him.

"Two broken tie-rods? No wonder this baby lost it. Never seen anything like it. One maybe, but not two."

"Take a closer look, Ed." Ollie pointed at the clearly exposed surface of the broken tie-rod. Jake looked over Ollie's other shoulder with no thought now of the precarious hanging vehicle.

"Look how smooth this rod is, three-fourths of the way through. But the last quarter is rough, like you'd expect a break to look. Same thing exactly on the other side."

Ed's jaw slackened and he went back to the other side to look. He let out a low whistle.

Only Jake was in the dark. "Excuse my ignorance, but what exactly is a tie-rod? And what are you saying?"

Ollie looked at Ed. With the simple eloquence of a man who knows his trade, Ed said, "The tie-rods connect the wheels and the steering box. They're what give you control over the car."

"What we're saying is," Ollie added, "the rods broke all right, and that's why the car crashed and rolled. But they only broke because they'd been cut three-quarters of the way through. With a plain old hacksaw I'd guess, though it could have been an electric saw, maybe a reciprocating saw with the right blade?"

Ed nodded his agreement.

"With slow driving, and no sudden turns or stresses on the tie-rods, the car would be okay. You wouldn't notice anything different, maybe just a little shake or something," Ollie said. "But once it got up a lot of speed, then had to make a sudden turn or swerve or hit a bad bump…"

Jake's brain went numb. A little later, in the distance he could hear Ollie telling Ed to keep this thing under his hat until further notice. Ed was disappointed he'd have to sit on this story for the moment, but gratified he was on the inside of something worthy of the Sunday night movie of the week.

Jake came back to reality when he felt Ollie's hand on his shoulder. His voice got a little raspier when he was making an important point.

"Don't know who wrote your little note, Jake, but whoever it was knew what he was talking about."

Jake stared at Ollie.

"The boys in the lab will have to confirm it, but I don't need an electron microscope to know the difference between a break and a cut. There's no doubt about it. It *wasn't* an accident. It was murder."

"We are not captives to time here, but your friend still is," Zyor explained. "Elyon permits us to enter his time and observe his most important and strategic moments. That is why we can see him now. He prides himself on being brave and in control, but he is confused and frightened."

"You seem to know Jake well."

"Remember, I stood by you. Whenever you were with him, I was there too."

"Of course. I still can't get used to the idea."

Zyor gave him an uncomprehending look as if he couldn't understand what was so difficult about a concept so basic to him and so clearly taught in Scripture—that angels surround and minister to the redeemed. Finally he said, "Your friend needs your prayers."

"I can pray for him here?"

"Of course you can pray for him here."

"I've never thought of praying from heaven."

"Does not Elyon's Book say Christ himself prays for Adam's race from heaven? And that the martyrs of the end times watch and react to the events on earth? And that the bowls of heaven are filled with the prayers of the saints?"

"Yes, but I thought those were just prayers offered on earth."

"The prayers of heaven and earth merge into one. God's people are God's people no matter where they are, and their prayers are prayers no matter where they are. Does not the Book say the prayer of a righteous person is effective?"

"Sure. I know that verse. I even taught a class on it once."

"I know. I was there."

Finney nodded sheepishly. "Right. I won't ask you to evaluate my lesson plan."

"But if the prayers of righteous imperfect ones on earth are effective, how much more the prayers of righteous saints made perfect in the very presence of Elyon? Your prayers have no more ended than your life has. You have been praying ever since you arrived. With every thought and word of gratitude and wonder expressed to Elyon you have prayed. Now it is time to intercede for those below."

Zyor paused, taking on the look of the tutor.

"In the dark world there were theological discussions about whether or not to pray for the dead."

"I remember."

"I often wanted to speak through the veil and say, 'There's a much more important subject you've never considered—whether or not the dead pray for you.' "

Finney grinned at the thought.

"It is not that men need ask those in heaven to pray for them. But they do pray, as Elyon allows them, the cloud of witnesses, to see the drama acted out on earth. Pray for your friend Jake. There is more facing him than just the disturbing circumstances he has now discovered, though they too will play a part in whatever is to come. He is being pursued by Elyon, and is under great attack from the powers of darkness. Two divergent paths lie before him. I do not know which path he will choose."

No sooner did Finney turn his thoughts to Jake than a window opened up and he saw him again, still sitting in that unmarked police car in the wrecking yard. Jake! Finney loved this man now more than ever. Never had he felt so sorry for Jake, confined to that world of death while Finney was here, breathing in life itself. It was difficult enough to be in the dark world at all—but the thought of Jake being so alone, without God and therefore without hope, was unimaginable.

"Your friend is like every man," Zyor said. "All that is within him cries for certainty, for purpose, and for truth. For life eternal. Yet all that his world offers him is uncertainty, purposelessness, deception. He walks in darkness, groping for the light. For a moment he sees it and is drawn by it, but as he moves toward the light, it hurts his eyes and he retreats back to the soothing but deadly comfort of the darkness. He listens to the voices of those who have lived so long in darkness that they believe man was born to be blind, that light is a myth, that darkness is all there is, and nothing lies beyond. They believe the lie, and they teach it. They try to create their own fires, with all the success of a man rubbing two sticks together in pouring rain. Your friend needs your prayers. Perhaps part of Elyon's purpose in bringing you here now is that your prayers for him may accomplish even more."

Finney turned toward the throne and dropped to his knees. Zyor did the same, piggybacking his requests on those of the believer-priest he had guarded in the Shadowlands.

CHAPTER EIGHT

J ake and Ollie sat quietly in the police car, overlooking the rusted metallic
panorama of the wrecking yard. The crumpled mass of wreckage seemed to
Jake an all too vivid picture of how life was destined to end.

"As soon as we get the car over to the police storage lot, I'll have the boys in
criminology take a look. I need their corroboration; the rods were cut, so I
can go with a murder investigation. I'll have a couple of guys go over the car,
every inch of it. Now that we know this isn't a hoax, I'll have them take a close look
at that yellow note card and envelope from our informer, and...Are you with me,
Jake?"

Jake was lost in thought. "Yeah, Ollie, sorry. This is just so...bizarre."

"Yeah. Guess I'm used to the bizarre, but I admit this one's a little creepy.
There's something straight forward about blowing somebody's head off or burying a
knife in them in the heat of the moment."

Jake shot Ollie an incredulous look he missed completely.

"But when somebody plans it out like this, gets under a car and cuts away...I
mean, children could have been killed, other motorists, all kinds of people. You get
callused in this job, you have to, but this is pretty scary stuff. And it leaves us with a
lot of guess work. Anyway, I'll have the boys pour ninhydrin on the envelope and
the card and see if we can get anything."

"Ninhydrin?"

"To check for fingerprints."

"Fingerprints? On an envelope that went through how many hands at the post
office and the *Tribune* and...?" Jake felt a little stupid as he considered for the first
time how much he had handled the letter.

"It's a long shot—most things are—but we have to try. If we could match the
same print from envelope and note card...Only you and the person who sent it
would have your fingerprints on the inside and outside, right? Sometimes we get a
good print inside the envelope where they hold it to lick the glue. If we get an
inside print, it could be the key to everything. Of course, the tip may have come
from someone with no prints on record. On the other hand, if we could find prints
under the car...Again, it's not likely, but you never know. If we get anything, AFIS
can do miracles."

"Afis?"

"Automatic Fingerprint Identification System. It's all computerized. In the old
days, even when we had good fingerprints, it was worthless unless we had a suspect.
Then, we'd pull their fingerprint files, if we had them, and we'd manually compare
the suspect's prints with the ones found at the crime scene."

"And now?"

"Now, and I mean only since 1990, if we get a good print or two, or even partials, we run them into AFIS, and it has every print on file in Oregon, Washington, California, and Nevada. We can get into other states too, but it's kind of a hassle outside your region. Now we don't have to have a suspect.

"We scan our prints fresh from the crime scene, and all of a sudden AFIS calls up Fred Swartz, arrested only one time for burglary in Reno in 1989, and we've got the creep. Of course, the print doesn't establish guilt, but it makes a definite link, and at least we know who to question." Ollie started to go on, but stopped when he looked at Jake, who seemed lost in himself.

Jake was watching Ed light up a cigarette, but his mind was forty years removed, in the old gray shed back behind his house, where Dad kept the lawnmower and garden tools and a secret bottle of whiskey that tasted like gasoline. Doc and Finney were with him. Each had swiped a pack of cigarettes from his parents, Doc his mom's Kents, Finney his dad's Camels. Jake contributed some Lucky Strikes he'd found on the school playground and hidden two weeks earlier at the bottom of his box of Superman comic books under his bed. They'd planned this for ten days. The three cronies smoked and choked and compared brands and said they liked one better than the other, though the truth was they all made Jake nauseous. But it was doing something with his friends, and that made it worthwhile, even when Mom smelled the smoke in his shirt and confronted him.

He denied the obvious truth and swore he'd never smoked, and the more she accused him the more stubborn and adamant his denial. She spanked him and for three whole weeks wouldn't let him play with his buddies, who were busy being punished themselves now that Jake's mom had called theirs, figuring it all out even though he'd refused to squeal on them.

"Jake? You there?"

"Yeah. Sorry, Ollie."

"I know this isn't easy."

"Ollie?"

"Yeah?"

"Who would want to kill Doc?"

"You're one step ahead of me, buddy. That's where you're going to help. I want a list from you tomorrow. Can we meet at your deli? One o'clock work for you? Okay, I want a list of every possible person or group that might hate your friend enough to do this. Somebody he ripped off. Somebody he made angry, real angry. Maybe botched a surgery and left somebody crippled?"

Jake shrugged his shoulders.

"Ex-wife? No? Present wife? Girlfriend he won't dump his wife to marry? Scorned women? Outraged husbands? Did he ever have an affair?"

Ollie saw Jake wince.

"He did, didn't he? More than one?"

Jake nodded, feeling as if he was betraying a friend.

"I want anybody he posed a threat to, anybody who didn't like him. Somebody he was costing money. Anything. Everything. Old grudges or new ones.

Doesn't have to be personal, either. Who stood to gain from his death in any way? This is brainstorming—everybody's fair game. If someone comes to mind and you think 'no, that's crazy' put 'em down anyway. We can always cut people off the list, but we pare it down later, not now. I want every possible suspect you can think of. Got it?"

"Yeah, I got it, chief. You sound like Winston dishing out an assignment. Ollie, listen, I really appreciate this. I know you must have a dozen cases that—"

"A half dozen on the back burner, one I can finish within a week. None as important as this one." Ollie put his hand on Jake's arm. "Listen, Jake, I'm not Mister Sentimental, okay? But if it wasn't for you I wouldn't even be a cop anymore. For all I know, I might be doing time with all the guys I put away. I owe you. Maybe now comes the pay back. Besides, it's my job. I've got a terrific sergeant who gives me first crack at the really good stuff. He gives me lots of latitude to choose what I really go after, which ones I do hands on, and which leftovers get fed to the new guys. Steve's a great partner. He'll cover for me, free up some extra hours. I don't know where it'll take us, but I'm going with this one. I want to get on it before the trail gets any colder. I'm going to expect you to do some stuff too, where you already have the contacts and might get better cooperation. Unless the physical evidence delivers more than I think it will, this isn't going to be a narrow investigation. We're going to have to go out there with a big net to catch this fish. You got the time to work with me?"

"The time? This is all I've got the time for. It's all that matters to me right now. I've lost the best friends I've ever had. I'm going after whoever did this, Ollie." Jake's face showed a visceral anger and determination, as if the warrior and hunter within had been awakened. "And when I get my hands on 'em, I swear I'll..."

"Wait a minute! *We'll* get 'em, okay, Jake? My badge gives me just a teensy more freedom to nail the bad guys, remember? 'Stop in the name of the *Trib*' just doesn't cut it, okay?"

Jake caught himself. Maybe he'd seen a few too many Eastwood and Stallone movies. But this was the only thing he could do for Doc and Finney. He was determined to do it.

"Listen, Jake, officially I can't work with you, but as long as we're discreet we can cooperate and share information. I'll give this everything I can, but murders don't take a holiday, so you'll have some time I won't. I trust you. You can investigate and interview, you know how to dig stuff up. You've got guts, contacts, and know-how. And pretty good instincts, although you drive a Mustang and I was never really a big Ford man. It goes without saying you're not the pro I am, so leave the heavyweight stuff to me, okay? But you're gonna have to be careful. It's too personal for you. That gives you energy, but it can mess you up. Show some restraint. Talk to me before you pull out an M-14 or a grenade launcher, okay?"

"Okay."

"Let's just coordinate our efforts, touch base, and go for it. And don't thank me anymore, Jake. I don't have to wonder whether you'd do it for me."

Jake nodded, and his eyes said the "thank you" Ollie had just waved off.

Big Ed lumbered across the yard like a grizzly bear, turning his head from side to side hoping someone would see him, so when they asked what he'd been doing he could say, "Police business. Can't discuss it. Investigation's in process." Hooked to his tow truck was a trailer with Doc's Suburban on it. Ed wore gloves now—Jake assumed this was at Ollie's request, at least he hoped so. Somehow it wasn't an encouraging thought to consider Ed might know better than Jake the importance of keeping his prints off evidence.

Ed reported directly to Ollie's window, like a waitress taking an order at an old A & W. He had the look of a man whose years watching Perry Mason and Matlock were finally paying off.

"Ed, you've been a terrific help. Just follow me over to the police vehicle salvage lot, on 23rd. You'll need my clearance to pull in your truck. Remember, not a word to anyone till I free this one up, okay? We're counting on your full cooperation."

Ed nodded eagerly, like an Old West saloon sweep who'd been deputized by the marshal to go get the Dalton gang. As Ed strutted off, so full of himself he could burst, Ollie started the car, waited for Ed to follow, and turned onto the freeway to head back downtown.

"Jake?"

"Yeah?"

"How come you guys drove Doc's car Sunday?"

"No particular reason. Usually just one of us goes out to get pizza. We flip a coin to decide. This time we ended up all going because…" Jake decided not to mention the quarter that didn't fall. It sounded too weird. "Well, we just decided to go together."

"So…say Finney had lost the flip. He would have driven his car to the pizza place?"

"No, probably not. See, we were at Finney's house, we usually are, so his car was blocked in. Same thing every Sunday. Doc usually pulls in last. If he doesn't, he parks in the front, so his car's free. Usually if Finney or I lose the flip, Doc tosses us his keys. He's so proud of his rig he likes us to drive it. I'd lost the last three coin flips, so I'd driven Doc's suburban three weeks in a row. One of us drove his car nine times out of ten, I suppose. Why? What are you thinking?"

"Just wondering. We've been assuming whoever did this was trying to kill Doc. But could he have been going after Finney?"

Jake started to shake his head no, then suddenly remembered.

"Wait a minute. Finney borrowed Doc's Suburban to move a photocopy machine to one of his stores. I hadn't thought of that. Yeah, Doc and Finney had switched cars for a day or two that week. Doc drove up in the Suburban Sunday, so Finney maybe got it back to him Friday or Saturday?"

Ollie nodded. "Okay. It's possible the tie-rods were cut when Finney had it, but they held together till Sunday. If he wasn't driving fast and making sharp curves there might not have been enough stress to break them."

"Yeah, okay, Finney wasn't that fast a driver, and if he was moving office machines…maybe he wouldn't have been taking hard turns."

"All right, rule number one in an investigation. Don't blind yourself to other possibilities just because your first assumption is more likely. The murderer could have been going for either of your friends, or both of them." Ollie hesitated. "And, of course, he could have been going for you."

"Me? If they wanted me, why not do their thing to my car? Why Doc's? And why not a bomb hooked up to the battery? Why a car at all? Why not poison my latté at the deli or knife me in the restroom...or send me a letter bomb?"

"Maybe because they wanted it to look like an accident. And because people are different. A pharmacist might poison someone. A mechanic might do something to a car. A chemistry major might send you the letter bomb. People think differently. That's why they kill differently."

Ollie pulled into the police salvage lot on 23rd, got out, showed his badge, and talked to the gate officer, who waved in the proud driver from Brownlee Towing. Ollie said a few more words to Ed, then hopped back in the car and headed downtown with Jake.

"Keep your car in a locked garage?" Ollie followed his line of thought as if he hadn't skipped a beat.

"My apartment has private parking. It's enclosed."

"Secure?"

"Yeah, I guess. They had some problems maybe a year ago, so there's a security guard who makes the rounds. He's not the Terminator, but he carries a gun and almost looks like he knows what he's doing. I don't think there's been a break in since he was hired. I'm on the ground floor, so sometimes I just pull in to the curb, twenty feet from my front door. But if you're talking about getting to my car, you know my M.O. I park all around the *Trib* during the day, usually on Morrison. My car's easy enough to spot. Anybody could get to it."

"Nobody's going to walk down Morrison carrying a saw and crawl underneath your car. This took some time. Had to be done some place that wasn't too conspicuous, not downtown curb parking with a gazillion people walking by. The high suspension on the Suburban would be easy to crawl under. In a residential area, could be done right in a driveway if someone had the guts. Say they staked you out on weekends, saw that three Sunday afternoons in a row, about the same time, you'd been driving Doc's Suburban by yourself. Maybe they assumed this was normal. It's hard to believe they would have done it right there in your friend's driveway, but it's possible. Busy neighborhood?"

"No."

"Much foot traffic on a Sunday afternoon?"

"Hardly any."

"Car easily visible from where you were watching the game?"

"No."

Ollie nodded. "Do-able. Whoever they were going for, they probably didn't care what happened to anybody else. Or maybe they were going for all of you, and were willing to take one or two or three at a time, whatever they happened to get."

This cast a cold chill on Jake. "If they were after me too, then that means their job isn't done yet."

"True. Not likely, but true. I'm just covering all the bases. Wouldn't hurt to keep your eyes open. It was Doc's car. It was probably just Doc they wanted. Probably."

Ollie was about to make the left turn toward the *Tribune*.

"Listen, Ollie, just drop me off on Morrison, at my car, will you? I'll come in and get an early start on my column tomorrow. Right now I want to get started on my lists."

"I should have some early stuff from the lab tomorrow. See you at the deli at one."

Jake nodded, carefully extracting his sore body from the car. He started to say "thanks again," but was looking at the rear end of the car. Ollie was gone.

Jake walked down Morrison, past the tobacco shop with the magazine racks encroaching on the sidewalk, past the locksmith, and past his own car, which still had twenty minutes left on the meter. This was his beat, his turf. Each familiar crack in the sidewalk, each piece of faded gang graffiti somehow helped him think. The familiar was the springboard to the unfamiliar, the mundane the path to the creative. His best columns were born gazing into cracks on this sidewalk.

Jake checked his watch. He knew if he stepped foot back in the *Tribune*, it would be another three hours before he could escape. He ambled toward the pay phone outside the convenience store forty feet past his car. He called Winston to tell him he wasn't feeling well. It wasn't a lie.

Across Morrison, in a blue Mercedes, a stocky, sandy-haired man in a business suit jotted notes at the bottom right hand page of an open notebook, propped up on a nifty mini-easel made just for this purpose. His left hand was holding compact Bushnell binoculars. The pages of the book had narrow columns on the left, filled with dates and times, and wide columns to the right, with detailed notations. The last three entries on the lower right read:

1:22 P.M.—Subject leaves side garage door of central police station, in brown unmarked police car. Middle-aged heavy set man driving. Probably plain clothes officer.

1:43 P.M.—Subject and officer pull into wrecking yard. Talked with worker, examined mangled car.

2:19 P.M.—Tow truck pulls wrecked car, follows subject and officer to police lot on 23rd.

The man turned the page and wrote at the top,

2:39 P.M.—Officer returns subject to Morrison, near his car. Subject walks to phone booth by 7/11. Makes call. Prefix 636, rest obscured.

He put down his pen quickly and pulled out on to Morrison, two cars behind Jake Woods.

The delicious scent of mozzarella, pepperoni, onions, and green peppers from tonight's Domino's delivery permeated every corner of Jake's apartment. Two empty twelve-ounce bottles of Budweiser sat on the lamp table beside him. He opened a third bottle, tempted to down it and its three remaining partners in the six pack, not because he desired them, but because a drunken stupor sounded good. *When the world looks like this, what's the point of being sober?* But he thought better of it and left the other three in the fridge, the investigation providing a good enough reason for sobriety.

Jake leaned his head backward on his favorite recliner, pale blue and worn to a frazzle, sagging back a few inches further on the left side than the right. Champ, his brown and white saucer-eyed springer spaniel, snaked around at his feet, nuzzling him and emitting occasional groans of ecstasy, making perfectly clear there was no other place he'd rather be than at his master's feet. An occasional crust of pizza hadn't hurt his feelings either.

Jake took his yellow pad, tore off a few dated scratchings, and wrote "Doc's enemies." Old enemies? High school and college rivals? Sure, but nothing serious. Doc picked up a few antagonists in Nam, got in some fights, but as far as Jake knew there'd been no contact for years. Medical school? Some teachers he couldn't stand, some academic competitors, nameless people with hurt egos because Doc beat them out for key positions. Hardly the stuff of murders. Then Jake remembered the Texas mom who hired someone to kill the girl who beat out her daughter for the cheerleading squad. And the bizarre interviews he'd conducted in the local "Hit Men 'R Us" plot to take out the figure skater's rival. Jake reconsidered and wrote, "Med school competitors."

Jake knew Doc had clashed with a few of his colleagues at the hospital. Jake scribbled "Dr. Morgan" and couldn't remember the other name, so underneath it wrote "Dr. Doe (blond anesthesiologist)."

Ever since he'd become chief of surgery Doc had sat on all kinds of committees, several of which he hated. Jake smirked as he thought about Doc on a committee. Action oriented, no nonsense, let's get the job done Doc. He'd faced off with some people on a few of those committees, but Jake didn't know their names, so made a note to check it out.

Most of what he knew about Doc's life on the job he'd picked up when dropping by to see him at the hospital. He knew the outside of Doc's daytime world, but not the inside. He doubted Betsy would know much more than he did. Maybe one of Doc's nurses would give him the inside scoop. Or Dr. Simpson, if he wasn't still sore at Jake for sneaking into ICU.

"Scorned women? Outraged husbands?" Ollie's question raised a world of possibilities. Doc had been with a number of women, some of them married. Jake knew two by name, from the athletic club. He wrote "Sarah Jensen/Husband" and underneath "Barbara Doe/Husband." He couldn't remember Barbara's last name, but he'd get it from Frieda at the club before meeting with Ollie tomorrow.

Jake felt embarrassed to put these names down. But Ollie was right—somebody planned this murder. And since no one obvious came to mind, it had to be someone who wasn't obvious, right? Jake jotted down a few more names of women Doc had been with, and descriptions for those he couldn't name. A few were nurses, at least one a doctor. One was a hospital volunteer, very young, a teenager at the time. If her father found out, or maybe a brother or boyfriend...Jake wrote down "Jorgenson girl/Father/Brother/Boyfriend."

What else had Ollie mentioned? Unhappy patients? Doc often groused about patient complaints. He'd testified for another doctor in a malpractice case. Who else would know about unhappy patients? Of course. Chief of surgery involved some administrative tasks, and Doc had a secretary, Mary Ann. Jake had chatted with her a dozen times. He'd call Mary Ann tonight. She could clue him in on committees and hospital politics.

Who else had cause to hate Doc? No one, unless... Jake froze. The protesters. Right wingers, anti-abortionists. They marched against the hospital all the time. Doc mentioned hate mail. He'd laughed about it, thought it was funny, or so he said. They'd beefed up security at the hospital. A few doctors who did abortions had their homes picketed, fliers had been sent to their neighbors. Jake used some information from Doc to write a column exposing people who imposed their morality on the privacy of families and neighborhoods. He had no patience for these people. Now he wondered if all these "don't murder the babies" people were capable of murdering a doctor. It had happened elsewhere. Why not here?

But Doc hadn't performed abortions for, what, maybe four years? When he became chief of surgery there was no reason to continue, and every reason not to. Jake remembered Doc commenting, "I got out of the abortion business at just the right time." Doc needed more status and respectability to advance his career. Jake remembered him saying he missed the money, but was glad to get out before all the heavy duty action at the clinics, and before it was popular to picket abortionist's homes.

This line of thought opened up new possibilities. Doc served on the committee that urged the hospital to test the abortion pill, RU-486. That was two years ago. Jake had driven by the abortion pill protesters in the parking lot a few times when picking up Doc. As chief of surgery, someone might have held him responsible for the abortion pill, maybe all abortions at the hospital. Someone with a long memory might finger him for past abortions. Could this be a case of vigilante justice—with some anti-abortionist fanatic acting as judge, jury, and executioner?

What about Ollie's idea they could have been after Jake too? His columns berating protests at doctor's homes and defending the testing of RU-486 had earned him lots of critical mail. Most of the letters were signed. Unfortunately, he'd thrown them away after reading the first few sentences. Otherwise, he could have given them to Ollie.

Jake needed specific names of anti-abortionists. Who were some of the nut cases that might do this? Where could he find out? Court records of lawsuits against protesters? *Tribune* clippings of clinic incidents? He could get those from Liz in the *Trib* library. Who could he talk to first hand? He knew plenty of pro-choice advocates on a first name basis. He didn't know any anti-abortionists by name, except...except Finney and Sue.

Finney had done his own sort of activism, approaching community businesses and persuading owners not to do business with the abortion clinics. He'd written a letter to the editor opposing the abortion pill. And didn't Sue do some volunteer work with one of these groups? Finney and Sue knew the anti-abortion crowd. She might get defensive, but he'd go to Sue. Find out who she knew, who might be capable of murdering Doc.

He sat there reflecting on what seemed more and more possible to him, that the murderer was a religious zealot trying to impose his morality on a society that didn't need or want it. A vigilante acting like the angel of death, but too cowardly to do it in the open. Something stirred inside him. He felt like the first few kernels of popcorn, just as they began to explode in rapid succession. It was something alien yet all too familiar, a thirst for justice, a lust for revenge. He thought of Hyuk, his Montagnard friend who went out to track down and get revenge on the man who killed his mother, wife and child. Like Hyuk, Jake would get whoever did this to his friends. The possibility it was a self-righteous religious fanatic threw gasoline on the spark of his rage.

Everything within him demanded justice and retribution. The rules of society didn't restrain his rage, they fueled it. All the rules seemed to protect the guilty and exploit the innocent. He'd sat in court too many times, when he was a reporter on the justice beat, to be anything but jaded about his country's legal system. The judges were cozy suburb dwellers content to keep releasing those who would rape someone else's wife or daughter, kill someone else's brother or father. Everyone applauded vigilante justice when the cause was right. Ollie was an officer of the law. He'd taken an oath to obey it. Jake had taken no such oath. The rules didn't apply in warfare. If it came down to it, he wouldn't let any rules keep his hands from the throat of the person who'd killed his friends.

In his mind's eye he pictured things that would in saner moments repulse him. But civilities meant nothing when good men were stripped of life with no chance to fight back. If only whoever did this had come forward with gun or knife. Then Doc and Finney could have faced their enemy, had a chance to draw blood. That it was a coward's assassination infuriated him even more.

An hour later Jake awoke from his furious trance. It was too late to make any phone calls now. He got up, stiff and sore from rage and recliner. He poured some milk and mixed it with chocolate, heating it in the microwave. He thought of Janet, with her favorite Cadbury mug she got on their trip to England, microwaving her nightly Lemon Zinger tea alongside his hot chocolate, begging him to watch a Bogart movie when he always had something else to do.

The unpleasant noise of the microwave fan brought him back to the moment. He turned off the kitchen light, shuffled to his bed, put down his mug on the night stand, took off slippers and clothes, and dropped back into his waterbed like he'd watched Lloyd Bridges drop back into the water in *Sea Hunt* thirty-five years ago. With Doc and Finney. He turned off the light and sipped his hot chocolate in the lonely darkness, convinced that if anyone in the universe ever had a reason to be angry, and a justification for getting revenge, it was he.

Across the street, a shadowy figure sitting in a car wrote in a notebook, "11:42 P.M.—Bedroom light turned off."

He was intoxicated not by mere feelings of joy, but by joy itself, a billion burning quasars of pure joy. All joy he had known on earth was like drinking from the partially contaminated lower waters, far from the source of the stream. Now he was drinking from the Source itself, the very fountain-head of Joy. This world was so potent and bright and overwhelming he felt it would have blinded and ripped his earthly body to shreds. The joy of heaven was like a volcanic explosion, spectacular and thrilling, but never subsiding. Not like a once-in-a-lifetime eclipse seen for a moment then gone forever, but an ongoing phenomenon, yet one whose familiarity bred neither contempt nor indifference. The longer he experienced it, the more potent it became, as if his capacity to experience joy was increasing by the moment, leaving the next instant always more rejuvenating than the previous. Like a blood transfusion, this admixture of joy invigorated him to explore the further joys of this new and marvelous world. Where should he go next, and what should he do? As always, he would ask his guide.

Finney could see the luminous wonder in the deep-set eyes of the mighty warrior, who seemed at times tutor, philosopher, bard, and poet. Suddenly he realized Zyor was gazing deep into his own eyes, as if he saw something equally remarkable within Finney.

"I long to understand what it means that you, my master, were created in his image. There is something of his very essence in you. Something that permits you to see things that elude my grasp. For now, at least." Zyor's voice took on a wistful tone as he added, "But I think perhaps forever. For there are things about Elyon's relationship with you, things which my kind shall always long to look into, which we may never understand.

"At the heart of the mystery, etched forever in my mind is that incredible day," Zyor's voice lowered to an intense whisper, "when Elyon stepped through the portal of eternity and left our world for yours. Creation was a wonder, but not a miracle. It pales in comparison to the true miracle, that he would become...one of you. The Creator becoming the creature. It could not be. And yet it was. It could not happen. And yet it did."

As he beheld the wonder in Zyor's eyes, Finney realized the angel was unconsciously demonstrating the very concept he had earlier expressed—the joy of learning, and the marvel of pondering what he might never understand.

"For a long time, as earth's history progressed, certain things seemed predictable. My comrades and I began to think we knew what would happen next, that we understood Elyon's plan. Then, in a moment, our presumption lay shattered. We realized we knew nothing of the ways of God. We had not comprehended the unfolding drama of redemption. It was a terrible realization to learn how little we knew, even having been with him for so long. Terrible, yet," and Finney saw a faint but distinct smile, "wonderful.

"He became one of you. Not merely like you as I myself have done, but one of you. Not for a moment, but for a lifetime...and for eternity. God became man. While Gabriel announced the miracle on earth, Michael announced it to us. I will never forget his words as he pointed through the portal and we gazed upon that teenage girl. You will meet her eventually, master Finney. She was lovely. She reminded me of your Angela."

The angel's fondness for Angela was unmistakable in the way he said her name. Finney was touched by the reminder Zyor had been there beside him when Angela was born and attended all her birthday parties and softball games. He'd been by her bed each night as Finney prayed with her. The valiant warrior, the loyal guardian, had come to love her. With sweet anticipation, Finney longed for the day he'd have the privilege of introducing Angie to Zyor.

In a voice that seemed to take on Michael's texture and tone, Zyor proclaimed the archangel's unforgettable words of old—"The unborn child now living in this Galilean peasant girl is the Creator of the universe."

"When Michael saw the shock on our faces," Zyor continued, "he added simply, 'Elyon has become a human child. The Son of God is now the Son of Man.'"

Finney marveled not only at what Zyor was telling him, but that the angel had never ceased to wonder at an event millions on earth affirmed in their doctrinal statements with such little wonder at all, with hardly more than a second thought. To Zyor Christmas was not making a list and shopping at a mall. It was the heart and soul of the cosmos itself.

"And just when we thought Elyon could not surpass this greatest miracle with another, there came the greater one." Zyor stood, and his voice trembled, not only with awe, but now with unmistakable anger.

"That little hill, where little men were permitted to do unspeakable things to Elyon's Son. My comrades and I jammed against the portal, begging permission to break through and strike down the cowards, to unleash the relentless wrath of heaven's army. We longed to raise our swords as one, to destroy every atom of the dark world. All that was in us thirsted for revenge. We ached to once and for all obliterate that cancer of rebellion against the Most High God."

For the first time Finney saw in Zyor seething anger, fierce rage erupting to the surface. The angel paced back and forth like a caged lion, seeming suddenly much taller and more powerful, no longer the gentle teacher. Finney backed out of his way as Zyor metamorphosed, appearing as a towering oak tree blown in a storm of wind and lightning, casting a menacing shadow and whipping out wildly with its branches.

"Here were these puny men obsessed with the offenses of others against them, while themselves committing the ultimate offense of the universe, driving nails through the flesh of God. We longed to make them eat the dust of the ground and vomit clay. Any one of us could have struck them all down, and we yearned to do it. Millions of us, legion upon legion, crowded forward, from every corner of heaven, pressing and pushing, crying out and begging leave to destroy those who would dare to curse and mock and savage the holy Lamb of God!"

Zyor's mighty voice echoed in Finney's ears, and he couldn't imagine there was anywhere in heaven outside its range. Zyor was completely lost in the memories of that day. Then suddenly it was over. The angel sat down, the anger subsiding as swiftly as it had materialized.

"But Michael would not permit us," Zyor said softly. "For Elyon would not permit him."

For a moment Finney thought he saw a tear in Zyor's eye, but told himself angels did not cry. Did they? Yet now it was clear. Zyor was touched by emotion Finney had assumed him incapable of. And something else was happening. Zyor was becoming a blur. Finney's own tears obscured his vision now. He too had gone back two thousand earth years, he had been there with Zyor, pushing against the portal, longing to go to earth to punish the enemies of God and rescue the Lamb. He too, in Zyor, had then fallen into a broken heap at the horrid realization that the Lamb must be left to suffer alone.

They both sat in silence now. Finney drew close to Zyor, with whom he now felt profoundly one. He realized worship came in many packages here, and this was yet another.

"We writhed in agony," Zyor continued. "We had never thought such pain possible here in the perfect realm. And yet we grew to know—though not completely understand—that all this was necessary to meet the demands of Elyon's justice and his love. He did not need us to rescue him. With a single word, with merely a thought, he could have unmade all men, destroyed the universe, purged all creation of the ugliness that nailed him to that cross. But he did not. He would not. He did not go there to be rescued. He went there to rescue."

Zyor buried his face in his hands. Finney noticed for the first time how huge and hard and calloused those hands looked, in stark contrast to the gentle softness of his face. Finney also realized in this quiet moment that the Bible's promise of no more crying or pain was indeed for a day yet to come.

As wonderful as this place is, Finney thought, *it cannot be everything that heaven will be until Elyon's plan is completed on earth.*

"I can say the words which attempt to explain what happened on that day when Elyon's Son died..." Zyor drew a deep breath. "But they are only words. I will never understand it. Yet I will never give up contemplating it. And I will never run out of time to do so, nor ever lack the company of those who share my quest and are eager to contemplate the wonder with me. And of all the adventures eternity will bring—most of which I can no more guess than you—the fact that Elyon was slain to buy the souls of men will overshadow everything. May his name be forever praised."

Zyor wound down what was less a discourse than a drama. "These, Master Finney, are things you will never fully understand either—yet I sense that in some ways you already understand them better than I. You are, after all, among those created in his image. Among those for whom he died. You are the bride of Christ; I am merely the servant who attends the wedding and rejoices for both bride and Groom. You are among the privileged people those in the far reaches of the universe marvel at, and shall marvel at for all eternity.

"If I look at you sometimes in apparent awe, remember it is because I know your kind and what you are capable of. I know how all the offenses you chronicle others having done against you pale in comparison to your offenses against the Almighty. How all the rage your people direct against others, and a billion times over, should be directed against each of you by Elyon, and for eternity. When you were first closed out of the Garden of God, I thought he was done with you. You have seen many things here that cause you wonder, and you have barely begun to see. But for me, the greatest wonder is simply that you are here at all.

"For I knew what you were before Elyon captured you, and I knew your transgressions on earth even after he first laid hold of you. I marvel at your transformation, which began on earth, from darkness to light. I have never known darkness, though some of my closest comrades once chose that path, before your world was born.

"Twisted and marred beyond recognition, you were transformed by his grace and empowered by his Spirit to live as a light in the midst of the darkest world the universe has ever known, or ever will. And so you lived, master Finney, not perfectly, but faithfully. And this you see now is only the beginning of the glory still to come."

Finney was at once warmed by the thought of his unspeakable privilege in being here, and chilled by the angel's dark and morbid description of the world he'd once thought of, rather fondly, as his home.

CHAPTER NINE

Jake sat at his newsroom desk, staring into his computer terminal, daring it to leave him columnless at deadline. Not once had it ever beat him. He'd been awake half the night thinking about the note and Ollie and the list. He had more distractions than ever to brush aside, but he knew he could do it, simply because he had to.

It was now 10:20. He had nearly an hour and a half left, which was still too much time to feel really pressured, though he honestly didn't know his next move. Jake could type eighty words a minute, and the spell checker would catch his errors, which meant ten minutes would produce the necessary eight hundred words. There would be a column. The only question was the question that motivated him, that made work fun—*how good* will this column be?

All Jake's columns informed readers, some deeply touched them, others challenged them, still others angered them. The only kind of column he considered a failure was the kind that didn't move the reader at all. The kind that just sat there on the page, or left the reader uncertain of the columnist's point. At the top of his terminal, lined with cracked yellow Scotch tape, was a note he'd seen ten years ago at the *Boston Globe:* "Better to offend a million readers than to confuse one."

He could get away with an occasional "no brainer" column, a really-doesn't-matter piece. This context of normalcy would accentuate the meteoric column, which might come every few weeks. These were the kind that got reprinted, photocopied, and posted on everything from refrigerators to faculty bulletin boards. But you couldn't hit a home run every time. There was room for singles, doubles, and triples. These made the strikeouts tolerable. People were more patient when they knew the guy at the plate was capable of hitting it out of the park, even if he didn't do it today.

Jake was a print celebrity, one of the *Trib's* most popular columnists. In his first years as a columnist he'd done local issues. Five years ago he'd moved to less geographically tied subjects, more issues of national concern, to increase the likelihood of getting syndicated. It worked. Creators Features, a young and aggressive syndicate, had picked him up nearly four years ago. Two of his three weekly columns—he got to choose which two—would go out through Creators to forty newspapers in nine western states, usually making it to print within a week of his original in the *Trib.* The third he made local, or at least regional enough that Pacific Northwest readers would still consider him one of their own. Today's column, whatever it was about, would be the local one. It took off some of the pressure knowing if he popped out, at least most of his fans wouldn't see it.

Striving for excellence had served him well in school, athletics, and the military. It created its own pressure, but he'd become used to it. Janet said he'd become addicted to the deadline, to coming up with something worthwhile under the threat of damnation if he didn't. He wondered now if life itself wasn't much the same, an opportunity to get something done, with a deadline appropriately enough called "death." Once the deadline arrived, there was no more chance to get it right. Come deadline, a column—perhaps even a life—was forever fixed, for better or for worse.

Jake resorted to a brief look at his file marked "Emergency," in the back of the top file drawer that supported the right side of his desk. These were his columns on ice, none of them great or he would have used them already. Given thirty minutes polish they'd be passable. But they were Jake's last resort, his insurance policy against coming up empty, and he didn't ever want to cash them in. Most would never escape their manila prison. In the newspaper business, ideas were perishables, coming and going like dandelion wisps in the wind. If not served up today, they'd be stored in the front of the refrigerator, then crowded toward the back, and finally—neglected until too old to recognize and too rancid to digest—unceremoniously tossed in the trash.

Jake looked at the familiar cork board backdrop above his work area, hoping to find something new, just a trigger, an idea that would launch him from the starting gate and keep him going. There was a picture of Doc, Finney, and him on a fishing trip. Next to it a photo of a giant sea turtle he'd taken with his underwater camera while diving in Oahu, in Turtle Canyon, two years ago. A few of his journalism awards, the ones small enough to be displayed in a seven-foot-wide workspace. Jake picked off and discarded a half dozen outdated phone messages pinned to the cork. One was a three-week-old message from Mrs. Best, the program director at the Vista Manor, asking him for the third time to come speak to the "residents" about what it was like to be a reporter. He'd never had time to call her back.

Then there was a picture of Carly. Sandy happened to look over just at this moment and notice Jake's sad-eyed, contemplative look. More than once she'd seen the same look as he gazed at the same picture.

Jake moved his eye from Carly to a letter next to her, dated five months earlier, in June. The writer was a woman deeply hurt by his column about a twenty-two-year-old boy who'd broken into a house and raped two girls. He'd suggested the boy was the product of poor parenting and societal neglect, that home and society alike bore responsibility for the poor self-esteem from which his crimes emerged. Of course, he'd not known the boy or his mother.

In this letter the mother assured him she'd done her best, and the pain of having a criminal son had been hard enough without him humiliating her in public. She said, "After all the years of trying so hard with a son who went bad, after being assured by my three other grown children that I was a good mom to all of them, including Billy, it struck me as strange you would feel the freedom, knowing absolutely nothing of me or my family, to say I am to blame for Billy's detestable actions. Most of my friends read your column. Fortunately, they know it was false. But my more casual acquaintances, those at work and in my apartment, they do not know, and they assume what you said was true, because 'they read it in the paper.' Please don't forget, Mr. Woods, that when I misjudge someone, it probably won't hurt them. When you misjudge you can hurt them irreparably. It's too late for me now, but I felt I should write in the hope you will think carefully before hurting others as you have me."

Jake had been disturbed and touched by the letter. He'd started to file it in his "keepers—bad" file, right behind his much larger "keepers—good" file. But then he decided to post it at his desk, to remind him not to be small, cruel, or flippant in his writing. It was a sort of self-imposed purgatory. It also served a remedial purpose—looking at it had prompted him to hold his tongue or make one more phone call to check the facts. He'd kept it up longer than he'd planned, partly because it impressed fellow reporters and visitors and bolstered his reputation as an honest, open-minded, soul-searching journalist who knew how to take criticism. More than once, when accused of bias and insensitivity, he referred to the letter on his wall, proving he wasn't arrogant and was open to correction.

Next to that letter was another, written by hand, with mixed capital and lower-case letters, all slanted, showing signs of carelessness and hurry. "Dear Mr. Woods, I see you're defending the filthy liberals again, faggots and all. Don't get too smug, you godless Fascist commie. You're going to Hell, and I for one am glad." The letter lacked only a "Sincerely yours" and a signature and return address.

Though it was two years old now, Jake displayed it proudly, partly because if anyone that sick and hateful was against him, it had to mean he was on the right side. Partly too because when he took on the religious right, which he often did, it reminded him who he was dealing with, and why he shouldn't hesitate to expose them for what they really were. It was maybe the most hateful letter he'd ever gotten, but he preferred its refreshingly forthright hatred to the pompous arrogant tripe other "conservative Christians" had sent him, cloaking their hatred and bigotry in words of "concern," "compassion," and "forgiveness."

Jake scanned the newsroom looking for inspiration. He saw a sea of heads bobbing on telephones, hovering over terminals. Though he couldn't see below shoulder level, he knew what lay beneath the horizon—hands busy on keyboards, reaching into file cabinets, digging through stacks of paper, bending paper clips, flipping through rolodexes. Besides the phone, the second most common fixture to rise above the horizon was the coffee cup. The few who despised coffee were inevitably tea or cola drinkers. One way or the other, caffeine fueled the newsroom. It fit the pressured, got-to-finish-by-deadline atmosphere, and helped explain why reporters and editors could sometimes be a testy and cranky lot. But the newsroom was full of more than its share of good-natured fun. Occasionally a hand would rise up to attempt a three-point bank shot at trash cans across the aisle. One reporter had his own Frisbee he occasionally let fly. More than a few desks contained dart guns and squirt guns. As Jake surveyed this self-contained world of the newsroom, smiles and frowns and rolled eyes and finger tapping dominated the landscape.

He looked down the aisle to Ray at city desk, whose job every morning was to punch in succession the twenty-three preprogrammed numbers on his telephone,

one button for each department at the police station. "Good morning, Ray at the *Trib*. Anything new?" Good newspapers didn't wait for news to come to them. They went after it. But this could be a strange business. He'd learned from Ray last month that he'd never been to the police station, only a few blocks away, never seen face to face a single one of the twenty-three voices he spoke to every morning.

The phones were their life lines, the air hoses that let them breathe in information. Breathe in info, breathe out articles. In the columnist's case, breathe in info, breathe out opinion. Reporters once spent a lot of their time on the streets, at the scene. Today, thanks to the phone, many stories didn't take them far from their desks. Three out of four reporters were on the phone in any ten minute period. Archie, the floor manager, told Jake the *Tribune* had over two hundred phone lines.

I've got to find out how big the phone bill is. Jake realized how hard up he was for a column to be sitting there thinking about a stupid phone bill. Then he considered that wasn't a bad idea—phones and journalism in the age of information. He jotted down a few words and stuffed a memo in his ideas file.

He saw Clarence Abernathy in the distance, maybe seventy feet away, headed to his desk in sports. Lois Sylman happened to walk by Clarence right at that moment, prompting Jake to laugh out loud. He could sense the animosity from here. Clarence was rough around the edges and not about to apologize for his gender. Lois was a feminist, the kind who believed if a man opened the door for her he was superior and condescending, and if he didn't he was rude and insensitive. Every man was Atilla the Hun or the village idiot. Lois had no room for the opposite sex except those that heeled for her like a pooch fresh out of obedience school, and there were a surprising number of these at the *Trib*. Clarence called them "men doing penance for the sin of being men." When Jake told him he should try smiling at Lois, he came back, "And get sued for sexual harassment?"

Though many of their views were different, the camaraderie he felt with Clarence was the closest thing to Doc or Finney he'd found in the newsroom. It was a grown up version of the all-male friendship he'd enjoyed since childhood. The childhood variety was replete with bold dares and great adventures, and in less exciting times, tossing rocks in the creek and sitting around the tree house making references to bodily secretions, excretions, odors, and sound effects. Come junior high, some of this was eclipsed by interest in girls, but no amount of Jade East or English Leather could change your genetic code. Dares and exploits led to crazy things like surfing on moving car bumpers and shooting arrows straight up, standing still, and seeing who flinched and who didn't. Some of the stunts they'd egged each other into made the military seem almost safe in comparison. In short, the three of them had spent a great deal of time proving they weren't women. Some male energy deep inside had pushed them to such things, and while sometimes exaggerated and often misdirected, it wasn't in and of itself bad. To Clarence, maleness wasn't a sin to be repented of, a curse to be revoked, or a disease to be cured. Jake liked that. He found it refreshing.

There were many coworkers here, both women and men, who believed men having a good time together was always at the expense of women. The only good men were the feminized ones. Clarence had captured ultra-feminist dogma beautifully one day after he and Jake had a run-in with Lois Sylman—"There's nothing wrong with men that can't be fixed by a good castration."

Ironically, Jake noticed, the men women actually admired were not these modern feminized males, but the partial throwbacks—those men who weren't total jerks but still showed the strength and toughness many dismissed as oppressive machismo. Like some of his colleagues, Jake found himself in the presence of *Trib* employees rolling his eyes at barbaric men who "just don't get it," then in his offhours, out of sight of the political correctness patrol, enjoying the company of that same sort of man. He'd considered writing a column on this subject, but only briefly, when he was ill or drunk, or both. When he came to his senses he'd realized too much was at stake. There were certain subjects you didn't touch if you valued your reputation or your longevity.

Jake winced when he saw the big old-style clock, white faced with black numbers and rim, just like the ones he remembered from grade school. 10:48. He had less than an hour. Utter lack of focus and direction told Jake he wouldn't come up with a column. Experience told him he would. The Pulitzer was not an issue here. *Play the hand you're dealt.* It was time to ante up, even if it meant bluffing. He knew how to write with a poker face.

Jake took one last look around the room, hoping for a vision. There was Martin over in his cubicle, turning around and glancing furtively across the room. Ah, good news. His chief competitor was also hung up. Martin's columns came out on Tuesdays, Thursdays, and Saturdays, so he and Jake shared Mondays, Wednesdays, and Fridays as their creation days. Susan Farley also shared the same days, but she focused on politics, and Jake felt no real competition with her. Martin was a general columnist, like Jake, and every subject was fair game for both. Seeing Martin's struggle vitalized Jake as a runner seeing signs of weakness in his challenger.

Jake jumped on the phone. While it rang he rehearsed his interview strategy, dormant for the last week. His technique, only partly conscious, was to challenge those he was sympathetic toward and to sound as sympathetic as possible to those he disagreed with. This gave him a feeling of objectivity, but more importantly, it drew out the best, most straightforward, and quotable responses.

"Jake Woods here. Can I have Barbara Betcher please?" Betcher was head of Oregon's chapter of the National Education Association. Since this was his local column, he'd decided to deal with some current education issues, including the teachers strike now in its second week, and the school voucher controversy.

"Hi, Barbara, Jake Woods. Fine. Listen, I'm short on time. So let me prime the pump. You know how sympathetic I am to education. I'm the first to say teachers are more important than professional athletes and all that, but I admit I'll pay a lot more to watch the 49ers play the Redskins then I will to go hear a junior high math teacher lecture on 'Exciting new ways to teach algebra.' " Barbara wasn't laughing, he noted. "The market is the market, and teachers are underpaid. But doesn't it just come with the territory? You get the perk of shorter days and a few months off, good benefits, you get the downside of being paid less than a plumber—doesn't it sort of even out?" Jake knew he'd fanned the flames.

"It's precisely that cavalier attitude that's hurting our children and our future." Boy, Barbara was grouchy today.

"Barbara, I think I know what you're thinking, but you have to say it. Exactly what was cavalier about what I said, and how does it hurt children?"

"People are willing to pay athletes and mechanics and plumbers more than they want to pay those entrusted with the care of their children. Which tells us their children are less important than their cars and pipes."

Jake typed, "mechanics and plumbers paid more, because value cars and pipes more."

"I hear you, Barbara. But what do you tell the taxpayer who says, look, I'm all for education, but I'm not happy with what my kid's getting now, or I haven't had kids in school for years and my property taxes have tripled since I moved here twenty years ago, and a huge amount of the money has gone to the schools, while the quality of education has only gotten worse."

"That's very selfish. And I challenge them to prove the schools aren't as good now as they used to be. That's unfair. They always point to declining test scores, but our state consistently scores in the top half nationally."

"But the scores are still bad, aren't they? I mean, Barbara, it's great to be in the top half, but if I can play the devil's advocate, just because other public schools are doing a worse job doesn't mean you're doing a good one, does it?"

"How can you blame us? Many of these children are being ignored and abused in their own homes. You think that doesn't affect their academic performance? And I resent your characterization of our schools as not doing a good job. Given our limited funding, we're doing a remarkable job."

"So the problem is lack of funds."

"Yes, of course it is. A good education requires good teachers and programs. Good teachers and programs require good funding. Also, funds represent community support. What message does it send our children when we vote down tax levies? And as for this voucher nonsense, if that legislation ever passed, how'd you like your tax money to go to schools for skinheads and Satan worshippers? I suppose you've been talking to the CARE group?"

"Not yet, but I intend to." Jake glanced at his watch. *Sure hope somebody's available!* He'd committed himself to this column now, for better or worse—there was no turning back.

"Okay, Barbara, I may call you back within the next thirty minutes. Could you stay near your phone?"

"Sure. Please do call back. And listen, I've got two pages of comparative pay scales and some excellent stuff exposing this tuition voucher thing for the scam it is. Also, a fact sheet on the CARE group that shows their hidden agenda is bootlegging religion into the classroom. I think you'd find it helpful. Can I fax it over?"

"Sure, as long as it comes quick. Still got the fax number?"

"Right here. I'll have it to you in five minutes."

Jake pressed the dial tone button and looked up the CARE group's number in a master list of city organizations compiled by the *Tribune*. He'd never called CARE. He'd seen Carl Mahoney quoted several times, and he knew before calling he didn't like the man.

"Citizens Advocating Responsible Education. How can I help you?" It was a woman's voice.

"Yeah, Jake Woods from the *Tribune*. Need to talk to Carl Mahoney."

"Hi. I'm Linda, Carl's wife. He's mowing the lawn right now."

"This isn't the CARE office?"

She laughed. "Yes, this is the CARE office, which happens to be in our laundry room. I'm doing the wash, so I'm near the phone or you would have gotten the answering machine. We're a grassroots movement, no fancy offices. Nobody gives us tax money to spend however we want."

Her voice sounded cheerful enough, but Jake rolled his eyes at the dig. He heard a loud noise.

"Hang on just a second. The washer's in spin cycle and it's clunking again."

"If you could just get Carl..."

Jake was too late. Rather than tapping his foot or reading one of a hundred miscellaneous papers on his desk, Jake resorted to his habit of typing random impressions on the screen, to be overwritten when he tapped the insert key and went into typeover mode. He typed, "Jake Woods's column will not appear today due to spin cycle problem."

"Sorry, Mr. Woods. I'm back. This old washer—"

"Listen, no offense, but I've got forty minutes to do this column, and I need to talk to your husband."

"Sure, Mr. Woods. I'll get him."

Jake's fingers busily typed, "Readers will be glad to know Carl Mahoney's wife went to pry him from his lawn mower exactly thirty-eight minutes before column deadline."

"Carl Mahoney here. What can I do for you, Mr. Woods?"

"Got just a few minutes to finish up a column on the teacher's strike and tax funding of schools. I've talked to the president of the teacher's union. I need another viewpoint."

"Well, thanks, it's nice to be called. I often read the other perspective, and it's good to have an opportunity to give ours."

He expects to be called on for an expert opinion when his office is in a laundry room and he's out mowing the lawn?

"Listen, can you just briefly tell me your position, what you stand for?"

"I'm pro-child and pro-education, though I've been labeled the opposite. I have no gripes with the teachers, not most of them anyway."

"Well, that's interesting, because everybody seems to think you do."

"Maybe that's because they don't read our materials or listen to what we're saying. My wife was a public school teacher for ten years, and she still subs once in a while. One of our concerns is that most of our tax money never ends up in the classroom. We're paying huge salaries and retirement programs for lots of administrators. Some of them do a good job, but when funds are limited we should be cutting some of the nonessential positions, not hamstringing our teachers."

"But I've heard you think our teachers are doing a poor job."

"Well, some of them are. Others are doing a great job. There just aren't any standards to assure quality. The NEA blocks every move to measure teachers' performance so the good ones can be rewarded and the bad ones can be helped to improve or weeded out. There's no occupation where job performance means less than among unionized school teachers. If public education was self-supporting or if it was on a level playing field with private schools, I wouldn't be concerned about it. Bad schools would improve or disappear, just like bad businesses do. Incompetent teachers would be fired just like in real life. But there's no incentive to improve, and the public always gets the blame—we're not providing enough money. But the truth is, there's some fundamental problems money doesn't help. It's like trying to put out a fire with gasoline. A lot of the taxpayers' money is being wasted."

Jake jotted down, "teachers incompetent, schools waste of taxpayers' money. Putting out fire with gas."

"Okay, what else?" *This guy's gripes would fill up the whole forum section.*

"What's the focus of your column?" Mahoney sounded nervous.

Jake rolled his eyes. "It's what I told you. I want to be fair, so I'm interviewing both sides."

"Okay, I needed to ask, because even though I've only been called by the *Tribune* twice before, I was misquoted both times."

Jake shook his head in disgust. *These bozos always think they're being misquoted. They just don't know how bad they sound till they see it in black and white.*

"Look, Mr. Mahoney, I'm not going to misquote you, and I'm running out of time. Can you just tell me a few more of your complaints?"

"I don't think of them as complaints, but we do have concerns. For one, test scores are way down. Studies show nearly half the people graduating from high school are functionally illiterate. But instead of teaching children to read, schools are pouring their energies into self-esteem and sex education and diversity training.

"Then there's sex education, where sex is divorced from morals and values. Kids are getting birth control from the schools, which isn't working, no matter what your moral perspective. Many of our schools will drive kids to get abortions when their parents know nothing about it."

Jake had jotted down a few key sentences, but now his fingers rested on the keyboard. *These guys always have to get abortion in somewhere.*

"Am I going too fast, Mr. Woods, or are you getting this?"

"You're doing fine. Keep going."

"Are you taping this?"

"Taping it? No, I'm just taking notes." Jake looked at his screen. He'd typed six partial sentences and a few phrases he'd fill in later, if he needed them.

"I'm just wondering how you could possibly write fast enough to get down what I'm saying."

"I'm not going to use all of it. That's not how it works." *This guy thinks I should get every pearl of wisdom dripping from his mouth!*

"I know you're not going to use it all. I'm just wondering how you're going to accurately reflect what I've said."

"Look, Mr. Mahoney, I'm taking notes with you the same way I take notes with Barbara Betcher from the NEA and everyone else. You don't get special treatment, okay? There's no plot to misrepresent you, if that's what you're thinking." *These people and their media conspiracies—what a bunch of loonies!* "I've got a column that has to be done in thirty-two minutes, and I certainly can't record you and have it transcribed."

"I understand. I'm just wanting it to be accurate. I hope when you look at your notes you'll remember what I said, in context. And the way I said it. I'm not asking you to agree with me—I'm just asking for fairness and accuracy."

Jake's face flushed red. "I've been a journalist over twenty years. I have a reputation for fairness and accuracy. If you don't want to continue the interview, fine, I'll just go with what I've got. But don't complain when most of the quotes are from the other side, if your side won't talk."

"I'm glad to continue the interview. I just want to be quoted accurately."

"You will be. Now, please, time's running out. Do you have anything more to say?"

Jake heard a sigh on the other end, and it irritated him.

"It's important for your readers to understand that if the public schools were a private enterprise and people were choosing them, that would be different. I mean, I might not like the car you buy or the mechanic you hire, but that's your choice, and it's none of my business. But if you choose a car and hire a mechanic and it's my money that pays for it, then I've got a right to give some input, right? If taxpayers think certain programs are faulty and destructive, and it's their money that's paying for them, they're entitled to say something about it. The public schools don't just belong to administrators, teachers, and the NEA. They belong to the public, and especially to parents."

"Are you saying public schools are destructive?" As Jake asked the question he typed in "programs faulty and destructive."

"Not generally. They're doing fine in a lot of areas. But in those I've mentioned, yes, sometimes they are destructive. I don't doubt the teachers are sincere, but value-free education is by nature destructive. No wonder kids have no regard for life, no wonder all the gang violence, when they're taught it's okay to throw someone off the life raft for the good of the others, or to kill innocent unborn children."

Here we go again.

"Schools certainly aren't the only ones to blame—we all are—but they have to take their fair share of blame too. I mean, if you can't talk about real values and standards higher than whatever kids happen to feel like at the moment, what's the point of ringing the opening bell? Don't we want the next generation to rise above us in their integrity and morality, rather than fall further down? Of course, I realize the first responsibility is with parents. We take that responsibility very seriously in our home, and I encourage all parents to do the same. That would sure make it a lot easier on our teachers. They've got a tough job."

Someone walked by and handed Jake the fax from Barbara Betcher. Jake nodded a quick thanks. The fax was filled with good stuff. Concise and quotable. Jake underlined a few things as Mahoney continued.

"Everybody knows the quality of any industry improves because of competition. But the NEA doesn't want competition. They want a monopoly. They think they have the right to teach our children whatever and however they want to, using them as guinea pigs for every liberal social experiment they can come up with. School vouchers would put them on a level playing field. By opposing vouchers to allow school choice, they're admitting they can't compete when put head to head with private schools."

"So you'd like to see public schools shut down?"

"No, of course not. All the good schools, public and private, would thrive. The only schools that would close are those that are so bad no parents would send their children there if they could afford any alternative. Should schools like that remain open? Why? We'd all be better if they were closed, wouldn't we? Meanwhile, all the other schools would get better. You have to offer a better product if people are going to buy it."

"Well, that's easy to say if you're in the middle or upper class. What about the poor and minorities? They'd be hurt most by school vouchers." Jake paraphrased the question from the NEA fax in front of him.

"Mr. Woods, are you serious? Haven't you read the polls? Poor and minority people favor the school voucher system in far greater numbers than the white middle and upper class, precisely because they're the ones who lack choice and are saddled with the worst public schools. They want their children to be able to go to schools like higher income people send theirs to, where they'll actually learn to read and write, and won't have to walk through drug deals between classes. I'd be glad to give you the names and telephone numbers of dozens of minority people who've gotten involved with our voucher efforts. They'd give you some great interviews."

"That's not necessary, Mr. Mahoney. This is just a column, not a feature article. By the way, you have kids, right? Where do they go to school?"

"They go to Good Shepherd School. Up until last year our oldest daughter went to Evergreen High, the public school down the street. Unfortunately, she was told she couldn't get a certificate of mastery unless she was able to demonstrate certain attitudes toward diversity that violated her convictions. So we put her back in a private school."

Jake felt the rush of adrenaline that comes with pivotal information. He typed, "Pulled kids from public school for religious reasons. Couldn't agree with diversity. Sends kids to church school. Evergreen nearby."

Mahoney sounded nervous again. "I hope you'll include in your column that 22 percent of NEA teachers, more than twice the national average, send their children to private schools. In Milwaukee, the figure is 50 percent. Obviously, they believe in having the choice to send their children to better schools. I applaud them for this. But why should the poor and minorities have to choose between paying tuition or paying the rent, and be forced to send their children where many public school teachers wouldn't dream of sending their own children? These people have the same hopes and desires for their kids as we do. Why should we force them to go to schools that aren't educating their children?"

Jake wasn't typing.

Mahoney paused. "Are you going to say something about this in your column?"

It's none of your business what I'm going to say. "Look, Mr. Mahoney, I don't know what's going to be in it."

"Okay. Well, I've got a stack of research here, Mr. Woods. Other states spend much less per student each year, and yet have much higher test scores than we do. Washington, DC, spends the highest amount of money per student in the country, and is exactly number 51 in test scores, the absolute worst. I've got a study here of the 170 public schools identified as the best in America, and their expenditures are way under the national average. It's an established fact there's no direct correlation between money spent and quality of education. Yet we're always told if we would only spend more money, everything would be okay. But it just isn't true. I'd be glad to send you this information, Mr. Woods. The statistics are straight from official agencies. They're not biased."

"Sorry, I just don't have the time to wade through a stack of papers from either side. I get the drift. Anything else?"

Jake had lost interest. He busily wrote and edited his story while Mahoney droned on. Finally he interrupted him.

"Okay, I've already given you more time than I gave Ms. Betcher. Any last shot you want to take?"

"Well, I don't have any shots I want to take at all. What I've said hasn't been shots, it's been honest opinions. I would say thanks to the many teachers who are doing such a great job, and I'd suggest to the schools they be open-minded and consider the advantages of instilling traditional values in kids, and getting back to the basics in the classrooms."

Jake typed a few more lines. "Okay, Mr. Mahoney. Thanks for your time."

"I'd be interested in your perspective on this issue, Mr. Woods."

"Read tomorrow's column and you'll get it. Thanks again." Jake hung up quickly. He didn't mean to be rude, but he was under deadline. Mahoney had used up too much of his time already.

It was 11:17 now, and the adrenaline was really flowing. He had to get this off by 11:35, 11:45 at the latest. At least he wasn't waiting for return calls today. He thought it should be a law, at least on Mondays, Wednesdays, and Fridays, that all important people stay by their phones—and off them—from 9:30 to 11:30 A.M.

After typing furiously, he pushed the word count key to check length. Good. He was at six hundred words already. He typed eight more sentences and got to seven hundred. It was time to call Barbara back.

"Jake Woods again. Barbara's expecting me." Ms. Betcher was on the line in five seconds. "Barbara, just wrapping it up. Talked to Carl Mahoney. Yeah, he's a real peach. Listen, I need your responses to a few of his statements. Okay, here's the first one—'public education isn't competitive with private education.'"

"That's ridiculous. We provide the finest education possible with our limited funding. Private schools are patronized by the wealthy. They close their doors to the poor, racial minorities, and handicapped children. They only let in privileged children, so at the end of the year they can say, 'See, our test scores are higher than public schools.' Our teachers are trained and certified. Theirs are glorified Sunday school teachers. Not competitive? In their dreams. Ridiculous."

So, Barbara, do you have any opinion on this. "Of course, I don't know that I'd want it said like that in print. But you hear what I'm saying, don't you Jake?"

"I do. Okay, here's another one," Jake said, searching the screen and finding the partial sentence "pay taxes, have right to say how they're spent in schools."

"Mahoney says, 'My tax money goes to the schools, so it's my right to control how that money is spent.'"

"The arrogance of these people! Who do they think they are? This isn't a company and he's not a stockholder. What about the silent majority who think we're doing a good job, and support us, or at least just leave us alone? They don't tell us how to run our schools. We've done some homework on this yahoo. Did you know Mahoney doesn't even send his kids to public school?"

"Yeah, I caught him on that."

"So what right does he have to tell us how to run a school system he's abandoned?"

"Hey, don't get mad at me, Barbara. I'm just asking the questions."

"I know. I'm not mad at you, Jake. These Bible-thumping fundamentalists just make my skin crawl. If they got their way, it would destroy education. Anything else you want me to respond to?"

"Nope, out of time. Thanks for standing by, Barbara. Good to talk with you."

"You got the fax, right?"

"Yeah, it was a big help. Thanks."

"Jake," Barbara sounded like a real pal now, "we're looking forward to you speaking at our conference in March. The NEA really appreciates the pro-child, pro-education stance of the *Trib,* and your column in particular. Keep up the good work. We'll all be looking for this column. Tomorrow's paper, right?"

"Right, assuming I finish it in the next ten minutes." 11:45 was like the empty sign on a gas gauge, but he wouldn't panic even then. You could squeeze out more miles by running on the fumes, and he could squeeze out more minutes, even if Winston grumped at him. *Winston's cute when he's crabby, anyway.*

Jake attacked the article, paragraph by paragraph. Now he had nine hundred words, and a hundred had to go. He heard the gun for the final lap and geared up for his finish-line kick.

CHAPTER TEN

J ake finished his column at 11:51, flirting as usual with his deadline. He pressed the send button, releasing it to Winston. His screen showed Winston was editing Martin's column. Jake sighed relief Martin hadn't been late. If Winston didn't have one of their columns by 11:35, he was on the prowl like a cougar, stalking his prey. Sometimes Jake hit the dump button when he saw the testy editor coming, or heard his growl, so he could say "I sent it to you," only to retrieve it and make a few more changes before Winston could work his way back to his office, sloughing off inquiries from the two-sided row of reporters.

Sometimes Jake waved his arms frantically and caught someone's attention, someone who understood the signal meant "stall Winston." Bart, the television critic, twenty feet away and facing Jake's work area, perpetually looked up at the three mini-TV screens bolted to the top rim of his cubicle. It was he, more often than not, whose attention Jake caught, and who pounced on Winston with some inane question, buying Jake the extra minute or two he needed. Such favors were commonly granted at the *Trib*. You never knew when you might need to call in your chips.

As he watched his screen, Winston exited Martin's column and sent it on to copyediting, next stop before layout and design. The terminal told Jake when Winston retrieved his column. Too late for touchups. He was supposed to stay by his desk for another fifteen minutes, in case Winston needed a conference, which he rarely did. Now it was kick back time. Jake was good for nothing the first few hours after a column. Coming to deadline with a job well done was as great a cause for celebration as coming empty-handed was cause for disgrace and regret. Usually the kick back began by taking the time to look at what others had written. Often he'd call up Martin's column and give it the once over, hoping it was mediocre at best. But not today. He'd read it as hard copy tomorrow.

The *Tribune's* bevy of columnists wasn't the close knit fraternity some newspaper groupies imagined. They rarely spent time together, perhaps believing they had more to lose than to gain by fraternizing and giving away ideas to those who seemed more like competitors than teammates. Columnists were an elite and privileged group. But he'd seen older columnists lose their touch, get replaced by the young bucks. The young ones genuinely admired them just as rookie pitchers admire the veteran hurler, but that admiration didn't stop them from bumping the veteran off the team if younger arms could do what his no longer could. Sometimes Jake felt the hot breath of younger reporters chasing after him, like hounds at his heels, turning phrases just so, in the hope that the *Trib* or some other newspaper would be so impressed they'd be offered the coveted role of columnist. It was an amazing thing, Jake thought, getting paid for doing what old men relish doing for free at lunch counters—giving an opinion on everything, solving the world's problems every day.

Jake highlighted one of the options on his screen and tapped into Clarence Abernathy's sports column. The notation showed it had been finished and to the editor by 11:30. Smart man, Clarence, since Hugh, the sports editor, had been an all-American linebacker. Clarence was Jake's favorite reading at the *Trib*—the only columnist Jake read word for word, every column. In the midst of some journalistic wannabes, Clarence brought a precision, clarity, and energy to his writing that Jake admired.

Twice a week Jake and Clarence's columns coincided, so they were in synchronous kickback modes together. Just a few weeks ago Jake distracted Pete Harman while Clarence commandeered Pete's keyboard and saved, under a different name, the article he'd been sweating over. Then he cleared the screen, making it look like Pete's entire morning's work had disappeared. He and Jake watched Pete's contortions from forty feet, while Clarence took a few pictures with fast film and a telephoto lens. After letting him try to figure out how he was going to explain it to his editor, the two fessed up. Thirty minutes later Clarence came back from the darkroom, and he and Jake presented Pete with an eight-by-ten blow up of the most mournful panicked look Pete's face had ever known.

Clarence was ten years younger than Jake and right where Jake had been at the same age, an ex-jock gym rat sports columnist with a loyal following. Jake knew if Clarence wanted to leave sports he'd make a top notch general columnist, and he'd told him so. In this case, Jake would welcome the competition. He and Clarence would sharpen each other if they ran head to head. Jake read the last paragraph of Clarence's column, smiling and saying under his breath, "You nailed him, Clarence. Another winner. Good job."

Jake heard the noon whistle from the old city hall five blocks away. One hour till lunch with Ollie. Time to set up some appointments. He knew both numbers by heart—Mary Ann at Doc's office number, Sue at Finney's home number. As he listened to the ring on Mary Ann's end, he wondered how long it would be before he forgot his friend's telephone numbers.

The calls went quickly. Fifty minutes to kill. Jake got up from his desk and headed to the staircase. Only one floor was above him, administration. It was the least familiar floor to Jake. He vaguely pictured lawyers strategizing, accountants calculating, and, most importantly, somebody issuing paychecks. But the heart of the floor was the huge plush office of Raylan Berkely, which he was familiar with. Like a star pupil shown off by the principal, Jake was called up there a couple of times a year, usually for a pat on the back, or to meet some VIP hobnobbing with Berkely or some prestigious editor the *Trib* was trying to woo from Chicago or Los Angeles.

But today Jake was going down. He descended one floor to advertising and circulation. The floor was busy, but less hectic or noisy than the newsroom, brighter and more cheery. Seeing all the people reminded him that of 1,400 *Trib* employees, only 350 were reporters, a few more counting stringers, part-time writers who worked from home. The *Trib* received three thousand phone calls a day, requiring a full staff just to answer, talk, summarize, and forward complaints and concerns about the paper's content, appearance, and delivery.

The *Trib* wouldn't happen without all these people in circulation, selling the paper, working with the supermarkets and convenience stores, recruiting delivery people, talking on the phone with potential subscribers. As Jake walked by one employee's desk, she assured an unhappy subscriber that the paperboy would be instructed to stop throwing the *Trib* in her swimming pool.

All that work, then we put the whole shootin' match in the hands of a twelve-year-old kid!

Advertising, into which Jake now strolled, was even more aesthetically pleasing. Interior design people had put in some time here and it showed. They'd never darkened the door of the newsroom, that was certain. But advertising had to deal with the high rollers, the big accounts whose advertising made the *Tribune* possible. Cheap as it was, a hundred pages of newsprint and all the labor that went into it wasn't paid for with a few coins from the buyers, not by a long shot. The best reporting in the world would never see the light of day without someone's tireless efforts selling ads.

Jake sneaked up on Maggie, his friend in advertising layout and design, pulling gently on her long auburn hair.

"Hi, Mag."

"Hey, Jake." She checked her watch. "Column finished, huh? Making your rounds?"

"Somebody's got to check up on you people down here." Jake pointed at the ad design on her computer screen. "You look like you're working hard, Mag. Grateful Dead coming to town?"

Stifled snickers surfaced from a few designers within ear shot.

"Let it drop, will you Jake? Look, it's been what, ten years?" Maggie smiled despite herself. Jake knew she enjoyed the ribbing. She'd drawn up a terrific ad for a Grateful Dead concert. She intended to place it in the Arts and Entertainment section, but somehow jotted down the wrong code and it ended up elsewhere—right in the middle of the obituaries.

Jake winked at Maggie and continued his rambling tour of the newspaper he loved. The tension between news and advertising had reached a fever pitch more than once. News always complained their "news hole" was shrinking smaller and smaller, gobbled up by advertising. In reality, there was a constant ratio of news to ads. That meant the more ads were sold, the larger the newspaper and therefore the larger the news hole. Most reporters could never grasp this, for some reason.

Every day editors learned how many total columns of print they'd been given to fill—national, state, city, sports, and so on. It didn't matter what stories were brewing. Each section had to fill its quota, no more, no less. That could mean cutting news items if not much advertising had been sold, or scurrying to get copy by calling up stringers or ransacking the wire services if too much advertising had been sold. It didn't matter how much or how little news happened today. The size of the paper was all determined by advertising sales.

Wandering aimlessly, poking his nose around this corner and that, he thought the irony of all this was most evident near Christmas and in the summer. Around Christmas, the flow of news slows considerably because lots of news sources—including government and education—go dormant. But advertising swells, forcing editors to scrounge for news, printing features and news items they'd never consider other times of the year. In summer, advertising slows and papers get thinner, meaning lots of good summer stories never go to print. Some advertising people resented the fact no ads were permitted in the first three pages. Some reporters resented ads intermixed with news anywhere. To Jake, it was a symbiotic union he'd never lost sleep over. He was a liberal, but not a socialist. He pondered the irony of journalists and their fashionable anti-capitalist bent, never seeming to grasp that their socialist ideas could have no audience apart from the consumption-oriented capitalism which bought them the very space to air their anti-market sentiments.

Now he headed for the staircase and walked down to the press room. He felt a note of sadness as he passed the floor that for decades housed the composing room, once a fixture at the *Trib* and every major newspaper. He had fond memories of the "dog houses," the rows and rows of double sided A-frame slats where dozens of cursing old men taped full pages of cut-and-paste printouts of text and pictures, putting them together, stripping on design lines and corrections and color separations before they were burned on to the metal plates. Some papers still used the old composing rooms, others were still in phase out, using them partially. The *Trib*, as of a year ago, had ended the phase out, and the last generation of newspaper composers got their pink slips. He thought nostalgically of Chester, the old makeup editor, who tweaked things by hand at the last moment, typing up and pasting on credit lines and corrections, not as straight as the always-perfect computer, but with the human touch.

The magic of pagination had changed everything. It eliminated the in-between steps, allowing newsroom computers to do layout and design, sending the finished product directly to where negatives were burned on to the steel plates, which were finally fixed on to the massive printing presses.

As he walked onto the huge open warehouse style floor, the unmistakable smell of newsprint hit him, that incomparable ambiance of paper and ink. With every step his feet felt the sticky tug of ink, settled from the air. It was quiet now, unearthly quiet, accentuated by the stark contrast to what it had been nine hours earlier and would soon be again. In a few hours the mammoth presses would be rolling, thundering at deafening levels, while men wearing earplugs yelled and signaled at each other. Jake often thought the press room was the perfect place for the hearing impaired, already so proficient with sign language.

In the center, a soundproof room was the one refuge from the noise, the eye of the hurricane, where instructions and conversations could take place. A few technicians stood in there now, discussing machinery problems. To Jake's right were a hundred rolls of newsprint, massive eighteen-hundred-pound rolls of paper, each seven miles long, yet so delicate that a single stone in a freight car could ruin an entire roll. Far too heavy to be moved by hand, the rolls traveled to the printers on conveyer belts. Five years ago a paper mill strike forced the *Trib* to run a half-size paper and under print the circulation. The paper buyer now bought rolls from six different suppliers in different parts of the region, insuring their eggs were no longer in one basket. It was unthinkable, unimaginable that the *Trib* would not be there on people's porches, in their boxes, featured on the newsstands, lying in the machines where hurried people plopped their coins.

Jake pawed through the huge garbage bins that hadn't been dumped since this morning's last printing, around 3:00 A.M. The evening edition printings started at 1:30, the first morning printing around 11:30 P.M. This was "the first draft," hauled by coffee drinking, country and western singing truckers to the far corners of the state before dawn. The second printing, around 1:00 A.M., was for closer outlying areas. The third printing, the metro edition, designed for the city dwellers, rolled off the tired presses from 2:30 till 4:00, followed by a nine hour slumber.

The metro edition not only had the benefit of late breaking news, with updates and details, but was the most accurate. Night editors, chugging down their third cups of coffee, dutifully caught errors in the first two editions, quickly correcting them before the third and final edition, which reached the most people anyway, and from which the most complaints came when something wasn't right. Final edition was the last shot—all that was good would be good forever, all that was wrong would have no chance to be redone. The corporate equivalent of each writer's deadline, final edition was one last chance to get it right. People being what they were, though, getting it just right was a pipe dream. So too many writers and too many papers, Jake thought, became content with the lousy and congratulated themselves for the mediocre.

Jake rummaged through the papers in the garbage bin, the five hundred papers wasted while the presses were adjusted. He found a sample front page of each of the first two morning editions, the ones he hadn't seen. Similar to the untrained eye, but Jake noticed in the later edition the extra details from Associated Press, the slightly smaller picture to make room for them, and the reworded headline. The headline had been changed from "Governor's reelection campaign questioned" to "Governor's campaign strategy still uncertain." The uninitiated would suppose the headline was changed to reflect greater accuracy. Jake knew it had been changed for one reason—the original had too much trapped white space. It just didn't look right. The different tone of the headlines would matter to the governor's friends and foes but probably had nothing to do with why the change was made.

Mistakes in the *Trib* used to drive Jake nuts, but no longer. How accurate can something be that comes out 365 days a year, in three to five editions a day, then is gone forever? You can't hold onto news until you're sure it's absolutely accurate, or by then it's old news and nobody cares. Nobody wants to eat a week old sandwich. Get it while it's hot. That's what it's about, Jake thought. There's a lot more truth than error, and you have to learn to live with the error.

The black smudges of the castaway papers covered his hands now, but Jake didn't mind. The huge bins of discarded newspaper, here today and gone tomorrow, commented on the industry, Jake thought. No matter how good or how bad what you wrote was, it wouldn't last. Within two days the column Jake had just finished laboring over would be strewn under bus seats, absorbing parakeet droppings, and starting winter fires. When he looked at it that way, his life seemed small, his job insignificant. It was hard to make too much of your insights when you realized no one in the next generation would be reading them, and those who would appreciate them most two days from now were vagrants seeking warmth on their favorite park benches.

Here today, gone tomorrow. Such was the newspaper. Such, it seemed to Jake, was life. Still leaning up against the bin full of smeared and trashed news and opinions, he thought about what Finney's pastor said about the brevity of life, and the heritage every man leaves. What would he leave behind after he was gone? What would the final edition of his life look like? How would other eyes, discerning eyes, read him? How would his life be measured by whatever audience ultimately mattered? Come deadline, what would the verdict be? Would his words outlast the paper they were written on?

Jake the newspaper man, recognized by a half dozen downtowners in the Main Street Deli, spread out his notes at the most remote table, up against the back wall. He'd just been served a turkey on whole-wheat for himself, a jumbo frank with extra onions and a large fry for his soon-to-arrive partner.

Ollie marched in the door right at 1:00, doing the familiar duck walk necessitated by his extra forty pounds. It wasn't obesity but the sort of surplus poundage some tough cops carry—not like the Pillsbury Doughboy but like the street-smart warrior who could head butt you around the room and toss you into the salad bar without breaking a sweat.

"Jake! You already ordered. Looks great!"

Ollie plopped down on the chair and was half way through the jumbo frank before Jake could ask "how's it going?"

Well, Ollie, nobody's gonna mistake you for Gandhi.

Ollie smacked his lips, wiped his mouth with a napkin, and asked Jake, "What's the difference between a catfish and a journalist?"

Jake rolled his eyes and shrugged.

"One's a scum-sucking bottom dweller. The other's a fish."

Jake sighed and smiled more than he intended to. Ollie was a master at recycling lawyer's jokes for reporters. Jake never took offense, especially knowing Ollie's history with the *Trib.*

"Okay, Jake, here's the deal. Tie-rod ends were cut—we knew that, but now it's official. That makes it homicide. The sarge said I could go with it. Got some details. Tie-rod on the passenger side was cut three-quarters of the way through, driver's side two-thirds. The passenger side was weaker, so it probably broke first, when your friend had to swerve or whatever. That would put instant stress on the driver's side tie-rod, snapping it off and sending the car out of control."

"Could you tell anything from the cut?"

"More than you'd guess." Ollie checked his notes. "It was a hacksaw blade, but not the low-grade type that comes with the saw. Could have been any old saw, but the blade itself was a Snap On cobalt steel blade, with twenty-four teeth, never used before."

"How do you know that?"

"It had the characteristic red smudge marks and not just trace amounts, but as much as could only come off in a first use. There's some uneven cuts where the blade slipped and only made one run, and they can tell how many teeth it had. I'll take their word for it. They're never wrong. With this kind of blade, a guy with a strong arm, lying on his back under a Suburban, could cut a rod three-quarters through in one-and-a-half to two minutes. The second one would take him longer because his arm would be tired. But if he got right at it he could have the whole thing done in five minutes."

"Come on, Ollie. How do you know all that?"

"Simple. I'm a hands on guy. I got hold of an identical tie-rod end this morning, set it up in a vise at the right height. I bought the identical hacksaw blade, cut the rods on the threads just like our guy did, lying on my back like he would have. I simulated the conditions, then sawed away and timed it. Of course, the guy probably wasn't the stud I am, so it might have taken him an extra few minutes, even accounting for all the adrenaline. I put myself in the part—always do that—so I had some adrenaline too. If I did this in a private garage, no sweat, but if I was in the open, on a back street or in a driveway, I'd be stopping, turning my head this way and that, looking and listening for approaching feet. If he did it in the middle of the night there'd be less risk of being seen, but more danger of sound carrying, so it'd be a trade-off. If it was dark he'd need a little penlight or something to get his saw on the right spot. One other thing would slow him down—probably added 50 percent to my cutting time. He'd have to keep checking to make sure he was cutting far enough but not too far. If he cut too far, nobody would get hurt because the car wouldn't get out of the driveway before it broke.

"So factoring all that in we're probably talking a ten minute job. No more, unless he had to freeze under there till someone walked by. The cutting makes more noise than I would have guessed. It would seem really loud to a guy under the car, terrified of being caught. Unless he was a pro, this guy's heart would be pounding like a jackhammer. But with average street background noise, nobody would hear unless they were within, say, thirty feet of the car. If it was done at an off time in a low foot traffic area it would be easy to get away with."

"I'm impressed."

Ollie shrugged. "It's my job."

"Fingerprints?"

"Yep. Conclusive."

"You're kidding."

"Nope."

"Ollie, stop toying with me. Conclusive fingerprints?"

"We know conclusively the killer was Homo sapiens. Unfortunately, the only prints were smudged, so that's all we know. But at least we can eliminate all other species. For instance, it definitely wasn't an orangutan."

Exasperated, Jake made strangling motions with his hands. "Ollie, how would you like to investigate your own homicide?"

"Hey, I once solved a case where orangutan prints were critical. You never know."

Jake wasn't going to bite. "Tell me now what you've got and what you haven't got or some other detective is going to find my prints all over your throat!"

"Touchy today, aren't we? Catching the PMS that's been going around? Okay, the only prints on the tie-rod or anywhere under the car were smudged. The weather's been perfect for long-term prints, nice and moist, so I had some hopes. And usually there's lots of oil accumulated underneath a car and clear prints are a possibility—but your friend's car was amazingly clean, even underneath."

"You didn't know Doc. Wouldn't surprise me if he polished the tie-rods every week."

"Aren't you going to ask me about the prints on the note card?"

"No, I'm not. You'll tell me if you want to."

"From the look of it, whoever sent the yellow card wasn't a heavy sweater and hadn't been eating onion rings, so I didn't expect good prints on it. Except yours of course. By the way, they need to get your prints to verify those beauties all over it are yours, but I assured them they were."

"Thanks."

"But anyway, besides your prints, there was a partial of a thumb and a perfect index finger. They ran AFIS and no match. So probably it's someone without a criminal record, unless it's in Lower Slobovia or something. But if we get a specific suspect, we can make a positive ID with that print. Meanwhile, Jimmy gave me odds that narrow the card's sender to half the human race."

Jake looked uncertain.

"He says it was probably a woman."

"How does he know that? From the fingerprints?"

"You can't tell gender from prints. What they found was a tiny particle. Little red thing that hung on the card, but you couldn't see it with the naked eye."

"And?"

"Guess."

"I don't have a clue."

"Go ahead and guess."

"Ollie, I'm gonna..."

"Fingernail polish."

"No kidding?"

"So, I figure...it was either a woman or a transvestite."

Ollie laughed hard and long at this one, and Jake cringed as everyone in the room turned and looked at them. Everyone except the one closest to them, a sandy-haired, stocky man in a business suit two tables over, whose head was buried in the morning issue of the *Trib* and whose eyes emerged only when tilting his head back to drink his wine cooler. Jake noticed it was his own favorite, Red Sangria.

"All right, here's the scoop," Ollie was keeping it down now. "The boys found two things under the car that could help us, and they're still looking them over in the lab. Both look recent. First, there were a few short hairs, black and gray mixture, caught in a few joints and crevices under the Suburban. Human hairs, not animal. From that picture of your friend you gave me, it definitely isn't his hair. I called his regular mechanic—there was a receipt in the glove compartment—and the guy hadn't worked on the car for five weeks, and his hair doesn't match either, so we figure it had to come from the perp. Even with the high suspension, it was a snug fit under there, assuming it wasn't hoisted up. So it would be easy to snag your hair. Could have come from the scalp or beard or mustache. So I told the guys, 'Thanks a lot, now we know it was a woman with nice red fingernails and a crewcut or a beard.'"

Jake rolled his eyes. "That's only if the person under the car was the one who sent the note. We don't know that, right?"

"Right. Actually, I doubt it was. If a woman sent the note, could be her husband or boyfriend who cut the tie-rod. A woman could have cut the tie-rods, but not likely. Cutting tie-rods is a man sort of thing and typing a neat little note on a yellow note card is a woman sort of thing, don't you think?"

"I outgrew sexual stereotypes years ago. I wouldn't know."

"Spoken like a true journalist. Don't let the realities of human nature sway you, huh?"

"You said there was another clue?"

"Right. A tiny snag of navy blue fabric. They found it way underneath, nearly four feet from the tie-rods. I think the perp snagged his sweat pants. Possibly sweatshirt, but my money's on pants. The guy's knee—or girl's knee if we've got a liberated short-haired female murderer—was bent up when he hacked away on the rods. I laid on my back under a Suburban to figure all this out, and it made sense. They're running more tests on the fabric. The hairs are another story. They have potential."

"Really? What can you do with hair?"

"Sometimes you can identify race. You can narrow down your suspects because you can conclusively prove hair isn't from certain people. You can say it's probably from this person, but hair doesn't usually nail anybody in court. It's hard to prove anything from a strand of hair, unless…" Ollie paused, as if to see if Jake knew the answer.

Jake shrugged his shoulders.

"Unless there's a follicle." He paused for effect. "Never would have thought we could still have a good one after ten days, but the moisture in the air saved the day. One of our hairs has a decent follicle."

"So?"

"So when you've got a follicle and it hasn't dried out or rotted, you can get a

DNA fingerprint."

"What's that?"

Ollie sighed. "Everybody has forty-six chromosomes, twenty-three from Mom and twenty-three from Dad." Ollie the biologist. "Each chromosome contains a hundred thousand genes. So the combination is absolutely unique. We use it when there's blood on a scene and to test semen in rape cases. It's expensive, but when you can make a positive match it's 100 percent reliable. In fact, the military now keeps a little genetic sample from every soldier, so even if there's not much left of the body, there won't be any more unknown corpses in battle. Would have ended a lot of uncertainties in Nam, huh?"

Jake nodded, thinking about missing soldiers who couldn't be identified because so little was left.

"Genetic fingerprinting? Interesting. Sounds like what we need."

"Hopefully, but only to nail an existing suspect. There's no master computer file that's got everybody's DNA fingerprint, so we have to go out and get them from suspects. But if we get to that point, we can ask for voluntary contributions. Of course, if we have enough evidence we can demand it. Even if we can't, though, we've got some pretty clever ways of getting it."

"What do you mean, voluntary contributions? If someone's guilty, they wouldn't volunteer."

"One time we had a rape and there was some dried semen on the woman's clothes. The genetic fingerprints proved the primary suspect was innocent. We had reason to believe the rapist lived in the same neighborhood, so we asked for voluntary blood tests from every guy on the block. They didn't have to cooperate, but of course if they refused they knew they'd become a suspect. Well, everyone agreed, but this one guy got a friend to do the blood test in his place. Almost got away with it. But we caught him, got a judge to order a blood test on the real guy, and sure enough, he was our perp. The test nailed him. The lab gives us a form, and at the bottom it computes the chances of any other human being having the same results. The answer is usually 'less than one in ten billion.' When you consider the population of the world, that's pretty conclusive, even to the most bleeding heart juror. The guy's in jail, probably earning a college degree as we speak."

"You've impressed me again, Ollie."

"Hey, your job isn't the only one that takes skill, you know."

"I'm realizing that. Maybe we're not wasting our tax money on you guys after all."

Ollie looked at Jake. "Well, I've done my part. So what do you have for me, detective?"

Jake handed over his lists, dispensing profuse disclaimers about how unlikely everybody was. Then he eyed his list of compromised women and their husbands.

"Wait a minute, Ollie. You think a man cut the tie-rods and a woman did the note card? How about this scenario? The woman's upset that her husband caused this accident, maybe she even loved the guy he killed—in fact, that's exactly why he killed him. Okay, so she finds out about it. Either she's angry or she has a conscience attack. Maybe she wants her husband or boyfriend or whoever to be caught, but doesn't want to come right out and be the one to nail him. Maybe because she's afraid of him or feels guilty because of her affair? So she sends me the note card."

"Great movie plot, Jake. You sound like a soap opera screenwriter. Actually, I like it. We'll take a close look at Doc's girlfriends and their men. Okay, what else?"

"I'm getting some info on anti-abortion activists. I called Sue, Finney's wife, and I'm meeting with her tomorrow morning. I meet with Mary Ann, Doc's secretary, this afternoon. I hope she can fill me in on the scene at the hospital. I'll get the doctors' names I left blank on your list. Then if I need to, I'll talk to Betsy, Doc's wife. But I just don't want to upset her, Ollie. Does she have to know there's a homicide investigation?"

Ollie paused a moment. "Maybe not quite yet, given the after-the-fact nature of this whole thing. Eventually, of course. I like these quiet investigations where there's no media pressure, so we can do our jobs without suspects hearing speculation and strategy on the six o'clock news. Or reading about it in some half-wit's column."

"Very funny."

"To the columnist maybe. Not to the detective."

As they headed toward the door, Ollie reached his right hand inside his suit jacket, to his Colt Police .45, fingering it, as was his habit whenever he went back on the street. He saw Jake watch him and couldn't resist a comment.

"Almost traded it in on a guns-for-toys exchange. But when push came to shove and the bad guys had me cornered in an alley, I thought, would I rather have this or a Ken doll? Ken's a real cutie, but hey, what can I say? I chose the .45."

Ollie and Jake walked out together at 2:05. The sandy-haired man in the business suit walked around the block to his blue Mercedes, jotted down some notes, and picked up his car phone.

Jake walked down the familiar corridor to Doc's office at Lifeline Hospital. He'd remembered it as bright and cheery. Today it was dark and gloomy. He walked into the front administrative office and turned to the right, to the head of surgery's office. While Mary Ann wrapped up a phone call, he looked with casual disinterest at a *Newsweek*, scanning the bylines to see who he knew. Often Jake chose the articles he read not by the subject, but by the writer.

Mary Ann, tall and slim with strikingly full and glimmering chestnut hair, had the face and body of a twenty-five-year-old receptionist and the tempered skills of a fifty-year-old office manager. Doc raved about her. As Jake recalled, she'd come to Lifeline six months ago after Doc's old secretary quit. Mary Ann had just moved to town and was overqualified for the job, but took it anyway. She was top flight. Smart. Diplomatic. "Savvy about hospital politics," Jake remembered him saying. Doc was blunt and sometimes abrasive and needed the equivalent of a press secretary to take off the sharp edges. Mary Ann was just the one. He could trust her with anything. That she was young, warm, and beautiful didn't hurt either.

"Jake," Mary Ann said. Her perfume preceded her as she walked toward him and extended her invitingly feminine right hand. "Welcome. I'm glad you called. I've thought about you often since...everything happened."

A lot of guys would feel it in their spines hearing Mary Ann say she'd been thinking of them. Jake realized he was one of those guys.

"Yeah, well...I guess it hasn't been easy for you, either."

"No, it hasn't. Just trying to keep my head above water while they get a new chief of surgery. Till then I have to do my job and half of what Greg did. I'm just hoping they won't assign me an open heart surgery!" She laughed. "So, what can I do for you, Jake?"

"Can we go somewhere more private?"

Mary Ann looked curious. "Sure. We could go in Greg's old office. Nobody's using it yet." She led the way.

Jake had the eerie sensation he was walking into a museum. Doc's books and wall hangings were right where Jake remembered them his last visit, maybe three weeks ago when he picked him up for an afternoon round of golf.

"I haven't had time to go through everything yet and get it all packed up for Greg's wife. I told her I'd be glad to do it, and she said no hurry."

Jake wished the office could be left as it was, but he realized businesses didn't keep memorial offices. Mary Ann waited attentively.

"Well, I don't know quite how to say this, and this is very confidential. Do you understand?"

"I understand confidential, if that's what you mean."

"Well, there's an investigation into Doc's...into Greg's death."

"Investigation?"

"It looks like it was murder."

Jake almost relished this moment because he was sure he could finally throw the unflappable Mary Ann for a loop. She did raise her eyebrows, but that was it. Now she looked skeptical.

"Murder?"

Jake recounted the note card and tie-rod story.

"So, you're conducting the investigation?" Mary Ann still sounded skeptical.

"Well, I'm just...sort of a go-fer. A homicide detective asked me to help."

"This isn't for a newspaper story is it?" Mary Ann squinted distastefully.

"Of course not. I'm in this because my best friends were killed, not for a byline." Jake sounded defensive, and he knew it.

"Okay. What do you want from me?"

"Information."

"Like what?"

"Like, did Doc have any unhappy patients you know of?"

"Everybody thought he was a terrific surgeon. There's always some gripes, but I never saw anything really serious."

"Nothing?"

"Not that I can think of. Did he mention any to you?"

"No, not really. I figured you'd know. No lawsuits or anything like that?"

"Malpractice? He had some a few years ago, I've heard. But nothing recent. It's rare for a doctor not to have them you know."

"So I've heard. Now this may get a little...touchy. Are there people who work here at the hospital that Doc had run-ins with?"

"All kinds of them," she laughed. "It might be easier to give you the list of those he didn't."

"I mean serious conflicts, where it might have gotten personal."

"As in, personal enough to kill him?"

"Look, we're just looking for names of people with an ax to grind against Doc. I'm talking about regular people, not terrorists or anything. Anyone come to mind?"

"Anyone who might be a criminal?" Mary Ann clearly resented the implication.

"Look, Mary Ann, maybe I'm not approaching this right. Please, I've been asked to do this by the homicide detective in charge of this investigation. If you don't want to talk to me, you can talk to him."

"No, that's all right. I'm sorry, Jake. I didn't mean to be difficult. I'm glad to help anyway I can. This is just a little, well different. Let me check the personnel roster. There's not a person who works here capable of killing him, but that's my opinion and you already know that, so let's go from there." Mary Ann ran her index finger down a computer printout.

"Well, Greg didn't like Dr. Carlton, and the feeling was mutual. Ditto with Dr. Morgan. And he refused to work with Dr. Dudley, he's an anesthesiologist. Greg said he was incompetent, almost lost a patient. Dudley claimed it was Greg's fault. There was an investigation, and no blame was assigned."

"Investigation?"

"Yeah, it came through the State Medical Board. That's where patient complaints are filed, and sometimes doctor's complaints about each other, if they're serious enough. I don't know the details. Haven't been here long enough. Maybe the patient advocate could tell you."

"Patient advocate?" Jake jotted down the note.

"Just down the hall. When patients have a complaint they often go to administration, and she's the contact. She listens to them, and if it's anything other than a misunderstanding she can help clear up, she refers them to the State Board, gives them the address and forms." Mary Ann paused. "Does this interest you?"

"Yes, it does. Please, keep going down the list."

"Well, Dr. Marsdon was on the ethics committee with Greg, and they were always duking it out. Marsdon has an opinion on everything, and Doc got fed up with him. Quit the committee. Marsdon seemed to have it out for him."

"Is Marsdon a tall red-headed guy?"

"Yes. You know him?"

"No, but I was with Doc when we passed by him in the hall one time. They shot some pretty chilling glares at each other. I asked Doc what was going on and he changed the subject."

"I don't know the whole story, but there was definitely bad blood."

"What can you tell me about the committees Doc was on?"

"Well, let's see, there were four, five counting the Ethics committee—the surgical committee, the quality assurance committee, the transplant committee, and the intensive care committee. He chaired a couple of them, at one time or another."

"What do they do in these committees?"

"They've all got their purpose statements. How effective they are is debatable. You know all the jokes about committees—a camel is a horse put together by a committee, and stuff like that? I've been told committees used to be a prestige thing here. Looked good on your resumé. Some doctors won't serve on them anymore. They're so tired of all the red tape everywhere. But there's still power there. You determine policy, make alliances. Trade votes."

"Vote trading?"

"Sure, it even happens on the Supreme Court. Ever read Woodward's *The Brethren?*"

"Yeah." Jake had once skimmed it in an airport bookstore, but it seemed the right response.

"I don't know how much I should be telling you, but a lot of people don't have a clue the political forces at work in a big hospital. It's pretty cut throat."

"In what way?"

"For one thing, administration and physicians sometimes are in real adversarial roles."

"Why?"

"Competition for the bottom line—money. Hospital management wants to capture physicians' incomes. Not all of it, but they want a great deal more than the doctors want to give. With all the health care changes, available dollars are even more limited. You can understand why doctors can't roll over and let everybody pick their pockets."

Mary Ann had the distinct sound of a legislative assistant—she did understand the politics. Jake could see why Doc admired her.

"Sometimes you get a few doctors together and they set up clinics competing with the hospital. They hire their own staffs. They figure, why should the pencil pushers and PR people get their money, when its their skills people want? Our CEO here is a businessman, not a doctor, and the doctors feel like military officers taking orders from civilians. It just doesn't sit well. Generally, they manage to get along, at least on the outside, but sometimes the lines get drawn. Like union and management battles I guess. Some people feel pulled two directions."

"Anyone in administration hostile to Doc?"

"Dr. Cooper, the CEO, for one."

"I thought you said he wasn't a doctor."

"He's a Ph.D. Believe me, that doesn't impress an MD! Greg used to say, 'He isn't a real doctor.' I heard he said it once to his face. You know Greg."

"Yeah. Anyone else you see on the list?"

Mary Ann moved down the rest of the alphabet. "Let's see. Reilly. No problems. Simpson. Greg liked him. Turner. Orthopedic surgeon. Greg didn't have much time for him, but no serious conflicts—at least, not that I know of."

She threw out a Dr. Walden as her last case where there was bad blood, assuring Jake once more none of these people were killers.

"Okay, one last question. What do you know about the anti-abortion people?"

"The kooks, you mean? Now there's some people who belong on a suspect list! They'd be capable of taking out anybody that crossed them. And Greg crossed them, big time."

"How?"

"Well, you know his part in the abortion pill discussions. They were out holding their stupid signs for months, trying to give the hospital a bad name. Same with fetal tissue research. Greg was instrumental in securing one of the research grants, and they didn't like it a bit. Why don't these people mind their own business and get a life?"

Jake shrugged his uncertainty. "Anything else they have against him? Maybe more recent?"

"Nothing that comes to mind." Mary Ann hesitated. "Well, is this confidential?"

"If it's pertinent I have to tell the police, but otherwise, yes, it's confidential."

"Okay, since he was your friend I guess I can trust you with it now, even though I'm willing to bet he never did. He was involved with a few late-term abortions. Perfectly legal, of course, but he didn't want anyone to know about them. The protesters go bananas over stuff like that. They can make life miserable for you. Greg didn't want anybody to know."

"Who did know?"

"A handful of doctors and a few nurses, I suppose. Plus somebody at one of the clinics that made the referrals. Most won't do them after twenty-four weeks, so they pass them on to hospitals."

"Twenty-four weeks?"

"Yeah, you know, the late-term stuff is pretty sickening, from what I've been told."

Jake wanted to change the subject. "Okay. Do you know any of these protesters by name? Especially any that might have contacted Doc personally?"

"No, not really. He got some letters. I took a few phone calls. Most were cordial on the outside, but you can sense the arrogance, the condemnation. These are self-righteous people. Loose cannons. I'd check them out for sure."

"Yeah, I plan to."

Jake jotted down some more notes, then headed out to the hallway. Mary Ann walked him out the door.

"Listen, Jake. I feel bad about how...uncooperative I may have seemed at first. I feel like I owe you one. How about I take you to dinner tomorrow night?"

Jake was taken off guard. "You don't owe me anything. I mean . . ."

"No, listen, it's a good excuse anyway. I've...well, I've thought before I'd enjoy getting to know you better. An office is such a stuffy place. I thought maybe we could have some fun together. How about tomorrow night?" Her bright warm smile took on new dimensions.

"Well, I'd be a fool to turn down that invitation. I'm working late at the *Trib* tomorrow afternoon. Probably can't leave till after 6:30."

"Perfect. I'll meet you at 7:00 downtown, say at Anthony's, on Fifth Street?"

"Uh, sure, Anthony's at 7:00."

Jake felt intoxicated by the combination of Mary Ann's perfume, her smile, and her graceful fingers with their crimson nails, now making themselves at home on his right shoulder.

"Great. I'll look forward to it, Jake. See you then."

Mary Ann waved coyly and returned to her desk. Jake watched her admiringly, then turned and walked toward the patient advocate office with a noticeably lighter step.

CHAPTER ELEVEN

After getting Little Finn off to school at 8:15, Sue Keels sat down in her bright warm kitchen, savoring her morning coffee and solitude. Sometimes Finney wouldn't leave for work till 9:00, and they'd enjoy those forty-five minutes together. The hardest times were waking up and reaching over to a husband who wasn't there, and preparing for a 6:00 dinner knowing Finney wasn't going to barge in the front door at 5:45 and meet her in the kitchen for a hug and kiss.

Jake had called last night and said he'd be there at 9:00. He sounded tense. It hadn't been easy for Sue—not at all—but she felt she had the resources to deal with her loss. She was afraid Jake didn't.

Sue opened up the *Tribune*, skimmed over the lead stories, and went to the forum section. There was Jake's column right on the front page, upper left. She read it faithfully, sometimes agreeing, often disagreeing. She glanced at Jake's sketched profile and smiled, noting the picture gave no hint of his graying sideburns and slightly receding hairline.

"We've got to update that sketch, Jake," she said aloud, eagerly digging into his column, titled, "Our Schools: Our Future."

> According to Barbara Betcher, head of Oregon's chapter of the National Education Association, our public schools face a funding crisis. She says a great deal of blame for children's problems has been laid at the feet of public schools when parental neglect and child abuse have risen dramatically.
>
> "The stability of the children's home environment affects their academic performance," Betcher says. "Given our limited funding, I think we're doing a remarkable job in the classroom."
>
> I got a very different picture from Carl Mahoney, head of Citizens Advocating Responsible Education (CARE), a right-wing group with a long history of battling public schools. Mahoney's reaction to raising teacher's salaries or any other increases in school funding? "It's like trying to put out a fire with gasoline."
>
> According to Mr. Mahoney, "Public education is inferior to private education." He claims "many school programs are harmful and destructive," citing declining test scores as proof. When I asked him about public schools that would close down if school vouchers became a reality, he said, "We'd all be better off if they *were* closed." As for the poor and minorities who would be hurt most by vouchers, Mr. Mahoney simply says "they wouldn't."
>
> Carl Mahoney is bothered that "morality," by which he means his

particular brand of morality, isn't the central focus in schools. He opposes birth control and abortion, and thinks schools shouldn't discuss such issues. Mr. Mahoney says "It's my tax money that goes to the public schools, so I have a right to control how it's spent."

Ms. Betcher says we should be proud our state test scores are better than the national average. She points out the deck is stacked toward higher test scores in private schools because they don't accept poor and minorities.

"Public schools accept everyone. Naturally, underprivileged children pull down test score averages, but every child deserves an education."

I agree with Mr. Mahoney that public schools have to set their sights high. I agree with Ms. Betcher that we must not discriminate by leaving out poor and minorities because they cannot afford our schools. That's the whole reason for tax-funded public schools in the first place, to assure an education for all children regardless of race, religion, sexual orientation or economic status.

Some may be surprised to know that though Mr. Mahoney lives just down the street from Evergreen School, he sends his children to a private fundamentalist school. That is his prerogative. But doesn't it raise some questions about his right to control the curriculum of schools he has chosen to give up on? If I handed in my resignation to the *Tribune* this week, accusing it of mismanagement, then came back in six months to tell the editors how to run this newspaper, should I be surprised if I wasn't given much credibility?

You and I pay taxes too, and Mr. Mahoney's taxes are a very small part of the total. But they aren't "his" taxes anyway. They are his debt to society. None of us has any more right to demand our schools do something our way than he has to tell the Highway Administration what roads to build and how they must build them. While private schools have the luxury of fostering whatever narrow set of beliefs they prefer, public schools don't. Funding our schools is basic to fostering the sense of healthy diversity and pluralistic thinking essential to the future of this country.

Mahoney advocates abstinence indoctrination, with its implicit conformity to fundamentalist Christian beliefs. No doubt he'd like to see creation taught instead of evolution. Again, it's his right to send his children to a private religious school. But it's not his right to try to turn our public schools, which his children don't even attend, into the mirror image of a fundamentalist school. The rest of us have rights too. That's what this country is about.

Do I want to spend more money on taxes? No. Do I support our schools? Yes. These may seem like conflicting priorities, but the choice is clear. Children are the future of our country. So instead of abandoning our schools and casting stones at those trying to help them, how about we try something else, something harder but a great deal more productive?

How about we choose to invest in our schools, reminding ourselves that an investment in our children is always the best investment in our future.

Sue put down the paper and sighed, "Oh, Jake." She shook her head slowly, both hands wrapped around her coffee cup, absorbing its warmth.

At 9:05 the door bell rang. Smiling, Sue opened the door to a typically rumpled Jake, with a brown v-neck sweater and casual maroon shirt underneath. Sue always had to fight the instinct to straighten his collars or volunteer to iron his shirts. After the two eyed each other a moment, she threw her arms around him and gave him a bear hug.

"Wow." Jake responded. "What will the neighbors think?"

"That some strange man is visiting me. And they'll be right," Sue laughed. "Come in, Jake. Sit down."

Sue pointed toward the living room, which looked exactly as it had twelve days earlier. Jake walked in, eerily looking around the room as if he expected some bats to suddenly dive bomb him. He avoided the couch where he'd last sat with his friends, choosing the rocking chair over by the coffee table. As he sat down his eyes dropped to the shiny but pockmarked hardwood surface.

"I put the quarter in my jewelry box," Sue volunteered. "For some reason I felt like hanging on to it."

"Yeah. I guess I almost expected it to be just sitting there on its side. Crazy thing, wasn't it?"

Sue nodded. "How's it been for you, Jake?"

"Listen, Sue. I'm sorry I haven't been over, and I haven't called you since the funeral. I..."

"I know, Jake. Don't even think about it. I am going to miss Sunday afternoons though."

"Yeah. Well, at least there's going to be a lot less clean up." Jake was instantly sorry he'd said it.

"I already miss cleaning up after you guys." Sue choked on her emotions, then tried to harness them with a smile. "I hope you can still come over once in a while, Jake. I'm no substitute for Finney or Doc, but I'd be glad to make popcorn, pass you a beer, and show you how little I know about football."

Jake smiled weakly.

"The kids miss you too. Little Finn's always talking about you."

"Yeah, I was thinking maybe I could take him to a ballgame or something."

"That'd be great. It would mean a lot to him. Me too."

"Yeah, I'll do that. I'll check my schedule and give him a call."

Jake cleared his throat even though he didn't need to.

"Listen, Sue, I've got to talk to you about something. It's a little strange—no, it's *really* strange—and I don't know any good way to get into it, so let me just tell you what happened."

Jake recounted the story of the yellow three-by-five card, his meetings with Ollie and the trip to the wrecking yard. Sue leaned forward, hanging on every word.

"The bottom line is, somebody was trying to kill Doc." Jake decided not to bring up the possibility they were trying to get him or Finney. She didn't need that.

Sue sat there, still from the shoulders up, rubbing her hands together as if they were frostbitten. "Just when you think life's getting as crazy as it can, it gets crazier."

Sue got up and went to the window. Jake couldn't see her face but knew she was crying. After several minutes of awkward silence, he started back in.

"Ollie wants me to come up with suspects. I mean, there's no one obvious, so I'm supposed to come up with anybody who had a conflict with Doc, an ax to grind. I've met with Mary Ann, you know, Doc's secretary? I got a few ideas from her. And I've got a few of my own."

"Who?"

Jake resisted an instinct to hold back, giving Sue the full list, "scorned women" and "betrayed husbands" and all. Jake could tell from Sue's expression she was aware of Doc's indiscretions. He wondered if it was sinking in that one of Doc's affairs might be the reason her own husband died. When it did, she'd have to be bitter. No, angry. Looking at Sue, he could imagine anger, but not bitterness.

"Jake, I'm glad you told me all this, scary as it is. What can I do to help?"

"Well, I have to ask you something. It's a little delicate, but..."

"You want me to go undercover as a prostitute to flush out the murderer?"

Jake laughed. "Well, not quite *that* delicate."

"Good."

"Ollie said I should check on anything, no matter how improbable. You know how Doc used to perform abortions? And he was on the committee that got the abortion pill and the fetal tissue research grant over at the hospital. And, this is confidential, but it appears he might have done some late-term abortions even recently."

Sue closed her eyes and sighed. The latter was obviously news to her.

"So I thought maybe one of the anti-abortion people might have...might have gone after Doc."

Sue looked at Jake in disbelief. "You're suggesting a prolifer murdered Doc and Finney?"

"No, not really, but Ollie wants every possibility."

Sue looked hurt. Her body language said she was holding her reaction in check. "So what are you asking me, Jake?"

"Well, I guess for some possible names."

"Is this like when actors were asked to turn over names of people in Hollywood that might be communists?"

"Sue, come on, I just—"

"You just want the names of people who object to children being killed because anybody who'd defend a vulnerable child is likely to be a murderer, is that it? Will the names be taken before a Senate committee, or were you just going to print them in your column and let other people harass them? Is this going to be the latest *Tribune* lynching of the politically incorrect?"

Sue's eyes blazed, and Jake tried to figure out where he'd gone wrong.

"It's not like that at all, Sue. It's just that Doc got some pretty hateful letters.

I've gotten a few myself. I know how you feel about this thing, and we've got some honest differences, okay? I'm not saying anybody you know did this, but *some*body did it. I'm just trying to find some possibilities, no matter how remote. But I can see this is too much for you." Jake started to get up. "I'll just—"

"Sit down, Jake." Sue felt awful and looked it.

"Yes'm." Jake reversed himself and fell back into the rocking chair.

"Jake, I'm sorry. I'm really sorry. My emotions are on my shirt sleeves. I blew it. Please forgive me."

"Look, Sue, you don't have to apologize."

"Yes, I do, Jake. Let me try to explain. I guess I get a little defensive about this stereotype that people like me are hateful. I know you didn't say that, but I'm used to having that laid on me. You probably didn't know that for the last six months or so I've been going down to the Lovepeace clinic once a week to counsel women as they go in. I'm just there to help, but people are always giving me obscene gestures. And *I've* been at Lifeline to protest RU-486. I never saw Doc there, to be honest I hoped I never would. I always went an hour after he went to work so I wouldn't have to face off with him. I've gotten to know these...'protesters.' The idea that one of them could possibly do such a thing is.... To be honest, it really offends me."

"Sue, I didn't mean—"

"I know you didn't, Jake. You're my friend. And you were always such a special friend to Finney."

Tears streamed down Sue's cheeks now, overcoming every effort to hold them back. Jake wished for a moment he was more like Finney, that he could reach out and touch and comfort her. But he couldn't. The trip across the living room was too long, comforting too foreign.

Sue grabbed the Kleenex beside the table lamp. "I've been buying this stuff in bulk," she laughed. "I keep it nearby in case something reminds me of Finney. Problem is, pretty much everything does.

"I'm okay now, Jake. Of course I'll help you. I don't know everybody in the different prolife groups, but I've got friends who do. If there's somebody vengeful or weird or something, somebody that could have done this, maybe they'd know. I'd be glad to introduce you to them, and you can ask them yourself."

"That's not necessary, Sue. I thought if you just happened to know a name or two..."

"What's wrong? Afraid to meet some Bible-banging fundamentalist bigots?" Sue grinned, good-naturedly baiting him.

"No, not afraid. Just not sure how helpful it would be."

"I think you'd be surprised at how down to earth and honest these people are. As long as we assure them nothing they say will get printed in the *Tribune*, most of them would love to meet you and help any way they could. It wouldn't go in the newspaper, would it?"

"Of course not." Sue's distrust for journalism irked him.

"On Mondays a dozen of us meet to pray for pregnant moms and their unborn babies. Most of us are women, but there's a few men too. We could meet right here next Monday morning at 7:00. I'll have coffee and donuts for you, Jake. Your favorite kind."

"Okay, why not? Monday will work." Trying too hard to act casual, Jake glanced nervously at his schedule book and wrote it in.

"Don't worry, Jake. Nobody's going to try to baptize you or anything."

"Thanks, Sue. That's reassuring." He started to get up.

"Can you stay a few more minutes?"

"Sure." He sat down again. "What's up?"

"I just read your column about Carl Mahoney."

"It wasn't really about Mahoney. I just quoted him on some things."

"What everybody's going to remember is about him. Listen, I know Carl and Linda Mahoney and their kids. They go to our church. Their kids go to our school. They're about the sweetest family you'd ever want to meet. I've never heard them say an unkind word. Sure, they have convictions, but that doesn't make them self-righteous rednecks, Jake."

"I didn't say they were, did I?"

"Yes, actually you did. Not in those words, of course. Jake, I don't know how else to say this, but you have a way of putting people down, putting labels on them. The truth is, the Carl Mahoney I've known for years is not the Carl Mahoney you portrayed in that column."

"Look, Sue, you didn't hear the interview. I asked him questions, he answered, I quoted his answers. Okay, I took issue with him. It was nothing personal."

"What do you think it's going to do to Carl and his family?"

"What do you mean?"

"Jake, come on. Words have an effect on people. Proverbs says, 'Life and death are in the power of the tongue.' My high school debate coach called what you did in your column setting up a straw man. You state the other person's position as if it were stupid, then that sets yours up to sound smart. And when your case isn't strong enough, you resort to ad hominem arguments, attacking the person's character."

"I know what ad hominem means." Sue was in lecture mode and Jake bristled at being lectured.

"You should, because that's exactly what you did with Carl. Once he's labeled as a right-wing extremist, people won't listen to him. So they won't have to deal with the common sense stuff he's saying."

"Are you finished?" Jake asked.

"Not quite. Actually, Jake, every day I read straw man and ad hominem arguments sprinkled throughout the *Tribune*. It isn't occasional anymore. It's constant. People with beliefs and values like the Mahoney's—and mine and Finney's—are misrepresented. I resent that, Jake. It's like you're tolerant of every position except ours. Your new term for moral conviction is 'bigotry.' I don't think it's right and I don't think it's fair. Why can't you just quote exactly what people say and stick to the facts?"

Jake rolled his eyes, digging in for another skirmish over media bias.

"Come on, Sue. Ever read a courtroom transcript? It's accurate, but incredibly boring. We have to select and summarize, cut to the heart of the issue as we see it. If we just record every word of an interview, it's way too long and it's deadly dull. Nobody would read it."

"I don't have to know every word, Jake. Just enough of them to get an accurate picture. And no offense, but when I read the paper I'm not interested in hearing the heart of the issue as the reporter sees it. I just want to know what happened, hear what people actually said, and have the freedom to come to my own conclusions. I'm tired of having to wade through the reporter's slant in search of the real facts."

"You do understand a column is supposed to be opinion?"

"Of course I understand that. I like to read columns, even those I disagree with. Give your opinion, give it sarcastically or forcefully if you want to. But you're not entitled to distort and take out of context. You're not entitled to misrepresent people's positions and integrity. I know Carl Mahoney's positions and I know his integrity. How come I didn't see either in your column?"

Jake started to respond, but Sue went right on, unfolding the morning *Tribune*. "Look at this, Jake. This article on legal efforts to prevent special minority status for homosexuals. First, it quotes the governor comparing the issue to Nazi Germany and the holocaust. Then, look at this lead quote that supposedly captures one side's position. 'Homosexuals are animals. They don't deserve to have any rights at all.' Jake, I've had dozens of discussions with supporters of this measure, and not once have I ever heard anything approaching this kind of hateful attitude. My bet is the woman was misquoted, but even if she wasn't it's grossly inaccurate to portray this as a typical attitude."

"Look, Sue, I know the reporter who wrote this. He's a nice guy. He wouldn't make this stuff up."

"I'm not saying he's not a nice guy, Jake. The drunk driver who killed Jenny was a nice guy. I'm just looking at the results."

"Look, Sue. We've got better things to do at the *Trib* than plot to overthrow the church or whatever it is you people think we're doing. While you send us letters telling us we're going to hell, your political adversaries send us nice concise press releases. They also return our phone calls, which your side often doesn't. Any wonder if they come off looking better?"

"I've never sent a letter like that and I hope you know it, Jake. And could it be past experience that makes people hesitate to return your phone calls? But maybe you're right—maybe we don't relate to the media the way we should. But help me with this, will you? Reading the *Trib* every day I keep getting the distinct feeling that to not be a bigot you have to believe every choice and every action is as good as every other one. The only way to avoid bigotry is to have no morals. And the one group it's okay to have hateful intolerant attitudes toward is Christian conservatives. Am I wrong? I really want to know, Jake. Tell me what you're thinking."

"What I'm thinking is, you don't like the message so you shoot the messenger. Journalists are just messengers. We tell people what's happening. If they don't like it, they blame us for it."

"Okay, I can identify with that. When I say abortion kills children, I'm just stating a scientific fact, but I feel like people get so angry at me, like it's my fault."

"That isn't what I had in mind."

"Of course it isn't. I'm just telling you I relate. When you say something that's true but unpopular, people take it out on you because they just don't want to deal with the truth."

"Right. So you understand our dilemma?"

"I understand your shoot-the-messenger analogy. What I disagree with is your application. If you carefully communicate what really happened and what was really said—like a messenger is supposed to—and then people blame you for it, then yes, they're being unreasonable. But I don't hear anyone blaming the media for the famine in Africa or the scandal on Wall Street. I certainly don't blame you for the mass murderers and the rapists. But what I'm saying is that often you *don't* do what messengers do. You don't just convey what actually happened or what was actually said. You don't just tell the truth. You put your own spin on it. You don't let the reader take the facts and relate his own values to it, you impose *your* values on it. Like the idea that anyone who believes homosexual behavior and abortion are wrong is a bigot."

"Well, Sue, if the shoe fits..."

"But does the shoe fit, Jake? Am I a bigot just because I believe what virtually everyone in this country recognized only forty years ago? Because I agree with Abraham Lincoln that homosexual acts and abortion are morally wrong? Is it wrong to believe there are some moral absolutes? Do we wake up every morning and take a new vote, and if 51 percent decide something that used to be wrong is now right, does that make the other 49 percent a bunch of narrow-minded hate-mongers?"

"Anyone knows it's wrong to hate people and discriminate against them. If people think you're a bigot, maybe it's because you make gays sound like they're garbage."

Sue stared at him, hurt and confused. "I've never thought or said *any*thing like that. Doc committed adultery and I believe it was morally wrong. But I still loved him, and I saw a lot of good in him. A person can engage in homosexual acts and I think it's wrong. But I still love him, and I know in many areas he may be a fine person. I believe homosexual acts are terribly destructive to him, that he should live by the right standard, and that's in his best interest. I honestly want what's best for him. When people steal or lie you tell them it's wrong. It isn't loving to tell them whatever they want to do is okay. It'll just destroy them. And hurt our whole society, our children and theirs."

"Sexual orientation is like race. You can't expect people to deny what they are."

"I can introduce you to a half dozen former homosexuals. Four of them go to our church. Want their names? You could write a column on them. No? I didn't think so. There are thousands of them around—people who used to practice homosexual acts and no longer do. But there's no former whites and former blacks and former Hispanics. Race and sexual practice aren't the same thing, Jake. People need hope. They need to hear there's right and wrong. And I believe God can change people and give them the strength to live by what's right."

"You make it sound so easy, your nice neat little Christian world. It's just not that easy, Sue."

"It's not easy at all. It never has been. But it's still true."

"You know how I felt about Finney—and about you. Forgive me if I'm blunt."

"Be blunt, Jake. I've always found it refreshing."

"All right. Don't you think you people do an awful lot of whining about media bias? You act like we're picking on you just because we don't share your beliefs. Like we sit around in smoke-filled rooms plotting your destruction. And the fact is, the *Trib* carries two syndicated conservatives, George Will and William F. Buckley. These guys make Ronald Reagan look like Chairman Mao. I mean, they probably thought Barry Goldwater was a communist. They're just as conservative as...well, as you are."

Sue laughed. "That bad, are they? Jake, you point to a couple of columns that run a few times a week in a paper so thick I can barely lift it with one hand anymore." She laughed, looking over her five foot even, barely one-hundred-pound frame. "I guess I'm a wimp, but you know what I mean."

"One thing you're not is a wimp, Sue."

"Anyway, my point is, where's the rest of the story? If you've got time, I can show you a half dozen other examples in today's paper alone."

"Sorry, Sue. I don't have time. And even if I did, we've got some basic philosophical differences that just aren't going to change. To you, it's all black and white. Well, the world has a lot of gray, and I'm just trying to do my job the best I can. I'm afraid the *Trib* is never going to suit your tastes no matter what we do."

"I don't expect you to agree with me, Jake. I was just hoping you'd understand. I'm afraid I've done a poor job communicating. I can come on pretty strong when I'm upset. Anyway, I hope you know I love you. I didn't mean anything personal."

Jake nodded. "I've really got to go."

"Jake, Little Finn asked me to give you something for him. Actually, it's a loan. But he wanted you to have it awhile." Sue handed Jake an old, well-worn leather covered book.

"Finney's Bible?" Jake had seen it on hunting trips, on the coffee table, at Finney's office. It was Finney's shadow. He never went far without it. Until a week ago Sunday.

"Yeah. Little Finn just loves to thumb through it. He reads all the notes Finney wrote in the margin. And he thought maybe you'd like to look at it. You know Little Finn."

"Yeah, I know Little Finn. Always trying to convert me, isn't he?"

"He thinks you're a worthy cause, Jake. That's another way he's like his dad. And mom."

"Well, okay. Tell him I'll take good care of it. I don't promise to read it, but I appreciate the thought."

Jake edged toward the door, feeling strangely awkward with a Bible in his hand.

"One more thing, Jake. You know how Finney was interviewed in that *Trib* article a few weeks ago? The one that quoted maybe half a dozen prolifers? I assume you read it?"

"Yeah?"

"Well, he felt he'd really been misquoted, and the most important things he'd said weren't reported at all."

I thought this discussion was over. "That's a common complaint. The interviewer can only use so much, and it's rarely what the person wants."

"I know. Finney understood that. But he wrote a letter to the editor. He stayed up late two nights in a row banging it out on his computer. He finished it early Sunday morning—the day of the accident...or whatever it was. It's been sitting on his dresser since then. I couldn't mail it. But since it was the last thing he ever wrote, and since it was going to the *Tribune*, I thought he'd want me to give it to you."

Sue stretched out her hand and gave the envelope to Jake. The *Trib's* address was neatly printed by Finney's laser printer. *Palatino, fourteen point,* Jake thought.

"Thanks, Sue. I've really got to run."

Jake, Bible and envelope in hand, walked out the door toward his car. He glanced around subconsciously, wondering if there was a proper way to carry a Bible. Like a brief case, a hunting rifle, or an infant? Oh, well. No one was watching him. At least, he didn't think so. As he walked out Sue's front door he heard the phone ring inside. They both waved a quick good-bye.

As Jake approached the door to his car, Sue picked up the kitchen phone. The woman on the other end was in tears. "Linda," Sue recognized the voice. "Are you all right? Yes, I read the column. Yeah, he's the one I know, one of our good friends. No, I'm sure it *wasn't* fair. In fact, I told him that just a few minutes ago."

Sue listened as Linda Mahoney told her of two angry phone calls they'd already received, one from a new next door neighbor, a school teacher deeply offended by Carl's "arrogant and nitpicky" attitude. Sue shook her head, wondering if Jake had any clue how his words affected people's lives.

Zyor, a master tutor, continued to guide Finney into a fuller understanding of heaven. Zyor explained he would later learn the skill of stepping across time as one steps across stones on a stream.

"One day you and I will not merely view the past, the great moments of history I was there to witness. But I will take you for a walk through those times. You will experience them as they actually happened."

To his surprise, the major object of Finney's study so far had been the events of his life on earth. When he would have been expecting to learn about the unknown, he was instead engaged in reinterpreting the known. The events that had flashed before him at death were not merely a summary of what had been, but an overview of a course of study he would need to master in heaven. Finney went back, reviewing his life, evaluating his choices, listening again to his words and seeing the powerful effects they had on people, for better and for worse. It was encouraging to see some of the previously unknown effects, but when he saw how he'd failed, sometimes even with Doc and Jake, it sobered him. Too often he'd been pigheaded and pushy, defensive when someone questioned his opinions.

He found himself looking at his life with a wholly new objectivity. It was almost as if he were watching Thornton Wilder's *Our Town*, understanding things from the outside that the characters in the town could not see from the inside. How strange, he thought, to be on the outside of his own life looking in. While he was moved by what he saw in his life's review, the passions within him were free of the whims of conditioning and biology. His emotions were now a trustworthy part of his mind, no longer a sometimes unreliable and manipulative propagandist trying to hold sway over it.

"I feel as if I were an artist, Zyor, and I painted my self-portrait, which was my life. At death I stepped off the canvas, and now for the first time I can see it, the whole picture. I can see it not as I saw it then, but as Elyon saw it. I don't like everything I see, but I can now see it as it truly was."

Zyor nodded his approval, as if this was the whole point—to see through God's eyes, the eyes of eternity.

"I'm eager to finish my orientation and move on to the greater wonders of Elyon's world. Yet I'm beginning to better understand the value of this reviewing process. When David was confronted by the prophet Nathan, he saw the point of the story only because he thought it was about someone else. It's much easier to see our lives, and learn from them, when we can see them from the outside."

"Exactly. You learn from the lives of others as you contemplate their stories. Now you are studying your own story, as you once studied *The Odyssey* in school. This time the story is real, not invented. You lived it. And now by reliving it you learn the lessons uniquely designed for you by Elyon. You rejoice in those you learned, complete those you began to learn but left unfinished, and now undertake for the first time those you never learned at all."

"I never realized how many of those there were."

"No man dies finished. Your first duty here is not to forget your life on earth but to understand it. You must milk it for all its meaning. Lessons not learned there must be learned now. Lessons learned there must be built upon now, as advanced mathematics must build on the simple. Inaccurate understandings must be cleared up. Elyon does not ignore such things, neither does he simply reverse their effects. Sin is gone, your mind is pure, but your understanding is not complete. Many lessons remain unlearned, and to share in heaven's wonder all must learn them. Elyon does not force feed. He teaches only the willing and the ready. That which you were unwilling to learn on earth you must now be willing to learn. As you've seen, it is not all easy. It will take time. But here you have time, and you do not have the hindrances of sin and blindness. You will not like everything you see about the past, but you will see, and that is what matters."

"Heaven is much more wonderful than I imagined. But this part is much more difficult than I would expect."

"Joy and ease are not the same. As you scanned your computer disk for viruses and removed damaged and obsolete files, so here your mind must be purged to free you for all this place offers. On earth there were things held to be true that were not, and things held not to be true that were. You wrote your life on earth. Now for the first time you are reading it. Those who lived it carefully will find more joy in their readings, as one finds more joy in good literature than in bad. Those who crafted their lives according to plan and purpose wrote books of enduring quality and depth. Those who did not have nothing to review but a hastily written first draft. They will see its flaws and weaknesses and superficiality, and wish they had written it more carefully. Of course, it is too late to edit it now. The deadline is past, and the edition is final. But it is not too late to learn from it. And learning the truth is central to heaven."

"The joy here is beyond description, Zyor. But I never thought of it as involving review and reflection. I thought we would look forever forward without ever looking back."

"But 'back' is where Elyon began his work in you. He will not give up on his creatures by abandoning the process he began. He will bring it to completion. As for joy, you cannot separate joy from truth. There is no joy in ignoring or denying truth. The rejection of truth is the rejection of joy. And by embracing truth, even truth that is difficult and unpleasant, we are made ready to fully embrace joy. Elyon's Book says you will yet stand before the judgment seat of Christ, giving an account for what you did while on earth.

"You come from a world where truth is obscured, shrouded, reinterpreted. The father of lies dominates, and the world order has become built around lies, which are mistaken for truths because the majority believe them, as if the universe were a democracy and truth subject to a vote. Men choose to believe certain things because they find them flattering, comfortable, and popular. But truth is seldom any of these. They choose to disbelieve other things because they are unflattering, uncomfortable, and unpopular. But none of these have any relevance to the question of truth."

"I suppose hell is the ultimate example of that?"

"Yes. No one wants it to be true, therefore men declare it is not. They might just as well vote on the law of gravity. Their confident consensus there is no law of gravity will be no consolation to the man who walks off the tenth story of a building. There *is* a hell. All roads cannot and do not lead to the same place. The heights of heaven's mountains are measured against the depth of hell's valleys. The joys of salvation are in contrast to the horrors of damnation that you and every one of your kind deserved, and but for Elyon's grace, would be doomed to experience for eternity.

"Men take their favorite lies and make them sound grand and noble by calling them 'truths.' But they cannot be truths, because they have been invented by men, and men have no power over truth. Truth by its nature prevails, and lies by their nature wither in truth's eternal fire. Every untruth, every half-truth, every pretense—no matter how fashionable and widely believed—shall be shown for what it is, declared a lie in the sight of all men for all time.

"High stakes give meaning to war, courtship, even to games. Heaven and hell are the high stakes that give meaning to life on earth. Man denies the stakes are real.

He says all life's roads lead to the same place, and that therefore it makes no difference which road men choose. But the truth remains the truth, unimpeded by the lie. The roads lead to very different places, opposite places, to infinite joy or infinite misery, to unimaginable glory or unimaginable tragedy. That is why a man's choice of roads could not be more important."

"The stakes *are* high," Finney responded. "And not only in the difference between heaven and hell, but of a Christian life well lived and poorly lived."

"You are learning, my master. It is time to return now to the study of your life on earth. As you relive it, as you listen again to the things the world told you, consider this. In the darkness, men can shine flashlights on a sundial and make it tell any time they want. But only the sun tells the true time. The flashlights are the changing and fleeting opinions of men. The sun is the eternal Word of God. Only God makes truth. Men either discover it or fail to discover it. They either interpret it rightly or interpret it wrongly. But they have no power to make truth or change it. For truth is no man's servant. Ultimately, the truth must become each person's friend or his enemy, his master or his judge."

CHAPTER TWELVE

J ake walked restlessly around the *Trib* newsroom again, looking for insight. His feelings about his profession ran deep but contradicted each other. He knew Sue's perception of journalists was inaccurate and unfair. Certainly the conscious journalistic bias she believed in didn't exist. The bordering-on-satanic conspiracy to hide or warp the truth, to silence or discredit Christians was a myth, one journalists could only laugh at or deeply resent, usually both.

He looked around him at Sandy and Jerry and others like them. They were good decent people, with lives and families and hopes and dreams of their own. The last thing they wanted to do was subvert or destroy their society. On the contrary, they'd become journalists because they believed society was worth preserving and improving, and they felt their values and ideas and skills could help. No less than Sue and her friends, they wanted their children to grow up in a better world.

Yet Jake knew some of what Sue had said was true. For the last few years he'd become increasingly cynical about his profession, much more than he dared let on to Sue. There was a great deal of politics in this newsroom, and a lot of it made its way into news stories. Most of it, he was convinced, was unconscious and incidental, but it was nonetheless real.

As he leaned against the wall near National desk's coffee pot, emptying his packet of cream and swirling it with a swizzle stick, his eyes landed on Debbie Sawyer. He remembered Debbie's feature stories years ago on the Clarence Thomas hearings. She'd painted it as a clear-cut issue of male sexism and harassment. Never mind fatal flaws in Hill's testimony. Never mind that virtually every person who knew both Hill and Thomas believed Thomas. Jake still wasn't sure who told the truth, but he remembered as if it was yesterday that anyone at the *Trib* who even raised the possibility that Hill rather than Thomas might be lying was labeled sexist. Accordingly, virtually every *Trib* article had been a Hill puff piece, leaving Thomas the unmistakable chauvinist villain.

Much as he eschewed Thomas's political views, Jake found it hard to swallow the presumption a conservative man was incapable of telling the truth and a liberal woman was incapable of lying. He'd started a column raising the possibility that it was Hill who had lied. He worked on it for several days, looking over his shoulder to be sure no one saw. Finally, he tore it up. It wasn't worth it. In the years since, he'd been ashamed of himself for not going through with that column. What the *Trib* did back then, Jake had to admit, wasn't journalism, it was advocacy, pure and simple. And by holding back, he'd become a silent partner in the travesty. That fact ate at him, even now.

As he read the *Trib*, he'd been seeing more and more of the reporter's presence in a story—once considered the ultimate no-no. Just last week Marty Hawes, a political reporter, had gone into a bar on 27th Street to ask what the common man thought of the former mayor who was considering running for governor. Jake happened to know Marty despised this man. He had a personal vendetta going back to some story they'd fought about years ago. So here was an article getting the opinion of the common man, and Hawes said something to the effect, "one man seemed to capture the consensus here when he said this candidate is a thief and a fraud, and you can't trust him any farther than you can throw him."

After reading it Jake thought, "Isn't that a coincidence? The common man thinks just like Marty."

In his journal he'd labeled it "journalistic ventriloquism." People became wooden dummies who said whatever the reporter wanted to say. Ask enough people and somebody will say it, you quote it, and no one ever sees the rest of your notes, if in fact you bothered jotting down the unwanted comments in the first place. He was glad to be a columnist, paid to give his opinion, not having to smuggle it in the back door.

From National's coffee station, leaning against the big red Coke machine, he could see almost the whole floor, over two hundred journalists at work this moment. He considered what a large percentage of his colleagues were divorced. Many had remarried and divorced again. The single were between marriages, the married between divorces. Jake, himself a statistic, held this against no one. But the fact remained that journalism was hard on the family. Reporters kept weird hours and long ones, and when they weren't working they were preoccupied with the thought of work. Jake's efforts to advance his career had taken a toll on his own marriage, he knew. And the atmosphere at the *Trib* was, well, open and free-wheeling. A lot of people thrown together, working next to each other, day after day, talking more with each other than with their husbands or wives. The thrill and rewards of work overshadowed the daily drudgery of home. A lot of romances, a lot of affairs. Most were short-lived, which made things a bit complicated, walking every day past people whose eyes you used to want to meet, and now you desperately want to avoid. Jake wasn't speculating. He'd experienced it first hand. But, he supposed, it wasn't that much different than any modern workplace. It had left him somewhat defensive in the "family values" debates, he had to admit.

Jake took his last gulp of coffee and summarized his musings. Journalists were like doctors, businessmen, mechanics, plumbers, attorneys, teachers, preachers, anyone. They were ordinary, imperfect people. There were those who cared deeply and did their best to be fair, and others who were arrogant and self-serving, using people to further their ideologies and careers. Journalism was no different than plumbing—except that it affected not only pipes and water flow but the minds and perceptions of society. Journalists were like everyone else—except that while others held in their hands pea shooters and slingshots, they happened to be holding a rocket launcher. Hence the saying, "Don't get in a word fight with someone who buys ink by the barrel."

It was a strategic position, Jake thought, one the careful could use to serve society, and the careless could badly abuse. He felt pleased to know he was part of the former group.

After a few more hours at his desk, Jake set out in his Mustang for a drive in the country, as he sometimes did to let a column gestate or to sort out the turns of life. Three years ago he'd taken such a drive to figure out whether he and Janet's marriage had a future. Two years ago he'd had to decide whether to take an attractive job offer with the *Boston Globe*. He still didn't really know why he hadn't. It was a great career move. But his friends and his...family...were here, and here was Oregon. He just couldn't bring himself to leave. If he had the same offer today, with Finney and Doc gone, he wondered if he'd reconsider it. Home had lost much of its draw.

It was a mid-November afternoon. The leaves were past their prime but still colorful on the country hillside, artfully herded by the gentle winds into piles up next to old barns and farmhouses. He took some new and different turns in the road today, tiring of the old paths, and curious where the new ones would lead. Barren roads beckoned ahead and receded behind, except for one car headed his same direction, barely visible in his rearview mirror had he looked carefully, which he didn't.

Tonight was his date with Mary Ann. He'd told her he'd be working late at the *Trib*, and had intended to until just an hour ago, when he was overcome with the compulsion to get out, to get away. And here he was, in the middle of nowhere, knowing where he'd been but not where he was going.

Farm houses, few and far between, dotted the landscape. Smoke trailed out chimneys, dissipating into nothingness. Such is life, Jake thought. Over a rolling hillside, he suddenly saw on the left side of the road a plotted area with a short wrought iron fence. It was a graveyard. For a moment Jake looked away and wanted to speed on by. It was the last thing he wanted to think about. But it was as if an unseen force compelled him to pull over.

He could see no one in any direction, just farmland surrounding this cemetery, which itself was bordered by tall willows and maple trees trying in vain to hold on to their remaining leaves. There was no church here. Perhaps once there had been. Perhaps this had been the center of a little town. Jake's face turned pale and clammy as he walked uncertainly to the edge of the graveyard. Suddenly it grew much darker. The hillside blocked the sun, and clouds obscured it as well, creating such an abrupt change it felt like an eclipse.

Black and white frames of Boris Karloff movies flickered in his mind, playing him as a private audience. Of all times to walk through a cemetery, a gloomy late afternoon twilight. This wasn't at all like the symmetrical rows of Memorial Military Cemetery, where his father was buried. Here there seemed no rhyme or reason, with tombstones as varied, random and tilted as life itself. This seemed a more accurate reflection of death than the mock precision of Memorial. Death was random and purposeless, so why not the harbingers of death?

Jake noted the loveliness of the late fall flowers. Stooping low over a purple chrysanthemum, he saw a tiny droplet of water turning the last remaining gleam of sunlight into a miniature rainbow.

How could death and life exist in such close proximity? What could explain such a living vibrant world languishing under the sentence of death? Death would ultimately defeat life, of that he felt certain. He could almost hear the sounds of warrior insects chewing greedily, their mandibles devouring the splendor of each flower, racing to destroy them before the cold did. The flowers would not last, could not last, and their transitory beauty saddened Jake. Nothing could last in this world of destruction and decay.

Melancholy overtook him. Tree branch shadows became long spidery fingers threatening to grab his ankles and pull him under ground, which itself became a carnivore, a salivating T-Rex wanting to eat him alive. He shook off the chill of the moment, sensing that beyond the silly superstitions of graveyards, something real, something dark and sinister, did not want him here, for whatever reason.

The variegated layout of this graveyard left every next step unpredictable. Behind the next tree or the next tall tombstone, who knew what he would find...or what would find him. He wished he'd not seen the mad slasher movies whose graveyard massacres flooded his mind now. Death was not as unrelated to life as he wanted to believe. It was quiet, deathly quiet. Where were the animal sounds that should inhabit places like these? It was as if lesser creatures were keeping respectful silence for man their master, whose remains lay here.

Who were these people whose bodies were assembled like dead butterflies in a collection? Did their lives matter? Did anyone care? The cemetery was abandoned. No fresh flowers, only wild ones. No freshly turned mounds of dirt to show a recent burial. Only tombstones worn by the elements, fractured by decade after decade of water invading and freezing in their cracks, sinking and tilting as the earth underneath them grew too tired to hold them up.

The most recent date on a gravestone Jake could see was 1909. Before World War I. Before his own father was born. He studied the names and found himself wanting to weave tales about them.

David Elijah Rothman, born July 3, 1898, died July 3, 1898. To be born and die the same day, to know this world so briefly. How did little David die? Of cholera? Of some disease that no longer existed or would now be easily treated? If David had been born ten years ago, would he still be alive now? Was it his fault that he was born too soon? What is the purpose in a child's death the day he was born? David had parents who loved him, who must have grieved terribly. Yes, there, that big tombstone with the military insignia...Robert Rothman, born September 15, 1858. Wasn't that around the Civil War? Did Robert's father fight in that war? Died November 2, 1908. Fifty years old. Jake shuddered. Robert had been Jake's age when he died.

Another stone, between father and child, belonged to Elizabeth Rothman, born June 12, 1869. Robert's wife and David's mother. Died—what was this? Died

August 20, 1898. At only twenty-nine? Did she die in childbirth? No, it was six weeks after David's birth and death. Jake shivered again, the cold moist air turning more frigid as the sun began to set. Did Elizabeth die of a broken heart at losing David?

What was the gravestone just the other side of Robert's? "Sarah Staley Rothman. Born April 3, 1835." Ah, this must be Robert's mother. She must have made the journey on the Oregon Trail with Robert and Elizabeth. "Died June 23, 1898." What? Only ten days before David was born and died. She didn't even get to see her grandson. And poor Robert. The man had his mother, son, and wife all taken from him in a two-month period.

The senselessness of it all saddened Jake. What possible explanation would suffice? Why would God, if there was a God, take a child from his mother's arms? And take a mother from a son who loved her enough not to leave her behind, but bring her with him down the Oregon Trail to the new land? And what kind of God would look at this man staggering in his grief, and then take his wife from him as well? How helpless and lonely he must have felt. As helpless and lonely—though perhaps not as angry—as Hyuk had felt at his own loss of mother, wife, and son.

Who knew or cared about the Rothman family? Who told their stories now? They were like pebbles dropped in a pond, whose ripples lasted only a moment. What difference had their lives made? None, it seemed to Jake. They were gone, long gone.

David's little monument had been worn smooth by the hard Oregon rains and winds. Jake bent down to read the words, the moist dirt soaking into his knee. For a moment, he started to get up, remembering these were the clothes he would wear to dinner with Mary Ann. But curiosity pulled him back down.

"David Elijah Rothman. Taken by his Lord as he left the womb, as Enoch, beloved of God, taken before his time." Then underneath, in small print, "Jesus said unto her, 'I am the resurrection and the Life: He that believeth in Me, though he were dead, yet shall he live.'"

Ah, the hope and faith of parents. These were not modern people. If they were they would have held no hope for what lies beyond. The God they believed in was obsolete. He'd been replaced by...by what, Jake wondered.

Elizabeth's monument was larger. Did Robert lay her body in the grave himself? Jake suspected he did. Back then people were not insulated from death by the middlemen, the funeral homes and undertakers, the brokers of death hired to keep the family at arm's length from the stark realities of the final end.

Jake imagined Robert, dressed in his best suit, worn only on Sundays to the house of God, riding in the buckboard, his family in tow to the church that probably stood on this very spot. Did Robert believe what the country preacher said? Did he read the black book quoted from on his infant son's grave? Or was the caretaker of the family faith really Elizabeth, the woman who taught the children virtue while the man plowed the fields and drank the whiskey and went to town to visit the saloon girls? Somehow he felt this assessment was wrong, that Robert was a man of faith, a man who believed and lived by a truth that shaped and guided a family he deeply loved. Still, did Robert manage to hold on to that faith after losing mother, son, and wife that cruel bitter summer?

Jake pulled out his pocketknife to scrape off the moss that had crept into the grooved letters on the gravestone of Elizabeth Rothman. Now the words, before obscured, became clear.

"Here lies the body of Elizabeth Rothman, beloved wife of Robert, mother of David. Until the resurrection." The smaller print below read, "All that are in the graves shall hear his voice, and shall come forth; they that have done good, unto the resurrection of life; and they that have done evil, unto the resurrection of damnation."

Robert must have written these words, this man who lived a hard life and trod his way through it in anticipation of a better life to come. Robert's own tombstone had no inscription beyond his name and the dates. Perhaps because he was the end of the family line, and no loved one was left to give tribute on his tombstone. Jake could only guess about this man's life. The only certainty was, it was a life now done. There was no revisionist history, no air brushing away the man and his warts and virtues. Whoever he had been, and wherever he had gone, his life here had been what it had been, no more and no less and no different.

Another tombstone caught his eye, this one all by itself, away from the Rothman cluster. It was dark and it looked newer and different than the rest. Jake read it, his eyes suddenly large and his heart pounding.

"Oh, my God," he cried aloud. It said, "Jake Woods."

Wait, no, "Jake Weads." He heaved a sigh of relief. But why? His name would one day be on such a stone. He knew the first date it would say, the date of his birth. But what would the second date say? Would it be thirty years from now, or ten, or five, or next year? Next week? Tomorrow? Today, before he left this place?

And what would his tombstone say? Who would care enough to write something? Who would know what to write? Would he want the words of some song like Frank Sinatra's "I Did It My Way"? Or John Lennon's "Imagine"? No, he was drawn to songs of greatness, songs with lasting meaning, songs such as those sung at Finney's funeral. But as he searched his memory, he could not remember the words of those songs, or even their names. He could, however, remember many songs of Lennon and Sinatra. Could one live his life by one set of songs and expect to be associated with another in his death?

Was there really a God? Was there really a book of life, with some names written in it and others not? Where were the Rothmans now? Were they right there, beneath his feet? Or were they somewhere else? Jake did not know. It saddened him to think he would never know.

An old friend watched with great interest Jake standing in the graveyard. He saw every move, read each inscription, felt as if he was right there with him. He was unable to read Jake's exact thoughts, yet he somehow sensed most of what was going through his mind. Zyor stood next to Finney, also intensely interested.

As Jake got in his car and drove back toward the city, the clear vision of the scene faded, as it often did when the strategic moments, the eternal hinges that demanded the attention and prayer of heaven's inhabitants, faded into the routine and normalcy of earthly life. Finney had been seeing Jake with greater frequency and hoped this indicated something significant.

Finney prayed aloud for Jake, then Zyor followed his lead. They prayed at length, sensing that Jake's next hours that evening would be hours of great warfare, with strategic and eternal importance.

After they had prayed, Zyor showed a slight smile and said to Finney, "Come with me."

"Gladly, my friend. Where are we going?"

"To meet some people whose company you will very much enjoy."

"Who?"

Zyor thought for a moment, as if trying to decide whether to tell him now or wait. He looked at Finney, not wanting to miss the first eruption of that ear-to-ear smile.

"Their names are the Rothmans—Sarah, Robert, Elizabeth, and David."

Jake arrived at Anthony's thirty minutes early. He went to spruce himself up in the elegant men's room since there was no time to go home and change. Jake paid more attention than he had in a long time to the face looking back at him from the mirror. It was an older face, the hair graying on the edges, receding in a way that made him look more like his father. Grooves cut across it like furrowed land. He looked weathered, like a lonely sea captain whose face had long borne the brunt of furious winds and pounding surf. Who was the man in the mirror? It troubled Jake that he didn't know the answer, and might find it only too late.

He bent over close to the mirror to inspect a discoloration on his skin. His warm breath fogged the mirror a moment, then he watched the fog shrink and disappear as quickly as it had come. Someone, he didn't remember who, had compared life to the warm breath that is here for a moment, then leaves. Life was moving quickly, too quickly. Fifty years old. He was already older than his father had been when Jake trudged off to boot camp. His dad had seemed so very old to him then. He'd died only five years later, at fifty. Fifty. Robert Rothman's age. His age.

Those who liked to spend money for lots of drinks and little food loved to spend their evenings at Anthony's. The *Trib's* restaurant critic raved about the food, but after the one time he'd taken Janet to Anthony's, Jake concluded he'd rather have a burger and onion rings at Lou's Diner anytime. Jake asked for a table with a view of the front door.

When his date came in, he caught his breath. Mary Ann glided into the room. Her ruby red silk dress, matching fingernails, and red spiked heels took over, as if the restaurant and its other patrons were merely black and white background existing to accentuate her presence, as if only she had been colorized. Her diamond necklace sparkled even in the low light. Jake didn't know much about clothes and jewelry, but he knew these had to cost a bundle.

In the hospital environment Mary Ann was a professional. Here she was all woman. Her desire for attention seemed strikingly evident, and the attention was well earned. She captured lots of eyes, not least of all Jake's. He rose to walk toward her, but she caught his eye and eagerly swept up to him, putting her right arm around him in a teasing squeeze and kissing him on the cheek. Jake knew he was now identified to everyone as the fortuitous companion of this stunning woman. Much as he normally eschewed public displays, he very much enjoyed the feeling.

"Hi, Jake. I'm famished. Hope you're ready for some fun tonight," Mary Ann clearly was. Jake pulled out her chair for her, and before he could sit she was effervescing.

"This is one of my favorite places. I just love the scallops here. Have you ever had them? No? Well, you just have to. They're wonderful."

After a few minutes of soaking in Mary Ann's appearance and imbibing her delicious scent, Jake found himself losing interest in the long string of small talk bubbling from her. His mind slipped into cruise control. Soon he was operating on instinct, saying "uh-huh," laughing and responding briefly at what he trusted were the right times.

His mind withdrew, thinking about Mary Ann and what she represented from his past. Her stylish clothes, her low neckline, her suggestive comments, and the way she carried herself was all too familiar. Twenty-five years ago he and Doc used to joke about what was then called "women's liberation," and later feminism. Women were "liberated" to sleep around like men, which was the liberation of every man's dream. Men didn't have to think of a woman's honor and purity anymore. Guys didn't have to feel responsible for seducing a girl because now she played the game too.

He remembered what they used to call sexually liberated women. "Easy chicks." "Whores." "Sluts." They called them by parts of their anatomy. They were things, not people. The women he'd always respected most were those who hadn't got swept away in the revolution. When he met her as a college freshman, Janet had been one of those. But the music and climate of the day, along with their freethinking professors, with Jake's eager help, wore down Janet along with what seemed like a whole generation of young women. They became "free"—free to be ogled and used by men, cheap characters in their bragging tales of conquest.

Janet and Jake had started having sex five months after they met and were living together by their junior year of college. Jake thought it was great. The privileges of marriage with none of the responsibilities. That was when he first learned to take Janet for granted. Now, after three years of divorce, he recalled how much he'd respected her their first date—a respect he'd lost the night she became one more easy girl. It surprised Jake to find himself thinking about such things when his mind and hormones should have been focused on the obvious.

"And she was wearing the most gorgeous dress. And you know who the man with her turned out to be?" Mary Ann continued at high speed, Jake still smiling and nodding and pretending he was interested, while following his own inner rabbit trail.

I've made a career of being a feminist, Jake recently confessed to his journal, the closest thing he had to a priest. Over the years he'd gone to the feminist marches, the prochoice rallies. He'd been hailed as one of those sensitive modern men. He loved the attention, the affirmation, the respect they gave him, and yes, the sex. He could play the role—the macho man, to get one kind of woman in bed, and the egalitarian man, to get another kind of woman in bed. For years he never admitted this hypocrisy. It was Finney who pointed it out to him, and when he did Jake steamed and fumed and even tried to commiserate with Doc, who only said, "So what? Who cares how you get 'em in the sack, as long as you do?"

"Jake? Jake! Earth to Jake! Are you ready to order?" Mary Ann laughed and the waiter gave a confused "do you need more time" look at Jake.

"Uh, I'm sorry. Guess my mind was wandering." After promising he'd eat a few of her scallops, Jake ordered prime rib, acting as if he came to places like Anthony's a lot, and trying hard but unsuccessfully to remember protocol at an establishment that boasted live musicians rather than a juke box.

"What's on your mind, Jake? Dreaming? Hope I'm in the dream." Mary Ann gave him a warm smile, squeezed his hand, then excused herself to use the ladies' room, leaving his mind to resume its wandering. It did, like a rushing stream, changing directions slightly with each rock.

In his sixteen years of marriage Jake had a number of one night stands and two affairs, and now he couldn't even put faces to some of the bodies he'd been in bed with. Janet had been hurt deeply by his indiscretions, from the *Playboys* and *Penthouse*s he'd stopped hiding to the trysts with women on out of town "investigative journalism" excursions. He knew she knew about those escapades as certainly as if he'd told her, which he hadn't.

Janet had protected herself the only way she knew how—telling herself it was somehow okay or she didn't care, then compensating or retaliating through indiscretions of her own that proved to herself she was still desirable. Always, of course, with "sensitive men," the kind the women who slept with Jake thought he was. These men were just like Jake, sensitive to the woman they wanted now, insensitive to the one they'd vowed before man and God to always love and cherish.

Why should a man marry a woman if she would give him all she was now and he was free to move on when he wished, harvesting women like a field of corn? Why take on the "in sickness" and "for worse" parts of the marriage vow when he could have her "in health" and "for better" and just take a walk if it became too much for him to handle?

Mary Ann returned, full-bodied hair bouncing and shining, a magnet attracting every man in the restaurant. Jake was disgusted with himself, sitting there ruminating and philosophizing, when he was with such a beautiful woman. He could have her tonight if he wanted her, and what sane man wouldn't? But despite himself, Jake kept thinking about where it would go, and especially where it wouldn't. He seemed to tire of women easily. He had tired of Janet, tired of her little annoying quirks that had once been cute and endearing. Tired of her habit of telling him in detail her dreams from the night before, as if such things should interest him. He had written a column once saying it should be illegal for spouses to tell their dreams, that there should be an 800 number to call for this kind of spousal abuse. He knew he'd hurt Janet's feelings, and she'd not mentioned her dreams for months afterward.

"You look great tonight, Jake."

Jake knew what he was supposed to say now. "Not as great as you, Mary Ann. You look...well, stunning."

Mary Ann blushed. There, they'd said it. They both looked great. Now, what was inside them? Doc would tell him he was crazy for even thinking this. If you could get a woman like Mary Ann in bed, what did it matter what was inside her? Suddenly Jake realized Doc and Mary Ann must have slept together. He knew Doc. And if he was reading Mary Ann right, the two of them couldn't have worked together long before their chemistry did the inevitable. Inevitable, that is, when there were no moral restraints to hold them back. Thinking of Betsy and the children, Janet and Carly, Finney and Sue and their family cast a dark shadow over what, Jake told himself, should have been a spine-tingling evening of fantasy and anticipation.

"You know that incredible ballroom at Floren's? Diana and Jason—Jason's her new boyfriend, this hunk that's a partner at Gleason, Underwood, and Dodge— they decide 'hey, let's get some action going here,' so they call over this waiter..."

Mary Ann was uneasy with gaps in the conversation, and Jake was contributing the gaps. He continued to nod, though he'd lost track of where Mary Ann had been and hadn't the slightest idea where she was going. Her voice was a distant echo, her words hovering in the air about him. He could grab them from the air when necessary and let them float away when not. Most of them floated.

He thought about sex, since it could be his tonight if he so decided. Even in the pre-herpes, pre-AIDS era, sleeping around was always a great fantasy, but never a fulfilling reality. After sex, the worst part was being in bed the rest of the night with someone you didn't know but had to pretend to feel comfortable with. There was something terribly sad and lonely about it. He felt so empty and awkward, like a man who's smoked a pack of cigarettes and has no use for the package. He just wants to toss it. But there it is, in bed beside him all night, waiting to face him in the morning. Would Mary Ann be such a package tonight?

Sex had become more and more a chore. "Are you HIV negative? Are you sure? Who's the last person you slept with? Do you know who he'd been sleeping with? Did you use a condom? Do you have a condom now?"

So much for the free and spontaneous love without consequences Jake had bought into in the sixties and seventies. It had given birth to the chaos and diseases of the eighties and nineties.

Again, Jake could hear Finney's voice. "God doesn't intend us to be promiscuous. All these diseases are just a reminder."

Not too subtle a reminder. So far six reporters at the *Trib* had died of AIDS, and others were wasting away before his eyes.

Sex was an anesthetic that for a short time made Jake forget how lonely he was.

But every time, as soon as the deed was done, his loneliness deepened. It was fulfilling only for the moment. And he wanted more from life than fleeting moments. But here was Mary Ann. Incredibly attractive. Clearly available. Not just available, but eager. Served up to him on a platter. The kind of woman who would have revved up his engines just a few years ago. She did now, but something was different. Before, he would have been figuring out how to get her in bed. Now he was trying to figure out how to avoid it.

Amazing how my strategy's changed, he thought, with some disappointment in himself.

Dessert was served, some fancy thing with a French name. Jake couldn't tell what it was even as he ate it. Mary Ann said, "Don't eat too much, Jake. I was thinking we could make some dessert of our own later on."

She smiled coyly, and it had the desired effect. Why not take her home with him or spend the night at her place? What would it really hurt?

Jake's mind was flooded with images of Janet early in their relationship. Their idealism, the hopeful and expectant anticipation that each new day would bring a great adventure. The thrill of just being together. The dreams they shared. If only he'd never had that experience. Perhaps then he could be satisfied with the superficial. But he knew better. He knew what it was to love, to laugh, and to dream with the woman of his dreams. But they'd lost it. He'd lost it. It seemed the ultimate tragedy to have your dreams dashed, to watch the wild stallion of love grow old like a broken down mare, ending up a crumpled heap at the glue factory.

They'd been idealistic, unrealistic, he'd decided. The concerns of career and self-advancement, which he told himself were for her as much as him, had overshadowed their love. He became an absentee husband, an out of touch father. The hundreds of photographs of Carly he took when she was a baby dwindled to dozens a year by the time she was in third grade, and virtually none when she reached junior high. Janet, with no interest or talent in picture taking, had become the family photographer, as well as the family everything-else. Jake just wasn't there. He always intended to slow down at work, spend more time at home, do more with the family, but it never happened. Work was more important than home. He'd said the opposite, even in his columns, but Janet reminded him that his schedule, his choices, didn't lie. They reflected his true priorities.

Many nights just before dozing off, he'd heard Janet's quiet sobs, but pretended not to notice. He didn't want one more late night guilt trip about how much she and Carly needed him. He couldn't make her understand most women were a lot worse off, and many would gladly trade places with her. She seemed less the girl he had pursued and married than a nervous, frightened, and critical middle-aged woman. He'd given up on the marriage. It took too much effort. The divorce seemed anticlimactic, a funeral taking place years after the death. He'd written a column about how divorce was the honest thing to do and often the best choice and didn't have to hurt the children. It had been a popular column.

"Jake. Jake, you're drifting again. It's okay if you're fantasizing, as long as I'm in the fantasy." Mary Ann giggled. "Oh, look. There's Dr. Henry from the hospital.

I'm going to go say 'hi.' Don't eat my dessert!" Mary Ann smiled and swept away.

"I won't."

He watched Mary Ann work her way across the room, admiring her walk. He thought of Finney, who years ago had seen a wall coming up between himself and Sue and determined to tear it down. Finney and Sue. How often he'd envied them and the freshness and vitality of their relationship. So had Janet. They offered hope. They sent the message that yes, a good marriage was possible. Marriage could last, marriage could survive, even thrive. But that was Finney. Always different. Always beating the odds.

Janet filed the papers, but it was Jake's divorce, and both knew it. He wanted out, he wanted the easier life. No commitment, no apologies, no regrets. It was a dignified divorce with all the modern mature no-fault trappings. "We're still friends, you know." "It was best for both of us." "It was best for Carly too." Yeah, right. He'd even gotten a "Congratulations on Your Divorce" card from Lenny at the *Tribune*. Everyone got a big kick out of it. Lenny had been divorced three times. He was the expert. "Happy Divorce"? Yeah, sure, they were all better off.

Mary Ann returned, talking on and on about this doctor, and how Doc said he was one of the best surgeons in town, and how he owned this incredibly beautiful mansion with an Olympic-sized swimming pool, and how she'd been there for a party once. Jake tried to pay better attention, feeling guilty his mind had been there so little.

When the check came, he put down his VISA, but she reminded him it was her treat and took her billfold out of her purse. Running her finger over the ridges, she selected from the row of cards a shiny American Express. A few minutes later she signed it off, refusing to let Jake even leave the tip. He inwardly groaned at the total, calculating that the tip alone could have paid for two full meals at Lou's Diner, plus milkshakes and coffee.

As they walked to the door, Mary Ann put her arm in his and pressed up against him, bumping her hip against his. His resolve began to weaken. She suggested since they both had cars he could follow her to her apartment. Her red-lipped smile beautifully framed her white teeth.

Almost ready to say "yes" to the suggestion and all that was sure to follow it, Jake thought again of Janet and Carly and Finney and Sue and Betsy and Doc, and the empty carton of cigarettes and the lonely feeling of waking up next to someone you don't know or love.

"Listen, Mary Ann. I really enjoyed having dinner with you. Thanks for treating me. Maybe we can do it again some time. But, as you could tell, I've got a lot on my mind, and I'm just not very good company right now."

Mary Ann promised, "I can take your mind off whatever it's on. Come over. I guarantee I'll make it worth your while." The way she said it and the look on her face backed up the claim.

"I'm sure you would, but I feel like I just need to go home alone."

Mary Ann looked confused and disappointed. "Well, it's your choice. It was fun being with you. Please call me. I'd love to do it again. You've got my number."

"Yeah. Thanks."

She pressed herself against him and kissed the edge of his lips. "Sure I can't change your mind?"

Jake swallowed hard. "No. Thanks. I need to go. See you."

Jake drove home, alternatively hating himself for being such a fool to let her go, then hating himself for being such a fool years ago when he let Janet and Carly go for what Mary Ann represented—pleasure without responsibility.

Jake sat in his recliner drinking hot chocolate and flipping pages in a Grisham novel before realizing he couldn't remember anything he'd read the last fifteen minutes. He wandered toward bed, turning off the last light. He listened to the steady Oregon rain drubbing the verandah, a sound he usually found comforting. Tonight it only reminded him of his aloneness.

Jake tossed to the right, then the left, and the waterbed shook at his frustrated sleeplessness. A hot tear fell onto his pillow, first one then another. He thought about the stains on the pillow case. No problem. They'd come out in the wash. Besides, if they didn't, who would ever see them?

CHAPTER THIRTEEN

The hearty aroma of dark Colombian coffee permeated Jake's apartment. It slowly weaned him from a deep sleep. His first regret-filled impulse was to drag himself out of bed and go through the morning shave and shower routine he could do in his sleep, and often had. Then came the oh-so-sweet realization that the coffee wasn't Colombian after all, it was Chocolate Macadamia Nut, which meant this was Saturday morning and he didn't have to get up.

Every weekday morning Jake's automatic coffee maker sprang into action at 6:15. His alarm rang at 6:30, giving the coffee a fifteen minute chance to awaken him slowly, civilly, before the alarm rudely took over. But he didn't set an alarm for weekends. Coffee came on quietly at 8:00. But often Jake wasn't up till 8:30 or 9:00. The brewing coffee was the only common element of weekends and weekdays. Yet even that was different. During the week it was dark Colombian. On Saturdays it was Swiss Almond or Chocolate Macadamia or whatever struck Jake's fancy at his weekly grocery shopping, where he selected and ground his coffee.

On a typical Saturday, he lounged around in his underwear or gym shorts till 11:00, postponing his shower until after a workout on his stair-stepper or cross country skiing machine. He'd catch up on his reading, maybe an old Ludlum or Hillerman or a new Clancy, check out a college ballgame or two. He felt the stubble on his face, prickly against his pillow case, and luxuriated in the fact that today no cold steel would touch his face, and no comb would attempt to bring order to the chaos that was his hair. There was no day like Saturday.

Jake turned over, extracting his face from its deep impression in the pillow and breathing deeply the coffee-flavored air. Suddenly a wet nose pressed against his neck. Champ knew it was Saturday too. Jake had little time for him on weekday mornings. But on Saturdays they were pals. The chocolate brown and white spaniel's nose, pressed up close against Jake's face, looked like a brown electrical outlet. Champ wormed his way under the covers and joyfully immersed himself in his master's morning scent.

"Your blood's getting too thin, fella," Jake teased. Champ had been spoiled by his inside habits, including these periodic pilgrimages under the covers of Jake's waterbed. Jake had named this Champ, the springer, after the golden retriever who spent many nights in Jake's sleeping bag thirty-five years ago, out in the backyard, under the stars. The original Champ, Jake pondered, was the only other being who'd regularly spent time with the three musketeers. That dog accompanied Jake, Doc, and Finney in their wonder years, from about third grade until high school, when he went the way of all dogs.

As he scratched Champ in all the best places, bringing groans of ecstasy, Jake remembered old Saturday mornings. Watching *Sky King* as he ate his Shredded Wheat biscuits. Sleeping in at college. Vietnam, where there were no Saturdays, and the coffee came in one flavor—black and full of grounds, and where the only filter was his own pursed lips. Then there were the Janet years, where the companion in bed wasn't a spaniel.

It was only thirteen days since that Sunday that had forever changed his life. It was no longer late fall but early winter, having made the transition in a day, like the seasons do in Oregon. The wind howled and cold blasts ruffled the base of the curtains at the sliding glass door to Jake's patio that came right off his bedroom. It was a houselike apartment, with accouterments that included fireplace and patio, without all the hassles of home ownership that no longer appealed to Jake. He leaned out of bed and pulled back the curtains, surprised and pleased to see a sheet of ice already covered the neighborhood and a dusty snow was falling.

How many times as a boy, on mornings that looked like this, had he hoped against hope the announcement would be made "East Benton Grade School is closed today." Then he and his buddies would launch into a day of sledding, snow ball fights, and frosty mischief, breaking only for Campbell's Cream of Chicken soup and Ritz Crackers compliments of Mom, who never had a day off.

Champ was now in the kitchen, loudly gulping water from his metal dish. Jake lay in his waterbed, leaning against a padded headrest, covers pulled up under his arms. On his chest lay yesterday's *New York Times* and a novel Sandy had given him. He knew the *Trib* was sitting out there in that long row of yellow paper boxes. Though five days a week he could get it free at work, he still subscribed. That way he could be more like the average reader, going through his paper-fetching routine, anticipating what awaited him within. He wanted the *Tribune* now, but he wasn't about to go get it. Not on a frigid Saturday, not yet. He opened the novel instead.

Jake had never been an avid fiction reader until the last few years. He'd tired of the "real world" of nonfiction, with all its senseless tragedies and unresolved issues. When he was younger and idealistic he'd had such hopes for the world, hopes those issues could be dealt with, the tragedies averted. Now the world seemed so dark, with all its kidnappers, rapists, muggers, child abusers, street gangs, drug dealers, and murderers, its endless parade of sadistic abductors and psychopaths, whose exploits were often rewarded with a made-for-TV movie. At least the killings in novels weren't real, and at least the story usually involved love and courage and ended with purpose and hope and something that could satisfy. Even if, in coming back to real life, one had to face the fact that love and hope were merely an illusion. The world no longer gave him reason for hope. Fiction provided a momentary escape from the nagging futility of life's purposelessness.

While Jake pretended to be glued to the pages of the novel, the brown spaniel slunk back up onto the foot of the bed, an inch at a time, as if afraid that any sudden move would tip off his master. Jake chuckled to himself.

"Come here, fella. You're not nearly as subtle as you think."

Champ's rich fur was getting thicker as the weather grew colder. He turned circles, getting ready to land, his tail wagging so hard, like a chopper blade, Jake felt the breeze. Just before plopping down he buried his nose into his master's neck. Neither the drinking water still dripping from his jowls nor the wet cold of his snout repulsed Jake. His presence was the welcome and familiar comfort of an old friend. Even more welcome these last few weeks than before, as friends were in short supply.

What was it about this dog that made Jake feel more comfortable than with most people? *He makes so few demands.* Maybe that was it. *He sees me at my worst and still loves me. No person could do that.* Finney had called it "unconditional love." He remembered his first Champ.

I could yell at that dog, threaten him, send him into ice water to fetch a stick, and he'd look at me like I'd done him the biggest favor in the world just because I recognized his existence.

Thoughts of Saturdays, snow, and dogs took Jake back to the old neighborhood, that few dozen square miles of Benton County, vintage fifties and sixties. He lay flat on the big hand-painted blue sled, "the clunker," with Finney stretched out on top of him, his red gloves clenching Jake's shoulders, visible in his peripheral vision. After a day of sledding, Jake's shoulders were bruised and sore from the vise grip of his buddies when they took a sudden turn or hit a bump and went flying. Jake loved the feeling, because he usually engineered it with a quick turn of the rudder. It was fun to be in control, dishing out the surprises to his friends. And the real thrill was when the unpredictable contours of the icy slope reminded him he wasn't in control after all.

Champ's rhythmic breathing and occasional contented sigh fueling his recollections, one wild ride in particular filled Jake's mind. With Finney on his back, Jake was frantically trying to avoid trees as they rocketed down Dead Man's Hill on the Swenson farm. Everything was a blur, and Jake could feel the frigid sting of icy needles flying into his face. He could see Doc down at the bottom of the hill, his oversized black coat prominent against the winter whitewash. His Polaroid camera in hand, like a war correspondent Doc waited to document what he hoped would be a major crash.

The snow had begun to melt, and there was a light rain, making for furious sledding on the slightest decline. Jake feared Dead Man's Hill would soon be renamed Dead Jake's Hill. As he flew down the hill too fast to scream, the icy crust suddenly cracked and his face was buried in the snow. But he still moved forward, plowing through snow as a diver through water. When he came to a stop, he suddenly panicked. He couldn't breathe. As if underwater, he instinctively pushed up to the surface, only to hit his head on something. In desperation he hit it harder, butting his head into it, and heard it crack. All of a sudden his head surfaced above the ice and he sucked in air. He shook his whole body and it too broke through the ice. He looked back and could see the hole he made when the sled went under the ice. It was at least twelve feet behind him! His momentum had carried him through the powdered snow under the ice.

Finney! Where was Finney? He heard Doc's shouts at the bottom of the hill. Was Finney hurt? Then he realized Doc was laughing. There he was, on his hands and knees, beside himself. The body with the blue coat—Finney—was sprawled out, hands and legs outstretched, still in motion, moving up the opposite hill, sliding back down to the low point and back up the base of Dead Man's Hill, losing just a little momentum with each pass. Finney's efforts to stop himself were futile. The ice had put him into perpetual motion. Finally the laws of physics prevailed, and gravity brought him to an ever-so-slow stop.

Jake wanted to get down the hill to his friends but wasn't about to get back on the clunker, still buried under the snow. Wanting to be in on the laughter, he stood and started toward them, realizing instantly he'd made a foolish mistake. He fell flat on his backside and headed feet first down the hill. Now he could hear Doc whooping it up again. Then he heard Finney's voice join Doc's, equally hysterical. Champ barked wildly, joining in on the fun.

Quicker than he thought possible, Jake was at their feet, streaming past them in a reenactment of Finney's wild ride. He could see Doc's red face, contorted with spasms of laughter. As Jake passed him on his next sweep, he kicked out his leg and caught Doc, who was now standing, on his left heel. This slowed down his own ride and sent Doc into a frantic tap dance to keep his balance. Finally, like a circus clown, he fell in a heap.

Now Finney broke into hysterics, so much so that he fell again. Within seconds, all three had settled together at the low point between Dead Man's Hill and Swenson's pasture, Champ zealously licking the frost off their faces. They were all three clutching each other, exhausted from the scare, breathless with gut-wrenching laughter. Jake had never felt so close to any friend. That day was one among many that had sealed their forever friendship.

Forever? Suddenly a gentle tug on his T-shirt brought Jake back to his bedroom. A dog's soulful eyes gazed at him curiously. Another Champ had taken the place of the first. But Finney and Doc were gone, and there was no one to take their place. There never would be. Jake's eyes blurred. He felt embarrassed, even though his only audience was a dog. He longed for Doc and Finney days, the innocent adventurous days of childhood. When life was simple, and you knew whose side you were on, and who was on your side. When friendship really did seem it would last forever.

Champ's eyes seemed a mirror reflection of Jake's, as close to shedding tears as Jake had ever seen them. Jake saw his own contorted face reflected in those eyes.

"It's okay, fella," he said, arms wrapped around the spaniel. "Everything's been crazy, hasn't it?"

Jake flipped on the alarm clock radio to his favorite oldies station. "Peggy Sue." "Rock Around the Clock." "I Get Around." From Chuck Berry to the Association, six of the "ten hits in a row" promised by the deejay aroused memories of places and people back in that little Oregon place and time. Nostalgia ran through his blood and warmed his extremities. His friends' deaths made the memories more painful, yet more rich.

After trying the novel for another ten minutes, he set it down in surrender to the thoughts that first tugged, then yanked at him. The investigation was like looking at all the fragments of a thousand piece puzzle with no master picture as a guide. He felt like he was a character in a novel, along with Ollie and Mary Ann and Sue and everybody on the suspect list. But Jake had no idea where the author, if there was an author, was taking this thing. There was no promise of a happy ending or even a successful one. He might go the rest of his life and not know who killed his friends.

Mary Ann's information on the doctors was interesting, but had led him nowhere. The patient advocate had been no help. While Doc had his share of complaining patients, the complaints weren't serious. Certainly nothing sufficient to generate the kind of grudge people killed for. He'd nosed around for leads on a few of Doc's girlfriends and their husbands or fathers, but nothing seemed very likely there either. The meeting with the abortion protesters at Sue's was coming up. Maybe he'd get the break he needed from them. He hoped the slowness of this Saturday would allow insight and direction to emerge. He'd try to let all the ingredients of the investigation mix around in the soup and simmer for a while.

Jake got up, walked across his Spartan living room, notably devoid of much-needed feminine touches. Once in the kitchen he poured twelve ounces of coffee in his oversized *Star Trek: The Next Generation* mug, and sank into the recliner. Saturday coffee couldn't be savored without reading something. He'd left his novel and *Times* in the bedroom. Lazily, he looked around for other options on the lamp table. There was Finney's Bible, with his envelope addressed to the *Tribune* on top, right next to the television remote control.

He pushed the remote's power button, then channel surfed, pausing at ESPN, a couple of journalists he knew on a C-Span symposium, more bad news for the day on CNN, and an old *Dick Van Dyke* on Nickelodeon. He flipped a few more channels and saw a religious huckster ranting and raving and proving true the old carny adage that a fool and his money are soon parted. Disgusted, he flipped a few more channels, then pushed off the power. Twenty-nine channels and nothing to hold his interest.

His eyes fell on Finney's letter again. Something had kept him from reading it after Sue gave it to him, and something pushed him away from it now. Yet something drew him too. What were his old friend's last written words?

Opening the envelope, Jake rehearsed what led to the letter—Holly Hannah's article on anti-abortion activists. As he recalled, Holly had interviewed a housewife or two and a couple of inarticulate full-time crusaders. Finney found his way in as a well-known businessman who'd thrown himself into the controversy. Jake didn't remember the details, only that he felt distinctly embarrassed for his friend as he read the article. While the two often disagreed, Jake knew Finney meant well. This was nowhere evident in the article. It was a different Finney—a mean-spirited chauvinist who wanted to control women and take away their rights. Jake shook his head and wondered why Finney had said what he did. It sounded so irrational and out of character.

Strangely, though, years of misunderstanding and bad press never changed Finney's convictions. *Nothing* seemed to change Finney's convictions. Jake shook his head in irked wonder. *You'd think a guy would eventually learn.* He'd never known a man who could be so open-minded and accepting on so many things, and so intractably dogmatic and unbending on others. If Finney had been misunderstood, Jake reasoned, he'd only brought it on himself.

The letter was a page and a half long, neatly printed in a font Jake didn't recognize. Finney had shown Jake a set of two hundred fonts he'd stored on his computer's hard disk. This must be one of them. Jake noted the letter was properly addressed and directed to the *Trib's* "Editorial Staff." Well, what did his old buddy have to say?

Dear Friends,

My reason for writing is your October 20 article, "The anti-abortion activists: who are they?"

First, I believe the semantics of your coverage would bias any neutral reader against the prolife position. The term "anti-abortion" is repeatedly used throughout the article—no less than twelve times. In contrast, the other position is always called "prochoice."

"Anti-abortion" sounds negative; "prochoice" sounds positive. It appears to me the *Tribune* refers to every other movement by what it calls itself, whether gays, feminists, environmentalists, or the "prochoice" movement. I don't know any prolife group that refers to itself as "anti-abortionist." It's always "prolife." So why is the prolife movement the conspicuous exception to your practice of calling groups by their actual names?

If you choose to use the term "anti-abortion," fairness suggests you should use "anti-life" to describe the other position. At the very least you should call it "pro-abortion." If you refrain from this out of courtesy to those holding the position, then please show the same courtesy to prolifers. I'm not asking for favoritism, just fairness.

My other concern is that in twenty years of reading the *Trib* almost every day, I have never once seen a picture of an aborted baby. The article seemed to silently agree with the prochoice advocate who first said the preborn baby was a mere "blob of tissue," then condemned the "anti-abortionists" for displaying those "bloody and intimidating pictures." But I don't understand. The *Tribune* showed photos of children dying in Vietnam and in the Middle East, Somalia and Rwanda. Why would you refuse to show the equally real and equally convincing pictures of children killed by abortion? And why, when some prolifer holds up such a picture, is she angrily condemned as if she were the one responsible for the very killing to which she is objecting?

Of course these are terrible pictures. Any picture of a dead baby is terrible—not because of the picture itself, but the reality it depicts. Prochoicers are against the pictures of killed babies. Prolifers are against the killing of the babies in the pictures.

Censoring these pictures from the debate is like censoring pictures of slaughtered baby seals from discussions about animal rights. How can citizens make an intelligent decision on any issue when vital information is withheld? Let both sides and let the media show whatever pictures they can verify as authentic and unretouched. Why should anyone be afraid of a level playing field for the truth? (Unless their own position isn't true.) If this is just a 'blob of tissue' and not a baby, why are we so opposed to looking at it?

Whoever controls the semantics, and censors the information shared with the audience, inevitably wins the debate. I'm not asking you to take my side. I'm just asking you to tell the truth. I'm asking you to give your readers the chance to make up their own minds based on an honest and unbiased presentation of scientific facts. I'm asking you to be fair.

Sincerely,
Finney Keels

Jake sighed. Reading this was like swallowing a big pill. It caught in his throat and left a terrible aftertaste. It was vintage Finney, all right. How could someone so sharp when it came to business be so naive and simplistic about complex social issues? Finney just didn't get it.

Jake examined Finney's familiar signature, which he'd seen evolve since they learned cursive in Mrs. Petersen's third-grade class. He put down the letter, gazing up at the ceiling with his head propped back on the recliner. He sat there a long time before he pushed down the foot rest, clutched his empty mug, and wandered toward the kitchen for a refill.

Jake took the miniature carton of French Vanilla creamer from his refrigerator, dumped a large helping in his cup, then picked up the coffee pot and poured it, watching the white liquid turn into a swirling sea of creamy brown. He breathed deeply, as if doing so would make him think more clearly about the investigation, and perhaps, more clearly about life.

The firm knock on the door startled Jake, yanking him from the semi-stupor his mind drifted in and out of on lazy Saturdays. He rushed to the bathroom mirror to be sure his face wasn't too scary. He noted the bloodshot eyes, the ragged stubble, the matted hair. *It could be worse.* As he walked to the door he added, *But not much.*

Jake opened his door, half expecting the landlord or somebody's lost relative. He was surprised to see two men in dark suits, both serious and important looking, their dignity and composure accentuating his own lack of both. The one, solidly built and fiftyish, was about Jake's height, with sandy red hair, wet and neatly combed. He held out a badge in a little leather case, just like in the movies. The other, jet black hair and deep tan, had a distinctively rugged look, like a man who'd worked his way into a respectable profession from a career that started as a night-club bouncer. Jake recognized them immediately but couldn't place where he'd seen them.

"Good afternoon, Mr. Woods. I'm Special Agent Colin Sutter, this is Agent Jeffrey Mayhew." Mayhew nodded dutifully, like the junior partner of a pair of Jehovah's Witnesses. "We're with the FBI." Jake stared at the badge. It looked authentic, though he didn't ever recall seeing a real one.

"We need to ask you to accompany us to our office. Or, we can talk with you here. But in any case, it's imperative that we talk immediately."

A moment before, he'd been gazing through a giant telescope and studying the distant wonders of Elyon's universe. But now Finney was thrust into what seemed another dimension, neither heaven nor earth. He felt like he was in a huge theater, viewing a curved screen. Like a planetarium, yet real, not simulated. He had the feeling he'd become much smaller, that he was inside of something—or someone. He was the face of the camera, intimately close to something magnificent on the verge.

Before him was a huge ball, being vigorously assaulted by swimming threads with tiny heads. Both ball and threads were parts of living beings, but not living beings themselves. The threads frantically searched for an opening to the ball, trying this place then that. In time they weakened, resigning themselves to failure, wilting into oblivion. One by one they fell off, until center stage switched to one, which showed hope and promise. Yes, it was penetrating, moving inside the ball, and somehow changing it, infusing it with life. Apart from each other, both ball and threads were incomplete. But together they produced something mysterious, something that felt to Finney like the magic of life.

Twenty-three grooves from the thread-shaped sperm joined with twenty-three grooves in the ball-shaped egg, meshing together like the two halves of a zipper. A great explosion produced a mighty sound and the full spectrum of colors, of what seemed galactic proportions, like a supernova. The two separate strands of twenty-three melded into a single seamless unit of forty-six, creating a unique genetic code that had never and would never be duplicated. Finney knew he was witnessing conception. It was the sound and spectrum of life. As Finney watched, a library of a thousand volumes, six hundred thousand printed pages of five hundred words per page, poured itself into a single strand of DNA.

Suddenly powerful singing enveloped him. He'd never heard the song before, but after hearing the chorus once, he knew it. It was a song about Elyon—his majesty, his greatness, and his power as Creator. Finney saw now he wasn't witnessing this remarkable event alone but was surrounded by many others who watched with equal fascination.

Finney stared at the ball that was now so much more than a ball. It was a person, fully a person, and her beauty transfixed him. Yes, *her*. He could read her genetic registry and knew this was a girl. Now a great angel, one of the special angels that continuously beholds the face of the Father, spoke forth a wondrous name, a name he had never heard, a name he felt he could never pronounce. It was the girl's name, her true name, no matter what she might be called on earth.

Finney felt exuberance. Joy. Exhilaration like he'd never known. A strong steady sound undergirded everything. He looked to find man or angel beating on a great drum. Surprisingly, he couldn't locate the sound's source.

To what could he compare what he now felt? It was several things at once. The joy of consummating his relationship with Sue, of being told there was a new life within her, of hearing in the doctor's office their children's heartbeats for the first time, of holding little Jenny and Angela and Finn in his arms.

Yes, of course, that was the sound he heard! The sound of a heartbeat, the child's heartbeat. He knew it would be almost three weeks before this magnificent creation would have a beating heart, but heaven anticipated the sound, providing it now for all to hear. And why not, for all that this child would ever be was there now in that single cell, not at all simple but incredibly complex, endowed with every bit of genetic information she would ever have, determining height, color of eyes, thickness of hair, and untold millions of invisible details of design. The child's heartbeat became a lovely melody, held up by the steady harmony of a more powerful beating sound, the sound of her mother's heart. Mother and child, harmony and melody. He realized this was a unique musical score, every pregnancy an original concerto.

There was another sound, like the approaching tide he'd heard so often at the beach, the Manzanita beach where his family spent so many wonderful vacations. The pounding of the surf. Waves. Yes, brain waves. Brain waves which couldn't be measured until forty days after this first day. The foreshadowed sound of those waves swept across the theater. Here was life before the signals by which life was measured in the dark world. All this girl would ever be she now was. Not potential, but actual. The life blood of Elyon had been poured out into her. And poured out for her. This was creation in his image, and redemption for his glory. Here before Finney's wide eyes the unfolding drama of redemption played out in the eloquent witness of one tiny person.

Finney's wonder exploded into joyful weeping, loud and unashamed. This wasn't the shadowy glimpse of joy he'd sometimes caught in the twilight world, but joy in its full and total sense, joy that exceeded his ability to contain it, a contagious joy caught from and passed on to all those around him. For Finney, in a moment's realization, had understood what this event was all about and why he had been so suddenly ushered to this place to observe *this* miracle of life's beginning, and not another. He looked around him at the smiles on the faces of both men and angels. He saw many familiar faces, some of the same ones who had been there at his entrance to heaven's birthing room. There was his mother and Jenny and...so many others. Of course. It all made sense.

The great concert moved to its climax, where Finney sensed it was his part to clash the cymbals at just the right moment. The moment now upon him, he raised his voice above the vibrant sounds of life rising from the new creation. He gestured at the colorful animated single-cell child, pulsating with life.

In the swirling tornado of color and sound, Finney shouted to all, "Do you see? Do you understand? My daughter, my child, is carrying a child. The tiny baby is Elyon's. She is Angela's. She is Bruce's. She is Sue's. And she is mine!" Tears formed in his eyes, refracting the colors of the new creation. "Behold, my granddaughter!"

Thunderous cheers and applause followed, but this was not yet the climax. The wonder of the moment overwhelmed Finney, his one hand firmly grasping Jenny's, the other his mother's. All eyes focused on the threesome, the family awaiting both completion and reunion. In an instant of insight, Finney was given the name Angela and Bruce would call the child, a name they'd not yet thought of, and he spoke that name and listened as words from his heart found their expression:

Karina, whose name means "gift":
Spawned in the sea of your Creator's consciousness,
Woven in the Artisan's loom,
Spun by the Potter, molded in his hands.

You are so much more than that world sees.
No aimless product of time, chance, and natural forces;
Destined to be ruler of beasts, not descendent of them;
Climax of Elyon's creative genius: the Magnum Opus of God.

As the simple watch must have a watchmaker,
So you must have a Creator,
An author of your genetic code,
A draftsman, architect, and builder of your soul.

A God so big the cosmos cannot contain him,
So small he too once slept in a mother's arms.
One day you will know that awesome mystery:
A baby born in a barn is Creator of all.

Bearer of God's likeness,
Object of his love,
Carved on his palm;
Apple of his eye.

When the stars collapse,
When the solar systems breath their last,
When the galaxies crumble with age,
You, Karina, will still be young.

So helpless there in your mother's protective shelter,
So vulnerable, susceptible to harm.
So frail and weak, dependent on your elders;
So unsuspecting of the ugliness that lies outside.

A sin-stained world, no longer Eden's paradise;
Torn and disfigured, marred by human will;

Testimony to man's indifference to his God.
Tombstone on the grave of human sin.

True, that world is dark,
Held in the grasp of the lord of darkness.
But dark, Karina, that your light might brighter shine,
That straining eyes might sooner turn toward your unfading radiance.

Answer to our prayers,
Fulfiller of our dreams.
You are Elyon's gift to us;
We give you back to him.

Ours to love,
But only His to possess;
For on your tiny shoulders will be borne
the reputation of the Creator's Son.

As a prism reveals
the manifold excellence of light,
May you project to a tarnished world
the multifaceted beauty of your Creator.

Our prayer, Karina,
Daughter of God:
That when eyes of men and angels gaze upon you,
They might always and only see Him.

Finney, his mother, and his daughter Jenny smiled broadly at each other. Heaven erupted into still greater applause, and once again they found themselves immersed in the contagious laughter of the kingdom.

As on the day of his entrance, Finney saw a bright and wonderful being standing at the back of the crowd, quietly orchestrating this marvelous event, his eyes on Finney, smiling his approval. And Finney knew when the celebration was over and the crowd dispersed, he would take another unforgettable walk with Elyon's Son, the Creator and Redeemer of this new child.

What was that name, that wonderful name the angel had called Karina? He could hear its echo in his mind, yet could neither pronounce it with his lips nor even remember exactly how it sounded. Now he knew why. It was Elyon's name for her. She would not be called by that name until she was given it by him, on a glorious day after she would be born into heaven, graduated into glory, joining her grandfather and her great-grandmother and her aunt, and whoever else migrated home before her.

He looked again at the fair fabric of Elyon's creation, this delicate living being. In another nine months she would be born, and in the Shadowlands they would say she had become. But she already was, before anyone on earth knew of the pregnancy.

Finney had been there to behold her becoming, when she was spoken into being by the Word of God. Birth would merely be passing through a door, a rite of passage.

Overwhelmed, Finney longed at once to hold this girl, to hold Angela, to hold Sue and Little Finn. And yet in the longing itself there was joy, as if the anticipation of the embrace of reunion were the embrace of reunion itself. So strong were his longings in that moment, though separated by the veil, Finney thought Sue must be able to feel his presence. But not with the clarity he felt hers.

Suddenly, the embrace he longed for was real and physical, for Jenny wrapped herself tightly around him, and Finney's mother made it a threesome again.

"O Daddy. Can you believe it? Look! Listen! Everyone's rejoicing. I have a niece. You have a granddaughter. Grandma has a great-granddaughter! Angela and Bruce don't even know! Mom's a grandma and she doesn't even suspect! I can't wait to see the expression on her face. And little Karina. I long to hold her. Let's pray that she'll be a great champion for Elyon."

Spontaneously, Jenny prayed aloud, head not bowed but looking toward the One who stood among them, who was always there in every nook and cranny of this vast realm, yet who sometimes focused his presence in one place, now this one.

"Protect her Lord. Give her mother—my sister!—and father your strength and wisdom. Let them know the privilege and responsibility that is theirs. Be with them in long and weary nights. Let them never think that any possession or opportunity or career compares in worth to this little one. Help them to see each moment invested in her is an investment in eternity!"

A chorus of "amens" erupted. Finney marveled that those of Zyor's great race would say "amen" to a prayer offered by his little Jenny, who was as pure and inno-cent—no, much more so—as ever on earth. Yet now, compared to him, Jenny was a veteran of the new world, knowing its ways far better than he. Finney was so proud of her. He hugged her tightly, and they both trembled with excitement at the advent of Angela's child.

After a while, Finney felt a hand on his shoulder, a great and mighty hand. It was Zyor.

"Congratulations, master. Angela is a godly young woman. You raised her to follow the Almighty. She will be a fine mother for this girl, as her mother was for her. And the father is a godly man—with your guidance, Angela chose him well. Elyon is pleased."

"Thank you, my friend. The sense of wonder is so strong. I fear I'll become cal-lous to it, that it will somehow grow old to me. Yet how many times have you seen a child conceived, and the wonder seems new and fresh to you. How can that be?"

"Here you do not grow callous to wondrous events. You deepen in your appre-ciation of them each time. You gain new insight into the old wonder, making the old wonder always new. You never 'get used to it.' It never 'gets old.' It is always wonderful, always fresh, as if it were the first time. And there is something else— each time you see a child conceived, it is a reminder of *the* child, *the* conception, *the* incarnation of Elyon's Son—the day God became man. Each child's conception is a sacrament, a symbol, an enactment of that greater drama."

Zyor's voice trembled. "And that is the wonder of wonders. Never shall we fully comprehend it; always shall we joyfully celebrate it. The applause you heard was not only for your granddaughter, but for the One who once became as your granddaughter now is, that you and she and any of Adam's race might have the privilege of being where you now are."

Finney, one arm around his daughter, the other around his mother, pondered the words of his old guardian. He thought fondly of Sue, of the years they'd shared together, and of how happy she would be when she learned Angela was carrying this child. He peered again in unmasked adoration through the window into Angela's womb, gazing upon this wondrous creation that those without eyes would call a mere blob of tissue.

The celebration was suddenly eclipsed by a realization that something was happening in the dark world, something somehow connected to him. Finney's mind went first to Jake, and then to Jake's teenage daughter Carly. Yes, that was it. Carly was in trouble, and Jake didn't know about it. But Finney was being called to prayer. He rushed to the portal.

CHAPTER FOURTEEN

J ake stood staring at the FBI badge. He'd spent enough time with police and military to know these two standing at his door were the genuine item. Right down to the formal politeness, the air of respect in addressing him as "sir," and even the use of the word *imperative*. Still, he wasn't going to let them intimidate him. His mentor Leonard once told him, "Show me someone with respect for authority and I'll show you a lousy reporter." Jake was not a lousy reporter.

He stood there silently, studying their eyes, assessing the situation, as they grew more uncomfortable. Good. They were probably genuine, but it would be stupid to let two strange men into his apartment. Yet if these guys wanted to take him, he knew they could. He could see the outline of their holsters strung under their suits, and it was obvious both of them put in their time in a weight room. He decided the best approach was to go along with them, but on his terms.

"Where's your office?" Jake ushered his best I'm-not-intimidated voice, as if Feds were always dropping by on the weekends and he was getting a little bored by it.

"The Federal Building on Fourth Street. Seventh floor."

"All right, I'll go. But I'll drive separately and follow you."

"No problem, Mr. Woods." Agent Sutter seemed gracious enough.

"Okay, give me ten minutes to take a shower and change."

"Sure. We'll wait outside." Jake wasn't going to offer them his living room, but it was nice of them to back off on their own.

Jake's adrenaline rushed as hot and hard as the shower water. Obviously these guys were on the case. What did they know? How much would they tell him? What did they want from him? He'd heard Feds often didn't let local police in on what they were doing. Did Ollie know about these guys? Jake was out of the shower and in his jeans and sweatshirt in five minutes. The whiskers would stay. On weekends Jake never shaved until his face itched, and it didn't. Besides, it would remind these guys he was a civilian, with all the rights and privileges thereto.

Jake grabbed a spiral notebook and pen and stepped out the door. Sutter and Mayhew were pacing on the apartment's front lawn, looking about as inconspicuous as two guys in full suits and trench coats could look on any Saturday afternoon outside an apartment complex.

"Ready," Jake said. "I'll pull out my car from that driveway over there." He pointed to the driveway exiting from the secured parking lot. Jake saw Mayhew eye his spiral notebook uncomfortably. *This could actually be fun.*

The car with federal plates pulled into one of many open spaces in front of the building, Jake following. The federal building looked unoccupied today. Agent

Sutter ran a card from his wallet through a scanner to gain entry to the front door, then nodded to the security officer manning the desk at the entry way. Sutter signed the log book. The officer looked bored, as though pulling the weekend shift was effortless but tiresome.

The three men entered the elevator and quietly rode to the seventh floor, where they turned to the right and snaked down a hallway to a room marked FBI. Sutter stuck in another coded card, a light turned green, and the door unlatched. The three walked in, past an office that said "Special Agent Sutter," and into a small conference room with a fancy tape recorder set up on the center table.

"Sit down, Mr. Woods." The chairs seemed new, virtually unused, and surprisingly comfortable for government issue.

"Coffee?" Sutter asked.

"Okay," Jake shrugged. Little did he know when he got up that morning he'd be served his third round of coffee by the FBI.

Agent Mayhew got the three coffees while Sutter sat down and took out a large notebook, which seemed to be a procedure manual of some sort.

Jake watched Sutter take a sip of coffee, coal black, from his transparent mug. Jake tried his own, which wasn't hot enough. *Viennese. Been in the pot too long.*

He studied Sutter's every move, trying to gain any advantage he could in a situation where the advantage was clearly not his. Trying to look more at home than he felt, this time he took a gulp of coffee. *Way too long.*

One deep draught of his own and Sutter moved the coffee aside like a man who wouldn't be coming back to it. He turned on the tape recorder second naturedly, like he'd gone through this routine before, then opened the clasps on a large bulky manila envelope. Without looking at the contents, he flipped them across the table to Jake.

"These may interest you, Mr. Woods."

He looked at the photographs. A five-by-seven of Jake entering the front door of his apartment. Another five-by-seven of him standing by the Mustang, plugging a meter on Morrison. An eight-by-ten of him jogging in the park. Another buying milk at the convenience store. Having lunch with Ollie at the deli. Standing by Doc's Suburban hoisted up at Ed's Garage. Jake felt his ears turn red. These were professional close-up photos any *Trib* photographer would be proud of.

"So much for the right of privacy. I suppose my phone's tapped too?"

"Nope. Could have, but I didn't think it was necessary." Sutter turned toward the microphone extending from the tape recorder. "Let the record indicate we are discussing the surveillance photos of Mr. Woods."

"Didn't think it was necessary? That's considerate of you to give some nominal recognition of constitutional rights."

Both sides knew this was more than a citizen who felt violated—it was the classic adversarial relationship between government authorities and the press.

"Don't you think you're overreacting a bit, Mr. Woods? It's perfectly legal to drive around the city and take photographs of people without their knowledge or permission. In fact, your newspaper does it all the time. You call it journalism, I believe. Have I heard you say something about the first amendment?"

"It *is* different and you know it. But why do I have the feeling it wouldn't make much difference to you whether it was legal or not?"

"We're a legal agency, Mr. Woods. We're here to uphold the law, not to break it, no matter what you've read about us. Or wrote about us, for that matter. Okay, I know it's unnerving to find out you've been followed. But I didn't have to tell you about this. I've laid the cards on the table. I'm being honest with you, in the hopes you'll be honest with me."

There was still one picture he hadn't shown Jake yet. It was face up but mostly covered by the envelope. Jake sensed Sutter was debating whether he should show it to him. Jake reached across the table, under the envelope, and pulled out the photo. Sutter didn't object. Jake saw a line of people in front of a coffin. *Of course.*

"You were at Doc's funeral, both of you. I saw you there."

"That's right."

"You don't respect much of anything, do you?"

"Just doing our job, Mr. Woods, like you do yours, even when people don't understand or like it. One of our associates took dozens of pictures at the funeral— it was a disguised camera with a silent shutter, so it didn't bother anyone. It's not uncommon for a murder to be committed by an acquaintance who makes a point of being at the funeral, either out of propriety or some twisted sense of curiosity or smugness. Like he wants to take one last look to be sure he did his job, or to congratulate himself. We studied the pictures to identify who was there, who should have been but wasn't, who shouldn't have been but was."

"What did you discover?"

"I'm not free to discuss with you, at least not now."

"You can't talk to me, but you want me to talk to you?"

"Look, Mr. Woods… Jake. We're on your team. Whether or not you believe it, that's the truth. We've been watching you partly for your own protection."

"Really?" Jake didn't hide his skepticism.

"Obviously you can guess some of the reason. We know you've been talking with Detective Chandler. We know everything he knows, and more. We also think you're in greater danger than you imagine."

"Danger? From whom?"

"That's where this gets a little tricky, Jake."

"How?"

"We can't divulge more information to you without some assurances of full confidentiality and cooperation."

"Forget it. I'm not going to agree to anything until I know exactly what's going on."

Agent Mayhew, leaning against the wall, crossed his arms.

"You *don't* agree and you might have to live with letting the boys who wasted your friends get away."

"Boys? As in more than one?"

"You get nothing else without agreeing to some conditions."

"Tell me what you want me to agree to. Maybe I'll think about it."

"Okay. Most of it's standard. It includes a commitment that you put nothing about this in print without our prior approval."

"Oh, is that all? Well, this is going to be easy, then. I won't agree to that. You can't tell me what I can write and what I can't."

"Spoken like a true reporter. But you have to play by the same rules everybody else does in this situation. You don't agree, then you head on home. We'll leave you alone, and you'll never figure it out. If we withdraw completely, you may not live to write again. We're under no obligation to tell you anything. It's a question of how much you want whoever killed your buddies. We're taking a big risk by talking to you. Signing the document is nonnegotiable."

Jake stared blankly. Inside he was starting to give a little, but wasn't about to show it.

"Look, Jake, on the confidentiality thing, I'm just talking about information you receive from us, or as a direct result of what we give you. If it's something you know without us, we have no control. You can do what you want with it. But if it's something we tell you, we're taking you on as a major security risk. You were in the army. You know how it works."

Jake had to admit it made sense. They were in the driver's seat. Without their information he might waste weeks going down blind alleys.

"Here's the paperwork. Sign it and we'll give you some info that should prove very helpful. We'll also ask you for some information and hope for your cooperation. You don't have to agree, but for your friends' sake we hope you do. Don't sign it and we can't do business. It's up to you."

He took a deep breath, as if putting his last card on the table. "Now here's the thing that's going to bug you the most. We've got a very important reason for it. You can't say anything about us *anyone*, including the local police. That includes Detective Chandler."

"Ollie? Why not? I'd trust him with my life. Which is more than I can say for you guys."

Mayhew didn't seem to appreciate the comment, but Sutter handled it in stride.

"As far as we know, Detective Chandler himself is no problem. But he has superiors he's obligated to report to. And if they became aware of some of this information it could compromise our investigation, maybe result in more people being killed. And the lowlifes who killed your friends could just disappear, and I don't mean with their throats cut, which wouldn't make any of us shed a tear. I mean disappear to some Caribbean island for the rest of their lives, sipping margaritas, or whatever they drink down there."

"You're saying you don't trust the police?"

"I'm saying there's good cops and there's bad cops. Most of them, maybe 98 percent of them are good cops, but it only takes one bad one to ruin this whole operation. If it was just Chandler we'd probably bring him in. He seems straight enough. But he's obligated to talk to his superiors. For everything Chandler learns there's a few sergeants and lieutenants and deputy chiefs and all kinds of people in the chain of command that are going to know, and probably a few assistants and secretaries, maybe even a custodian who looks over what's on the desks. There are leaks over there, Woods. We know that the hard way. Leaks that relate directly to our situation here."

"Look, I'm working with Ollie. He trusts me, and I trust him. If I can't talk to him about this, forget it. What's going to keep me from walking right now and telling him the whole thing?"

Agent Mayhew squirmed.

"Nothing, Woods. You can do that very thing. In fact, we know it's a chance we're taking. But if you do, the only thing you'll know is the FBI is on this. You won't know what we know. All you'll know is because you refused to cooperate, the chances will be much better that your friends' killers will live to be a ripe old age while all that's left of your buddies is food for the night crawlers."

Sutter's insensitivity rubbed Jake the wrong way, yet had its desired effect. What did he have to lose? Better to have info he couldn't directly give Ollie than have no info at all.

"Okay, Sutter. Let's see what your document says."

Agent Sutter passed over a single paragraph, typewriter style Courier, about thirteen point. It was stuffy but surprisingly jargon-free, as if written by a reporter rather than a lawyer. Still, any editor would have pared it down, shortened the sentences and cleared away some of the fog:

> Special Agent Colin G. Sutter of the United States Federal Bureau of Investigation has been authorized to reveal classified information to Jake Harvey Woods. It is understood that Mr. Woods' revealing of this information to any person or persons could severely compromise an ongoing criminal investigation. After being given this information Mr. Woods is free to choose not to cooperate in the investigation, but he is not free at any time to divulge, in print or in conversation or in any other way, any information released to him by federal agents pertaining to said investigation. In signing this document Mr. Woods agrees that if he does divulge any such information to anyone for any reason—including officers of any other legal agency—he would be interfering with a criminal investigation and violating section 793 of Title Eighteen of the National Security Act. In the event of such a violation he understands he will be prosecuted to the full extent of the law.

Jake leaned back. "I take it this means you don't want me to talk?"

Sutter smiled. Mayhew didn't.

I may not be free to divulge this information, but nothing tells me I'm not free to act on it. And if at some point Ollie sees me act on it, well, that's not the same thing as telling him, is it?

"I don't suppose you'd let me consult my attorney before I sign this?" Actually, Jake didn't have an attorney. The truth was, he'd started despising lawyers twenty years before it became popular to despise them.

"I am not authorized to divulge any information to your attorney, Mr. Woods. Chances are *you* don't trust your attorney. Why should we? It's the 'need to know.' As a former army officer you understand that, don't you?"

The need to know. The cornerstone of military intelligence and security. But why did these guys need *Jake* to know any of this? What was their angle? There was always an angle.

"All right." Jake picked up Sutter's pen and signed the paper on the line above his typed name, Jake Harvey Woods. "But I'm adding a little note."

Jake scribbled out a final sentence at the bottom: "Agent Sutter and I have agreed this contract does not apply to any information which has already come to my attention, or which comes to my attention independently of that given to me by the FBI." He handed it to Sutter.

Agent Sutter read it, smiled and mumbled, "Very good." He initialed his approval, then set the document aside.

"I don't suppose I get a copy of anything?" Jake pointed at the document and the tape recorder, still rolling.

Sutter looked at him to see if he was joking. "I'm sure you can understand we don't make triplicates and run these things up flagpoles? If you had any documentation of today's meeting it could compromise all of us."

"Right, sure. I don't suppose Agent Mayhew is a notary public?"

Mayhew made a point of not smiling.

"All right, Jake. Here's our situation. We're going to tell you certain things and ask you certain things. We'll lay our cards on the table first. I hope our show of good faith will convince you full cooperation is in all our best interests."

Jake gave his best you'll-have-to-convince-me look.

"For fifteen years, my specialty with the FBI has been organized crime. The last two years Agent Mayhew has been my partner."

Your silent partner, Jake mused.

"For eight months we've been investigating a new strategy of organized crime in this city. It parallels similar movements in at least eight other cities, probably as many as fifteen. We have every reason to believe these movements will continue to grow. The more entrenched they become, the more difficult it will be to deal with them."

Jake's casual front vanished. He made no pretense of disinterest as Sutter continued.

"One of our divisions maintains constant surveillance at major airports. Simply by tracing arrivals and departures of known figures in organized crime, we can tell when and where something new is brewing. These guys don't trust communication over the telephone. We've often got them tapped and they know it. Obviously, they can't use letters or faxes or telegrams, because those are easily intercepted and copied. Besides, these are hands-on guys, not just figure heads. They maintain a legal distance from everything, which is why they're not behind bars, but to keep in control they have to see their people working on site. That sends them the message they're not in the dark, and they can herd them into line if necessary, remind them who's boss. Anyway, eight months ago something new started brewing in this city. We didn't know what, but departures and arrivals told us it was big. So big I've gotten a few calls from the director himself."

The director of the FBI?

"We don't know everything, obviously, or we wouldn't be talking to you. But we do know it involves pharmaceuticals and medical facilities, including certain physicians. It appears to involve your friend, Dr. Lowell."

Jake flashed a disgusted look at Sutter. "Doc? Organized crime? Come on, Sutter. What kind of fool do you take me for? Doc working for the Mafia? Give me a break!"

Sutter studied Jake's reaction with some interest. He sat back as if preparing to give a lecture he'd had to give before.

"Mr. Woods, I thought with your background as an investigative journalist, you'd have a better understanding of organized crime. Perhaps I need to give you a thumbnail sketch to show you what we're dealing with here."

"Please do." Jake's voice carried more than a hint of sarcasm.

"The most common misperception of organized crime is the image of Al Capone or the Godfather. Guys who look like Marlon Brando, with raspy voices and Italian accents, surrounded by muscle men named Vito, carrying submachine guns and planting horse heads in people's beds."

Mayhew snorted, in apparent disdain for ignoramuses like Jake. Sutter sent Mayhew a stiff look intended to remind him they needed to show respect for their "guest."

"What you have to understand about organized crime is that gangsters and racketeers of that sort are dinosaurs. They really existed, but now they're nearly extinct. So people think organized crime is extinct too. Well, it isn't. Organized crime isn't a function of one place or segment or era in society, it's a simple function of human nature. It goes where the profits are. And it does it in the most effective way, which today is quiet, low profile, infiltrating and expanding, never identifying itself as what it is. It never looks like Chicago in the twenties. If it did, it would be recognized and derailed."

Sutter stopped, as if wanting Jake to show he was interested.

"Go on. I'm listening."

"What it looks like today is just another money-making opportunity some entrepreneur came up with on his own, with no ties to anyone or anything else. It presents itself as a lucky chance to make some money on the side without really hurting anybody. It thrives on the guy in the opportunity seat thinking he's been given the shaft by the system, that he deserves this break, that he'd be a moron to pass it up. Besides, he tells himself he's *really* doing it for the wife and kids and grandkids, so he can give them what they want and retire earlier and spend more quality time with them.

"The point is, organized crime has diversified, and it doesn't have one single kingpin nationally or even regionally. It has competing segments. And there's all kinds of entrepreneurs that don't have a long history in organized crime, maybe no history at all. They just see a money-making opportunity and organize what amounts to their own little syndicate with them in charge. So organized crime is really just an umbrella term for every attempt to generate and control profit in the context of legitimate enterprises, by moving out into fringe areas, gray areas, illegal or borderline legal involvements. The grayer the better."

"So what does that have to do with—"

"I'm getting to your friend, Dr. Lowell. Bear with me. You need to hear this."

"Okay." Jake sounded skeptical, but not as skeptical as he was trying to sound.

"During prohibition, the profit was in bootlegging. But alcohol isn't much of an opportunity now. Gambling and prostitution are still big bucks, so organized crime's still there. There's big money in professional sports, so they've managed to fix some fights, have an occasional game thrown, but it's rare because sports are too much in the public eye. Drugs, now that's been a real windfall. Easily processed, easily transported, tremendous value in small packages. But what you have to understand about organized crime is, these guys are always looking for something new, and something clean. They prefer to stay away from the illegal stuff. Some of them are community leaders, family men, church-goers. They just want the money and the power. They'd rather be associated with respectable stuff. These guys don't wear pinstriped suits and call each other Bugsy and Babyface. They wear business suits and call each other Bob and Jim and work out next to each other at the health club."

Jake looked at Sutter, wanting to challenge him, but realizing this agent knew a great deal more than he did in this area. It made him feel good to know he was being trusted with important information, that he was being "brought in" to an FBI investigation. Still, he wasn't going to buy into it that easily.

"So, you're saying these guys appear respectable enough that people can get involved without realizing who they are?"

"Exactly. It all goes back to Meyer Lansky. Know the name?"

"I've heard it."

"Lansky was a businessman. He proposed a working agreement where territories were laid out so the gangs could stop hassling each other and there'd be more profits for everyone. That became the Syndicate. The Syndicate realized prostitution and gambling and bootlegging and other criminal activities were too confining and dangerous. So it moved into the labor movement. Then into food products, taverns and bars, restaurants, securities, real estate, vending machines, garment manufacturing, produce, garbage disposal, securities, the Waterfront, you name it. They're always looking for something new where they can flex their muscles. Something where there's big money."

Sutter checked out Jake's expression. The cockiness had melted. He was listening intently.

"So where you gonna go today that's new, Jake? Where's the big money? Big salaries, big facilities, big grants? Unlimited future, yet change and uncertainty that spells opportunity?"

Jake gave a questioning look and shrugged. Agent Sutter was in the driver's seat and clearly knew where he was going. Jake didn't.

"Medicine. Health care. Look at today's upper class. I don't just mean the really wealthy, I mean the country club set, the people who live in the three-thousand-square-foot houses in the suburbs and drive the BMWs and give their kids private tennis lessons. What do they have to worry about? Primarily, just their health, right? How do they spend their discretionary income? Health foods and vitamins and exercise equipment and health club memberships. And when they get sick, they'll pay anything to get the best medical care. Everybody's concerned about their health, right? I mean, your health is all you've got. That's what opened the door to pharmaceuticals."

"What do you mean?"

"Specialized drugs are big money. The latest medical technology is always big money. So, naturally, unscrupulous people are getting in on the edges, buying some research, manipulating some results, pumping up certain companies, deflating others. But the inroads in medicine didn't used to be as strong as they were in other legit enterprises. There's been something about the medical community that didn't make it as vulnerable as the waterfront and trucking. It's had kind of a moral wall protecting it. Sacred oaths to protect life and all that. And because health care's been relatively uncorrupted in the past, it just leaves more room for the flood-tide."

"Flood-tide?"

"The wrong kind of people moving in. Making some tempting offers. That's where your friend comes in. He met with some people, outwardly respectable people, but with known links to the bad guys. We've been tailing them for months, seeing who they spent their time with. And guess what? One of them made at least three contacts with your friend."

Jake started to say, "That doesn't prove anything," but instead asked, "What did they talk about?" He felt he'd betrayed Doc by his choice of responses.

"We don't know yet. We were hoping you might be able to tell us."

Sutter studied Jake's face like a palm reader examining a palm. "First, we need to know if you've ever seen or heard anything that substantiates what I've just told you."

"That's easy. It's all brand new to me. I don't think I believe it, but I've certainly never seen anything that makes me think it's true."

Even as he said it, Jake realized he was lying. He was believing a lot of this, and he *had* been aware of what seemed like a large windfall of money Doc had been spending the past year. He'd wondered about it several times. Doc seemed under more pressure at work, often complaining about unfair medical regulations and health care revisions and how they were "trying to cut doctors off at the knees."

"So there's nothing you've come across related to the car wreck that points the finger to organized crime?"

"No."

"Okay, I just have to be clear on this. Second, we know you're working on this case too, and no one knew your friend as well as you. We'd like you to tell us what you know, or at least what you suspect."

Here it was, finally. The FBI had a lot of puzzle pieces, but they just weren't fitting together. They needed him.

"If you want anything official on the investigation, you'll have to go to Detective Chandler."

"I've already explained why we can't do that." Sutter looked exasperated. "Look, twice in the last year the FBI has talked with ranking police personnel in this city, and twice vital information has leaked to organized crime. There's either a collaborator or somebody with an awful big mouth. We just can't take the chance of them even knowing we're on their tail. The director himself called that shot. No contact with the police. So, what can you tell me?"

"Well, maybe you can tell me what you know I know, so I don't bore you."

"We know about the yellow card. We know about the car, the tie-rods. We know a lot more, but please, bore us, will you? We want you to bore us."

Jake hesitated, but figured they'd been honest with him and it couldn't hurt to help them. This wasn't like giving a scoop to another newspaper. He wanted Doc and Finney's killer nailed, and these might be the pros to help nail them.

"Well, I can tell you there's a lot of other people who could have had motives. A right-wing fanatic, opposed to Doc because he's done abortions or promoted the abortion pill."

Even as he said it he thought of "pharmaceuticals" and noted Sutter's slightly raised eyebrow.

"It could be somebody else with a personal vendetta against him. You know, someone unhappy with a surgery he did on them."

"They'd have to be awfully unhappy. I mean you don't kill somebody because your stitches show." Now Sutter was skeptical. "More likely because you've crossed them or threatened to squawk."

"It's even possible someone was going after my other friend, Finney, or me."

"We've thought of that. Our surveillance on you was originally for information, but we've told our agents to give you protection too. Other people are tailing you, we know that. But if they wanted you dead, they've had ample opportunity. We give it a 95 percent chance that Dr. Lowell was the sole target. The kingpins probably ordered a hit by an out-of-town trigger man who's long gone, although I've got to admit using a hacksaw isn't their style. Who knows? Anyway, you're probably not in danger. But we'd hate to be proven wrong by a bullet in your head."

"Yeah, I'm not real excited about that either."

"Who else have you talked to? What else have you found out?"

The photos and the surveillance told him they knew exactly where he'd been, so he figured he'd better tell them the general stuff. He told them about talking to Sue and Mary Ann. That he'd be talking to some of the abortion protesters next week. He even told them about the possibility of betrayed husbands or women scorned. He decided it was a little late to be protecting Doc's reputation.

After another forty minutes of probing and note taking, Sutter put down his pen.

"Jake, we appreciate your honesty. I'd like to ask your ongoing cooperation. We're going to be contacting you periodically. We'll update you on our investigation, tell you everything we're authorized to. In return, we'd like you to update us on what you know. You could come across exactly what we need to put these guys away."

"So, do I just drop by to chat? Or do I wave a red hanky to your surveillance guys?"

Sutter smiled. "It's essential you don't come by here, or you could blow the investigation. You didn't ask about the other people tailing you."

"I was working up to it."

"Our surveillance agents, Mayhew's been one of them, have noticed some of the same bystanders happen to show up around you in different parts of town. Not a coincidence. Today they weren't around, I don't know why, so we made our move. They didn't tail us here. We have ways of knowing. Bottom line, I'm not even going to give you our phone number. It's just too risky. We'll call you regularly, at your office usually. Until then, be careful. And, please, remember your agreement. We wouldn't want to prosecute you, but we would if you forced our hand."

Mayhew nodded, as if doing so put real weight behind Sutter's threat.

"Remember, we're on the same team, Jake. We want to get the guys that took out your friends. We want them as bad as you do."

Somehow Jake doubted that, but he was sure Sutter meant it anyway.

"Okay. Am I free to go?"

"Of course. We'll escort you out."

CHAPTER FIFTEEN

t was 2:45 Monday afternoon, three hours after Jake finished his column. He dreaded what awaited him in fifteen minutes. But first he had to return a call to Ollie.

"Detective Chandler would like you to hold a minute, Mr. Woods." It was the familiar voice of the detective bureau receptionist.

"Sure."

"Actually, his exact words were, 'Tell him to hold on to his shorts, I'm coming.'" Jake smiled. He was enough of a regular now she felt free to actually quote Ollie.

No stranger to holding, Jake used the time to contemplate his bizarre weekend. Despite his initial skepticism, there was no doubting Sutter and Mayhew were FBI. And as wild as the organized crime scenario sounded at first, the more Sutter explained it, the more it had the ring of truth. From his years as an investigative reporter, Jake had developed a gut instinct about what was true and what wasn't. The FBI's hypothesis was disturbing but plausible.

Meanwhile he had other, more ordinary suspects to pursue. Now he also had the added dimension of looking over his shoulder, realizing at any time he could be followed not only by FBI agents, his self-appointed guardian angels, but others, potentially ruthless people fully capable of playing hard ball if they didn't like his nosing around. The game took on a new complexion. The stakes had been raised.

"Chandler here."

"Your favorite reporter checking in for duty."

"Try again. That doesn't carry much weight. Sort of like favorite tax collector."

"Understood. What's up?"

"I'm snowed under, that's what's up. Crime takes no holiday. I remember when murders used to be rare in this city. I'm having a hard time recalling which leads go with which investigation. Let's see, you're on the strangled high-class hooker case, right?"

"Funny, Ollie."

"Okay, I got the file. Hang on."

Jake noticed Ollie's voice, usually loud despite its thinness, reduce almost to a whisper. Obviously he didn't want to advertise he was sharing information with anyone outside the department. Jake realized again Ollie was taking a risk trusting him, which made him feel even worse about holding back on the FBI's involvement. But what choice did he have?

"More news from the boys in crime lab. They've really earned their bagels on this one. You know that little piece of fabric they found under the car? Well, they identified the fabric type—80 percent cotton, 20 percent polyester. They say it's a basic sweatshirt type material, which narrows it down to a few million items. But they ran a chemical analysis and identified the dye lot."

Ollie paused as if Jake should immediately respond.

"Which means...?"

Ollie sighed, as a master with a slow pupil.

"Which means, every manufacturer keeps detailed records on clothing it produces, including dye lot information and what retail stores it sells the clothing to. That's no big help if it's a line of clothing sold to lots of different stores everywhere, or if it's sold to one national chain, say K-Mart, and they ship it all over the place. All you know then is your killer could have bought his clothes in Orlando, Florida or Gresham, Oregon or three hundred other cities in between. But our strand of fabric was much more isolated. This particular dye lot was processed by a small manufacturer and all sent to Regent's."

"Regent's? That's just a local chain, isn't it?"

"Exactly. Only five stores, every one within twenty miles of where we sit."

"So, what does that prove?"

"It doesn't prove anything. But it strongly suggests whoever did it is local. Shops locally, lives locally. Bought his blue sweat shirt or sweat pants at Regent's."

"Uh-huh."

"You don't sound too excited. Well, granted, it doesn't tell us a lot, but it's one more piece in the puzzle. If we come up with suspects we can watch them, study their shopping habits, maybe even find our blue sweats with a nice little hole, maybe an oil stain." Jake could almost hear Ollie salivate. "But we've got a long way to go here. Got anything more for me, Jake?"

"Nope, sorry. Listen, I've got to run to a meeting. I'll call you if I come up with anything. And thanks for telling me this stuff. I really appreciate it."

Jake hung up under a load of guilt. He wanted to discuss everything with Ollie. But he'd vowed not to. He'd have to sift all this out for himself. How did Ollie's new evidence jibe with the FBI's theory of an out-of-town hit man hired by organized crime? Besides, he still couldn't picture a hit man with a hack saw. On the other hand, maybe that was the whole point—if a head shot was an obvious professional murder, why not stage an apparent accident which, even if discovered, would look like the job of an amateur? Jake could make a case for every possibility, but nothing seemed right. His head spun like one of those carnival squirrel cages he and Doc and Finney used to cram into every summer at the Benton County Fair.

Normally he'd be column brainstorming, sneaking out early to play some golf, or taking an extra long walk in the city this clear crisp afternoon. Instead, he found himself walking toward a *Trib* conference room, to one of his least favorite activities, made all the more odious by this rare November sunshine flooding into the *Trib* from every outside window. Jake shook his head in resignation. A committee meeting.

Managing editor Jess Foley presided at the long rectangular table in the *Trib*'s biggest editorial conference room. Every day he met with all the *Trib*'s department heads, getting fifteen to twenty of their nominations for what deserved to make A-1.

Exactly one would get the top billing, the main headline, and four or five others would get a less prominent role on page one, expanding on later pages. The prototype diplomat, Jess showed the same respect for the Travel and Living and Sports departments as he did for Metro, Foreign, Politics, and Business. Jess wasn't a curmudgeon like Winston, but shared the same dedication to the newspaper, and a much larger picture of how the components worked together. If the *Tribune* was a symphony orchestra, Jess Foley was the conductor. He also chaired a few key committees, including the one now assembled.

"Okay, first let's welcome our newest member. Everybody knows Jake, right? We thought it was about time we got a general columnist on the committee. We need opinions here, and columnists have opinions to spare. Welcome, Jake."

Jake nodded. Most of the eight others smiled, especially Clarence, his favorite sports columnist and occasional partner in pranks. Jake had known for a month he'd be joining this committee, but with every spare moment off the job going to the investigation he didn't need anything new right now. Nonetheless, here he sat on the "Multicultural Concerns Committee," with only a vague understanding of what it did.

"Whenever we add a new member, it's a good time to remind ourselves what we're about." Jess sounded like a college professor working with a group of masters students.

"Two years ago we were getting a lot of feedback from groups that felt slighted and misrepresented. That's when we started diversity training for editors, then reporters. At first this was voluntary, as you recall, but we found those who didn't choose to attend needed it most. We needed some sort of structure to assure diversity was being respected. Hence, this committee. As you know, some other papers are doing the same, and it seems to be working well."

"So," Jess eyeballed Jake now, "we try to stay on top of what's coming down the pike in our different departments, things that could affect the image of minority groups. Also, we evaluate what's already in print and give input to editors and reporters when necessary. We're a diverse group ourselves, and I think we've done well to arrive at as much consensus as we have, all things considered."

Jess looked down now, and from a few facial expressions Jake caught his first clues this committee was not a big happy family. Clarence in particular seemed uncomfortable.

"Anyway Jake, you'll get a feel for what we do here. Jump in any time. Okay, Peter, let's start with a report on the New York conference."

Peter Sallont, a promising young reporter assigned to politics, struck Jake as someone making a mark at the *Trib*. Peter made no bones about his sexual orientation, right down to his bumper sticker, "Gay and Proud of It." He'd written a few pieces on the homosexual rights issue, including the one Sue complained about. Jake wasn't about to tell Sue Peter was gay. She'd never understand.

"Well, seven of us from the *Trib*, including three on this committee, got back Saturday from The National Lesbian and Gay Journalists Association conference." Peter spoke excitedly. "Myra and Pamela and I all agree it was incredible, a real highlight. It was a great investment on the part of the *Trib* to send us."

Peter looked at two women Jake didn't know. Both smiled and nodded their agreement.

"A $40,000 grant from the *New York Times* underwrote the conference. It was attended and co-sponsored by evening news anchors from NBC, CBS, PBS, CNN, and representatives from *Time*, *USA Today*, *Newsday*, and Knight-Ridder, among others. All sorts of key newspapers were represented. There's six hundred gay journalists in the Association, and it's growing rapidly. The networks and newspapers all pledged they'll continue to recruit and hire more gays and lesbians. It was tremendous. We're all looking forward to going back next year and bringing some others from the *Trib*."

Myra and Pamela added a few comments, while Jake watched Peter unfold a full page from section D of the *Trib*, from a few days earlier.

"Jess, this seems a good time to point out this piece on the history of AIDS. Some of it's okay, especially the parts about condom use and how everyone can get AIDS, young or old, heterosexual or homosexual. But there's a few sentences here that are totally out of line."

Nods from Pamela and Myra and a couple of others accompanied this, suggesting to Jake it had been discussed before the meeting.

"Listen to this—'The AIDS epidemic originally surfaced in the gay community in 1981, and at first was largely confined to the most promiscuous gay males. It spread primarily through anal intercourse with numerous sexual partners, and was greatly exacerbated by the disease ridden climate of gay bath houses in larger cities, notably New York and San Francisco. This same environment had already produced a meteoric rise in herpes, syphilis and gonorrhea, as well as lesser known STDs, and now became the fountainhead of AIDS. The deadly disease started spreading outside the gay community as homosexuals shared needles, donated blood and were involved in sexual relationships with bisexuals, who in turn spread the disease to exclusive heterosexuals.'"

Peter looked at the committee as if nothing more need be said.

Jess asked, "So your concern is, it blames the gay community for AIDS?"

"That's exactly what it does. Now, as I said, the rest of the article is pretty good, but that paragraph just feeds the prejudices of the 'AIDS is a judgment from God' crowd. I got a number of calls from people who were offended. I noticed some letters on the editorial page too."

Again, there was a chorus of nods.

"What's your recommendation, Peter?"

"That we send a memo to the reporter and editor involved and caution them to be more careful in the future. This is something that shouldn't have been written in the first place, and should never have slipped by the editor. If they're not sure what's appropriate and what isn't, they should submit it to us beforehand. That's what we're here for."

"Okay, does the memo sound good to everybody?" Most of the heads nodded. Jake noticed Clarence's didn't. "Peter, would you draft it for us? Maybe you and I can just sign it on behalf of the committee. I may follow up personally, with the editor at least. That okay?" The same heads nodded again.

Pamela added, "I'd suggest we send them to one of the Gay Understanding Workshops. A lot of businesses are doing them for their employees. They're all over the city."

"Good idea," Peter said. "The Gay Task Force has a list of all the scheduled workshops in the next few months. I'll enclose them with the memo. Maybe I'll give them some of the materials we picked up in New York too."

Jess looked down at his legal pad. "Okay, Jody, what have you got?" Jody Mendez was a talented reporter from Metro.

"With the Domingo trial coming up we've got some concerns. The race riots were the context for this thing, and it isn't fair to talk about Domingo's alleged crimes without dealing with the community's responsibility for creating the racial climate that produced Domingo's actions."

Domingo was half Hispanic, half black, and had been claimed by both communities, Jake recalled.

"Agreed," Myra added. "We need some balance. People are still stinging from *Trib* pieces that seemed to justify police brutality against Hispanics and African-Americans."

After a moment's pause, Clarence spoke up. "Well, I always tell myself I'm going to be quiet, but it never works. Several of you are thinking this, but you won't say it, so I will. Namely, when has this paper *ever* justified police brutality? In every editorial and column and news piece I've ever seen, we've bent over backwards to condemn police brutality. If anything, we've managed to get cops saddled with the brutality label when there's been no solid evidence."

A few angry glances left Clarence apparently unfazed. *Ollie would like this guy.*

"The implication that we've got to make up for being pro-police brutality in the past is ridiculous. As for the Domingo situation, when a black man beats the tar out of a black shop owner while pulling off an armed robbery in a black community, how can you call that the product of racial indignation? It's his own race for crying out loud! The man is a *criminal*, not a victim! And let's not forget that one of the two officers accused of brutality was black—who knows, maybe he was especially mad because it was a black victim. I know it's not customary to be concerned about the *victim's* race, but it's worth a thought."

"The purpose of this committee is to be sensitive to minority concerns," Myra responded. "We know the pain they're feeling. We've seen the rage and we understand why it erupts in violence." She looked Clarence right in the eyes. "Maybe if some of us here were more in touch with our people we'd understand that."

Clarence sighed deeply. "It's now time for my regular reminder that the color of my skin is coal black. In fact, since some of you consider skin color a proof of credibility, a quick look around the room shows I'm the most credible person here."

Jake chuckled, then stopped abruptly, embarrassed when he realized he was the only one laughing.

"Now, I realize the fact I'm a heterosexual male makes me suspect, but please rest assured this is not shoe polish, and I am truly a black man, the descendent of Kentucky slaves. I grew up three blocks from where Domingo murdered the store owner, and I have two sisters and a brother who still live in that neighborhood. It could just as easily have been them, or one of my nephews or nieces that got wasted. I'm not out of touch with those people. In fact, the ones I know who live there are all *outraged* at the murder. They believe Domingo's guilty as sin and deserves the gas chamber, what do you think about that? To them Domingo isn't a political symbol representing the angst of an oppressed people, he's just a bad apple, a vicious criminal. They don't want him to be a role model or poster child of black rage. They believe nobody should let 'racial tension' justify the murder of innocent people—black, brown, white, or purple."

"You may be black on the outside Mr. Abernathy, but it's pretty clear what you are on the inside." It was Myra again. "Hundreds of years of abuse and oppression and put downs and you act like we're supposed to forget it all. Well, some people don't have it as easy as you do."

Jake could see the tension in the room wasn't newborn but had picked up where it left off in previous meetings.

"Listen to yourself." Jake thought he could see steam rising from Clarence's forehead. "You're saying we're entitled to be racist. People were racist against us, so now *we* can be racist, is that it? White people labeled us all bad, so now we can label them all bad. And who suffers for this? Not white people. Good ones and bad ones, they still sleep at night, no matter how much we blame them. It's *our* people who suffer, that's who. We're the welfare society's permanent underclass, dependent on the doles from every liberal politician, white or black, that comes along. Our women are paid to have children but not be married, then paid to get abortions. Two out of every three black children in this country are born out of wedlock, and don't give me that look like I'm being judgmental. The fact is, these children need fathers. We teach our men that women and children don't need them, and they believe us. Our leaders sit and blame everybody else for what their ancestors did to our ancestors, and every time some criminals beat people up and sell drugs and steal a stereo it's because they've been victimized. When are we going to stop the blame and teach our young men to take responsibility?

"Wipe that shocked self-righteous look off your face, Myra. You're so used to acting like a victim you don't know how to be anything else."

Several outraged groans didn't deter Clarence a bit.

"You know what I want for the black community, for *my* community? I want it to blend in with everybody else. I want it to excel and prosper like the Vietnamese and Japanese and East Indians. They're not smarter than we are, they're not better than we are. It's just that they're not content to live off welfare, eating society's leftovers. They're out there working hard and keeping their kids in school, off drugs, and out of gangs. Exactly like my sister and her family are trying to do in a community where sleazeballs like Domingo are killing kids with drugs and guns."

Clarence looked hard in Myra's eyes. "We've got to quit talking about our skin color, quit considering it an asset or a liability, and learn how to get color blind and just be good decent citizens, and raise our families to do right and succeed! And let's quit talking about our 'African-American leaders.' First, I'm not African. I'm American. My ancestors were African, but this is my country. Second, I want leaders I can respect and follow—I don't care what color their skin is. Nobody talks about 'Japanese leaders' and 'Vietnamese leaders' and 'Romanian leaders.' That's because they're just Americans. And that's what I am. Most blacks I know are fed up with being a special interest group or guinea pigs for patronizing liberal programs, as if we had some deficiency and can't make it like the others. Well, we can, I tell you."

"Look, Clarence." This was a light-skinned black man Jake recognized as the Arts and Entertainment department editor. "Misty is with the Native American Journalists Association. And even though you quit the National Association of Black Journalists, I'm proud to still be a member. So don't go telling the rest of us how to solve the problems of minorities. I think we know a little about that—"

"Amazingly little, if you ask me, Jeremy. And you know *exactly* why I quit the NABJ. It's because it was the National Association of *Liberal* Black Journalists. I got tired of going to meetings and hearing nothing but moaning and complaining and why people should be hired just because they belong to a certain race. I happen to believe that we really *are* equal, and we can compete on the level of other journalists, without special favors. I'm sick and tired of gender journalism and sexual journalism and race journalism—I just want plain old journalism. And to be honest I'm also sick and tired of being lumped in with the homosexual community, as if being black and committing sodomy were moral equivalents."

Pamela gasped, Peter blushed. Jake had mixed feelings, but the boredom he'd prepared himself for seemed nowhere in sight.

Clarence now looked around the room with pleading eyes, which occasionally fell on Jake.

"The discussions at these Black Journalist meetings were nothing like the discussions my extended family has on weekends and holidays. The people I know are the backbone of the black community, the hard workers, the people who make no excuses, who stay in school, go to church, work to improve their community rather than collect somebody's guilt money because their ancestors were persecuted by a bunch of bigots. I'll say it again—my goal is to be color blind, but the NABJ is nothing but color conscious."

"Okay, Clarence, we've heard this before," Jeremy said. "It's got nothing to do with our agenda today. The point is—"

"The point is, this committee is doing exactly what's at the heart of racism—it's focusing on differences, on racial identity, as if that was what made a person a person. Well, it isn't. I'm black and I'm glad to be, wouldn't want to be anything else, don't want to be white or act white. But that doesn't make me worse or better or more needy or less needy than anyone else, and I'm tired of being treated as if it did! All this multiculturalism just emphasizes differences and creates hostilities between people. Remember the melting pot concept? We need to come together as Americans. Anything less is pure racism."

Several started to respond at once. Sensing the meeting was about to deteriorate into a bar room brawl, Jess raised his hand in a conciliatory gesture.

"Okay, folks, I'm afraid we're getting pretty far afield. I know we have some philosophical differences, but we're not going to resolve them here. Let's move on. Please. Pamela, you wanted some time."

"Right. A friend in Metro caught wind of an upcoming article that's going to portray Rape Crisis Centers as some sort of feminist indoctrination center or lesbian recruiting ground." Several rolled their eyes and laughed.

"I've got a friend who works at one of the centers being investigated, and she says the reporter is setting this up like it's a big time scandal. I don't know the time table on the story, but I think somebody needs to cool the reporter's jets!"

"Now wait a minute." It was Misty, the American Indian reporter. "I'm not sure that's entirely fair. Have you talked to Heather Ashley? She's the one doing the article, right? I know Heather. She's a feminist. She had some friends go to a few of the Rape Crisis Centers and they told her the same thing. She wasn't looking for this story, she didn't like it at all, but it came to her. She went to the meetings herself and found this constant inundation with anti-male anti-heterosexual propaganda."

Several people shot looks at Misty, and she backpedaled.

"Well, I'm not saying it *was* propaganda, just that it sort of seemed like it. Heather told me some women aren't just getting counseling, they're being introduced to a sexual subculture. In some cases, women in counseling are ending up in sexual relationships with their counselors. Isn't that violating professional ethics? Isn't that exploiting a vulnerable woman?"

"The sexual orientation of the workers isn't an issue, unless you're homophobic," Pamela replied. "And if it seems anti-male, consider the fact that these women have been raped by men. I wouldn't expect men to be made the hero of the plot, would you? And it's not like they're changing anybody's sexual orientation. Nobody made me a lesbian—it's just the way I am. It's irrational and naive to think someone can be persuaded to be gay."

Jake hoped Clarence wouldn't jump in, but he did.

"But you used to be married to a man, didn't you, Pamela? Didn't you tell us once you were married to this creep, and then you had your first lesbian relationship in your thirties?"

"Yes, but—"

"So you changed, right? I mean, at very least you changed your behavior. The point is, these women have been raped. They're going to be extremely vulnerable to anti-male sentiment. Is it right to take advantage of their situation to manipulate them for personal or political gain?"

"The stench of homophobia is growing here." It was Myra. "What's wrong, Clarence? Afraid we're conspiring to take over the country?"

Laughter filled the room. Jake noted it wasn't good-natured and light-hearted, but cynical, almost acidic.

"Do you seriously think the *Trib* could get away with an article like this?" Peter asked. "It'll fall right into the hands of the right-wing bigots. And the gay community won't stand for it. Expect boycotts and pickets, loss of advertising revenues, and major loss of credibility among your most loyal readers."

Peter looked at Jess. "The *Trib* is going to suffer if this thing gets printed."

"I thought we did stories because they were true and important," Clarence said. "Who cares what political views they further or don't further? Who cares about economic threats as long as our research is sound and we stick to the facts? You didn't care when Christian groups staged a boycott because of what they thought was anti-Christian bigotry in the *Trib*."

You're not one to give up easily, Clarence, I'll grant you that.

"Well, I for one certainly care how the gay community thinks about the *Trib*," Peter replied. "I didn't become a reporter to be part of a paper that fuels the fires of prejudice."

"And I didn't become a reporter to have important stories stuffed and censored because they didn't fit somebody's agenda." Clarence was adamant. "Are you saying all lesbians are automatically good, that they never do a bad thing just because they're lesbians?"

"Of course not, but—"

"Then what's so bad about somebody reading an article that suggests *some* lesbians may be doing the wrong thing? I mean heterosexuals sometimes do the wrong thing, and we show that in the *Trib* all the time. And we've had a number of pieces showing the wonderful contributions gay people make to our community. Why not show they're just like everybody else, some good, some bad?"

"Because you're going to promote bigotry," Peter said, with evident sincerity. "We have a responsibility for how people interpret what we write."

"I thought we just had a responsibility to tell the truth and let people draw their own conclusions. Why do we have to make them draw *our* conclusions? Because our conclusions are right, is that it? So we need to make them think like us, even if the only way we can do that is by withholding critical information from them?" Clarence's tone was blistering, and the overall temperature of the room was stifling to Jake.

"Look," Jess jumped in again, less a chairman now than a referee. "Let's take a vote on this thing. I see three options. One is to leave it alone. Two is to have the reporter continue her investigation, but caution her and her editor to balance any negative portrayal with some positives. Three is to recommend spiking the story entirely. Okay, option one, story go on as is?"

Clarence raised his hand, with a sad and lonely look, and didn't seem surprised no other hand went up.

"Okay. Option two, go ahead but with a caution to balance?"

Jake raised his hand, assuming most other hands would come up too. Only Misty's hand went up, raised half way, accompanied by a pained and sheepish look.

"And option three, kill it?" The other six hands went up, minus Jess who didn't vote.

"Okay, we recommend spiking it. I'll tell her editor, let's see, that would be Patsy. She can work it through with Heather."

"Just like that?" Jake asked.

"Well, we've got to move on. How else would you like us to handle it, Jake, if not by vote?"

"Maybe we should hear what the writer has to say, why she feels this is an important story. Or just trust the writer and editor to work it out."

Jess's eyes implored Jake not to pursue it. "Our job is to represent the multicultural aspect of the issue. We're looking out for the overall effect on the gay community. Besides, it's only a recommendation."

"What he's saying, Jake," Clarence interjected, "is that we're the censorship committee. Get used to it. Killing stories is what we do here. It's 'only a recommendation,' but of the dozens of recommendations we've made in my six months on this committee, every single one has been followed. Correct me if I'm wrong."

"If looks could kill" was too mild an expression for some of the looks directed at Clarence. But no one spoke up to correct him.

"Look, tensions are a little high," Jess said. "Let's take a break and shake it off. Get some fresh air. We've got three or four other stories to discuss. Let's be back in ten minutes."

The room cleared like a bomb scene, only to have several small groups reassemble in the hallway. Only Jake and Clarence were left in their chairs. Clarence looked deep in thought, then said to Jake, "I have this soothing effect on people. Have you noticed?"

Jake laughed heartily, welcoming the release of tension.

"Careful, Jake. You laughed at something I said earlier too. You're allowed a spiteful laugh, a disgusted chortle, but no good-natured laughter. Laughter is a form of approval. You don't want to be caught approving of my viewpoint, not on this committee."

"Come on, Clarence. It's not that bad."

Clarence looked glum.

"Is it?"

"I call this the hyphenation committee, Jake. Multi-culturalism, African-American, Hispanic-American, Indian-American, Homo-sexual. I wonder what this country's first two hundred years would have been like if people were divided into groups like this. Italian-Americans with Italian-American studies at the universities, Russian immigrants studying Russian history instead of American history, Irish-Americans hired according to quotas, multicultural police making sure every newspaper had its proportionate number of Swedes. There never would have been a United States of America. There would be no melting pot, just a bunch of special interests groups looking out for themselves and not caring about everybody else.

"Look out in the hallway at our subgroups. This isn't a committee of journalists, Jake. It's a committee of lobbyists. We're not here to see accurate information gets printed. We're here to do the opposite. We're here to protect and promote our particular constituencies. I'm telling you, we're just a bunch of lobbyists."

"I admit I was surprised at the vote, but—"

"Jake, the vote is *always* like that, except you threw in a new wrinkle by voting as a moderate, along with Misty, who surprises everybody once in a while. I'm the conservative. The rest are intractable liberals, with an occasional defection by one of them, usually with apologies. The control they have over other reporters and editors is incredible. Take that paragraph on the history of AIDS. What no one pointed out was, it was completely factual. It was the truth! Why can't we tell people what's objectively, demonstrably true? Because it might affect their opinion of the gay community? I read that article—the rest of it did the usual obeisance to the gay lobby. Now we can't allow even a single *paragraph* to appear, if someone could possibly even question the responsibility of some of the gay community as a result. We don't *dare* let readers use their brains and reach their own conclusions!"

"Listen, Clarence, I hear you. Frankly, I don't want to be on this committee. I'd rather go do something else, like have a root canal. But these people are just trying to do their job. Don't you think you should cut them a little slack?"

Clarence calmed down a little, pausing long enough to take a deep breath. "Don't get me wrong, Jake. I don't mind working with homosexuals. Peter and Pamela and even Myra, these are people I can get along with fine, if they just get off their soapbox. They're certainly nice enough. Peter and Pamela anyway. But nice doesn't always mean *right*, does it? You say they're just trying to do their job? That's the whole point. They're *not* doing their job. I don't make an issue at work out of my sexual practices, and I don't appreciate anyone else making an issue of theirs. If it doesn't matter, fine, then let's quit talking about it. Why keep cramming it down everybody's throat?

"You want me to accept them as people, fine, no problem. I do. They're people with the same rights as you and me. I don't try to force them to accept my beliefs and my way of life and frankly I'm tired of the constant pressure to accept and endorse theirs. Coming out of the closet is one thing, but making a constant issue of what's in the closet is another. Maybe some things *belong* in the closet, ever think of that? To me pluralism means you can agree to disagree, but they won't tolerate disagreement. If you don't endorse their behavior you're a no good bigot, a homophobe, a hatemonger. To put it in terms a modern school kid would understand, if this committee was adrift on a life raft and determined they didn't have enough room for everyone, do you think they'd have *any* hesitation deciding who to put overboard? Man, I'd be treading water right now."

"You really think it's that bad, that it's affecting their integrity as journalists?"

Clarence sighed, giving Jake a "you really don't get it, do you" look that raised his defenses.

"Let me ask you a question, Jake. Suppose there was a Catholic therapy group, run by priests, and it set up a Rape Crisis Counseling Center. Suppose a number of women attending the center reported they'd ended up in bed with the same priests who counseled them. First of all, that story would never have surfaced on this committee because there's no one here to represent Catholics or fundamentalists or even nonreligious conservatives." Clarence reached out his hand toward Jake. "If we're interested in representing minorities, how come we only choose certain ones? How come we don't get an evangelical or a Catholic? Because we only want politically correct minorities.

"Anyway, suppose someone had brought up exactly the same story, but with Catholic priests doing the victimizing. There would have been no discussion. *Of course* we'd investigate the story. And if it's true, we'd print it, and probably with a bit of glee, don't you think? It'd be A-1, with follow-ups in Metro for days. It's news, isn't it? And if it makes the Catholics look bad, that's their problem. We're not here to protect the image of Catholics, that's what we'd say. We're here to tell the truth, let the chips fall where they may. Every one of us would have voted to tell that story, including me. So what's the difference? We want to protect the image of one group and we don't care a rat's hind end about the other one. That's the only difference."

"They did put you on the committee didn't they, Clarence? Doesn't that tell you something?"

"I was put here because I'm black, and since I was in sports nobody knew I was a conservative. Now that they know, it's too late, and I'm just Uncle Tom. You should have heard Jess introduce me the first week. Called me one of the finest sports writers the *Trib's* ever had. Now I'm a traitor to the cause. Journalists are supposed to be mindless reflexive liberals, and I'm not. So what do you think my chances are of ever being a general columnist, like you? Now that they know my true colors, think they'll let me loose with opinions on anything but sports? Man, when I'm sixty-five I'll put in my last day at this paper philosophizing about new developments at the International Badminton Tournament."

Clarence put his big right hand to his forehead, still beading with sweat. "Jake, that bottle of Tylenol still in your desk? I need a couple."

"Yeah, it's extra strength. I'll get it for you."

Clarence waved him off. "Nah, I'll get 'em myself, thanks. Extra strength? Yeah, that's what I need. Besides, Jake, you shouldn't be seen walking with me. We don't want to tarnish your image. You're already a heterosexual white male, which is one rung down from being a convicted rapist with leprosy. Don't make it any worse on yourself by appearing to be sympathetic to me. I'll just move on down the road."

Clarence forced a broad grin and shuffled out of the room with perfect rhythm, as if he were a minstrel. Jake watched this man, a good man, trying to keep his humor in a beloved vocation that seemed to have shifted underneath his feet.

CHAPTER SIXTEEN

J ake took his last sip of coffee early Tuesday morning, washed it out in the sink, and headed toward his front door. The phone rang. It was a private number, but even then Jake let the answering machine screen his calls. If he didn't want to talk—he rarely did—he just let it go, as he did now. After the fourth ring he heard his own voice say, "Leave a message after the beep."

"Jake? Jake, it's Janet. If you're there, please pick up the phone. It's an emergency."

Like a coiled spring, Jake vaulted to the phone, ten feet away, before Janet could start her next sentence.

"Janet? It's me. What happened?"

"Carly needs you, Jake. She won't call you, but she needs you. She's so confused. I found a note..." Janet's voice broke and the intensity of her sob alarmed Jake.

"What kind of note?"

He could hear her muffled groan, and tried not to be impatient, but was. "Janet—what does the note say?"

"It's a suicide note. If I hadn't come into her room and found it..."

The knife poised above Jake from the moment he heard Janet say "emergency" now dropped and pierced his chest at the word "suicide."

"Where's Carly now?"

"She's here, in the living room, just sitting on the couch in her bathrobe. I won't let her out of my sight. We've been talking, but..."

"Was this note for real? Was it maybe just an attention-getter?" Jake remembered the interview he'd done with the psychologist who said all suicide threats must be taken seriously, but some were only attempts to get attention.

"It was for real. I'm certain."

"But...I thought she was happy. Her grades are good, she was playing volleyball, and on the speech team, right?" All this was hearsay. He'd learned none of it from Carly.

"There's more that you don't know, Jake. A lot more. It's not good. She's in trouble. I really can't talk about it now, not on the phone."

"Janet, what is it? Bad enough that she wants to kill herself, and you can't tell me?"

"Oh, Jake, I don't know what to do. She needs help. More than I can give her. She needs...a dad."

The words "a dad," rather than "her dad," opened a puncture wound. She needed a dad because she hadn't had her dad. He'd been off charming a million strangers while neglecting his own daughter. Of course, Janet didn't say that. She didn't have to.

"I'll be right over. Stay with her. It'll be okay."

"Please hurry. We need you. I mean, she needs you. But drive carefully, Jake." It was an old habit, saying "drive carefully, Jake."

"Okay, I'm on my way." Jake tried to sound more composed than he was.

He moved as fast as he could and still convince himself he wasn't panicking. He scanned the room to see what else he might need, as if he were heading out on survival camp. His eyes hesitated at Finney's Bible by the recliner, still unopened since Sue gave it to him at Little Finn's request. It cried out to him that it could help in a time of crisis, and this was clearly a crisis. *But I don't even know what to do with it.* Jake left it sitting there, grabbed his keys and wallet from their place on the mantle, and charged out the door, not losing the extra two seconds by checking if it locked behind him.

As he hopped in the Mustang, Jake prepared himself. It had been a long time since he'd seen Carly, not counting Finney's funeral. Longer than he could admit to himself. And even then, the last few times they'd only said hello and endured a brief superficial conversation.

I'm rusty at being a dad, Jake acknowledged to himself. *I haven't had a lot of practice.*

As he wove through traffic, Jake considered, with some irony and self-flagellation, that if this was an interview on teen suicide or with a teenage drug addict, he'd know exactly what to do.

It's real life and my own daughter I don't know how to deal with.

He considered with some embarrassment how many times he'd administered treatment to society's ills from a distance, with no real empathy for the situation. Now he was in the situation. And while he knew this was one of the most important missions he'd ever gone on, he felt woefully unprepared and ill-equipped. He felt like he was going out in a Southeast Asian jungle naked and unarmed.

Carly looked at the apartment floor, maintaining steady eye contact with two knot holes in the hardwood. She made a point of avoiding her father's gaze, not realizing it wasn't there anyway because he was busy avoiding hers. Janet sat looking back and forth from one to the other, finally giving in reluctantly to the role which had always fallen to her, the role of go-between.

"Carly, I think you need to tell your father what happened."

Carly paused, just for a moment, then blurted out, "Somebody raped me. And I'm pregnant."

She said it defiantly, as if she resented having to say it, but refused to sugar coat it to make it go down easier.

After an initial few seconds of shock, angry fire rushed out of Jake. "Who? Who did this to you? I'll kill him."

For the first time, Carly's eyes rose to meet Jake's, and he expected some appreciative look in response to his fatherly protectiveness. What he saw instead was anger as intense as his own. *Good, let her anger come out against this monster. She needs to express herself.*

"Who do you think you are?"

Jake was stunned to realize he was the object of the anger.

"You waltz back into my life just when I'm done with it, to tell me I should keep living. Where were you before? That's why you came, isn't it, to tell me I'm stupid to think about suicide? Well, you don't know anything about me, nothing, do you understand?"

Jake rocked backward, and a deeply wounded Carly pounced on his show of weakness.

"You hear I've been raped and what do you care about? Me? No. You only care about wasting the guy who did it. Why? Because he violated your property, and that gives you some macho right to blow him away? Well, I'm not your property. You junked me three years ago, so don't try to pretend you have a part in my life anymore. You're not going to get any medals of honor here, Mr. Famous Journalist who knows all the answers."

As if reaching the culmination of a well-prepared closing argument, Carly spewed out, "I'm not your daughter. I'm a person. And I didn't ask you to come here. So get out. I don't want you here. Get out!"

Carly threw a couch pillow at him and marched into her bedroom, slamming the door so hard it shook the whole apartment.

Jake sank back into the couch in stunned speechlessness. The blow left him numb. For a moment his defenses rose. How dare she blame him for her problems? But something in him realized she was right, at least in part. The soldier in him wanted to shoot the enemy, and it had taken his focus off the dying girl who needed a medic.

Jake didn't know what to say. Not to Carly, not to Janet. He could come up with an eight-hundred-word column every time he needed to. But he couldn't think of eight words that would work here. He would be silent now, not as a strategy, not as the best course of action, but because he knew no other course of action. He was clueless how to handle this situation. He knew what faced him now had festered over many years. There was no one-hour fix for this. Perhaps no fix at all.

Jake was too ashamed to look across the room at Janet, this woman who knew his intimate habits, down to his insufferable snores and drooling on the pillow. He remembered how he longed for her in Nam, how the thought of her kept him going. He remembered how they felt when Carly was born, the wonder of this infant child. He remembered all the hopes and dreams for her, the wrestling on the carpet, the time she hid in the clothes hamper and popped open the lid when he and Janet were reading in bed. He thought about all Carly's school programs and YMCA volleyball. And he remembered how, in backing away from Janet and the marriage, he had ultimately backed away from her too.

When he first moved out he'd made a point of not missing Carly's activities, to prove to himself and to everyone that divorce need not hurt a parent's relationship with his child. But over the months, when he'd take her out for ice cream and movies, it seemed they had less and less to say to each other. Increasingly, his efforts seemed strained, more and more like a pretense to both of them. So he'd drifted, letting weeks and finally months go by between phone calls, then not calling because he was embarrassed it had been so long. It was the same with his mother, in the retirement home on the other side of the city. He didn't visit her because when he did her eyes always asked him, "Why has it been so long?"

Finally Jake dared to look at Janet, with whom he'd shared so many dreams now broken. Not only the dreams for her marriage, but now the dreams for her daughter had become a nightmare. She was looking Jake's direction, but not at him really. He saw the hurt. Disappointment. Disillusionment. The death of a vision. He felt certain she was wondering how two people who loved each other so much could produce beautiful Carly, the fruit of their love, and see it come down to a day when she hated her own life enough to take it, and hated her father enough to tell him she wanted nothing to do with him.

Jake knew there was more in Carly than hate. It was because she loved him so much and needed him so profoundly that his abandonment had hurt her so deeply. In some ways, her hatred would be easier to bear than admitting his own neglect.

The past haunted him. Somehow sitting in this living room, under these conditions, didn't allow him escape. As much as Janet had been hurt by the betrayal of Jake's affairs, she'd been willing to forgive and go on. But he had not. To him the final affair was the setting of a new sail. He didn't expect it to last, and it hadn't. But it cemented that what he wanted in life was no longer in this marriage and family.

Over the years he'd fired his share of verbal heavy weaponry at her, the shrapnel digging deep in her flesh and spirit, wounding her. But mostly it hadn't been smoke and fury, but slow death. The wall between them had gradually risen, cemented by the mortar of indifference, until only a stranger was left on the other side. They'd become tired, lacking the fiery passion to scale the wall and find each other again. But it was especially Jake who'd become tired. And restless.

Honesty compelled him to divorce Janet, or so he said, and there was some pride that he did it amiably, giving her the best car, her choice of furniture, and half the bank account, and offering her the house, though she elected to move out to the apartment, saying the house would be too much work for her. He'd read trendy books such as *Open Marriage* and *No Fault Divorce,* convincing himself he had the right to be happy, the right to get what he wanted out of life. It was all very contemporary. Like anyone with good self-esteem, he just wanted to be true to himself. It would be better for everyone if he was. Really.

Finney, in his inimitable way, gentle but oh-so-firm, had reminded Jake, "Your marriage vows said nothing about being true to yourself. What they said was, you'd be true to Janet. You committed yourself to her welfare, not your own. That was a sacred commitment. It should govern your decisions. Don't turn your back on your family."

Jake, though, had convinced himself the divorce was the best thing for Janet and Carly. After all, Carly would be much better off with one parent in the home than with two who couldn't get along, or weren't compatible, or didn't share the same life goals. So he'd been told, and so he'd told himself, and so he'd told others. That's why he so deeply resented the "two-parent families are better" flap with the vice president and Murphy Brown, which was going on right when he was divorcing Janet. He didn't want to hear that sanctimonious self-righteous gibberish from the right-wing crowd, and he'd shot it down in his column more than once.

As he sat there on a couch that had once been his, seeing the crushed remains of a wife who had once been his, and hearing through a closed door the hot bitter sobs of a daughter who had once been his, he realized in a moment of breathtaking clarity that everything he had told himself to justify the divorce, no the desertion, had been a lie. All of it. He doubted the realization would last, but here and now it was self-evident.

"She's out of the shower now," Janet said. "Drying her hair. Should be out in a few minutes. I asked her to come back out and talk with us, and to...give you a chance."

"Thanks," Jake replied weakly. "Is she out of danger? I mean, I know you took the razor blades, but you can't guard her every moment. I'd be glad to stay if I could do anything. I'd stay up all night."

Suddenly his face was wet, and Janet was just a blur. "I'd do anything for her, Janet, anything. I'm so sorry."

He buried his face in his hands and wept, for the third time Janet could ever remember. The first was on a day they both perpetually pushed from their minds, a day during college when they'd visited a clinic that would forever determine the composition and perhaps the ultimate destiny of their family. The second was at Finney's funeral, when she'd looked down the row and seen him during the slide presentation. Each time had in common loss and grief. And missed opportunity. This time there was also a heightened sense of failure.

Jake told himself he would gladly give up every journalism award he'd ever received in exchange for a relationship with his daughter.

Janet came to his side, his tears pulling her to him. She put her hand on the back of his neck.

"Oh, Jake."

She couldn't get out more. He felt the flood of her tears spilling on his right pant leg.

"All those plans we had for our family. We never thought it would turn out like this."

Janet hugged Jake, for the first time in perhaps four years. They looked into each others eyes just for a moment. Suddenly Janet noticed a tiny reflected image in Jake's eyes.

"Carly!" Janet said, with too much alarm, as if she'd been caught doing something wrong. Jake and Janet quickly drew away from each other.

Carly looked at them curiously. Then, as if trying to decide whether to maintain or relinquish her anger, the edges of her mouth went into a soft smile.

"It's okay. Don't feel like you've been caught. I'm only your daughter." The smile was weak, but sincere. "I guess the fact that I'm here suggests the two of you did your share of hugging in the past."

Janet blushed and gave a contrived look of admonishment, tremendously relieved at Carly's smile. She hadn't seen her smile or heard her witty comments for weeks. Jake's face was red, partly from crying, partly from embarrassment.

Carly walked forward slowly, making a deliberate choice where to sit. She chose the rocking chair, across the coffee table from the couch where her parents were sitting. Janet started to get up to move to another chair, but Carly said, "No, Mom. Stay where you are. Since this is all about me and my mixed up life, at least I should be able to assign the seating."

"Sure, honey." No one was in the mood to argue with Carly right now.

"To tell you the truth, it feels good to see my parents sitting near each other. It's been a very long time." Her voice broke.

Janet started to get up again, this time to put her arms around Carly. But she stuck out her arm.

"No, Mom. I'm okay. Please stay there with him." Jake noticed she didn't say "Dad," and it stung.

"Well," Carly was looking at Jake now, "I'm not going to apologize for what I said to you. I've felt it for a long time."

Jake nodded as if to say "I understand," thinking it was better not to say the words.

"But I've decided to tell you the truth. The lie didn't work the way I wanted it to, and no other lie seems as good. So we'll just give the truth a try and see what happens."

Janet and Jake both looked confused.

"I am pregnant. But I wasn't raped."

Carly waited a moment to let it sink in. "I guess that's bad news and good news. But I said I was raped because I just didn't want the blame. Or Michael to get the blame. But when you," she was looking at Jake, "wanted to put on your guerrilla fatigues and toss hand grenades at potential rapists, the lie got a little too big for me."

Both parents had questions, but neither was about to attempt to take the floor.

"I've known I was pregnant for a few weeks. Three days ago we decided to just take care of it. You know what I mean. I assumed I'd have to get you to sign something since I'm under eighteen, like when I had my ears pierced. But we found out we didn't need your permission. Everything seemed so easy. But I just couldn't do it. Michael is angry at me. He says if I won't get the abortion, we're through. He loves me, but he...how did he put it? He's just not ready to be committed to me, and certainly not ready to have a baby. Of course," and her already sarcastic voice suddenly turned bitter, "every time we've had sex he's been quick to assure me his commitment is deep and lifelong.

"So, maybe some of my anger at you"—Carly looked at Jake—"is coming from what I feel about Michael. Right now I think all men are jerks. They say things they don't mean. They make promises they don't keep."

There was no misinterpreting the last sentence. Jake had not kept his explicit promises made at an altar twenty-four years ago, or the implicit promises to be there every parent makes to his children. All three of them were painfully aware of that.

"I guess I should explain my decision about the abortion. When I first found out I was pregnant I thought it was my only choice. Isn't that funny? Prochoice, but I thought there was just one choice. I read all kinds of stuff on the subject. Some I'd collected for a speech on abortion. Some I got from the school clinic. All of it said abortion was okay. Then I pulled out a few of your columns," Carly said to her father, "and those made me think it was okay too."

Jake was surprised she'd seen his columns on this subject, much less saved them. It had been six months since he'd done a column on abortion.

"Then I talked to a few teachers at school. One said I shouldn't do anything without talking to Mom, but the other two said I should just get the abortion. One of them offered to drive me to the clinic herself—she's done it for a few of my friends. She said the clinic owner is a personal friend of hers, and everything is totally professional. She gave me literature from the clinic."

Carly held up two bright, attractive brochures she'd brought out from her bedroom.

"I almost went through with it. But something held me back. I know both of you are prochoice. And I'm prochoice, or at least I was. But something kept haunting me. I have two friends who say abortion is the worse thing they've ever done. Both of them say they'll never do it again. One's in counseling, and she tried to kill herself. Like I almost did."

Carly looked down, as if wondering how to continue. "But there's something else. Something really strange. I've never told anybody about it."

Jake and Janet sat forward on the front edge of the couch, bookend parental images.

"Almost a year ago I was watching the late news on a Saturday night. I never watch it, you know that Mom. But the state volleyball finals had been that day, so I stayed up. Just before sports, they showed a group of people standing outside an abortion clinic. And one of them was holding a Bible. I thought, 'What a weirdo.' Then all of a sudden I realized who it was. It was Uncle Finney, and Aunt Sue was right next to him.

"I was taping the whole news in case I wanted to run back the volleyball clips. So I went back and listened to the abortion clinic part five times. Uncle Finney read something from the Bible, you know that big old herky Bible he used to carry around. Something about how God creates all of us and has a purpose for our lives, and how we shouldn't kill children just because they're inconvenient, but we should speak up for people who can't speak up for themselves, and that's why they were at the clinic.

"Well, I still have that videotape. For some reason I saved it. Four nights ago, the night before Michael was going to drive me to get the abortion, I went back and watched it again. Uncle Finney looked right into the camera. It's as if he was looking right at me. This is going to sound weird but, I swear it was like he was there in the room. I could swear I heard him say my name. 'Carly'—he had a special way of saying my name, a slight accent like nobody else—'Carly, please let your baby live.'

"It freaked me out. I ran it back to see if it was really on the tape. Of course, it wasn't. I thought I was going crazy. But I couldn't get it off my mind."

Carly looked at her parents to assess their reaction. Janet was wide eyed, Jake slack jawed. It sounded so crazy, but Carly had never been crazy before.

"That's when I decided I couldn't go through with it. No matter how much it messed up my college plans, my volleyball scholarship, and my life in general. I started thinking, what if I had come along at a time that was inconvenient for my parents? Would I want them to kill me? I just couldn't punish an innocent child for my stupid mistake."

Janet and Jake kept their eyes from each other. Jake realized this wasn't Finney and Sue's conviction Carly had acted on. It was her own. He felt something toward her he'd never remembered feeling before, not just love, but respect. She seemed less the spoiled and self-indulged girl used to having everything go her way. She'd made a hard decision. The tears that came now were tears of pride in his little girl. But something she'd said mingled pain with the pride, and he suspected Janet's pain was even deeper.

"And the truth is, Mom, the suicide note you read was written two days before the abortion was scheduled. You know me. I have to express my thoughts, so I got an early start. I figured after I finished the letter, got the wording just right, then I'd wait till after the abortion and kill myself. I just wanted to turn off all the noise in my head. I was reading the *Final Exit* book and trying to decide the best method— something that would be painless for me and wouldn't be too messy for you. There were lots of ideas, but it was hard to choose."

Janet turned white as a ghost. "Carly, what are you talking about? What book?"

"*Final Exit*. You know, the one written by the head of the Hemlock Society. Hang on a second."

She went to her room and got the book, looking at the author's name as she walked back in.

"Yeah, Derek Humphrey, that's it. You know the guy, he's been on *Donahue* and *Oprah* and everybody for years. He helped his wife commit suicide."

"What are you doing reading a book like that? Where did you get it?"

"Checked it out of the school library."

"You got it from school?"

"Well, it's not like I couldn't have gotten it somewhere else. I first started reading it at Waldenbooks a few years ago. It had all these different ways you could take your life, page after page—sort of a menu approach. It was a bestseller. Don't you remember? Your ex-husband knows all about it."

"Yeah, I know about it," Jake said weakly .

"In fact, you wrote about it. Which is what first made me notice it at Waldenbooks. You remember your column?"

"Yeah, sort of." Jake remembered well, but he could feel Janet's accusing stare and he was trying to wriggle out from under it.

"See my bookmark? Look familiar?" Carly showed Jake the yellow strip of old newsprint. He recognized it as his column.

"I quoted it in a speech that got me second place at district. I'll read your last paragraph:

> While those who resist progress and all that is new and different are sure to take offense at this book, the first amendment says it needs to be available. Those with terminal illnesses, those who are tired of life and feel useless, must be empowered to pursue death with dignity if they so choose. This may not be a path we would choose. But we cannot, we dare not impose our personal values on the rest of society. Some will find in *Final Exit* an affirming and helpful means of carrying out their own agenda for their lives. We need to support suffering people as they consider all options, including the option of choosing how they wish to leave this world. In their hour of need, we have no right to deprive them of the know-how offered in this book, nor to judge them if they choose to find their relief by exiting this life in the time and way that seems best to them."

The words hung in the air, accentuated by the silence.

"You said that?" Janet finally asked.

"Not about Carly. Not about a teenager. I meant for older people, for the handicapped or terminally ill."

"I was terminally depressed, Dad. I was suffering. All the options seemed so hard. Suicide was the easiest. At first, I decided against razor blades, but I came back to them. At one point I narrowed it down to one particular poison or carbon monoxide—I have the pages marked. Do you want to see...?"

"No! I don't want to hear anymore." Janet jumped up, grabbed the book, and started ripping it to pieces.

Realizing she'd laid too much on her mom, Carly reached her arm around her, but Janet thought she wanted the book. "No, don't even touch it." She threw the mangled book in the fireplace.

Still hanging out of the book was Jake's column. Only three feet from the fireplace, he watched the yellow paper, both his sketch and his words, turn brown, then black, and line by line become a puff of smoke that disappeared forever into nothingness.

"I'm sorry," Carly said. "I'm sorry I've upset both of you. I didn't finish, and I should have. I wrote the note two days before the abortion was scheduled. Since I canceled the abortion, I haven't had any thoughts of suicide. Just because I haven't felt like living doesn't mean he doesn't deserve a chance to live. Besides, he needs me."

Janet stood numbly. All three of them were surprised to see Jake at Carly's side, his arms around her, tears flowing.

"We need you too, sweetheart. I need you." Much as he hurt, it was the closest thing to home Jake had felt for years.

* * *

"There is a man I want you to meet, master Finney. His name is Zeke."

They hadn't walked long before Finney saw a coal black face, animated and cut with deep lines of character. The man waved at Zyor.

"Master Zeke, I would like you to meet Finney. He is a novice."

"Welcome to Elyon's place. May you find eternal rest and pleasure as you live for his glory."

Now that the formal greeting was done, Zeke took on a distinctly casual appearance, as if kicking back with old friends. He even slapped Zyor on the back, which seemed to Finney an overly familiar gesture to such an awesome being, but Zyor didn't seem to mind.

"Finney and I have been speaking of the days on earth, treasures in heaven, and the rooms Elyon's Son prepares for his own."

A big smile broke out on Zeke's face, as if this was a favorite subject.

"This is something Zeke knows much about, master Finney. I served him on earth some time ago, before I was assigned to you. I saw his life, and I know Zeke's room in the great city will be large, very large. His reward will be great."

Zeke handled the compliment well, with only slight embarrassment. He said to Finney, "It was easier for me in many ways. See, I was a slave."

Finney's eyes grew big. "A slave—and you say it was easier?"

"Oh, there was much that was very hard. To live in poverty. For my wife to be used by the one I had to call master. To have two of my children taken from me when they got old enough to plow a field. That was the hardest—much harder than the beatings.

"I survived the whippings by taking my mind from earth and putting it here. I couldn't read very well, but I did memorize a lot of the Good Book. And I thought about it all day, in the cotton fields, and whenever Nancy was mistreated and whenever I wanted to kill somebody for what they did to my mother and wife and children."

"It must have been terrible."

"Sometimes. But I had my joys. The love of family. What could be sweeter than that? The smell of a good plate of beans. Lilacs in the spring. A gentle breeze. The feel of fresh cold river water going down your dry throat in the summer. But best of all was just thinking about this place here. A few times, when it was hardest, God gave me visions of heaven. I thought they were just dreams. But as soon as I got here I knew they'd been visions because what I saw was here. It was this place, and the place to come, the new heavens and new earth—at least, I think so, because some things I haven't seen here yet.

"This was my home. The other place was like a rented room. I knew I was just passin' through, and when you're just passin' through you don't get too attached. We loved those Scriptures that said this was our home. We loved the reminders we were pilgrims, aliens, strangers in a foreign country. 'Our citizenship is in heaven, from which we await a Savior.'" Zeke laughed. "I said that verse so many times a day, Elyon himself must have gotten tired of it, and he wrote it!"

Finney laughed right along with Zeke, and even Zyor seemed to find humor in it.

"See, Finney, for all the same reasons the rich and comfortable loved their homes on earth and didn't relish the thought of leaving them, we looked forward to the final day and the long tomorrow. That's the reason for our songs—'Swing low, sweet chariot, comin' for to carry me home.'"

Now Zeke broke into song, his beautiful baritone resonating with emotion. "'Soon I will be done with the troubles of the world, goin' home to live wid God. No more weepin' and a wailin', I'm goin to live wid God.'"

Finney saw, in his mind's eye, Zeke standing in torn clothes, working in a field, back bent from fourteen-hour days. This often happened when he met new friends here—their bodies were windows to their character, and their character had been molded by their past on earth. So when one became familiar with another, he always learned the story of how he had served Elyon on earth. Finney was constantly reminded that no one's life in the other world was forgotten and irrelevant, but had ongoing and vital links to his identity in this one.

"That song was on your lips when you left the dark world," Zyor said to Zeke.

"Was it now? I didn't know that. You never told me."

"There is much I have not told you yet, old friend. And there is no hurry here."

Zeke looked at Finney. "We were privileged, you and I. Zyor was an ace of a guardian."

"The best," Finney replied.

"I longed for your freedom, Master Zeke." Zyor's head hung now, and in a flash he moved from sadness to fury.

"Every time they whipped you I begged Elyon to let me break their arms. Twice he let me strike them, only twice in forty years. I agonized when I could not hold back those who hunted you down or defeat the evil spirits that compelled them."

Finney now saw Zeke running across a river, with a pack of dogs and six men, rifles in hand, chasing him.

"And if you'd succeeded, I wouldn't have come to Elyon's world when I did, which would have been my loss."

Finney watched Zeke's right shoulder explode, blood discoloring the foliage. But somehow he kept running, and for some reason the dogs ran another direction.

"I made it to the railroad. They were the kindest white people I ever met—present company excepted, Mister Finney. It was good to die in their arms, rather than be eaten by the dogs in the woods and paraded home as another captured nigger. They had sad eyes in the railroad. And that made me trust them. The sad-eyed people knew pain, and often they knew Elyon. The steely-eyed ones, they thought they had life by the tail. They'd sooner spit on you than give you the time o' day. I feel sorry for them now. My hardship was just for a time. Theirs is for eternity. And here I am. Ol' Zeke. Walkin' the streets of heaven with the likes of Zyor and Finney. And Zyor calls me 'Master.' You think it didn't take a while to get over that one?"

Zeke let out the heartiest laugh Finney had heard since coming to heaven.

"So don't fret about not being able to save me, Zyor. Elyon is sovereign over the smallest things, from the hairs on your head to the flip of a coin. There's a purpose in everything. Even if we don't understand it till we get here."

Suddenly something inside him seized hold of Zeke.

"The birthing room. I've got to go to the birthing room. Somebody's comin'! Are you with me, gents?"

Zyor and Finney moved rapidly alongside Zeke. The journey was a long one by earth's standards, but no sooner had they gotten moving than they were there, as if the speed of thought took over and their sense of urgency created a shortcut through heaven's version of space and time.

On the other side of the portal was a tiny black boy lying in an all-white hospital bed, his mother and father holding each others' hands and clutching on to the boy, as if to keep him from going anywhere. Finney could feel heaven's tug on the boy, and his spirit seemed to be pushing toward the portal by its own will.

"That's Bobby. He's got leukemia. Been hard on his ma and pa. He's suffered pretty bad, though they've sure taken good care of him. Doctor's have come a long way since my time, but when a little one hurts, everyone hurts."

I know, Finney thought. His mind went back to Jenny's death. Suddenly he wanted to go find her and hug her again.

"I knew it would be soon," Zeke said. "He caught a glimpse of me three days ago by his time. He saw me in this robe and thought I was an angel!"

Zeke angled his elbow upwards and poked Zyor in the ribs. The angel gave an almost-grin, as if it were a human ability he couldn't quite get right, but wanted to.

"Me, an angel! When he woke up for a minute, you know what he said? He said, 'Mama, I saw an angel. And, Mama, he was black!'"

Zeke laughed heartily again.

"To me, these angels up here look like they've taken on a middle eastern dark brown. But I guess Bobby expected white. His mama got the biggest kick out of the black angel. She's told everybody. When someone's dyin', people need something to laugh at. Of course, they all thought he was delirious. They never knew he really saw me. Me, the black angel!"

Zeke whooped, and a lot more laughter joined his. Finney realized the room was now crowded with people, most of them black, all of them indescribably beautiful, wearing their character on the outside as if it were a bride's wedding dress. He caught impressions of great stories, great suffering, and great joy. He wanted to experience their stories now, but reminded himself "there is no hurry here."

Zeke pressed forward and leaned over in expectation, pointing and leaning so far into the portal Finney wondered if his hand would appear on the other side.

"Zyor knows this, Mister Finney, but I should tell you. That woman there is my great granddaughter, and Bobby is my great great grandson. Me and Nancy used to pray for our children and their children's children, that they would know better days. And Elyon blessed us with all these good people you see here. I'm the patriarch of this whole bunch! I was here in this room to greet every one of them. I guess you'd say I was the midwife, eh Zy?"

His elbow flew at the big angel again. Finney had never imagined anyone calling him Zy, but there was no complaint.

"There's Nancy now! Get over here, woman! Bobby can't come till you're here with me. That was Elyon's promise to us, remember?"

Nancy was strikingly beautiful. Elyon had obviously used her hardships to make her into someone very special.

Looking at Finney, Zeke explained, "Elyon said to us, 'You were faithful to me. In every generation of your line there will be some who will follow me, and it will be your honor, both of you, to welcome them to my world.'

"I've been longin' to hold little Bobby. He's suffered enough. It's time for rest. It's time for him to be able to run and play, and to eat and drink without tubes. It's time, Elyon, it's time, all-wise God."

Zeke's voice was now strong and focused and carried authority.

"Please, my God, bring him home now. Pull up the anchor and let him sail 'cross the lake. Now, Elyon, please bring him to us now!"

Nancy sighed her heartfelt agreement with the prayer.

Suddenly there was a mad rush of wind. The portal to the dark world strained and twisted. It was like the final stage of labor. Finney now saw the view from heaven's side of the birthing room. A huge warriorlike figure slipped through to the side, out of the limelight, quietly welcomed and congratulated by Zyor and several other angels. Suddenly there was Bobby, popping through the portal into Zeke's arms. He wore not the blue hospital gown but a beautiful white robe that fit perfectly, as if sown precisely for him and no one else. His eyes grew big, and he reached his tiny hand up to touch Zeke's craggy face. A tear ran down Zeke's cheek. Bobby caught it on his index finger and looked at it. Zeke held him tight.

"Welcome to heaven, Bobby."

Bobby smiled wonderfully. "It doesn't hurt any more." He looked at Zeke and asked, "Are you Jesus?"

There were several hearty laughs, Nancy's the loudest.

"No, Bobby," Zeke replied. "Once you see Jesus, you'll know there's no face like his."

"I know who you are," Bobby said. "You're the angel!"

The whole crowd laughed this time, and Zeke threw Bobby up into the air and caught him. He giggled and giggled. Everyone came up close to touch and hold the boy, in the way that you do someone you've loved and watched and prayed for from afar, but never been able to touch till now. Finney stepped back to give them room, feeling privileged to witness such intimate moments. Nancy held Bobby the longest, before surrendering him back to Zeke.

Suddenly there was a bright light and a powerful but gentle presence, divine and yet fully human. It was Elyon's Son. Everyone turned toward him in wonder, dropping on their knees. Zeke was right. There was no face like his. He was shorter than the angels, man-sized. Yet those hands had towed heavy lumber up a long lonely hill, and eons before had fashioned the galaxies themselves. The sheer force of his presence dwarfed the mightiest angel. Strangely, his eyes were moist and heavy. Finney realized the Carpenter had just gone through the agony with Bobby and his family.

"Rise, my friends. I come to join your celebration. It's time to prepare a special feast. Bobby has arrived!"

The Christ's eyes held those of the child, whose jaw hung open in wonder, his pearly white teeth perfectly matching his robe.

"You can't hold him forever, Zeke. Give him to me!"

Zeke reverently held out the child, and the Creator and Lover of children took him into his arms. Turning only to say "we will see you all at the feast," he walked away with Bobby.

Where they went, Finney did not know, though he watched as Elyon's Son put Bobby to the ground for the first time, and the boy took his first uncertain Bambi steps in heaven, followed by running and jumping and yelling and falling without being hurt, wildly flailing arms he hadn't had the strength to lift in a year.

Finney thought of the time he had spent alone with Elyon's Son after his own birth into this world. It was the most wonderful experience he'd ever had. He could only rejoice for Bobby at the undivided attention he was now receiving. Yet here all attention was Elyon's attention, and Finney drew closer to him every day, not only through their direct interaction, but through the indescribable way he spoke to him through each of his creatures, both men and angels.

Zeke looked back at the portal. For a moment his joy was tempered by what he saw. Bobby's parents wept.

"This is the hard part. We understand what they as yet cannot. They're going to miss him terribly. Lead us in prayer for them, will you, Finney?"

Finney prayed, he wasn't sure how long, his thoughts linking with others to put invisible arms around Bobby's family. He well remembered the day he and Sue and Angie and Little Finn had lost someone so dear to them they thought they couldn't bear to survive another hour. Elyon and his people had comforted them. And now, at last, he'd been reunited with Jenny. He was no longer on the underside of the tapestry, where all you could see were the snarls and knots and frays. He was now on the top side, where he saw the beautiful work of art woven by the Master Artist.

"O God, give them strength to trust you and walk with you despite the blows from the last enemy, Death. Help them to know you understand how it feels to have your son suffer and die. Help them to anticipate the glorious reunion with Bobby."

As he finished the prayer, it occurred to Finney that after Jenny's death, his mother had no doubt prayed for him and Sue, just as he and Zeke and Nancy and Zyor prayed for Bobby's parents. He made a mental note—with no fear of forgetting—to join Zeke and Nancy in the birthing room for each reunion between Bobby and his family members.

Suddenly he caught a glimpse of Jake, Janet, and Carly in an apartment living room in another world. He prayed for them, longing for them to one day experience the great reunion.

Some of the crowd began to disperse, several excitedly making arrangements, deciding the feast would have to be just so, and saying Bobby hadn't eaten a normal earth meal for so long, and wait until he was served not only the best food in the universe but discovered his vastly improved capacity to taste.

Zeke and Nancy stayed where they were, exchanging hugs and handshakes and backslaps with dozens of great-grandmothers and great-aunts and great-uncles, all chattering on and on about the goodness of Elyon, and how another of their family had come home.

CHAPTER SEVENTEEN

T he seventeen-year-old girl put down the book, heavily underlined. She had considered her options carefully. While this one was messy, it was at least fast. She looked through the medicine cabinet and found the hidden pack of blades for Mom's old-style razor. Carly removed one of the blades, looking at it carefully to be sure it was new and sharp.

She sat on the edge of the bathtub. Her eyes were empty. The will to live was gone and in its place was a power from somewhere else, a power that gave her the will to die. Deliberately she lowered the blade to her wrist, to just the right place the book had described.

With a sudden slashing motion she chose death over life. Blood gushed from her wrist, which she'd been careful to hold over the bathtub, wanting to make as little mess as possible for her mother. Carly turned pale and slumped into the tub, her life flowing down the drain.

Suddenly, with a strength that shouldn't have been in her, she looked toward someone at the bathroom door, someone watching her, and screamed, "You did this to me. It's your fault. I hate you! I hate you!"

"Carly! No! No! Don't! Carly!" Jake jumped out of bed, turned a circle, and ran to his door, flipping on the overhead light and frantically looking back into his room. Champ was on alert, trying to find the enemy, not sure whether to bark or at what. Jake kept looking around the room and saw the clock that said 4:30 A.M.

Then he stepped quickly to his bathroom, turned on the glaring light, and looked in the bright white tub. It was empty. He sat on the bathtub's edge. For some reason he turned on the water. He sat motionless for five minutes while the water ran.

Jake pulled up close against the curb right before Sue's driveway, tucking in next to the familiar maple tree. He remembered when the tree was young and small, back when Finney and Sue had moved here twenty years ago. Now it towered, still looking majestic despite losing more of itself every day to the ravages of late fall. Even as he watched, a yellowish-purple leaf fell, sashaying its way down, picking up one gentle gust after another, like a hang glider trying to catch the right current to postpone its inevitable appointment with the ground. It was mid-November, and a shivery Oregon winter took its turn at the season's helm.

Jake sat in the Mustang reviewing the morning's events. He'd called Janet at 6:45 to make sure Carly was okay, asking her to check in on the room where her little girl slept, just to make sure. Janet could sense something in his voice, she always could, but of course he didn't tell her about the dream. He said he was just checking. She said that was nice, but sounded worried about him. He hadn't gone back to bed since the dream, and felt like he never would.

Still a few minutes early and not eager to go in, he got out and looked at the maple tree, pondering whether it was really possible someone stooped over by this tree, then crawled under Doc's Suburban. Someone with an ordinary hacksaw and an extraordinary thirst to kill. Jake examined the concrete driveway, wishing the ground could talk and wondering what story it would tell. He wasn't looking forward to walking into a room of anti-abortionists, where everyone would suddenly quit talking about him and stare, then try to gang up and convert him.

This feeling was reinforced as he looked at the familiar black and yellow bumper sticker on the Hyundai Finney used to drive, parked right in front of him. "My Boss is a Jewish Carpenter."

"Hi dere, Unca Jake!" The unmistakable voice brought light music to air that was otherwise heavy and dark.

"Hi dere, Little Finn!" Finn jumped up at Jake with the same abandon Champ showed when Jake returned from out-of-town trips. Unlike Champ, however, Little Finn was getting bigger. As Jake braced to catch Finn's weight, he realized again his back and side were still sore from the accident.

"I'm gettin' ready for school. And I'm fixin' my own breakfast 'cause Mom has her prayer meetin'."

"Really? Whatcha fixin' for breakfast, guy?"

"Honey Nut Cheerios!" Little Finn said it almost reverently, with all the pride he'd have if he were fixing strawberry crepes and eggs Benedict for a champagne brunch.

"Wow, sounds good!"

"I'll make a bowl for you too!"

"Uh, no thanks, Finn. Already had breakfast." That was a lie. For some reason Jake felt funny telling even a harmless lie to this child.

"Bet you got room for dose donuts Mom got, dough. She says dey're your *favorites*." It tickled Jake the way Finn's oval eyes grew when he shared inside information.

"Well, there's always room for a donut."

"Unca Jake, guess what?"

"What?"

"It's about my sister, Angie."

"What about Angie?"

"She's gonna have a baby!" Finn jumped in the air to accentuate the point.

"No kidding! Hey, congratulations. Now *you're* going to be an unca!" Jake thought a moment. "Hey, Finn, how about I take you to a basketball game some time soon?"

"No kiddin'! Hey, datted be great, Unca Jake! Wait till I tell Mom!"

Little Finn started to run into the house, but turned around, ran back, and grabbed Jake's hand, pulling him, yanking him on to the porch.

"Mom's goin' to New York next Thursday to see Aunt Adele."

That was Little Finn—a bottomless pit of random information. *Wait a minute. New York? Thursday?*

Sue met Jake at the door, giving him a hug. "Jake, good to have you. Come on in." Sue held his hand, leading him into the familiar living room.

"Jake, this is Betty Brenner, Suzanne Largo, and Tom and Zoe Sellars. This is Jake Woods, one of my best friends. He was like a brother to Finney."

The introduction touched Jake. Their differences were never enough to alienate Finney or Sue from him.

"Hi, Jake. Read your column all the time. Glad to meet you." Tom Sellars extended his hand.

I notice you said you read *my column, not that you like it,* Jake thought, returning the firm grip.

The ladies also said they were glad to meet him, and by that time Sue had him seated on the recliner with his favorite Seahawk Sunday afternoon coffee mug, filled with dark Colombian Supremo. Now she was back with a tray of donuts, with old-fashioned buttermilks stacked to the side she offered Jake.

Right on target again. At least the morning won't be a total loss.

Several others marched in, warmly greeted by all, and within five minutes Jake was in a crowded living room with sixteen people. Among them was Alan Weber, Finney's friend, the pastor who spoke at his funeral.

Sue got things going. "I've told just a few of you the purpose of this meeting. I didn't want to scare you off."

Not the most reassuring way to start, Sue.

"I want you to know Jake and I don't always agree, but I trust him, and what he's going to tell you is the truth. You can be honest with him. He's not here to get a story for the *Trib*. This relates to Finney and our friend Dr. Lowell. Jake, I guess the floor is yours."

"Well, first let me say thanks for coming. And let me ask you a favor. Please keep confidential what I'm about to tell you. That's *very* important."

A few of them nodded, but Jake was skeptical. He remembered with embarrassment a few times he'd printed information intended to be confidential. He knew he couldn't control these people. Trusting them made him nervous.

"In fact, it's so important that if any of you don't feel comfortable agreeing to absolute confidentiality, I have to ask you to leave now before we go further."

No takers. Everyone sat still. Jake drew a deep breath.

"All right, the situation is this. We have reason to believe—no, I should say we know with absolute certainty that Finney and Doc, Dr. Lowell, were murdered."

Jake's words stunned everyone in the room. A few of the women generated quick tears, and the two sitting on either side of Sue reached out and took her hands. There was a certain gratification here to a veteran reporter. He'd hooked his audience with his lead, and they were his.

"Someone sabotaged Dr. Lowell's car. I'm not a homicide detective, of course, but for years I was an investigative journalist. Because these men were my good friends, I'm doing what I can to assist one of the police detectives. And Sue's right, this isn't for a story or a column or anything. We just want to find out who did it."

Jake paused, trying to think of how to phrase what he had to say next. Sue bailed him out.

"Jake has been asked by the homicide detective to come up with a list of names, no matter how unlikely, of anyone who had any reason to dislike Dr. Lowell or to act against him in any way. He's got a long list of people, and they may all be innocent. But as we all know, some of the first people who might come to mind as enemies of Dr. Lowell would be, well, active prolifers."

"Are you saying we're...suspects?" Betty Largo asked incredulously.

"No, not at all," Jake reassured her. "What I'm wondering is if you know of people that have been particularly upset with Dr. Lowell. Maybe someone who has threatened him or screamed at him, pushed him, written him a letter, stalked him, done anything violent or spoken of doing something violent."

There was a long pause, then Tom Sellars spoke. "Mr. Woods, I think you have the wrong impression about us. In fact, since I've read your column regularly for years I can say without a doubt you have the wrong impression. I know there have been some violent things happen around the country, but our group, like the vast majority of prolife groups, is committed to nonviolence. That's why we oppose abortion in the first place, because it's violent."

"I don't believe there's one of us who would even consider doing anything violent," Betty added. "We're just there to tell women the truth and offer them alternatives to abortion."

"Maybe it would help," Suzanne's voice had an edge of defensiveness, "if you understood what we're doing at the clinics." She opened a piece of literature with a picture of an unborn baby.

Here comes the propaganda. Jake steeled himself, reluctantly looking at the soft rose-colored picture with the delicate eyes, ears, mouth, nose, fingers, and toes.

"In the abortion clinics they say this isn't a baby, it's just a mass of tissue. Well, my husband's a doctor, and I'm a nurse, like Sue. What they tell women isn't true. We think they deserve to know the truth. So we educate and offer alternatives. That's it. We're not there to take revenge on anybody."

"Look, this is a tough issue for all of us." Alan Weber spoke now, and it was obvious to Jake his voice was respected in this group. "And it must be *really* tough for Jake meeting here with us. Put yourself in his place. He's lost his two closest friends. I golfed with the three of them once, and there was something special about their friendship. And now Jake's just trying to find out the truth. There's no hidden agenda here. I trust Sue and Jake on this. We don't need to be defensive or apologetic about anything, and neither does Jake. He's trying to find out the truth, and we're committed to the truth in everything, aren't we? So, Jake, don't feel bad asking us for help. As for me, there's only one guy I've ever met in prolife circles that I could even imagine doing something like this. He's not part of any established group, but I met him at a rally last year. I think I've got his name at my office. Anyway, I know where I can get it. I doubt seriously he would even consider doing something like this, but I guess there's no harm in checking him out."

"Thanks. I really appreciate that."

A woman in her midforties spoke up now. "I met Dr. Lowell once, maybe a year and a half ago, over at the hospital, when we were protesting their experiments with RU-486. I remember at first he just had a smile on his face, seemed sort of smug, and he drove by us as if we weren't there. But after a few weeks, when we didn't go away, he got agitated. He shook his fist at us, and once he swerved as if to run us over. I don't think he really meant to do it, but it was pretty scary. I admit I don't understand how a doctor can know the medical facts and just go right ahead and kill babies anyway, but I can tell you this—I had no hatred for Dr. Lowell. None whatsoever. In fact, we used to pray for him, right there on the sidewalk. We prayed that God would open his eyes to the truth. It may sound funny to you, but I can honestly say we loved him."

"You asked if we knew of anyone who might have written him a letter," Betty said. "I know *I* did, but it wasn't a threatening letter. It was a letter reminding him of his oaths to protect life and not to take it. I know a lot of us are labeled as being emotional about this issue. But then, we're convinced that unborn babies are no less precious than born ones. They're just a little smaller, weaker, more vulnerable. They're in need of protection. And for some of us, at least three of us I know of in this room, it's closer to home than that." Her eyes watered.

"I suppose everyone here but you," Betty was looking right at Jake now, "knows I had two abortions, one early, one late. I didn't know, Mr. Woods, or maybe I just deceived myself. I went to Planned Parenthood, and they assured me abortion was a simple procedure, the solution to all my problems. So I did it. Two years later I did it again. I went through the anxiety attacks, the suicidal thoughts, the dreams of my babies asking me why, the whole nine yards. After years of suffering and depression, I discovered from reading a women's magazine that it was Post-Abortion Stress Syndrome."

Her lip was trembling now. "So if it seems like some of us can get a little emotional now and then, I guess it's because the deaths of little children is a pretty emotional thing. And I thought about Dr. Lowell a lot, because...he was the one who did my second abortion."

The woman next to her reached over to comfort Betty, and Jake caught the look of surprise in Sue's eyes.

One of the three men in the room, middle-aged, dressed in a business suit, said, "To be honest, there was one guy who used to come down to the hospital and sort of cause trouble. Several times he raised his voice at Dr. Lowell. One day he rolled down his window and they started yelling at each other. Frankly, I was embarrassed, and I took the man aside. I told him if he couldn't hold his temper to please stay home and do something else. He stopped coming. I don't want to say his name here, and I have a feeling it's the same guy Alan's thinking of. But anyway I'll write it down for you, as long as you understand I don't think he would have done it."

"Yeah, I appreciate it. That would help."

"You know," Tom Sellars said, "there's another angle I think you should consider. I never approach the women, my wife does that, but if men come to the clinics—boyfriends or husbands—I talk to them. I've seen a couple of guys I didn't talk to come back, and I've heard them say they're going to make the clinic pay for what they did to their wife or their baby. It's been pretty scary. I don't have any names for you. All I can tell you is, I have a firm commitment to nonviolence, but some of these guys who've had violence done to their wives or babies don't share that same commitment."

"A question, Mr. Woods." This was from a young woman, maybe twenty-five, who looked about six months pregnant.

"Yes?"

"Have you asked yourself if someone involved with Dr. Lowell in abortions or RU-486 was responsible for this?"

"What do you mean?"

"Well, to be blunt, these are people who make their living killing innocent children. Isn't it possible that they might be capable of killing adults also?"

Jake raised his eyebrows. "I don't think that's very likely."

"None of this seems very likely, does it? But I have another question. Is it possible someone knew Finney was going to be in that car?"

Jake hesitated. "The police have considered that possibility, but its very unlikely." No reaction from Sue.

"Well, I've heard some terrible things said about Finney by some very hostile abortion advocates. People I've seen scream and push, bite and pull hair at peaceful prolife protests. And I certainly wouldn't eliminate anyone who works in the abortion business. They're callused to the value of life. And even if Doctor Lowell was the target, maybe he knew somebody botched an abortion and they wanted to cover it up. Or maybe there was a fight over profits. Maybe one of his own coworkers turned against him. Are you checking on the doctors he worked with?"

"Well, yes we are, but I don't really think physicians are the kind of people who would do something like this."

"Look, Mr. Woods," this was a man, sixtyish, dressed in classy casuals, a man with an air of dignity and professionalism Jake had immediately noticed. "The name's Jim Barnes. Dr. Barnes, OB-GYN, I used to perform abortions. Don't kid yourself. Doctors are like everybody else, we just went to school longer and wear white coats. You tell yourself you're doing this for the women, but the truth is you'd get out of it in a second if it wasn't for the money. I mean, I used to pocket a thousand dollars for half a day's work, then spend the afternoon on the golf course. In this state a full-time abortionist makes three times the salary of a typical OB-GYN. To put it bluntly, there's a lot more money in taking babies out of the world than bringing them into it. You're never on call because abortion is an elective surgery, not an emergency. And once you start making the big bucks you get addicted. I did. You keep raising your lifestyle, and now you've got payments on a summer home, a golf club membership, a boat. You can't afford to go back to a normal salary.

"What I'm saying is, it's easy to get in and stay in, and the next thing you know you're rationalizing and justifying and cutting corners in the rest of your practice. Abortion isn't good for doctors. It brings out the worst in them. Are doctors capable of murder? Of course they are. No, it isn't likely, but don't rule it out because you think doctors are morally superior to everyone else. They're not. We're not."

After another thirty minutes of discussion, Jake wasn't getting exactly what he came for, but he was getting insight into this group of people. He'd always thought of Finney and Sue as exceptions to the rule of the self-righteous, ignorant religious bigots. But once they got over their initial defensiveness, he began to wonder if he may have misjudged some of these people. They seemed intelligent, thoughtful, and caring. Funny, he thought, that in all his years of meeting with all kinds of groups and constituencies, he had never once spent even an hour just talking with and listening to people of this persuasion.

Everyone but Dr. Barnes left promptly at 8:00 A.M. While Sue was saying good-bye to the last people at the door, Barnes looked at Jake.

"I had something I didn't want to ask in front of the group. Did your friend ever talk with you about doing abortions?"

"Not really. Why?"

"Well, there's no way I can really describe what it means to be an abortionist. It's the opposite of being a doctor."

Jake shot a questioning look.

"I'm very serious, and I speak from experience. The Hippocratic oath was to forever separate killing and healing in the medical profession. I brought you a copy of the oath, and at the bottom is the Declaration of Geneva, after World War II, when the Nazi doctors brought shame to the medical profession."

Jake looked at the neatly printed page, Times Roman, large print, maybe 15 point. At the bottom he read, "Declaration of Geneva, 1948: 'I will maintain the utmost respect for human life, from the time of conception; even under threat, I will not use my medical knowledge contrary to the laws of humanity.'"

"Okay, Dr. Barnes. Thank you. I need to get to the paper to work on a column and—"

"Hang on just a second. This is an article from an American Medical Association journal. It's on abortionists and what goes on inside abortion clinics. You can read it later. And this is the AMA's official position on abortionists, issued back in 1871. It's fascinating. You really need to read it."

Why do these people always have to peddle their little propaganda pieces, as though I don't have enough to read already?

"The bottom line, Jake, is that abortionists are the bottom feeders of medicine. Other doctors joke about them. They make big money, but they get marginalized, and it grates on them. Some of them get real angry. Most are hurting bad inside. Remember, I know. I used to be one. I understand what your friend was living under. It affects your attitude, your character, your values. I know what it did to me, to my marriage, my family, everything. I'm just now finally getting healed up."

"Well, doctor, I'm happy for you. But I do need to get going here. Thanks for the stuff."

"One last thing, Jake, and I'm out of your hair. There's a psychiatrist friend of mine who's been a big help to me. Post-Traumatic Stress Syndrome is his specialty. He works with a lot of Vietnam vets, and he's spent tons of time with men and women traumatized by abortion. He's a friend now, but I got to know him as his patient. Anyway, Dr. Scanlon could be an important resource for you. He's worked with potentially violent people on both sides of the abortion issue, right here in this city. If you want to pursue whether your friend was murdered because of the abortion connection, he's the man you need to see."

With no intention to follow up, Jake said, "Okay. Scanlon. Maybe I'll look him up some time."

"I've got his card right here. And I've got some good news. Dr. Scanlon's incredibly busy, not to mention expensive." He chuckled. "But I just happen to have a 3:00 appointment with him today, and I'd like to give it to you."

"No, really that's not necessary."

"Look, Jake, if you want some answers, this is the guy, and you're not going to get to see him on your own for a long time. Frankly, I'd like to take my wife for a long drive this afternoon. I'll call him and tell him you'll be there at 3:00 to take my place. Okay?"

Jake looked at the address on the business card. "Well, it's only five blocks from the *Tribune*. I guess I could make it. If you're serious, I'll take you up on it."

"Great. I get a monthly bill from Dr. Scanlon, so this will just be my little contribution to the investigation. I owe a lot more than that to Finney. He was one of the most..." He cleared his throat and the words stopped coming.

Finney had that effect on people, didn't he?

With Barnes gone, Jake, Sue, and Little Finn chatted a few minutes. The little guy's mini-bus taking him to the special school pulled into the driveway at 8:20.

"'Bye, Unca Jake. What time you pickin' me up for the game Friday?"

"About a quarter till six?" Jake looked at Sue for approval and got it. "I'll take you out for a hamburger first."

"And *French* fries?" Finn asked, as if it would be a dream come true. He was now close enough to the little bus that other wide-eyed children, most of them with Down's Syndrome, could hear through their open windows.

"Hey, French fries, onion rings, a chocolate malt, you name it, bud!"

Jake laughed, Sue beamed, Finn was walking on a cloud as he skipped up the steps, gesturing and pointing at Jake, no doubt telling everyone on the bus that Jake wrote for the newspaper, and was one of his dad's best friends, and was taking him to the game Friday, and was even going to buy him *French* fries.

What is it about this kid? He takes the weight of the world off your shoulders.

Finn's sheer delight in life, his wonder in seeing the universe through a different set of eyes, was something Jake wondered if every person was meant to have, but very few experienced.

Jake saw one car he hadn't noticed when surrounded by the others. "Hey, is that Angela's car?"

"Yeah, Bruce is out of town on business this weekend, so she came back to spend the night. We're so excited about her baby! Come on up and say hi to her. She sneaked down for a donut, so I know she's up."

As they walked up the stairs, Jake said, "Finn said something about you going to New York next week?"

"Yeah, Thursday at 8:00. I'm going to see my sister Adele. She felt so bad she didn't make it out to the funeral, but she was flat on her back. I thought I'd go spend a long weekend with her."

"Great. You can use the break. Enjoy it."

"I plan to. Okay, Angela!" Sue looked first in Angela's old bedroom, then in the office and sewing room, where she found her behind Finney's computer.

"I saw you sneak down for that donut! Somebody wants to say hi."

"Hi, Uncle Jake!" Angela got up and gave Jake the from-the-heart hug Sue had patented.

"Hi, Angie. Congratulations on the pregnancy. I'm happy for you."

"Yeah, Mom and I are just a *little* excited!"

"What you working on?"

"Bad time to ask. I'm stuck on something."

"Hey, I thought you were your daddy's girl with computers."

"Well, usually I am. I've been calling up and printing out all of Dad's files. He kept a journal on here, and even some of his letters, the personal ones, are really special. I want to have every word he wrote that's in this computer. I want my son or daughter to be able to read what their grandfather wrote." Angela's voice broke, and Sue was next to her like Velcro.

Jake quietly contemplated the heritage Finney had passed on to his family. He thought of Carly, of how good it was to be with her the other day, tough as it was. If he had died along with Finney and Doc, as he should have, how would she remember her dad? What kind of legacy would he have left her? He shuddered at the thought.

"You'll have to excuse a couple of emotional females, Jake. Anyway, Angie, you were talking about the problem?"

"Well, I've got hundreds of pages printed out," she pointed to the neat three-inch-thick pile of computer paper, frayed sprocket holes on the sides, flowing out of the dot matrix computer. "But there's one group of files, saved in a special directory named 'COD.' I guess that stands for code, because there's only four files in it and they're all locked."

"Locked?"

"Yeah, look. When I try to call it up from any word processor or file manager, this is what I get."

Angela double clicked the mouse and a box appeared, labeled "Password," with the message "Enter password for file."

"There's fifteen spaces and you'd have to have the exact combination to unlock the file. I've tried all kinds of stuff Dad might use, and I get nothing."

"Interesting. These are the only password protected files?" Jake asked.

"Yep. And it's not like Dad. You know, we've spent a lot of time on the computer together. We'd hack around in all his programs, on the modem, in Compuserve, whatever, and I've never known him to protect a file. Why would he? He never kept anything from any of us. In fact," Angela grinned, "if he would have wanted to keep something secret from *Mom*, just having it on the computer would have been enough. No password was needed."

Sue looked at Angela in mock offense. "It's true, Jake. I'm not sure I know how to turn the darn thing on."

"But it's really got me curious, because I can access the general file info, and the dates of all four files are recent. All in October. Two were the week before Dad died."

Sue looked admiringly at her daughter. "Anyway, you got out a pile of your dad's stuff. I'm looking forward to going through it. I've already reread all Finney's love letters and birthday cards. I need some new material!"

Jake cleared his throat. "Well, I've really got to run. Great to see you, Angie. And thanks for inviting me this morning, Sue. I better get in some hours at the *Trib* before my afternoon appointment." Jake still couldn't believe he was going to see a shrink.

As they walked down the stairs toward the front door, Sue asked, "So how do you feel about the investigation, Jake?"

"Honestly? Like it's taking on a life of its own."

CHAPTER EIGHTEEN

F inney relished one of the greatest dynamics of heaven—being freed from the preoccupation with self. On earth he had to work hard to be unselfish. Here it came naturally, for he was immersed in something infinitely greater than himself, and it was the greater that gave meaning and purpose to himself, the lessor. He imagined how silly it would be to sit at a great feast with all the most interesting people who have ever lived, and to choose to spend the evening contemplating oneself instead. Nothing wrong with self, but in the face of such multifaceted wonder, who would want to pay it much attention? In one of Elyon's endless ironies, in this unselfish state Finney found the greatest pleasure and happiness he'd ever known. From this vantage point he could see clearly that those who pursue holiness can find both holiness and happiness, while those who pursue happiness can find neither.

The nearest experiences he'd had on earth were forgetting himself in a powerful storm or a great piece of music or in making love with his wife. In reading a great story, he'd sometimes lost all consciousness of both time and self. The joy was in ceasing to exist outside the story and finding himself no longer on the outside looking in but on the inside. This was the liberating glory of heaven. He was finally on the inside.

The new perspective infatuated him still. It was as if he'd been standing on the sidelines at half-time of a football game, watching the band form letters but not being able to see the words they spelled out. Now he'd gone up in the stands. By going to Elyon's Word on earth, Finney had been able to gain enough perspective to see life differently. Now he saw it completely differently and, as if someone had at long last adjusted a television antenna just right, with stunning clarity.

"I'm flooded with memories of earth, Zyor. People and things I thought I'd forgotten rush at me, sweep me up. They seem more real now than then."

The towering angel nodded. "Then you were looking through a dark glass. Now you see clearly. Not completely, but clearly. You cannot recall what you haven't heard or read or experienced. Have you noticed you understand my explanations much more readily in those areas you meditated on and lived out while on earth? Every moment that you invested in thinking the thoughts that matter and living the life that mattered, you brought with you into this world. And now you are able to build on it."

"Then some have a fuller understanding here than others?"

Zyor paused like a kindergarten teacher, considering best how to explain this to a sharp young mind that was like a blank slate longing to be chalked.

"If you take five students who graduate from high school and go to college, they are all in the same place, are they not? They are all in college. But they do not begin evenly, do they? They bring what they have learned, and what they have learned is determined by the choices they have made, by how they have invested their time, how they have lived before coming to college. So it is here. Those who wait till they come here to begin exploring the depths of Elyon's nature start behind and never catch up. Their joy is full, of course, but their capacity is less. A gallon jug that is full contains much more than a pint jug that is equally full. Elyon's Book says of your people, 'We are God's workmanship, created in Christ Jesus to do good works, which God prepared in advance for us to do.' One's capacity is inevitably less here when he has chosen not to do what Elyon appointed him to do in the other world."

"I knew our lives there were critical. I told others they were. But they were more critical than I ever realized."

"Many of your people do not understand this. When they filled their mind with what was ungodly, it damaged their capacity to worship and drew them away from the things of God. This led to other choices that sucked their lives of meaning and contentment. They come here to Elyon's realm fully covered by the blood of Christ, or they could not come at all. Yet they are woefully unprepared." Zyor said it painfully.

"It takes a great deal of time to orient them. They simply are not ready. As you have seen, it is not automatic. Elyon decreed wisdom and folly, blessing and curse, choice and consequence. If life on earth has any meaning at all, it must have effects that outlast it."

"I always believed what we thought and did there had eternal effects, but I could never understand how it worked. I thought we'd all be alike the moment we die, that forgiveness was the great equalizer."

"Earth was heaven's womb, Elyon's nursery," Zyor said. "His children's lives continue from the old realm to the new. What was done in that world has great bearing on this one. All your people must be resuited for this realm, and some are more prepared for it than others. It is not a question of forgiveness. It is a question of choices made after forgiveness, of how his children invested their lives, whether in the treasury of earth or the treasury of heaven. Forgiveness was the beginning of the story but not its end. Forgiveness does not nullify the law of the harvest, the reality of choice and consequence. It does not negate your life in the other world, nor does it make your choices there moot and irrelevant. Earth was heaven's dress rehearsal. Rather, it was act one of the great play itself. And as such, what happened on earth's stage will forever matter.

"Of course, you will not be tarnished by the acts of selfishness and cruelty in the old world, his grace will see to that. But the scars on his hands and feet will testify to the price that had to be paid. And the fact that others will cast their crowns at his feet will remind all that they too could have brought him more glory had they lived more for him and less for themselves. No act of kindness and love will be overlooked, all will be enshrined for eternity."

"Everyone who gives even a drink of water to one of these little ones in my name," Finney quoted, "shall not lose his reward."

"Exactly, Master Finney. You are becoming the teacher." Zyor was obviously pleased.

"And it is not just that such acts will be remembered, it is that they will always be. Elyon walks backward and forward in time as easily as we walk a garden path one way then the other. We too are allowed to step back in time to reflect on what has been as if it were now happening."

"What do you mean, Zyor?"

"Your life on earth is like a phonograph record or a videotape, played and replayed. Like broadcasts of radio and television programs projected out into space, earthly lives do not dissipate. Stand now on Alpha Centauri's ring world, and you can see live what happened on earth four years ago. Go to the third planet of Pollux, look toward earth, and you can watch the events of what you called World War II. Stand now on Rigel's second orb of ice and you can watch the Middle Ages unfold. From Yargos, eighth planet of Wezen, you can watch the life of Christ as it is now unfolding.

"Human events have permanence. None of them are lost in space and time. They are projected outward at the speed of light, for all eternity. But that done for the glory of Christ will be sifted out from all the others, as gold nuggets are separated out in pans from the sand and mud, and then displayed for all to see and to celebrate. In eternity we shall consider and cherish those acts done for him. And we will not merely be passive viewers but active participants. Some day I will take you back to relive moments in history, to experience and study and enjoy these things as they actually happened."

The thought of walking back through time to explore as one might explore the woods or a cave thrilled Finney. But he was perplexed.

"I suppose I thought we wouldn't look backward here, only forward."

"But we must look backward as a reference point for our worship of Elyon's Son. That is why his Book speaks of the memorials in the heavenly city, eternal reminders of the twelve tribes and the Lamb's apostles and the great exploits of men and women of old. Heaven is not a place to forget great acts of faith done on earth, but to remember them. Elyon's book says, 'A scroll of remembrance was written in his presence concerning those who feared the Lord and honored his name.' What did you believe this meant?"

"I...don't remember reading it."

"It is found in Malachi. You will want to read it."

"Yes, I will."

Zyor looked at Finney. "I sometimes heard you call your life there a 'window of opportunity.' It was an accurate term, an inspired one. You knew it to be true, but its truth was far deeper than you understood. Look back with me."

Suddenly a little cloud formed and a hole several feet across showed him a man (somehow he knew it was Moses) his stylus in his hand, carefully inscribing words on a clay tablet. The words were Psalm 90, most ancient of the psalms.

As if the ages between had not been, Finney saw himself on his knees late one night, wearing faded jeans, his old Bible open in front of him. From his view in heaven, he now looked over his own shoulder, staring at the words of Moses' psalm.

Lord, you have been our dwelling place
    throughout all generations.
Before the mountains were born
    or you brought forth the earth and the world,
    from everlasting to everlasting you are God.

He heard his own voice from the past saying, "Lord, Moses says here to establish, to make permanent, the work of our hands. He says to ask you to 'teach us to number our days that we may gain a heart of wisdom.' I don't know how long you'll keep me here. How long I'll have with Sue and Jenny and Angela and Little Finn. God, help me to live this life as I should, to use this brief window of opportunity to make a difference for eternity. I give you all that I am and all I have, my money, my possessions, my life, even my family. I confess my pride and selfishness and laziness. I need your strength and wisdom to live as I should. Help me Lord, to invest my life in what will matter forever. Teach me to number my days that I may live wisely, that I may live every day in light of eternity. I ask all this in the powerful name of Jesus. Amen."

As Finney watched himself pray, he noticed a great shadow kneeling beside him. He said aloud to Zyor, "There was no one there that night. Sue and the children were in bed."

Yet there, unmistakably, was someone else, a huge imposing figure at his side, praying as earnestly as he himself.

"Zyor...it's you."

"Yes, it was just as you see now. But you lacked the vision then to see things as they really were."

Zyor and Finney both felt something the same moment. "It is time for us to pray again," Zyor said. "Your friend is in the thick of a great battle, a battle with stakes far greater than he imagines."

It was Jake's first appointment with a psychiatrist, and he was already certain it would be his last. He'd interviewed a few psychiatrists on various topics, but this was different. Now he was standing in for a former abortionist to meet with a shrink to get some insights on the kind of person who might kill a doctor. Jake shook his head. It was all too weird.

Looking around the waiting room, Jake imagined someone here had attended some conference on the importance of bright cheerful colors when you're dealing with people on the far edge of sanity. He noticed his hands wringing together. He'd never been a smoker, but for a moment he thought how useful it would be to have something to do with his hands.

Jake looked at his watch. Ten minutes till 3:00. Compulsive reader that he was, he searched the table for material. He saw an issue of *Esquire* with a cover story called "Men and Abortion." It was a couple years old, but there were two copies of the same issue lying right next to each other. Why? A powerful voice within told him not to read the article, but he opened to it anyway.

The article was billed as twelve men speaking candidly on the price they paid because of abortion. Some agreed to the decision to abort, some didn't. Some, like the first man, pushed his will on his girlfriend:

> "It's her body, but I had her brainwashed. I made all the decisions. Once it was over, we never talked about it again. We kept our mouths shut. She did have some real prophetic words, though. She said, 'Wagner, you're going to regret this all your life.' I told her, 'No, no.' But inside me something would spark and cling to that. She was right. I'll never forget it. I'll never forgive myself."

Most of the men talked about the disastrous effects on the relationship with their girlfriend or wife. One lamented,

> "Abortion is presented to you as something that is easy to do. It doesn't take very long. It doesn't cost very much money nowadays, for a middle-class person. You say, 'Well, it's okay.' But it wasn't okay. It left a scar, and that scar had to be treated tenderly and worked on in order for us to get on with our lives. I don't think abortion is easy for anybody. The people who say it's easy either don't want to face the pain of it or haven't been through it, because it's really a tough experience."

Jake squirmed uncomfortably, but he was hooked. He read next the words of a married man:

> "We tried to figure out why we weren't getting along so well. It occurred to one of us that it was a year since the abortion. That was the first time we realized that we felt we had killed something we had made together and that it would have been alive and might have been our child. We talked and shared how disturbed about it we both had been. We hadn't known that we were angry and upset and hadn't been willing to face the facts."

Jake thought about walking out of this psychiatrist's office that had brought him face to face with something in his past, a monster in his soul that he'd managed to push back and hide from the light of reality. But there was one more man left, and he felt compelled to read his story:

> "I've had a heck of a time dealing with it, actually. To this day I still think about it. I'll go to bed and I'll think about it and say to myself, 'Man, what a terrible thing to do. What a cop-out. You don't trade human life for material niceties.' Which is what I was doing, because I was hoping for a better future, more goods I could buy.

"I don't have a good rationalization for it either. I've come to believe more and more that the baby in the womb is just that—a human life. I wish I didn't. I wish I could make myself believe differently, but I can't. It would make it easier to deal with mentally. When you have the opposite view and you go through with the abortion anyway, well, that's worse than anything.

"So, you see, I'm kind of stuck. She did it for me. I feel like I murdered somebody. I wish I could do it over again, if I could just go back in time and relive those years. If she'd had the child, even if we'd got married and everything, it wouldn't have been that bad. I've seen other people do it. Reality's such a pain sometimes, you know?"

Jake sat quietly in the chair, glad no one else was in the waiting room, no one's eyes to keep his own from meeting. *Reality's such a pain sometimes, you know?*

Five minutes later a well-dressed professional stepped out of his office and warmly extended a hand.

"Mr. Woods? Welcome! Harvey Scanlon. Jim Barnes called and told me about your situation. I rarely have stand-in patients, but I'm flexible! Jim told me to give you his time for whatever you had on your mind. Come in."

It didn't take a psychiatrist to see how preoccupied Jake was. "Are you all right, Mr. Woods?"

"Uh, yeah, sure. I...was just reading a disturbing article."

"Oh? Which one?"

"Esquire." *I'm here for information, Doctor. Don't get so nosy.*

"Men and abortion?"

"Yeah."

The doctor nodded knowingly, with what Jake presumed was self-congratulation.

"It's amazing how many men have a nerve touched with that one. But think about it. With over thirty million abortions, there have to be maybe fifteen or twenty million men who have lost their children in the last twenty-two years. That doesn't even count fathers and brothers and other sons of the aborted women. In the last five years I've discovered how many men have been traumatized by abortion, and I'm just scratching the surface. Our fatherly instincts go much deeper than we suspect. I'm afraid the old expression 'an abortion is between a woman and her doctor' is a myth."

"A myth? How do you mean?"

"Well, a few people are left out of the formula, don't you think? I suppose the most obvious person is the baby. But we've also totally ignored the baby's father. As men we have deep loyalties to our women and to any children we father. When those loyalties are encouraged and maintained we're at our best. But when those loyalties are violated or ignored we're at our worst. Over a million fathers each year either demand abortion, decide on it, or turn the other way while it happens.

Others object to it but are powerless to stop it. The psychological effects are profound in any case—except perhaps in the man who is totally irresponsible, who has no conscience at all. For the rest of us, it's profoundly negative. It's complicity in violating and killing the very women and children we were designed to protect."

Jake wasn't sure what he was expecting in the doctor, but this wasn't it.

"Forgive me, Dr. Scanlon, but I'm of the persuasion abortion is just another elective surgery on a woman's body, like a tonsillectomy or a root canal. It's up to her, no one else."

"Haven't given it much thought, have you?"

"Pardon me?" *Who does this guy think he is?*

"Mr. Woods, no offense intended, but anyone who minimizes abortion as you did is simply ignorant of the facts, biological and psychological. I don't mean to get us off on the wrong foot. You're the one who came to me, and I'll be glad to answer your questions. I'm not trying to take a political position on abortion, or even a moral one. I'm not an activist like my friend Dr. Barnes. I'm just a professional who deals with the realities intense traumas bring into people's lives. But as a professional I can tell you without reservation that when you say abortion is like a root canal or an appendectomy, you just couldn't be more wrong."

Jake stared at him blankly. If this was a battle of wits, he was feeling badly unarmed.

"Have you ever heard of Women Exploited by Abortion?"

Jake shook his head.

"It's an organization with over thirty thousand members in more than one hundred chapters across the United States, with affiliate groups in at least nine other countries. I'm familiar with a half dozen other post-abortion support and recovery groups, but I've never come across support groups for those who've had tonsillectomies and root canals. Why? Abortion takes a toll that normal surgeries don't. People don't suffer a sense of loss at tonsils they no longer have. People do suffer a sense of loss at a child they no longer have. If they don't come to terms with that loss, Mr. Woods, it will haunt them, interfere with their relationships, desensitize them. It'll do all kinds of destructive things that people like myself have to show them in a mirror to help bring them healing."

Jake flipped open his notebook. The doctor waited silently, dropping the uncomfortable subject.

"Doctor, did Dr. Barnes tell you what I'm after—any possible suspects in the killing of my friend Dr. Lowell?"

"Yes, tragic situation. As I understand it, it's possible the doctor's involvement in abortions was connected to the murder?"

"Maybe. We can't be certain. We know that emotions run very high with this issue." For some reason, Jake avoided saying the word "abortion."

"Precisely, Mr. Woods. Considerably higher, say, than with root canals and tonsillectomies?"

"Touché, Doctor. Obviously, you know your field better than I do."

"I know it from several angles. One from the women, who tend to react one way. One from the men, who react another. I counsel and lead support groups for both. But in the last three years there's been a third group. Doctors and nurses who do abortions. There are five of them that have come to me for counseling, from three different clinics. Dr. Barnes was the first."

"No kidding. Five?"

"Yes. My reputation is as a therapist, not a prolifer. They think they can trust me, and they're right."

Dr. Scanlon looked down at a yellow legal pad, where he'd scratched some notes.

"Mr. Woods, there's a lot of ground to cover. If you don't mind, I'd like to give you a thumbnail sketch of how abortion affects people, and the potential for violent response against a doctor."

"Sure. I'm all ears."

"Let's begin with the women. Those who've had abortions are nine times more likely to attempt suicide than women in the general population. Many women are incapacitated by grief following their abortions. Some are very angry at the doctor. Given the right kind of woman—I guess I should say the wrong kind—there's no doubt in my mind she'd be capable of violence against the man she's convinced deceived her and took her money to kill her baby. It's like somebody blowing away a drug dealer because he got them or their friend or their sister hooked. Or like the women who've killed men who molested their children. I've learned not to underestimate what a woman will do because somebody has wronged her child."

"You really think a woman who was given an abortion, say by Dr. Lowell, might be capable of killing him?"

"It's possible, certainly. It would be rare of course, but the sheer numbers of women getting abortions has to be considered. Suppose only one in a million would do an act of violence against a doctor. That would account for thirty such acts of violence in the last twenty years. In fact, I've personally counseled with two different women who had a revenge fixation, one on a doctor and one on a Planned Parenthood counselor."

"No kidding?"

"Sure. They believe they were lied to, deliberately deceived and used. Their lives seemed ruined, and the thought of that doctor or counselor just going right on with their lives was infuriating. Obviously, I can't divulge much more due to doctor-patient confidentiality, but I assure you we're talking very serious situations."

"But Doc—Dr. Lowell—he stopped doing abortions several years ago when he became chief of surgery at Lifeline. If someone was going to kill him for doing abortions, wouldn't they have done it sooner?"

"Maybe, but not necessarily. There's a denial following abortion that can go on for years. If people don't get the help they need, a profound psychological deterioration can take place. It may culminate in a realization of what the abortion really was. Then there's a tremendous sense of guilt, and sometimes anger. Over time that anger can become severe bitterness. Some people, most people, internalize all this and seem content just to destroy themselves. But some externalize it and want to destroy others, psychologically or even physically. Did you know studies show parents who have abortions are much more likely to abuse their other children?"

Jake shook his head.

"And it makes sense when you think about it. If it was okay to kill this child up to the day of his birth, what's so bad about just slapping around the same child a few months or a few years later?"

Jake swallowed hard. "Doctor, can we get back to the traumatic stress syndrome, or wherever you were going?"

"Certainly. People are much more familiar with post-traumatic stress syndrome for Vietnam vets than they are for the same syndrome experienced by aborted women, even though the numbers of women are far greater. But when you start talking about anything that could make abortion appear bad or dangerous, the media just won't cover it. So people don't know about it."

Jake didn't want to hear the media blamed for one more thing, but he didn't know how to argue with the doctor, so he let it go.

"Let me give you some background. In the early eighties I started working with a lot of Vietnam vets, guys with post-traumatic stress disorder. I felt for them because I served in Nam. Maybe that's why you're one of my favorite columnists. I always enjoy it when you talk about Nam."

"Thanks."

"So we both understand what it was like to lose friends, to wonder why they came home in a box and we came home on a plane. I don't know if you ever killed someone?"

Jake nodded.

"At close range?"

"One."

"Me too. One. But one was all it took, wasn't it?"

Jake nodded again.

"So, I counseled these guys, did some group interaction, accomplished some very positive things for them and for myself. I researched, read, consulted everywhere on post-traumatic stress disorder. It was like that eye-opening thing alcoholics discover in AA—a world that relates to you, that explains inexplicable behavior, that shows you're not alone. This was ten years ago. When meeting with one of the guys, I found he seemed to have gotten over Vietnam. Now he was strung out on something else, but with exactly the same symptoms. It finally surfaced. He'd gotten his girlfriend pregnant and paid for her abortion. He was angry at the doctor and violently angry at himself. He felt like you'd feel if you'd beaten up a little kid, as if he'd killed his own son or daughter. It was frightening. At the time I was prochoice. To be honest, I'd never thought it through."

Jake stared at the floor.

"I'd had some women suffering the same thing, but it was that guy who pushed me to make the obvious link to post-traumatic stress disorder. That led to some research, some referrals, and eventually to what's developed into a specialty, of sorts. Even the American Psychiatric Association, which is very prochoice, officially recognizes abortion can lead to post-traumatic stress disorder. It can be triggered by all sorts of little things, even the sound of a vacuum cleaner."

"A vacuum cleaner?"

"It sounds like the vacuum machine used for suction abortions. It's like a Vietnam vet hearing a loud noise and all of a sudden he's under the table."

"I understand." Jake had hit the deck twice after Vietnam, once ten years later at an amusement park. He remembered trying to explain his reaction to little Carly as he wiped the dust off his shirt.

"Think about it, Mr. Woods. One and a half million abortions are performed in this country every year. Suppose only 1 percent were seriously traumatized. It's much higher, but if it was only 1 percent, that would be fifteen thousand women a year."

Jake's thoughts drifted to Janet. He thought about her emotional distress, her near breakdown. At the time, he was bothered by her weakness, ashamed of it. The doctors had never figured out the cause. For the first time he wondered if...

"Women rake themselves over the coals for this. They need forgiveness, Jake. Desperately. But so many of them don't know where to find it. That's where I can help them as a Christian in a way that all the psychology and medicine in the world can never help them. They need the grace of God. They need the forgiveness of Christ. I can't give it to them, but I can point them to him."

The message Jake had once just associated with Finney and Sue now seemed to be coming at him wherever he went. And part of his past he'd stuffed deep inside pursued him relentlessly.

"Bottom line? An enraged woman is certainly capable of retaliating against the doctor she believes violated her." Scanlon paused. "But to be honest, I think the more likely candidate is a man."

"Why?"

"You read the *Esquire* interviews?"

Jake nodded.

"What those interviews don't talk about is the violence thing. It gets back to something I said before. Men are very physical in their desire to protect, and in their desire to avenge injustice, especially injustice against women and children under their care. If a sister or mother or daughter or son is raped or killed, there's a profound compulsion to take revenge. Maybe part of it is needing to compensate for his own failure to protect. Look at the men's movement."

"What about it?"

"You've got all these guys feeling like they want to get in touch with their masculinity. They're tired of acting like emasculated wimps. I'm afraid we could be on the verge of a violent backlash of men against these doctors and clinics. Who knows? What happened to your friend could be that very thing."

Jake sat silently, his mind drifting from Doc's death to Janet, to himself, to a cold winter day at a clinic almost thirty years ago. Sensing his inward journey, Dr. Scanlon was silent.

"One last thing, doctor," Jake said. "You talked about clinic workers having problems."

"There's often a veneer of hardness on abortionists. Beneath the veneer, though, they suffer guilt, which manifests itself in destructive behavior. Studies and interviews show abortionists and abortion clinic employees have extremely high rates of nightmares, alcoholism, drug abuse, and family problems leading to divorce. Dr. Barnes has been through it personally, and I've seen it in the abortionists I've counseled. I'd like to tell you more, but because of the relatively small numbers of them in this city, I'm afraid I could violate confidentiality. Besides, it's almost 4:00."

"Already?"

"Time flies when you're havin' fun, huh?" Dr. Scanlon laughed.

"Listen, Jake. At 4:00 I've got a therapy group in our conference room. It's five men dealing with, guess what? Post-abortion stress syndrome. We know each other well, been together three months. My guess is they'd welcome you to visit the group, maybe ask them some questions."

"No, I really couldn't..."

"Why not? You can get some tremendous insights from them. Might be really helpful."

"Yeah, but..."

"Please. I have an ulterior motive, Jake. Other than the *Esquire* feature and a few others, I've never seen anyone deal with the effect of abortion on men. I know you're focused on an investigation now, but my hope is, if you see this thing up close you'll write a column on it, bring it into the public eye."

"Well, I don't know."

"They're probably all here by now. I'll ask if it's okay with them if you join us. Back in a minute." Scanlon headed to the door.

"Uh, okay."

Jake had the distinct feeling this whole day was going according to someone else's plan. He knew for certain it was not going according to his.

CHAPTER NINETEEN

The five men in Dr. Scanlon's therapy room were an odd assortment. Two wore business suits. Jake assumed they'd come straight from downtown office jobs. From the cut of the suits he guessed one, the graying midfifties one on the left end of the couch, was a corporate executive. The other, on the opposite end, the meticulous ruddy-faced Ivy Leaguer with gleaming wire-rimmed glasses, had to be a lawyer. A tall long-faced man in old saggy Levis and tattered Reeboks sat on the same elegant white flecked couch, between the suits.

In a separate chair that matched the couch sat a young man, perhaps twenty-five, in off-white slacks and a Green Bay Packers sweatshirt. The other, in an identical chair, was a very big man with powerful shoulders, dressed in gray slacks and a maroon sweater with an open collared gray dress shirt underneath.

Dr. Scanlon pointed Jake to a third matching chair. Then the doctor took what appeared to be his customary seat at the far end, a sculptured wooden chair next to a coffee table, where he put down his notepad and pen.

"Gentlemen, Jake Woods. Some of you read his column in the *Tribune*. Nothing you say today will leave this room without your specific permission, unless it's sufficiently disguised to preclude any possible identification. Right, Jake?"

"Absolutely."

"I'm not going to ask you to introduce yourselves, but feel free to use first names, and if you want to allude to your occupation or background or whatever, that's fine. In other words, the usual ground rules apply.

"The guys have agreed to have you here, Jake, because one of the things we've discovered is that we all share a desire to get the word out on this thing. We wish we'd heard about it ourselves, and maybe things would have been different." Scanlon turned his eyes from Jake back to the others.

"So, I think the best thing we can do is, everybody share your own story briefly. Bob, why don't you start?" Bob was the man in the suit Jake had labeled the corporate executive.

"Well, my wife got pregnant when she was forty. The whole idea cramped my style. Our youngest was in high school, and we were on the verge of freedom. We knew we wouldn't have more children, and...suddenly, there we were. I felt like we didn't have the energy to start over. I was kind of embarrassed, too. Kids are okay, in a limited quantity and at a certain time in your life, but in my circles it's frowned on to have too many or have them too late. We already had three, and the childbearing years were long past.

"The pregnancy surprised Donna, but I could see she was pleased. She told me later *of course* she was pleased, the way every woman is when she's pregnant because she knows she was uniquely made to be a mother, and this is her highest destiny."

He looked tentatively at Jake, knowing he'd said something that might sound suspect.

"Keep in mind I'm quoting Donna, that's what she told me. I know it doesn't fit what we generally think about women anymore, but that's what she said...after it was too late.

"I wasn't just disappointed, I was determined to stop this situation in its tracks. I started talking about the risks to Donna, said she was too old, that the baby could be deformed, that a child deserved younger parents, and on and on. I even got the doctor to tell her the chances were higher for Down's Syndrome and all kinds of horrible things, even though the truth was it was still a very small risk. It was all an excuse, of course. I just didn't want the inconvenience.

"Donna turned sullen, but she knew I always get my way, so she went along with the abortion. That was six years ago. Our life hasn't been the same since. As she put it, part of her died the day she got the abortion. When she craved my love and support, I wasn't there for her or the baby. She needed me to stand with her, to reassure her, to be proud of her, to be excited about *our* baby. She told me later I'd refused to even acknowledge it was a child, much less *my* child. She said I didn't want a baby that was the ultimate expression of our marriage, our love for each other. And she was right on all accounts. She took it personally. It hurt her... *I* hurt her...more deeply than anything I could ever imagine.

"After the abortion came the attempts at compensation. I took her to Hawaii, bought her a new BMW, tried to prove my love with money. But I'd already shown her what I was made of. I wasn't a man. I was a coward, a self-centered pig."

Jake moved back in his chair at this blunt self-characterization of a man he'd never have suspected would think of himself in such terms.

"She lost respect for me, totally. She finally told me that. And she lost respect for herself too. She was terrified our other kids would find out, still is. She feels she couldn't face them if they knew we killed their little brother or sister. I tell you, the last few years have been hell."

A man obviously used to being in control, he shook his head at how out of control life had become.

"Ditto," the guy in the Packers sweatshirt chimed in. "We were on the front end of a family, but it was the same story for us. We were going to get married, but not yet. I didn't feel we were ready. Besides, we wanted Sally to work so we could combine our incomes and get a decent house. The baby was there and I should have taken the responsibility, but I wanted a house first. Funny, we got our house, but no children to live in it. Sally can't have children now. We found out that happens after abortions sometimes. They can cause infertility. It was mentioned in the fine print on that long form we signed, but of course we didn't read it. Who wants to think about it? You just want it over with. We weren't willing to take the child that was given us, so we can never have another one. If it wasn't so tragic, it'd be funny, huh?"

He was looking at Jake, but Jake didn't respond.

"We've gone through a lot of serious problems. I've been angry, really angry. For a long time I blamed the clinic. I wanted to kill those jerks, because they had to know better. Things have improved since we both started therapy, but you look back and always think how it could have been. We're on an adoption waiting list now, have been for three years. Strange to be waiting so long when so many people are getting abortions every day. I want to say, 'Hey, save yourself incredible misery, make us ecstatically happy, and let a child live and grow up in a home where he'll be loved.' Sounds like an 'everybody wins' situation to me. I'm so tired of hearing people talk about unwanted children when we've *desperately* wanted a child for years."

There was a long silence. Dr. Scanlon seemed comfortable with the silence, much more than Jake. Finally the doctor nodded at the man on the middle of the couch.

"Clay?"

The lanky, long-faced guy in the old Levis and Reeboks appeared almost in a daze. He said nothing for some time, long enough that Jake doubted whether Clay had heard the doctor say his name. Then suddenly he looked up and asked in a slow and measured, almost self-tortured voice, "Do you remember the date? I always remember the date. July 14, 1991. I didn't remember the date till a year later. Didn't even think about it. Till I came home from my swing shift at the store and found my wife lying on the floor next to an empty pill bottle. I called 911 and they came and took her in, pumped her stomach. The doctor said, 'We've put Mrs. Dalinger on suicide watch.' My wife on suicide watch."

Clay hung his head as if the disbelief was as fresh today as back then.

"When I asked her why she did this, she told me it was the one year anniversary of the abortion. She was hurt that I didn't even know it. I didn't think anybody kept track of dates like that—I mean, it wasn't like a birthday or Christmas. She kept saying 'Our baby would be walking by now,' and then 'She'd probably be saying Mama now.' It was torture. She wouldn't forget. By then I couldn't forget either. I guess you'd say we became obsessed, right Doc?"

Doctor Scanlon gave an affirming look.

"Five months after the anniversary of the abortion she left me. December 14, 1991. I tried to see her, but she got a restraining order. She wouldn't talk to me. She was drinking all the time and getting into drugs. I tried to talk her into getting help, but she wouldn't. She said she could never put the abortion behind her unless she put me behind her. Got a restraining order against me, said I was bugging her. And then..."

Clay suddenly let loose a sob from deep inside. Twenty seconds later he spoke again. "July 14, 1993. The second anniversary of the abortion. They found her in her apartment. She killed herself."

Jake felt like he'd been slapped in the face. Everyone knew this story but him. Yet there wasn't a dry eye, not even Dr. Scanlon's. Everyone waited for Clay to regain his composure.

"So I lost her. I lost Janet. Because of that stinking abortion."

"Did you say Janet?" Jake blurted it out, and was immediately sorry.

"Yeah. Why?" Clay's eyes looked defensive and suspicious.

"Oh, nothing. I know a Janet, a different Janet. I just happened to be thinking about her. Sorry. Go on."

Clay looked at Jake uncertainly. Jake sat embarrassed and self-conscious. He consoled himself that if ever he'd been with a group of men where he didn't have to protect his image, it was this one.

"We both decided to get the abortion," Clay continued, "but I could have talked her out of it. I know I could have. I didn't know better, I honestly didn't, I swear to God I didn't. They told us it wasn't a real baby, that it was a blob of flesh. Two or three weeks later I was in line at the supermarket and I saw the cover of *Life* magazine. August 1991. Funny how all these dates stick in my mind now. As I stood waiting to buy a gallon of milk and a six pack, I looked at the pictures inside the magazine. They had to do a price check for the woman in front of me, and I was stuck in line flipping through that magazine, picture after picture. I read the captions. And I knew without a doubt 'it' wasn't an it. It was a he or she, a real baby. There was no doubt. Heartbeat, brain waves, fingers, toes. It was a baby."

The word *baby* hung out in the center of the room as if suspended from the ceiling. Jake's chest felt like a thousand-pound weight was pressing against it. He didn't remember the date. He wondered if Janet did.

With a zombie-like expression Clay said to Jake, "Tell the men."

Jake gave him a questioning look.

"In your newspaper, tell the men that they lie to you. They lie to your girl friend, they lie to your wife, and they lie to you, and you don't find out till it's too late. Tell them. Somebody has to tell them."

Clay wasn't crying. He seemed a hollow man who had no tears left. Almost as an afterthought, he added, "And they lie about your mother too."

His mother? What did his mother have to do with it?

Dr. Scanlon paused almost as if he was going to ask Clay to elaborate, but instead he looked over at the guy in the maroon sweater, who was quietly sobbing. The crying was incongruous; this was the man in the group Jake would have picked out as the resident stud. Now probably in his early thirties, he was easily 6'5" and 270 pounds of muscle. His impossibly broad shoulders looked even broader as he hunched them forward into the room, powerful arms propped under his square jaw and thick neck. Obviously a college football player, Jake guessed maybe from Nebraska or Ohio State, where they grew the farm boys so big half the team looked like the product of selective breeding.

The thought of football brought up images of Doc and Finney, high school football, and the state championship. Then more football with his buddies at Bosworth College. And the last twenty years as weekend warriors, playing football or shooting hoops over at City Park, and being stiff and sore for the next three days, but not admitting it. Competing together, working together, sweating together, laughing together. It stung him violently, he missed "together" so much.

The big man shook his head softly toward Dr. Scanlon and riveted his eyes to the floor. Jake felt a sense of loss. He really wanted to hear this man's story. The wanting surprised him. This was exactly the kind of situation he'd always dreaded. It repulsed him, this touchy-feely stuff. It seemed effeminate and self-indulgent. Years ago he'd heard and read that as a modern man he was supposed to make himself sensitive and vulnerable. He even tried it for a few weeks. But he decided it wasn't for him. *Women* were sensitive and vulnerable. He was a man. If he ever decided that wasn't good enough, he could always have a sex change operation.

As he'd read about the men's movement, guys getting around in circles beating drums and telling their stories to each other, it had seemed so silly. Yet here and now, in this room, something tugged at him, drew him in. He felt something here he'd felt with Doc and Finney. Something he'd felt in sports, high school and college, and in the military. Almost daily in that one year in Nam, that year when the world was reduced to the man on his right and the man on his left. These men in this room—Bob the executive and Clay the sad one and the nameless athlete and the other two—perhaps had nothing else in common, but their experiences made them soul-mates, threw them together as Jake had been thrown together with Slider, Harvey, Chavez, and others in that Asian jungle. There was something surfacing in this room that society had denied men, stripped away from them. And there was something oddly refreshing and therapeutic about it. Jake pondered all this in the continued silence of the room, a silence he began to grow more comfortable with.

Finally, the fifth man, the one in wire-rimmed glasses Jake had pegged as a lawyer, spoke up.

"Well, for me it was two abortions, two different girls. One in high school, the other in college. I told myself I was doing the responsible thing. My dad paid for the first one, I paid for the second. I told myself I was protecting their reputations. That's funny. I guess the way you protect a girl's reputation is to not sleep with her in the first place, huh? But that was the way of the sixties. 'Free love, free sex.' What a joke. Have it now, pay for it later, that's what it really was. And no one ever told me about the interest rates, and how they keep accumulating the rest of your life, and you can never pay off that debt."

He cleared his throat again and laughed half-heartedly. "There's an irony in that, now that I'm a tax attorney."

Bingo.

"It didn't hit me until our ten-year high school reunion. I was so glad to be with everybody again. See, I'd gone back east to college, so I'd missed all the homecomings and everything. I had such great memories of high school. I was student body president, all-state point guard, the whole deal. It was local boy makes good in the big time. Then at the reunion I saw Linda, she'd been a cheerleader—you know, the storybook romance. But the moment I saw her there was such an emptiness, such a shame between us. It took my breath away. I was totally unprepared. My wife was talking to someone else at the other corner of the room, and I was so glad because I couldn't stand the idea of her and Linda even meeting each other.

"Everybody standing around Linda and I kept saying they were so surprised the two of us didn't end up together, and we still made such a cute couple. But both of us were *so* uncomfortable. When people backed away I started talking about superficial stuff, just like a guy, right?"

A couple of the men chuckled.

"Then she started crying. I could tell she was thinking about…our secret. Then she came right out and said it—'Do you ever think about our baby?'

"It blew me away. I was angry. It spoiled the whole reunion for me. I'd lived with this denial, always pushing it out of my mind. Whenever the prochoice issue came up, in college or at work or anywhere, I'd wax eloquent about the woman's right to choose, like I was some great women's advocate. And I'd refuse to listen to any evidence to the contrary. The truth was I was trying to convince myself. I even joined a prochoice march and screamed at a group of prolifers. What's that Shakespeare line? 'Methinks the lady doth protest too much'? Sometimes we argue most heatedly for things we want to believe but really don't. I wanted to believe what my sign and my bumper sticker said, because if it wasn't true, it meant I had killed two innocent children. I just couldn't live with that.

"I guess I should explain the second abortion. It was with my wife, our junior year of college, a year before we were married. When we get introduced somewhere I always cringe when someone asks 'And how many children do you have?' My wife says one, but I know what she's thinking, even though we never talk about it, I mean *never*. She's thinking what I'm thinking. The answer is really two. There were two of them. But now there's just one. If you had a child who died as a six-year-old, you could say 'We have one child now, our daughter, but we had a son who died a few years ago.' People would say 'I'm sorry,' but you wouldn't be hiding anything. They'd know the truth. But we can't tell them the truth. We have to lie. Because how can you admit the reason the other child died?"

Jake felt connected to this man. His honesty, his ability to express himself. He was the sort of man who could have been his friend. Jake realized as he sat there he hadn't had many close friends, and since Doc and Finney had died there was almost no one. Who was his closest friend, who could he really talk to? Ollie? Or Clarence—yeah, maybe Clarence. He missed feeling part of a platoon, being with men who shared the same sense of mission and destiny, who depended on each other to make it through the day and the night.

"Our daughter is in seventh grade now. Her brother or sister would be a freshman in high school. I wonder if he'd be a basketball player, like I was. Or a four-point student like his mom. Maybe he'd find the cure for cancer or AIDS. I've found it real hard to bond with my daughter. Dr. Scanlon helped me see I've guarded myself against a close relationship with her because of what I did to my other children. At first that made no sense to me, but now it does. It's hard for some parents to fully give themselves to one child when they've taken the life of another. It's hard for me. I love her so much, but I have a real hard time showing it."

There was no mass of tears welling up, just one single tear that worked its way down his cheek in slow motion. He didn't wipe it away, didn't even seem aware of it.

Jake thought of Carly again. Carly, to whom he'd never really given himself.

The man in the maroon sweater, the mammoth one, was unexpectedly drawn into the forum by something the lawyer said. His voice was just as Jake had anticipated it, deep and rich with a mild country flavor.

"I had a friend whose child died of leukemia. Only seven years old. It would be awfully hard to lose a child like that, but at least my friend can treasure the memories and tell himself he did what he could to give that child life. He was there for his boy those seven years. And if he had it to do over again, he wouldn't do it differently.

"But when you're the one who took the life, not cancer but you, then it's different. We've experienced the Lord's forgiveness now. We know we'll see our baby some day. But it's been a hard road, still is sometimes. I just wish somebody would have told us about it. There was no one outside the clinic when we went there. No one. I see these pictures of prolife people standing outside the clinics now. I've never gone back to one since the abortion—I won't even drive by, those buildings give me the creeps. It's like the setting for a horror movie or something. But whenever I see these prolifers on the news, I say to myself, *Where were you back then?* Why wasn't there somebody to warn us, somebody to tell us the truth? Maybe we would have listened. I don't know, but I'd like to think we would have."

His head was back on the platform of his big palms, face down, propped up by his arms, elbows dug into his huge thighs.

Dr. Scanlon paused and looked around, as if checking to see if anyone had something to add.

"Well, Jake, those are the stories, in a thumbnail. I guess it gives you an idea what this is about. Have any questions you'd like to ask?"

Jake shook his head no, then thought a moment and looked up.

"Wait. Yeah. Lots of questions. I'd like to know more how you guys come to terms with this. How do you get past the denial? How do you forgive yourself? How do you learn to talk about it? How do you help your wife, or your ex-wife? How do you overcome that distance from your other child you were talking about?"

Jake surveyed the room, for the first time really looking in each man's eyes. "Yeah, I guess I've got lots of questions."

All the men stayed late, none seemed eager to leave. For the next hour Jake listened to the answers, sometimes scribbling down things that were said, but for the most part his pen hung limp between his fingers. He listened with an interest that went far deeper than journalism, far deeper than the investigation, neither of which, for the moment, occupied his mind.

"This place is so much more magnificent than earth, and so different. Yet I expected it to be more unlike earth than it is. It's not as much unearth as it is perfect earth. There's still a body, but a wonderful body; still a physical world, but not one that confines or imprisons, one that liberates. And there still seems to be a sense of time passing."

"You ask much at once," Zyor responded. "As for time, eternity is neither endless time nor the end of time. It is the transmutation of time. It is all times at once and all places at once, where every time and place is as accessible as goods on a store shelf or books in a library. Our Sovereign is the lamb 'slain from before the foundation of the world.' Before time was, all that time would bring existed in the eternal mind of Elyon. And he shares it with his creatures. The accessibility of all times and all places is another reason why heaven must always be the very opposite of boring."

It was obvious to Finney that Zyor still hadn't gotten over his earlier question related to boredom.

"As to another part of your question, Elyon's Book speaks of the new heavens and the new earth. 'New' does not mean fundamentally different, but vastly superior. Think of your own experience on earth, Master Finney. A new car did not mean a car without a steering wheel, seats and doors and tires. It meant a better version of what you already had. This is a physical world because it was made for you, and you are not only a spiritual but a physical being. The body he made you was not a mistake, but a sovereign design. You do not change your species here—you become all God intended your kind to be. You are not an animal, body without spirit, and neither are you an angel, spirit without body. You are both."

Finney raised his eyebrows. Zyor's comment about being "without body" seemed strange coming from such an imposing body.

"I take on this body to function in a realm of space and time, to participate in a place made for you. But it is not a part of me. I merely occupy it. Have you noticed how similar this body is to those of my brethren? Or how this body seems different on my kind than yours? It is because I merely inhabit it. It is not part of me. I am spirit capable of taking on body. You, however, are spirit and body integrated into one. That which you take for granted—for instance, inhaling with your body the fragrance of a flower and having it move your spirit—is something I have never experienced, and cannot.

"You could not bring your old body to this world, for it was unsuited. But you are now clothed in a temporary body that allows you to experience this world, all the while awaiting the reclothing, the merger into your new and eternal body. On earth you did not long to be *un*clothed, but *re*clothed. Man's rebellion against Elyon doomed your old body to decay and death. Your soul was purified through Christ, but your body remained under corruption. Hence you had to experience the unnatural separation from it that is death."

"But isn't the spiritual superior to the physical?" Finney asked. "Doesn't the physical confine and inhibit the spiritual?"

"Many believe spirit is good and body is bad, and therefore imagine heaven as the abode of disembodied spirits. But you are human, made to be soul and body in one. Death is an aberration—two things separated that belong together as one. That is why your people await the resurrection, the rejoining of what was meant to be together. You will not be complete until the resurrection, where your soul again merges with body, this time in perfect unity.

"Elyon promises you a spiritual body. As your physical body allowed you to move and travel and participate on earth, so your spiritual body will allow you to do the same in heaven. The spiritual body is much more than physical, but it is physical. That is why Elyon's Son, in the prototype resurrection body, walked and talked and ate and was grasped and held by his disciples."

"Won't such a body limit the expression of the soul?"

"On the contrary. It will liberate it. The soul without the body is not free to participate in the glories of the material worlds Elyon creates at will. That is why I must take on a body here. But to take it on and shed it is very different than being one with it. Hence, your abilities to fully participate in the material world far exceed mine and always will."

"I wondered once how our souls would come from the east and west and sit at a table and eat with Abraham, Isaac, and Jacob," Finney said. "I have eaten since coming here, but I have not been hungry. Yet the food was delicious, in a way I would have supposed impossible without hunger. Still, I desired the food, I savored the smell and delighted in the taste, more intense and satisfying than anything I had on earth."

"The great banquet feast could not be more spiritual, nor could it be more physical. The two are not at odds. You are free from need here, but you are also free to enjoy what you used to need—food and work and rest and exercise. It is, in a sense never envisioned by the phrase on earth, 'the best of both worlds.' Your longings on earth were the hunger pangs that prepared you to forever enjoy the feasts of heaven. Your resurrection body will allow you not simply to behold and appreciate beauty as you do now, but to fully enter it and participate in it, to plumb its very depths. Have you noticed here that you recognize people more from their character than their body?"

"Yes, from the moment I arrived."

"On earth the body hid the spirit. In heaven the body reveals the spirit. But even on earth you could sometimes see the spirit in the face, could you not?"

"Yes. In the eyes, especially. You could sometimes see the depth of a person, his love, his compassion, his honesty, his suffering, his thirst for justice or longing for peace. Or his shallowness, selfishness, greed, dishonesty, hostility, indifference. Someone said the eyes are a window to the soul."

"Yes. Here it is more transparent. The whole body is a window to the soul. And because the souls have been purified, what you see in someone is often unique, but never frightening, always compelling."

"In my mother I see the beauty of age, in my daughter the beauty of youth. But how can this be? There's no age here. Is there?"

"Agelessness does not eliminate ages, rather it embraces all ages. Every age anyone ever was on earth, he is now, here, to someone. Your mother's mother sees in her the sort of youthfulness you see in your daughter. Your mother sees you as a boy she might want to take into her lap, your daughter sees you as an older man whose lap she might want to crawl up in. They are capable of seeing you in other ways, and will, but each cherishes you in special ways. This is not an illusion, it is real. Everyone is to everyone else their *true* selves, yet each person will focus on an aspect of others most familiar or fascinating, that means the most to them. Everyone sees truly and accurately, but not identically."

"But I am still a man here, and everyone I see is clearly male or female, more distinctly in fact than on earth. I had thought perhaps there would be no gender here. I had read that we would all be...like angels, like you."

Zyor looked immensely surprised at this.

"You are like us in that you do not marry and bear children here. But as for your being a man, what else would you be? Elyon may unmake what men make, but he does not unmake what *he* makes. He made you male, as he made your mother and wife and daughters female. Gender is not merely a component of your being to be added in or extracted and discarded. It is an essential part of who you are. You were not a neuter soul in a man's body. As you were a man in every cell of your body, so you were and are a man in every facet of your soul, for the two are ultimately designed as one. Your sexuality is innate. Manhood pervades your very being, just as womanhood pervades Susan and Jenny and Angela. Elyon redeems fallen maleness and fallen femaleness, but he does not ignore or dispose of what he himself designed.

"Part of the grandeur of heaven's music is the melody of the female set to the harmony of the male. No one here will ever resist or reject the gender within him. What woman would want to be other than woman when her womanhood is the very glory of Elyon? And what man would want to be other than man when Elyon intended for him to be nothing else? The multifaceted dimensions of Elyon's character are fully reflected neither in the man nor the woman, but only in the two together. The two genders shall never war against each other here, any more than hydrogen would war against oxygen in a vain attempt to be water by itself. Both are redeemed and completed, both will find in the other the perfect complement Elyon intended from the beginning. You experienced a foretaste of that mystical union on earth, in your marriage with Sue. It prepared you for a dimension of heaven many come unprepared for, never having known the sacred dimensions and distinctions of male and female."

Zyor's powerful body suddenly seemed far less awesome than that which would one day be Finney's.

"You shall be all man was meant to be, in full strength and full sensitivity, in full power and full compassion, never one sacrificed for the other, each fully realized in the other. You shall be what man was meant to be, and what he has yet been only once, in the perfect spiritual body that is Elyon's Son. Your resurrection body will be the body and soul of a man. It could be nothing else, master Finney, for by the decree of none less than God himself you were, are, and ever shall be a man."

Jake stopped at Morely's Market on his way home from Scanlon's office. While dozens of cars circled the front parking lot in search of a space, he smugly pulled around the back of the building. He stopped in his favorite parking place, unmarked by yellow lines or anything else.

Morely had given Jake night parking privileges in the back where deliveries were made during the day. At night there were just a few employee cars, most of which he recognized, maybe all but the brownish late model Volvo. The back of the store was still, dark and quiet, an eerie contrast to the perpetual motion, glaring headlights, and commotion at the front of the building. Jake hopped out into the darkness, using as his beacon the store light shining through the wired window of the employee entrance. He carefully climbed the concrete stairs, then pushed the button by the door. The back room manager on duty peered through the window, smiled, and let Jake in.

Jake bought his usual coffee, turkey pot pies, cereal, diet pop, eggs, soup, crackers, and a few other miscellaneous items. As he shopped, he pondered the day. What more could be crammed in it? He looked forward to getting back home, wrestling with Champ, and maybe writing in his journal to help crystallize his thoughts. Jake paid at the front of the store, then turned and headed to the back again, a plastic grocery bag in each hand. Congratulating his good fortune in avoiding the zoo of the front parking lot, he stepped out the back door, pausing a moment to introduce his eyes to the darkness, then slowly stepped down the stairs.

Without warning he noticed out of the corner of his eye a shadowy image, eerily like the Statue of Liberty. He felt a stunning blow to the back of his neck. As he crumpled to the asphalt, he heard the crash of soup cans and the cracking of eggs. He turned his face toward the source of the blow, the back of his head still on the ground. Jake looked up at his stocky assailant who appeared, as best he could tell in the shadows, to be wearing a ski-mask.

The man's strong arms raised something over his head again, something long and thick—it appeared to be a baseball bat. The apparent target was Jake's head, which lay vulnerable on the bare asphalt. Jake braced himself, but the man seemed in no rush to finish him off, giving him time to think, *I'm going to die.* And then a corollary. *But I'm not ready.*

Why was his attacker hesitating? Each second allowed Jake time to regain his wits. His neck and shoulders throbbing, he lay perfectly still, to give no hint there was any fight left in him. He readied himself to move his head out of the bat's path, which seemed now more like an executioner's ax, the ski mask being the modern equivalent to the medieval executioner's black hood. Jake visualized catching the attacker off balance, then rolling toward his legs and tripping him to the ground where he would take him on in a fair fight, one he could hope to win. The bat was poised for what seemed an eternity. Did the masked man have second thoughts? Or was he savoring the smell of murder as he might a fresh cup of coffee before drinking? Suddenly the thick arms, fully extended, tilted slightly back and the broad chest inhaled. The ax was about to fall. Jake tensed, knowing that making his move—if indeed he *could* move—too fast or too slow would be equally deadly.

The surface between the assailant's feet and Jake's head suddenly exploded like a Claymore mine, followed by a rush of deafening sound. Jake instinctively closed his eyes and covered his face with his hands. He felt sharp edges of splintered asphalt cutting into his exposed flesh.

When he opened his eyes, ears still ringing from the explosion, he saw the stocky man running, like a panicked animal, still clinging to his bat, flailing away at his side. In a moment the darkness swallowed the shadowy figure, and the two became one.

Suddenly another figure was at his side. A hand reached down and pulled him up, rougher than he could have wished. Jake's head swam. He saw a hand only a foot from his face. The hand held a gun, pointing into the darkness. It was a huge piece, a .44 Magnum.

"You okay, Woods?"

"What?" The voice seemed familiar. "Mayhew?"

Jake was confused a moment, then realized he was still being followed by the FBI. Agent Mayhew had drawn duty.

"I could have nailed the creep on the dead run, but the Bureau frowns on shooting people in the back, even when they've tried to waste somebody. You're lucky I was on your tail, Woods."

"Yeah. Thanks, Mayhew. I really mean it. I owe you." Jake felt a little guilty for his previous hostility toward Mayhew and Sutter and the Feds.

Mayhew seemed uncomfortable with the whole thing and obviously wasn't as trained in aiding victims in crisis as he was at using his gun. "Want a ride home? Need to go to the hospital?"

Jake moved his neck around, feeling the back of his shoulders with his hands. "No. A hot shower sounds good though. Maybe you could help me pick up my groceries?"

"Yeah, sure." Mayhew looked painfully out of place collecting dented soup cans and sorting out cracked eggs from uncracked, but seemed to be a good sport about the whole thing.

Once Jake and his groceries were in his car, Mayhew said, "I'll follow you home."

Jake drove home very slowly, applying the brakes quickly with every shifting shadow. It embarrassed him, knowing Mayhew saw how edgy he was. After parking his car in the apartment lot, he waved and nodded thanks to Mayhew and headed inside. He knew Janet would have insisted he go to the hospital, but that wasn't Jake's style. Janet—what made him think of her again?

As Jake turned the key in the lock he noticed Mayhew, across the street, settle in to the front seat of his car just like it was his living room. The night was hopefully over for Jake, but Mayhew was still on duty, watching over him sleeplessly.

Not exactly my image of a guardian angel. But Jake had to admit he'd been a little hard on Mayhew. Sure, he was no Rhodes scholar, and wasn't Mr. Congeniality, but he'd just saved his life. For the first time, this "invasion of privacy" seemed a very welcome and comforting presence.

After he picked out a dozen slivers of asphalt from his hands and face, Jake took off his pants and shirt, still damp from being laid flat in the parking lot, and stepped into the shower. He let the stream of hot water pound on his neck and upper back, turning up the knob for maximum water pressure and losing himself in the steamy deluge.

After drying off, Jake searched through drawers and cabinets for some kind of soothing ointment to rub into his neck. If Janet were here she'd know what to use and exactly where to find it. Finally he gave up looking, put on old sweatpants and a sweatshirt, and sat quietly in the muted darkness of his living room.

Was death a door or a hole? He'd come perilously close to finding out just an hour ago. He felt more determined than ever to solve the mystery of his friends' deaths. He wondered if death resented this intrusion on its domain and might claim him before he found the answer.

Jake went to his bedroom closet. He got up on his tiptoes and reached to the far left back of the shelf above his hanging clothes. He found it. The Walther P38, a World War II trophy his father had brought back from Europe. Then he went over to his dresser and reached into the top drawer. He pulled out the black five-inch-long metal clip, looking through the round holes in the side to see it had three bullets. He started to shove the clip into the Walther, then stopped, reaching back into the dresser drawer to fetch a little cloth sack. He dumped out the bullets on the bed. They were gold shelled and bronze capped. They looked dull and old. They were. He picked one up and squinted to read the "43" engraved across from the "9MM." Jake soberly contemplated the history he held in his hands. These bullets had come with the gun, made in Nazi Germany in 1938, when it replaced the Luger as the standard Nazi sidearm.

When Jake would take the Walther on hunting trips with Doc and Finney, he'd always shoot new 9MM shells, throwing in just a couple of the old '43 bullets, saving the other few dozen as precious relics. He'd shot off the last of his new rounds, so all he had now was this sack of antiques. But not one of the dozen he'd fired over the years had failed. Fifty-year-old ammo that could still fire. Legendary German craftsmanship. He looked closely at the gun, cocking it, examining the chamber, the barrel, pulling back the hammer. He detected the faint scent of gunpowder buried beneath the strong smell of metal coated with WD-40, with which he'd cleaned the gun after using it on a hunting trip—the last of its kind with his friends, it occurred to him.

He broke down the gun, made sure all parts were clean and well oiled. He moved it back and forth from one hand to another, refamiliarizing himself with it, as he might a tennis racquet he hadn't held for a long time. Then he pointed at the center of the bed and dry fired, squeezing the trigger and imagining the water bed's explosion if a bullet had been in the chamber. He remembered the countless dozens of plastic pop bottles he and Doc and Finney had filled with water, then wasted in target practice on those hunting trips. Doc had joked that if the three of them were ever attacked by two-liter pop bottles filled with water, the bottles wouldn't stand a chance.

Carefully and methodically, Jake loaded five more bullets into the clip, making eight total, then shoved it up into the Walther. It glided smoothly into place. He hesitated, then after a moment's thought pulled back the chamber, loading the first bullet. He positioned the safety, then studied the gun again, wondering as he often had about the man it had been issued to. Who was he? Did he understand what the Third Reich was about? Had he sincerely bought into what had once appeared a virtuous social vision that had originated, and finally culminated, in the very pit of hell? How many civilians had been threatened by this gun? How many ruthlessly killed? Had the soldier who carried it unloaded the trains at Auschwitz? Was his uniform soiled by the human ashes that fell like snowflakes? Did he escort women and children into the chambers of the Nazi doctors, who in the name of medicine committed such unspeakable crimes against humanity? Did he go home to his own wife and children, leading a "normal" life and denying his complicity in an evil that murdered children and women and old people?

Where was the man whose gun this had been? A young soldier then could still be alive now. And even if he'd died, the question remained unanswered. *Where is he now?*

The throbbing pain in Jake's neck reminded him the stakes had been raised. He wasn't merely an object of someone's curiosity. He was in someone's way. He would have to be ready. Mayhew and Sutter couldn't always be there for him. He would have to defend himself.

He placed the gun carefully on the floor next to the right side of his bed, the side he still slept on as a matter of habit, though Janet had not been on its other side for nearly four years. He turned out the lights.

Suddenly Jake reached down to the floor, grabbed the gun, flicked off the safety with his thumb, and pointed the barrel toward the open door of his room.

He repeated the drill three more times, until satisfied. Then he tried to sleep.

CHAPTER TWENTY

Ollie's message on Jake's home answering machine had asked him to call him at his office around 6:00 the next morning. It was 6:02 now, and Jake dialed the special number that bypassed the precinct switchboard. He was stiff and sore, but knew he couldn't tell Ollie what had happened last night without bringing in Mayhew and the FBI.

"Ollie's Sub Sandwiches. Our special today is the *Tribune*. It's 100 percent bologna. How may I help you?"

"For starters, you can tell me what you're doing there so early."

"It's been a zoo, Jake. The body count's incredible. Street gangs are at it again, and we got a couple of weird yuppie killings yesterday, no robbery or anything. We've had a rash of those lately. Some of them are hooked up at the hospital, but they're brain dead. It's pathetic. The city's going to hell in a hand basket. I'm considering retiring. Maybe take up the easy life, write a crime column or something."

"Yeah, right. You'd really fit in at the *Trib*, Ollie."

"Well, I'll probably get sent to another murder scene before lunch, so I'll make this quick. I interviewed the two anti-abortion guys, you know, the names you gave me? Don't think there's anything there. One of them's a few sandwiches short of a picnic, but I think he's harmless. I got my eye on them, but I'd be surprised if either had any connection to the murder. There's still some doctors low on our list I haven't contacted. Frankly, I don't think I could get to them for a couple of weeks. I mean, I'm still on the case, but I can't put it over all these fresh cases that keep getting thrown on me. Just wanted to shoot straight with you. I'm giving it all the time I can, but things are crazy right now."

"I understand, Ollie. Can I help?"

"I don't know. Maybe contact a few of these doctors on the list? Let's see. There's Marsdon. Maybe Simpson, although he's low priority. You're still checking out the angry husband angle, right?"

"Yeah, but it hasn't amounted to anything. Some guys who could have gotten mad, sure, but no one I could picture doing this."

"But somebody did do it, Jake. And we'll find him. If I could just get the rest of the killers to take a few weeks off, we might find him a lot sooner."

Sue Keels waited in line on the ramp leading to the 747, her carry-on slung over her left shoulder, while her right arm awkwardly held up her boarding pass and struggled with the heavier-than-usual purse that dangled from her elbow. Every time she put down her carry-on the line moved another twelve inches, so she moved with it just to prove she was awake. She shuffled forward, staring at the boarding pass again, still not understanding why the agent rewrote her ticket.

Angela had dropped her off at the airport. She reassured Sue she'd pick up Little Finn from school and he'd have a blast staying with her and Bruce while Sue was gone. Since Finney left, Angie had become an even closer friend, more like a peer than ever before. How she wished Finney could witness Angie's pregnancy. Their first grandchild. Finney would have been so proud. Sue's eyes misted up.

"Hello," the flight attendant greeted her warmly, looked at her boarding pass and said, "4A—to your left, ma'am. Up here."

"But...that's first class, isn't it?"

"Yes, ma'am. This is a first-class ticket."

"But I bought the cheapest fare there was."

"Well, somebody must like you. If I were you I wouldn't make a fuss about it!"

"I guess not. I've never flown first class before."

"Well, a 747's the place to start. You'll love it."

Sue wandered into the cavernous first class, looking this way and that as if she'd crept into the holy of holies and some offended inhabitant of this sanctuary might chase her out or strike her dead. She tentatively sat down in 4A, then stretched out her legs till she was almost horizontal, giggling because she still couldn't touch the back of the seat in front of her. Two flight attendants appeared, offering her juice and snacks and magazines and pillows and blankets and things she didn't know airplanes carried.

Sue still couldn't figure it out, but she knew enough to say, *Thank you, Lord!* In a funny sort of way she wondered if Finney had pulled some strings for her from up above, just to tell her he approved of her getting away.

As the long line of commoners trudged back into coach, Sue felt like royalty, walking to the base of the spiral staircase leading to the upper deck of the 747. Seeing her gazing up with childlike wonder, the flight attendant smiled and said, "You're welcome to climb up and take a look." She did. It was amazing, this compartment. It reminded her of her secret space in the attic where she had kept her dolls, and her friends gathered. *Little Finn would love this,* she thought. And thinking of how delighted he would be with it made it seem all the more delightful to her. Being around one of the special ones, like Finn, made you see how special life was. The unexpected little things such as...somehow ending up in first class!

Sue climbed back down and settled into her seat, which was really a nicely padded recliner. She popped the footrest in and out, decided she could easily sleep up here but wouldn't want to. It was too much fun. She wished the nearly five-hour flight was even longer. She closed her eyes and enjoyed the light air blowing on her face.

Sue was still sprawled out like a junior high girl at a slumber party when suddenly, standing by the seat next to her, a gruff voice barked, "Madam! No slouching on the seats!"

Startled and embarrassed, Sue straightened up, expecting to see the pilot. What she saw took her totally off guard.

"Jake! What in the world?"

Jake smiled broadly. "You didn't think I was going to let you fly all the way to New York by yourself, did you?"

"Jake, what's going on? Why...?"

"I've had this trip on the calendar for months. Going back to New York for a journalism conference and to see an old friend, my mentor. Ever told you about Leonard? Anyway, at your house when you said you were leaving eight o'clock Thursday for New York, I knew we were on the same flight."

"But how did you...?"

"Well, I don't usually fly first class. But I've got a stack of frequent flyer coupons, and you can use them to upgrade. I had enough for both of us, so I called and had them change your ticket, but told them to surprise you. I guess it worked, huh?"

"It sure did!"

Sue threw her arms around Jake, with all the warmth of an adoring sister. For a moment it made Jake wish he'd had a sister, though somehow he doubted she would have adored him. He cringed from the pain in his neck and shoulders, which were still tender from the supermarket mugging. He hoped Sue hadn't noticed.

"Jake, that was so thoughtful of you. And the best part is just having time with you. We can catch up!"

"I saw Angie in the terminal and told her all about this. She screeched and giggled and hugged me, the whole nine yards. You'd think she was your clone!"

Excited, Sue chattered on and on. She told him how she and Janet had a slumber party with Betsy, wearing pajamas, eating popcorn, and watching old movies. Betsy was having a rough time, and they'd tried to cheer her. Jake couldn't imagine Betsy having better friends than Sue and Janet.

After they'd settled in and chatted awhile, and Jake thought the last passengers had boarded, a large sixtyish man in an expensive dark blue suit made his way to 3C, the aisle seat across from Jake and one row up. Accompanied by an attractive short-haired woman, dressed in a snazzy business suit, he walked with a self-important swagger. He took off his suit coat and handed it to the flight attendant as if she were his personal valet, then perused first class like a man who expected to be recognized, and who wanted to see if anyone of any importance would be traveling with him. No one registered until his eyes fell on Jake.

"Jake Woods? The columnist?"

Jake looked up from the *Sports Illustrated* he'd just opened, then groaned inwardly.

"Good morning, Senator. How are you?"

Senator Rupert Colby. Chairman of the Ethics Committee. A legend in his own mind. He'd never forget how impressed the senator had been with himself when he last interviewed him a few years ago.

"Connie, this is Jake Woods of the *Tribune*. Jake, this is my lovely assistant, Connie Lang."

"Nice to meet you, Ms. Lang. This is my good friend, Sue Keels. We happened to end up on the same flight."

The senator winked at Jake. "A happy coincidence, I'm sure." He looked at Sue, admiring her in a way that irritated Jake, as a big brother is irritated when someone looks at his little sister as though she were a piece of meat.

"A lovely traveling companion, Ms. Keels. Mr. Woods is a fortunate man." The senator turned and looked at Connie, seated next to him, and grinned slyly at Jake, "As am I."

The senator beckoned for a flight attendant, with a hint of annoyance that he'd been seated all of thirty seconds and hadn't yet been served a cocktail. The flight attendant, thirty and attractive, with a Barbie-like neatness and precision, responded immediately.

"What can I do for you, sir?"

"Several things come to mind, darling, but a Bloody Mary will do for starters." The senator's eyes wandered all over the woman.

Don't you know the rules have changed, Senator? You want a sexual harassment lawsuit? It occurred to Jake that the senator just didn't get it, that he saw himself as a real charmer the ladies just loved.

Jake had to smile at what was brewing there in the intimacy of first class. Without even looking at Sue he knew she was thoroughly unimpressed with the senior senator. After a bit of small talk and a smooth take off, Jake settled back to some casual conversation. He usually read nonstop on flights, often pulling out his notebook computer to work on a column. But he really enjoyed talking with Sue. In an eerie sort of way, it was like talking to Finney. The two of them were like one, so in tune with each other, and since Finney's death Jake felt to be around Sue was somehow to be around Finney. Not so with Doc and Betsy. Their lives just didn't have that connection. Much as Betsy loved Doc, there didn't seem much of him in her.

There was something else Jake liked about being with Sue. In the last three years he'd had some flings with women, but never the unique dimension of friendship with the other half of the race, friendship unthreatened by romance and therefore devoid of scheming and manipulating and hurt feelings. He enjoyed that kind of friendship.

Jake stood up and looked out the windows of the airplane, as if somehow it would allow him to see everything in perspective. A few days away might let him get a fresh jump on the investigation. What was he missing? Or Ollie? Or Sutter? It was so aggravating not to be able to put all their heads together. He sat quietly, going over and over the raw information as if it might suddenly come together as in the last ten minutes of a mystery movie, and he could say "of course" and get the bad guys once and for all. But did real life ever end in such a satisfying way?

After twenty minutes of being further spoiled with first-class service, Senator Colby turned in his spacious seat, which he filled to overflowing. Jake noticed. *The prima donna is about to speak.*

In a bombastic voice he said, "So, Jake, still putting the right wingers in their place, I see!" He chortled as if this were the cleverest thing people had heard all day.

"Uh, yeah, sometimes, I guess." This was just the sort of praise Jake didn't want right here and now. He wished he was on the other side of Sue so he could see her reaction without having to turn and look. It was profoundly uncomfortable sitting between her and the senator, like being trapped between the front lines of two armies in which the slightest flinch would trigger the inevitable skirmish. He had the distinct feeling shots were going to be whizzing by his head, and he wished he could dig a trench and get low.

"Don't be modest. You nail those bigots with the best of them."

"Well, I try to be fair."

"Fair? If they had their way they'd put the cause of women back a century. Well, we're not going to let them do that in the senate!" Colby looked around first class as if he were stumping for his campaign and expected some applause.

"Senator." Sue's voice was sweet, but Jake cringed because he didn't have to guess where she was going to take this.

"Yes, ma'am. Sue, wasn't it?"

"Yes, Senator."

"Call me Rupert, ma'am. I'd be honored if such a pretty thing as you would call me Rupert."

"Senator, what do you mean about putting the cause of women back a century?"

"I suppose primarily, of course, I mean the abortion issue."

"Well, were you aware Senator that all the pioneer feminists, including Susan B. Anthony, were totally opposed to abortion? That they regarded it as the killing of innocent children and completely degrading to women?"

"Well, I doubt they thought of it in those terms..."

"But they did, Senator. It's a fact. I've read their writings. That's exactly what they thought. Their solution to the abortion problem was to offer women support and alternatives so children could be saved. So, I'm wondering, why did you vote for the legislation that would effectively put Crisis Pregnancy Centers out of business?"

"Well, because...they're just thinly disguised right-to-life organizations."

"Have you ever visited one, seen first hand how it operates? Talked to the staff members and volunteers? Talked to the women who've gotten help and assistance and love and guidance from these centers?"

"Well, I'm a busy man, Sue. I don't have time to go check out everything first hand. But I've been fully briefed on their activities."

"By whom?"

"Well, I've received information from Planned Parenthood and the National Organization of Women, among others."

"Yes, that's what I thought. Senator, I *have* seen these centers. I've volunteered in one, gone through the training, met with lots of desperate women we've been able to help. I could make some phone calls, ask around, and with their permission I could easily give you the names of dozens and dozens of grateful women who were helped immensely at Crisis Pregnancy Centers and Birthrights and all sorts of similar organizations. Would you like me to give you a list so you could get some first-hand knowledge?"

"Well, you can send me a list, of course, but I have to honestly tell you I'm very busy, and I trust my sources on these centers, even if you don't."

"Surely you know Planned Parenthood is the largest abortion provider in this country. They make huge amounts of money from performing abortions. Obviously, they're not going to be objective about other groups. The Crisis Pregnancy Centers offer counseling, classes, financial support, blankets and cribs, adoption information. The unborn are the poorest, weakest, and most vulnerable people in society. I don't understand how anyone with a conscience could oppose women being offered the choice of bringing those children into the world."

"I would remind you, ma'am, that my party has always stood for the rights of the poor and needy, and—"

"And I would remind you, sir, that your party was the party of slavery. It patronized the poor and said the slaves were better off in bondage. And now you make it sound like unborn children are better off dead. You've got two million families wanting to adopt, and yet you want children eliminated, and then you turn around and pretend you're being virtuous and compassionate."

Whew! It was vintage Sue.

"Planned Parenthood's motto is my motto—'Every child a wanted child.'"

"Oh, I agree. Every child a wanted child. Now how would you finish the sentence?"

"Excuse me?"

"Every child a wanted child...so what?"

"I'm not sure I follow you."

"Okay, here's how I finish the sentence.'Every child a wanted child, so let's learn to want children more. And let's work to promote adoption and cut through the red tape so we can get children into the hands of all the people wanting to adopt, people who very much want these children. Now, how do you finish the sentence?"

"Well, I'm not sure that I..."

"All right, then I'll finish it for you. 'Every child a wanted child, so let's identify those who may not be wanted and kill them before they're born.' If you were honest, Senator, your slogan really means, 'Every unwanted child a dead child.'"

Jake looked at Sue, not sure whether this was audacity or raw courage. She reminded him so much of Finney in his confrontations with Doc.

"I've never said any such thing."

"Of course, you don't say it. You use nice-sounding words, but it doesn't change the reality. For instance, I've heard you say you want abortion to be rare, that abortion is a heart-wrenching decision. My question is, why? What's wrong with abortion?"

The senator looked surprised, as though he'd never been asked that question. "Well, it's...it's not a pleasant thing, and it's a difficult decision for a woman to have to make."

"What's so unpleasant about it, Senator? If it's just a blob of tissue, like a cancer or something, a woman should be glad to get rid of it. Why is it such a difficult decision? I mean, if your appendix or a kidney stone or something is making your life miserable, you just have it removed, get rid of it. It's not a difficult decision at all."

"Well, it's not the same thing really."

"What's different about it?"

"Well, when it's your own child..." The moment the senator said it, Jake could tell he wished he hadn't.

"Exactly, Senator. That's the whole point, isn't it? The truth is, what makes abortion so difficult is it takes an innocent human life. The only good reason I can think of for abortion being a heart-wrenching decision, for wanting it to be rare, is exactly the same reason why any one with a conscience should oppose anyone having an abortion—it kills an innocent child."

"Well, that's how you see it, but—"

"Senator, think about it. Listen to yourself. You know it's true. You're the one who said it's different, that it's a woman's own child."

"Perhaps I said it wrong."

"No, you said it right. That's what I don't understand. You sit on the senate ethics committee, yet you stand on the wrong side of the greatest ethical issue of our time."

The senator bristled. "You're not being rational here. I think it's clear we're getting nowhere. I don't think you'd be so self-righteous and judgmental if you'd been raped or forced to give birth to some deformed child who'd be better off never coming into the world."

"You mean, like a Down's Syndrome child?"

"Yes, exactly. It's easy for people who haven't been there to impose their value judgments on everyone else."

Colby, you're a dead man, Jake thought, with a certain amount of pleasure.

"I do have a Down's Syndrome child, Senator. I wish he was here so you could meet him. He and his friends are precious and delighted to be alive. It's not easy raising a handicapped child. He requires extra attention and effort. When he was born the doctor said, 'I'm sorry,' like we hadn't had a real baby or something. It was hard on us, I don't deny it, but when they wrapped him in the blanket and handed him to my husband, he looked in our baby's eyes and smiled ear to ear, and he put him up close to me. And do you know what my husband said to me, Senator? He said, 'This one will need our love even more than the others.'" Sue choked a little as she said it.

Jake remembered Finn's birth and how touched he'd been at Finney and Sue's response to what to him had seemed such a tragedy.

"We believed that not only were we what our son needed, he was just what we needed, and God had a reason for bringing us together. We've met many families who've drawn together and found joy and strength in having a child with mental and physical handicaps. I've checked around, and you might be interested in knowing there's not a single organization of parents of mentally retarded children that has ever endorsed abortion."

"Well, that might be, but you still need to understand that—"

"What you need to understand is that a handicapped child is still a child. Look at the telethons, the March of Dimes, the United Way ads. We sponsor the Special Olympics and cheer on the Down's Syndrome competitors. We talk about the joy and inspiration they bring us. Then what do we do when we hear a woman is carrying one of these very children? We say 'kill it before it's born.' Most people think there's something wrong with my son. Well, I don't expect you to understand this, but I can tell you there's something very right about him. The truth is, something is wrong with us, Senator. Badly wrong."

"Well, I can see we're not going to resolve this issue on the plane." The senator started to turn back around, when his assistant popped her head over the padded headrest.

"Look, the senator is a widely respected women's rights advocate, and he deserves your thanks, not your accusations."

"A women's rights advocate? I've noticed how he looks at you, how he leers at the stewardess, how he flirts with women."

Shut up, Sue.

"I wonder what kind of respect that shows for his wife? You do remember your wife, Senator, the mother of your children? The one you pose with in the campaign pictures?"

The senator turned red, then pale, and suddenly noticed that every person in first class had put down his reading material. Even the flight attendants were watching and listening to every word.

"Let me tell you both something. My husband died six weeks ago. He was one of those prolife men you'd accuse of being anti-women. Well, he treated me and every other woman he knew with dignity and respect. And he gave his time and his money to help them, to give them other choices besides killing their babies. He didn't flirt with them, sleep around with them, then give them three hundred dollars for an abortion like you probably would, Senator. And you have the audacity to sit there and say he didn't respect women and you do? Well, you may be fooling yourself and your aid and a lot of the voters and the *Tribune* and everybody else, but you're not fooling me!"

Sue grabbed the in-flight magazine and glared at it, like Supergirl using her x-ray vision. Hot tears flowed down her cheeks.

All of first class sat stunned and silent.

Almost a minute went by before Jake dared to look over at Sue. A few seconds later he leaned over and whispered gently, "Your magazine's upside down."

Sue looked, and sure enough it was. With an embarrassed giggle, she turned it right side up.

"Sorry, Jake. I lost my temper."

"I noticed."

"Why are we whispering?"

"Let's keep whispering, Sue." Jake was barely audible. "I think it will make a more pleasant trip for everyone."

"I really am sorry, Jake. Here you get me in first class and I pick a fight with a senator. Please forgive me."

"Don't apologize. I don't ever remember seeing the senator foam at the mouth and wet his pants in the same conversation." Jake chuckled, and Sue turned various shades of red.

The flight attendant, the one the senator had made the suggestive comment to, came over to Sue.

"Can I get you anything ma'am? Here's some extra peanuts, a champagne, a few chocolates."

She'd gone through the store of goodies and brought one of everything to Sue. Without asking, she filled a champagne glass and gave it to Sue, who accepted it with thanks.

"Anything you want, ma'am. Really," the flight attendant continued, in a whisper. "We all appreciate what you just did. He's a jerk. Besides," she winked at her, "it was a lot better than any in-flight movie we've ever had."

Zyor led Finney into a great hall that opened into an expansive meadow. It was disorienting, because the hall, gigantic as it had appeared on the outside, was only a fraction the size of the meadow within. And before he had entered, behind the hall he'd seen a landscape much different than what he saw now. Like many of heaven's doors, it seemed to lead to a world of its own, a world within a world.

Thousands were gathering here, looking toward someone who was speaking. Whenever he paused in his speech, as if for a translation, little discussions broke out everywhere. Those of Michael's race answered the questions of heaven's students, Finney among them. Finney noticed many in the crowd were heaven's young children, like himself. Once explanations were made, attention went back to the one up front like iron filings drawn to a magnet, and he resumed speaking as if there had been no interruption.

There was no rudeness to these midcourse discussions. On the contrary, it was the intense interest in every word of the speaker that prompted them. Finney remembered the two distinctly different kinds of whispers in school classes. One kind was born of boredom and disinterest, where students sought escape from what the instructor was saying. But the other was born of profound interest, which compelled a student to comment to his fellow students or to ask clarifying questions.

Here no one asked the dutiful question, "Will this be on the quiz?" Everyone listened because he wanted to learn. What flowed from the speaker was fresh water to a thirsty mind. Finney was again exhilarated by his vastly improved ability to retain, yet challenged that every new thing in this lecture seemed eminently significant and worthy of retaining.

Finney was engrossed in the speaker's words, which seemed a direct extension of his life. This one had the wisdom of a thousand mentors. Finney was inexplicably drawn to him and kept asking himself who he was. His face seemed almost a hybrid of child's face and angel's face. Why was this face so familiar? Finney gasped.

He knew this face! It was the face of Little Finn! But Finn was still back on earth. And yet...

Of course, Finney thought. It was his face, the pure delighted face of what was called on earth the Down's Syndrome child. This professor around whom gathered the students of heaven, some of them once professors on earth, was a Down's child, rather a man with the enduring qualities of a child. How had he obtained such wisdom and eloquence? Was it from his long residence here in Elyon's world? From an intimate acquaintance with Elyon that preceded his entrance to this world? Finney theorized he might even be part of a unique order of being, a special strain of Adam's race. Not a genetic accident, inferior to the norm, but one challenged in some conventional senses yet in profound and invisible ways superior to the norm.

He listened as the man, this eternally young man, spoke. Even the texture of his voice reminded him of Little Finn, and Finney marveled at his words:

"When our Lord Christ walked in the dark world, we are told 'People were also bringing babies to Jesus to have him touch them. When the disciples saw this, they rebuked them. But Jesus called the children to him and said, 'Let the little children come to me, and do not hinder them, for the kingdom of God belongs to such as these. I tell you the truth, anyone who will not receive the kingdom of God like a little child will never enter it.'

"Again, Christ said, 'I tell you the truth, unless you change and become like little children, you will never enter the kingdom of heaven. Therefore, whoever humbles himself like this child is the greatest in the kingdom of heaven. And whoever welcomes a little child like this in my name welcomes me. But if anyone causes one of these little ones who believe in me to sin, it would be better for him to have a large millstone hung around his neck and to be drowned in the depths of the sea.'

"On another occasion, we are told, 'He took a little child and had him stand among them. Taking him in his arms, he said to them, 'Whoever welcomes this little child in my name welcomes me; and whoever welcomes me welcomes the one who sent me. For he who is least among you all—he is the greatest.'

"To those who wanted to silence the praise of children, Jesus responded, 'Have you never read, "From the lips of children and infants you have ordained praise"?' Again, Jesus said, 'I praise you, Father, Lord of heaven and earth, because you have hidden these things from the wise and learned, and revealed them to little children.'"

The young man surveyed the audience and seemed to achieve the impossible by establishing eye contact with all the thousands at once.

"I who stand before you today, and all those of my kind, are testimonies to the truth written in still another place: 'But God chose the foolish things of the world to shame the wise; God chose the weak things of the world to shame the strong.'"

Finney found himself wondering if Little Finn would someday occupy this role of teacher in the new world, and if he would have the privilege of sitting at his son's feet. The thought caused his spine to tingle, and even as he wondered it, he knew the answer would be yes. Finney listened in rapt attention as the young man moved on to develop the favorite theme of heaven:

"Elyon's Son is Alpha and Omega, beginning and end. As he was at the beginning, so he is now, and at what men call the end, so he will yet be. He sees that coming end as one more beginning, the beginning of a new world. It will be built on the foundation of his character, defined by the cornerstone of his grace. It has been conceived by the master Architect, drawn out with the meticulous pen of the great Engineer, and will be constructed with the skilled hands of the Builder. The hands, pure and strong, the hands scarred for eternity, the hands of the Carpenter."

The child's voice became more powerful with every sentence, his angelic face racked with synchronous joy and pain, the latter at the reference to the scarred hands.

"The Carpenter of Nazareth, building the house of faith, joining with the mortar of heaven apostles and prophets, fishermen and seamstresses, farmers and shepherds, bricklayers and teachers, businessmen, homemakers, and nurses."

Finney felt he was beholding the beauty of a great river, watching the current and its white caps highlighting rocks and fallen trees buried beneath. But now there was a change, for he had fallen in the river, was caught up in the current, surrounded by the rushing sounds of moving water, dragging him pell-mell down the rapids. Thrown into the currents of a divine and awful momentum, he felt one part of what he once knew as consuming fear—the exhilaration of being lost in something far greater than himself, the feeling at the top of the roller coaster, about to fall into the abyss. Yet he did not feel the other part of consuming fear, the loathing of the horrors of destruction. Only after adjusting to the flow of the current, Finney could again evaluate what he was not simply watching, but was now a full-fledged participant in.

This child had been "handicapped" in the other world. Handicapped and unable to deal with life in conventional ways. He could never make much money, never hope to be *Time* magazine's Man of the Year. The majority, on knowing what he was, would elect to take his life before he was born, or let him die of neglect afterwards. But here in Elyon's realm his value was so obvious it showed such thoughts to be unspeakably evil, unthinkable to the sane mind.

On earth he would not qualify for a seat on the orchestra. But here and now, he was the conductor, surrounded by rapt and attentive musicians, ready to do his bidding. Finney could see the coat and tails, the flying hands and baton. He felt the line between audience and orchestra blur until there was no audience now, only orchestra, conductor, music. Melodies and harmonies. And yet, there was an audience. An audience so great and all encompassing that Finney had been no more aware of it a moment before than a fish is aware of water. But the conductor was intensely aware of the audience and bent upon finding approval in its eyes.

Feverishly, Finney played his instrument. What it was he could not say, though it seemed as much like him as his ear-to-ear smile. He could hear it now, its sounds blending into the whole. One member would solo, and then another, and then the power of the whole dominated again. The attention of the orchestra was always on the piece, at once carefully composed and directed with discipline, yet wonderfully free and spontaneous. He sensed this piece of music had been played countless thousands or millions of times, yet never like this, and therefore never before. Finney soloed now, the orchestra creating a splendid and dazzling background to the focused and inspired rendition of his singular part.

There *was* an audience. It was the Audience of One. And the sense of his approval swept through the orchestra and its delighted childlike conductor in a profound sense of joy and completion. The orchestra played on. The Master was pleased. And for the moment, and for ever, that was all that mattered.

CHAPTER TWENTY-ONE

J ake crammed his verbal foot in the door of the clinic, first with the reception-ist, then a nurse, in an attempt to get the doctor on the phone. In shameless journalistic fashion (actually, it was a honed skill he took pride in), he'd used everything from "urgent" to "I'm calling from New York" to "it's a highly confidential official matter." He'd been on hold five minutes.

"Marsdon here. This better be good, Mr. Woods."

"Yes, Dr. Marsdon. Thanks for talking to me. I'm calling from New York and—"

"I don't care if you're calling from the Sistine Chapel. What's this about? I've got patients waiting."

"It's about Dr. Greg Lowell. There's an investigation into his death."

Marsdon paused. "If I talk to anyone, it wouldn't be a reporter."

"This isn't for publication. I'm assisting Police Detective Ollie Chandler in his investigation." Jake knew the detective department brass wouldn't appreciate his self-promotion to assistant detective, but desperate times called for desperate mea-sures.

"A reporter assisting the police?" Marsdon asked skeptically. "How about I just call your Detective Chandler and ask him?"

"Good idea. He'll vouch for me. Look, I fly home tonight. If I come by your clinic tomorrow afternoon, is there a chance I can grab you for half an hour?"

Marsdon laughed. "Oh sure, I've got plenty of time."

Jake felt as if he were about to lose a fish he'd expected to reel in. Finally Marsdon sighed and said, "Okay, Woods, I'll call Detective Chandler and see if this is for real. If so, I'll try to squeeze you in between patients, sometime after 2:00. You'll get fifteen minutes max. Bring something to read. Could be a long wait."

"Thanks, doctor, I really appreciate your..." Jake stopped self-consciously when he realized there was no one on the other end of the line.

Jake checked his watch, cursing to himself because he had so little time. He rushed to catch a cab over to 43rd Street, to the *New York Times* building. He need-ed perspective and in that building was a man he'd gone to for perspective for the past twenty years.

A half dozen different newspapers, all today's, were strewn across an eight-foot counter that served no other purpose. Next to the *New York Times,* Jake saw the *New York Daily News* and the *Wall Street Journal,* three out of the five U.S. papers with circulations over a million. They were joined by *Newsday* and the *New York Post,* themselves reaching over a half million. New York was the center of American journalism, the fountainhead from which a nation's information and worldview flowed. *The Washington Post* distinguished itself as the only "outside" publication on the counter. Several of the papers had been marked with heavy red lines and circles, while two others had headlines and opening paragraphs highlighted in yellow.

The room was cluttered, yet suggested its own peculiar order if the observer understood the master of the place, Cornelius Leonard. Jake talked to his old mentor on the phone at least once a month, but it had been two years since he'd been in Leonard's New York office. He felt like an eager devotee who'd been too long away from a holy place. He drank in every sight, sound, and smell of Leonard's inner sanctum.

The slow burn of the cigar in the transparent ashtray left a vapor permeating the room. The gray-haired codger nodding and occasionally barking into the telephone looked maybe sixty, but Jake knew he had to be seventy-five. He appeared almost ordinary, even a little quaint with his retirement-center-vintage, open-collared white shirt and red suspenders, but he was anything but ordinary. He was one of the last, and one of the best, of a dying breed—a crusty, fearless, investigative journalist devoted to the pursuit of the truth, no matter who it incriminated and who it exonerated. His investigations had brought down whole families of organized crime, and he had lived to tell the story

Leonard had been hated, maligned, and feared by the powerful. In the back of his top file drawer he still kept two files, both bulging, marked simply "Death Threats." Once his hair grayed, he'd been promoted to a sort of journalism hall of fame, and even many who had suffered at the hands of his printed words gave him begrudging respect, as pitchers who hated Babe Ruth years later bragged they had faced him from the mound.

Leonard's secretary let Jake in while the master was still on the phone. Leonard gestured, indicating Jake should make himself at home. The invitation to browse was more welcome here than anywhere. Leonard's walls were lined with framed exposés and stories, most of them front pagers. Many had been picked up by other major dailies, so among his trophies were feature stories in the *Washington Post, Boston Globe, Chicago Tribune, Los Angeles Times,* and *Miami Herald.* His stories had broken into magazines ranging from *Atlantic Monthly,* to the *New Yorker,* to *Life, Look,* the *Saturday Evening Post,* the *Village Voice, Rolling Stone,* and *Lady's Home Journal.* He'd never come to them, hat in hand, like most writers. They came to him, all of them. But none of his magazine articles found a place on his wall. When Jake once asked him why, his simple answer summed up the man himself— "They're not newspapers. I'm a newspaper man. Always have been, always will be. I don't care much about anything else."

Jake looked reverently at Leonard's impossibly crowded walls. They were a private museum of journalism, most written by Leonard himself. Some news clips went back to the forties, many were from the fifties and sixties, a few, long after his official retirement, trickled right into the nineties. Subjects included the Korean War, Bay of Pigs, JFK's assassination, the Mafia, Patty Hearst, Charles Manson, Kent State, Woodstock, Bobby Kennedy, Martin Luther King, Vietnam, and Watergate. Civil rights pieces were everywhere. Those yellow and brownish headlines, most underneath glass but some exposed to the room's air, injected their distinct fragrance into the room. The cleaning lady dismissed it as the bothersome stale smell of old paper, but to Leonard, and to Jake, it was the sweet fragrance of aged newsprint, as appealing to the trained palate as a vintage wine.

Jake gazed nostalgically at a familiar quote, written in calligraphy, hung next to Leonard's prize-winning article on the South American drug czars, the earliest of its kind. "The power to mold the future of the republic will be in the hands of the journalists of future generations." Below the quote was the name, Joseph Pulitzer.

Next to it was a little "Hawker" pin from the *Times*, one of Leonard's most prized possessions. Leonard had begun in the newspaper business the way he was convinced everyone should—hawking newspapers on the street for a nickel apiece. This, Leonard had reminded Jake, was back when people were honest enough that many newspapers had "honor boxes," open newspaper vending receptacles where the buyer was trusted not to take any more than he paid for, and at the end of the day the seller wasn't a single nickel short. Nowadays, Leonard lamented, even the locked vending machines weren't safe, often rifled for a handful of quarters to feed video games.

Leonard cleared his throat and rolled his eyes and gestured palm up to Jake, indicating whoever was on the other end of the line was droning on and on. Winking at Jake, Leonard suddenly took on an urgent tone. "Look, Roger, I've got something hot here. A major lead that could go cold on me. Yeah, I was sure you'd know how it is. Gotta run. Talk to you later."

In a single motion he slammed down the phone and swung his right hand across the huge desk. He picked up his cigar with the left hand, drew in deeply, and stood there with his firm right hand on Jake's, eyeing him with the satisfaction of a colonel inspecting the troops.

Leonard stood five and a half feet tall, though Jake thought he must have lost another inch since he'd seen him last. Many famous bodies were a lot more impressive, Jake thought, but they'd all come and gone. None of them had shaped journalism, and in turn the country, the way this man had. The mind was still as firm as the grip, and the tongue as sharp as ever. Leonard still struck a powerful image.

"Woods! Long time. I see you've been doing well out there. Some of your columns are good, as good as columns can be compared to real reporting, I mean. Maybe you'll make those west coast papers competitive yet!"

"Thanks, Leonard...I think." No one called Leonard by his first name. Jake had to think to remember it was Cornelius.

"How was your conference?"

"All right. Nothing life-changing. I'd hoped to get here earlier."

"Okay, Woods, how much time before you head to the airport?"

"Should be out of here a little before five."

"All right." Leonard clasped his hands together. "We've got an hour before you hail a cab. Enough to get started. You said you had some things on your mind— what are they?"

That was Leonard. No small talk. He once told Jake, "Cut the extraneous talk and you'll buy yourself two more hours a day to be a reporter. It's like extending your career ten years without having to live a day longer."

"Actually, Leonard, I've got a lot on my mind. I'm concerned about some trends at the *Tribune*. I see certain stories spiked and others edited into oblivion because they might offend certain special interests groups. If we write a piece that knocks religious fundamentalists, we pride ourselves we've done tough, honest reporting and don't give a fig about reprisals. We pass around the critical mail as if it were a badge of honor proving how fearless we are."

Leonard nodded intently, listening carefully to every word.

"But if we do a piece that offends gay groups or feminists or environmentalists or whoever, then we do penance, have special editorial meetings, establish sensitivity groups, promise to hire more reporters of that color or persuasion or orientation, and vow to be more careful in the future. This has been sneaking up on us for ten years, and I'm just now waking up to it. I don't like what I'm seeing, Leonard. We stay away from stories, good stories, if they look like they could show a negative side to certain groups. Yet we seem to take delight in nailing others. We've become so selective, so partisan, so...political."

Jake surprised himself with his own words, as if someone else had said them. He sounded more like Finney or Clarence than himself.

"We used to take delight in nailing everybody, Jake. That was the fun of it. One week we'd nail a gangster, then the cops, then management, then labor, then the Republicans, then the Democrats. Nobody felt safe. If they liked what we did one day, the next day we'd put their rear ends to the fire. Sure, you had to do meticulous research, check and double check your story. But the reward was in catching the fat cats with their pants down." Leonard chuckled with obvious glee, then his craggy face turned sour and somber.

"But now things are different. Not just at the *Trib*, either. Every paper I visit, somebody pulls me over in the corner, looks around to make sure the thought police don't hear him, then tells me the same story. It makes me sick. Newspapers pussyfooting around, kissing up to this group and that one as if they were, well what you said...politicians."

Leonard said the word with disgust, as if on an occupational scale it was somewhere, say, below serial killer.

Leonard waved his cigar hand at the counter under the window, covered with newspapers. "Almost every daily in the country has a half dozen major stories a week we never would have let in forty years ago. They read like press releases from special interests groups. What's really scary is, sometimes that's exactly what they are. Want an example? Okay. I still read five dailies almost cover to cover, every day. Remember the gay rights march in DC, the big one in '93? Three of the five papers said there were a million marchers, even though the DC park police estimated 300,000. Every beltway journalist knows that's the official estimate, the one you always use."

Leonard paced now like a prosecuting attorney. "It wasn't my beat, but since it was front page, I thought, what's with this? So I checked around and got hold of the press releases sent to all the papers by the gay and lesbian groups. Well, they said there would be a million people there. That was just a guess, of course. It was obviously way off. But the papers used the figure anyway, as if it were true. I looked closely and saw a couple of the reporters had virtually plagiarized whole paragraphs from these press releases. Right down to the wording comparing it to the civil rights marches, and the treatment of gays and lesbians being the great ethical issue of our day, and the monumental importance of the march in fighting bigotry and all that."

Leonard looked around the room as though he was ready to spit, but there was no appropriate receptacle, so he continued.

"Can you imagine? They took the one million figure from a press release! They just ignored the actual figures, I guess because they were too low for their tastes. And that's the whole problem. The facts hardly matter anymore. 'One million' gave credibility and importance to the march—it wouldn't do to say 'Less than one-third of the predicted numbers showed up to march for gay rights in the nation's capital.' It would have been true, of course, but it just wouldn't do."

Leonard sat on the front of his desk now, leaning toward Jake. "I mean, the *Today* show and a bunch of television stations used the one million figure, but what do you expect? 'Television journalism'—there's an oxymoron if ever there was one. These are the people who put explosives on cars so they'll blow up for the camera, then use the footage to prove how dangerous the car is. Or the Minnesota station that did a special report on underage drinking, and the TV crew bought these teenagers two cases of beer so they could film them drinking. You know I'm against capital punishment, but I'm willing to make an exception for people who do that to journalism.

"You expect this nonsense with television, because everybody figures 'let's do whatever it takes to get ratings.' But the printed page is different, Woods. We've got to have some integrity. Instead of holding the television news teams accountable for these farces, we're following their lead. Like McNews over there." Leonard gestured toward a marked up issue of *USA Today* on the side of his desk.

"I found out one of these reporters with a front-page story about the gay march is a gay activist who marched in the parade. Not as an observer, a participant! I know for a fact the same thing has happened at the *Post*—reporters have joined in the pro-choice marches. I mean, I'm as pro-choice and pro-gay as anybody, but how can you march advocating one position, then deal with the story with any objectivity? In the old days the reporters that pulled those kind of stunts would have been keelhauled. I mean, it would have been a scandal, Jake—using your post as a journalist to shamelessly promote your own cause, and lying to boot. Their editors and their peers would have lost trust and respect, and the other daily in town would have hung them out to dry in front of the public. Nowadays?" Leonard thought about it. "They probably got an award for excellence in journalism and invitations to speak at banquets."

"You're not helping me with this, you know, Leonard. I was hoping you'd tell me it was just the *Trib*, that the overall state of journalism is a lot better than what I'm seeing."

"You know what bugs the heck out of me? When I point out this stuff to people and they act like I'm betraying the cause. I was a liberal before these half-wits were born. You know what it used to mean to be liberal? It meant to be open-minded, to not buy into the status quo just because it's the status quo. Well now, guess what? We're the status quo! I've always liked to read stuff that challenges my perspective. Like the *National Review*. Usually I don't agree with the Review, but on some issues it makes a lot of sense. Used to be people didn't think anything to see the *National Review* on my desk. Now I see their raised eyebrows and you know what I feel like? I feel like a little boy whose mother caught him with a *Playboy*. They've been taught it's a sin to consider anything that violates their creed. Their viewpoints are so weak they can't even stand up to scrutiny. The liberalism we've got in the newsroom today is different than old-time liberalism. It's a house of cards, where you don't dare let one card topple."

Leonard paced the floor, as if each step clarified his next sentence. "You know what really hurts us now? In the old days there was always the second major newspaper in town. If the other paper was more fair and accurate than we were, we'd lose readers and credibility and money. Our competitors were a real pain. But we knew we weren't the only game in town, and that keeps you from getting smug and arrogant. People had a choice. You had to earn their loyalty. But today there's no one to keep us honest. Almost every major city in America used to have at least two dailies, often more. Take Austin, Texas. My dad worked there for three years when I was a boy. It had fifty thousand people then. You know how many daily newspapers it had? Six. Now it has half a million people and only one daily. It's the same story everywhere. I do a lecture on this. Fifteen hundred cities with daily papers in America, and less than fifty have local daily competitors. It's like a monopoly on ideas."

Leonard ran his hand back through his thinning gray hair, as troubled as Jake had ever seen him.

"I don't know how to break this to you, Leonard, but the *Trib's* got a multicultural concerns committee, and somehow I got on it."

Leonard groaned. "Those committees are springing up all over the place. They started with the sensitivity training, which is the absolute worst thing you can do to journalists. We get sensitive to certain people, and then we don't take them to task. We stop doing journalism and resort to protection and advocacy. Now the seminars aren't enough, we have to have committees. Multiculturalism? Diversity? Let people worship diversity or Buddha or Christ or anything else they want, but keep it out of the newsroom!"

Jake was surprised at how similar Leonard's analysis was to Clarence's, despite their radically different beliefs. Leonard flicked the butt of his cigar in the ashtray and hopped off his desk in an agitated motion.

"I don't even take the invitations to speak at journalism schools anymore, not many of them anyway. It's a bunch of clones, an army of automatons. The saddest part is they think they're thinking for themselves. You know why they think so? Because they've been told they're thinking for themselves! The real problem with journalism schools is they're located on college campuses. So they're in the shadow of all those speech codes and sensitive language and all that hogwash. The journalism department becomes an extension of the college's philosophy of 'don't say anything that could offend the wrong people.' Offenders go to sensitivity training until they repeat the party line like a bunch of zombies. What a place to learn journalism! We grab hold of one perspective, and we get as dogmatic and preachy as the religious right!"

"An interesting comparison."

"It's true. We're so much like the church in the Middle Ages it's scary. Anybody who comes up with unpopular data or discoveries or ideas is like Galileo, a heretic. Instead of looking at the facts, researching and investigating them, we reject them because we don't want to believe what they're saying. They didn't want to know the earth revolved around the sun, so they wouldn't listen. We don't like discoveries that could discredit our world view. So we don't listen."

Leonard paced more furiously, in a well-worn section of carpet he'd obviously walked many times before.

"The more I think about that analogy, the more I like it. Young newspaper reporters are as indoctrinated as any religious fundamentalist. Most of them don't know how to think. They come out of journalism schools believing a good story is any combination of homelessness, AIDS, crack babies, single mothers, and some social program that's being unfairly cut. It's formula news, just like romance and science fiction and westerns and gothic—it has to have certain ingredients. Stories have to have a victim, and if there isn't a real victim you have to find one. People are never lazy and it's never their fault. It's always some businessman or landlord or citizens or the community who's exploiting them or isn't doing enough. We're social workers masquerading as journalists."

Leonard looked at his watch. "We've got twenty-five minutes left. I need some coffee, Jake."

Leonard kept right on talking as he walked toward the lunch room across the massive newsroom, three or four times bigger than the *Trib's*. Like any newspaper man he was always aware of the clock, always aware of limited space into which the maximum story had to be stuffed.

The two stretched their legs and enjoyed the familiar and comforting environment of the newsroom, the background music for both of their lives. After pouring two cups, Leonard sat on the edge of the Formica countertop, took a sip, and looked at Jake in an almost fatherly way, as if he were talking to a young son about the facts of life.

"Fairness used to be our goal. But now we decide in advance which side deserves to be treated fair. To be fair to the wrong side is actually to do the wrong thing because their values could end up being advanced. And the 'right side'—we can't critically analyze them because if we did, some readers might not sympathize with their agenda."

Leonard looked at a half dozen reporters sitting around the room, a few of whom appeared to have overheard him. Self-consciously he gestured a "Let's go" to

Jake. Clearly he didn't want others hearing this discussion. That was fine with Jake. Neither did he. Leonard went to the door, heading back toward his office.

"Something on my wall I want to show you." They reentered Leonard's office, where he immediately became animated again and led the way to the left of his window, behind his desk. He pointed to some papers thumbtacked to a cork bulletin board.

"Here's Robert Bazell of NBC. He says, 'Objectivity is a fallacy. There are different opinions, but you don't have to give them equal weight.' Linda Ellerbe says, 'Any reporter who tells you he's objective is lying to you.' Leonard pointed at a statement highlighted in yellow. "Tom Oliphant of the *Washington Post* says, 'There's no such thing as objectivity, so there's no use wasting time striving for it.'

"On the one hand, I applaud their honesty. At least they're admitting they aren't objective. But I resent that they've given up on objectivity, that they feel no compulsion to even try. Just look at the narrative style of a lot of lead articles, you know, that Gay Talese or Tom Wolfe fiction-feel. It's like storytelling. When your goal isn't just to relate the facts but tell a good story, it's a quick slide from fact to fiction. Reporters know a story has to be engaging and readable but it doesn't have to be entirely factual. And once you depart from the facts, the writer's moral prism inevitably refracts the story."

Leonard wasn't just responding to Jake's concerns. He'd been plagued by the same thing, and had given it a great deal more thought.

"There may be no ultimate moral standards, Jake. I really don't know. But I do know that whenever we go beyond reporting a group of abortion-rights marchers had a march, and then write as if we know their moral cause is right, we've ceased to be objective. We've become preachers, indoctrinators, propagandists. Just as much as the religious right. We're not looking for readers, we're looking for converts. We're dispensers of doctrine. The committees, like this one you're on, they're like little church councils that determine orthodoxy and heresy."

Jake stood up, wanting to inject a little hope into the dialogue. "We've got a guy named Clarence. He's a real comer. You should hear him, Leonard. He's a conservative, a black guy. I guess I'm supposed to say African-American now. But Clarence doesn't care. To him, skin color doesn't matter one way or the other. They don't know what to do with him at the *Trib*. He's sharp, one of the best writers we've got and he won't kiss anybody's feet, or any other part of their anatomy. It's hurting his career, but I think he's too good to be held down. He's on the Multicultural Committee with me. Actually, he's the one who makes the meetings worth going to."

"Hope he sticks it out. A lot of good people just get fed up and leave." Leonard rubbed what looked like a day's growth of salt and pepper beard.

"Then there's the hiring quotas, spoken and unspoken," Jake added. "The *Trib* committed itself seven years ago to having at least 10 percent homosexuals on staff, and we achieved it, even surpassed it. Then next thing you know the Guttmacher study comes out proving homosexuals are less than 2 percent of the population. So now we've got over five times the homosexual representation society does. To be honest, it never bothered me till recently. And it still wouldn't bother me if it didn't tilt the *Trib*. But it definitely does."

Both men instinctively looked at the door, barely ajar. Leonard went over and closed it.

"The philosophy behind all these quotas is the same, Jake. It's like the only way we can insure fair treatment of every group is to have every group represented. What happens is exactly the opposite. We hire people now not just because they can write well and do good research and are disciplined and energetic, but because they're part of a certain group. So now it's like having that group as an in-house censor, telling us what is and is not sensitive, what is and is not acceptable. One of our basic goals in the old journalism was to train writers to separate themselves from their vested interests. Now we hire people precisely because of their vested interests. Some of these people are good reporters, but some are there to make the paper an arm of some cause. And that compromises the integrity of the paper. If they want to go serve their cause, fine, let them join the ACLU or NOW or the Church of the Hokey Pokey or whatever, but get out of journalism!"

Jake recounted to Leonard the story of the rape crisis center piece killed by the *Trib's* multicultural committee, feeling some shame he hadn't voted completely with Clarence to let the story stand. "I guess my point is, advocacy doesn't just happen in writing stories, but in selecting them."

Leonard nodded. "And you think other reporters don't get the message? This woman had maybe invested twenty or thirty hours on that story. She probably used some of her own time. Think she'll do it again? Why bother? Save your investigative skills for something you know will make it in, like scandals in the Salvation Army. It's censorship with a capital C. Most of it's self-imposed, but that's the worst kind of censorship. Why waste your time and energy on a story that's so politically incorrect it doesn't have a chance of seeing the light of day? What's the point?"

"Exactly. I thought the same thing after that meeting."

"I mean, reporters are only human. We want to be liked. I remember Susan Okie at the *Post*. She wrote a story that wasn't even about abortion, it was about new methods to save premature babies. Some of the other reporters took her aside and warned her this kind of story wasn't good for the abortion rights movement. Never mind that it was 100 percent true. Susan said she felt herded back in line."

"When did all this happen, Leonard? I feel like I'm just catching on."

"It's been gradual. The sixties were part of it, of course. Then came Watergate. Everybody hated Nixon. So did I. Then we threw the bum out. And who pulled it off? Two journalists. All of a sudden journalism had a new image, Woodward and Bernstein, or more precisely, Robert Redford and Dustin Hoffman. Journalists were movers and shakers, shapers of public opinion. Now we had power to dethrone people, to change the shape of politics. I deal with this in one of my lectures. Did you know that in the single decade between 1968 and 1978 enrollment in journalism schools quadrupled? Everybody was a Woodward and Bernstein wannabe. Journalism was no longer showing the world what it was. Now it was making the world what we thought it should be."

Jake got up. "I've got ten minutes, Leonard. While we walk to the elevator, let me throw one more thing at you. I've got a friend who insists conservative Christians are portrayed unfairly in the media. I've always thought she was whining, looking for special treatment. She says she's not, and though she overreacts sometimes, generally she's pretty fair minded, and she's hard to ignore. She can show me article after article where Christians are linked with censorship, bigotry, hatred, child abuse, you name it. At first, I always had an explanation. I told her it was her imagination, or coincidence, or an exception, or that it really wasn't as bad as she made it out to be. But she makes a good case. And, of course, I know a lot she doesn't. If she heard some of my inside conversations at the *Trib*, she'd really flip. What do you think? Any truth to her complaints?"

As they stood outside the elevator door, Leonard took another deep puff from his third cigar, almost as if he needed an extra boost of nicotine to take him down this path.

"Jake, I'm not a religious man. I waver between agnosticism and atheism. I haven't darkened the door of a church in forty years, and I don't plan to. Frankly, I don't have a lot of sympathy for religion. Keep that in mind as I answer your question.

"Okay, back in the eighties they did the Lichter studies, which showed 90 percent of journalists didn't go to church, more than half thought adultery and homosexuality were okay, the whole deal. Journalism was radically more liberal than the country as a whole. Most us knew that, but now it was official.

"Then, you remember the flap in '93 when the *Washington Post* described the religious right as 'poor, uneducated and easy to command.' After all these people came forward with their PhDs to prove they weren't complete morons, the *Post* apologized. But the reporter explained he'd meant no offense, he simply thought this description was a universally accepted one. And the truth is, among journalists, it was, and it is. How else could that statement make it through all the layers of editing? No one even saw the red flag. Pure and simple, religion is associated with the Dark Ages, the bad old days. Look at Ted Turner. Owns a network and one of the most influential voices shaping the news, and he tells a group of broadcasters Christianity is just a 'religion for losers.'

"My point is, nobody could get away with saying that about anything but Christianity. But the thing is, who built all the hospitals and rescue missions in this city? It wasn't the ACLU or NOW, that's for sure. It was Christians. I've got a sister and a couple of nephews who are conservative Christians. I disagree with them, but they aren't hypocrites. The thing your friend has to come to terms with is that people like her have no standing. There's no legislation granting them special protection from being fired because of their convictions or lifestyles. There's no proposals making it a special crime to harass Christians or hate Christians. There's no sensitivity training sessions to help people understand that fundamentalists are people too. And I don't even have to ask if they're represented with the others on your multicultural committee. They never are."

"You're right. They're not." Leonard's certainty about this unsettled Jake.

The elevator door finally opened and the two walked inside, Jake feeling relieved no one else was on board. Leonard didn't miss a beat.

"Okay, that's one side of it. Here's the other side. Frankly, a lot of it's their own fault. First, they abandoned journalism. They quote those statistics and say we're lots more liberal than your average Joe living in South Dakota. True. I admit it. So what? Who told them they couldn't be journalists? If we're such heathens, why didn't they send their children to be missionaries at America's newspapers instead of sending them to Africa? It's a free country, so don't come whining when you cop out and then it doesn't go your way.

"Not only that, but some of them treat journalists like we're the devil. I mean, who takes the journalist to lunch? You know, I can't remember the last time I had a casual conversation with one of these conservative Christians, except my sister and her boys at holiday dinners. Sure, a few people have called and bawled me out, sent me some angry letters. But that's the only contact I have with them, ever.

"Meanwhile, I've had all sorts of lunches with abortion rights people and homosexual leaders and feminists and liberals of every variety. I don't let them pick up the tab, ethics and all that. I'm not beholden to them, don't get me wrong. But I'm sympathetic to them. I rub shoulders with these people. They tell me their stories. I play cards with a guy on the ACLU board. I speak at liberal colleges. How many invitations do you think I get to speak at Christian colleges or seminaries? How many Christian magazines ask me for an interview? How many of the abortion protesters invite me to lunch? Where am I going to bump into these people? At church? Don't hold your breath! Next time I'm in a church will probably be my own funeral."

They walked out of the elevator together, heading for the front door of the *Times,* and out to the sidewalk.

"I've told this friend of mine," Jake said, "the Christian, that I get tired of the conspiracy theories. Some of them seem to think journalists sit around in smoke-filled rooms doing incantations to the devil and trying to figure out how to crucify Christians and bring the country to moral ruin. I admit we're biased, but most of us are still trying to do what's right. They can't seem to accept that. When somebody treats me like I'm the antichrist or something, it's pretty hard to take them seriously."

Leonard laughed. "I know exactly what you're saying, believe me I know. My sister used to talk about the newspaper's 'ungodly humanist agenda,' as if editorial meetings consist of choosing the stories for the day based on what's most ungodly and anti-Christian. But she's helped me understand why it seems that way to Christian people. We finally came to something we can agree on—that the only conspiracy in journalism is the conspiracy of shared values."

"What does that mean?"

"Well, I'm a liberal, so are you. Most of us in this business are. So, naturally, if I share the same values of the feminists in NOW or the ACLU or the NEA or the Hemlock Society or the Gay Task Force, I'm going to be sympathetic to their agenda and portray it in a positive way. If I don't share the same values of the Christian Coalition or the Catholics or the local Baptist church—and I don't—obviously I'm not going to portray them and their agenda as positively. So even though I don't sit down in that smoke-filled room with NOW and the ACLU, often I'm going to sound like I did. Of course, that's not a conspiracy in the conscious sense. It's just an unconscious alignment that exists no matter how objective I try to be. It's a 'conspiracy of shared values.' That's why we need true diversity in this business. And that's why it's too bad the Christians have largely abandoned it."

"Interesting." As usual, Leonard was making Jake think.

"People like your friend don't know how to play the game, Jake. Things have changed. When I first became a reporter after the war, I was in a middle-sized town and I knew half the pastors and priests. The mayor was a deacon at the Baptist church, the chief of police was a conservative Christian. I had contact with these people—they were leaders in the community. Now it seems they're all out in their evangelical ghettos, and they stick their heads out just long enough to yell at the rest of us and tell us what a mess we're making of everything. Their books and magazines just talk to themselves. They don't talk to people like me. Then they wonder why I don't understand them. Of course I don't understand them. They don't understand me either. Sunday morning I play eighteen holes of golf while they sit in an uncomfortable bench and listen to someone make them feel guilty. Do I understand that? No!

"I pride myself on being objective, Jake. I know I have strong biases, but I can usually set them aside to understand someone else. But in some ways, I suppose it would be as hard for me to put a positive spin on an anti-abortionist as on a Ku Klux Klanner. Maybe I'd feel differently if I knew them better, if I understood why they believe what they do. But I don't. When I do a story on cocaine addiction, I'm not going to balance it by finding someone who says cocaine addiction is good. Some things we just accept as right or wrong, and don't feel the need to balance them. If we're convinced abortion and homosexuality are right, why balance our treatment of them?"

Jake knew he had to get his cab quickly, but he held back, wanting to be with Leonard as long as possible.

"Bottom line? Your friend has a legitimate gripe. She's part of a group that's a lot larger than most of the special interests. But it's like their time is past. Christians had their day in the sun and it's over. The nation chose another direction, lots of other directions. People resent their efforts to regain power after giving it up so long ago. So now fundamentalist Christians are always fair game for a good journalistic kick in the teeth. Gays and abortion rights activists are never fair game. If someone takes on a minority, it's persecution. If someone takes on conservative Christians, it's about time they got their comeuppance. If the gays or feminists or abortion people get on our case and boycott our paper, it's reasonable action in response to rights deprivation. If the Christian conservatives boycott us, it's attempted censorship. They can't win."

With a wry smile he added, "Not that I want them to win. But I do wish there wasn't such an adversarial role between them and us. We all want truth and justice and a better society. Maybe if we talked more we'd find out we could work together better."

Leonard seemed to suddenly realize he'd come to his last words with Jake. "You know, I've read the biographies of Greeley, Hearst, Pulitzer, and other great newspaper men. Most of them died lonely and miserable—suspicious, jaded, wondering whether they'd accomplished anything of value. That's not how I want to go out, Jake. It's a very unsettling thing to have thought my life was dedicated to something noble, and now to wonder sometimes how much I contributed to the chaos."

Jake saw something he couldn't remember ever having seen before. Tears in Leonard's eyes.

"What do you mean, Leonard?"

"I mean, I was on the forefront of opposing the old moral standards. I thought they were old fashioned and unnecessary. I helped portray them as that. And I supported the new, revolutionary ideas, thinking they were best for society. Well, I won, Jake. We won. We managed to change the way our society thinks and lives. But now I look around at the incredible violence, teenagers packing weapons to school, drive-by shootings, gangs, rape, drugs, AIDS, child abuse, and on and on. And I ask myself, what went wrong? And the only answer I can come up with is that we tore down the old standards but left no standards in their place. Maybe...maybe we had no standards to offer."

Jake desperately wanted to stay and talk longer, but he knew he had to get to the airport. He stepped up to the edge of the sidewalk, facing traffic, and raised his hand to hail a cab, New York style. He wanted to tell Leonard about the investigation, but he really couldn't. He wanted to share his important journey with someone so important to him. There was so much he wanted to say. But he was out of time.

Hearing Leonard standing there, reflecting back on his life as if it were done, he wondered if he'd ever see his mentor again. For a moment Jake wanted to put his arms around Leonard, like he'd never done to his own father. He sensed Leonard wanted to put his arms around him like he'd probably never done to his own son. Both hoped the other would. Neither did.

A beat up taxi slowed to the curb, running over the curbside debris. A wind-blown page of newspaper—Jake couldn't tell which one—stuck to its back right tire, as toilet paper stuck to the shoe of an unsuspecting pedestrian exiting a restroom. The driver gave Jake an impatient what-about-it look. Jake nodded.

"Good-bye, Leonard. Thanks for your time. It means...a lot to me."

"Thanks for coming by to see me, Jake. I wish it could have been longer. Take care of yourself."

As the taxi drove off, Jake turned to look through the rear window, to catch one last glimpse of a powerful culture-shaping giant. He saw instead a sad looking little old man with slouched shoulders and sagging jowls, staring bewilderedly down a dirty New York street.

CHAPTER TWENTY-TWO

T he platform glimmered in the piercing light emanating from the throne. Made of materials unfamiliar to Finney, the platform seemed to have the raw strength of steel, but the flexibility and natural beauty of wood. A huge, attentive crowd had gathered, sprawling out as far as the eye could see in every direction. Finney thought of a gathering he'd attended in Washington DC, which filled the huge Ellipse in the great mall, then spilled over Constitution Avenue, and up toward the Washington Monument. But this assembly was thousands of times larger, at least.

Voices everywhere merged into a single hum of excitement. Finney zeroed in on snatches of dialogue here and there. Never had he heard such fascinating conversations. He felt connected to everyone in the crowd, as if they were old friends sitting in the same living room.

Sort of a galactic-sized "small group," he thought. As Elyon's Book said, "a great multitude that no one could count, from every nation, tribe, people and language, standing before the throne and in front of the Lamb."

Diversity. One of the great wonders of Elyon's creation.

In his creative genius, Elyon had built the unity of the universe not on the unwilling conformity of identical components, but on the voluntary yielding to one another of diverse components. On earth this meant two different genders, many different races and cultures and languages. Different personalities, gifts, interests, and callings, but all with one unifying center of gravity, all resulting in the glory of God and the common good of man. Diversity not as an aberration from Elyon's created order, but in perfect harmony with it. Every component had placed itself under his lordship, creating an overriding unity that transcended the diversity. The unity was to be celebrated, and the diversity appreciated.

A woman on the platform began singing with a lighter-than-air voice that seemed at first to waft and float. But it became steadily stronger and more focused. The voice was as clear and audible to those in the back of the crowd, many miles away, as to those only feet from the front.

The words of the song were familiar, though the tune was new, an intoxicating melody. It struck Finney that he was drawn not to the singer but to the object of the song, not to the performer but the one for whom she performed. The woman's focus was so clearly on Elyon and not on herself that the magnetism of her voice drew the crowd to God alone.

"You are worthy to take the scroll and to open its seals, because you were slain, and with your blood you purchased men for God from every tribe and language and people and nation. You have made them to be a kingdom and priests to serve our God, and they will reign on the earth."

Many of Michael's legions seemed to appear from nowhere, some striding forward, some coming down from above, some appearing to come from beyond the far side of the throne. It appeared to Finney there were untold thousands of them, ten thousand times ten thousand. They encircled Elyon's throne, and sang in a loud voice, "Worthy is the Lamb, who was slain, to receive power and wealth and wisdom and strength and honor and glory and praise!"

This vast choir sang with a quality of voice and richness of harmony that reflected either effortless perfection or disciplined and lengthy rehearsal, Finney was uncertain which.

Suddenly an explosion of sound pierced the air from behind and around him. Finney shook and trembled from the impact. He realized his old body could not have endured its force any more than it could endure a moment in the bowels of an erupting volcano. He was almost alarmed, though it was a welcome alarm, like the exhilaration of a surprise drop on a thrill ride. For a moment he still did not understand, then realized what the explosive force was—the united voices of the crowd. Everyone was singing now, with an impetus that actually pushed him forward toward the throne.

The angels still sang up front, but Finney could barely hear them now over the combined voice of the audience. He realized that rather than the greatest choir ever assembled, which he had at first thought, the countless thousands of angels in the front were merely the small worship ensemble. This "little group" was leading untold millions of others in a powerful hymn of praise.

Finney thought every creature in heaven must be singing the words that burst with a significance beyond anything he had understood on earth: "To him who sits on the throne and to the Lamb be praise and honor and glory and power, for ever and ever!"

The decibel level rose far above the roar of a jet engine, yet it did not hurt his ears, but soothed them.

To be part of something so big, so right, so much what he was made for, filled Finney's heart with inexpressible joy. How long the worship lasted, or whether indeed time passed at all, Finney could not say, nor did he care. Caught up as he was, preoccupied as he was, he lost touch with all else. He was utterly lost in the majesty of praise. Every thought was of Elyon, every energy directed to his throne.

This was what man and woman were made for, he thought, and though they were made for more as well, everything else—no matter how glorious and exhilarating—was so dim and remote in comparison as to be meaningless.

The air was thick with the glory of God. Finney breathed it in greedily as a man sucks in air after surfacing from a deep underwater dive.

"Second room on your left, Mr. Woods. Dr. Marsdon said he'd be there shortly."

Jake walked down the hall at Lifeline Health Clinic, right next to the hospital. He'd been waiting nearly two hours, feeling the three hour jet-lag, which always seemed worse coming back than going. He walked into the room, white and sterile, the walls bright with crisp colorful medical posters, featuring muscles and veins and arteries and bones as if they were works of art. And so they seemed, an intricate work of art with design and purpose. But Jake reminded himself of what he believed, that the human body was simply the product of time and chance and natural forces. It could not, therefore, reflect a plan or design. Funny how it seemed to.

Medical centers, Jake pondered, testified that if there was a plan, something had gone badly wrong. Not only the bodies racked by cancer and ravaged by age, but even the aches and pains of his own "healthy" body, not to mention the stretched bottom two buttons of his shirt. He was getting older, and his most diligent efforts at exercise might postpone his death a little longer, but nothing could break his appointment with that final day. He wasn't used to such thoughts, but all that had happened recently served as a constant reminder of his mortality.

Jake looked over to the three-pocket transparent magazine rack, featuring the kinds of magazines he hated. "Hypochondriac Monthly" he muttered to himself, summarizing his view of health magazines. The door flew open and startled him, as if he'd been caught doing something wrong. A tall red-headed man stared at him blankly.

"Dr. Marsdon? Jake Woods. Thanks for taking the time to meet with me."

"All right Woods, the detective told me I could trust you, that everything I say is confidential. So what can I do for you?" Marsdon was businesslike but friendlier than he'd been on the phone.

"Look, Doctor, I know you didn't get along very well with Greg Lowell."

"That's an understatement."

Jake waited for an explanation, but none came. "Could you tell me why?"

Marsdon hesitated. "Exactly why are they investigating Lowell's death?"

"This is confidential, but the police believe he was murdered."

Marsdon's stone face showed a flicker of surprise. Obviously, Ollie hadn't told him.

"Who gave you my name?"

"Someone on the staff, I don't remember who, said you worked with him on a committee." Jake lied, not wanting to get Mary Ann in trouble. "If he was doing something controversial we need to know. Anything that would make him unpopular."

Marsdon leaned up against the examining table, relaxing slightly. "Unpopular? Well, he wasn't popular with me, I'll tell you that. You're not going to like this, but you asked for it. Our problems began when we were both on the ethics committee. I brought a concern from another physician, and Lowell didn't like it. This physician wanted to remain anonymous. He saw serious flaws in the system, related to our lists of people waiting for transplants. In many cases these are life and death situations. Yet there's no objective way to handle who gets priority."

"I'm not sure I follow."

"Say six people are waiting for a kidney transplant. It's not a simple first come first served situation, like taking a number at Baskin-Robbins. There's lots of other factors. If number one on the list can go another four months without this kidney, and number three is failing—is going to die without it—then the doctors involved might bump him up the list, and number one becomes number two. In fact, there are times where it's to a patient's advantage to show signs of rapid failing. Medicine is geared to the emergency, to the critical demand.

"But let's say the needs are equally critical. Number one didn't respond to his beeper, so we go to number two. But he's a middle-age man with grown kids and number three is a young mother with three little kids. Well, what if the person calling wants to help the young mother? Maybe dial the wrong number for patient two, so you can say he didn't answer either? Then go on to patient three, the one you really want to get the kidney. Not that this happens, but the point is it could. More and more of our decisions determine who lives and who dies. It's that simple. Demand is far greater than supply. Next thing you know people are going to be selling their body parts to provide for their families—or selling their family's body parts to provide for themselves."

Jake's face registered disbelief.

"I'm serious. Medical journals have been talking about this for years. They're calling for compensating people for noncritical organs and paying the donor's family for critical organs. Since the doctors and hospitals and everybody are making money on this thing, they say it's only ethical to pay donor's families. Can you imagine the implications of that? The temptation to not only stop spending money on a dying relative, but making money from selling him off?

"And what about the pressure on doctors? We used to minimize the conflict of interest between potential donors and recipients by maintaining a strict separation between doctors working with the dying and those working in transplants. But with health care changes, the lines have blurred. Which gets me back to the doctor who came to me with the concern in the first place. He said people were getting bumped up and down on the waiting lists with no discussion except between two or three doctors. And with superficial explanations he wasn't sure were valid. Is that controversial enough for you?"

"Uh...yeah, I guess so."

"Your friend, Dr. Lowell, was in on several of these decisions. They seemed almost arbitrary. I mean, let's face it, we've got major potential for abuse here. If person number five on the list is your sister's husband, you've got vested interests in bumping him to the top. Or if he's been a jerk to your sister but has a million dollar life insurance policy, you might want to bump him down. So several of us felt like we needed to establish much clearer criteria for rearranging the priority lists and to have more than just a few physicians involved in the decision.

"Some on the committee, Dr. Lowell the most outspoken, said this was just bureaucratic red tape. They said they wouldn't practice medicine by committee, that they were the experts and needed to be free to make judgment calls. I could see some of his points, but I didn't like his attitude. We butted heads and kept butting heads again and again till he finally quit the committee, just two months ago. Then he spread the word we were a bunch of pencil pushers trying to make everybody do it our way."

"Sounds like a tough situation, doctor."

"It's a terrible situation. It's rationed health care. Who gets it, who doesn't? Everyone's looking to cut costs. From a financial point of view, sick and injured people are just living too long. There's no delicate way to say it. And it's all so arbitrary. Thirty years ago doctors would have quit before they'd let a patient die. Now it's common to withhold food and water for low quality of life situations. We've got people in the hospital right now who are being starved to death or are dying of thirst. By deliberate decision. Doctors and family members concurring. And that's without even touching physician-assisted suicide. Not that I favor keeping people alive against their will. But it's all so complicated."

Jake soaked in the picture. Maybe it merited a column after all.

"You see why we need ethics, Mr. Woods? Well, your friend didn't. But without ethics, money and convenience and selfishness are going to be the only considerations. Nearly 20 percent of the patients in ICU have DNR orders—do not resuscitate. Sometimes these are appropriate, other times I wonder. Are we just trying to make bed space, move people in and out as if this was a restaurant? Are we after their organs? Nobody's going to admit it, but we all know it's a factor. You want other controversial areas Dr. Lowell was involved in? How about fetal tissue research?"

"I've heard Doc was involved in it."

"He was all for it, no reservations. When the president took the ban off it several years ago, Lifeline was right there, your friend in the thick of it—not actually doing the research, but pushing it. So suddenly we're not just doing abortions, we're tinkering with their parts, cannibalizing them to patch up adults. The anti-abortion people don't like it, I'll tell you that. They on your list of suspects? I thought so.

"Any way, the same thing's been done with anencephalic infants, but there's not enough of them. There's lots of aborted babies. But it takes maybe three to eight fetuses to treat Parkinson's disease or diabetes. I read that to treat every person in this country with diabetes would require something like twelve million fetuses. We're way short. Some places pay winos to give blood. Next thing you know we'll be paying women to get pregnant and have an abortion, and we'll justify it by saying look how much it helps Parkinson's and diabetes patients. And even if it's illegal, demand still stimulates supply and forces up the price. A black market is inevitable. Somebody wants to make bucks? Get pregnant, get an abortion, walk away with cash.

"But American abortions won't be enough. Where will we go? People are already looking at the Third World. Since fetal tissue research was legalized in '93, we've been importing fetuses from Russia. Offer somebody American dollars, more than they might make in five years, to have an abortion. And why stop with treating diseases? Why not use fetal gums with teeth buds to give someone new teeth? Or fetal skin to replace scarred facial skin? Or fetal scalp with hair follicles to treat balding?"

"Sounds like *Brave New World*."

"You don't know the half of it. A Scottish scientist perfected a method to take eggs from the ovaries of aborted female fetuses, fertilize them, and implant them in the wombs of infertile women, who will then give birth. You realize what that means?"

"I'm not sure."

"You're going to have children growing up whose real mother never existed. Well, that's not quite right. Children whose real mother was never born. How'd you like to explain that to a kid? 'Your mom was a dead baby.' Or 'In order for you to exist, your mother had to be killed before she was born.' It's bizarre, Woods. I'm no psychiatrist, but there's got to be confusion and guilt here. We've got people saying this is unnatural and immoral, that you shouldn't commandeer someone else's reproductive capacity without their permission. But whose permission are we talking about? The fetus has no legal rights. So why are we worried about violating them? I'm prochoice. Almost all of us on the committee are. Why should we be more offended about the idea of a fetus bearing offspring than the idea of killing that fetus in the first place? I honestly don't know the answer.

"*Brave New World,* you said? Tomorrow the issue will be conceiving fetuses for no other reason than to furnish body parts for transplants. When it becomes possible to incubate an embryo to maturity, some entrepreneur will start a fetus farm, breeding hundreds and thousands of them for nothing but spare parts. That's why ethics committees are so vital. We've got to think this stuff through or pretty soon we won't be that much different than the Nazi doctors."

"But how can you decide what's right and what's wrong? What standards will people agree on?" Jake's interest went beyond the scope of the investigation.

"That's precisely the problem. Try chairing an ethics committee when the people on it have no shared foundation for ethics. Everybody's got their own sense of what's right and wrong. If one of the doctors on the committee saw a made-for-TV movie on euthanasia last night, it might be the primary influence on his input to the committee today. So you've got some Hollywood screenwriter and producer setting the ethical direction of Lifeline Medical Center. Life and death decisions deserve a more profound deliberation than what you get on *Oprah* or in *People* magazine.

"Forgive my skepticism, Mr. Woods, but working on an ethics committee with people like your friend is a little like trying to make blueprints for a building with people who disagree on how many inches are in a foot and how many feet are in a yard...and whether the foundation should be made of concrete or Jell-O."

Jake understood, much more than he would have a few months ago. "I had a friend who used to say we've lost our 'moral compass.' People used to agree certain basics were right and wrong, nonnegotiable. But no longer."

"Exactly. Call it natural law, the Judeo-Christian ethic, conscience, tradition, common sense, or whatever you want. And several countries are further down the line. In Holland someone proposed a television game show called 'A Matter of Life or Death.' The idea was to have a studio audience decide which of two patients should receive life-saving medical treatment. Lots of people were outraged. But you know how it hit me? With the government taking over health care, doctors are constantly being pressured to make tough decisions to cut costs. My question is, how much more qualified are bureaucrats and physicians to decide who lives and who dies than a TV studio audience?"

Marsdon hesitated. "I've said a lot more than I was going to. This is confidential between you and the police, right? No surprise article or anything?"

"Completely confidential. I'm not taking notes. I'm not doing an article, at least not now. If I ever do I'd ask you for an interview. Anything you tell me now is strictly off limits."

"Okay. Good." Marsdon paused, obviously relieved. But Jake sensed this was a man with a lot pent up inside. He needed to talk.

"Do you know how much latitude we're given as physicians in deciding life and death situations? Living Wills are getting looser and looser. They're subject to family and physician interpretation. There's all kinds of different factors to weigh in declaring which organ donors are technically dead and which aren't. Of course, the truth is they have to still be alive in the case of every transplant. The doctor can't wait till their organs stop, then go in to get them because cell and tissue damage happens so fast, all you've got is a dead organ."

Jake looked confused.

"Do I have to spell out what that means? We have to pretend people are dead so we can take their organs. They're not really dead—it's just that they're near death, they're dying or in our opinion they have minimal hope of recovery. But that's not the same as dead. We call them HBCDs—heart-beating cadaver donors. That's why brain death is such a convenient standard. We can still live by the dead donor rule. We've just changed the definition of dead. Still another thing Dr. Lowell and I argued about."

"I've never even thought about most of these things, Doctor."

"Few people have. *JAMA*, the *Journal of the American Medical Association*, published a study on brain death and organ retrieval. I made copies for the whole ethics committee—Dr. Lowell would have gotten one. I've cited it in several papers and lectures of my own. The study showed only one out of three physicians and nurses were able to correctly identify the medical and legal criteria for determining death. Six out of ten had no consistent or coherent definition of death. And, get this, one out of five held a concept of death that defines patients in persistent vegetative states as dead. Which makes every case of their recovery a resurrection, I suppose. As our definition of death changes and fluctuates, the potential for abuse and bad judgment calls is magnified. I just don't think your friend understood the problem. He wasn't alone, which is the really scary part."

"Scary in what way?"

"Look, we've got all kinds of definitions of PVS around. Persistent Vegetative State. I'll give you one example. There's a brain condition called de-efferented, or locked-in syndrome. Not only is vocal control lost, there's a total lack of ability to communicate or control responses. But the cause isn't cognitive failure, it's paralysis. The fact is, EEGs don't distinguish between vegetative and locked-in patients. Sure, if a careful neurological study is done by an expert, he can tell the difference. But somebody has to order the test. And who has time and money for this stuff anymore with the health care situation? The inclination is to give up and say, 'Nah, she's a vegetable. Let's just call her brain dead and get on with it.' Especially since we can get a healthy organ out of her to save someone else.

"It's a lot easier to give up on person A when you tell yourself you're helping person B. It's not a pretty picture, Mr. Woods. I've been thinking about resigning from the ethics committee myself. Maybe getting out of medicine entirely. Become a plumber or something. Anyway, I've got patients waiting."

"This has been helpful, Doctor. Anything else you can tell me about Greg Lowell?"

Marsdon sighed. "Only that he was highly respected. We had our differences, major ones, but I don't mean to assail your friend's memory. He was a colleague. He had the brains and hands of a great surgeon. At times, to be blunt, I wasn't sure about his heart. But maybe that's unfair. We're all under stress in this field. The rules are changing on us, and a lot of us are getting tired of it. One moment we have to get permission to blow our noses, the next we're given the power of gods. Greg was frustrated. So am I. At another time and place, maybe on another committee, I might have seen him differently. I'm sorry he's gone."

CHAPTER TWENTY-THREE

J ake had been back in town a week. He'd written two of his three columns on
media bias, using illustrations he'd gotten from Leonard and a number he put
together on his own. He was careful to leave Leonard's name out of it, since
reporters are allowed to take chances with their careers but not each others'.
    Media bias was an okay subject as long as it didn't get specific, but Jake had
gotten very specific. Some of the illustrations hit close to home. The routine
over-inflating of attendance figures at gay and abortion rights marches were one
among dozens of illustrations that were provable, but Jake wasn't sure what kind of
reaction they'd get him inside the *Trib*. Anyway, Winston did no more than raise
his eyebrows and verify that the second article would be Jake's last on the subject. It
could have been a lot worse.
    Dr. Marsdon's input had been interesting and possibly valuable. Jake had
shared it first with Ollie, then after giving him a two-day head start, with Sutter.
This was his way of consoling himself that while he needed to help both investigators, he'd go the extra mile for Ollie when he could.
    When Jake came into the office he saw the message on his terminal to drop by
and see Jess Foley around two. He approached Foley's office right on the hour, but
saw through the big windows of the conference room next to his office that he was
still buried in the editorial powwow for the first evening edition. Jess saw Jake and
beckoned him in. That was Foley's style. He was an open-door type of guy who
often invited reporters in to see how editorial worked, thinking it made them better
when they saw the big picture. Jake agreed.
    "Hi, Jake. Sorry, we're running late here. Hope you don't mind sitting in?"
    Jake didn't mind at all. Several heads around the room nodded at him, though
Jake thought he detected an unusual coolness from two of the editors. Probably just
his imagination.
    "Okay, so far in section A we've got National nine pages, Metro fifteen, Foreign
eight." As he did every day, Jess was slicing up the *Trib* like a piece of pie to a group
of hungry children.
    Jake enjoyed visiting the "desk," the collective term for the editorial team. Most
of the top editors were in the room—city desk, foreign desk, metro desk, sports,
arts and entertainment, forum, the head of the graphic arts section, and a few others, twelve in all. So many of the crucial decisions were made here, decisions that
elated or crushed reporters the way decisions made behind the closed doors of a
parents' bedroom elated or crushed children.
    Posted prominently on a huge bulletin board were the front pages of each sec-
tion of the latest edition of the *Trib*. Jake knew the meeting had begun with a group

analysis in which the editors expressed their opinions of page layout and article selection. This served to highlight certain editorial choices, encouraging good work and critiquing the not so good. Section editors learned from each others' expertise this way.

Strewn across the counter next to Jake's chair were a few dailies and three biweekly newspapers from the suburbs. The papers quietly testified to the fact there wasn't much originality in journalism. There are no copyrights on ideas. The cardinal rule in journalism is to do it first, but if you don't do it first, at least do it better. Though there was no daily competitor to the *Trib*, Jess felt they could always learn from what the smaller papers were doing.

Jess looked at a yellow legal pad full of scratchings. "Wanda, still an embargo on CANCER?"

"Yeah, it's the usual with the *New England Journal*. If the public gets it before the doctors, they hit the roof. Tomorrow evening's edition is our first shot at the story."

"Yeah, right. Just checking. We could use it today. How much copy?"

"Three columns, easy, maybe four."

"Not that much in news—wish we had it today. Katie, how about that standalone for page one? You know, the early December tree with the last few leaves falling, by the water fountain."

"Keegan would be thrilled."

"Let's surprise him."

Every photographer's dream. A page one stand-alone, unrelated to any story, chosen purely for the merits of the picture itself.

Barbie, Jess's personal assistant, suddenly barged in the door with the unmistakable air of breaking news.

"We've got a plane crash in Seattle. A DC8. Just happened. All the networks are on it. Too soon for the wire services. We're making some calls. Looks pretty bad."

Jess groaned. "Great. Right when it looked like an easy set up. Get some g.a.'s on it fast," Jess said to Barbie. "Pull somebody if you have to. Maybe Denise or Christy? We need some quick action, phone interviews, direct contact stuff, anything that's different from everybody else, okay?"

"Right. What do you think of trying to make a connection with that last DC8 crash? Wasn't long ago. Any similarities, an aircraft design problem, that sort of angle?"

"Great idea, Barbie. Check the morgue. But have Liz do the work, okay? All extra hands on CRASH."

"Got it." Barbie was gone, but the last glow on her face betrayed an adrenaline high from the combination of breaking news and imminent deadline.

"Okay, CRASH is a definite page one. It'll bump FLU or RESIGNATION, but we'll have to see which. Probably RESIGNATION." Jess spoke the editorial language of slugs, the one-word name for stories.

"The stand-alone is definitely gone—what Keegan doesn't know won't hurt him. Joan, what will this do to our total pages?"

"I'll call advertising. You know the standing orders. We lose all airline ads the first twenty-four hours after a crash, or when the crash is still on page one. Don't know how many ads we had. If it's an average day, we'll lose a page or two of news. Probably same tomorrow."

Jake considered the irony. Huge news, but a shrinking news hole.

Jess shook his head. "We used to print the extra news pages even without the ads, but the budget's so tight now the bean counters upstairs say we can't."

Jess looked down the table to the only face Jake didn't recognize. "Okay, this probably means Metro loses two pages. Sorry, Fae. Your first week on Metro and we're already killing you. I'd tell you we'll make it up to you, but I'd be lying."

Fae gave a phony smile and made exaggerated hand motions crossing out a few stories. "I had some nice little briefs in a package. They would have made you proud. This probably kills UNSOLVED, the Dykstra murder case. Tomorrow is its anniversary. Don't suppose it could go in two years and one day after the original?"

Jess looked sympathetic, but only for a moment, shaking his head. He turned to Perry, the National desk editor. "National gets a page one with CRASH, but you probably reinherit RESIGNATION for back pages, so make room."

He looked at Wanda wryly. "Like I was saying, sure glad they put an embargo on CANCER. We haven't got room for it!"

The domino effect. Jake loved the relative safety of the opinion pages. Though he sometimes got shelved in syndication, in the last five years he'd only been bumped twice at the *Trib*. It was three columns a week, eight hundred words a column, as dependable as Winston's bad moods.

"All right," Jess sounded like a general giving his last word to the troops. "I want special attention to headlines. They've been getting a little flabby. Taut. Concise. Grab the reader. Okay? And all the adjustments don't change deadline. Nothing changes deadline. No excuses. Got it?"

The meeting abruptly done, everybody cleared out like it was a bomb scene, and Jess and Jake were alone in the room. Headlines and deadlines. The newspaper business in a nutshell.

"Good job, Jess. You sure know how to run this ship."

"Thanks." Jess paused, confirming Jake's fears the subject might be uncomfortable. "Listen, I just wanted to ask, are things...okay with you?"

"What do you mean?"

"Well, since your friends died and all."

"It's been tough, but I'm okay, yeah. Why?"

"Well, I don't know. I've heard some people talking. No big deal, but they're noticing a difference in your columns."

"What kind of difference?"

"Well, maybe not as hard-hitting. You know how good you've always been at taking on the right wing. It's kind of your hallmark. It's okay to talk about media bias, but you've done it twice, and you need to be careful or you'll give the impression it's a real problem at the *Trib*. And there's been other things recently, just little things here and there that seem...not really like you."

"What's not like me? I'm a general columnist, right? I've always been told the sky's the limit. Variety. Don't just do what everybody else does. I think the media bias columns made people feel good knowing we're honest enough to recognize it."

"It's just, coupled with some other things, I'm getting the feeling you're changing your style. What you've been talking about is okay, I guess, but it's not you, not your strength, Jake. People are used to a certain flavor in your columns. I don't know what I'm saying, really. Just wanted to make sure everything's okay for you."

"Hey, I'm fine. I've been doing some thinking about a lot of things lately, but I'm the same guy. Okay, maybe I haven't been hitting as hard against conservatives lately. I'm just trying to be a little more fair, check out my facts, try to understand what they're really saying. Look, Jess, if you've got a specific problem with any of my columns, let's talk."

"Nothing specific. Just noticed a little shift, actually not as much me as some of the others around here. That's all. It's probably not important. On the being fair thing, that's fine, but don't forget you're a columnist. You're supposed to take people on. Hit 'em hard. Don't lose your nerve."

"I'm not losing my nerve. That's why I took on media bias. That takes a lot more nerve around here than facing off with right wingers. And how come fair is a word we use with groups we agree with, but when we're talking about conservatives, trying to be fair is losing your nerve?"

"Look, Jake, don't get so defensive. I just thought I should say something before...well, I just thought I should. Look, I better get on this crash thing. Never ends, does it?" Jess turned and was out the door.

"No. It doesn't."

Jake worked late at his desk, trying to think of column ideas to prove to Jess and everyone else he was still as good as ever, that he wasn't going soft or whatever it was they were thinking.

It was six-thirty now, already a dark and rainy night. He'd spent the last thirty minutes looking at street lights reflecting on the wet streets of the city below. He didn't feel like going home. Jake walked to his car, past the loading dock where things were settling down after the second evening edition had been shuttled out. He got into his car, and just before buckling up, he opened the glove compartment, sucking out the faint smell of WD-40. He gave the Walther P38 a reassuring touch, then shut the glove box, wondering whether he needed a concealed weapon permit to keep a gun in his car. He'd never done this before.

Jake drove across town, past adult bookstores and tattoo parlors, to a place he hadn't been in months. There it was. Lou's Diner. It was straight out of the fifties, unmolested by the wheels of progress. There had been no progress in this side of town for decades.

Whenever Jake came to Lou's he almost expected to see Reggie trying to get Veronica to go for a spin in his new convertible, Betty batting her eyelashes at Archie, and Jughead eating three king-size burgers. There to his left was the old juke box, titles faded with time. Lou's still had its Elvis records, Beach Boys, and a strange hybrid of pop favorites. The labels were faded and worn. Lou's Diner wasn't a yuppie nostalgia place that had new copies of the oldies. It didn't have CDs of the greatest hits of the fifties and sixties. It had the same 45s that Lou bought back in the fifties and sixties. Only the most damaged had been taken out. Somehow the others had survived. Lou's didn't pretend to be from another era. It *was* from another era. Finney dubbed it "The Diner Time Forgot."

When Lou's health failed, there was talk the place would close down. Jake heard three or four businessmen discuss buying it just to keep it open. "I don't care if we lose money," a Computer Tech Systems executive had commented. "I've just got to have a place where I can get a decent hamburger and milkshake." His friend, dressed in a business suit worth more than cars Jake had owned, said, "Yeah, I know what you mean. One more power lunch at the Marriott, or 'Today's special with shrimp' and I'm going to take over this place myself."

As it turned out, no such rescue was needed. Lou's son, Rory, left his meatpacking business and took over. It was as if Rory·had been biding his time, maybe trying to get up a nestegg, knowing it was his duty, his destiny to take over Lou's Diner. He was the heir apparent.

It had been ten years now since Lou had died, and nothing at Lou's Diner ever changed. Rory would often point to Lou's picture on the wall—standing beside Buddy Holly and the Crickets—and begin, "You know, Dad used to say..."

Jake, Finney, and Doc had been there often together. Other times Jake came with one or the other of them. Who needed a time machine, when there was Lou's Diner? Maybe that's why he was here tonight. Maybe it would take him closer to his friends.

"Jake, it's great to see you. It's been what, a couple months? I'm so sorry about your buddies. Man, what a shock. You guys were the three amigos, eh?"

"Yeah. Yeah, we were. Thanks, Rory. Good to see you too."

"Hey, I read your column yesterday."

"Yeah? What did you think?"

"I really liked it. Kind of surprised me though. Didn't really sound like you."

"Thanks, Rory." Just what he needed to hear.

"Start with a cafe mocha, Jake?"

Jake smiled and nodded. Okay, so Lou's had made one concession to the modern world, and that with Jake's urging. At first Rory had balked at all this strange talk about frothed milk and flavorings and little chocolate covered coffee beans, but when Jake explained the gourmet coffee phenomenon and how it could draw in business, Rory checked into it. He didn't understand the craze, but he did understand profit margins. Within a week he bought the full equipment and was selling espressos, cappuccinos, lattés, the whole nine yards. Within a few months he was even pronouncing their names correctly. The new profits kept the business afloat, and Rory thanked Jake for it every time he saw him. He refused to take Jake's money for coffee—every cup, single or double, regular or grande, any added flavor he wanted, was on the house. Typically, Jake left Lou's with a major caffeine buzz.

After serving up the mocha, Rory took Jake's order and went back to the kitchen to fix up the burger, fries, and shake in Lou's patented way.

Jake sat evaluating, thinking of Ollie and Sutter and Mary Ann and Dr. Scanlon and Dr. Marsdon. His thoughts went to Janet and Carly. Much as he didn't want to admit it, he had several life struggles on his hands at once. The investigation was only one of them.

Amazing how your friends' deaths make you stop and think about life. Guess it makes sense. Why wait till life's over to think about how you should have lived?

Long after his remaining fries had assumed room temperature, Jake stared off into space. Without asking, Rory had served him two more coffees, first a caramel mocha, this one an almond latté. There'd be no danger of him sleeping tonight.

Finally, at about eight-thirty, he went to the front counter cash register, the old type that looked like it weighed two hundred pounds. He and Rory reiterated how good it was to see each other again. As Jake headed out the door, Rory said again how sorry he was about Doc and Finney. "What a shock. You see these guys, and a few days later they're gone. It's over. Finito."

"Later, Rory. Take care of yourself." As Jake walked by his table, he reached in his pocket and grabbed three quarters, then tossed them on the white-speckled table, on which quarters had been falling before they had Washington engraved on them. One of the quarters came up heads, another tails, and Jake looked back as the third spun and wobbled as if unsure how to land. Finally it succumbed, as everything eventually must, but by this time Jake had walked too far to see if it had come up heads or tails. Was life really so random? Or was there a controlling hand behind the flip of a coin? Or did anyone have the power to challenge the flip and change the course of his life?

Jake strolled back to his car, watching the shadowy images in the darkness, a few hookers putting on their care-free act, empty men heading from one porno shop to the next, pathetic people with no clue what life was really about. Jake wondered now if he understood it any better than they.

Jake was almost home when he realized what Rory had said. "You see these guys, and a few days later they're gone." What did he mean "a few days later"?

Jake made a sudden U-turn, so sudden he caught a clear head-on view of the driver of the Mercedes following him at what had been a discreet distance. He saw the surprised look on Mayhew's face. Mayhew tailing him again? That's right. He pulled the evening shift.

Jake had to know what Rory meant. He hadn't been at Lou's with Doc and Finney, or either of them since…well, it had to be six weeks before they died. *A few days?*

It took fifteen minutes for Jake to get back to Lou's. He barged in the front door, then saw from behind the white outfit busing a table.

"Rory?"

"Sorry, Mr. Jake. Mr. Rory gone. Go right after you did. I close tonight. Take a message for Mr. Rory?"

It was Chang, the brilliant Chinese student from the University. He'd been there six months and already spoke English better than Jake spoke Spanish after four years of classes.

"Uh, no thanks, Chang. Listen, I've got to get hold of Mr. Rory, I mean, Mr. Santelli. I mean, Rory. Look, do you have his home number?"

"Okay, Mr. Jake. Mr. Rory not mind, for you. I get you number of his telephone. Okay, Mr. Jake?"

"Yeah, okay, great. Thanks, Chang." Jake resisted the urge to call him Mr. Chang.

"Here is number, Mr. Jake. Mr. Rory live only few minutes away. Probably home already. You use this phone if want to. Not long distance. No problem."

"Thanks, Chang."

It was an old rotary phone, and Jake had the distinct impression it was the same phone he'd used to call home to Janet before Carly was born. It was probably an antique even then.

"Yeah, Rory. Jake Woods. Listen, did you tell me you had seen my two buddies not long before they died? You did? No kidding? Did you hear anything they were talking about? Yeah? Look, Rory, can I come to your house? How do I get there? Fifth to Thompson—by the Chevy dealer? 5106. Yeah, okay, I'll find it. On my way."

Jake took off again, after waving at Mayhew, parked across the street and back about sixty feet. Why had Doc and Finney met? What were they talking about? And why wasn't Jake invited? Rory told him it was a real serious talk. Why hadn't either of them mentioned it to him? What was going on? Did it relate to the accident? (*Murder*, Jake kept correcting himself.)

Jake's mind raced, trying to put together the puzzle. Now he stood on the Santelli doorstep.

"Oh, you must be Jake Woods. Hi, I'm Maria, Rory's wife. Don't think we've ever met, but I know all about you. I just loved your column on health food. It was really funny."

As Maria pulled him in the door—literally—Jake tried to remember a column about health food. He'd never written one. And his columns weren't funny, not deliberately anyway. But it didn't matter. Maria was talking about Boston cream pie, and how it was a new recipe but she hoped he'd like it.

"Jake, so glad you came," Rory said. "Maria's been dying to meet you ever since she read your column on health food."

"It was hilarious," Maria said. "Funniest thing I ever read."

"Thanks."

"Cecily, Robert, come here. There you are. This is Mr. Jake Woods, a very famous writer. And a friend of your grandfather's and mine. And a very good customer." Rory winked at Cecily, who looked about Carly's age, and said, "He gives very good tips."

Jake had never thought about Rory's family. Rory was a one-dimensional fixture in his world, like the holodeck images on *Star Trek: The Next Generation*, as if when Jake left Lou's Diner, Rory didn't have a life. He existed just to round out one little corner of Jake's world. Open-minded as he liked to think of himself, Jake was beginning to realize he seldom saw any place or anything from someone else's point of view. He was always the main character. The rest of the world had a supporting role or no role at all. It struck him as a strange and selfish way to live.

After they had their pie, and Rory and Maria brought Jake up to date on Cecily's soccer and Robert's water polo and their academic achievements and college plans, Maria was in the kitchen with the dishes and Jake was peering over a cup of coffee (*not another one,* he thought) at Rory, who finally said, "Now, you were wondering about your friends."

"Please, tell me everything you remember. It could be important."

"Well one of them, the doctor, he was very serious. I think he invited your friend Finney to meet him. He got there first. Seemed very nervous. I didn't hear very much, and I don't want you to think I'm an eavesdropper. Now, if my wife Maria had been there, she'd be telling you every word."

Jake wished she had been there.

"But I do know that the doctor was scared."

"You mean he looked scared?"

"Not just that. I heard him say he was scared. That maybe he'd gone too far."

"Gone too far?"

"I think so—maybe those weren't the exact words, but it was like that. And something about being involved with the wrong kind of people. I wondered if maybe he was into gambling or something a little shady. Whenever I came up to pour them some coffee, they got real quiet, so I backed off and let them alone."

"Did you see anything else?"

"It wasn't a busy night. Don't think we did a hundred dollars business. I noticed Mr. Finney reached into his coat pocket and pulled out a little book and read to the doctor."

"That must have been his Bible. He carried a little one in his coat pocket."

"Yeah, I thought it was a Bible. Well, the doctor didn't seem to like it. He waved his hand at Mr. Finney several times. I heard him say, 'I don't need this.' And Mr. Finney said, 'This is exactly what you need.'"

"Then what happened?"

"Well, Mr. Finney managed to calm the doctor down, but he seemed to get very..."

"Yes?"

"Well, stubborn. Like Finney was trying to help him but he didn't want his help. I heard him say, in kind of a loud voice, a gruff voice, something like 'I don't need anybody's help.' But it was very strange to me. Because it seemed like he very much did need someone's help. And Mr. Finney seemed eager to help him, but the doctor wanted nothing to do with it."

"Maybe he wanted a different kind of help than Finney was willing to give him." Jake thought for a moment. "Things must have been bad for him to call Finney in the first place."

"They were friends, weren't they?"

"Sure. But Doc is...was a very proud man."

"Yes, I could see that. When they were done..."

"Yes?"

"When they were done, the doctor seemed eager to leave. And Mr. Finney had tears in his eyes, and put his arms around the doctor and gave him a big hug. I remember because...it reminded me of my father's hugs. When you grow up in an Italian family you get used to hugs. I miss my father's hugs."

Jake nodded, surprised he wasn't more impatient when Rory got off track.

"You know, I do remember one other thing. It struck me as kind of funny."

"What's that?"

"The Doctor said it right at the end, and he must have said it three times, like it was very important to him. I guess that's why I remember. He said, 'Forget everything I said, Finney. Erase your files.'"

Erase your files?

"Thanks, Rory. Thanks a lot." Jake grabbed his coat, stuck his head in the kitchen to thank Maria.

"You have to write another one of those health food columns. That was so funny."

"Okay, maybe I will, Maria. Thanks again for a great piece of pie." Jake took off in his car, not waving to Mayhew this time, reminding himself that somebody else, maybe somebody with a baseball bat, might be following him too.

"Jake, you're full of surprises. First these incredible columns, and now you're dropping in on me ten o'clock at night?"

"Sorry Sue, but—"

"Hey, don't apologize. I'm delighted to see you."

Little Finn stuck his head out of the bedroom and called, "Hi dere, Unca Jake."

"Hi dere, Little Finn. Get back in bed, buddy. Sorry I woke you up."

Sue pointed to the couch. "Sit down, Jake. What's going on?"

"Sue, did Finney ever talk to Doc on his modem? You know, like E-mail?"

"Yeah, sometimes. They both had Compuserve. They left messages for each other once in a while. I remember Finney said, this wasn't that long ago, he got an E-mail message from Doc, that Doc wanted to meet him for dinner the next night. I thought dinner was kind of funny, seemed like lunch was more typical. And I really thought it was funny to have two grown men typing messages to each other when they could just pick up the phone and talk. Must be a man thing or something. Anyway, Finney sounded concerned. I asked what was wrong. He told me he wished he could talk to me, but he'd promised Doc he wouldn't. I was afraid it had to do with Betsy. Maybe that Doc was thinking of divorcing her."

"Do you know where they went for dinner?"

"Sure. Finney had onion rings. He never has onion rings anywhere except—"

"Lou's."

"Right. What is it, Jake?"

"Maybe nothing. Remember those files Angela said were coded?"

"Sure. She was really frustrated. Whenever she tried to call them up, it said to enter the password, and she had no idea what it was. She never got into them. Why?"

"Mind if I turn on the computer and try some passwords?"

"Sure, Jake. It's all yours. Have at it. If you need any technical help though, count me out!"

Jake bounded up the steps, turned on the computer, and found the locked files in the subdirectory COD, which he suddenly realized might be Doc spelled backwards. An hour passed and Jake had tried everything from Doc to Sue to the name of Finney's first dog, brother, eighth-grade teacher, company commander in Nam, mother's maiden name, name of his church and pastor and dozens of other words. He even tried CSLEWIS, Finney's favorite author. No luck. It could be anything.

Sue set down a cup of coffee. He cringed at the almost lethal caffeine level already in his system, but sipped it anyway. Maybe it would contain the magic insight LSD users sought in the sixties.

"JAKE?"

"Yeah?"

"No." Sue laughed. "I mean JAKE. Try JAKE."

Jake typed in his name and hit the Enter button, not even looking, knowing he would see "The Password is Incorrect. Cannot Open the Document." Instead, with no fanfare, a screen full of legible material appeared.

"That's it! We're in!" Jake felt gratified that in this secret communication between the two friends, it was the third friend who came to Finney's mind.

"Okay, there's four documents. The first has a different format. The date's October 10."

Jake scanned it and said with some disappointment, "Looks like a theological discussion."

"They used to go back and forth sometimes. Finney said Doc was more comfortable on a keyboard than face to face. But I wouldn't think Finney would consider it secret. What does it say?"

Jake started reading. "Okay, this file has both sides of the dialogue. I don't think you'll have a tough time figuring out who's who." Jake read aloud:

"I want no part of any God who would send people to hell."

"Do you want any part of a God who suffered and died so any one who accepts his gift can go to heaven instead?"

"No, I don't. I don't buy into your idea of heaven and hell anyway."

"It's not my idea. I'd never have come up with it. It's God's idea."

"You say 'God' but all the evidence says there is no God. This 'Jesus is the only way' stuff is just another fundamentalist guilt-producer."

"I think if what you said were true, you'd have no reason to press your point so hard. You'd be less defensive, less hostile. I feel like you're trying to convince yourself, not me. Like the louder and longer you say untrue things, the greater the chance you can make them true."

"What is truth? Truth is relative. It's whatever you want it to be. You have your truth, I have mine."

"And if what you call 'my truth' turns out to be *the* truth, how will your truth help you out? In fact, if the Bible is right, your truth isn't true at all. It's nothing but wishful thinking. Or worse, it's a lie from the pit of hell."

"Get off this hell trip, will you? I'm not going to be intimidated into serving your God. I like being a pagan. If you want to believe all that non-sense to make you feel better—why it would is beyond me—go ahead. I'm signing off, Finn. I've had enough for one night."

Jake looked at Sue, then clicked the computer mouse and again entered his own name as the code. It worked perfectly.

"October 18. This is just Finney's side of the conversation. Looks like a response to something Doc sent him." Jake took a deep breath and started reading aloud.

> "Doc, thanks for sending me the note. I'm using a password so my copy will remain confidential. Unless you erase our correspondence entire-ly, you'll want to do the same.
>
> "I understand your preference talking about this situation on a key-board rather than face to face. This is a serious dilemma and I want to help you however I can.
>
> "In answer to your question, I believe the only thing to do is to come forward and confess what you've done. You say it could mean the end of your career, but your conscience is more important than your career. Infinitely more important. A woman died, and you said what you did would be interpreted as violating your oaths. Built into every person is a sense of accountability, a fundamental belief that good will be rewarded and evil will be punished. God is talking to you, Doc. You've got to listen and respond.
>
> "Much as I hurt for you, for your sake I'm glad you can still feel this pain. It means your conscience isn't seared. But you must act upon it. Our capacity to rationalize is unlimited—I know mine is. Remember how you told me the first abortion was the worst, but after awhile it didn't affect you anymore? The same will happen with this if you allow it, Doc. You must not allow it. Jesus will freely forgive you, and so will your family and friends. But if you don't respond to his prompting, you'll desensitize your conscience. You'll tell yourself this was okay.
>
> "I've honored your wish and haven't told anyone, even Sue or Jake. I'm in this with you every step of the way. I'll do everything to help you make the right decision and face the consequences."

Jake and Sue looked at each other wide eyed. Jake clicked the mouse again and typed in the password.

"Here's the second one. October 20. Two days later."

"I understand what you're saying, Doc, but I can't agree. From a human point of view it seems to make sense to lie, to cover up. But ultimately it won't work, because you have to live with yourself and above all, you have to give an account to God. I know Betsy has a Bible. Please look up Jeremiah 17:10 and 1 Peter 4:5. I'm not preaching at you—this is truth you need to hear.

"You can't protect the other doctor from what he's done. Yes, by turning in yourself you turn him in. I understand that, but you do him no favor by allowing him to do it again. How many other doctors might get lured into this? I'll stand next to you, help you personally, help with your family, financially, in any and every way I can. But I beg of you, Doc, don't let this slide. Please, old friend, in your heart you know what's right. Do it."

Sue folded her arms in her bathrobe, chilled by these words. "Jake, I don't understand. Do you know what they're talking about?"

"I'm not sure, but I have some ideas. I'll tell you what I can. First, let's read the last letter. This one's October 23, the night before they met at Lou's for dinner. Just three days before the accident."

"Doc, thanks for letting me borrow your Suburban. I need a 'man's rig' to move those copy machines. I'm glad you want to talk face to face at Lou's tomorrow night. But if you've made up your mind not to come forward, I implore you to reconsider. You can't cover up from the one person who ultimately matters. Hebrews 4:13 says, 'Nothing in all creation is hidden from God's sight. Everything is uncovered and laid bare before him to whom we must give account.'

"You say you won't do this again, yet when I ask you if you'll give back the money, you say it doesn't work that way, and you may as well keep it. Can't you see yourself rationalizing? Now that you've done this, can't they keep coming back with attractive offers, or threats to turn you in unless you do it for them again? Only by confessing to the truth can you take away their greatest hold on you. If you don't go to the police, the situation can only get worse.

"You're at a crossroads, Doc. It's not too late to do what's right."

Jake stared into the computer screen. Sue gently put her hand on his shoulder. Both were thinking the same thing.

Now it is too late.

t had been a sleepless night, climaxed with a midnight call to Ollie. Jake made computer printouts at Finney's and faxed them to Ollie at his home. It was a windfall discovery, maybe the break they needed. Doc had been involved in some unethical medical procedure with a woman. The woman died, of what they didn't know. Doc had been paid, and another doctor was involved. Who and why? And someone was capable of leaning on the doctors to try to get them to do it again.

So what was it? They were closer to the truth, but still had too many possibilities to keep straight. Maybe Ollie could sort them out. Eventually Jake would need to get all this info to Sutter. But until he made his regular check-in call, Ollie would have the jump.

The phone rang at 7:20 as Jake was savoring his last half cup of Colombian before heading to a couple of interviews, one of them a biggie. It had to be Winston.

Grabbing the phone, Jake jumped right in, "Yes, Winston, I'm remembering the appointment with the commissioner—anything else you want to nag me about?"

A young uncertain voice broke the moment of silence. "Uh, hello? Dad? Is that you?"

Jake's cocky jive turned to embarrassed concern. "Carly? Hi, honey. I was expecting someone else. Winston from the paper sometimes calls...never mind. What's up?"

"Well, I'm afraid it's more bad news. But you don't have to race over this time. I'm not...well, I'm not going to do anything stupid. It's just something I wanted to tell you face to face. Could you drop by sometime? It doesn't have to be now."

Jake sensed now was exactly when it had to be.

"Sure, honey. I'll just make some quick calls, change a few appointments, and—"

"You don't need to do that, I just..."

"No, sweetheart, I want to do that. I really do. I just need a few minutes. I can be there by 8:15. Is that okay? Will you be all right till then?"

"I'll be fine, Dad." The hollow sound in her voice said she was far from fine. "I'll see you then. And...thanks." Her voice broke in the middle of the "thanks," but she hung up before Jake could say more.

Jake's mind went into warp drive. He wouldn't allow himself the luxury to think about Carly's problem till he cleared out his schedule.

Who's my contact at the commissioner's office? Jake racked his brain. *Oh yeah,*

Brady. How could I forget? The commish's banty rooster. He had Brady's direct office line. He hoped he was already in.

"Jake Woods here, Brady. Listen, I have to cancel my appointment with the commissioner. Something just came up. Sorry. I'll call back later to reschedule."

"Mr. Woods," Brady cleared his throat as if about to say something very important. "The commissioner is a very busy man. Many people are waiting to meet with him. When someone makes an appointment, it is customary that it be kept. I'm afraid it will be a few weeks before we can reschedule."

"Well, that's okay with me, Brady. I was thinking of taking a positive slant on the commissioner's plan to use tax money for the park blocks' cleanup, but I'm sure I can get an interview tomorrow with Councilman Fredericks. I understand he takes a different position."

"Wait. One moment. Yes, I have good news, Mr. Woods. I just noticed an opening tomorrow afternoon at two o'clock. Would that be workable?"

"Yes, thanks Brady, that would be workable. More than workable—it would be peachy keen," Jake said it with a broad grin, mocking the bigger-than-life pasted smile he'd seen Brady shine when he was sending the "everything's just dandy" message. "Glad that opening just happened to pop up." Jake's right index finger punched the disconnect right after the word "up."

Jake couldn't resist taking jabs at bureaucrats like Brady. *Self-important little weasel.* Jake learned long ago how to stroke the ego to get what he wanted. When that didn't work, veiled threats were the next step. The commissioner was a pompous buffoon, and Brady was his insufferable lapdog, but the project was worthy and, well, it was one more local column. He could use a few winners right about now.

Jake knocked off two other calls just as quickly, then let his mind go where it wanted.

What's going on with Carly? The news can't be as bad as last time—it doesn't get much worse than pregnant and suicidal. She sounded really troubled, but not desperate. *Is something wrong with the baby?*

Jake scanned the room one last time to see what he should bring. There was Finney's Bible again, right where it had been three weeks ago when he rushed out to see Carly. Jake hesitated, recalling how Carly had seen Finney and his Bible on that newscast and the profound effect it had on her. He picked up the Bible, but he felt silly, as if he were clutching a magic potion or an Old West miracle elixir to cure cholera. With mixed feelings, he put it back on the table.

Jake wove through the traffic and made it to Janet and Carly's apartment by 8:05. He knocked, expecting Janet to answer. It was Carly.

"Hi, Dad. Thanks for coming. Mom's already at work. She's getting off to pick me up at ten."

"Pick you up?"

"I'm going to the doctor. We decided to get a second opinion."

"Something's wrong with the baby?"

"Maybe. We don't know. But the main problem isn't the baby. It's me."

"What is it, Charli?" His old pet name for Carly, unused for at least three years, popped out, surprising them both.

Carly fidgeted. She looked like someone poised to dive into ice cold water. She'd welcome any reason to postpone this, but her determined look told Jake she was going to go through with it.

"This is awfully hard to say, especially to your father." Carly took a deep breath and dove in. "They offered us some tests at school, medical tests. I took one. And they say..." She looked away, her eyes showing hurt and hopelessness. "They say I have the HIV."

Like a wrecking ball swinging from a demolition crane, the words bowled Jake over. "Carly, I... Are you sure?"

"They're sure. We're going to a doctor today to find out if they're right. I think they are."

Jake wanted to reach out and embrace Carly, but he didn't feel entitled. So he just stood there uncomfortably, about three feet from her, nervously exchanging glances between her and the floor.

"What makes you think they're right, Carly?"

"Because Michael, you know, my old boyfriend, he has it. And we...we were together quite a bit." Carly hung her head. This was tough to say to a father, even a modern liberal father.

Jake felt hurt that some boy was so intimate with his daughter—intimate enough to give her the most dreaded disease—and he had never even met him. Then the anger started to kick in. *I don't even know what this jerk looks like.*

Jake wanted to ask Carly where Michael got it, but restrained himself, remembering how angry she was at his response last time. Besides, he figured her need to be listened to was greater than his need to know.

"Honey, I'm really sorry." Where were the right words when he needed them? He felt so inadequate, even stupid, as he awkwardly put his arms around her at last. The moment he did it seemed clearly right, and he wondered why it was so hard to do the right thing.

Carly stood quietly, soaking in the hug. It warmed Jake that it obviously meant so much to her to be in her daddy's arms. Once again, at least for this moment, he felt like a real father.

Finally, Jake pulled back. In the stillness, the haunting question rose again, and Jake tried to express it without tipping off the anger he felt. "How is Michael?"

"Michael has AIDS. He's dying."

"Full-blown AIDS?"

Carly nodded. "And Dad, you're going to think I'm really dumb."

"Dumb?"

"I knew he had the HIV. I knew it."

"And you still had sex with him?"

Carly withdrew a few inches, hurt at Jake's bluntness and his obvious agreement that she'd been dumb.

"We used a condom every time. But when I got pregnant, I figured if the condom didn't stop that, it might not have kept me from getting AIDS. That's why I took the test. I thought I was okay, but wanted to make sure. I was wrong. I'm not okay."

"You're saying Michael knew he had the HIV all along? And he deliberately put you at risk?" Jake was flabbergasted and didn't try to disguise it.

"At least he was honest enough to tell me," Carly came to Michael's defense. "Two other kids at school know they have it and never even told their lovers."

Jake recoiled at the word *lovers*. It seemed so out of place coming from his little girl. Shouldn't such a word be reserved for adults? Carly was just a child, an innocent seventeen-year-old. She'd gotten her driver's license only eight months ago. How had she been dragged into this world of adult passions and choices? A world where people said they loved someone, then put that person's life in jeopardy to gratify their own desires.

"Michael first told me about his condition back when we were just good friends. But the more time we spent together the closer we got. One night he started...taking off my clothes."

Carly's head dropped again. She was miserable saying this, but she had apparently determined to tell her story to her father.

Jake was just as uncomfortable. Both father and daughter had been taught they weren't supposed to be embarrassed about this subject. Yet both were, especially under these circumstances.

"I told him I couldn't have sex with him because of the HIV. He asked if I wanted to. I didn't know what else to say, so I said 'Yes, but not tonight.' I guess I was tired of being known as 'The Last American Virgin.'"

Jake's expression told Carly he didn't get it.

"That's the name of a movie—a couple of my friends started calling me that after we rented it. I got so tired of it, I guess I just wanted to sound like I was with it, anyway, so I told Michael yes, I guessed I wanted to have sex. But I thought I was safe saying it. I mean, I didn't think we'd ever really do it because of the disease."

Jake's heart broke to hear the desperation and vulnerability in her childlike voice. Carly paused, exploring Jake's face to see if she should continue. What she saw convinced her she should.

"The next day we went to the school nurse and got condoms. Michael had already told her how I was feeling. She showed us how to put on the condoms. I mean, on a...sort of model, or something. In a school assembly they had a drama where they practiced putting condoms on bananas. Everybody laughed. You should have seen all the jokes in the cafeteria. But when it was just Michael and me and the nurse, it was a lot more uncomfortable."

Jake disciplined himself not to let his shock or anger reach his face. It was like playing poker, trying to hide the worst possible hand. He didn't want to betray what he was feeling for fear he would shut Carly off. Besides, none of the hostility he felt was toward her.

"She said this was the way to have safe sex. If we used a condom, we'd be safe. If we ever wanted more, she had a file drawer full of them. She has one of those condom trees on her desk, you know, like the surgeon general? She joked about all the different colors and flavors. Michael laughed and squeezed my hand. I thought she was pretty cool too."

This is a school nurse? Helping our kids do things that can bring them under a death sentence?

"Of course, it wasn't the first time I'd held a condom. The Planned Parenthood people came into class last year and passed around condoms to everybody. They said, 'Try them on your fingers if you want to.' Michael and I were still just friends, but he handed one to me and whispered a joke about maybe trying it out together sometime. I was embarrassed at first, but you know, you get used to it with everybody talking about it all the time. They said most kids have sex, so it's normal. You don't want to be the weird one. They just said, be sure you do it safely."

Carly's voice suddenly went up a few decibels, and Jake thought he heard in her some of the anger he was feeling.

"I can't believe I'm telling you all this. Maybe it's because Michael and I don't talk anymore. It's over between us. And my counselor at school, my health teacher, who was one of my best friends—at least I used to think so—we don't talk either. And my friends are all into rally and the Snowball Dance, and trying out for club volleyball. I guess I won't be playing volleyball anymore, even after the pregnancy." Carly's heart sank, as still another domino fell.

"All this is so hard on Mom, and except for her, I don't have anyone else to talk to about this but you. Or maybe it's that all of a sudden I just don't know how much longer I'll have to talk to anyone about anything."

"I'm glad you're talking to me, Carly. I haven't been much of a father, especially the last few years. But it's like what I said about the baby—I want to be there for you now and help anyway I can."

There, I said it. Jake felt relieved, and he was pleased to see Carly's sad drooping lips turn up slightly at the corners.

Jake could tell there was something important about this teacher Carly mentioned, so he took the opening and jumped in. "Why don't you and your teacher friend talk anymore?"

"I guess...it's because I don't trust her anymore. See, I told her Michael had the HIV. And I told her how he got it." Jake wanted to ask, but the time wasn't right. "And I told her I was thinking I shouldn't have sex with him, and maybe I shouldn't let the relationship go any further, but..."

"But what did she say?"

"Well, she's Michael's counselor too. She said she knew he loved me very much. That he'd shown his love by telling me he had the HIV. And maybe it would really hurt him if I said no to him."

"She actually said that?"

"I can't quote her exact words," Carly said defensively. Jake stepped back and sat down in the recliner, lessening the intensity. "That's the definite impression I had, though. She told me abstinence was okay for some kids, but sex was part of a mature relationship, so most people want to experience it together before they decide whether this is the right person or not. She said with the old way, people got married and discovered too late that they weren't...you know, compatible. So she said it was my choice, and the really important thing was to not have unsafe sex. She said there was no right or wrong decision, it was whatever I felt comfortable with. I'm sure she thought she was doing me a favor."

"But...?"

"But all she did was put more pressure on me. I expected her to say 'No, stay away from him, don't go steady with him' or at least 'Whatever you do, don't have sex with him.' To be honest, that's what I was hoping she'd say. She kept telling me I had to be true to myself and my own values, but I kept thinking, what does that mean? I just wanted her to tell me what the right values were."

Carly looked at Jake with pleading eyes that made him want to do anything in the universe to make her feel better.

"Daddy, I didn't want to have sex with him, I really didn't. Not only because I was afraid of the virus, but I just didn't want to. Do you understand what I'm saying?"

"Of course I do, honey. I totally understand."

What Jake didn't understand was who this irresponsible teacher thought she was to pressure his daughter into having sex at all, much less potentially deadly sex.

"When Ms. Beal said what she did"—Carly paused for a moment, as if unsure whether she should have said the teacher's name—"I was more confused than when I came in. I don't know what my values are—and if I did, how would I know if they were right anyway? I mean if nothing is right or wrong, how do you ever know what to do?"

How does a teenage kid know what to do? How does anyone know what to do anymore?

"I met with the teacher"—Jake noticed Carly didn't say her name again, but he wasn't forgetting—"during my study hall, just a few hours before Michael took me to see the school nurse. Then he asked me to come to his house that night. His parents were out of town. He sort of had it planned."

Jake felt nausea at the thought of a strategy leading up to his daughter's loss of virginity. He also felt shame as he remembered doing the same thing with other girls in college, including Janet.

"He took me into his parents bedroom." Suddenly Carly clutched her mid-section and fell to her knees, startling Jake. He jumped out of the recliner and knelt at her side.

Carly clung to Jake like she had after her terrifying bike accident as a nine-year-old. "Oh, Daddy, it was terrible. I was so scared. And the worst part was seeing his parents' wedding picture on the wall. It didn't seem right. It just didn't seem right."

That's because it wasn't right.

Everything within Jake rose up in rebellion against the permissive attitude toward sex that he'd bought and sold his whole adult life. He'd been on the side of the sexual revolution, but the cause had betrayed him. It had littered the landscape with too many corpses. The thought that Carly, sweet innocent Carly, would become one of them was more than he could bear.

"Michael kept telling me everything was okay. Just before we…went all the way, I told him I didn't feel right about it. He argued with me and claimed that the teacher and school nurse wouldn't have said it was okay if it wasn't. He said, 'Remember where we got the condoms? Do you think they'd be giving us stuff at school if it was bad for us? If you won't trust me, at least trust them.'"

Carly pressed on with the story, in Jake's arms, her eyes looking down on the floor behind him.

"He kept telling me everything was safe and that I'd feel much better after we made love. He was wrong. I didn't feel better. I felt used and betrayed. And like a really lousy lover, too. I wasn't like the women in the movies. He wasn't very gentle and I was just so scared. And afterwards I was ashamed, Daddy. I was so ashamed that my clothes were off and that I'd done such a bad job."

Carly sobbed again. Jake didn't know what to do except hold her tighter and stroke her hair. After a few minutes she sat down and resumed her story.

"I realized immediately that 'losing your virginity' was exactly the right phrase. I'd lost something precious. Those romance novels Mom reads and the ones I got from the school library, and the sitcoms and the movies, they make it sound so wonderful. Then, when my virginity was gone, it surprised me I felt such a terrible loss, like the death of a close friend. I'd begun to think of it as a burden, but once I could never have it again, I realized that all along it had been…a treasure."

Carly sounded to Jake like she was reciting something.

"What I just said, more or less, was right out of my journal. I've gone back and reread it more times than I can count."

Jake didn't know Carly kept a journal, like he did. There was a lot he didn't know about this girl. His eyes moistened again as he envisioned her pouring out her heart to that journal in the middle of the night, after she'd lost something so precious to her.

"The strangest thing," Carly went on, "was that I thought so much about it afterward. I thought about my future husband. And I knew Michael wouldn't be the one. I felt like I'd cheated on my mate. And I thought, I wonder if the man I'm going to marry is sleeping with some girl right now that he's always going to compare me to."

Carly laughed bitterly. "I guess there's no danger of that now, is there? I'll never even have a husband!"

The torrent of tears was unstoppable. Jake knelt down next to her chair and pulled Carly's face right up to his. It seemed important they see each other's tears. The streams from Carly's face joined with those from Jake's and flowed down on their clothes. Neither had a thought to go look for a Kleenex. Both were wrecks and neither cared.

Jake felt sure that some of this she hadn't even shared with Janet. Maybe there were things a girl needs to tell her father and no one else. The thought had never occurred to Jake until this moment.

"Anyway, from then on, Michael wanted to do it all the time. He wanted to do it in the car, and once even at school. It got a little better for me—I guess I should say it wasn't as terrible as the first time. But it was never what you see in the movies, not even close. It was like we were little kids pretending we were Tom Cruise and Madonna, or something. It was a joke. But it wasn't funny."

By now every new revelation was to Jake like another shot of Novocain to a man already numb. He could feel the presence of the needle, but couldn't sense anything more. The pain had exceeded his ability to feel it.

"We used the condoms every time at first. Then once we didn't have one and it seemed okay to do it anyway. Once you get going, it's pretty hard to stop. At least we didn't. I mean, Michael and I can't even keep our rooms clean or floss our teeth," Carly laughed, "so it's not like we're going to always do the responsible thing with a stupid condom!"

Safe sex for teens suddenly seemed absurdly self-contradictory in a way Jake had never realized.

"When Ms. Beal saw us in the hall she'd say things like, 'Hope everything's going well with you two.' A few times she even winked at us. Almost like she was the godmother of our sexual relationship, like she was getting her kicks from it. It really started to bug me. One time in health class she made some joke about sex being fun, and caught my eye as if to say 'isn't it fun, Carly?' I was so embarrassed. I started avoiding her and we haven't talked since I told her I was pregnant, and she suggested the abortion. When I decided to have the baby I could tell she disapproved, like I ruined my whole life or something, but by then I wasn't feeling so good about her either.

"Well, there it is, Daddy. True confessions from your little girl. I remember my flub-up in the fifth-grade Christmas play and how it made it into your column. I sure hope this one stays out of the newspaper."

It shocked Jake that she remembered a column from six years ago he had forgotten completely. Obviously, he'd embarrassed her.

"Carly. You mean so much more to me than a stupid column. I would never do that. I'm sorry if I did it before."

"I was just kidding. I didn't think you would."

Several seconds of silence brought Jake to the question he'd put on the back burner.

"Honey, you mentioned Ms. Beal knew how Michael had gotten the HIV. Do you want to talk about it?"

"No. But if you want me to, I will."

Jake nodded and braced himself.

"Michael got it from a guy. He doesn't know who, exactly. That's the worst part. It could have been a few dozen different guys. Most of them...Michael doesn't even know their names."

Carly hung her head again, embarrassed for Michael, and more embarrassed for herself.

"Michael is a homosexual?" Jake couldn't hide his shock.

"He says he's not really a homosexual, he's bisexual. Ms. Beal told him the bisexual thing wasn't abnormal or anything. She told me the same thing—'some people are born homosexual, some heterosexual, some bisexual. It's a diversity thing. It's not wrong, it's just the way it is,' she said. That's her favorite line—'It's not wrong, it's just the way it is.'"

"No right or wrong, no standards, no moral responsibility for anything, huh?" Jake's voice dripped with cynicism and resentment. Had there been a nearby voodoo doll in the image of Ms. Beal, Jake would have riddled it with needles, enjoying every puncture.

"Excuse me. Isn't this Mister Broadminded, Mr. Free-thinking Liberal I'm talking to? I've read your columns on the homosexual lifestyle. You say it's perfectly acceptable, and you call people bigots who say otherwise."

Carly seemed to almost relish Jake's stunned look. "Well," she was pushing now, "am I right or wrong?"

"Uh, I wouldn't put it quite the way you said it," Jake was running for cover and he knew it. Carly was ready, and with a determined look started to reach for something on the coffee table.

"At least, I wouldn't put it that way if I were writing it now."

"So you feel differently on these things when it gets closer to home?"

This sweet little girl knows how to put the knife to you. He couldn't help admiring her for it.

"Yes, to be honest," Jake replied. "But it's not just that, Carly. I've been rethinking a lot of things. But this isn't about me, it's about you."

"Oh, no, Dad, it's about you, too, more than you think. I'm not blaming you for anything, but I've got to tell you what happened. I didn't know what to think about Michael's homosexuality. I only knew it seemed wrong, even though at school the teachers and a lot of the kids seem to think it's okay. But it hurt me. It hurt me because it seemed bad for Michael and I knew it was bad for me. Little did I know just how bad it would turn out."

Carly stared lifelessly at her hands. Noticing how tense they were, she stretched them out in an attempt to relax.

"Still, I kept telling myself that maybe it really was okay. That it was okay to be 'bi', that the condoms were okay, that having sex was okay. It was uncomfortable talking to Mom, and I wouldn't dream of calling you. But it was you I went to."

"I don't understand."

"My trusty scrapbook," Carly said, pulling a large green notebook off the coffee table. "I keep this in my room, by the side of my bed, but I brought it out here since you were coming. I didn't just read your article on *The Final Exit.* I've read every word you've written in the last three years." Carly looked Jake right in the eyes.

"You look surprised. Well, with you pretty much staying out of my life since the divorce, reading your column was the one way I had to get a letter from my dad, three times a week. Sometimes I pretended it wasn't for a million other people, just for me. I saved every one of them."

Jake felt tinges of warmth, regret, and dread at the same time.

"So when I was looking for answers, I went to my scrapbook and used my yellow highlighter on everything you said about sex and morals and right and wrong. Like what you wrote saying no one had the right to try to keep pornography away from people, first amendment and all that. And that sex outside marriage was all right. And that homosexual acts are okay too."

Carly laid the book on Jake's lap, pointing to some of the highlighted passages. *She'd make a great prosecutor.*

"And after reading your stuff, I decided I needed to be more open-minded," Carly said. "I mean, what kid wants to be more conservative than her dad, right? Well, I became more open-minded all right. And now I'm going to die."

The sheer force of her words suffocated him. He gasped for breath.

Carly wasn't angry like she'd been three weeks ago. She had the settled look of someone who'd finally said something she needed to say for a long time. She had arrived at the predetermined punch line. It was over. She quietly stood up, turned and went to the bathroom, closing the door behind her. Jake heard the water running. He pictured her washing her flushed and tear-drenched face.

Carly's punch line left him reeling. He sensed a need to fully confess his wrong and ask for forgiveness and help. But just as he began to give in to the responsibility he bore for all this, something happened. He didn't analyze it, but it was as if some force deep inside him pushed its way to the fore, sending a flood of denial to derail his admission of guilt. Jake's mind was suddenly swimming in a deluge of thoughts that were his, yet not from him:

I wasn't writing guidance for lovelorn teenagers. It's not a "Dear Jakey" column. I was writing for adults, consenting adults with sense enough to see the whole picture. I can't take the blame for what happened to Carly. The adults who talked with her and gave her the condoms were to blame. That school nurse. And Ms. Beal...

Jake's defensiveness roared into a mighty wind, bursting into flame his smoldering rage. *She was there to hand out condoms to my daughter, willing to drive my daughter to an abortion clinic. But where is she now? Her life's going on. My little girl's going to die.*

The sound of someone at the door startled Jake. A key turned in the lock. Jake swept around instinctively, hands in front of him ready to defend or attack, as if responding to the threat of an enemy in an Asian jungle. He was surprised to see Janet come in the door, and self-consciously moved out of his combat posture. He looked at his watch. Ten o'clock already?

Janet looked up and seemed even more surprised to see him. "Jake?" Not seeing her daughter, and sensing his tension, she looked around the apartment and with a loud panicky voice, called out, "Carly?"

"It's okay, Mom," Carly came out of the bathroom, running a towel over her face. "I called him. I've told him everything. I mean, about Michael and...the virus."

Janet looked surprised but relieved. "Well, I'm glad you told him. I think it's best."

There was an awkward silence before Janet asked Carly, "Are you ready to go?"

"Not quite. I'll be a few minutes—need a quick makeup job." Carly headed back to the bathroom and shut the door. Though Jake was miserable, a load seemed to have lifted from Carly.

Jake and Janet were left alone, both pale, weak, and drained, except for the undercurrent of rage in Jake that Janet's presence momentarily subdued. Jake felt he should give her a hug or something, but somehow he couldn't. Something seemed different about Janet. Her face had more lines, and her lower lip looked rough and swollen, as if it had been bitten hard. Her eyes watered, like someone who needed to cry but didn't have any tears left.

Staring vacantly, she said to Jake, "It keeps getting worse, doesn't it?"

Jake nodded. They were standing four feet apart, each looking like someone who needed someone else to reach out to him, neither feeling the strength to be the first to reach.

After a few more awkward moments, Jake said, "I've got to go, Janet. There's something I have to do."

Janet's probing look cut through Jake's calm and measured voice. She knew it was too calm and measured. She hadn't forgotten that look in his eyes either. Jake was angry, and someone was going to pay. Janet felt relieved it wasn't she or Carly, but feared for whoever it was.

Jake was out the door before Janet could say more. As he raced down the apartment steps, the volcanic anger within him swirled as in a lidded cauldron, a pressure cooker poised for eruption. Jake knew right where he wanted to be when it blew.

CHAPTER TWENTY-FIVE

The soldier embarked on a top priority mission that could wait for no one, and from which nothing could deter him. He swerved in and out of traffic, and within fifteen minutes pulled into the only space open in the front parking lot of Monroe High. The car next to him sported two bumper stickers—"Just Say No to Drugs" and "D.A.R.E. to Keep Your Kids Off Drugs." He didn't care about the "Reserved for Faculty" sign in front of his parking space. He was here to engage the enemy.

Jake started to leap out of the car a fraction of a second before he flipped back the handle to release the door. The pain in his left shoulder fueled his scorching anger, making one more thing for which he would blame Ms. Beal.

Like a race walker, with determined and efficient strides, Jake marched to the front office. Papers rustled at the receptionist's desk as he pushed the glass door open. His abrupt and exaggerated movements attracted startled gazes from all over the office.

Diane Koos recognized Jake's profile from his column sketch. She'd met him when he spoke at commencement a few years ago.

"Hello, Mr. Woods," she said in a calm voice. "How can I help you?"

Rather than defuse the time bomb that was Jake Woods, her casual and friendly tone only accelerated the countdown. Though sincere, in Jake's eyes she was condescending and pretentious.

"You can help me by telling me where that witch Beal is."

"Mr. Woods, perhaps you should sit down. I don't think..."

"I don't care what you think. Tell me where she is now."

Faced with this alternative, Diane Koos said something she'd later regret. "Well, I believe she's teaching health this period, in room 203. She'll be done in another fifteen minutes, and I'll arrange with her to meet you. Now if you'll just sit—"

By then Jake was gone.

"Mr. Woods, wait, you can't just...she's not done."

"She'll be done when I get there," Jake said, by this time out the office door and headed to the classroom.

Class skippers and hall wanderers parted in front of Jake. He'd only been in the classroom halls once, to speak to the journalism class, but he quickly found the 200 hall. Within moments he saw 203 on his left, door closed. Without breaking stride Jake yanked open the door and barged into the room.

He had expected to be in the back of the room, looking over students' shoulders to eyeball their teacher at the front. He planned to zero in on his target from a distance. Not having run reconnaissance, however, Jake discovered he was in the front of the class, looking into the eyes of twenty-five students, and standing only a few feet from Ms. Beal.

This wasn't a good beginning. He'd entered with all the grace of a junkyard dog, and now here he was. Jake quickly scoped out the room. On the board over his right shoulder was written "Good Sex is Safe and Consensual." On the teacher's desk were a half dozen different colors and textures of condoms, a diaphragm, IUD, and packets of birth control pills, laid out neatly on a tray to be passed around the class. Next to them were brochures from Planned Parenthood and a local abortion clinic. Jake recognized the distinctive design immediately because Carly showed him the same brochure when she'd said she was pregnant.

After a startled pause, a polite but strong voice fired Jake's direction. It seemed out of place coming from the stylishly dressed petite blond. "Excuse me," Ms. Beal said, "we have a class going on here. Can I help you find—"

"I'm Carly Woods's father. I've got some things to say to you."

"Oh, hello, Mr. Woods. I'm glad to meet you," Ms. Beal said, but the expression on her face wasn't so sure. "I'll be done here in just a few minutes and then we can talk."

"I'm not waiting." Jake loaded and fired his first round. "We'll talk now. Who do you think you are giving my daughter and her jerk of a boyfriend your filthy rubbers? She's dying. And it's your fault. How does it feel to give a death sentence to a teenage girl?"

The blood drained from the teacher's face, only to be quickly replenished by a crimson rush.

"Mr. Woods, I'm not responsible for your daughter's choices. I tried to save her life by helping her have safe sex. If I hadn't, she'd have gotten AIDS long ago. And," this was her heavy artillery, "it's not my fault you weren't there for your daughter. Don't blame me for your failure as a parent."

My failure?" The truth hit close to home, but coming from this woman it was too much. "This isn't about me, Ms. Beal. It's about you. You're the one that's been brainwashing my daughter—and all these kids who think they're getting the truth from you." Jake, an imposing figure for the twelve inches he stood above Ms. Beal, waved a big left arm at the class.

"Mr. Woods, I—"

"You told her staying away from sex was unrealistic. You told her she could have sex without worrying as long as she just carried your magic condoms. Do you get a commission for every one you distribute," Jake shouted, "or do you own the whole stinkin' rubber company?"

A few gasps and a brave chuckle surfaced. Jake felt he'd scored a few points. The twenty-five Monroe students couldn't have been paying better attention than if they had been told the class would end with a quiz and anyone flunking it would be executed by firing squad.

"I teach these students because I care about them. Get your head out of the sand, Mr. Woods. Teenagers have sex. That's a reality. So do we let them die, or do we do what's best for them, even if head-in-the-sand moralists don't like it?" Ms.

Beal was hitting some targets herself.

"Yeah, right," Jake came back. "But it's not the moralists who are dying from AIDS. It's you free-thinking, whatever comes natural, no self-control, have sex if you feel like it types. And the kids you lied to, and the innocent babies, they're the ones dying."

Jake surprised himself by throwing in the abortion issue. *Where did that come from?* It didn't escape Ms. Beal's notice.

"What are you, some right-to-life fanatic? I thought you were a journalist, not a right-wing preacher! Now get out of my—"

Jake picked up the contraceptive tray with all the samples, holding it out as evidence toward Ms. Beal.

"I suppose you're offering these kids clean needles and teaching them how to take safe drug injections? After all, they're going to do drugs anyway, so it's your job to teach them how to do it safely. God knows their parents are too stupid to teach them how to do drugs the right way."

Ms. Beal was so furious she started a sentence three times. Jake wasn't going to give her a fourth try. Pointing an accusing finger he said, "Why don't you tell them, 'Just say no to sex.' Why not give their parents bumper stickers that say 'DARE to keep your kids off sex?' Instead of teaching them how to dodge cars and sending them out on the freeway, why don't you teach them to stay off the freeway in the first place?"

Jake realized most of what he was saying he'd heard from Finney and Sue. Apparently it made a deeper impression than he'd realized, but for the moment he was grateful. It was good ammo, and he felt like he was taking this hill from the enemy.

"And," Jake continued his charge, "why don't you tell them about all the studies and people's experiences that say sex before marriage is bad for your mental health, that it increases the probability of divorce and family breakdown and serious problems with children. If you won't tell them, let me. I should know. I ruined my own marriage."

It startled Jake to hear himself say this. His admission gave Ms. Beal the opening she needed. Her voice was trembling, but her words were measured.

"Don't project your guilt onto me or these students. Being a lousy husband and parent is your problem. And don't you dare hang some Puritan morality around our necks and try to make us feel guilty just because we happen to think sex is natural and good."

Jake was loading his next round. "Why don't you stop dragging these kids down to your moral level, Ms. Beal? I hear you get your kicks out of being Monroe's Patron Saint of Teen Sex!"

"How dare you! My choices and the choices of these students are none of your business, Mr. Woods. You have no right to take over this classroom and spout off your ignorant hateful propaganda."

"But you have the right to spout off *your* propaganda every day?" Jake had no intention of retreating. "How about some equal time? I know I'm just a lowly ignoramus parent and all, and I have a lot of nerve to think my daughter is more my business than yours. I mean, you're paid to take care of these kids, we parents just take care of them for free. You think you know what's best for them? Well, when my little girl dies, just remember it was you who killed her, just as surely as if you gave her a loaded gun and helped her pull the trigger!"

"You—"

"I'm not finished, Ms. Beal. How many other kids in this school will die because they've bought your sales pitch? How many are already HIV positive and don't have a clue? How many carry around their industrial strength condoms thinking a stupid little piece of latex will save their lives? Why don't you try telling the truth, even if it goes against your ideology? I ought to sue you. Maybe Carly and I *will* sue you. You make me sick."

"Get out, get out of my classroom—you have no right to be here!" The normally confident and composed Ms. Beal was screaming now. A gob of spittle landed on her otherwise impeccable red lapel.

Jake pointed to the classroom. "Our children should be able to trust you, Ms. Beal. And Carly did. She trusted you, and now she has this plague. And you haven't even visited her. You're too busy raising up your next crop of victims."

He raised his voice on the last sentence to make sure Ms. Beal heard him twenty feet down the hall, where she was now running the other direction. Jake's head of steam dissipated as the object of his scorn receded. Suddenly, for the first time, he felt embarrassed.

Jake glanced self-consciously at the class. They looked as if they were posed for a 1914 photograph, where the shutter was opened for five seconds so everyone had to be perfectly still. No gum chewing, no sound of tearing paper, no packing and unpacking of books, no looking at the clock. Nothing. Jake realized he had the most captive audience of his life, and he owed them an explanation.

"Uh, hello class. Any questions?"

There was a ripple of nervous laughter.

One girl half raised her hand, big brown eyes heavy with water. Jake recognized her—hadn't he seen her with Carly when he bumped into her at the mall?

"Is Carly really going to die?"

"Well, some people have the HIV for years before getting AIDS. But usually...yes, Carly's probably going to die. Eventually, we all are." Once again he surprised himself. "Life here is short. It's like...a window of opportunity. And what we do here really matters. Don't waste your life. Maybe some accident or something will happen, but this isn't an accident. It's a choice. Don't choose to throw your life away on this safe sex myth. Or any other myth."

Jake felt a story emerge from deep inside him. "When I was in college I felt pressured to have sex. Not that I didn't want to, but there's a right time and place. And I did it at the wrong time and place, and kept doing it. And the people who seemed 'with it,' they kept saying it was okay. But you know what? It wasn't like in the movies. It didn't satisfy. I felt empty. And I started using people. I didn't respect the girls I slept with and I didn't respect myself. Do any of you know what I mean?"

Several heads nodded.

"I even used my reputation as a defender of women's rights to get girls in bed with me." It sounded so crass. But it was true, so he said it.

"Some of you know better. I never went to church as a kid. I still don't. But if you were taught sex should be reserved for marriage, don't ever apologize for it. It's right. I never thought I'd admit it, but deep inside I've known it for years. It's right. And because it's right it's also smart. It's the best way to live. A good friend taught me that.

"And that's what good friends do. They tell you the truth. They don't buy into the lies we're always being told. Look, I know about lies. I should. I work for a newspaper. Most of what we say is true, but in some of the most important areas of life, we tell the truth selectively, and sometimes the bottom-line impression is misleading, sometimes a downright lie. I've done it for years. But I'm not going to do it anymore."

Jake heard himself make a vow he hadn't composed till that very moment.

"Listen kids, I need to apologize. I shouldn't have barged in here like this." He smiled sheepishly. "You have to admit it wasn't your basic boring class, but still, I shouldn't have. I meant every word I said. And Ms. Beal may mean well—I'm sure she does—but I think she's dead wrong. I've interviewed lots of people, seen lots of life, and I think she couldn't be more wrong than she is. And one day you'll know that. I can only pray"—*why did I say that word*—"I can only *hope* that you won't have to learn the hard way like I did. Or Carly..."

Jake turned away and buried his face in his hands. He didn't know how long he'd stood there before feeling a gentle but firm hand grasp his arm. Turning, he saw a blurry Mr. French, the principal who seemed so pleased to meet him when he spoke at commencement, but was so obviously upset to see him now.

Mr. French turned him toward the door, quietly saying, "This isn't the place, Mr. Woods. Come with me."

Almost as an afterthought, the principal turned and said to the somber students, "Class dismissed."

Jake saw the room full of kids, most still in shock, a few crying, all very quiet. They slowly got up. One strangely familiar looking girl walked up briskly and caught Jake and Mr. French in the hallway. It was Molly, Doc's daughter. He'd seen her at the funeral or he wouldn't have recognized her now. She looked so old, her face hardened. Her short skirt, low-cut blouse, and lavish make-up made a statement he didn't want to hear right now.

"Hi, Molly. How are you?" Jake had seen her often over the years when he'd dropped by to pick up Doc, but realized now he didn't really know her. She'd never been a person to him, just Doc's daughter.

"There's something I just don't get," Molly said. Her forceful presence and determined approach reminded Jake of Doc as much as her piercing eyes, auburn hair, and olive complexion. Her intensity even convinced Mr. French to delay his determined march away from the classroom.

"What's that, Molly?"

"Carly made a presentation in this class, and she read from one of your columns. Ms. Beal thought it was so good she made copies for the whole class. I have it right here." Molly pulled out the goldenrod photocopy from her folder.

Jake recognized the distinctive heading with his profile sketch from the *Tribune*. It was titled "Let's Face the Facts about Teen Sex." The date was eleven months earlier. He couldn't remember exactly what he said, but he did recall some lively discussions with Finney and Sue about this column.

"It talks about why schools ought to pass out condoms to kids, to keep them from getting AIDS," Molly said. Looking down to scan the paper, she went on. "You said we should be realistic that lots of kids are going to have sex. That sexual activity isn't for everyone, but kids have the right to choose whether to be sexually active, and schools must teach them their options, since most parents don't bother. Here, I'll read the last part word for word. You said, 'Parents have no right to sacrifice their kids' lives by interfering with our schools' efforts to teach responsible sex. Just because the religious beliefs of a minority make them uncomfortable with sex in general and birth control in particular is no reason for the rest of us to punish our nation's children by denying them the necessary education and equipment for safe sex.'"

Molly looked Jake in the eyes. "Do you remember writing this?"

Jake remembered. He wished he didn't. He stared at the cracks between the off-white floor tiles, wishing they would suck him into oblivion.

"So what gives you the right to yell at Ms. Beal? Everything she's told us is the same stuff Dad said, the same stuff you say in your columns. You wrote it," Molly's voice shook with anger, "maybe you better go back and read it."

She shoved the paper in Jake's face. Reluctantly, not wanting to even touch it, he took it from her.

Everything about Molly's accusing tone suggested a story of personal pain was behind it. Jake started to respond, but she'd already turned away and headed down the hall. Mr. French resumed ushering him away.

Starting to think about what he'd wished he'd said to Molly, he said to himself, *No, this isn't about her, it's about me.*

He'd denied his own guilt and hypocrisy when Carly confronted him with his columns. He'd taken the focus off his responsibility by casting the blame on Ms. Beal. Now Molly had put her finger on his guilt again. This time he couldn't escape it and refused to try. He wouldn't let a voice, his own or any other, succeed in justifying himself again.

Jake realized his feet had stopped moving. He heard someone say something. It was Mr. French.

"Sit down, Mr. Woods. Obviously, we need to talk."

"I am reminded of another event, Master Finney, one I witnessed while on earth. Two men owned farms side by side. One was a bitter atheist, the other a devout Christian. The atheist was constantly annoyed at the Christian for his trust in God. So one winter the atheist said to him, 'Let's plant our crops as usual this spring, each the same number of acres. We'll both work hard, you your six days and I seven. You pray to your God and I'll curse him. Then come October, let's see who has the bigger crop.' When October came the atheist was delighted because his crop was larger. 'See, you fool,' he taunted, 'what do you have to say for your God now?' The other farmer replied, 'My God doesn't settle all his accounts in October.'

"And so it is, Master Finney. Elyon will settle all accounts. Some will begin to be settled in the other world, but the final settlement will not be on that side of death, but here on this side. You were right when you talked on earth about living in light of eternity and having only one chance to do so. Many will deeply regret their lives on earth and wish they could live them over again. But there is no second chance for unbelievers to go back and trust in Christ. Neither is there a second chance for believers to go back and live for Christ. Second chances sometimes come on earth, but they are always limited in time and opportunity. Whether through death or final alienation or something else, the doors always close on second chances.

"And that is why Elyon gave you his Book. So you could know the truth the first time around. So you could know the judgment that awaits you, when there are no more second chances. So you could know what Elyon required of you while still on earth. So you would not have to wait until you died to learn how you should have lived."

After pausing quietly to consider these truths, Finney and Zyor moved together toward the portal, not speaking a word. Once again they felt compelled to intercede for someone still living in the world of second chances.

Jake sat home, lonely and miserable. As he reflected back on the day, he felt hurt, depressed, and embarrassed. His own father hadn't been there for him, and he faced the fact he hadn't been there for his daughter. No, it was worse. At least his father had never walked out on his mother as he'd walked out on Janet. Somehow, in a way he had denied before, his desertion of his child's mother was the greatest possible betrayal of the child herself.

Carly and Molly both confronting him with his columns had caused much soul-searching. He found himself wondering about many things he'd believed for years, and the foundation—or lack of foundation—on which those beliefs had been built. He thought about Janet, Carly, and his mother. He saw the disastrous consequences of his beliefs and lifestyle choices. They had cost him his marriage, his relationship with his mother and daughter, and now they would cost even his daughter's life. As Finney might have put it, he was reaping what he had sown.

Worse yet, he had not only embraced these beliefs, he had propagated them through his columns, his speeches, and his conversations. He had not only failed in the important things in life, he had led others down a path that would lead to the same kind of failure.

As clumsy and inappropriate as his attempt to stand up for Carly had been, there was some inexplicable sense of rightness about it. He'd come to her aid and defense too late, to be sure, but he had come nonetheless. If she knew how he did it—and inevitably she'd find out—she'd be embarrassed, maybe miffed at him. Yet perhaps she would see that in his belated, inexperienced, and fumbling way, he had tried to do for her what fathers throughout the ages have tried to do for their children—defend, protect, and go to battle against those who dared to wound them.

Unfortunately, in Carly's case the one inflicting the wound wasn't just Ms. Beal. The deeper wound had been at his own hand.

Jake wished he had a chance to do it over again, this father thing. And yet he knew himself well enough to know he'd probably mess it all up one more time. He was still who he was. What would change? He'd just fail Carly a second time, wouldn't he? Could either of them endure the encore?

Finney's Bible, there on the lamp table by the recliner, seemed to call to Jake as if it were more than an inanimate object. It unnerved him. Finally he picked it up and gingerly opened the flyleaf, with the feelings of an explorer about to enter a cavern for the first time, having only a faint idea of what he might discover within. He sensed some of it contained perilous dangers, but felt willing to take that risk for the rewards that might await him. How much worse could things get?

Jotted in various places, with different colors of ink, were sayings such as, "Christians aren't perfect, just forgiven," and "Hammer away, you hostile hands; your hammers break, God's Anvil stands." At the top of the second page the word Bible had been turned into an acrostic, reading "Basic Instructions Before Leaving Earth." Underneath it, nicely typed and printed in Times Roman, were various quotes Finney had assembled, printed, then taped in this prominent place. The yellow tape suggested he'd done all this years ago. Jake read a couple of them with interest:

"I must take care, on the one hand, never to despise, or be unthankful for, these earthly blessings, and on the other, never to mistake them for the something else of which they are only a kind of copy, or echo, or mirage. I must keep alive in myself the desire for my true country, which I shall not find till after death."—C. S. Lewis

"He is no fool who gives what he cannot keep to gain what he cannot lose."—Jim Elliot

"Let no one apologize for the powerful emphasis Christianity lays upon the doctrine of the world to come. Right there lies its immense superiority to everything else within the whole sphere of human thought or experience. When Christ arose from death and ascended into heaven He established forever three important facts, namely, that this world has been condemned to ultimate dissolution, that the human spirit persists beyond the grave and that there is indeed a world to come. We do well to think of the long tomorrow."—A. W. Tozer.

The long tomorrow. That's the big question, isn't it? What awaits us in the long tomorrow?

He read another sentence at the bottom, written in Finney's distinctive hand. "When all else fails, read the Directions."

Jake smiled wryly, remembering all the times on vacations and outings when he was lost and Janet accused him of being proud and stubborn because he refused to stop and ask directions. He always thought he knew the way, and if he didn't he wasn't about to admit it to someone else. He knew the answers, Jake realized, to innumerable questions. But to the questions that ultimately mattered, he had no answers.

Jake sat back in his recliner, and with a profound feeling of failure combined with a faint glimmer of hope, he began—as a man relieved to finally admit he's lost—to read the Directions.

CHAPTER TWENTY-SIX

J ake labored over his column with uncharacteristic nervousness. As he typed the sentences that magically appeared on his terminal, he found himself turning his head to be sure no one was watching. Today he felt as Leonard had described it, like a boy in class hiding a *Playboy* behind his textbook.

He was startled by a hand on his back. It was Guy, a city politics reporter.

"Jake, you're not actually doing your column, are you? It's only nine. You put in a full three hours and they'll have to pay you overtime."

It was the usual good-natured ribbing of columnists, who were *Tribune* heavyweights, but had a rep for keeping lightweight schedules.

Jake quickly turned and blocked Guy's line of sight to his screen. "More on my mind than usual. This might be a tough one to write, so thought I'd get a jump on it."

"What's it about?"

"Oh, I don't know. Condoms in schools, that sort of thing."

"You've done pieces like that before. This a new slant?"

"Yeah, I guess you could say that."

"Well, prudes everywhere are out there just waiting for you to infuriate them. Don't disappoint 'em! See ya later."

"Later." Jake's voice was uncharacteristically limp. He listened as his seventh call of the day came in on his telephone recorder. He was screening for the rare one he needed to take.

"Jake? Sutter. I need to talk. Pick up that phone, will you?"

Jake hesitated a moment then picked up the phone, instinctively whispering as he never did for other calls. "Look, I'm busy, Sutter. I've got a real job."

"Is that what you call it?" Sutter chuckled. He seemed to find humor in everything.

"I'm on deadline. Make it quick."

"Tried to call you yesterday, but no answer. Just wondering if you found anything out at the high school. What's your lead there anyway? Think the water polo team was involved in the murder?" Sutter snorted, pleased at his wit. "Not holding out on me, are you?"

Jake sighed, tired of Sutter knowing everywhere he went. "The school had to do with my daughter. I do have a life besides the investigation."

"Sure, okay. But you've been running in and out of diners, making late night trips to your friend's house. You must have something for me, Jake."

"I do." Jake gave Sutter a quick synopsis of the locked files and told him he'd fax over Finney's computer papers as soon as they got off.

"What about you, Sutter? Anything for me?"

"Yeah. How about we get together?"

"Look, maybe tomorrow. Not today. If you've got anything, tell me over the phone. Nobody would have it bugged but you."

"What I've got you're not going to like, but here it is, and it fits perfectly with the new stuff you uncovered. We've run traces on some complicated financial transactions. They take off from a bogus company set up by our friends in organized crime. And they land in the back yard of your friend, Dr. Lowell. He took at least one payoff, maybe more, just as your computer files suggest."

"What was the payoff for?"

"No details yet. We have a few ideas. And when I go over your faxes I think some stuff may rise to the top. There's more, but not over the phone."

Sutter had piqued Jake's curiosity.

"Okay. How about you meet me in the deli at one tomorrow? The one where you were pretending to read the *Trib* and drinking your Red Sangria? You know, when you were eavesdropping on me and Ollie. Remember?"

Sutter laughed. "I wondered if you ever put that together."

"Don't mistake me for a complete moron, Sutter."

"I don't, Jake. Believe me, I don't. One more thing, and I hate to say it. The Bureau's got an operation going on somewhere else, a big one, and I've got to pull surveillance on you for a couple of days. Mayhew flew out last night. The two other agents who've been sharing duty on you have to take a hike too. I fought the brass on it, but they have to set priorities with limited personnel, and this time you got bumped."

"That's reassuring."

"Look, they've only made one move on you, right? And our guys haven't seen 'em on you for over a week—that's a lot of coffee and donuts and sore rear ends for nothing. Besides, they don't know we're not still on your tail. They've been timid since the episode behind the market, and remembering Mayhew's .44 Magnum isn't going to make them braver. Hey, it may just be one guy anyway—Mr. Baseball didn't have any backup, right? By the time anybody notices, our guys will be back on the job. Your own little guardian angels."

"Okay, Sutter. I'm not going to sweat it." *What difference would it make if I did?*

"Good. Just be careful. See you at the deli at one tomorrow. And we'll make sure no one's eavesdropping!" Jake cut off Sutter's good-natured laugh when he hung up his phone.

Once again Jake undertook the mental discipline of setting aside the latest distraction to concentrate on the task at hand. He typed for another thirty minutes, identifying with asterisks parts where he needed hard data and further development. In the past he'd always called Planned Parenthood on this subject. He did so again, got lots of opinions, but they didn't have documentation on most of the things he was looking for. He called Barbara Betcher at NEA. She had some strong feelings, but again not the hard data he needed. He took a deep breath and decided to call Carl Mahoney at CARE. Jake had a vague impression from his interview two months ago that Mahoney might have some studies he needed.

Jake dialed his number, smiling as he recalled his last episode with Mrs. Mahoney and the spin cycle. This time a man answered the phone.

"Citizens Advocating Responsible Education. Carl Mahoney speaking."

"Yeah, Carl. Jake Woods from the *Tribune*."

There was a pause. "Uh-huh."

People's voices usually picked up and showed life when they heard Jake's name. He knew it was a bad sign that Mahoney's did not.

"Carl, I'd like to ask you a few questions."

"Excuse me, Mr. Woods, but I need to tell you I'm pressing the record button on my answering machine. Our conversation is now being taped. I'm not sure if I'm required to tell you this or not, but I wanted you to know."

"Um...why are you taping our conversation?"

"It's a practice I started after the last time you called me, actually. You were the third person from the *Tribune* who misquoted me. This is a protective measure."

"I misquoted you?"

"I'm going to assume you're shooting straight with me, but I find it difficult to believe you don't know how you portrayed me in that column. I received hate mail and two phone threats. Even my kids got hassled because their dad supposedly said some things I didn't say. Or if I did say them, you took them out of context."

"Well, if that's true, it certainly wasn't deliberate."

"First, it *is* true. Anyone listening to our last conversation then reading your column would know that. Second, while I appreciate your saying it wasn't deliberate, that doesn't reassure me. If anything, it frightens me."

"Why would it frighten you?"

"Because if it had been deliberate, then you could apologize and promise not to do it again. But if it wasn't deliberate, if you did it unconsciously, then you'll just do it again, because it comes naturally. I mean no offense, but that's how I see it."

"Well, Mr. Mahoney, I don't quite know what to say."

Jake considered apologizing, but admitting wrong was seldom good policy. Especially not when you were being taped!

"I understand you have strong beliefs, Mr. Woods, as I do. Those beliefs are very different. Maybe it would be hard for me to communicate your beliefs fairly, but I'd like to think I could quote you accurately, then take issue with you honestly, in a way that showed respect for you as a person."

"And you felt I didn't show you respect?"

"That's right. Don't think this is a matter of hurt feelings. If my feelings were easily hurt I'd just go with the crowd. But when I take the lumps, I want it to be for what I really believe and really said and how I really said it. Since your last interview, and a few other misrepresentations, I've been on the defensive, doing damage control, putting out fires. I've had to repeatedly refute your caricature of me. I had a speaking engagement canceled because they read your column and found out 'what kind of person I really am.' I just don't think you understand how you can mess up somebody's life. You move right on to the next column, but we have to pick up the pieces. Can you understand that?"

"Well, yeah, I guess so. I can see you're upset. I'll do my best to quote you accurately, Mr. Mahoney."

"I'm sorry, but our board has made a list of four or five media people who have badly misrepresented us, and they've instructed me not to grant them more interviews. I'm afraid you're on the list."

"But...you've already been talking to me. And you're taping the interview, right?"

"I'm taping our conversation in which I'm explaining why I can't grant you an interview. I turned on the tape lest you misrepresent my explanation. To be honest—and I'm probably crazy to say this—an attorney told me the tape won't do much good anyway. Suing the media for libel or slander is pointless unless you can prove what was said is false *and* that there was deliberate malice. If I had a tape of our last interview, I could prove you misrepresented me. As I understand the law, though, all you'd have to do is say you intended no harm. Unless I could prove otherwise, the case would be closed. Am I right?"

"Well, I'm not sure it's quite that simple, but yes, that's basically accurate."

"But whether or not you had malice, the harm still stands. I rear ended someone last month. I didn't intend to smash into his car, but I did. There was no malice, but I was still liable for the damage. But it doesn't seem to work that way with you people. You're immune. The tape recording is a small consolation, but what good will it do? Even if I have proof you misquote me, how do I get it into people's hands? A half million people read what you said about me—is that the *Trib's* circulation? I'd be lucky to reach a few hundred."

"Mr. Mahoney, I probably shouldn't say 'I was wrong' and 'I'm sorry,' especially not on tape. But as a show of good faith, I'll do it. I was wrong and I'm sorry. It wasn't malicious, but I believe you when you say damage was done. I'm truly sorry."

"Well...thank you. It doesn't undo the damage, but it does make me feel better. To be honest, a correction or retraction would make me feel a lot better than your apology, but I'm not unrealistic. I know you won't do that."

Mahoney paused, as if there was a faint hope Jake might say he would. Jake didn't even consider it. It was too late, it would make him look too bad, and Winston would never go for it anyway. Mahoney was right and Jake knew it. His apology was sincere, but it did nothing to correct any damage.

"It's like the old saying, 'Fool me once, shame on you; fool me twice, shame on me.' I want to trust you, Mr. Woods, but after what happened last time, I'd be a fool to. If I sound like I'm a little gun shy, remember you're not the only one I've had this experience with."

"Well, I can see where you're coming from, Mr. Mahoney. I understand your decision not to do the interview, but I think you may be surprised when you see the column."

"Really? Well, we'll see."

"Anyway, let me ask you this. Do you have some material on Planned Parenthood, birth control education, school clinics, condom distribution in schools, that sort of thing? I've got files full of stuff from the other point of view. Do you have anything you can fax me in the next hour?"

There was a pause, as if Carl Mahoney wasn't sure if this was some kind of trick. "Well...okay. Give me fifteen minutes and I could get together lots of pertinent stuff, government studies, independent research, all kinds of data."

"That's exactly what I'm looking for. I appreciate your help. I owe you for this, and again I'm sorry about last time."

"Okay, well, thank you. I'll fax this stuff over pronto. What's your fax number?"

Jake gave him the number and seconds later was staring at the screen, pondering the indictment Mahoney had laid on him. He was surprised he hadn't been more defensive. Mahoney was wrong thinking he'd done anything deliberate. But he needed to take the accusation seriously. He looked at the letter from the woman, pinned up on his wall, the mother he'd unfairly accused in the column about her criminal son. What was it Mahoney had said? "Whether you intended it or not, the harm stands." And, "You move on to the next column, but we have to pick up the pieces."

Jake had a queasy feeling, like maybe after this column, he'd be the one picking up the pieces.

Ten minutes later he walked to the common fax machine in his area. A call just came in, and the waxy white sheets were slowly emerging. Good, it was from Mahoney. He started reading the first few pages, without tearing them away from the machine. He looked through the research and statistics and started marking pertinent items with his pen. *Yeah, this is exactly what I'm looking for.* He could fill in the asterisks with hard data now. But lots of people weren't going to like it.

After another hour of pounding the keys, editing and rewriting, Jake finally had a column, eight hundred words. He'd had to cut it in half and decided to remove the hard data after all and save it for another column, assuming he'd still be working here. He just summarized the main facts and appealed to the reader's common sense. He sat back to read it start to finish, trying to put himself in the place of his readers:

What I'm about to say will be controversial. That's an enlightening commentary on our times, since what I'm saying also happens to be indisputably true.

Here it is: The true biological cause of teen pregnancies is not the absence of birth control. You'd never know this from the literature and television programs and columns on the subject, but it's true nonetheless.

Teen pregnancy isn't caused by the absence of anything. It's caused by the presence of something—teenage sexual activity.

Here's something equally controversial: The true biological cause of the spread of AIDS is not the lack of condoms or sterile needles. It's not the lack of anything, except the lack of training, determination and self-discipline to abstain from sex and drugs.

In other words, it's not what we're not doing that's gotten us in trouble.

It's what we are doing.

Planned Parenthood has had a profound influence on the young people of America for two decades now, bringing birth control training into our school classrooms. Guess what's happened in that same twenty-year period. The rate of teen pregnancy and sexually transmitted diseases has skyrocketed. Why? Well, one clue is this statement from a recent president of Planned Parenthood: "We are not going to be an organization promoting celibacy or chastity."

It appears some things are worse than disease and death. For certain adults, teenagers abstaining from sex seems to be one of them.

By its massive distribution of birth control and its efforts to make premarital sex seem normal and exciting, Planned Parenthood and the mainstream media have promoted the illusion of "safe sex." They've obscured all the traditional reasons for teenagers not to have sex. Consequently, the number of teenagers having sex has risen dramatically.

This has resulted not only in increased unwanted pregnancies and STDs, but in emotional scars in children not mature enough to handle the psychological dynamics and responsibilities of sexual intimacy. Planned Parenthood, and many school nurses and health teachers who take their cues from the recognized sexperts, believe it's naive to expect to teach fifteen-year-olds to abstain from sex. Which is no different than saying teenagers can't be taught to abstain from drugs.

Instead of recognizing the basic flaw in its approach, Planned Parenthood points to the rise in teen pregnancy and STDs as proof for the strategic importance of its further efforts with teenagers. But their efforts can't succeed without curtailing the root of all teen pregnancy, which is, once again, teen sexual activity.

Imagine if Planned Parenthood were put in charge of children's traffic safety. They would devote their efforts to teaching children the art of dodging cars rather than teaching them to stay off the freeway in the first place. They would argue with great conviction that the cause of children being run over on the freeway is they've not been trained to jump aside quickly enough when an eighteen-wheeler bears down on them. They'd point to the tragedy of increasing teen freeway fatalities, claiming it's naive to think teenagers can stay off the road. Then they'd demand more tax money and classroom time to teach our children how to juke and jive their way around the freeway.

Since we've accepted the Planned Parenthood strategy, why stop here? Let's put them in charge of preventing wife abuse. Then they can set up programs to distribute boxing gloves to every husband in America.

Well, young people, here's the message that's been so buried and obscured by the foolishness of your elders, myself included:

You can fail to use condoms 100% of the time, and still have a 0% chance of getting pregnant or contracting STDs. All you have to do is abstain from sex. This is not impossible. People in many cultures throughout recorded history have done it for a good part of their lives. I even managed to do it for the first twenty years of my life. Now I wish I would have waited until I was twenty-six, when I got married. In this age of enlightenment and achievement and self-determination, surely you can abstain from sex with the same kind of discipline you exercise in athletics, doing homework, saying no to drugs, and getting out of bed when the alarm goes off.

Of course, many adults are convinced you cannot do this. They think of you as mindless animals whose lives must be driven by hormones and desires, not by reason and moral values and self-discipline. I know. I used to think that way. Recent events have helped me see how wrong I was.

My suggestion is simple, kids. Don't listen to us. Listen to what you know is true. There are many good reasons for waiting until marriage to have sex. Staying alive is only one of them.

Jake looked at the clock. 11:25. Winston would love to have his column so early. But there was no way he would let Winston see this until 11:50, when it was too late to make substantive changes. He couldn't get up and wander or Winston would see he wasn't at his desk and come over and check on him. He'd have to sit there, pretending he was still at work.

For the next twenty-five minutes Jake stared at his screen and thought about a lot of things. Carly and his experience at the school. Janet and the mistakes they started making twenty-eight years ago, and the profound effects it had on them since, many of which he was only now realizing. His talks with Leonard and Clarence and his concerns about journalism. Carl Mahoney's words were freshest in his mind. They pointed out things not just in his profession but in himself that he found disturbing. The wait until 11:50 felt like an eternity. After releasing the column, he sat quietly, thinking about nothing and everything.

At 11:55, Winston stepped out his office and yelled, "Woods!"

As he walked the gauntlet, someone mumbled, "Wow. I'll have to read your column, Jake. Must be a real winner!"

Winston's voice boomed before Jake could shut the door behind him. "What's going on, Woods?"

"What do you mean?"

"Don't get smart with me. What do you think you're doing?" Winston waved at his terminal, possessed by Jake's column.

"I'm writing a column. That's what I'm paid for."

"Come on. This is an attack piece on a respected organization. And it makes the schools sound like they're morons. Reading this you'd think everybody out there but the conservatives are trying to kill our children or something."

"Isn't that a bit of an overreaction, Winston?"

"Overreaction? You want overreaction? I'm trying to save you from two hundred phone calls and a deluge of mail, some of which will be retractions of their previous letters that wished you to get well soon."

"I can handle the backlash."

Winston sighed. "Look, Jake, you must have something else we can run instead? Buy us time so we can talk about it tomorrow?"

"Sorry. That's all I've got." Jake had a dozen half-baked pieces Winston would have preferred, but he wasn't about to offer them. "It's just an opinion piece, Winston. This is a newspaper, as in there isn't just one position we can take, right? Can't we have some different opinions once in a while?"

Winston bristled at the implication of censorship. "Look, Woods, you know that's not the issue. George Will could write this and I wouldn't think twice about it. But not you. It sounds like somebody got to you or something. Like you've been...I don't know, unduly influenced. Or maybe this is a grudge column, like somebody at Planned Parenthood called you a name and this is your way of getting back. It doesn't sound authentic, especially not after those two columns on media bias. You sound like a preacher. It's like somebody took an old Pat Buchanan column and put your name on it."

"Really? So, I'm as much a stereotypical liberal as they are conservatives, huh?"

"In a word, yes."

"So if a conservative columnist—I know this is hard to imagine since we've carried so very few of them—submitted a piece supporting Planned Parenthood, you'd say 'Let's not print it, it sounds suspect, like somebody got to him.' Is that what you'd say?"

Winston rolled his eyes. "I don't have time for this. Okay, Woods, it's your reputation. See if I care what happens. Get out of here. Go talk to a defense attorney, or someone who knows damage control. Cop a temporary insanity plea. Tell them you hit your head in the accident and your brains haven't settled yet, or some of them oozed out your ear!"

Winston waved his arm toward the door with the sense of a king who'd offered a subject a pardon, which he'd refused.

"Yes, sir. Thanks for your usual gentleness and understanding."

Jake closed the door to Winston's curses, which escaped through the crack into the array of cubicles.

Jake wandered back to his desk, avoiding eye contact with what he knew were a lot of questioning stares and feisty smiles. He realized that as soon as his column was released to layout, a bunch of eager eyes would be reading it on their terminals. As he got back to his desk, his phone was ringing.

"Jake Woods."

"Winston." The voice wasn't quite as gruff as forty seconds ago.

"Miss me already, Winston? Want me to come back so you can yell at me some more?"

"No need. I can yell at you over the phone." Winston's tone suddenly got as soft as Jake had ever heard it. "Seriously, Jake. I'm going to print this thing, but let me take out the references to Planned Parenthood. Let's just refer to this as a philosophy some people believe. No need to offend a certain group. Okay?"

"Not okay, Winston. Planned Parenthood is an identifiable group, well known as a major organization promoting this philosophy. I'd be playing games not mentioning them. Whenever I've talked about them positively I mention them by name, and there's never been a problem. I think we've got to mention them by name now too. Otherwise it's just too vague and general. If I had a beef with the Catholic Church or the Christian Coalition or one of the local right-wing groups, we'd call them by name, wouldn't we? We always do. We'd say it was a mistake not to. Thanks for trying to run interference for me, but I'm a big boy, Winston."

"Suit yourself." The phone slammed. Somehow Jake wondered if the force of the slam was a fitting commentary on the column.

Zyor led Finney into a great hall, with displays of writings, ancient books and modern, scrolls and parchments and letters, the old ones written in ornate hand, the new ones crisply typed. It was heaven's Hall of Writings. This sacred place held what was written in the dark world that would be forever enshrined in the Kingdom of Light.

A monk walked up to the podium, and Zyor whispered to Jake the name by which he might recognize him from earth. "Francis Xavier." Finney did not recognize the name but listened intently.

One of Zyor's kind handed the monk a parchment he'd written the original on. He looked at it fondly for a moment, as if he'd never imagined the scrawlings of that one ordinary day would be heard by anyone but himself and his God. He looked away from the writing, set his eyes directly on the throne of the Lamb, toward which the podium pointed. He gazed over the heads of the immediate audience to a greater Audience beyond. Without looking back down, he spoke the words as one speaks to his beloved.

Oh, God, I love thee.
Not that my poor love might win me entrance to thy heaven above,
nor yet that strangers to thy love must know
the bitterness of everlasting woe.

But, Jesus, thou art mine and I am thine,
clasped to thy bosom by thy arms divine,
who on the cruel cross for me hast borne
the pain, the tears and man's unpitying scorn.

No thought can fathom and no tongue express
thy grief, thy toil, thy anguish measureless.
Thy death, O lamb of God, the undefiled,
and all for me, thy wayward sinful child.

Not for the hope of glory or reward,
but even as thou hast loved me, Lord,
I love Thee, and wilt love Thee and adore,
who art my King, my God, forevermore.

Person after person stood to read, with periods of rest between, allowing all to contemplate the message and experience the communion elicited in the writing. There were letters written by parents to children, and children to parents. Letters to husbands, wives, friends, pastors. Letters to the editor. Articles and columns written by journalists. Each was followed by thoughtful applause and earnest noddings. Some, like Finney, had never heard these readings before; others perhaps had heard them often, but on hearing them again felt as much or more joy as the first time.

Finney sensed the program was leading to its climax. The others had been praised by Elyon for their writings before, though they never tired of his praise. But here came a little boy. Finney knew somehow it was his first time doing a reading in this great hall. He was, like Finney, a newcomer. He had in his hand a paper he'd written for his third-grade class. He held the wide-ruled notebook page he'd first written it on, but it had a different look, as if it had been transformed into the parchment of heaven that would never deteriorate.

A moderator, an angel, held up his hand and explained this had been a school assignment where the teacher had asked the students to write about someone they loved. They turned in the assignment and later would read it to the class. But suddenly, as if there were a large screen video projection in midair, everyone was seeing the teacher, not angry but with a worried look, examining Jeffrey's paper and explaining to him, "Jeffrey, remember I said it had to be a real person, not someone imaginary."

Jeffrey, the Jeffrey in the projection of what actually happened on earth, looked surprised. "Jesus is a real person."

The teacher kindly explained there would be other assignments where the class could write about Santa Claus or Spider Man or any character they wanted, and perhaps he should save Jesus for them. Jeffrey explained he wanted to write about Jesus now because Jesus really was his best friend. What followed was a conversation Jeffrey had never seen, now broadcast in heaven. The teacher was talking to the principal, and they were saying something about the separation of church and state, and how the ACLU got upset about such things, and how it could get them in trouble. The principal concluded, 'Give him credit for the assignment. Just don't let him read it to the class.' The next day, other students gave their readings, but before Jeffrey was called on, they were out of time and had to move on to mathematics. The image vanished, and the focus returned to the Hall of Writings.

The moderator said, "Now, at last, we are all eager to listen to Jeffrey read his essay."

The boy cleared his throat, then proudly projected his voice. "'Someone I love,' by Jeffrey Montgomery." He flashed the incomparable smile of a child about to recite an original composition.

"I love Jesus. He is my best friend. He likes it when I do good things. He doesn't like it when I do bad things. But he always forgives me when I ask him to. He died to take away the bad things I've done. But he is still alive and I talk to him every day. He talks to me too, through his Bible, and sometimes even when I'm not reading the Bible, I can tell he's talking to me in a quiet voice. Even though I can't exactly hear the words, I know what he's saying. And some day my Mom and Dad say I'm going to heaven where he lives. And you can too if you just ask him to forgive your sins, like I have. I have a lot of nice friends, but Jesus is my best friend. Jesus can be your best friend too."

Suddenly there was the sound of thunder and an earthquake. All heaven shook, and Finney grabbed the pillar next to him, looking at Zyor for an answer. What was it? What had happened? All eyes turned to the great throne of heaven, at which Jeffrey was already looking. There was the Audience of One, not sitting but standing. And then Finney watched as his hands clapped together again, and the ground and buildings gave and shook like a plywood shack in a wind storm.

Angels and humans joined in the applause, though Jeffrey could not hear the meager noise they made, for the sound that came from the throne overpowered them. And then a voice cut through the air like lightening. The voice too shook the ground, each word creating its own tremor. "Well done, my good and faithful son."

All heaven bowed along with the boy who had so deeply touched the One who had made the universe itself with less fanfare than he now devoted to this child. Suddenly he was there on the stage. Lifting him high above his head, he said to the wide-eyed delighted boy, "Well done, Jeffrey."

The hall was evacuated, Finney leaving with the rest, for what followed was private and sacred. What the two would talk about, where they would go, what they would do was between them only. And should Jeffrey decide to tell others, it would be only for the joy of it, only to relive and recount it, to exult in the fellowship and friendship of which the strongest version on earth had been but an impoverished foreshadow.

As he walked out of the hall, Finney turned back and took one last look in the boy's eyes, filled with wonder and delight. The faint taste of these realities that the boy might have occasionally known in the Shadowlands had now erupted into all the flavors of heaven. Boy and God-man were turning circles on the stage, the boy laughing as never before. The deep, hearty laugh of the Ancient of Days and the high, squeaky laugh of heaven's new child, melded into one.

Finney knew the immense delight that flooded him now came not just from the boy, but from the God-man. The pleasure taken *in* Elyon was exceeded only by the pleasure taken *by* Elyon.

Finney pondered that if the atmosphere of earth was nitrogen and oxygen, and the atmosphere of hell was sulfur and acid, then the atmosphere of heaven was joy and delight.

Jake sat next to Little Finn, looking at the wonder in his eyes, which held his attention more than the basketball game. The Blazers were ahead by twenty-five. It'd been a yawner since the first quarter. Nothing like playing an expansion team to catch up on your sleep. Jake had canceled this boy's night out twice since making the promise weeks ago, but this time he had followed through. Little Finn was one nonstop smile after the other, saying 'what a shot' and cheering at lay-ups even Jake could make. A child's joy. Jake tried to remember far enough back, before reality—or was it cynicism—had eclipsed his own ability to see wonder in the little things of life. Or even the big ones.

"Unca Jake! Do you dink my dad saw dat shot? I'll bet Jesus opens up windows in heaven and let's ya see dings down here. Dat was a good one to see, huh!"

Jake hadn't even seen the shot. "Yeah, Finn." *Poor kid. He's out of touch with reality. Maybe he's better off. Reality's not so great anyway.*

He'd sat in this same section often with Doc and Finney, and Little Finn had come along a few times. But now it was just the two of them, Little Finn and Unca Jake. Five minutes left on the clock, and not one Blazer starter left in the game. Jake got antsy.

"Hey, bud, I got an idea. If we sneak out now, we'll miss the traffic jam, and I'll take you to Lou's Diner for a milkshake. Whadaya say?"

Little Finn' s eyes shone as if Jake had offered him a trip to Disney World. "A milkshake? Sure, Unca Jake!"

They'd driven through the golden arches on the way to the game, but just had time to grab a burger and fries and two waters. Jake didn't offer Little Finn a milkshake then because he didn't want it all over the front seat of his car.

Jake led the way to the aisle and down the stairs, out to the Coliseum's walkways and across the parking lot, holding Finn's hand and running in the light rain. This was all as big a thrill to Finn as the ball game and the milkshake. Jake was cheap enough not to pay for parking, and had a favorite little spot on grass near an off-ramp where he tucked in his car. The spot was seldom taken, largely because it was a real stretch to even see it as a spot. Only a journalist would be bold enough to park there, Jake told himself. He even left his press pass visible on the dashboard in case a cop considering a citation might be fooled into thinking he parked there only because he was hot on the trail of some critical story. As if that would impress a cop. But it didn't keep Jake from trying, and not once had he been ticketed.

He took pleasure from Little Finn's squeals of delight as they jumped over curbs and ran across streets and out into the weeds beyond the sidewalk. With his free hand, Jake fumbled for his car keys in his coat pocket. He dropped them, and they landed in some tall grass. The rain was pelting down now and Jake motioned to Little Finn.

"Go ahead, bud. I'll catch up with you."

Finn smiled and took off for the car, still some distance away, lumbering in his unique Special Olympics style, while Jake leaned over and searched the soaking plant life for his keys.

When he was about forty feet from the car, Little Finn saw the passenger-side door was open. Someone in a dark trenchcoat was leaning into the car. Little Finn assumed the best, thinking some helpful person was doing Jake a favor, maybe turning off his lights or returning something to the car, or even locking it up for him.

"Hi dere!" Finn yelled.

The man was startled, banging his head on the door frame. He had something in his hand, which he shoved in his pocket, and reached for something else with his other hand. It was too dark and rainy to see him clearly, though for some reason Finn thought he might have seen him before. The man stared at Finn, deciding what to do.

Jake had just found his keys when he heard the gun shot. He sprinted toward his car where he could barely see Little Finn running from it, and something else in a heap on the ground beside it. But the runner he'd assumed was Finn didn't look right. He ran into the street and turned the opposite direction, running like a sprinter, not a Down's Syndrome boy. And he was wearing a trenchcoat. The silent, utterly still lump on the ground...it must be Little Finn.

Frightened and pleading, to whom he didn't know, Jake ran the last sixty feet as fast as he could, sliding as he got to Finn, almost falling on his body lying there so perfectly on its back. The body was motionless, and Jake prepared himself for the worst. It was hard to see in the rain and shadows. He put his face close to the angelic face lying there helplessly in the cold and wet.

"Hi dere, Unca Jake!"

"Little Finn! Little Finn! Are you okay?" Not waiting for an answer, Jake pulled Finn up and got him into the car. Despite the shadows, the street lights showed chipped paint on the edge of the Mustang's passenger door. Somebody had slim-jimmed it. Jake ran around to the driver's door, which Finn had already unlocked, and hopped inside. Both were soaked.

"Are you sure you're okay, Finn? You weren't shot? Did he hit you?"

This was Little Finn's big moment, and he was poised as if a whole hunting party were assembled around a campfire, eager to hear every detail of the most amazing story ever. And to Finn, as with most of his stories, that's exactly what this was.

"Da man pushed me down," his eyes were big, "but it didn't hurt very much, and den I heard a noise like a big firecracker. You know, da kind dat's illegal in Oregon and you haf to go up to Washington to buy dem, and Kenny Olson got in big trouble for having one in Oregon, and—"

"I know, I know, Finn. Then what happened?"

"Well, I just laid there 'cause I was a little scared—not too scared but sorta pretty bad scared—and den I heard you comin' and yellin' and I just laid there 'cause on TV dey say you're not 'posed to move a body till you're sure it's okay, and I wasn't sure my body was okay yet. I saw dis man with his head in your car and I didn't know..."

As Finn launched into a repeat of the story, Jake hugged him, then turned on the overhead light and looked around his car. There'd been nothing inside but what was still there—the McDonald's sack with wrappers and fry boxes and unopened ketchups inside. The tape deck was intact. They'd arrived just in time. No harm done but the chipped paint. Unless...he grabbed for the glove box door and yanked it opened. The Walther was gone. The thief had made off with a loaded Nazi sidearm.

* * *

"Yeah. Got it. But there may be a problem." The man was out of breath.

"Problem?" The voice sounded like it was battling a migraine and didn't want to hear about problems.

"The kid may have seen me."

"What kid?"

"The retard. He took him to the basketball game and that's where it happened. It was dark and rainy and the kid might not have gotten a good view, but he could have."

"The subject never saw you?"

"No. Not him."

"Are you absolutely sure?"

"Positive. Just the kid. What should I do?"

"You've done enough for one night." The migraine sounded worse. "I'll check with the men upstairs. For now, leave the kid alone. We may have to deal with him later."

CHAPTER TWENTY-SEVEN

S pecial Agent Sutter's plate was clean before Jake took the first bite of his turkey on whole wheat. Sutter's Red Sangria was half gone, Jake's still unopened. After some opening small talk, Jake told him about the stolen Walther.

"The worst part is, it was kind of a keepsake. My father left it. Didn't really give it to me. Just died, and I ended up with it."

"A Nazi gun, huh? You're probably right about the street punk. Still, it could be Babe Ruth and his buddies didn't want you armed." Babe Ruth was Sutter's nickname for the guy who'd used Jake for batting practice.

"How would they know I had a gun in the glove box? Never kept one there before."

Sutter shrugged. "Tomorrow afternoon we get back Mayhew and at least another agent, maybe two, and we'll be your shadow again. Till then just don't get isolated. Stay around people. No back parking lots, okay? I'm serious, Jake. I don't want you getting hurt."

Jake smiled. "Gee, Sutter, I've grown kind of fond of you too."

"Yeah? Well, it doesn't mean we're going to the prom together, okay? And when this is over, to be honest, I've told you more than I had to, and some of the guys at the Bureau wouldn't appreciate it. So if we ever lift the restrictions on this thing and you write your memoirs, don't hang your old friend Sutter out to dry, okay?"

While Jake took a few sips of Sangria and his first bite of turkey, Sutter looked over some notes, staring at them, seeming to correlate this fact with that, as seasoned investigators do. He reminded Jake of Ollie. Finally, Sutter spoke.

"Okay, like I told you on the phone yesterday, a lot of money showed up in one of your friend's bank accounts six months ago, through some really complicated routes. That fits with your computer files. But since yesterday we found out it happened twice. Could have been a two-part payoff or two separate payoffs. We're working on it."

"You know what it was for?"

"Marsdon gave you the answer, if you think about it. It was simple, really. All Dr. Lowell had to do was move someone's name up the list."

"Which list?" Jake pushed aside his sandwich.

"The heart transplant list. I've got the papers from someone inside at the hospital. Nine people were waiting for a heart transplant. A guy—a rich guy—found out three months ago he could live another ten years or more with a new heart, but without it he'd be dead in two months. The problem is, he was number nine, and his name probably wouldn't come up for six months, depending on if he's lucky enough for nine donors with healthy hearts to die before he does. And it's hard to get your average guy off the street to volunteer to give you his heart, know what I mean?"

Sutter chuckled at his little joke. Jake didn't find it funny.

"So, anyway, he decides it's worth a half million dollars to get his name bumped up."

"A half million dollars?"

"Not much money when you consider the alternative. You can't take it with you, remember?"

"You're saying Doc took a bribe?"

"Yes, but not in the direct way that would be crass and unconscionable, you understand, not like a politician would do. There's a broker, a middle man. That's where the organization comes in, the entrepreneurs, the opportunists—the new rendition of organized crime I told you about. See, this guy that wants the heart tells his story to his lawyer, who says he knows a guy, probably one of his other clients, who knows a guy that might be able to help. This guy calls the rich guy and offers to be the middle man, for a modest commission, of course. A straight out deal between patient and doctor is too risky, too...obvious. The rich guy needs this middleman, his contacts, his credentials. The deal would never work without him."

"Sutter, is this stuff for real?" It confirmed Jake's worst suspicions, fit perfectly with Finney's letters to Doc, but it still sounded so incredible.

"Absolutely. The broker could be a health professional himself or maybe a crooked lawyer, pardon the redundancy. He needs to be able to assure a doctor that other doctors are doing this, everyone's doing this, he's just the last to find out about it. The doctor resists it at first, but finally decides he'd be a fool to miss out on the opportunity. After all, there's a list, and the doctors are given control of the list. They decide whose case is most critical and most deserves the next available heart or kidney or whatever. He rationalizes, tells himself, 'Hey, I'd probably bump this guy up anyway even if I hadn't been contacted. We do it all the time, so what does it hurt if I get a little from the deal? The government already steals half my paycheck and now it's limiting my income. Why not? The patient's happy, I'm happy. Nobody's hurt, and nobody's the wiser.'"

"I just can't believe Doc would do it." Jake was trying to sound more certain than he felt.

"Why? Was your friend some kind of saint or something?"

"No, but he was a decent guy. He'd try to do the right thing."

"Sure. But what's right and what's wrong? Is it really so clear, so cut and dried? And even if they know better, are doctors so morally superior to everyone else? No one seems surprised if a businessman takes advantage of a windfall opportunity that might be a little shady. Why can't a doctor? Can't they cut corners? Can't they cheat like everybody else?"

The word cheat hit Jake hard. He remembered Finney talking about the breakdown of families and society. He'd said, "A man who cheats on his wife will cheat on anybody. If you violate the highest vows you've ever taken, lesser vows are sure to topple." At the time it seemed judgmental and unfair. Now it seemed prophetic.

"Why would Doc do it?"

Sutter shrugged. "He needed the money, I guess. Most of them do, you know. That's what makes the industry so vulnerable. On the one hand, there's the change in ethics, the decisions for some to live and some to die, the financial and pragmatic considerations in health care. On the other hand, there's all the new health regulations and changes related to the shift toward national health care. The doctor's profit margins are thinning down. They've got mortgages, with payments bigger than your whole monthly paycheck. They've got their kids in private schools, they work hard, they're on call half their lives. They don't want to drive Hyundais; they want to drive BMWs.

"But their take home keeps shrinking, and they're convinced the health care system is only going to make it worse. Socialism doesn't make things better, that's the attitude. They went into huge debt to get through medical school, with the promise of a big capitalistic payoff, but the rules have been changed on them. Some are fighting back publicly, others are fighting back behind the scenes, taking advantage of quiet opportunities. Your friend was one of them."

"What happened? Do you know the details? We know at least one other doctor was involved, right?"

"Right. Your friend's note makes that clear. Somebody got to him, maybe the other doctor. Or maybe your friend got in first. Anyway, somebody credible suggested your friend could think of a good medical reason to bump this guy up the list. He did. Don't know if he agonized over it or just did it like you'd pick up a hundred dollar bill lying in the street. Meanwhile they got him money coming from different directions. That part was professional. The pros have accountants who work overtime shifting money in and out of this account and this company so anyone trying to trace it will die of old age or fatigue first. It doesn't appear to have been that tough for your friend. He had only a few other doctors, at most a small committee, he had to explain himself to. Maybe he said it related to compatibility or age or body weight or timing or rare blood type, who knows? I'm not a doctor. Anyway, they bought it."

"But if he was doing what the bad guys wanted, why would they kill him?"

"That's what we need to know. And that's why I'm telling you all this. We don't normally give out this info, you know. I need you to talk to me, Jake, whenever you find something out. Leads, possibilities, new info, just like the computer file. We'd have never come up with that. FBI just doesn't march into private homes and do that, not when we're trying to stay low profile. We've had progress, but it's the kind of thing where they could hear our footsteps and bail out. We could come up empty if we don't get our case together and make our move soon.

"Anyway, you asked why'd they kill him? Maybe he held out for more money. Maybe he refused to do it again. Once you're on the payroll you're expected to play ball. If you're no longer an asset, you're a liability. That's how it works. Maybe his conscience was acting up. Maybe he talked to a priest, or looked like he was going to confess. Omerta."

"What?"

"Omerta. It's the old syndicate term. The code of silence. It's their way of saying, 'You talk, you die.' They make clear, usually after you've already got your hands dirty and it's too late to back out, that if you talk, they'll kill you. And that's another reason they do so well. These days most people don't think anything's worth dying for. Guess you can hardly blame them, huh?"

Jake nodded and was disturbed that he had. Nothing worth dying for? He'd once heard a general say, "If nothing's worth dying for, nothing's worth living for."

Maybe that was it, maybe the sickness of this society that screamed out to all but the hopelessly deaf was the product of believing nothing was worth dying for. And therefore nothing was worth living for.

Jake and Sutter went their separate ways. Jake headed to feed the meter, carrying on his shoulders a weight no man should have to bear alone.

Jake came back to a note in Jerry's handwriting, taped on the middle of his screen, the only guaranteed place a journalist will look. Jerry saw him return and explained from across the divider.

"I answered your phone. Your machine didn't seem to be working, so I thought what the heck, it could be the president. It was bigger. A reporter from the *LA Times*. He wants an interview. You must be more important than I realized."

"An interview? About what?"

"Didn't say, and I didn't pry, either. You know me. I'm too much of a professional. I may eavesdrop when you call him back though."

"Thanks, Jerry."

"Hey, that's why I'm here. Can I get coffee? Shine your shoes? Fetch you a newspaper?"

"You could shut up for a few minutes," Jake said with mock irritation.

"Oh, sure, no problem. Shut up? Just say the word, Mr. Bigshot columnist doing an interview with the *LA Times*. For you? Anything."

Jerry continued to mumble under his breath. Next to being the human thesaurus, this was one of his most endearing features. He was one of many reasons Jake loved working at the *Trib*.

Jake picked up the gray phone and raised his left shoulder to cradle it against his neck, while his fingers pounded out the ten numbers with the same rapid skill he punched computer keys. He looked at Jerry's note.

"Yeah, can I speak to Frank Harmes?" He looked at Jerry, who was listening intently. "Sounds like he's got a secretary."

"Hey, I answered your phone, remember? I don't care if it is the *Times*, no reporter has a secretary. No way."

"Frank Harmes here."

"Yeah, Frank. Jake Woods at the *Trib*. My secretary gave me your message."

Jerry rolled his eyes.

"Oh, great, thanks for calling me back, Jake. Secretary, huh? Wow. Before I forget, Cornelius Leonard sends his greetings. Just saw him yesterday. He was here for some meeting with the big wigs. They introduced him to some of us in the newsroom."

"No kidding? I just saw Leonard in New York."

"Somebody was saying something about your column on condoms and people's reactions, and Mr. Leonard said he knew you. You've got a rep as one of the best columnists on the coast. People like your stuff. And this column seems quite a bend in the road, so it's really piqued some interest. Mr. Leonard suggested I call you. Just a second. I've got it here on my desk somewhere. You know what it's like."

"Believe me, I know." Jake looked at the piles on his desk. Nothing a little kerosene and a lighter couldn't fix.

"Before I forget, how big's the syndication? How many papers you in?"

"Last I heard, forty. Creators Features tells me there's a dozen more considering it."

"No kidding? That's great. Congratulations. Yeah, okay, here it is. By the way, Leonard got a charge out of this."

"Really?"

"Yeah, he says you really kicked up the dust this time."

"He's right."

"He also said he's proud of you. Takes courage to take on the big boys, he said."

"What can I do for you, Frank?"

"Well, just a few quick questions about what you wrote here. First, you allude to something, where is it? Okay, you say, 'I used to think that way. Recent events have helped me to see how wrong I was.' What recent events are you referring to?"

"Just some personal experiences. I saw first hand in a school situation how some kids' lives were affected by condom distribution and the basic 'all sex is okay' philosophy. It wasn't good."

"And you think the school was wrong to pass out condoms even to the sexually active kids who could get AIDS?"

"Well, my point is, our first responsibility is to help them see why they shouldn't be sexually active. I don't think it's right to pass out condoms and send the message to go ahead and do the behavior that spreads HIV in the first place. A lot of what's passing for birth control education is irresponsible because it neglects or minimizes the one alternative that's 100 percent effective in preventing what we all say we want to prevent."

"And this position represents some sort of conversion on your part, doesn't it? I mean, you've never had a reputation for being a conservative, have you?"

"I've had a change in thinking, like I said in the article, if that's what you mean. I'm not saying I'm a conservative. In some areas I'm liberal, others conservative. I don't care what the label is, I just said what I believe."

"Could you tell me a little more about this experience with the school?"

"No, sorry. It's personal. Not for publication." The moment Jerry heard this, he got up and took a walk. Jake appreciated it.

"Can you talk off the record?" Harmes asked.

"Just between us, right?" *As if there were some other meaning to off the record.* Jake felt a little silly.

"Right."

"Okay...my daughter was given condoms and what amounted to encouragement to have sex by a school nurse and a teacher. I went down there to...talk to the teacher and find out what was going on. I didn't like what I saw."

"And...what about your daughter?"

Jake hesitated, but the guy was in Los Angeles and no one else was going to know. "Again, off the record, she's pregnant and has the HIV."

"No kidding?" The voice conveyed a sense of pleasure in having discovered something big.

This guy's starting to bug me. "Listen, Frank, I'm pretty busy and to be honest, I don't feel like talking about this. It's pretty draining stuff. And I'm still getting lots of grief on my column. I need to go."

"Just a couple more questions. Why—"

"Sorry, gotta go. Good to talk with you."

Jake hung up and sat motionless. He was offended at this reporter's insensitivity. What did he care about Carly? To him she was only an interesting dynamic, a piece in a puzzle, whose misery had been for him just a source of stimulation. Jake wondered how often he had grabbed hold of people's tragedies with equal pleasure, using someone else's pain to fuel a story.

Frank would be frustrated to have to sit on the information. Jake was just glad he understood the business well enough to have stipulated "off the record." Too many people depended on a journalist's sense of discretion to leave out what was obviously harmful to innocent people. Jake learned long ago such discretion couldn't be depended upon. Sometimes it didn't exist.

Thinking back he remembered several cases where he passed on personal information that had made for a great story, without regard for others' feelings. When people had been hurt, he was sorry but felt they were overreacting. The news was the news, and people had the right to know. More particularly, the journalist had the right—and the duty—to tell.

Jake spent the afternoon trying to put out fires. Someone had organized a phone campaign to hound him. They were all saying the same things, using the same language, as though reading from a script. There must have been a mailing or a mass fax. People who hadn't even read the column were referring to someone else's summary and interpretation of it, but whenever Jake asked where it came from they wouldn't tell him. Some worked at Planned Parenthood, some were school teachers, several were NEA executives, including Barbara Betcher, who said she and her group couldn't believe Jake had been used as "a tool of the religious right." He had done "untold damage" through his "irresponsible" column.

Jake was struck with the sheer arrogance of these responses. Whenever he would ask for any hard evidence or statistics to refute what he'd said, invariably they had none to offer and seemed offended or mystified that he was even asking.

One leader of a local feminist group called and warned him that unless he printed a retraction they would be forced to withdraw their invitation to speak at a businesswomen's breakfast a week from Saturday. He'd forgotten about the breakfast and didn't feel like going anyway. Because she was surly, and Jake was weary, he couldn't resist pulling her chain.

"So you're threatening me, is that it? I write one column you don't like, and I'm dog meat? If I don't parrot your creed, say just what you want, then you break the commitment you made, what...six months ago? How would you distinguish this phone call from intolerance? Or an attempt at censorship?"

She went ballistic. Jake pulled the phone eight inches from his ear. Sandy, eyebrows raised, heard every word, including a few that made her blush. When the caller finally ran out of breath Jake said, "To tell you the truth, I wasn't looking forward to your breakfast anyway. Josephine's makes runny omelets, and I'm tired of those flaky little croissants. Besides, I don't know if I want to identify with a group that throws a tizzy fit when a journalist chooses to exercise the first amendment!"

Just as she was launching a new barrage, Jake hung up, a triumphant smile on his face. He grabbed a black marking pen, opened his appointment book to next Saturday, and put a thick line through the speaking engagement. Then he picked up a pencil and wrote below it, "Ask Carly out to breakfast."

His mail stacks were three times the usual size. Everyone who generally loved his columns hated this one, and everyone who generally hated them loved this one. He felt somewhat betrayed by those who would turn on him for just one column that he felt was accurate and fair, as if one aberration from the accepted dogma represented a permanent fall from grace unless he recanted.

He was equally amazed at those he'd offended for years who now rallied to his defense and didn't seem to hold his previous columns against him. Jake felt his world being turned upside down.

The next day Jake had been at his desk almost three hours when Clarence wandered over to him, holding masthead down what Jake assumed was the morning *Trib*.

"How's my man doin' today?" He slapped a greeting on Jake's hand.

"I'm surviving. Barely." Jake heard the battle fatigue in his own voice.

"I came to ask if I can take my hero to lunch. Writing that column makes anything you did in Vietnam pale in comparison. Plus, I've done some reconnaissance, and my sources say you could use a body guard. The word is, there's some snipers setting up right in this newsroom. I don't mean to worry you, but I've seen some M-14s and a 40-millimeter grenade launcher aimed at your cubicle. And radar has picked up enemy aircraft from the NEA, ACLU, NOW, and NARAL. Just stay close to me, man. They wouldn't dare hit a black man. From a distance they'd assume I was a liberal!"

Clarence's warm smile and hearty slap on the back were truly welcome.

"Lunch sounds great, Clarence."

"Good. They'll expect us to take the elevator, but we'll double back and duck down the stairs. Seriously, Jake, I figured you could use some company." Clarence was suddenly solemn. "And this isn't going to help things."

He flipped over the newspaper in his hand and flopped it on Jake's desk. It was the *Los Angeles Times.*

"D3," Clarence said.

Jake hadn't given another thought to the call from the *Times.* "The guy didn't portray me as a hero, huh? It was a three-minute interview, with a minute and a half off the record. I didn't think I gave him enough ammo to do me much damage."

Clarence gave a blank look. He obviously wanted to be there when Jake read it. Jake's heart raced. *What did this guy say? He was nice enough, knew Leonard—he didn't sound antagonistic.*

Even as he thought it, Jake kicked himself for being so naive. How many people had he won over with a congenial voice and agreeable interview style, only to crucify them in print?

There it was. "Columnist's Family Problems Cause Belief Shift."
No. No, he didn't. He couldn't have.

Popular *Oregon Tribune* columnist Jake Woods, syndicated in forty western newspapers, including the *Los Angeles Times,* surprised his readers two days ago with a column attacking Planned Parenthood.

"It was mean-spirited and totally false," Vicki Noonan of California Planned Parenthood said. "It's amazing a journalist could just repeat this right-wing propaganda as if it were true."

When I asked Mr. Woods to explain his position, he said he now believes it is "morally wrong to pass out condoms, even if doing so saves the lives of young people." His explanation was simply "they shouldn't be sexually active." He also said, "I believe public schools are acting irresponsibly by giving attention to sex education." In the interview he referred to some sort of personal "conversion" that has influenced his thinking.

Woods has been a firm supporter of schools teaching young people how to avoid pregnancy and STDs, but in his controversial column he said, "recent events have helped me to see how wrong I was."

What were these recent events, which are not specified in the column? Woods says they involve his teenager daughter, who became sexually active, got pregnant, and contracted the HIV. Woods believes the public school and its teachers, as well as Planned Parenthood, are to blame for what happened to his daughter.

Another Planned Parenthood spokesperson, Marla Krueger, said, "I'm genuinely sorry for this personal tragedy in Mr. Woods' family. But instead of attacking those who are doing the most to help, I hope Mr. Woods will use his influence to help other children avoid the hazards of unsafe sex."

Jake sat in perplexed silence. After ten seconds he said in a shaky voice, "Clarence. All that about my daughter? It was all off the record, every word. I clarified that two or three times, and he agreed to it. He lied to me. He betrayed my confidence...and I've betrayed my daughter. My God, Clarence, she was suicidal about this thing. Now it's all out in the *Times.* What am I going to do?"

His anger toward the *Times* reporter burned hot, but for the first time he could remember his broken heart laid a stronger hold on him than his anger.

Clarence knelt down, there was no place to sit, and looked at him sympathetically.

"And he twisted the rest of what I said. The words, most of them, were mine, but they're completely out of context. Conversion was his word, not mine. How could anyone with a conscience do this? He set me up, talking about Leonard, made me feel like he wasn't going to trash me. Why didn't I tape it? I should have taped it, then I could call the *Times's* publisher and play it for him and get this jerk fired."

Even as he said it, he knew there was no chance of that. The reporter would say he didn't remember or didn't understand. He'd be sorry, but say Jake should have been more clear. It would be the word of one reporter on the wrong side of a position against another on the right side—or rather, "just doing his job." This was a reporter who would never need anything from Jake again. He'd gotten his story, scored his points. He didn't need Jake to like him.

"Jake, have you ever violated someone's confidence to make a good story?"

"Maybe if it wasn't completely clear, or if it was really necessary, but not like this."

"Difference in degree, but not in kind?"

Jake shrugged and nodded lamely. He did understand, and it bothered him that he did. There was a built-in protection in the shared values and politics of his profession. Once he'd stepped outside those shared values, he'd become fair game. That was his problem, and he'd have to live with it. What he couldn't handle was Carly suffering for his naiveté.

Clarence was sympathetic. "Even the bad ones don't usually pull that on other journalists—sort of honor among thieves, I guess. Usually it's just done to mortals, not fellow members of the pantheon. You don't want to cross someone in a position to throw lightning bolts back at you. I had it happen once myself—the off the record thing, I mean. The twisting and out of context stuff, well, that's par for the course. That goes without saying, given my political incorrectness. I guess you haven't been on this side of things enough to be on guard, have you? Well, it could be worse. Remember that hospital chaplain that got fired when Jamiesen printed his off the record support of the 'no special rights for homosexuals' ballot measure? At least you've still got your job."

Jake didn't answer, and right now having his job was no consolation. He just sat there staring, thinking of Carly's fifth-grade flub-up in the Christmas play and wondering how he was going to explain this to her. And to Janet.

"Journalism's like fishing, Jake. It's a lot of fun as long as you're holding the pole. The fish's point of view is a bit different, isn't it? Come on. Let's go for a walk."

Clarence's coal-black hand made a striking impression on the shoulder of Jake's off-white sweater.

"It's times like this when you need to get as far away from a newspaper as possible, just so you can breathe some clean air."

CHAPTER TWENTY-EIGHT

The holiday music from the Mustang's stereo and the bell ringers along the sidewalk gave way to the business-as-usual sounds of the newsroom, which didn't change for any holiday season, other than an occasional card or wreath taped to the side of someone's terminal.

Jake had gone to Carly and apologized profusely about the fiasco with the *Times* story. She was embarrassed, but said, "I don't really know anyone in Los Angeles. I guess it doesn't matter that much what they think about me."

To Jake it mattered and he had groveled, but Carly was surprisingly quick to forgive him. If only he could forgive himself. If only he had it to do over, he swore he'd never violate his daughter's trust again.

Jake pawed through his huge pile of mail, sorting all the materials from manila envelopes he'd received the last two weeks. The first batch was all from the Pacific Northwest in response to the original *Tribune* printing of the "condom" column. The second batch was from all over the west, from Colorado, Wyoming, Arizona, New Mexico, and lots from California. Those had started coming in a week later, after syndication prints. The response was phenomenal. While an inner voice said "don't be a fool; leave it alone," he felt compelled to come back to this subject that had buried him in reader responses.

He jotted down a rough outline of items he wanted to address, then hunkered down in his chair and rattled off a lot of words quickly, as if firing from a bunker. Twenty minutes later he stopped. He pressed the "home" key, popping the cursor back to the beginning of the column, and eagerly started reading.

An interesting thing happened after my recent column about condom distribution being a poor solution to teen pregnancy and STDs. I received many supportive letters, and innumerable copies of studies and reports validating my points. But I also received the largest number of name-calling letters I've ever seen. Some of these names intrigued me. One was "religious bigot." This struck me as strange, since I'm not a religious person, and there was nothing religious in the column.

Another was "homophobe." I reread my column, since I didn't remember saying anything about homosexuality. In fact, I hadn't! Given this level of interest and agitation, I've decided to put on my flak jacket and tackle this subject again.

Several years ago our surgeon general made a classic statement. (I'm embarrassed to say that at the time I defended her for it.) She said, "Driver education tells kids what to do in the front of the car, and we should be telling them what to do in the back of the car."

She referred, of course, not to abstaining from sex, but to using condoms when having sex. (It wasn't too much later the president's AIDS czar blamed our problems on "Victorian morality." Huh?)

What doctors know and our children should too is that wearing a condom takes a few bullets out of the gun's cylinder. But when you're playing Russian roulette, eventually the one or two bullets left in the chamber will kill you. The solution is not to better the odds in Russian roulette. It is to stop playing it. That means sexual abstinence, as curiously offensive as that concept seems to be.

Four days ago I watched the television program "Prime Time Live." It featured schools that arrange for female students to have Norplant (a five-year birth control device) surgically implanted beneath their skin, without parental permission. What caught my attention was that they interviewed three eighth-grade girls who were sexually active. The interviewer asked if they would do anything different if they could start over. All three said they would wait until they were married to have sex. They were all very sorry they hadn't.

Amazingly, the interviewer did not follow up on the girls' deep regrets at their lost virginity. It was the perfect opportunity—totally missed because of the program's focus—to feature the concept some call "secondary virginity." If sexual activity for teens is psychologically harmful and physically dangerous, and studies confirm it is, we must offer them a chance to go back, to start over with new values and commitments. We should offer them help in developing their self-control, help them to "just say no" to sex as we help them to "just say no" to drugs. And to realize that even if you said "yes" before, you can say "no" from now on.

Recently Hollywood has gotten behind the Russian roulette "safe sex" programs. Yes, the same Hollywood which routinely shows teenagers hopping in the sack with each other. The same Hollywood which makes millions on teen sex and violence films. Given its track record, when Hollywood supports one side in this debate, perhaps it should be enough to convince us to throw our lot with the other side. (Why is it so politically fashionable to be concerned about polluting rivers but so unfashionable to be concerned about polluting minds?)

Various abstinence centered programs have sprung up across the country, and a number of readers sent me copies of the curricula. Much of it looks very good. And it gives students a real choice. If they want to, they can still choose the Hollywood way, the Planned Parenthood way. But if they do, at least they should know what they're choosing. They should know the profound physical and psychological risks. They should also know there's a better way. They should understand the advantages of "saved sex" over "safe sex."

Alley cats and rodents engage in sex with any available partner and no thought of consequences. What raises us above animals is our capacity for understanding, insight and foresight. We understand how life works, that there are long-range consequences of our decisions. There is not only today. There is tomorrow. Perhaps it's time more of us—both parents and children—learn to live not just for today, but for tomorrow.

Jake sat back, curious at what he'd read. He'd written instinctively, without much pause for thought. The thought was there all right, but it had formulated on its own, simmering beneath the surface. The full shape and intensity of it hadn't been clear until Jake read the words that emerged from him. For some reason, they frightened him.

He pressed the word count button. 750. Good. Now he could go back and edit, polish it up, add a few lines. Maybe make it sound a little less...whatever. He'd better make it good. Winston and Jess weren't going to be happy he was addressing this subject again, even though it got a huge response before, which was normally what editors wanted from a column.

For the next hour he whittled away. At 11:46 he pressed the save and send buttons, and the column whipped through the network wires to wait briefly for Winston.

At 12:10 Jake relaxed, surprised Winston hadn't called him in. He glanced down the aisle to his office, and his heart skipped a beat as he saw Jess standing across the desk from Winston. There could be any number of reasons, Jake realized. Why did he think they were discussing him?

Suddenly he felt a hand on his right shoulder and heard a voice saying, "Is this the Reverend Jake Woods?" Jake knew what the face would look like before he turned and saw it.

"CLABERN!" Jake called Clarence by his computer handle. "What's up? And what's with the Reverend? Come to confess your sins?"

"Neither of us has time for that. Actually, I just read your column." Clarence whistled. "Man, you got everybody talkin'. I heard somebody say you must have had an out of body experience after the accident or something. Like you met God and now you're trying to make him like you. Reverend Woods, that's what they're calling you." Clarence was clearly enjoying this.

"Why? Just for talking common sense? What's that got to do with being religious?"

"Hey, don't get chaffed with me, Rev. You're preachin' to the choir. I'm on your team, remember? I just wish I'd written that piece. I've been trying to figure out how to work that kind of stuff into a sports column. Got a few ideas to bounce off you. How about we talk over lunch?"

"Great." Jake looked down to see Jess and Winston still talking intently. "I feel like a drive. Ever been to Lou's Diner?"

"Lou's Diner? Never heard of it. Which makes me a little suspicious."

"You're in for a treat. It's on me."

They small-talked till they got to Lou's and ordered. Rory was delighted to see

Jake. When he heard Clarence was a sports columnist he told him all about Cecily's soccer and Robert's water polo, and how he and Maria loved to watch their kids' games, and how the whole family was going to be together all day for Christmas and it was his favorite time of year. In turn, Clarence told Rory all about his wife and kids. Jake had never asked Clarence much about them. Finally, the demands of work pulled Rory from the much-preferred socializing. He left to cook the order, but only after he brought over a cappuccino and latté, on the house.

"Refreshing guy. I like him." Clarence said. "This place is like a throwback to the past."

"The diner time forgot."

"Yeah, exactly. It reminds me of a conversation with Jess just the other day. We were discussing my goal to get out of sports columns into political or general or any place I could talk about some serious stuff. He told me nobody doubts my skills, but they question some of my beliefs and politics, though he said it differently—I forget how—so it would still sound open-minded.

"Anyway, Jess looked at me and said, 'Aren't you afraid of these religious right groups and all their political goals?' I replied—and this probably seals my professional fate at the *Trib*—'No, why should I be?'

"He looked at me like I was crazy and said, 'They're convinced their way is the right way, they're so dogmatic, and they're so...intolerant.' First, I pointed out that those holding the opposite positions are just as convinced they're right and just as dogmatic. I asked him, 'So is dogmatism and intolerance made better just because you don't believe in God, or made worse because you do?' Then I said something that never occurred to me till that moment."

"What? If it's good, I'll steal it from you."

"You're welcome to it. I said, 'I've read through the letters from Focus on the Family that lay out all the values they support. I've read through the political goals and proposed legislation the conservative Christian groups have come up with. And the truth is, if they got their way on every single thing they want—and of course they never will—but if they did, then you know what the bottom line would be? America would just look a lot more like the country I was born in than the country it's become.' So I told Jess, 'If you're asking me which country I prefer, the answer is, the one I was born in.'"

"Never thought of it that way."

"Me neither. Of course, the America I grew up in was far from perfect, and the religious conservatives aren't right about everything. But when you compare their agenda and the country it gave us to the country the secular liberals have given us the last thirty years, well, which would your children be safer in? Which did they get a better education in? Which one did more families stay together in, spend time together, communicate and become close knit? Which let the black community pull itself up by its bootstraps and compete and get good jobs, like my daddy and uncles did, and which has lulled so many blacks into a permanent underclass? Sure, there was a lot of racism, but there still is. We're being treated differently, and our children are in gangs, killing each other, because they've got no incentives, no direction, no role models. No fathers. And they won't even let us use our tax money to send our children to decent schools."

Clarence had talked like this before, but for the first time Jake felt that much of what he was saying was right on target.

"That's what I mean about sitting in this place, Jake. It's like it brings back the values of days past, when we were growing up. The days of Ozzie and Harriet and Ward and June Cleaver and Donna Reed. You know, before Freddy Kruegger, Madonna, and Howard Stern. It's a world I wish my kids could grow up in, instead of walking through weapons detectors at school and getting inundated with R-rated movies and being fitted for birth control devices when half of them can't even read by the time they graduate."

"Does all this relate to your column idea?"

"Yeah, it does. It's the whole sports role model thing. The best athletes are black, let's face it." Jake smiled at Clarence's directness.

"Ten percent of the population and eighty percent of the NBA, with an occasional white guy who beats the genetic odds. Meanwhile the schools these guys went to are passing out condoms and Norplant and you name it with no parental permission, just like you said in your column. Not many credible people are showing the alternative of responsibility, abstinence, saving yourself for marriage. Well, the guys in sports are the role models. Nobody's more credible than they are. Every boy wants to be like them. And make no mistake, if these boys aren't taught something radically different than what they're growing up with now, they're going to be dead or in jail, and they're going to take down a lot of women and children and other young men with them. I want to challenge these athletes to bring this message back to the 'hood."

"Are enough athletes living that way themselves to convince kids to do the same?"

"More and more. You don't have as much Wilt Chamberlain and Magic Johnson stuff going on now. More out of fear than anything, for some of the guys, but fear's better than nothing. It's a start. And you've got guys like A. C. Green and some others. But we need three or four in every city, with every pro team. Do you realize what that could do for boys, black and white? Anyway, I'm thinking of raising up that challenge in my Sunday column after Christmas. Maybe the family aspect of Christmas will grease the skids. What do you think?"

"I think you're a brave man. Or maybe a little stupid." Jake grinned. It was fun to be on the outside looking in.

"Takes one to know one, huh? Here's where it really gets controversial. People will agree with the need for strong role models. But I'm going to link the absence of fathers to the abortion issue."

"How? What's the link?"

"Simple. Men are told when they get a woman pregnant it isn't their baby, it's just hers. They're told they have no say if they want the baby to live. Spousal consent is an offensive concept to abortion rights people. Men have no rights concerning the babies they've fathered. But, Jake, we all know rights and responsibilities go hand in hand. You can't separate them. So, when we tell men they have no rights, we're really telling them they have no responsibilities.

"How can we say, 'You have no right to stand up for the welfare of this child,' then expect them to take any responsibility whatsoever for the child if the mother decides to let him live? You can't have it both ways. Either the father has rights *and* responsibilities for the child, or he has neither rights nor responsibilities for the child.

"So what do we have as a result of believing this abortion propaganda? A bunch of irresponsible men. They've been taught they're not needed in the home, women and children can get along fine without them—*better* because the government gives them a paycheck as long as they don't marry the father. So the men can go get a woman pregnant, then move on to the next woman and do the same thing, instead of settling down, getting a job, and supporting their family. If they decide they want to take responsibility, which is what they should want, they're told it's none of their business, it's the woman's baby, not theirs."

Clarence looked at Jake. "Okay, what do you think?"

"Three months ago I would have said you were off base. I would have thought maybe you'd lost it. Now, I don't know. No, actually I do know. You're making perfect sense."

"Scary, isn't it?"

"More than you can believe. But are you really going to bootleg all this into a sports column?"

"Why not? Who are the sports figures? Young virile men, lots of them black men, looked on as role models by black boys and young men. As a sports columnist, as a black man myself—and still virile I might add—can't I challenge these guys to stand up on this issue?"

"Can't hurt to try. What's there to lose...other than your reputation and your career?"

"You talk like a man speaking from experience."

Jake studied the onion ring in his hand. "Yeah."

Jake came in to the *Trib* at 10:00 A.M. the next day, December 23. Among the responses were a few cheerful "Merry Christmases." He also caught several strange looks that he interpreted as stemming from personal offense or genuine concern about his mental health. He also saw a few smiles and nods of approval, several from people whose names he couldn't remember. The looks felt like covert acknowledgments made by one undercover agent to another, signaling a sense of camaraderie they didn't openly display in the hostile environment they'd managed to infiltrate.

"Messages waiting" greeted him at his desk. The "top priority" memo from Jess was terse.

"Back off on your moralistic columns, Jake. You're getting too preachy. Winston and I decided to let this column go. Now we're taking the heat for you. Tone it down. Go back to what made us assign you to columns in the first place. You know we've always given you every latitude in the past, but this isn't a religion column. We already carry Bill Buckley, and you're not him. I hope I've made myself clear."

Jake was shocked. It was the sternest rebuke from Jess he'd ever received. Jess never pulled a trump card like this. What did he mean he was taking the heat for Jake? Then the light turned on. The publisher. Of course. Raylan Berkely was upset. And why not? His wife was on the Planned Parenthood board, active in NOW. It was one thing to carry a few columnists that challenged political correctness. It was something else to employ one. That was too much like complicity. Berkely hadn't come to Jake—he prided himself on non-interference with the newsroom. But now he was coming down on Jake's superiors, twisting their arms to twist his.

Jake thought of showing the note to Clarence, it related so closely to their discussion. He decided against it for the moment. He reread the note. Not a religion column? Of course it wasn't. Did he say anything about religion in the column? He called it back up and reread it on his screen. No, it was just facts and common sense conclusions. What was religious about that—unless religion was also facts and common sense, a supposition he knew was not widely held at the *Trib*. And Jess was right—they had always given him latitude in the past.

Until now.

Jake had crossed a line. The line was not obscenity or inaccuracy or vengeance or damaging the reputation of an innocent person. The line was certain moral beliefs and their overt or implied criticism of popular institutions. Ironically, Jake pondered, these same moral beliefs were once widely accepted by the culture. Now they were so alien as to constitute a major threat. In the open-minded world of some of his journalistic superiors and peers, they were met with all the fear and distrust and sense of mortal danger as an alien invasion in a sci-fi flick.

Jake pressed the button on his recording machine. Two positive and three negative calls concerning his column. The next message was direct and to the point.

"Jake Woods? Barbara Betcher, NEA. The executive committee met this morning. We're formally withdrawing our invitation for you to speak at our spring banquet. Your columns have been attacking some of the very things we stand for. There are plenty of speakers sympathetic to education and to our children—we don't need someone who's not. I hope this is just a phase you're going through. For your sake and everybody else's, we all hope you shake it soon. Real soon."

"Merry Christmas to you too, Barbara," Jake said aloud. He shook his head, marveling at the short memories of those who had only a few months ago appeared so loyal to him. Why did they feel so betrayed? Maybe it was his own fault for serving as their mouthpiece, rehashing their propaganda when he'd thought of himself as truly independent. Had he been willing to obscure the truth to serve what he considered a good cause, and unwilling to tell the truth when it served what he considered a bad cause?

It wasn't the responses of Planned Parenthood and Barbara Betcher that bothered him most. It was the responses of some of his colleagues, including those on the multiculturalism committee. They confirmed all too clearly that the religion of political correctness, of which he had been a dutiful if unthinking priest, had come to truly dominate the mainstream of his profession. Unbelievers, such as syndicated conservatives who had never been part of this religion, were scorned but given a begrudging respect. The greatest scorn was reserved for someone who had been on the inside and now dared to betray the religion, to defect from its sacred creeds and violate its dogmas. Jake had become a heretic. The rising smoke from his terminal, message machine, and mailbox promised he would face the fires all heretics must face.

At 6:06 A.M. on October 28, Gregory Victor Lowell had exited his temporary residence. He'd been unconscious his last hours, but on leaving his body his faculties immediately sharpened. Time had passed, if time still was. The time or day on earth was unknown and irrelevant here. Wherever here was.

For the first moments Doc thought he was dreaming. This was the only possible explanation for his conscious appraisal of his body lying on a hospital bed. He felt free, liberated, relieved, as one who had escaped from the confinement of the body. But this changed almost instantly as he sized up the situation.

He was out of his body, which meant he was dead. He realized in a flash of insight he had been wrong all those years in thinking that life ended with death. He had said there was no soul, but a soul is exactly what he was and had been all along. He had not ceased to exist. Indeed, the very idea of a person ceasing to exist was ludicrous. People did not die, they merely relocated from one place to another. Such an exit could never be mistaken for a move from existence to nonexistence except by shortsighted, egocentric people in one room who thought that whenever someone went into another they must no longer exist.

This new world, if indeed he had arrived there—and he desperately hoped he had not—did not seem unreal but much more real than the old world. A sickening feeling of foreboding gripped him; he was unprepared for this realm. And it was now too late to prepare.

Doc knew instinctively that whatever lay ahead of him would never end. This truth was self-evident. He felt embarrassed and foolish he had ever thought otherwise.

How could I have been so deceived?

Yet even as he asked the question, he knew he had been willingly deceived because of how he wanted to live and what he wanted to believe—and because of how he did not want to live and what he did not want to believe.

What had Finney told him? "The reason you don't want to believe in a Creator is because then you'd have to believe in a Judge—and you don't want to think you'll be held accountable for how you've lived. But there is, and you will be."

This irritated him before, and it irritated him now. Who was Finney to preach to him?

Doc looked around uneasily, trying to get his bearings. Where were the others? He could see or hear no one. A flood of proud and confident words from the past rushed over him. The party where he said, "I'd rather be in hell with intelligent people than in heaven with a bunch of Christians." The times he'd quoted Mark Twain—"It's heaven for atmosphere and hell for company." His retort to Finney—"I'd rather be anywhere with anyone than to be with a herd of narrow-minded fundamentalists and their narrow-minded God."

Finney's life and words haunted Doc now even more than they had on earth. His mind flashed back to a conversation two years earlier. It was more than a memory, with the fuzzy edges memories have. It was like a videotape, vivid and complete to the detail. Doc could remember every word, every sound, every feeling. It was relived in his mind, moment by moment, as if it were happening right now. And that made it all the more painful.

While looking for a pen on Finney's desk at his house, Doc's eyes fell on a receipt. It showed Finney had recently given a large sum of money to feed the hungry in an African country. Doc was irritated, and he let Finney know it, waving the receipt in front of his face as if it were incriminating evidence.

"Don't you know that money isn't going to solve the problem? Those people are going to die anyway. You're just prolonging their agony. It's a foolish waste of hard-earned money."

"Well, Doc," Finney came back, "I'm sure those people think their lives and the lives of their children are just as important as ours. All that I am and all that I have belongs to someone else. It's his money, not mine, and I think that's where he wanted me to put it. You call it foolish. I think it's wise. I guess some day we'll both find out who was right."

"Think about your own family," Doc responded. "You could have given them a terrific vacation with that money. Or invested in a mutual fund that would help pay their way through college. And what about Little Finn? His condition is permanent—he might have some big expenses down the line. And what about your retirement—are you going to have enough for you and Sue? Look, buddy, I appreciate generosity as much as the next guy, but let's get real. You can't save the whole world. Think ahead, for crying out loud."

"That's exactly what I'm doing, Doc. You're thinking thirty years ahead. I'm trying to think thirty million years ahead."

Doc's familiar *Twilight Zone* whistle had filled the air. He looked at Finney with a combination of pity and scorn.

"I'm serious, Doc."

"That's what scares me. There's a place in our psych ward reserved in your name. They're all serious, too. Have you considered therapy?"

Finney's look of concern for him bothered Doc as much as anything. It seemed so arrogant and condescending.

"You talk about foolish," Finney said. "Foolish is not planning for your eternal future. Jesus told about a rich man who stored up treasures on earth but didn't prepare for eternity. And God said to him, 'You fool, this night your life is required of you. Now who will get all you've laid up for yourself?'"

"Not the church, if I can help it!"

"Come on, Doc. Leave the church out of it. This isn't about the church, it's about you and God. I admire your accomplishments. You've worked hard, earned a lot of respect, a lot of influence, and a whole lot of money. I've been in your cheering section, you know that. But there's a lot more to life than all that."

"Like what? Here and now is all there is, old buddy."

"Do you really believe that, Doc? Come on. You're more than an animal. You're an eternal human being. You're going to live forever. And what you do now has bearing on eternity."

"I don't believe that for a minute. I reject it. So what do you say to that?"

"Your rejection doesn't change reality. You are who you are, and God is who he is. And he did what he did for you on the cross. Nothing you think or say will ever change any of that."

"I didn't ask for anyone to go to the cross for me—I pay my own way. I don't want your religion; it's a pacifier for fools. And I don't want any part of your God."

"I'd rather be judged a fool by you for the moment, than be judged a fool by God for eternity." Finney eyes pleaded with him. "Doc, don't say you'd rather pay your own way. You may get your wish. It's called hell. God not being there is what will make it hell."

Doc shivered as the scenario played itself out in his mind. It was so real, as if he had actually gone back and relived it. "A fool for eternity." Finney's words haunted him.

Where was everybody? Doc had never felt so utterly alone. He was waiting for someone to come, a citizen of this realm to orient him, to explain the ground rules, the boundaries and opportunities of this world. There was an invisible fence. He could sense it. A limiting wall that could not be penetrated. An iron curtain locking him in, preventing any escape. This was confinement. Much worse, it was solitary confinement. He kept hoping it was only temporary.

The more he thought, the angrier Doc became. *How could God do this to me? If God was a God of love, he would offer me a way out.*

He would not allow himself to realize God's love had indeed made a way out, and at immense cost to himself. Or to realize this way had been explained to him many times, by one of his best friends and others as well. He had rejected the way. He wanted another way, a way that would not force him to confess to wrongdoing. A way that would recognize and reward his goodness, those he had helped, his contribution to humanity. A way that didn't require him to crawl on his knees like a sniveling beggar. He would find his own way. He always had before.

Yet even as he said this to himself, he sensed the ropes slipping through his hands. Verses of the Bible he had tried to ignore, thrust upon him by Finney, flashed back into his mind. Jesus said, "I am the way, the truth and the life—no man comes to the Father but by me." No other way. "Neither is there any other name under heaven given among men, whereby we must be saved." No other way. It was God's way or none.

Very well, Doc thought. *Then none it will be.*

He would have to make the best of this world. Anything would be better than the alternative. At least there would be no rules and church services and hypocrite evangelists and pansy angels and interminable do-gooder boredom.

The aloneness was becoming stifling. He could hear nothing, feel nothing, see nothing, sense nothing. He had only himself. He considered the unthinkable—that this was not a phase, a part of a transition, but the final destination. That this was hell. Or at least the beginning of hell.

He felt a burning. A fury welled up inside him. Anger and bitterness, unfocused hostility, frustration leading him to lash out. But there was no one to lash out at. No incompetent nurse, no demented patient, no Christian bigot, no wife, no children. And there was no audience to convince he was being treated unjustly. No one to cower in fear at the power of the great athlete, the scholar, the renowned doctor, the skilled surgeon. No one to admire the champion of women's rights who courageously provided them abortions.

Abortion—there was no longer a lack of clarity, no longer a pretense. It was killing children. He had known all along that's exactly what it was. What else could it be? The images of mutilated babies consumed his mind.

The pain began to sink in deeper, creating a desperate desire for relief. It was a pain far worse than any he had ever felt before. Doc thought of all the times he had loosely used the word *hell*. "I had a hell of a day in surgery." "Jake and I raised hell that weekend in Miami." Even "War is hell."

No, this was hell; all else paled in comparison. And this was only the first hour of hell, and there was no calendar to check off the days until the sentence was finished. How could he endure even a day, much less an eternal night? How long would tomorrow be? He could not bear the thought of it.

But if he could escape, what was the alternative? Heaven? The thought of being there sickened him. To be under those rules, that constant self-righteous oppression, would be intolerable. More intolerable, even, than this place. Yes, the doors of hell were locked all right, but they were locked from the inside. If God attempted to enter this world, Doc would double bolt the door and put his shoulder against it. This was his place, his world. God had no right to intrude.

Doc thirsted for help, but not redemption. He hungered for hope, but not righteousness. He longed for friendship, but not with those who followed God. He could see in his mind's eye Dante's sign that hung over the entrance to hell's inferno. "Abandon hope all ye who enter here."

Already his last shred of hope was fleeing from him. He panicked. He had lived by goals and aspirations and hopes. But here there was room for none of these. He had lived by the pursuit of excellence. Here there was no excellence to pursue. Here there was nothing.

Where were the great people Twain said would inhabit hell? There were no great people here. No people at all. No company of the damned with whom to commiserate and strategize an escape, like in all the prison movies. Commiseration is the one desirable element of suffering, and hell had nothing desirable to offer. No camaraderie. No family. No sports, no music, no movies. Not even a television to watch a sitcom or laugh at those phony preachers.

Doc had fantasized that if there was a hell, it would be like a pirate ship where the most shrewd and powerful would rise to the top. Better to be a captain in hell than a harp strumming eunuch in heaven. If there were Hitlers and child murderers here, which he doubted, he would just stay away from them. He would find the great men of hell, join their fraternity, work his way to the top. Yet even as he thought this, he sensed it was not true. He would never again see another human being. Except one day there would be a long and terrible line leading to judgment.

The God he insisted did not exist, and he did not want or need, had granted him his wish—to have him once and for all out of his life. He realized now there was no life without the Creator and Sustainer of Life. This was existence, not life. This was eternal death. For a moment Doc was filled with grief, but it was quickly replaced with anger and outrage, much deeper than before. How dare God do this to him?

Suddenly he heard a sound, a terrible sound, so awful it proved him wrong when he'd thought that any sound would be welcome. It was an almost human sound, but more like an animal writhing in agony. A sound of moaning building to a horrible scream. It went on and on, torturing him, its only consolation the fact that someone or something else must be here with him.

Suddenly he realized the terrible truth—the scream was his. He was still alone, and there could be no comfort in this hideous scream. The animal nature of it shocked him. He had once put his hope in the thought that he was but an animal, a higher one, but he'd always known he was something more. Now he felt he was becoming something less.

He had rejected heaven's call to selflessness for hell's call to selfishness. And why not? What could matter more than self? He would not let go of himself, entrust himself to the will of another. He wanted to set the ground rules, for himself and others. He wanted control. But now he felt out of control. No one was reporting to him. When he still had opportunity to choose, he had chosen a path he could not turn back from now.

He would gladly spit in the face of God, if only he could do it without looking at him. To look at that face would be hell itself. He could not imagine even a moment in his presence. He longed for relief, yet said to himself, "If the door to heaven were opened I would run from it. No hell could be worse than the hell of hearing narrow-minded Christians say 'I told you so.'"

In his mind's eye, from what source he did not know, he could now see that coming day of change from the state he now found himself in. He saw a great kingdom, a thousand year reign of unparalleled peace on earth. But the one who ruled was...no, it could not be. The carpenter from Nazareth? The self-proclaimed God of the Christians? And with him, ruling with him, were none other than the Christian bigots themselves. How could this be? What gave them the right to control and oppress the inhabitants of the world?

And at the end of that thousand years, he could see a great parade. No, not a parade. A march. A march of criminals, prisoners of an oppressive government, champions of freedom unjustly accused, going one by one in front of a great white throne. He could see himself marching along with many others, each to stand before a terrible judge, a tyrant, a despot. They were no doubt to be punished for their progressive ideas.

Doc saw many ordinary people. No one seemed to recognize him. He did not stand out from the crowd. He was just another person. No one else cared. Every mind was directed inward at itself and its plan to deny or escape or accuse or blame others for its choices.

But no denial would work, for Doc could see great books being opened, books that had accurately logged every thought and word and deed. These books were what would determine his future, and he realized they contained adulteries, lies, and betrayals of his wife and children, as well as neglect and failure to guide them into truth and integrity. But he had given them plenty of material things that should more than compensate, he was sure, if the Judge was fair. Doc would defend himself before the court of heaven. He would appeal to the jury, a jury of his peers, and they would be won over by his eloquence. They would let him off.

But hard as he looked, he couldn't locate a jury anywhere. Only the Judge.

There was one Book beside these other books. It was written in a strange language, but somehow he could read it. The Lamb's Book of Life. It contained the names of people who were as guilty as all the others, but who would be pardoned because they had bowed their knees to One who had been slain for their crimes. Doc could see many names in that book, names of people from every nation. A few he recognized. There was Finney's, and each member of his family. Why were some names there and others not? This was intolerable discrimination.

His name was not there. He had made sure it would not be. Why would he want it to be? He was glad he had not seen Jake's name either, though he knew he'd seen but a tiny fraction of the names there. *At least Jake and I will be together,* he thought, he hoped. As soon as he thought it he realized it was not true. Even if they were together in hell, it would be in utter misery. But misery loves company, and there was love of nothing in hell. Even if Jake were here they would not be together. He was alone. All alone. For eternity. Grief and rage warred with each other for control of his mind. Hell was not just confinement, but a growing cancer, gnawing at him, eating away at him, devouring him.

The most frightening thing in the scene that ran through his mind was people bowing their knees before the One who sat on the throne. The sheer power and magnitude of the Judge seemed to fall upon them, and every knee bowed, not out of repentance or loving submission, but out of inability to bear the weight of judgment laid upon them. Doc shuddered at the thought of his knee touching the ground before such a tyrant. No. He would not allow it. And yet...many once mighty men further up in the line were falling to their knees in terror.

The future scene vanished from his mind as inexplicably as it had come. He turned his memory to his days on earth, but panicked as he found it increasingly hard to remember what had happened there. He wanted to, for memories of what he had accomplished, things he had done, awards he had won, were at least a distraction, something to occupy his mind, a sort of solace. But everything was closing out on him, leaving nothing but the desperate reality of the moment.

He wanted to think of something else, anything else. But all he could think of was timeless unending aloneness. An eternal fire fueled by hate and bitterness and...yes, and bigotry toward those he had loved to call bigots, hate toward those he had called hatemongers. He rejected all that was not himself. And all that was left was himself, a shrinking shriveled version of himself that could not thrive without the presence of the Other he so despised. Now, finally, the self he had loved he began to despise.

Words from the past haunted him. "But the fact is, there is a God and you will stand before him." No! The thought of suicide came to him. Physician-assisted suicide, he mused, still thinking of himself as a doctor, though there was no one here to heal, neither was there the power to heal.

Yes, I'll end this. I'll just go to sleep. I'll cheat death and hell.

He had no tool with which to inflict harm on himself, nor did this body, though capable of great suffering, seem capable of being harmed. His body was like a bush that burned but was not consumed. The pain that could neither end nor be relieved seared his mind, now in a fearful craze.

Thirst without water to quench it. Hunger without food to satisfy it. Loneliness without company to assuage it. There was no God here. He'd gotten his wish. On earth he'd managed to reject God while still getting in on so many of the blessings and provisions of God. But it was now clear, excruciatingly clear, the absence of God meant the absence of all God gives. No one could have good without the God who is the source of all good. No God, no good. Forever.

Doc was overwhelmed with the horror of it all. Doctor Gregory Lowell had wanted a world where no one else was in charge, where no order was forced upon him. He had finally gotten it.

He missed the sound of laughter. There was no laughter here. There could be no laughter where there was no hope. The awful realization descended on him that there was no storyline here. No opening scene, no developing plot, no climax, no resolution. No character development. No travel, no movement. Only constant nothingness, going nowhere. This was Doc's first day in hell. And he knew, despite every protestation erupting from within him, that every day would be the same, and of his days here there could be no end. Excruciating eternal boredom. It was all so terribly unfair.

For a moment he longed to be in heaven, to be in the very presence of God. But he could not allow this God-hunger to continue. He could not face God's existence, much less his goodness and justice, and the commentary it made on all the inexorable choices that had shaped his life in the other world, and determined his destiny here.

A wave of something came across him. He sensed it was some extension of the presence of an omnipotent God, like a wind blowing through the deserts of hell. It was the same presence that in heaven caused men to be filled with joy and awe and love. But here even God's love felt like wrath and his joy like torture. The consuming fire of God that was purity and goodness and comfort to those who loved the light was blinding searing punishment to those who loved the darkness. The same fire of God that was life-giving warmth in heaven, drawing all to huddle around it rejoicing, here was a destructive life-consuming inferno compelling all to flee in terror.

"Get away from me! Get away!"

In horror and revulsion Doc tried to escape the One who had finally consented to withdraw from him, but even then could not finally be escaped. God's very existence was a mortal insult, an eternal slap in his face. It was not enough for God to withdraw. He must cease to exist. If only God were no longer God, this misery would be endurable.

Hell was merely heaven refused. Denial had always been Doc's solace, and now that he could not deny the reality of the Other, his only solace was gone. Once you left earth there was no spin or twist on the truth, no angle on it, only the truth itself. As Finney's heaven had started on earth, so Doc's hell had started there. Now he was experiencing its final fruition.

No end. No sleep. No escape. Questions pointed their mocking bony fingers at him. Why had he been so sure about what he did not know? Why had he been so stubborn, insisting on being his own god, living by his own rules? He'd been a fool, and would remain a fool, for all eternity.

No, no, no! I am not a fool. Finney *was the fool. It was Finney. Not me. Not me! Not me!*

CHAPTER TWENTY-NINE

J ake left the *Trib* at 3:30, December 23, not at all in the holiday spirit. He was bone weary of putting out fires, making explanations, and second-guessing everyone's looks and glances. How could he focus on turning out decent columns when his mind was torn between the controversies springing up around him and the perplexing mystery of his friends' murder? He decided to drive home the long way, the way that took him by Lifeline Medical Center.

He passed by the clinic where he'd talked with Marsdon, then drove in the hospital entrance about three hundred feet further, parking in the same row as when he came to meet with Mary Ann. Part of him wanted to drop by Doc's old office and see her, to be with her, maybe ask her to dinner and then...who knows? He decided instead to go back to ICU, where his friends had spent their last moments on earth and where his life had taken such a wild turn from which it now threatened never to regain control. Maybe he'd bump into Simpson or one of two or three doctors on his list neither he nor Ollie had found time to talk with yet. Maybe fate would connect him with somebody, anybody, who could fill in the blanks, link him with just the right piece of information about Doc and who might have taken him out.

Jake wandered into the ICU waiting room, reliving in vivid detail all that happened there the day after the accident. He sat staring at the security door he'd sneaked through eight weeks ago, as if it might magically open and yield the missing pieces to the puzzle.

Suddenly two nurses burst out the door. Both seemed upset, one puffy eyed, as if she'd been crying. He thought he recognized her. Jake followed them out to the hallway. They turned a corner into a recessed area, where they stopped, thinking they were outside anyone's hearing.

"I'm so tired of it, Laura! Wheeling in bodies right and left, pressured to make room for more. It's starting to feel more like warehouse inventory than health care."

"I know, I know. But that's the way it is. It's nobody's fault. There's nothing we can do about it, Robin."

Robin. Of course. It was Doc's ICU nurse, the one Dr. Simpson bawled out after Jake infiltrated the hallowed halls of ICU.

"The shift's almost over. Call it a day, all right? I've got to get back in there."

Robin said thanks, and the other nurse marched back to ICU, past Jake. He walked up to Robin as if he hadn't been eavesdropping. The moment she recognized Jake, Nurse Robin froze.

"Why are you here? You came to talk?"

Jake looked at her, puzzled. She was nervous, suspicious, uptight. The stress of being an ICU nurse was taking its toll. "Uh, just taking a stroll, but if you've got a minute, maybe we could chat. Want to sit down somewhere?"

Just then two doctors rounded the corner, startling Robin. *She's a basket case.* Jake recognized one of the doctors. Simpson. *That's who I need to talk to. What a stroke of luck.*

"Dr. Simpson?"

Simpson and the other doctor stopped and turned around, both busy, weary and in no mood to be waylaid in the hall. Simpson stared at Jake just a moment before the light of recognition turned on.

"Woods? Jake Woods. How are you, Jake?" The initial ice melted into warmth as Simpson seemed to take pride in introducing the well-known columnist to his colleague, making it sound as though he and Jake were old buddies. It helped that the other doctor lit up on hearing Jake's name.

After the three chatted a minute, Jake remembered Robin. He turned to tell her he'd catch her some other time, but she'd already left. It was no surprise. Anyone that nervous wouldn't want to hang around two doctors and a journalist.

"Dr. Simpson, any chance I could talk to you for just five minutes?"

Simpson said, "Okay. Sure."

The other doctor (Jake had already forgotten his name) said it was good to meet him and headed off down the hallway. Simpson directed Jake around the corner to a reasonably private bench in the hallway. Once they were seated, Jake cut right to the heart.

"There's an investigation into Greg Lowell's death. It wasn't an accident."

Simpson turned pale. "What? What are you telling me?"

"I'm telling you somebody murdered Greg."

"Murdered him?" Unnerved, Simpson stared at Jake, making him reconsider his tactics. Maybe he had been too blunt.

"Yes. That's right."

"But...how do you know?"

"Somebody cut the tie-rods on his car. The police are certain it was deliberate."

Simpson caught his breath, and finally started to relax. "That's terrible. But what can I do for you?"

"This isn't for a story. I'm helping out a police detective, who's a friend of mine. I've talked with a few other doctors. Can you tell me about anyone who didn't get along with Doc?"

"Well, I got along with him as well as anyone. He was strong willed, for sure, but we all are. You had to let some things slide and focus on his positive side, which far outweighed the negatives. His skills were incredible. He was maybe the finest surgeon I ever worked with. We did a few transplants together, and when something would start to go wrong, you could hear panic in other doctors' voices, but never his. The guy was unflappable. People who didn't get along with him? Sure, I can toss out some names, for what it's worth. Not that anyone who works at this hospital would sabotage somebody's car!"

Simpson came up with now familiar names, with similar assessments to those he'd gotten from Mary Ann and the others.

"Then there was Dr. Marsdon."

"What about Marsdon?"

"There's a guy who hated Greg's guts. Major conflict. All the time. Marsdon's a bureaucrat at heart. Greg was the type to do what was necessary. Get the job done. He was my kind of doctor." He looked at Jake. "You come up with some other leads outside the hospital?"

When Jake mentioned abortion, fetal tissue research, and RU-486, Simpson really lit up.

"Now I think you're on to something! Those people couldn't stand Greg. You just look at those picket signs. You think they're not happy he's dead? It's hard to believe anybody would kill him, but if anybody would, it would be them. Listen, Jake, I've got to run. Hope you find the guy that messed with Greg's car."

"Thanks, Dr. Simpson."

"It's Barry. Glad you've recovered so well, Jake. You look a lot better than when I last saw you sneaking around ICU!"

"Don't remind me. And thanks again."

Jake caught a whiff of morning coffee, saw the light peeking through his bedroom miniblinds, and took his first blurry-eyed look at the big red digits of the clock. 8:42 A.M. About two hours later than he expected. It was December 24.

Every year with the *Trib,* Jake had worked on Christmas Eve day. But this year he said no. He recycled an old holiday column and left it at that. His thoughts had returned to childhood and how special this day had been. And how special it had been for three women in his life, none of whom he shared the holidays with any longer—Mom, Janet, and Carly.

In his childhood, this had been the big day of the year for the Woods family, with turkey and stuffing and potatoes cooking all day, and the big dinner about four or five o'clock. Aunts and uncles and grandmas and grandpas were joined by single people with no family around, who were adopted for the day. Presents were opened at six, because they couldn't fend off the begging children any longer. It was a day of conversation, laughter, and game playing, especially Parcheesi and Monopoly, and for the adults, Pinochle.

Jake recalled his brother Bryce throwing a handful of snack mix in his face after Jake had put a hotel on Park Place and Bryce landed on it and went broke. Jake reached for the nearest thing to retaliate with, grabbing his glass of Byerly's orange soda. Jake's initial thrill in watching Bryce's white T-shirt turn orange turned to horror when the rest of the splash soaked into Mom's white and red Christmas tablecloth.

Jake and Bryce were not close, as brothers go, but having been in the trenches together, having killed and rescued each other in war games in the ten acres of wheat behind the house, there would always be a bond. Jake thought about Bryce and his wife Carol, and kids Jennifer, Brian, and...what was the youngest one's name? Jake was embarrassed he couldn't remember, and it nailed home how much he'd lost touch with family.

Ever since Mom's Alzheimer's had flared up, family contact had become rare and perfunctory. Bryce called occasionally. He'd ask, "How's Mom?" Jake would say, "Not much change," not volunteering he hadn't visited her for two months. Of course, Bryce hadn't seen her for a year. A thousand miles away, sure, but he flew on business trips all the time. He could come see Mom if he wanted to. Living in the same city, though, Jake knew his excuses were lamer than Bryce's.

Mom was the glue of the family. Not Dad, who could take or leave Christmas, never remembered a birthday, didn't even know which presents were from him since Mom had picked them out. Not Jake or Bryce, whose lives revolved around friends and sports and school activities, then later military and college and getting started in business and having their own families. Even after Dad had died, Mom always got them together for Christmas and made phone calls on birthdays. But as her health failed, especially her mind, the glue lost its adhesive, and the Woods family gradually broke out of Mom's orbit.

Mom was Christmas. Dad's only job was to bring home the tree. Even that Mom picked out because Dad didn't have the taste or the patience to make a good choice.

I'll never forget that pathetic noble fir he brought home one year. A smile came to his lips as he remembered Mom trying to find a few branches that would hold up the ornaments.

She had no help in the kitchen. No help with the dishes. Dad sat all day reading the paper and swapping stories with the old folks, Jake and Bryce coming in and out with their muddy tennis shoes and playing games and tossing snacks and orange soda.

Mom was always cheerful on the holidays. She hummed "Santa Claus Is Coming to Town" and a few sacred songs as well, but Jake couldn't remember which ones. Except "Silent Night." Jake was surprised he could remember as many of the words as he did. They'd sung it in grade school choir, and it stuck with him, though church had never been part of his Christmas.

Still lying in bed, Jake realized he'd been singing. "Silent night, holy night, all is calm, all is bright, 'round yon virgin, mother and child, holy infant so tender and mild. Sleep in heavenly peace, sleep in heavenly peace."

There was something calming and reassuring about these words. But something profoundly disturbing as well. Who was this "holy infant" to offer heavenly peace? To promise calm in a world full of turmoil, abuse, and death? How could he expect anyone to believe him? Yet there were those who did believe, with all their hearts. People such as Finney and Sue. Finney.

Where are you now, old friend?

Jake had no plans for the day. Mom was in no condition to make plans, hadn't been for three Christmases now, and without her none would be made. Sue had invited him to join her and Little Finn and Angela and the extended family later that night, but his day was free. He'd been looking forward to sitting around, doing nothing, catching up on his reading, maybe watching a movie or two on tape. He'd looked forward to not shaving, getting dressed, or leaving the house.

But now he was in the bathroom shaving and humming "Silent Night" and thinking about the words. After a long hot shower, he put on some casual clothes, grabbed his wallet and keys, and headed for the door.

I wonder if Mom will recognize me.

It was Christmas Day now, and Jake was alone. His time with his mother yesterday morning had been difficult at first, but the longer he'd stayed the more at home he'd become. He even met a few of his mother's friends, which he'd never had time to do before.

Last night he'd been with Sue, Little Finn, Angela and her husband Bruce. Their first Christmas without Finney. There had been tears, but lots of laughter. The laughter in that family came from deep inside. They celebrated Christmas as if they had some inside knowledge of what it really meant.

The investigation's shadow hung over him. Perhaps Jake would spend the rest of his life speculating on who killed his friends and why, never knowing for sure, and never seeing the killer brought to justice. To think that someone could get away with this. Where was justice in this world? It was frustrating to be out of control, to not be in charge, to know he wasn't calling the shots. Maybe nobody was. He was tired of it. He wanted answers and he wanted them soon.

He sat back in his frayed blue recliner, molded perfectly to his shape and sitting position. The surround sound and big screen of his home entertainment system presented impressive reruns of the new starship Enterprise blasting through space, with Captain Jean-Luc Picard at the helm, accompanied by his trusted friends and advisors. The journey into the unknown, the exploration of the undiscovered country appealed to something deep inside Jake. It wasn't just his desire to escape, but his longing to understand the universe, to know what if anything lies beyond, to discover and interact with worlds and peoples far greater than his own. To find a planet, perhaps a whole galaxy, untainted by the ravages and ruin of earth. It seemed a childish fantasy, but it was a fantasy he would gladly choose over the reality he knew.

Two more hours of television left him hungry for something that satisfied. Jake opened Finney's Bible for the second time. He flipped his way through it, like a pioneer hiking through virgin territory, seeing new terrain from every new viewpoint. He was amazed at all the underlining, circled words, lines connecting words and verses to each other. He read the notes and the verses, seeking to understand. Often he was pleased he could, though he suspected Finney saw deeper and more profound connections than he. He looked at each page as if it were an ancient treasure map, with the scrawlings of Magellan in the margins.

Jake's mind drifted, holding Finney's Bible triggering thoughts of his old friend. He was awakening to the crackle of an early morning campfire. He crawled out of his Cutter's-scented sleeping bag and stuck his head out of the tent to get a deeper whiff of the savory smell of frying bacon. Finney looked and laughed.

"Morning, bud! You look like you need a jump start. I'll pour you a Cappuccino."

Finney brought over a cup of fire-roasted coffee that should have tasted terrible, but didn't. Then Finney ruffled Jake's matted hair. Funny how he remembered that. Jake missed not just the sight of his friend, but his smell and touch.

Why did they go on those hunting trips together? Was it the spontaneity, the differentness, the departure from the routine? The adventure, the danger (minimal though it was) of the wild? Or was it just an excuse to stay up late with people you loved? Yeah, that was it, though you couldn't just come right out and say you "loved" those guys. It was being with friends where there was nothing to do but talk and tell stories and hold on to this something special you knew you had together. You could accomplish a lot of the same thing just setting up a tent in the back yard.

His mind drifted back to his friend's most valued possession, the ancient book on his lap. These pages so cram full of notes revealed Finney's view of the Bible, Jake thought. He saw it not as a relic to be enshrined, but bread to be consumed. Every scratching of the pen represented time spent in thought and prayer. Finney would read the *Tribune* to see how people were living. He would read the Bible to see how people should be living.

Jake suddenly remembered the letter. About a year ago Finney had written him a letter, not long after the infamous duck hunting disaster when Finney and Doc almost came to blows. He remembered how bad Finney felt. He wrote to Jake, to let him know why he felt as he did. Jake had put that letter somewhere. He'd thrown away some other notes—"Finney's evangelistic notes" he'd labeled them—but not this one. Perhaps he instinctively realized that if one day Finney was gone, he could always remember him from this letter.

Jake got up from his recliner and scanned the bookshelf. Finally, yes, there it was, folded into a book Finney had given him at the same time—*Mere Christianity* by C. S. Lewis. Jake had never opened the book. It had served only to preserve the letter.

The letter was three typewritten pages long. It was a typical Finney-looking letter, beautiful on the page, having been labored over on his computer and printed out on his laser printer. Jake imagined him writing it late one sleepless night just after the hunting trip.

Dear Jake,

Sorry about the "duck hunting disaster," as you so aptly dubbed it. I find myself between the proverbial rock and hard place. I feel compelled to act according to what I believe, yet it troubles me to know this makes things so uncomfortable for you.

At the truck stop, I believed I had to warn Doc not to do something so wrong and destructive to him and his family. I got angry and said things I shouldn't have. I asked both of you to forgive me then, and ask you again now. I'm sending a letter to Doc too. I don't want to jeopardize the rich friendship we've always enjoyed.

I've decided to lay out for you in this letter the core of my beliefs. Before you say "Not again," hang on. I want to share them with you, then leave the ball in your court. I can't promise I'll never bring anything up again, but I do promise I'll try never to push anything on you. Agreed? So please indulge me and read this. Like you, sometimes I need to put what I believe in writing. (Unlike you, though, nobody's willing to pay me for it!)

You've wondered aloud more than once why I spend my Sunday mornings in church. Well, it's not to honor the dead, that's for sure. Church isn't a memorial service for a dead man. It's a worship service for a risen Lord. This isn't about being religious. This is about Jesus. I believe what the Bible says about him. I believe the Bible isn't a bunch of fairy tales, but precisely what it claims to be—a serious record of history, written by reliable eye-witnesses. These included some real skeptics, who despite themselves just couldn't ignore what they saw and heard.

This Jesus has changed my life. You told me once you thought I was just fine before I became a Christian. I appreciate it, old buddy, but in my heart I know differently. Even back then I knew something vital was missing, though on the outside most people thought I was okay.

I believe Jesus was and is God, that he's alive and is coming again. I believe he died on a cross for my sins, but that means nothing unless the Jesus who died on that cross was who he claimed to be. He claimed to be the Savior of the world.

You're probably thinking, "To believe all this, don't you have to check your brains at the door and throw out common sense?" You know me well enough to know I've never been easily convinced of anything. I don't believe things just because I want to, only when I'm convinced there's a compelling reason.

I grant there's a lot of foolishness and insincerity that passes itself off as "Christian," but that doesn't invalidate real Christianity, any more than counterfeit bills invalidate real money. The truth is real Christians are just ordinary people who've accepted the grace of God.

Jake, I'm asking you to read the book I'm giving you—*Mere Christianity* by C. S. Lewis. I've mentioned him before. An agnostic Oxford professor, Lewis was so intellectually honest that he forced himself to weigh the evidence for the Christian faith, never expecting to be swayed by it. As he studied the biblical accounts, he was disturbed to conclude they were authentic, that they were written as history, not fable. Despite his deep desire to disbelieve, he found himself believing. This is how he described his conversion:

"You must picture me alone in that room in Magdalen, night after night, feeling, whenever my mind lifted even for a second from my work, the steady, unrelenting approach of Him whom I so earnestly desired not to meet. That which I greatly feared had at last come upon me. Finally I gave in, and admitted that God was God, and knelt and prayed: perhaps, that night, the most dejected and reluctant convert in all England."

Later he began to find great joy in his new faith. But it was reason, it was the evidence that compelled him to believe even when he didn't want to.

Many people have said, "Well, I don't believe Jesus was really God, but I do think he was a great man and a fine moral teacher." You've said this yourself, haven't you, Jake? But as Lewis says in *Mere Christianity*, Jesus claimed to be much more than that. He claimed to be the only way to heaven. I won't say any more about this here, except to ask you to read what I've highlighted on pages 55 and 56.

God created us to know him and to find great joy in our relationship with him and each other. But he gave us free choice, and we chose to rebel against him. The Bible says "all have sinned and fall short of the glory of God" and "the wages of sin is death" (Romans 3:23; 6:23). It says God is holy, that he's so utterly righteous he has to judge sin. Somebody has to pay the price. Either we pay the price, through an eternity in hell, or Jesus pays the price for us. It's just that simple, Jake.

Remember when we were playing ball in front of Swenson's? Mrs. Swenson set up that old card table and put out the lemonade for us, and then she and Mr. Swenson sat and watched us. Doc was pitching, and you knocked one of his pitches right through old man Bronson's second story window. He was mowing his lawn and saw the whole thing. Our mouths were hanging open, and suddenly he was running at us like crazy.

Well, you know what happened next. Mr. Swenson comes out in front of us and tries to calm Bronson down. Finally, he takes out his wallet and gives the guy what seemed like a fortune—wasn't it a $20 bill? And Bronson walks away satisfied. We were off the hook. I don't think we had three dollars between us. Mr. Swenson saved our necks by paying the debt for us.

Jesus died for our sins, but his death doesn't guarantee forgiveness for everyone. What it guarantees is the availability of forgiveness to everyone. If you want it, it's yours: "Whoever is thirsty, let him come; and whoever wishes, let him take the free gift of the water of life" (Revelation 22:17). Christ offers the gift of forgiveness and eternal life, but we must choose to accept it or it isn't ours.

Death is the one certain thing in all of our lives. No intelligent person would face death without seriously examining the claims of Jesus. Don't turn away from Christ until you've taken a close look at him. Once you do, I think your mind will be forever changed. So, let's see some of that open-mindedness good liberals are supposed to have. Are you open-minded enough to give Jesus a chance before the deadline's past?

I hope it doesn't make you uncomfortable to know I pray for you every day, Jake. I have for years. I don't want our friendship to end when our life here does. If I leave this world first, one of the greatest joys I can think of is being in heaven to greet you when you arrive.

I only hope you'll look past my inadequacies and failings and not hold them against the God I'm telling you about. I don't want to get in the way of you or Doc coming to know Him. If I can ever be of help to you in this or anything else, please call on me, Jake. I'll be there. I promise.

Your friend,

Underneath was Finney's distinctive signature, the "F" a block rather than cursive, the "n's" blending together into what looked like an "m," and the "y" going straight down the page as if it had fallen down an elevator shaft.

I miss you, Finn.

For the next fifteen minutes, Jake was in another world, a world of memories and questions and conflict. When he returned, he discovered Finney's letter still in his hands, wrinkled by his grip. He carefully smoothed it out, folded it, and put it back in the envelope.

Jake went into the kitchen and put on some Macadamia Nut decaf, poured his first cup, then added French vanilla cream. He walked back to the old recliner and sat down with his coffee in one hand and a book in the other. He opened *Mere Christianity* to page 55 and read:

> I am trying here to prevent anyone saying the really foolish thing that people often say about him: "I'm ready to accept Jesus as a great moral teacher, but I don't accept his claim to be God." That is the one thing we must not say. A man who was merely a man and said the sort of things Jesus said would not be a great moral teacher. He would either be a lunatic—on a level with the man who says he is a poached egg—or else he would be the Devil of hell. You must make your choice. Either this man was, and is, the Son of God: or else a madman or something worse. You can shut him up for a fool, you can spit at him and kill him as a demon; or you can fall at his feet and call him Lord and God. But let us not come with any patronizing nonsense about his being a great human teacher. He has not left that open to us. He did not intend to.

Jake put the book down on his lap and, lost in thought, stared at nothing for the next several minutes. Then he picked the book up again, turned to the front, and started reading. He read it as a man reads something written by an old friend.

CHAPTER THIRTY

You've taught me so much, Zyor. This place is wonderful, much more wonderful than I had even dreamed. And, besides Elyon himself, you've been the most wonderful part of it. I'm so glad we're here together, finally able to talk face to face as friends."

"I am but a tiny part of your life here, which has just begun, and has endless eons of joyous adventure ahead." The mighty one's face softened into its most childlike features. "But I am honored you believe that part significant."

"At last," Finney added.

"Master?"

"You didn't say 'At last you believe that part significant,' but you must have felt it. All those years you served me. You protected me from death and injury in situations I never knew. I remember when I was seven—I fell into Benton Stream and hit my head on that rock. No one could figure out how I'd kept from drowning. It was you, wasn't it?"

The gigantic warrior nodded like a sheepish child. "I begged Elyon to let me carry you to land. He said his purpose for you on earth was not done and granted my request. It was one of only three times I was allowed to physically touch you. I will never forget that day."

"You fought to keep me from temptation," Finney said, "and when I foolishly walked headlong into it you fought to bring me through it faithful to Elyon. I gave God credit, and I know that's all you wanted. I also gave myself some credit, and my family and friends and church. But never once did I give you any credit, faithful friend."

Finney reached his arm up to Zyor's mammoth shoulders, accentuating how thin his perfect human body was, compared to this tender warrior's. "I'm truly sorry, Zyor, for Elyon's Book told me your kind were spirits sent to minister to my kind. It spoke of angels guarding us. But in the shadows of that world such thoughts somehow seemed unreal to me. As we used to say, I just didn't get it. Please forgive my blindness, dear friend."

The angel's resemblance to a bashful child kept growing. Finney grinned dimple to dimple again, feeling as if he were looking at a little boy—though this one was ten feet tall—blanching at the praise of his father. Zyor's head hung low in a way that made Finney think of Barney, the Tennessee mountain boy in his platoon. He almost expected Zyor to say "Ah, shucks, it weren't nuthin'."

That precious expression on his face. *Yes, it's like Little Finn. Just like Little Finn.*

"It is mine to serve," Zyor said. "The servant seeks ultimate approval only from the Audience of One."

Zyor said the word "One" with such reverence there could be no doubt of whom he spoke. Yet these words seemed rehearsed, as if they came straight out of some angelic handbook designed to keep Elyon's messengers focused and on track. Finney sensed Zyor must have said the words to himself many times in the dark world, as he worked so hard to defend someone who didn't even know he existed.

"And it is the beckon of that One I now must follow," Zyor said with sudden urgency and determination. "That is why I must leave you."

"Leave me? How can you leave? My orientation isn't over, is it? This is our home, Zyor. Why would you leave?"

"My home is wherever my Lord sends me."

"But where is he sending you?"

"To the front lines, where a warrior belongs when the battle rages. There will be time to celebrate later, time to tell great stories of valor, of campaigns won and lost, of struggles and weariness and victory. The time now is to do these things, not to speak of having done them. You no longer need me. Others do."

Zyor looked at Finney. "I am a warrior. The years by your side on earth were good, though never easy. And my time with you here has been a great privilege. It is so like Elyon to give us goodness beyond what we imagine. First and last, beginning and end, King of Kings and Lord of Lords, may his name be forever praised."

The giant's acclaim for Elyon was so spontaneous and absorbing that it sometimes seemed a continuous interruption to his train of thought. Yet Finney could see that the focal point, the overriding theme of this world was Elyon. Not his creations, not his plans, but Elyon himself—the virtues of his character, manifested in the greatness of his deeds. He was the magnet that drew all things to himself, the center of gravity, the reference point, the anchor and foundation of all. Elyon was the subject matter of heaven. Everything else was a temporary interruption, a brief digression. That was why no conversation could go far without erupting into praise.

"Zyor, I understand you are a warrior. But I thought your years of battle were done. Where exactly are you going?"

Zyor's voice was now resolute and intense, with a strength of will that almost overwhelmed Finney.

"I go where the battle rages. I go to the one place in the universe that dares to challenge the lordship of Elyon."

"Earth! You're going back to earth?"

The angel did not need to nod assent. Finney knew it was true.

"But why? I thought I was your assignment. I thought your tour of duty was over." Finney vividly recalled the emotions he felt returning from his one year in Vietnam. Not the least was relief—to have done your job and to now be able to enjoy the privileges of home. Surely after all those years on earth, Zyor had earned such relief.

"I was assigned to others centuries before you were born," Zyor replied. "And I was assigned to you as long as needed. You are no longer in danger, but others are. I too thought you were my final charge before the dark world breathes its last. But while Elyon is faithful, he is not predictable. He sends me back for another assignment. He has told me I am the best one to do it. I am...honored."

Finney could see Zyor was flooded with vivid memories of his recent commission from the Commander.

"But I thought it was time for you to rest." Even as he said it, Finney realized he could not and would not try to interfere with Elyon's plans. But he was troubled not only at the thought his new friend was going to leave him, but of his return to that most dark and dangerous place.

"I have rested. I have been renewed. To walk with you and Zeke and others, to have you see me and speak with me after all these years has been great refreshment. So it has been to worship Elyon in the great assembly. But I belong in the battle. Like all good warriors I long for peace. But when I know war rages, that my brothers—and those they serve—struggle and suffer at the hands of the twisted ones, I cannot hold back the longing to join them in battle. I have restrained that longing, for I had to, thinking Elyon would not send me back. Now that I know he beckons me, my heart pounds for the battle, my arms ache to raise Galeed again."

Finney understood Galeed must be Zyor's sword. He realized for the first time that Zyor wasn't carrying a sword, that he had never seen him with one. This world needed no sword, but the hazards of the dark world demanded one.

"What will your job be, Zyor?"

"I must take the place of one of my brothers who has been injured, who is in far greater need of rest than I."

"Injured? What do you mean? Isn't your race immortal?"

"We are immortal but not invulnerable. We can be hurt, injured, worn out, overpowered for a season. Like you, we are finite."

"Were you ever hurt when protecting me, Zyor?"

Zyor's face contorted, and for just a moment Finney saw in his eyes the desperate pain of an injured animal. "Yes...more than once. But once more than any other."

"Can you tell me when?"

"It was at a time in your life you well remember." Zyor paused and thought. "Yes, I believe I am permitted to tell you. But not now. When my assignment is over. When I come back to Elyon's presence and yours. But I am on the dark world's time now. I must go quickly."

Zyor thrust his arm outward and upward, and from nowhere a great glimmering sword flew into his right hand, a sword as long as Finney was tall. It looked white hot, as if newly forged in heaven's foundry. Yet Finney knew it was more ancient than the earth itself.

So this is Galeed.

He was in awe at the sight of the gentle scholar turned fierce warrior who now stood before him. The lights of heaven bounced off the perfect surface of the blade. Finney saw Zyor's powerful physique mirrored on Galeed, the sword seeming more an extension of the warrior's right arm than a weapon held by it.

Finney realized with astonishment that this very instrument, in the hands of this soldier, had been raised in his defense many times on earth. Yet he could remember not so much as a gleam of light reflecting from it as Zyor, his advocate and champion, had cut through the ranks of Elyon's enemies, guarding Finney through his darkest moments and most desperate battles in the fallen world.

Finney felt his last moments with Zyor slipping away as the last grains of sand in an hour glass.

"Where will you go? Will I be able to watch you?"

"You will be allowed to see me, at least at times—for the attention of heaven is focused upon earth until it becomes Elyon's footstool. It will please our Sovereign to hear your prayers on behalf of me and my charge, prayers now unhindered by the shadows. I go to serve a new master, while serving only the one Master, whom to serve is life itself. Better than ever before, you understand the battle I go to fight."

Finney just then noticed crowds of Zyor's brothers, close to a hundred of them, now surrounding them, pressing closer to bid their comrade good-bye and wish him well. Zyor smiled with satisfaction at the tribute paid by the presence of his allies. He grasped mighty hand to mighty hand in an ancient camaraderie with warriors who knew firsthand the dangers and stakes of the dark world's mortal combat.

Zyor's stern and determined face showed vulnerability and need. In a soft and almost pensive voice he asked Finney, "My master, would you do me the honor of pronouncing a blessing for me as I embark to the Shadowlands?"

Finney wondered if there was a formula for such an occasion, recorded in some heavenly book of blessings. But he said the first words that came to mind, projecting his voice with boldness and clarity.

"Zyor, servant of the Most High, may you go to the dark world in the light and strength of Elyon. May you serve your new charge as faithfully as you served me—for you could do no greater. As surely as I will testify forever of the grace of Elyon, I will always tell others of his faithful warrior who guarded my life by day and night, though I did not know it. Besides Elyon's own name—and the names of Susan, Jennifer, Angela, and Little Finn—yours, mighty Zyor, shall ever be most prominent in my heart and on my lips. Go in the grace and power of Elyon's only Son."

"You honor me, my master and friend."

"No more than you deserve. I can never repay you, but my prayers will be with you, even if there are times when I am not allowed to see you at work. I don't know who you go to serve, but he is fortunate, as was I."

"Thank you, Master Finney. Your words are food and drink to me, for in your approval I feel the approval of Elyon. But in one thing you are wrong—you do know the one I go to serve."

Finney looked surprised. "Someone famous?"

Zyor gazed one last time into Finney's eyes. "His name is Jake Woods."

A flash of light blinded Finney, and a roar of thunder, created by the clash of earth's atmosphere with heaven's, momentarily left him deaf. As quickly as that, Zyor had gone through the portal and charged forward to the forbidden planet that had once seemed home to Finney. It was as if the giant had been violently swallowed by another realm hostile to all Zyor was and represented.

For a moment, Finney thought he could hear the shout of a great warrior, the clash of blade against blade, and the horrible screeching of powerful but wicked beings. Just as suddenly, there was silence.

The hundred angels around him fell to their knees, interceding for their comrade. Finney fell to his knees also, praying both for the servant and the one he had been sent to. He could only marvel that two beings for whom he felt such deep affection and loyalty, Zyor and Jake, were about to walk side by side.

In all his years with Finney, Zyor had been near Jake often and had surely learned much about him. *No wonder Elyon considers him ideal for the task.*

As he prayed for two dear friends, it struck Finney as terribly ironic that Jake, unspeakably privileged as he was, would not have the slightest idea that he was now under the vigilant and unsleeping watch of a valiant warrior from another universe.

After continuing to read the C. S. Lewis book and contemplating Finney's letter some more, Jake fell asleep with a great deal on his mind this fifty-first Christmas of his life. He wasn't one to have vivid dreams. Those had always been reserved for Janet. The only dreams he ever remembered were those that took him back to Nam, that featured grenades and Harvey from Zionsville, and Jimmy from Pensacola, and Hyuk and his dead wife and mother and son, and Victor Charlie and his AK-47 and his deep brown eyes, sliding from this life to the next as Jake felt death itself whiz by his left ear.

But tonight Jake dreamed vividly and much differently than ever before. He was fighting in a great boxing ring, in front of a huge audience. He was the challenger, vastly overmatched by the Champ. He punched, but kept hitting air—the Champ was too quick. He was also powerful, muscles hard as tempered steel. His reach easily ten inches longer than Jake's, the Champ kept landing punch after punch, until Jake's face was a bloody pulp.

To his horror Jake realized there was no space between rounds. Worse, there was no referee, no one to stop the fight. Some buffoonish men in self-made referee's outfits would periodically creep into the ring to stop the bout, trying to talk big but dispensing gibberish. One declared Jake the winner, blabbering on and on, quoting German theologians and the *New York Times,* saying "God is dead. Man is the Champion."

The Champ looked at this ridiculous figure as one looks at an insane person spouting bizarre things, unsure whether to laugh or cry.

Another referee jumped up and cried to Jake, "God is cheating, the fight is fixed, you're being used." He too tried to declare Jake the winner. Still another, as in an ongoing parade of circus clowns, jumped in and said, "It isn't a fair fight—who does God think he is lording it over man?"

With a roar like a Lion and a quick brush of his hand, the Champion knocked each of these busybodies over the ropes, not bothering to see where they landed. He kept his eye on Jake, not out of fear—it was obvious he feared no man and had no reason to—but out of great personal interest.

Another jab to the chin. Another blow to the midsection. Here came a heart stopping haymaker right to the chest, splashing sweat two rows into the crowd. But Jake would not give up. He would not surrender. Ten count after ten count, he kept getting back up. Football and boot camp and Nam and thousands of deadlines had taught him how to keep going when by all rights he shouldn't.

The stifling heat of the center ring and the sweaty smell of worn canvas threatened to overwhelm the queasy challenger, but he would fight until he could no longer lift an arm. Jake looked to see the steely determination and thirst for blood in the eyes of the Champ. It wasn't there. He realized he hadn't looked in those eyes before. He'd only imagined the Champ's ill-will toward him, seeing what he expected to see, not what was there. Now for the first time he looked, really looked. He saw strength, incredible strength, but he also saw goodness, kindness, compassion. He saw strength under control—the essence of manhood. Omnipotence governed by goodness and purpose—the essence of godhood. He saw an opponent who did not want to be an opponent. An adversary who had declared himself a friend, who was fighting only at Jake's insistence. One who wanted to be in Jake's corner, if only Jake would surrender, would recognize and acknowledge him to whom the belt and the title already belonged.

But Jake had learned to fight, no matter what. To admit defeat was the ultimate insult, an unthinkable blow to his self-esteem. Jake heard voices in the crowd, many of them unfamiliar. It was like standing in the international terminals at Kennedy airport, hearing languages he'd never heard before. He caught a glance of people in robes, wearing sandals, some with no shoes, wearing tree bark on their feet. They had all colors of skin, all kinds of clothing.

Now another man stepped into the ring, wearing a collar, holding a black book. It appeared to be a Bible, but a very small one, which Jake intuitively knew had been edited down from the original to include only the sayings this man liked. He'd ridded it of all he found offensive. This time the Champ could not refrain from a comment. His eyes were full of rage, not toward Jake, but toward the minister-referee.

"You dare to try to soften the blows of the Almighty? You dare to edit my Book, to dilute my Word? To deceive and prolong the agony of this one I love? Stay out of the ring, you who would cross the sea to produce a convert and make him twice as much a child of hell as yourself. This isn't about you, it's about him and me. It's between the two of us. Depart from me!"

With a flick of a hand, he knocked the man three rows back.

Jake took advantage of his opponent's distraction and landed a solid blow to the Champ's midsection. His hand and wrist burned. His opponent did not flinch. Jake had given his best shot, but the Champ was unaffected. The Champ's eyes didn't burn with rage now, but were filled with a cool sadness.

This opponent was like no other. Jake had defeated adversaries on the field, in debate, in the classroom, in the rice paddies. He had defeated writers and editors, candidates and sports heroes, ministers and judges. With pen and typewriter, computer terminal and phone call and column, he had made them all eat dust. No matter what they said, he always had the last word. Not this time, not with this One.

This One would have the last word. This One was the last word.

Suddenly Jake noticed his opponent was bleeding, and from the strangest places—from his hands and feet and from a long wound in his side. Why? Jake had hardly touched him. Yet somehow Jake knew he had once joined others, a myriad of others, in a galactic-sized mob that beat this man senseless. These wounds were the reopening of old ones, ancient wounds inflicted upon the Champion before the dawn of time. He was bleeding profusely. It amazed Jake, and moved him, that one so powerful was capable of bleeding.

A wraith now dared to ring the bell and declare the round over, as if he had authority to do so. One piercing side glance from the Champion and the wraith frantically flew to the far end of the arena, cowering like a dog expecting a whipping, begging for mercy yet wanting nothing of mercy but on his own terms, pathetically drooling and slobbering. He wore an old sweat-drenched robe that declared he was champion of the universe.

A gang of equally wretched beings surrounded him and whined and whimpered continuous tales of how unfair and cruel the Champion had been to them all. The irony hit Jake with the force and sting of a bullwhip—a world full of little self-important gods, self-proclaimed champions. But only One was worthy of the title.

Jake retreated to his corner, looking for solace and help, but there was no one there. He'd been abandoned. Where were the coaches who said his teams were the best, his commander who said his company was the finest, his philosophy professor who applauded him, his psychology instructor who told him he was so competent, his journalism professors and editors and admiring public who had told him he was the best, that no one was better?

Where was Doc now? And Finney? He'd always counted on having them in his corner. Doc's voice he could no longer hear, but Jake swore he could hear Finney's voice. Yes, there he was, a few rows back. But he was saying all the wrong things, Finney-like things. He seemed to be rooting for Jake's good, but he kept calling on him to throw in the towel and bow to the Champion. To lose his life that he might find it.

Jake's arms fell limp, slapping against his sweat-drenched sides. Overcome with fatigue, drained of everything, he was finally willing to give up and die.

"Go ahead," he spoke to the Champion. "You've won. Go ahead and kill me."

Jake closed his battered swollen eyes, anticipating the blow from which he would never awake.

But the blow did not come. And now there was someone in his corner, a coach offering mouthwash and a towel and leading the blinded challenger to the comfort of the stool. A manager wishing him the best and willing to do anything to help him, to relieve his pain, to help recondition him and get him back in the ring fighting opponents of his own caliber in his own weight class. There was no shame in this, he assured him. Everything would be all right. Tears and blood and sweat blurred the manager's image beyond recognition, but having been abandoned to his misery, any help was now welcome.

As his eyes were tended and cleaned, vision began to return. But wait, his comforter's hands and feet were bleeding. What was *he* doing in Jake's corner? Was there no escaping him? Who was this...this hound of heaven who relentlessly pursued him, who relentlessly pummeled him, who relentlessly loved him?

"No more. I meant what I said. I give up. I am so tired, so sick of myself, so tired of living life by my rules and not yours. You win. I accept your terms of surrender, whatever they are. Take my life...or use it, whatever you wish."

Jake cried, at first in despair, but then with heartfelt relief. The coach sprayed the astringent over his swollen gums, lifted the Gatorade to his parched lips. He held Jake's head in his strong hands. Jake's neck muscles could no longer bear the weight, but he felt the Champion's strength where he had none.

The irony pierced Jake's soul. Of all people, the one helping was the One he had always resisted. Those who had claimed to be Jake's advocates were nowhere to be found. Those who had heralded him and bet on his ability to win had slunk out the door, disgusted at his loss, yet powerless to help him win. Those who had tried to make the rules, to bend them, to tip the advantage to him, were all gone, caring nothing for him now that he belonged to someone else.

One voice and only one voice responded. "I have stopped, as I have longed to stop, for finally you have bowed your knee to me. You have turned from certain death and chosen eternal life. I am your God and also your friend."

Jake's eyes began to focus. No one was there but the One. He had the fierce strength of a lion, the vulnerable warmth of a lamb. He was all God and all man.

He carried Jake to the center of the ring and gently lifted his rubbery arm alongside his own.

"I have won for both of us, Jake. In the defeat that bloodied my hands and feet and side, there is victory for you. In the defeat that now bloodies your life you have entered into the victory I bought with my blood. I have redeemed you, my son. Heaven will be the place of our eternal celebration. Welcome to my family. In losing to me you have won the battle for life."

And Jake, for one wonderful moment, knew that the dream was not a dream, or that if a dream, it was much more. It was a dream with a life of its own. A dream that had reached out to him from another place and touched him in a way that would leave him never the same.

Jake gasped, bolting up wide awake, as if he had not just been asleep, but held in sleep, and was now abruptly released. He was soaked. Certain he was dripping with his own blood, he grabbed for the reading light, but it wasn't in the right place. He found himself instead pawing a lamp, then grimacing as its brightness harpooned his eyes.

No, it wasn't blood. He was dripping with sweat, panting and exhausted. Why was he in the living room? And fully clothed? It was a dream, Jake thought. It was, and yet it wasn't. As his heart began to calm from the great leap from one world to another, some of the dream's vivid details began to leave him.

He looked at the clock on the VCR. 3:38 A.M., December 26. He'd never gone to bed. He'd fallen asleep reading in the recliner; he vaguely remembered turning off the light as he drifted into unconsciousness. He started to sit back down on the recliner, then instead slipped down on his knees in front of it.

He went back to his thoughts and prayers hours earlier when he'd read Finney's letter, and the book by Lewis, and the verses from the Bible. His thoughts went again to his friend Hyuk, who had failed to protect his mother, wife, and child. Though Hyuk was not to blame, Jake finally admitted that in his case there was no one to blame but himself. He had been given the job of loving and protecting and leading his family. In failing to do so he had betrayed them, and also betrayed the one who had created him and assigned him the duty he had shirked. He would have died for his buddies in Nam, yet he had failed to live for those to whom his obligation was greatest, those who had needed him the most.

Only a coward would make a baby pay for his mistake. He confessed his sin of abortion. Only a liar would cheat on his wife and leave her. He confessed his sins of adultery and divorce. Only a selfish fool would fail to be there for a daughter who needed him. He confessed his sin of desertion. Only an ingrate would turn away from a mother who had made untold sacrifices for him. He confessed his sin of dishonor and neglect. Only a sinner would reject the truth and resist God's grace to stubbornly live his own way. He confessed his sin of willful unbelief.

No amount of rationalization made it right to abandon and neglect and violate sacred promises to those it was his duty to love and defend and care for. He'd been wrong, dead wrong, and he knew it. No excuses. He didn't have the goodness or the power to live right, and for the first time, he knew that too.

Jake, who'd never even admitted to his mother he'd smoked out in the toolshed, now admitted far greater offenses to God. He took full responsibility and asked for the power to live right. There was relief in the confession. He wasn't good enough to do life on his own. He no longer had to pretend to be.

In a place far away, yet very close, an old friend applauded and raced around wildly, hugging men, some whose names he didn't yet know, and angels who marveled at the depth of human emotion. He yelled triumphantly and heralded the good news, incredibly wonderful good news. Finally, he fell on his knees in ecstatic praise, but soon was on his feet again, celebrating in uninhibited and unrestrained rejoicing, of the sort that no one who has spent his life confined to the dark world can begin to understand. Joining him were cadres of angels, rejoicing with him in a miracle that had never lost its wonder...rejoicing that one more child of Adam had become a child of God.

Janet and Carly had been at Jake's apartment three hours, since 6:00 in the evening. It was a cold, white New Year's Eve day, but none of them had felt so warm in years. They'd been engrossed in conversation, telling stories of the old days, including family camping disasters that now seemed hilarious, but which Janet and Carly reminded Jake hadn't amused him at the time.

"Was I really that grouchy?"

They looked at each other, smiling like a couple of Cheshire cats, and at the same moment said, "Yeah, you really were." They giggled like school girls.

"Why do I feel like you're ganging up on me?" But he didn't really. What he felt was something refreshing and startling, something old and yet very new. Something that brought into sharp focus what he'd been missing the last three years. Something connected directly with the events of the previous week, the dream and the things he'd said on his knees on this very living room floor.

"I hate to say it, but we've got to go," Janet's voice hinted she wanted to be talked out of it.

"So soon?" Jake asked, his disappointment obviously genuine. Janet was astounded. To feel wanted by Jake seemed so...foreign.

"How about I run out and get that gallon of milk so we can have some hot chocolate first?" Jake asked. "Mom always made us hot chocolate on New Year's Eve."

It sounded so childish, so vulnerable. So unlike Jake. He didn't notice, but Janet did.

"Come with me, will you, Carly?"

"Sure, Dad."

"Want to join us, Janet?"

"No thanks, you two go. I'll stay where it's warm. How about some eggnog too? That's what we used to drink on New Year's Eve."

"Great. Eggnog it is."

"Button up your coat, sweetheart."

"Yes, mother dear." Looking at Jake, Carly added, "If it wasn't for Mom I'd never think to button my coat when it's twenty degrees outside!"

"That's what mom's are for," Janet said only half jokingly.

As Jake opened the door, a drift fell inward and white powder blew into the living room. He shut it and looked at the surprised faces. Champ, always hanging around the front door, had several snowflakes still on his snout. All three laughed.

"What in the world," Jake muttered, and went to the window. "It must have snowed four more inches since you came. It's a whiteout. I can't even see down the street." He turned on the TV. Regular programming had been interrupted.

"The snowstorm is crippling the city. No public transportation is operating. Cars have been abandoned in the middle of main roads. Visibility is almost zero. The word is, if you're warm and you have food and you don't absolutely have to travel, stay where you are!"

Carly and Janet looked at Jake.

"Well," he said, "we're warm, and we have food. And you don't absolutely have to travel, do you?"

"We don't want to impose, Jake."

"No problem. You two can have the bedroom, and Champ and I'll sleep out here on the couch. It's comfortable. He'll love it."

"Looks like this is turning into a New Year's party," Carly said brightly. "But I've got a bag in the car I need to bring in."

"I'll get it," Jake said.

"I'll go with you. This is fun."

With the streetlights reflecting brightly off the white blanket of snow, they walked out what Jake guessed was the pathway from the apartment to the sidewalk, laughing because they had no clue what was grass and what was pathway, and it made no difference. Impressive snow drifts pinned down the car, and they were almost wading now.

Jake managed to get into Janet's car from the least impeded access, the front passenger side, and reached over into the back of the car. He grabbed the bag, pulled it out, and turned and asked, "Is this all you wan—"

A snowball hit him right in the mouth. He could feel the cold on his teeth. Only ten feet away, but hard to see her expression in the whirling snow, was the perpetrator, stooped over and quickly making another snowball.

"Hey, wait a minute. I've got a handful of—" Another shot to the face.

"Where did you learn to throw like that?" Jake asked with unfeigned admiration.

"Five years of softball, third base," came Carly's reply, immediately followed with a shot that skimmed Jake's right ear.

Jake remembered the softball, but didn't remember her being so accurate. Throwing down the bag, he said, "Well, this is where my combat experience will pay off, young lady!"

As he stooped over to scoop up a handful of snow, he felt another snowball whack him on the shoulder. "Hit four times before I even load up," he muttered. "This was an ambush." *This girl's as good as Doc or Finney ever were.*

With two packed projectiles in hand, Jake let loose and barely missed Carly. "You're a smaller target."

"That's your problem," and just as she said it Jake's second snowball hit her in the throat, dropping down inside the front of her coat. Jake laughed uproariously and taunted, "You should have listened to your mother and buttoned that top button, young lady!"

He stooped for more ammo and before he could look back up, she was on him, knocking him off balance and pushing him to the ground, face first.

"Hey," he cried out with feigned indignation. "This was outlawed at the Geneva Convention."

He reached out and pulled her right leg out from under her and she fell backwards into the deep snow. Deep enough, Jake knew, there was no danger of injuring her or the baby.

"Well, that should be outlawed. Knocking ladies on their keisters, I mean. Pregnant ladies!"

"Well, ladies don't usually attack their elders."

They both sat for a moment in the snow, catching their breath and laughing, then realizing how cold it was.

"Truce. Time to go in." Jake got up and extended his hand to Carly. She took it, then wrapped her legs around his and knocked him back down, laughing like Jake hadn't heard in years.

"You are vicious!"

By the time Jake could get up, Carly had grabbed her bag and was half way to the front door. When he got within a few feet of the door, he heard her latch it, just like he would have done.

This girl has great combat instincts.

Jake pressed his head against the door and pounded, yelling, "Open this door or I'll call 1-800-dad-abuse."

"Sure. I'll open the door. All you have to do is say, 'I surrender. Carly wins.'"

"Like Winston Churchill, I will never give up...never, never, *never* give up."

"Then you and Churchill will never, never, *never* get in!"

Jake heard through the door two females laughing uproariously. He smiled broadly.

He explored his options, but the spare key was hidden under a rock buried under the snow, and it just wasn't worth the dig in the icy cold.

"Okay, I surrender. Carly wins. She doesn't fight fair, but she wins."

The door opened wide, and Jake, with clumps of snow falling from him, jumped in before she could change her mind.

"Jake, you're a mess!" Janet cried.

"Hey, wait a minute, it was your daughter who..."

"I couldn't believe he'd attack me like that, Mom. Throwing snowballs at a helpless young girl."

"Helpless? You should have seen her. She could win the Cy Young Award!"

"She beat you, huh Jake?"

"Yeah, she did." Jake laughed. "Actually, she beat me bad." And he couldn't have been happier.

Janet was kneeling in front of the fireplace, just starting a fire.

"Change your clothes and get dry, you two. I found some cider. I'll heat it up. It'll do just as well as chocolate or eggnog."

"Great idea, Mom. But what do I change into? Nothing in my bag but shoes and socks."

"I'm sure your father has lots of clothes. You're good at improvising."

"Getting into Daddy's closet? This could be fun." Carly was in Jake's room in an instant.

"Take anything you want, just let me get first grab. You owe me that much after kicking my tail out there. I'll change in the bathroom and you can have my room."

As Jake changed his clothes, he felt a childlike excitement he hadn't felt in years, many years. He came out to the smell of warm cider and popcorn and the crackle of a fire. That was Janet—in ten minutes she'd transformed Jake's apartment into a home.

While Jake sat down by the fire, Janet joined Carly in his bedroom. They came out modeling two outrageous outfits, both with overbig flannel shirts, Janet in fishing hipwaders and Jake's huge clod hoppers, and Carly topped with a Mets cap and rounded out with battery-heated hunting socks she thought were hilarious. Champ barked and barked and nibbled at the girls' feet, his way of joining in. Jake picked up a flashlight and shined it all over the room, sending Champ crashing into everything pursuing the light, as if he really thought he could catch it. They laughed until they wore out from laughing.

Janet went to bed first, partly because the warmth and laughter had made her contentedly tired, partly because she wanted Carly and Jake to have more time alone. A couple of hours later she got up to use the bathroom and saw two shadows in front of the fire, close to each other, talking softly. It was nearly one in the morning.

After Janet went back to bed, she didn't close the door all the way. She could just make out the words coming from the living room.

"I had the weirdest dream the other night," Carly said. "Want to hear it?"

"Sure," Jake said, smiling as he thought of how much she was like Janet, who'd always relished recounting her dreams to him, even though he'd usually not been interested.

Muffled laughter came from the bedroom. They looked at each other and smiled, realizing they had an eavesdropper.

"I just hope your dreams are half as interesting as your mom's always were," Jake said loudly.

Carly poked her head up over the couch and said, "Mom, I'll try to speak up so you don't have to strain to hear us."

More laughter, as if muffled by a pillow, made its way from the bedroom to the living room. Then Janet came out and joined them. The springer spaniel's tail wagged frantically. A dog takes his happiness from the happiness of the people around him. Champ had never been more happy.

The daughter told her dream. And then the mother told a dream of her own. And then both listened breathlessly as the father told his.

CHAPTER THIRTY-ONE

Ollie and Jake couldn't meet for lunch, so they arranged a midafternoon walk in the downtown park blocks. It was warmer than it had been for weeks, and the snow melted as they walked. Ollie jumped right into the topic at hand.

"When we first started talking this anti-abortion possibility I sent a note to Jeb Larson—he's our best arson detective. Well, he's been buried in other stuff and finally uncovered my note. Came in this morning and gave me the skinny on all the abortion clinic incidents in town. Boy, did I get an earful."

"More suspects?"

"It wasn't what I expected." Ollie eyed a bench and sat down, Jake next to him. Then he paged through a manila file folder.

"Jeb's got this big file of newspaper clippings. He copied a few of them for me. Here's one—Los Angeles, 1988: 'Prochoice activist Frank Mendiola pleaded guilty to charges of telephoning a series of bomb threats to local abortion clinics. He says he made the calls to arouse public sympathy for abortion rights and to motivate the media to come down with a harder line on people who harass the clinics.'"

"The guy who did it was prochoice?"

"Yeah, and that's just the beginning. Here's another one in Concord, California, where a Planned Parenthood abortion clinic was burnt down. The first few clippings quote all the Planned Parenthood people blaming the anti-abortion groups, milking it for all it's worth, and I guess you can't blame them. But here's the other clipping, from a month later, when police arrested David Martin, who lived across the street from the clinic. He admitted he set the fire because he was 'ticked off' at prolife protesters and hoped they'd be blamed. Jeb says the guy got his wish. His buddy in arson down in Concord, the one that sent him the clippings, tells him most people still think the prolifers did it, even after the case was solved.

"Here's one in Redding caused by a portable electric fan. And here's a couple done to cover burglaries. Jeb says some of these are just accidents or random arsons—I mean lots of hamburger joints burn down but nobody assumes it's done by vegetarians and animal rights activists.

"Now here's a classic, Portland back in 1985. Package bombs were sent through the mail to three abortion clinics and a Planned Parenthood clinic. Major bad press for the anti-abortion people, attempts at court injunctions against them, the whole deal. But the case was quietly solved. The perp was a guy named Batson, who was caught only because a bomb he was making exploded and took off part of his arm. The evidence tied him to the package bombs and another abortion clinic bombing. He was convicted and went to prison. Turns out he had no connections at all with the prolifers. Know what his motive was?"

"No."

"His girlfriend had gotten an abortion without his knowledge. He was taking revenge on the people he says 'killed his baby.' Interesting, huh? Then there's a clinic bombing in Florida they linked to organized crime."

"Organized crime?" Jake jumped at the term.

"Yeah, it's not real clear, but the mob wanted in on the action, or was already in on it. They wanted kickbacks, sold protection. They were on this clinic's payroll, and somebody didn't cough up the dough. So, good-bye clinic."

Jake grabbed the opportunity. "Ollie, do you think organized crime could be in on Doc and Finney's murder?"

"What?" Ollie looked at him strangely. "You been watching *The Untouchables* or something?"

"Just wondering."

"Seriously, where'd you come up with that idea?"

"Nowhere, really. You said anything was fair game when it came to suspects."

"Well, I draw the line at Al Capone and Frank Nitti."

Jake felt guilty for lying but tried not to show it.

"Anyway, the clinic stories go on, and these are just cases that happened to be solved. Most we'll never know what really happened. But here's what's really interesting on the home front. There have been four bombings or arsons at abortion clinics in this city the past ten years. All four are officially unsolved. I stress the word officially."

"What's your point, Ollie?"

"Officially a murder is unsolved until there's a conviction, even if I really know who did it. Same with arson and bombing. Jeb says he'd bet the farm he knows who did two of the four unsolveds. Case number one, July 1991. It's 5:00 A.M., an hour before anyone ever comes to this clinic. The owner of the clinic, the main abortionist, happens to be there. He smells something funny. He puts out the fire. It's front page news—naturally, anti-abortionists get the blame."

"So Jeb goes in as the arson detective, finds the incendiary device, runs a fingerprint check, and guess what? The only fingerprints on it belong to the owner of the clinic—luckily his prints were on file. Jeb asks the owner if he ever touched it. The guys says 'no way.' Jeb says, 'So why is your fingerprint on it?' and the guy just about loses his dentures. Then he says, 'Oh yeah, maybe I touched it after I put the fire out.' Jeb asks why. I mean, people stay away from that sort of thing, besides it would still be hot. Why would you touch it, or if you did, why would you forget or lie and say you hadn't? Well, Jeb's conclusion was, it was insurance fraud. The guy got public sympathy, made his enemies look bad, and got a new roof, which he needed anyway."

"No kidding?"

"No kidding." Ollie was flipping through his notes again. "Then there's the biggest clinic in town. May 1993, just after that abortionist was killed down in Pensacola. Some guy hears a ruckus and looks out his window and happens to see somebody throw something through a window of the clinic. He saw a long-haired man in a white shirt running from the clinic, but it was too dark for a positive ID. Those abortion protesters are the short-haired type, but naturally everybody assumed they did it. Know what Jeb says?"

"No, but I bet you're going to tell me."

"For a price."

"Okay, I'll buy you a hot dog next time we meet for lunch."

"I was thinking a Häagen-Dazs from that vender headin' this way."

Jake looked up and saw the vender in the distance.

"Okay, okay. It's yours. What does Jeb say?"

"This guy called the fire department, they were there in three minutes, and there was only damage to one room and one machine in that room. The ultra-sound."

"So?"

"So, Jeb's daughter is a nurse over at Lifeline. He had dinner at her place a week later and the fire comes up. He mentions the ultrasound, and she says, 'What a coincidence. They've been sending their patients over to us the last month because their ultra-sound doesn't work.' So, guess whose insurance company got them a new ultrasound?"

Jake shook his head in amazement. "What did Jeb do?"

"Nothing. Insurance companies have their own investigators. That's not Jeb's job."

"So they got away with it?'

"As far as I know. Who can prove it? It could have been a coincidence. Any way you look at it they come out smellin' like a rose."

"You don't sound too impressed with the abortion business."

"I guess I see too much violence in my job. I have to look at bloody pictures every day. You get callous to it, you have to, but a few times it's been babies. That's the worst. And when I see those pictures the protesters show, I know they're real. They look like things I've seen. And there's something in me that always makes me want to get the jerks that kill little kids. Not that I have a lot of sympathy for these demonstrators either. The whole thing just bugs me, that's all."

"What about the other two cases?"

"One was a zero. No clues, no witnesses. Could have been an anti-abortionist, could have been another inside job, who knows? But the other was very interesting. It was at the Downtown Feminist Women's Center. Four years ago."

"That was the clinic Doc worked at. And I think that was about the time he quit. He might have still been there."

"You know what else? There was an incident at that clinic during business hours the same day it got torched. Besides a few people hanging around passing out literature, there was a guy, tall guy, marijuana tattoo on his right bicep, who just walked into the clinic and started yelling. I've got a copy of the police report right here. By the time the cops got there the guy was gone. Took off on foot. They couldn't even book him, so we don't even know if his fingerprints are on file. He definitely wasn't with the protesters. His language was like a drunken sailor's." Ollie paused for effect. "I've saved the best for last, Jake. He came to blows with someone at the clinic."

"Yeah?"

"One of the doctors came out of a back room and this guy was on him. Three guesses who the doctor was."

"Doc?"

"You got it. Your friend got in a couple good licks on the guy, but not before he took him down and ripped up his clothes. The guy ran off, and Doc left for the day. The report says while the perp was in your friend's face, he kept yelling 'You killed my baby.' I imagine the doctor was pretty shook."

"Doc never told me that." Jake wondered how many other things about that part of his life Doc never told him. "Are you saying that same night this guy came back and torched the clinic?"

"Somebody did. I'd lay money on him, wouldn't you?"

"But what are the chances? I mean...this was over four years ago? You think this guy would wait this long if he was going to go after Doc?"

"Don't know. But it makes for an interesting thought, doesn't it?"

"Yeah, it does." Jake hesitated a moment. "Ollie, do you think Jeb would talk to me about this stuff? I mean, if I wanted to use it for a column some time?"

Ollie gave Jake a measured stare, as if analyzing a machine that wasn't working properly. "I've been meaning to talk to you about your columns. Is it my imagination, or are you going through some kind of change? Like male menopause or something?"

"Or something, Ollie. I'd like to talk to you about it, but first I've got to get some stuff worked out in my own head. Meanwhile, would Jeb talk to me?"

"Well, he'd have to downplay a lot of what he told me, especially his theories on the two incidents here in town, the ones he's convinced were deliberate. The department would have his neck if that came out. But most of this stuff is public domain, newspaper articles and other stuff. If I asked him, vouched for you, I'll bet he'd help you as much as he could, maybe be an 'anonymous police detective source.' Want me to ask?"

"Yeah, I'd really appreciate that, Ollie. I've never heard this stuff before, and nothing like it has ever been in the *Trib*, that's for sure. I'd like to tackle it, maybe after a few weeks of background research. Give Jeb my number, will you? Tell him there's a hot dog with kraut in it for him."

"In that case I may tag along." Ollie stood up and waved his hand at a vendor coming his way. "Meanwhile, I hear a Coffee & Almond Crunch calling my name."

"Sue? It's Jake."

"Hi, Jake! I've been thinking a lot about you lately. Haven't talked to you since Christmas. How are you?"

"Okay. Listen, Little Finn's not off to school yet, is he?"

"No. Want to talk to him?"

"No, that's okay. You usually read my column after he goes off to school, don't you?"

"Yep, every Tuesday and Thursday morning over coffee, like clockwork. And recently I can hardly wait to see what you're going to shock me with next. I keep looking back at the byline to make sure it's really your column."

"You're not the first person who's mentioned that."

"The other day, though, I figured it all out."

"What's that?"

"I figured out your whole scam."

"Scam?"

"Yeah. Suddenly it dawned on me. Finney didn't really die. He's holed up in Jake's apartment as his ghostwriter!"

"*Ghost*writer, huh?"

"Well, I didn't mean it that way." Sue laughed. "Seriously, Jake, I've been wanting to call you, but to be honest I didn't want to say the wrong thing. I'm afraid if you keep hearing me say how pleased I am with your columns you'll have to rethink them and maybe run a retraction or something! Anyway, I'm just so proud of you. I can't wait to get together and talk."

"Yeah, let's do that. I've got a lot to tell you. Some of it's good news. For now, I just want to be sure you read my column today. My phone's already ringing, and there's an uproar down here, and I thought...well, to be honest, I guess I wanted to ask you to pray for me."

Sue's coffee cup dropped to its saucer, and coffee lapped over on her blouse. "Jake, are you all right? Well, of course you're all right, I didn't mean to imply... Jake, really, are you all right?"

Jake laughed. Sue could hear the strain in his voice, but also a strange calm.

"It's that shocking, huh? You pray for me all these years and maybe it starts to have just a little effect and you can't believe it. You think I've gone off the deep end. You're a real woman of faith, Sue!"

"Jake, I don't know what to say."

"Obviously. Just read the column. But don't get your hopes up. It's not *The Confessions of St. Augustine* or anything. I have to deal with issues in the column— there's nothing spiritual in it, not directly anyway. Just something that Carly and I experienced last week when we spent the day together. But please. I was serious. Do pray for me. I need it, Sue. I've got an important meeting this afternoon, and I'm...nervous. Rome is burning around me down here, and I'm not sure whether to turn on the fire extinguishers or just sit back and fiddle."

"I will pray, Jake. But first I'm reading this column! I'll call you back."

Sue tore open the *Trib* to the Forum section and went straight to Jake's picture and column:

Last week I went into the local county library with my seventeen-year-old daughter, Carly. As we walked in the front door, there in the free literature rack were multiple copies of two homosexual newspapers. In addition to their schedules of gay activities, these newspapers are filled with homo-erotic pictures and advertisements of people seeking sexual partners. The ads often state a preference for "young" partners.

The newspapers also contain various 800 numbers to "get you in touch with other hot guys." They contain pay-by-the-minute sex simulation 900 numbers. They tell you where you can go to see homosexual X-rated movies right here in town, and "meet new friends." "All Boy's Company," advertised with a bare-chested young man, is billed as our state's "largest male escort service." It promises to provide you with "stunning guys as young as eighteen." (Am I missing something, or is this not-so-thinly-veiled prostitution—which is illegal?)

I went to the librarian and nicely pointed out these materials to her. I explained I didn't think the library was the place to distribute them. I'm a journalist—nobody's bigger on the first amendment than I am. But when it comes to distributing phone numbers and addresses of those soliciting sex, it just seemed a bit outside the scope of services of a tax-funded public library.

The librarian seemed uneasy, but assured me "we have to carry these newspapers." She gave me a complaint form to fill out and mail to the main library, which I did. Just yesterday I got my reply from Linda Colter, the director of libraries for Lytle County. Ms. Colter assures me "these publications provide important information for members of the gay and lesbian community and others interested in that community." She points out, "A library's collection mirrors society." They will continue to make these newspapers available, in multiple quantities, at all our county libraries.

I'm delighted our libraries carry a diversity of opinions, including many with which I disagree. This is America. But the director's statement, "A library's collection mirrors society" isn't entirely accurate. Society contains racism, but the library doesn't mirror it by circulating the *Skinhead Monthly*. Society has organizations of pedophiles, but the library doesn't pass out child molesting literature with phone numbers of available children. Society has drugs, but the library doesn't pass out information on where to buy drugs in this city. Society has a lot of people, both heterosexual and homosexual, looking for younger and more attractive sex partners, but our libraries have never felt compelled to assist them in linking up. Not until now.

I think back to myself and my two best friends, growing up thirty-five or forty years ago, dropped off by our parents at the town library. I suppose they knew we could sneak a look at naked pygmies in *National Geographic,* but what would they have thought—what would we have thought—if the library put into our hands printed materials containing sensuous pictures and specific sexual propositions from men in the area, complete with phone numbers and mail boxes?

Carly, from whom I've learned a lot the last few months, helped me think this through. We talked about all the lonely confused young people looking for love and attention, paging through these newspapers. Flattered they're "wanted," or just curious, how many young people might go ahead and call one of these numbers? Carly thinks some will.

I understand, of course, that such newspapers exist, and anyone can pick one up in a gay bar. Fine. But most of us don't send our children to gay bars. We *do* send them to the county library. As far as I know, the library doesn't carry *Hustler* and child pornography, so perhaps this same responsible willingness to self-censor could be applied to these newspapers without fatally wounding the first amendment.

This isn't just a homosexual issue. I would also object to the library passing out newspapers full of heteroerotic pictures, advertisements for escorts, 900 sex lines, and want-ad solicitations for heterosexual sex partners. Surely sexual propositions geared to the young aren't appropriate just because they're made by homosexuals, are they?

Realistic parents know that in a free society there will be any number of people wanting to sway and seduce our children. Many of us, though, will not think it unreasonable that our tax-funded county library refrain from serving as their distribution arm.

I realize that in the shadow of the political correctness that substitutes labeling and name-calling for intelligent dialogue, I will be dismissed by many as a homophobic puritanical bigot, or a religious nut. To be honest, that's exactly how I've labeled people many times myself in this very column. I hope to refrain from such labeling in the future.

I finish with just one question for those determined to take the path of political correctness to its ultimate embrace of any and all forms of diversity. If today our tax-funded libraries say they *must* provide our children with newspapers containing erotic pictures, prostitution services and solicitations for sex partners, what will they feel they *must* provide for our children tomorrow?

Sue set down the newspaper, folding it almost reverently, then quietly got down on her knees.

The stocky man walked by Jake Woods's car on Morrison, nonchalantly staking it out, watching who might be watching him. The steady foot traffic served more as a cover for his actions than a deterrent to them. The modern mind-your-own-business city people focused on their own concerns, and really didn't care about the man leaning down to pick up a quarter he'd dropped. While he picked up the quarter with his left hand, his right hand slipped under the side of the Mustang, moving the device in his palm until it attached securely to the undercarriage. He put the quarter in his pocket and disappeared into the flow of pedestrians.

* * *

Three o'clock. Time for the multiculturalism committee meeting. Jake was nervous. This time he had a few things for the agenda. He came at the last moment and sat by Clarence. There always seemed to be a seat or two open by Clarence.

Jess Foley started the meeting.

"We've gotten a number of letters saying we're not being fair and balanced in our treatment of both sides of the so-called 'No Special Rights for Homosexuals' campaign." Jess waved his hand. "I know, I know, a lot of us object to the terminology. We've made that clear in our coverage, I think. When we ran that front page letter from the publisher against the proposal last week, it made some waves. We'd never done anything like that before, and a lot of people seem to have resented it, think it demonstrates a lack of objectivity on our part. My question is, can we find any good points made by the other side without compromising how deeply we feel about it? Anything to make us come across a bit more objective and balanced?"

There was an awkward silence, until Pamela said, "That's like asking for a balanced view of the holocaust."

Jake took a deep breath and jumped in.

"I'm glad you raised this issue, Jess. I agree we should try to be more objective on this thing. As for comparisons to the holocaust, don't they trivialize the real holocaust? I mean, the holocaust wasn't about whether those who do certain sexual acts deserve preference in employment and housing. It was about herding people into rail cars, dumping them at death camps, stripping them naked, and murdering them with poison gas. Am I missing something, or is this comparison totally out of line? If we stigmatize people as Nazis just because they don't want to be forced to hire a homosexual as their church choir director, is that objective journalism?"

Several started to respond at once.

"Hold it, hold it." Jess stuck his finger in the dam. "This issue has dominated our discussion the last two meetings, and I don't want to get into it again. Most of us, myself included, have deep feelings against this piece of legislation. Fine. Let's just try to get a little balanced coverage in there, if possible. Now let's move on. What else have we got today?"

"Sorry, Jess," Peter Sallant said, "but in the last month *homosexual* has appeared on the Forum page nearly a dozen times. The correct term is *gay*. That's what the movement calls itself and that's what we need to call it. Somebody over in Forum needs to watch it more carefully."

Clarence asked, "How many of the dozen references were made in editorials or columns, and how many in letters to the editor?"

"Some were in letters, the others were in a column...ironically, written by someone who's a member of this committee. Jake, I have to say that column on gay literature at the library was incredibly bigoted and demeaning. I'd hope you'd be more sensitive than this. That's the kind of article that stirs up violence. We've got a hate crime commission trying to get on top of this thing, and then you write a hate piece like that. Who knows what some homophobe's going to do? Maybe bomb a library?"

Jake started to respond, but Clarence beat him to it. "Bomb a library? Give me a break, Peter. And 'hate piece'? Lay off the guilt trips, will you? You're concerned about the column's effects, but you don't seem to care whether or not it was true. Was *anything* Jake said inaccurate? Remember, he didn't go out looking to write that column. He was just a father going with his daughter to the county library and he gets this stuff shoved down his throat...and hers. What's he supposed to do? Show me just one thing in that column that was hateful."

Clarence didn't pause long enough for anyone to take him up on the offer.

"And as for *homosexual*, he shouldn't be forced to use *gay* any more than you should be forced to use *sodomite*."

He was looking at Peter, Pamela, and Myra. Several gasps surfaced, but Clarence went right on.

"Well, look it up, for crying out loud. That used to be the standard term. Okay, I can live using *homosexual*, which sounds pretty neutral. But to tell our reporters or columnists they have to say *gay* is totally out of line. And as for the letters to the editor, what are you thinking, Peter? Are we going to start censoring the public now? We can coerce ourselves to be politically correct—we shouldn't but we can—but we can't control our readers."

Clarence looked around the room, astounded at the silence. "Well, can we?"

"We all know there's a selection process as to which letters are printed," Myra said. "If people use offensive and bigoted language, we're responsible to screen it. We have no obligation whatsoever to print someone's letter. Either we change the words or we don't print the letters, as far as I'm concerned."

"Now that this subject's come up," Jake interjected, "I had a friend who was interviewed by the *Trib* maybe three months ago. He used the term *prolife* a number of times in the interview, but in the article, *prolife* was changed to *anti-abortion*."

"So?" Myra looked at him and shrugged her shoulders.

"So...that's not what he said. It was a misquote. It was wrong. Untrue. False." Jake kept coming up with synonyms because Myra's expression told him she wasn't getting the point.

"Jake, you know it's *Trib* policy not to use *prolife*," Jeremy said. "We always say *anti-abortion*. That's nothing new."

"*We* do, but we weren't quoting ourselves. We were quoting someone else. I'm not sure I believe we're having this discussion. What right do we have to put our words in someone else's mouth? And if we're concerned about other special interests groups, how come we don't try to be sensitive to prolifers?"

After a long pause, Jenny Mendez said, "Maybe because they're not oppressed. For that matter, they've been responsible for a lot of the oppressing."

"Now there's a bigoted statement if I've ever heard one. At least you're admitting we're being unfair. We've singled them out, haven't we? We're retaliating against them because we don't like what they stand for. They haven't been oppressed as much as some groups, so we'll make up for it by oppressing them ourselves, is that it? Not blatantly, just in subtle ways, semantics and terminology. We have these standards of fairness and we apply them to everyone except groups we don't like."

His discussions with Leonard and Clarence and Sue and his thoughts of the last months welled up inside Jake. Then he remembered something Finney had said in the letter that never made it to the *Trib*.

"Didn't I just hear someone say we should call a group what it calls itself? Fine. What do the prolifers call themselves? Prolifers. So why do we call them anti-abortionists? What do evangelical Christians call themselves? Evangelical Christians. So why are we always calling them right-wing fundamentalists and things like that? I just don't get it. And for that matter, since this multiculturalism committee exists to foster fairness toward various groups, why are other groups represented while conservative Christians aren't?"

"Clarence is a Christian, isn't he?" Jess Foley asked. "And he's conservative."

Several guffaws suggested Jess had made an understatement.

"Sure," Jake said. "But that's not why you put him on the committee, is it? Isn't he here because he's black—I mean, 'African-American'? Whenever he's represented a Christian position, at least since I've been on this committee, everybody gets angry and starts name calling. We've had, what, a half dozen sensitivity training sessions for reporters the last few years? I've been at three or four of them, but not once has anyone talked about being sensitive to religious people, people who believe in God, and church or prayer. Most of us are already much more sensitive to the other groups than to them. Why shouldn't we learn how to be sensitive to them too?"

"Well, listening to you preach at us and reading your column recently, it's pretty clear the right-wing fundamentalists now have *two* representatives on this committee." It was Myra again, and she made no attempt to hide her disgust.

"Listen, Myra, I have no intention of representing fundamentalists or anybody else," Jake's heart was racing, but his voice remained calm. "I just want fairness and objectivity. I don't want special treatment for anybody. Not for Christians, not for gays, not for whites, blacks, feminists, liberals, conservatives, or anybody else. I just want good journalism. And in most cases I think we do a good job. But on some issues the *Trib* is perilously close to becoming a newsletter that advocates certain causes. How about we go back to making the truth our only cause?"

"Jake," Pamela said, "I've always respected you as a columnist." Jake sensed the unspoken words were *until now*. "And I don't mean anything personal by this. But several of us have been talking, and we're all hearing the same concerns about your column. I don't know what's happened, but obviously something has. You've been violating a number of the principles this committee stands for. Your presence on the committee is ironic at best, and it hurts all our credibility. To be honest, it's embarrassing to have a committee member who's the most striking example of violating what the committee stands for. We've got a *Tribune* diversity and multicultural manual some of us put together."

Pamela slid the inch-thick manual across the table to Jake.

"It was passed out to every *Trib* reporter and editor last year. Have you even read it? If you're going to serve on this committee, you'd better! And for what it's worth, I'm not the publisher or the managing editor, but if I were you I'd reevaluate your columns, unless you want to get moved to the religion page. I have no problem with faith or religion—I'm a religious person myself—but this intolerance has got to go. And, Jess, frankly I think before anyone is allowed to serve on this committee in the future, we need to see a signed statement that they've read this manual and agree with it in principle. Otherwise, what's the point?"

"What's the point of having diversity on the diversity committee, isn't that what you're saying?" Clarence shook his head in dismay. "I can't believe you people. This is the most nondiverse committee I've ever seen. With one or two exceptions, nothing is diverse but our sexual practices and our skin color. What you want, Pamela, is a monolithically liberal committee that embraces certain beliefs and lifestyles that by definition Bible-believing Christians cannot embrace, since the Bible doesn't embrace them. Oh, religion is okay with you, as long as it's religion without moral standards. Faith is fine as long as it isn't faith in any truth that violates the current party line. What really frosts you isn't religion or faith, it's the idea that God could actually have some firm opinions on what's right and wrong, and might be unwilling to change them just because we want them changed.

"Don't you see the hypocrisy of this committee and what it's trying to do? The censorship? The threat to the first amendment?"

Clarence looked across the group and sensed that, for the most part, they didn't see any of this at all.

"Journalists have always fought to get Big Brother off our backs. And what's this committee? Big Brother, pure and simple. We're the censors with our neat little speech codes. We pounce on any expression of real diversity that steps on the toes of the special interest groups we represent.

"I want to get one thing straight here. When he came on this committee, Jake had a rep as a liberal, and that was great, right? But now maybe he's changing some of his positions, or at least questioning the status quo. So he's a traitor to your cause. Which proves you have a cause beyond just doing your job at the *Trib*. So now Pamela wants to make sure the diversity committee doesn't have any ideological diversity by making people sign a statement of allegiance to a particular ideology. This isn't a committee, people. It's just a bunch of lobbyists crusading for political correctness!"

Six voices responded at once, at varying levels of volume and hostility. Jess stood up, waved his arms, and said, "Let's take a break. No, let's just break for the day, okay? I don't want this turning into another barroom brawl! Let's all just take a Valium. Next week we'll start by discussing Pamela's proposal on the diversity manual. Meanwhile, get back to work. We've got a newspaper to put out!"

The group dispersed even more quickly than usual. Jake and Clarence were left again, but this time Jess stayed behind a moment. He looked at them both, exasperated and disappointed, like Jake's fourth-grade teacher looked when she caught him and Finney carving their initials on their desks. He was about to say something to them, then thought better of it. He shrugged his shoulders and walked out of the room.

Less experienced in this situation than Clarence, Jake just sat there, feeling a profound sense of not being at home. He didn't doubt the truth of what he'd said, but his yearning to be accepted was stronger than he wanted to admit. He remembered how good it used to feel to be on the common wavelength, to be liked and respected by most of the people who had just marched out of the room.

Finney saw from a distance the great city, ascending so high that even with his greatly sharpened vision it was a strain to clearly see the top. The city appeared complete from a distance, but apparently was still under construction. Finney hadn't been told the city was off limits—there was no need for rules here—but something written on his heart told him the time wasn't yet right for him to go there. For now, he could only stare and wonder and imagine how a city that looked so huge and so beautiful so far away must look up close.

Finney had been busily occupied watching through the portal as Zyor labored to clear a path for Elyon's message to reach Jake's heart. In the moment of Elyon's triumph his friend had raised Galeed, looking toward heaven where he knew his brethren watched and rejoiced with him, where Finney danced unrestrained. But the respite was only momentary, for the twisted angels of the dark world were outraged at his redemption and redoubled their attacks on Jake. Finney had been praying ceaselessly, yet he was not weary but energized.

Finney spoke to Elyon, as he often did, not just when interceding but as a man speaks to his friend.

"I understand as never before the Scriptures describing Christians as aliens and strangers and pilgrims on earth. That place was not my home. I spent my time living in a rented room, on borrowed time. My body was weak, my vision impaired, my mind under attack. I was tempted and worn down. But everything is different now. This is the world for which you made me, the place I feel completely at home. With less than this I could never again be satisfied. Thank you, Father, for bringing me home. I realize now the best reason for loving the old world was that sometimes, in its grandest moments, it seemed a little like this one."

In Elyon's realm, Finney knew he was yet an infant, nursing on the milk of wonder, gaining strength and coordination that he might embark as a toddler into a universe bigger and more beautiful than anything he'd ever imagined. Yet just as he had once felt a part of him had gone from earth to heaven when his mother died, and again when Jenny left him, Finney couldn't help but feel a part of him had gone back from heaven to earth with Zyor. Indeed, a part of him had always remained there with his family, for whom he found himself praying so often.

In a sense, he envied Zyor's proximity to his loved ones. But he knew this, not that, was his home, and they must come to him rather than he to them. He longed for the Great Reunion. He longed to hold them all again, to play with them as one could play only in the unrestrained pleasures of heaven, to journey and explore with them, to tell stories and sing Elyon's praises together. Meanwhile, he must be content to peer down into their world whenever he was allowed, so that he could witness their lives and cheer them on in their pilgrimage.

Finney began to understand what Zyor had said, that heaven's focus was, in a way he would never have expected, still on earth. Finney had moved from the playing field to the stands, where he was part of a great cloud of witnesses, whose role was to watch and root for and pray for those who would finish the game. As a relay runner, he'd grabbed hold of the baton passed to him and had passed it on to others. Those who went before him had been faithful. Those who came behind him, who now carried the baton, must prove faithful too. The baton must never be dropped.

"Seeing you gaze on the great city reminds me of something I once witnessed in the dark world."

Finney, thinking he was alone, turned to see the voice's source. As he turned he recalled the fear that could accompany surprise on earth. Here there was still surprise, but no fear. The voice belonged to Jaltor, one of Zyor's closest companions, who had first returned Zyor's salute on his return from the dark world. Though everyone in this place was welcome company, a close friend of his close friend was especially cherished.

"Jaltor! Hello. Please, tell me what you saw."

"A man and his wife, I was her guardian, returned after many years as missionaries in Africa. It was before airplanes, back when the voyage was by ship, and took months. When they finally arrived back in America, there was great cheering from the shore, and for a few moments their hearts were lifted. But soon they realized the cheering was all for a Hollywood actor on board their ship. There was no one to meet them. The man was very disappointed and struggled with bitterness. He lamented, 'After all these years serving God, after all the sacrifices, there is no one to greet us? This is our homecoming?' But his wife, my charge, squeezed his hand and reminded him this—'We shouldn't expect a homecoming until we come home. This world is not our home. Our homecoming will be in a far better place.'"

"You must have been proud of her."

"I was. I took her into the birthing room for her homecoming and was there with her five years later to greet her husband at his." Jaltor sounded deeply satisfied, like a soldier who'd accomplished his mission. He pointed now to the great city that occupied Finney's attention.

"Your home will be in that city. The Carpenter from Nazareth is the builder. You provided the construction materials."

Not understanding completely, Finney said, "Tell me more."

"Jesus told you, 'In my Father's house are many rooms; I go to prepare a place for you, that where I am you may be also.' Do you remember how you prepared a special room for Jenny and Angela and Little Finn?"

"Yes. But how did you know that?"

"I was there in each case."

"You were?"

"A guardian must stay close to the one to whom he is assigned."

"But Zyor was my guardian."

"Yes, but I was Jenny's guardian. I was with her while she still lived inside

Susan, so I witnessed all your preparations for her, and for the others."

"No! Really? I didn't know, Jaltor. That's wonderful." Finney spontaneously hugged his giant friend, who returned his embrace in a warrior's restrained sort of way.

"And that is the nature of heaven, is it not? That you are always learning something new and wonderful. Do you remember how you and Susan chose the wallpaper, the cradle, the crib, the baby swing? All the effort you put into it? Elyon's Son prepares a room for every child that arrives in his world. Your home is now ready, for your life on earth is done.

"The great city will eventually be moved to the New Earth, but only after the King has reigned on earth a thousand years. It is all written in the Book."

Jaltor turned his eyes toward the city and spoke in measured tones.

"I too have been praying for your friend Jake. The day you died Elyon sent me to talk with him in the hospital. He didn't know who I was, but we talked of your death and his. Even as we speak, the Carpenter has been preparing a place for him. The work of Jesus on the cross bought him the place. His first baby steps of faithfulness are already being laid up as reward to furnish the place. Jake will join us here. Perhaps it will be soon."

CHAPTER THIRTY-TWO

Mornin', Jake."

It was Nellie, one of the clerks from administration. Nellie spent her mid-morning hours delivering mail to reporter's boxes. When there was too much mail to fit in the boxes, she delivered it directly to the reporter's desk. Seeing Nellie at your desk was either good news or bad. It meant your story or column had touched a nerve. Jake had been seeing a lot of Nellie lately.

She handed Jake five neat packets of mail, each with a rubber band around it.

"Pushed some more buttons, didn't you?"

Jake nodded sheepishly. "Thanks, Nellie. Sorry to create more work for you."

"It was worth it, Jake. Thank you for that column on those library news-papers. It stimulated a great discussion at our dinner table. Just like your abstinence articles. You got us thinking. Keep it up!"

"I appreciate the feedback." He didn't know Nellie that well, though she'd worked there almost as long as he had. For the first time ever, he felt a tinge of regret at not having gotten to know her better.

It was now the third day after his latest controversial column. This gave people one day to read the column, a second to write a fresh-in-the-mind and from-the-gut response, and the third for the post office to get it to the *Trib*. And judging from telephone calls and faxes the last two days, Jake figured they were split down the middle—warm support and unconditional commendation on the one hand; outrage and condemnation on the other. Maybe one out of five, at most, would be mixed reviews. It wouldn't hit syndication for several days yet.

He opened the first letter. No "Dear Mr. Woods." It was a page full of profanities. There was something oddly refreshing about honest, to-the-point hate mail. No hypocrisy and forced politeness. Too many letters ripped you to shreds, then closed off "Sincerely yours."

As Jake opened another piece of mail, his phone rang. After vacillating whether or not to answer, he picked it up just after the second ring.

"Jake? Sutter here. You alone? Nobody's listening?"

It was Sutter, all right, but Jake had never heard him so excited. "I'm sure you'd know, Sutter. I'd be the last to hear if I'm being bugged."

"Very funny. This call was intended as a favor. Maybe I'll just forget it."

"No. Sorry. Just a little testy right now. What's up?"

"Major stuff." Sutter's voice oozed with fervor. "We've had the big break-through, finally. I can't explain on the phone. But if all goes well in the next few hours, I'll take you on a victory march through the whole federal building tomor-row. The beers will be on me."

"Sutter, what is it? Tell me!"

"We're outside of town, maybe a forty-minute drive, wrapping up a big surveillance. Just got off the phone with the director himself. That's why I called. It should be safe for you to join us if you follow my instructions to the letter. You might make it here in time to see it all come down. Interested?"

"You bet I'm interested. Where do I meet you?"

"First the customary vow of silence. No contacts with anyone, absolutely anyone at the *Tribune*, the police station or anywhere else, or the whole thing is off. Got it?"

"Got it, Sutter. Just tell me how to get there."

"It's in a cabin, pretty remote, out in the Hillsdale area. You know the Broder Road turn off, near Sedway, by that old country store?"

"Sure, I've done some hunting out that way, a little fishing too. Bought worms at that store."

"Okay, this is an old hunting cabin. About five miles past the store, take the third dirt road on the left. That road takes you back another three miles into some thick trees. Don't stop anywhere in the area, the store or anywhere else. We've got reasons. We're right on the verge, Woods. I'm taking a risk calling you, but you've been a big help. And they were your buddies."

"Okay, Sutter, thanks. I'm on my way. Be there in forty minutes. Don't do anything without me."

Jake kept pulling up his right foot every time he got above sixty-five. It wouldn't do to waste time or draw attention to himself by getting a speeding ticket. He had the feeling of going out on a mission, and the macho hope of getting his hands on the enemy. He turned by the country store, just closing for the evening. It was dusk.

Jake drove the five miles, found the third dirt road, and made the first two miles faster than you would if you cared about kicking up mud on your car. He slowed down for the final mile, not wanting to draw attention to his arrival.

There ahead of him was a light behind curtains in an old cabin, with a brownish late model Volvo parked down below. It wasn't Sutter's car, but Jake remembered seeing it somewhere. It didn't have federal license plates, which made sense. Surveillance work was hard enough without that kind of giveaway. Jake thought of all those television and movie detectives tailing people in their bright red sports cars that screamed "look at me."

Jake drove up slowly now, noting a shadow on the shade. Mayhew's profile. He parked his car and hurried toward the cabin. Just before he got to the door, Mayhew opened it, to show he couldn't be caught by surprise, Jake supposed.

Mayhew's suit coat was snug enough for Jake to see the impression of his Smith & Wesson .44 Magnum, artillery in the form of a sidearm, a formidable weapon to have on your side in a skirmish. The two exchanged glances and nods, neither warm to the other, though Jake hadn't forgotten Mayhew saving his life.

Inside the room Sutter was turned away from the door, peering intently through huge binoculars. From having dabbled in astronomy years ago, Jake recognized them as Celestron 20x80mm, powerful low-light lenses. He surmised the dual lenses would provide much better eye relief than a single barreled scope for long-term surveillance of whatever they were there for.

Sutter turned around. "Oh, hi Woods. Grab a seat. Have a Red Sangria. Be with you in a second. Yeah, Charlie, we're lookin' good, lookin' good."

Charlie? Jake noted a momentary look of surprise on Mayhew's face as well. Maybe Sutter was just talking to himself.

Jake sat down by four empty bottles of Red Sangria, and another unopened four pack, sitting next to Sutter's familiar burgundy briefcase. It struck him strange that FBI guys would drink on the job. Sutter seemed in no hurry, which irritated Jake since he'd broken his tail to get there.

"So...I'm here now, Sutter. Remember me? The guy you wanted over here pronto?"

No response, which irritated Jake more.

"What are you looking at?"

"Oh, you'd probably rather not know."

"What do you mean by that?"

"Pretty much what he said, bozo," Agent Mayhew said with a smirk.

"Breaking your vow of silence I see, Mayhew. Try not to dominate the conversation, will you?"

"Smart guy. You're gonna be changing your tune pretty soon."

This language alarmed Jake. It was totally out of character, an inexcusable departure from the respectful professionalism of the FBI, even for Mayhew.

What's going on here? Jake looked at Sutter for an answer.

"You'll have to excuse Charlie. This whole thing hasn't been as easy for him. He never got the leads in his high school plays. Not sure he even went to high school."

Jake stared blankly. "What are you talking about, Sutter?"

Sutter smiled broadly, enjoying drawing this out, like he was eating a pecan pie à la mode and postponing the last scrumptious bite.

Jake, still standing in the middle of the room, made a quick move Sutter's direction, then slowed when he saw Mayhew reach toward his shoulder holster.

Charlie? He couldn't remember Mayhew's first name from the day Sutter introduced him but he was certain it wasn't Charlie. Jake walked over to the binoculars, looking out into the now twilight. There was barely enough light to make out two images, a few feet square, propped up on rough easels of some sort, maybe thirty yards away. They were targets, both of which had been shot repeatedly, with a half dozen bullet holes within a few inches of the bull's-eyes.

"Not bad, huh, Woods? We're talking handguns, not rifles. Mine's on the left, Charlie's the right. We figure I got six out of ten kills at thirty yards, and he got eight out of ten. He's always been just a hair more gifted in that area." Sutter smiled at Charlie as if they were old fraternity brothers.

"Well, it takes all kinds, doesn't it, Woods? I mean, what's that the *Tribune's* always saying? Celebrate diversity? Yeah, that's us. I guess my dramatic talents more than compensate for two less kills out of ten, eh Charlie?"

Mayhew shrugged, with a conspicuous lack of affection.

"Why do you keep calling him Charlie?"

"Good for you, Woods. You're not as dumb as you look. Come to think of it, no one's as dumb as you look."

Sutter laughed hysterically.

"Yeah, I believe 'Jeffrey Mayhew' was the name I gave you. Rather dignified, don't you think? Made it up myself. Sounds English, doesn't it? I also like 'Colin Sutter,' don't you? Almost wish it was my real name."

Sutter, or whoever he was, watched Jake closely, enjoying his reaction.

"I'm calling him by his real name, Woods, because now there's no need to call him anything else. The production's over. It's a little game we play once in a while. We give out the man's real name toward the very end. It raises the stakes, heightens the senses, increases his motivation to be sure the man who heard his name doesn't repeat it to anybody. Of course, I don't think Charlie really needs any extra motivation with you. I don't think he likes you very much. Never has."

Charlie glared at Jake, eyes riveted to him. Lifeless eyes. That was it, of course. Charlie was a professional killer. And as the reality Jake guarded himself from sunk in, he realized that this man, unlike most of the scared young men on the other side in that Asian jungle, was going to very much enjoy killing him.

Jake asked the obvious question that bordered now on stupid. "You're not FBI?"

Sutter laughed hard and long, then looked at Charlie.

"Catches on quick, doesn't he? No wonder he's such a big-time journalist. Bet he just figured out Nixon was a crook!"

Both men laughed now, Sutter carelessly like a junior high boy, Mayhew ruthlessly like a particularly cruel junior high boy, but with the trained and focused stare of a professional assassin, his eyes not flinching from Jake.

"Listen, talk to me would you? I deserve that much. I helped you, didn't I?" Jake's nerves were real, but his survival instinct told him to act more confused and frightened than he was, not to let it appear he could offer any threat of resistance.

"That's very funny, Woods. We don't owe you nothin'. Well...wait a minute, I take that back. When he heard I was assigned to you, one of our associates gave you a lot of credit on the capital punishment issue. Told me it was narrowly banned by the voters, as I recall. Lots of people wanted it pretty bad, with all the guys getting off murder sentences after a few years watching TV at the pen. But you spoke out against the death penalty, said it was barbaric. Who knows? Maybe you swayed enough people to make the difference.

"Anyway, one of our best men was on death row eight years ago when the whole thing got overturned. And guess what? Six months ago he got out. He's a friend of ours, and very good at what he does. He's gone back to work and hasn't lost his touch. A few afternoons of target practice and he was first string again. So, I guess we do owe you, Woods, and I'm one to pay my debts. Right, Charlie? When Jake Woods joins his friends under the dirt I don't want him saying I didn't pay my debts."

Sutter rambled like an insane man.

"Take a deep breath and rest easy, Woods." Sutter gestured out at the twilight.

"I'd like it to get a little darker before we kill you. So, you have questions? How can I help you?"

"Who are you?"

Sutter laughed profusely, plopping himself on the edge of the table opposite Jake, while "Charlie" stood guard.

"Well, you're right. We're not the FBI. The truth is—we're the CIA!"

Sutter was delighted with his little joke. Even Charlie's chiseled face cracked a smile.

Good, Jake thought. *Get relaxed, get overconfident, think you're dealing with a coward. Good.*

"Since you're not going to repeat this, I admit I'm pretty proud of our little scam. Getting the use of the office in the federal building was a little tricky, but it's amazing the favors you can call in when people think you're someone else. Parts of the federal building are amazingly unsecured, once you show some good ID. Badges, wall hangings, business cards, official papers. Shoot, you can make half of those with your own computer and printers, alter some military surplus stuff, and you're in business."

Sutter flashed his badge again.

"This is the real thing, an FBI badge, confiscated from a man in the line of duty, God rest his soul. Not that it needed to be authentic, right? Not for you, anyway. Unless you're more of an expert in FBI ID than I take you for."

Jake felt like a real sucker.

"Why'd you follow me?"

"Started right after the funeral. Just in case you got wind of something. Being a mucky muck reporter and everything, we figured somebody might tip you off or you could figure out something on your own. One of our guys was on you in the deli the day you opened up the envelope and the yellow note card fell out. From the look on your face and the fact you went straight to the police, he figured something big was up. He followed you to the wrecking yard, took the pictures. Even got a view of one of the cut tie rods in the enlargement. We knew it was murder. But we still didn't know who. The big guys met the next few days and debated what to do."

Sutter strutted around the room like he was big stuff.

"With you investigating anyway, and since you were pals with a police detective, we figured let's take a risk and make contact to see what you come up with. That's when we conjured up the FBI story. We kept following you because you were out there in the trenches, conducting our investigation for us. We had to keep tabs on you. If you started going places and meeting people we didn't like, we had to know. In our business, knowledge is survival. We took a risk with you. You put money into General Motors, you keep your eye on how it's doing. You watch your investment. You were our investment."

"But...who were the other people following me?"

Sutter laughed again, grating on Jake.

"There were no other people."

"But..." Jake stopped, not sure how to phrase it, to Sutter's delight.

"Part of the smoke and mirrors. A little embellishment to endear us to you, maybe make you grateful for our protection. Grateful people cooperate."

"But the guy that tried to kill me behind the store?"

"I was hoping you'd ask."

Sutter gleefully reached in his briefcase and pulled out a crumpled up blue ski mask. Jake realized instantly the stocky man in the shadows was built exactly like Sutter. And with a sick feeling in the pit of his stomach he remembered where he'd first seen the late model brown Volvo now in front of the cabin. It had been parked near the employee cars behind the supermarket. After assaulting him, supposedly scared by Mayhew's gun fire, Sutter had run into the darkness, only to walk back and drive off after Jake and Mayhew left.

"Another role I played with consummate expertise, if I do say so myself. It takes a lot of skill to hit a man with a baseball bat hard enough to incapacitate him, but not so hard as to knock him unconscious. I've had to practice on a lot of people to get it just right. Some of them never woke up!"

Sutter guffawed, like a man so full of himself he imagines everything he says is clever and entertaining.

"I did my job perfectly. Of course, Charlie was a bit slow on the draw. I had to hold that bat up forever. I felt like I was carrying the Olympic torch or something."

Mayhew didn't smile. He just twirled something around between his fingers, something metallic, with a dull burnished gold look. Jake recognized it as a shell. A huge .44 Magnum shell. The same hardware that had comforted him when he came in the door had the opposite effect now. It all came down to whose side the Magnum was on, and Jake knew now it wasn't his.

"Just call me Don Vito Corelone." Sutter did a bad imitation of Brando in *The Godfather.* "Okay, so I'm not the don. I'm one of his trusty lieutenants. I told you I was in touch with the director himself. Oh, I'm sorry—did you think I was talking about the director of the *FBI?*" Sutter snorted.

"I don't believe it. Why'd you tell me all that stuff about organized crime if you're part of it?"

"You were already investigating. We figured in checking around the hospital you might get some ideas from a few of the doctors or somebody. So, why not get you sworn to secrecy on the organized crime angle in case something came out? Besides, I had to sound bona fide, had to make you believe in me, trust me. I'm a bit of a history buff. Unlike Charlie here, I do some pretty serious reading. Probably read half a dozen books on organized crime, and at least a couple on the FBI. I gave you accurate background information, most of it not vital but some important stuff sprinkled in. I hoped it would sound authentic enough to convince you to reciprocate. And you did. When Mayhew came to your rescue, you owed us your life. It made you more willing to talk to us, tell us everything we needed to know about your investigation, and what the police were coming up with. Reinforced your commitment to keep your mouth shut about us, like you agreed. That was the plan."

Charlie, alias Agent Mayhew, glared at Jake. Pretending to save his life hadn't produced any emotional bonding between the two. Jake imagined Mayhew had probably been disappointed to play the part of the rescuer and would have been much more comfortable swinging the bat. He was likely going to get that chance in the next few minutes.

"It's true, my approach to these things is a little unorthodox. I made a few of our superiors nervous. Some of them think I talk too much, if you can imagine that."

Charlie looked like he agreed, but Sutter was oblivious.

"But I get results. My experience with lying—and I have told an occasional untruth—has taught me it's too easy to get tripped up. You get details wrong, you start sounding phony. People get suspicious, then they hold back. What I told you had to have the ring of truth. So most of what I told you *was* true, with just enough misleading info sprinkled in to protect our rears in case you violated our little contract. And the more I told you, the more you told me. I never could have gotten that stuff from Marsdon or the psychologist, much less the things you let slip from the police investigation. And even if you talked to your detective friend, I knew we were covered. You couldn't prove anything. Besides, we were on you. If it looked like you were going to tell anybody, we could take you out any time. No problem."

Jake knew he had to keep a clear mind, buying as much time to strategize as he possibly could.

"Why did you kill Doc and Finney?"

"You still don't get it, do you?" Sutter paused. "We didn't."

"What?"

"Yeah, I feel almost guilty, closest thing to a confession I've made in years. Charlie doesn't frequent church very much himself, do you Charlie? We do seem to end up at a lot of funerals, though. See, we really didn't know who killed your friends, or we'd never have set this thing up with you in the first place. Unlike you and the police, we suspected foul play immediately. I guess we've got an eye for it. It could have been an accident, but the timing was lousy. Really lousy. It smelled like somebody took him out and wanted everybody, especially us, to think accident. We're in the business of making 'accidents' happen. The odds in the betting pool were two to one against an accident. In any case, we had to know."

"Why?"

"Your friend was a key man. He had lots of power, lots of potential. A man of influence, confident, secure, a real leader. We got him to get his hands dirty, then we knew he was ours. We were watching him, of course, and we knew we'd have to take him out if he went soft on us. But the boys at the top were thrilled with the doctor. No way they'd ordered a hit. It's like, you spend a few years training a guy on the job, and he finally starts to really pay off, and then you lose your investment. And the people we work for don't like to lose investments. We had to know who did it. In our line of work, you can't afford not to know who. Or next week you're history, with them laying flowers on your grave and saying what a great guy you were."

Jake was genuinely interested and tried hard to look it. Sutter clearly enjoyed playing to an audience. That meant more time to stay alive.

"At first the big guys thought it might have been someone in our own circle taking things into his own hands. Like I said, we were watching your friend. He gave us a few scares. Talking a little too seriously with that other friend of yours, though we weren't sure exactly what he was saying. We were afraid he was having a conscience attack, but it looked like he was getting over it, and we figured things would settle in for a nice long-term relationship in the heart, lung, and kidney markets—sort of the pork bellies and soybeans of the medical exchange."

Sutter lost it again and was acting more and more like a drunk. *Can only four wine coolers do this to a guy?*

"Of course, if we found it was one of our boys acting on his own, we'd have to discipline him. Severely. But within a few days we'd shaken everybody down and knew it wasn't an inside job. We were clean as a whistle. Then we figured it could be another group moving in on our operation. You never know about that. See, organized crime isn't the tight little knitting circle you might imagine. We've got all kinds of people, lots of them successful business people, established professionals, trying to break into this medical thing. It's a real bonanza. People will pay big bucks to go on living.

"So maybe a competitor was trying to get in on the act. Maybe they knew Dr. Lowell was our foothold and decided to terminate him. Set us back so they could get a jump with someone else. If so, we had to know. But we'd run out of leads, hit a dead end within a few days of the wreck. We needed hard facts. Oh, we could have eventually found where the car was towed, checked it out, but then what? We don't have a crime lab, fingerprints on computer, all that stuff. That's where you came in."

"Why me?"

"After a lot of discussion—and it still wasn't unanimous—the brass decided to make contact with you. If you helped us, great. If we helped you, the police could nail them, get 'em out of the way for us. Or if they got off easy, we'd take care of them. In fact, even if they went to prison, we might take 'em out there. Send a message, you know. Piece o' cake.

"I asked you about organized crime to see if your detective friend suspected anything. It was a great opportunity to find out if they were on to our operation, even slightly. If they were, we would've been on the suspect list. I mean, he wouldn't be stupid enough to tell us one way or another, so we had to come up with somebody who was. Who better than a reporter?"

Jake avoided eye contact with Charlie but sensed he was getting eager to do what he did best.

"Of course, we were relieved when you told us nobody even suspected organized crime—that told us our operation was still undercover. But if another group made the hit, the cops didn't suspect them either. Your friend's computer files came a little too close to home. I don't mind telling you it made me nervous, and now the cops know more than we wish they did. But it was a risk we had to take."

"So who did do it?"

It was just about pitch dark now, and Jake didn't want the conversation winding down.

"We still don't know. Your buddy will keep working on it after you're gone. If he solves it, he nails the guys who set back our operation. If not, we lose nothing. Well, maybe not nothing. We knew all along we were telling you too much. But that was the beauty of it. You took the vow of silence. Our own little Omerta. But now you've outlived your usefulness. Remember the saying. 'If you're no longer an asset, you're a liability'? Well, you're no longer an asset, Woods, and we have only one game plan for liabilities. 'You talk, you die.' Only this is the preventative version. 'You die, so you don't talk!'"

Jake had never felt like such a fool for keeping a promise. He'd broken plenty of others he should have kept. Why had he kept one he should have broken?

"Come on, Woods, lighten up. Don't look so shocked. It's just our own little euthanasia plan—when people's lives become too expensive for us, we put them out of their misery. Kevorkian style, but no consent required. Just think of us as your doctor, or your family member who's tired of paying the medical bills. You understand, don't you Jake? We don't want any hard feelings. We've become...sort of attached to you. You know, male bonding and all that."

Sutter laughed again, this time more deliberately, relishing the moment in his perverse way, squeezing out its juices and savoring them.

The dim overhead light caught Sutter's eyes, which seemed to Jake to have undergone a transformation. The eyes were coal black, lifeless, ruthless, deadly. Shark eyes. *Why didn't I notice them before?* The eyes seemed subhuman, animal eyes, vicious and uncaring, without conscience, without moral reference points. The eyes of a predator, alive but mechanical. His giddiness was no sign of softness, but an idiosyncrasy of an utterly ruthless man.

"Besides, Jake"—he said Jake's name with pronounced sarcasm, rubbing in the facade of a personal relationship—"we don't want you to have to live with that thing Vietnam vets have. What do you call it? Survivor guilt syndrome? You know, how come you lived when your friends died? You should have died too. Well...now you will."

"But..."

"This is now what we professionals call the pleading, bargaining stage, sometimes known as the procrastination stage. What would you like to say? What can you offer me in exchange for your life? You're not rich, I know that. Perhaps a favorable column? The promise to quote me fairly and accurately? A year's subscription to the *Tribune*? Ah, I have it. You could write my biography. Now that's a tempting offer. Well, what is it, Woods?"

"You can't expect to get away with this. If I'm murdered—"

"Oh, but we do expect to get away with it. We have before. Why shouldn't we this time? Besides, this isn't going to be known as a murder, just a permanent disappearance. Sure, your detective friend will be suspicious, but you didn't tell him or anybody else you were coming here, did you? Good boy, we knew we could trust you. Even if they knew there was foul play, who will they suspect? Somebody who hates your column? Some group you've insulted? Nobody's going to suspect us—they don't even know we exist! We've got a perfect place to bury you, don't we Charlie? They won't find your body for another fifty years when they turn these woods into a housing development. Nobody will remember Jake Woods then. Nobody will care!"

Sutter reached into his briefcase again, its raised lid shielding Jake from its contents. His hand wrapped in a white handkerchief, he lifted something out, something with a familiar scent, and said, "By the way. Have I thanked you for the Walther? A Nazi gun, you said. I'm impressed. I'm handling it carefully, 'cause we're thinking of possible uses for it. What's wrong, Jake? You look surprised. We didn't want you armed, just in case we had to face off with you prematurely. Tell him about it, Charlie."

Mayhew shook his head.

"Okay, I'm not shy. Charlie's good with a slim-jim. Took him all of twenty seconds to get in your car. Said he didn't think you'd leave the game early. Would have done the job earlier, but if you can believe this, he sat in his car listening to the game on the radio, waiting for the rain to stop. Never did, so he finally got out and went to work. That dopey kid freaked him out so much that when he started running away, he squeezed the trigger and almost shot off his own foot. He could break in the car any time, and he waits till you're coming back—'cause he didn't want to get wet!"

Sutter rolled his eyes with an exasperated good-help-is-hard-to-find expression. Charlie did not appreciate the ribbing, and no doubt wished he'd never told Sutter what happened that night.

"But how'd you know I had the gun in my car?"

"We didn't. But you're a vet and you hunt. Obviously you've got a hand gun. And after being attacked behind the supermarket, it was a good bet you'd start packing it. Besides, staging the break-in the day before you and I had a meeting was a timely reminder you should talk with your friends before your enemies took you out."

Sutter glanced across the room.

"What do you say, Charlie? Should we flip to see who does the honors?"

Charlie didn't look happy with this arrangement. Apparently he assumed the job would be his. Sutter reached in his pants pocket and pulled out a quarter.

"Call it." The quarter flipped over and over in the air, as if in slow motion. "Heads" Charlie called anxiously, clearly concerned he might lose. The quarter landed on the old, beat up, oil-cloth covered table, bouncing twice and awkwardly tripping over a big crease.

Sutter swept up the coin before Charlie could even see it. "Heads it is." Sutter shook his head. "Charlie always wins the toss."

Jake had the impression Sutter always made Charlie the winner—maybe because Charlie enjoyed this part of his work, or maybe so in case of a conviction, Sutter would only be an accomplice. That way Sutter might spend even less time away from his work or his retirement home.

Charlie drew his .44 Magnum, the barrel looking to Jake as wide as a cannon. He wondered why no gun had been drawn earlier, then realized they didn't consider him a serious threat. The gun fit comfortably in Charlie's right hand, as if it had spent a great deal of time there. He waved it toward the door. For the first time Jake could remember, Charlie smiled so broadly he could see his teeth.

"Time to take a walk, Woods."

Jake knew he was probably going to die, and in a strange way felt he was ready to die for the first time in his life, yet not ready, because he now had a stronger reason for living than he'd ever known. If he did die, he was determined it wouldn't be without a fight.

"See ya, boys. Don't be gone too long now," Sutter chuckled, walking toward the table and loosening his tie like he deserved to kick back after pulling off a major coup.

Jake knew there was no reason for a shooter to take him any further from the cabin than to avoid a mess some visitor was likely to see. And no doubt about it, the .44 would make a real mess. Jake had to make his move soon, somewhere between stepping out of Sutter's range of sight and getting maybe thirty feet from the house. Charlie might toy with him first, and he might not. He couldn't count on it, and even if he did, the first blow or shot would likely cripple him. He decided the moment he stepped out the door would be the moment of greatest surprise.

As Jake stepped out under the threshold, he looked back suddenly toward Sutter, successfully shifting Charlie's eyes back also. Sutter was taking his first big suck on a fresh wine cooler. At the moment Charlie's eyes left him, Jake swung his left arm up at the porch light, knocking it loose and shattering the bulb. The explosion of light was followed by intense blackness. Jake knew his only hope was that Charlie would be unable to see in the sudden dark long enough for him to get a lead into the trees.

Charlie didn't wait more than a second to start shooting. He shot blindly into the black, seeing nothing but the image of the light bulb burned into his retinas. The sound of the .44 was deafening, especially the first two shots, fired while Jake was within ten feet. Charlie swore and yelled, and if he'd been able to see Jake, could easily have killed him. Had he been quiet he could have heard Jake running close alongside the house. But quiet Charlie was too angry to be still the one time he most needed to be.

The path most natural for an escapee to run—straight from the house toward the cars or the close edge of the woods—was riddled with gunshots and flying dirt clods. The getaway path's logic was exactly what kept Jake from choosing it. Instead he ran laterally, pressed up against the side of the cabin.

By now Jake was beyond the edge of the house and running into increasingly thick trees. He slowed down enough not to hurt himself as he brushed off one tree and then the next, his hands and face breaking off the dead, brittle, quarter-inch branches of the trees, most of them Douglas firs.

He heard Sutter yell "Shut up," and stopped in his tracks, just a moment too late. A few twigs broke under his feet. Two shots glanced by him, one to his right, the other making a dull thud two feet to his left. Quickly he stepped behind the nearest fir tree, closing his eyes tight to accelerate their adjustment to the dark.

His opponents had two distinct advantages over him. There were two of them; and they had guns. On the other hand, there were lots of trees for cover; and they would have to find him. There were eleven hours of darkness ahead, and the ones who best used the darkness would win this battle. The next minute, Jake surmised, was critical, a minute in which they were still by the front of the house with the lights from the inside retarding their night eyes. He was closing his or squinting and looking away from the house to cultivate his advantage.

He could hear Sutter and Charlie arguing and knew they weren't listening for noise to shoot at. He moved slowly back from the tree and kept it squarely between him and the cabin. He backed into the next tree and stepped behind it, then repeated his backward motion. He tested the ground as he walked, seeking out the spongy, moss-covered soil, trying to avoid the crack of brittle branches and leaves. He looked into the darkness, willing his eyes to see more. He saw dimly, then stooped low and felt two pieces of dead wood, each about twelve inches long and an inch thick. The more he looked at them the more they took on shapes. It came back to him from Vietnam. You can see much better in the dark than you think, but you have to orient yourself to the subtle hues of the night. It's an art more than a science, an art he once knew well, and now tried to regain.

He was now ninety feet from the house, seventy feet into the woods. He supposed his enemies to be on the edge of that circle of soft light emanating from the cabin. He figured his eyes were adjusted at least a minute ahead of theirs. Straining to make sure he didn't hit overhanging limbs, he threw one of the pieces of wood about twenty feet, poising the other in ready position. As he'd hoped, the moment it hit the ground, a gun fired at it, and at that very moment, trusting the sound of the Magnum had desensitized their ears, Jake quickly moved back several feet the opposite direction. Even as he did so he threw the other piece, this time higher and farther along the same plane, so it would sound like he was moving the opposite way. Again the wood hit, this time both men fired at the sound, and again he moved backward several feet more.

The window of opportunity for such a bold effort was largely gone now. If they kept moving away from the house, soon they'd be seeing almost as well as he could. They might catch sight of his arm throwing the wood, or see the trajectory of the wood and fire not at its landing but at its launching. He could hear them rushing toward where they'd fired. He heard them talking and swearing. They supposed they had wounded him. They knew he was unarmed and that they should get him while he was close, while they still had their advantage.

He kicked himself for not buying another gun to keep in the car and for going into the cabin unarmed. But he'd never repaired the Browning, his other handgun, and you didn't just haul your hunting rifle around in the trunk. Not that he could get to it now anyway. Besides, who would have thought it? These were supposed to be the good guys. How easily they'd deceived him. He had less confidence than ever in his ability to discern what was true.

What was his next move? From hunting and fishing he knew this area better than his pursuers, and the darkness favored the hunted more than the hunters. He'd almost certainly get away from them. But no. By the time he emerged some place miles away where he could call the police, Sutter and Mayhew would be long gone, never to reappear. He felt certain of it. One might show up in Miami, the other in Chicago. Or they'd stay around town and finish him off. More likely, someone else would be hired to take him out, and they'd get a nice telegram in Miami telling them he'd bit it. It might just look like another accident. And as Doc's accident took Finney's life, Jake's could take Carly's or Little Finn's or anybody's. He wasn't going to let that happen. As they chased after him now, they'd think his only goal would be escape. They wouldn't expect him to choose to face them rather than run. That might provide the element of surprise he needed.

Were they lying when they said they didn't kill his friends? Certainly they'd killed other people's friends. For the moment he chose to believe they were lying, that they had killed his friends too. While his instinct for self-preservation was strong, the thought of revenge for his friends—revenge on these arrogant phonies who had fooled him so completely—energized him to a new level. It was like being in Vietnam again, but this time he had something personal against the enemy.

He knew Victor Charlie might think he was serving his country, might have wondered about what was right. Not this Charlie. And not Sutter. They were serving themselves and the ruthless men they worked for. No one had drafted them. They'd volunteered for this noxious duty and happily made a career of it. They knew what was right. They just chose to violate it. They joked about right and wrong, made a mockery of justice. Maybe Jake had helped this "associate" of theirs with his columns against capital punishment. They wouldn't be so lucky. They might not live to face trial. Then no one could get them off.

Jake found a dense, gnarly piece of hardwood that could serve as a club. He would pick up a new and better weapon every time he found it, abandoning the old unless he could carry both. Jake smelled something he'd forgotten had so distinct an odor. It was the smell of mud, and not far away.

He would find it now and take on his next advantage. He would blend into the darkness. And soon, very soon, it wouldn't just be Charlie hunting Jake. Jake would be hunting Charlie. And he would kill him, or die trying.

CHAPTER THIRTY-THREE

J ake moved stealthily, now a hundred yards from the cabin. His pursuers still
tracked him on the line of the wood he had thrown, leaving them now maybe
sixty yards from him.

His nose led him down a mossy slope to a low spot that had become a sink
hole. It was a bed of dark mud. He rubbed the soft cool camouflage over his
clothes and face and arms. He applied it smoothly, over every inch of his body,
to be sure it was uniform, that none of the worn white bleach marks of his jeans
surfaced.

His white Nikes were mud polished now, but he had to watch them. When
they scraped against a twig, a white glow showed through, all the more conspicuous
in the darkness. He wished now he hadn't dressed so casual for work. His brown
loafers or black dress shoes would blend much better into the darkness. Still, the
tennis shoes were ideal for moving. As long as they didn't show up and get him
killed.

Jake rested, sitting, getting his breathing under control. He felt as though he
was in that Asian jungle again, but this time too cold rather than too hot. He tried
to think of Sutter and Mayhew in subhuman terms, a technique that made war easier. That's why they'd called the enemy dinks, slopes, and zipperheads. It was hardest to take a human life when you acknowledged it was human. You might pause
and think, hesitate just a moment, and in the hesitation be killed. Mayhew and
Sutter were vermin, scum, trash that needed to be disposed of. And he was the
garbage man, the exterminator. He could see himself choking the life out of them,
getting hold of their guns and blowing their brains out. He could do it. He *would*
do it. He'd have to.

Jake noticed that what he'd thought was a moonless night really wasn't. The
clouds were thick, but he could see the sliver of a moon threatening to pierce them.
It was already low over the western sky. He looked forward to it going down.
Moonlight always favored the guys with the guns. He needed the full dark of night
to execute his plan.

He was surprised how easily he could distinguish not only objects but shades of
light and darkness. It was like a black and white television screen—there was no
color, but there was contrast.

Jake studied the terrain. This whole area was muddy, showing footprints much
more clearly than the mossy turf that left only slight foot impressions, or the floor
litter of leaves and twigs that left no discernible tracks at all, unless you were Daniel
Boone, and Sutter and Mayhew weren't. From an eight-inch length of wood, just
over an inch thick, he now fashioned a sort of dagger, sharpening it as best he could

on a tapered rock. He would carry this tucked in his belt, the club in his right hand.

Suddenly he saw two flashlights coming at him from the house. The ground was wet enough Sutter and Charlie could easily see Jake's tracks going along the house and into the woods. They'd realize he'd never been where they were shooting. They'd know they'd been lured off the track, that Jake was farther out this direction. The tracks would vary from deep and obvious, to shallow, to nonexistent. Good news for a man who wanted to escape. A problem for him, since he needed to get them to this muddy area to execute his plan. He'd have to lure them here.

The two flashlight beams indicated the men were still traveling side by side, working their way his direction, finding an occasional footprint. It was slow going for them.

Jake refused to look directly at the flashlights as they moved slowly in expanding circles, Sutter and Charlie studying the ground for the next track. If they caught him in their beam he was dead. But there was a flip side. If he stayed outside those beams, he would see them much better than they could see him.

They were now forty yards away, looking behind trees big enough to obscure him, then stopping to listen. Jake practiced his reach to the bulky hilt of the rough dagger blade stuffed in his belt. He swung his makeshift club in the darkness to get used to its feel. It made a soft swoosh, like a sword, the sound accentuated by the darkness. If it hit its target, he imagined, it wouldn't make the smooth, cutting sound of a blade piercing skin, but the dull thud of a bludgeon crunching bone.

A twig snapped under Jake's feet. The men stood still and the flashlights turned his way, with only a too-thin young fir directly between him and them. The lights were about to shine directly on him when Jake heard a louder noise some distance away.

The flashlights moved in unison away from where he stood, and he quickly ducked behind a larger tree, just in time to watch two flashlight beams catch a pair of frightened eyes in the darkness. Five rounds of ammo exploded, three from a .44 Magnum, thunderously loud and made all the louder by the tranquil quiet of the dark.

The deer fell lifeless, dead before it hit the ground, innocent yet brutally condemned. It had died that he might live. Yet he still could die—and would, if he made the slightest mistake again.

While his enemies went to check out the deer, Jake walked another five feet away from them to a Douglas fir near the muddy clearing, its lowest branches twenty feet above the ground. He scraped his feet against the spongy carpet, quietly digging it up and leaving footprints in the soil underneath. These tracks would be obvious to Charlie and Sutter. Then, walking as softly as he could on clumps of moss and fallen needles, he worked his way to a different tree, a hemlock he'd carefully chosen.

The hemlock, at the very edge of the clearing, had been exposed to sunlight. Unlike the large firs that dominated this forest, it had strong limbs beginning six feet from the ground, allowing him an easy climb up. He could see that about thirty feet up, its branches barely intermingled with the Douglas fir he'd tromped around.

He picked up a heavy stick and stuck one end down the back of his pants. With his dagger in his belt and his club wedged in the front left side of his pants, he was loaded down, but his hands were free.

While Sutter and Charlie worked their way back from the deer to where they'd last seen his tracks, Jake scurried up the hemlock. At about thirty feet up, he edged his way out one thick branch and over to the fir's adjoining branches. Then he climbed down to the fir's lowest branches, positioning himself directly over the most obvious tracks he'd made. Then, when his enemies were standing still maybe seventy feet away, he took out the stick he'd stuck down the back of his pants and heaved it to the ground.

He heard the crackling and the thud he'd hoped for, and so had they. The .44 fired again. They moved rapidly, the two flashlights quickly closing in until they were just a few feet away. The two men weren't talking, and he disciplined himself not to widen his eyes for a better look. They came right under the tree where Jake awaited them.

They were looking around now, checking out the torn turf and the muddy footprints, just as he'd hoped. He planned to fall right on one of them while reaching out to strike the other with his club. But something was wrong. This wasn't two men side by side, each carrying a flashlight. It was one man, Sutter, holding a flashlight in each hand.

He'd underestimated them. Charlie must be holding back in case Jake attacked Sutter. Then Charlie would get the easy kill.

Sutter stopped now, studying the footprints, failing to see where they went from there. He pointed both lights to the ground, while Charlie hung back, somewhere in the darkness. If Sutter pointed one of his lights up to search the tree above him, Charlie would have an easy target. But there was no reason to. It would never occur to him to search branches twenty feet up an unclimbable tree. At least, that's what Jake counted on.

Sutter had been beneath him several seconds, first kneeling, now standing again. Jake couldn't expect to have another chance like this. He'd have to improvise. He heaved his trusty club nearly forty feet behind Sutter, hoping it would also fall behind Charlie, the next best thing to striking him in the head. Then he quickly pulled out his dagger and slid off the limb. As he fell, he heard a shot and hoped Charlie was shooting at the sound of the club, not at the shape now falling toward Sutter.

As a diving osprey might view a fish in the water below, Jake focused in on Sutter in the fleeting moment of the fall. Just before impact, Sutter pointed the flashlights and looked expectantly back to the gun fire, perhaps believing Charlie had finished the hunt.

A sudden move by Sutter and Jake would have fallen to the ground like a sky-diver with a defective parachute. But he froze, and Jake landed with his full weight on Sutter's neck and shoulders, wrapping his arms around him as he fell. Sutter's body folded under Jake's weight. He heard the sickening sound of bones crunching as he pounded him into the ground, Sutter breaking Jake's fall at a terrible price to himself.

Jake's first act on the ground was to turn off one flashlight and heave the other away. He saw it land, blink out, then flicker. He reached into Sutter's jacket to get his gun, but it wasn't there. He frantically frisked him, unsure if Charlie would be misled by the thrown flashlight or would zero in on Jake at the bottom of the tree. He couldn't find a gun, and he was running out of time.

Sutter was no longer in this fight, but he wasn't completely unconscious. His soft moaning would draw Charlie to him, flashlight or not. Jake thought of taking the dagger and burying it in Sutter's chest, but the weapon wasn't sharp enough, and something restrained him from the impulse. Jake took the remaining flashlight, a long-handled metal type, like a night watchman's, and cracked it hard across Sutter's skull. The moaning stopped.

Jake moved away quickly. The only thing that saved him from a spate of .44s was the darkness and Charlie's uncertainty as to which sounds were coming from Sutter and which from Jake. He didn't think Charlie would relish explaining to his superiors how he killed his own man trying to get the other.

Jake stood behind the widest tree only twenty-five feet from Sutter and assessed his situation. He'd lost his club, gained a flashlight, and taken out half the enemy. He was still at a disadvantage, but now he had the luxury of focusing on only one enemy. That never happened in Vietnam. As long as you were outside your camp you never had an accurate count of the enemy. There could always be one more lurking in the shadows, ready to take you out the moment you thought you'd won. Jake finally had only one enemy to deal with.

His eyes were still burning, as if someone had taken a flash picture. He couldn't keep himself from having them wide open as he was falling, and he'd seen too much flashlight close up. Jake saw a figure slowly materialize on the back side of the sputtering flashlight. Charlie's gun was extended in the cold steady way of the professional. In the flickering glow, Charlie presented a clear profile. It would have been his last, Jake thought, if only he'd been able to find Sutter's gun.

Charlie picked up the light and started pointing it around. Jake hid sideways behind his twenty-inch fir. There was no room for error. He'd have given his retirement funds for just three more inches.

The shaft of light kept flickering eerily in Charlie's hand. The bad contact from Jake's throw gave the impression the flashlight was trying to decide which side it would serve in the conflict. For a moment it worked perfectly again. It slowly swept a fifty-foot semicircle, came to Jake's tree, and stopped. The sole light in this forest was focused directly on his tree, only thirty feet from where Charlie stood.

Jake sensed this might be it, that Charlie was seeing the edge of his mud-encrusted jacket, or that the climb and scuffle had made all sorts of scrapes on his white shoes and a part of them was showing at the bottom of the tree. He couldn't lower his eyes to look lest the slightest movement give him away.

Then the light moved on again, with an air of uncertainty, flickering for a moment, to the soft curses of its holder. Now it was pointed at the ground, near

Charlie's feet. While he closed his eyes again to court the night vision, Jake imagined Charlie's light shining on the pathetic pile of flesh and broken bone that was his partner.

He heard the whisper. "Michael." There was no pretense out here anymore. Even if these two got away, at least he had a couple of first names to hand to Ollie, if that was worth anything. But it wasn't enough. He didn't want their names. He wanted them. He had to take them out.

Charlie let loose a cocky insulting laugh and spoke to Jake as if he knew right where he was. "You stupid idiot. You didn't even get his gun. It was right here in his belt!"

His belt! If only he'd had a second longer to look.

"You're a coward, Woods. Come on out and fight like a man."

There was something ironic about being called a coward by a man who thirty minutes ago had led you out of a cabin unarmed to put a bullet through your head.

"You're never going to make it, Woods. Come out and face me now or I raise the stakes. I know where your daughter lives. You probably don't care if I kill your ex-wife, but I bet you don't want me to kill your daughter, do you? That's right, I followed you to their apartment one night. It's on Elm, across from the 7-Eleven. Second floor, number 219. It's not more than twenty minutes from here."

He paused to let the revelation sink in. It had its desired effect. Jake was suddenly frightened to the bone.

"Think about it, Woods. There's no phone in the cabin, probably no phone anywhere for miles. Think you can run and get a cop there before I kill your daughter? I bet I could stop for a Slurpee, rob that 7-Eleven, play a few video games, and still take her out an hour before the cops got there. Maybe I'll drop by that retard's house and blow him away too. I don't think he got a good look at me, but you can't be too careful. Yeah, I better take 'em both out. Maybe the retard first, then the girl. Or maybe I'll flip to see which one goes first. A hundred to one you can't stop me, Woods. But first, a little clean-up."

Daring to peek around the tree, Jake could see Charlie, flashlight on the ground, pull something white out of his coat pocket. He jerked his head back and winced as he heard the shot, not as loud as a .44, followed immediately by another. For a moment he'd assumed they were aimed at him, at a protruding sleeve or pant-leg or shoe.

But Charlie was pointing at Sutter. Two shots to his head at close range. A professional ending for a man who prided himself on being a professional. Jake could see the white handkerchief. For some reason, Charlie wrapped the gun in it and put it back in his coat pocket. Then he reached—Jake could hear more than see it—in his shoulder holster for his Magnum. Jake heard him reloading.

"I'm leaving now, Woods. Hope you've made peace with your daughter. I look forward to meeting her in about twenty minutes. I'll send your greetings to her and the retard. Since I've got so much time to kill—Michael would like that, 'time to kill'—maybe I'll have some fun with her before I scramble her brains."

Jake heard his receding footsteps.

"You're a two-bit punk," Jake yelled desperately. "You can't even finish me off!"

Despite the risk to himself, he had to keep Charlie from leaving. His grip was so tight on the flashlight his whole arm throbbed. Everything within him wanted to run wildly at Charlie. He felt as though he could take three bullets in the chest and still have enough rage left to break Charlie's neck. He was willing enough to die, but if he didn't play this right, Carly would die. Maybe Little Finn. Possibly Janet or Sue. He couldn't allow it. He'd put Carly and Janet through enough suffering. This time he had to save them from it. He owed them that, and more.

Charlie pointed his flashlight alternately at three trees, each about four feet apart. Jake was behind the middle tree. The flashlight was flickering again, now off, now on. Finally, swearing at it a final time, Charlie threw it to the ground.

The sliver of moon was long gone. The cabin was so far away its light couldn't be seen, at least not from Jake's vantage point. There were no other cabins, houses, cars, anything. It was pitch black. Jake's hearing was acute. He should be able to hear Charlie coming toward him.

Jake shivered, realizing now why Charlie wasn't moving. Why should he? He was taking away Jake's only remaining advantage. He was waiting to let his eyes adjust to the dark. He was watching the three trees and listening, knowing Jake was behind one of them, knowing his Magnum could let loose six rounds, and at this range, even in the dark, would probably bury at least two of them in Jake.

Charlie waited quietly what seemed another ten minutes, though it was really only three. He was coming now, night eyes and all. He was good—maybe not Kung Fu walking on rice paper, but there was no more sound than a slight broken twig every few feet. Jake could tell he was coming at the middle tree, his tree. Jake felt cold, his neck and shoulders stiff and painful from the fall and from standing stock-still behind the tree so long. He was ready to spring, wanting to let loose, knowing if he was a second too soon or too late, he would leave this world for the next.

Jake waited for the exact moment, then whipped the flashlight around in his right hand, turning it on and sticking it into what he hoped were Charlie's eyes. He held it only for a moment, then let go, knowing gunfire would follow. First there was Charlie's yelp of surprise and pain from the needles of light, then the gunshots.

Jake bolted around the other side of the tree, pulling his dagger out of his belt. Charlie was doing the dance of panic, eyes stinging, shooting at the flashlight on the ground. One shot blacked it out completely, but by this time Charlie had a dull dagger attacking his lower ribs, and Jake's left arm was around his neck.

The two rolled on the ground. The gun fired off two more times, and then Jake heard the welcome click. Empty. A real knife would have finished the fight. This one only pierced the skin.

Jake held a tight headlock while Charlie flailed and threw himself everywhere. Jake moved to a choke hold. He thought he could make him pass out, but Charlie broke free. He was ten years younger than Jake and very strong. Then Charlie grabbed something from his lower right pantleg and charged like an angry wild bull, knocking Jake on his back. Charlie had something in his hand he was flailing at Jake from above. At first Jake thought it was the empty gun, and he raised his left arm to fend off the blow. But it didn't have the dull throbbing impact of a gun used as a bludgeon. Instead it pierced his arm, painfully, and warm liquid splashed Jake's face.

Jake was in agony as Charlie pulled out the knife and raised it to strike a second blow. But Jake managed to let loose with a hard right to Charlie's face, breaking his nose. Jake was suddenly up and on top of him, striking Charlie repeatedly, telling himself this man was a killer, that he'd probably killed his friends and had threatened to kill Carly and Little Finn. He hit him again and again.

Finally he realized Charlie was unconscious. Jake's hands were wet, soaking wet. They smelled like blood. Had he hit Charlie that hard? No, it was *his* blood. Jake felt terribly weak. He was losing blood, a lot of it. He pulled the handkerchief from Charlie's suit pocket, taking out the gun wrapped in it, the gun that smelled of WD-40. The other gun. Charlie had forgotten it, and so had he.

He wrapped the handkerchief around his wound. It wasn't enough. He tore out lining from Charlie's suit to apply more pressure, to hold it tight. The task was getting harder. He was getting weaker. He wanted to sleep. Instinctively he knew sleeping now would be like sleeping in the Arctic cold, where you'd never wake up. He bandaged himself with everything he could.

If he died out here, Charlie would recover eventually and get away. Maybe he would still go after Carly. He couldn't let that happen. Jake held Charlie's knife in his right arm. He considered plunging it into Charlie's heart, or maybe severing his jugular, an execution for past crimes and a prevention of future ones. He reached for the other gun. He could finish Charlie off the way he'd finished Sutter, and who knows how many others.

But as he lay in the darkness he realized he wasn't the judge and executioner of these men, though thirty minutes ago he would have been glad to play the role. He'd come within an inch of eternity for the second time in two months, and before the hour was over would likely be there. Sutter hadn't been ready for what was on the other side. By human standards, he was made of better stuff than Sutter, but he knew he no more deserved to be in the presence of God than these two.

With startling clarity he considered the irony that he was about to die. What would he do if he had one last day or month or year to live in this world? He thought of the time he'd spent reading Finney's Bible, and how he'd found himself believing it. And about the Presence he'd felt with him. He thought of Janet and the abortion and the affairs, and Carly, and how he'd failed her. He thought of his mother and how he'd neglected her. As he lay in mud and moss and sweat, he felt the deepest sense of unworthiness he'd ever known. But with it he felt something else—forgiven—and with it came a freeing sense of peace. If he did not make it, if the lonely forest was where the abandoned shell of his body would lie, then he thanked God in the cold darkness that he was ready to face the long tomorrow.

He knew he was in no condition to walk. He might stagger thirty feet, but he would never make it back to the car. He gathered his remaining strength, took off Charlie's belt, and tied his hands tightly behind his back. He took off his own belt and tied Charlie's feet. He tore some more strips from the lining of Charlie's suit and tied them tight to reinforce the bind of the belts. He was determined that if he died here tonight, Charlie would not get far.

Jake reapplied pressure to his aching arm. The bandages were wet, very wet. Perhaps an artery had been severed. He would die here then. He was deeply sorry for the legacy he was leaving, successful by human standards, but what he now regarded as a failure by the only standards that mattered. Still, he felt that strange peace, knowing his entrance to the world beyond had been purchased by the flowing blood of another. In his final weeks on earth, at least, he'd done some things pleasing to the One whose opinion really mattered.

And he felt something else. He felt again that he was not alone lying in that darkness. Though he could not see well, and his vision was getting dimmer by the moment, there was someone else nearby whose eyes penetrated the darkness and strove to reach out and touch him. There was the presence of a Savior within, and a God in heaven above, but there was someone else too, someone close and wanting to be closer.

He heard a strange sound, as if someone had pried open a closed door and rushed through it. The mysterious sound was followed by another, a deep and almost other-worldly voice that seemed strangely comforting.

Memories of early childhood began to rush through his mind, as if it were a videotape of his life stuck on fast forward. As his grip on his arm relaxed and the deadly flow of blood resumed, for just a moment before losing consciousness Jake thought he saw and felt a powerful hand grab hold of his wounded arm.

CHAPTER THIRTY-FOUR

J ake woke up in the hospital for the second time in just over three months. This time he woke peacefully, dry and warm. How did he get here? Sore and weak, he began to remember the skirmish in the dark. He chose not to press the button and call a nurse, but to lie still, reorienting himself until he could perhaps ask an intelligent question and understand the answer. The clock told him it was two-thirty, and the sunshine coming in through the window told him it was afternoon.

A nurse passed by his room, glancing in as a matter of habit. She did a double take when she saw Jake's eyes were open.

"Hello, Mr. Woods! Someone's been waiting for you to wake up. I'll send him in."

Jake smiled as Ollie walked in the door, finishing off a sandwich from the hospital cafeteria or maybe from a vending machine. His spiral notebook was in tow. This wasn't just a friendly visit.

"Jake. First, I'm glad you're not dead. Okay, now that we've got the niceties out of the way, I want the whole story, from the beginning. You've got a lot of explaining to do. How'd you get mixed up with these guys? And how'd you end up mud wrestling with them in the woods?"

Ollie didn't like being in the dark, and he wanted Jake's answers now.

"Wait a minute, Ollie. First I want to know how I got here. Last I knew I was bleeding to death in the woods. I thought next time I woke up maybe I'd be seeing angels. Instead, I'm looking at your ugly mug."

"You're just jealous, Woods. Any angel would kill to have a kisser like this." Ollie ran his hand over his face as if it belonged to a Greek god.

"As for how you got here, forget it. You tell your story first, and if I'm satisfied, I'll fill you in on the rest. I'm the cop, remember? In addition to everything else, you led me to another homicide. Talk, mister."

"Your sensitivity to my condition is touching, Ollie. Where's the doctor who always comes in and says, 'I'm sorry, the patient is in no condition to talk right now. He needs his rest'?"

"I showed that doctor my badge, and when he still objected I kicked his rear into a broom closet. Unless you want to join him I'd start talking now."

"Okay, Ollie. But you're not going to like it. I owe you a big apology."

He backed up and told the whole story, from the Saturday afternoon Sutter and Mayhew paid him their first visit and took him to their phony office at the federal building.

"Okay, the FBI badges I can buy. But an office in the federal building? How'd they pull that off?"

Ollie jotted down a note and circled it prominently for follow up.

"Somebody thought they were doing a favor for the Feds, like this was a sting operation or something. I don't think it was somebody working for them. Just some sucker who fell for an elaborate ruse."

Jake blushed. Speaking of suckers...

"Thanks for your analysis, Detective Woods, but leave the investigation to us, okay? And don't quit your day job either. As for the federal building, somebody's head's gonna roll over there. It's just like the Feds, though. Everybody's got secrets from everybody else, so they can't double check security the way they ought to."

"What about Sutter and Mayhew?"

"Who? Oh, your forest friends? Bad dudes. I guess you found that out, didn't you? Before we go further I have to ask you, who killed Michael Fredericks?"

"You mean Sutter? Mayhew killed him. His real name isn't Mayhew, it's Charlie something."

"Charlie Nambag. Sounds like Scumbag doesn't it? We ran both their prints and the computer took all of two seconds before it started coughing up their rap lists. Charlie's couldn't fit on one screen. He's a real prince of a guy. Been paroled twice when he should have spent the rest of his life in jail. Don't I recall a column or two where you told the rest of us we needed to be more understanding of these troubled criminals? Feel any different now that one almost took you out?"

"A lot of things feel different, Ollie."

Ollie jotted down a few notes and looked Jake right in the eyes.

"Charlie says you killed Fredericks."

"What?"

"Problem is, we found that old Walther you showed me a few years ago. Guess what? The bullets that killed Sutter came from your gun. I even found the two shells out there. 1943? Cripes, Jake, ever consider buying some new ammo?"

"Charlie shot him. He must have used my gun. He stole it from my car."

"How come you had a gun in your car?"

"It's a long story, Ollie. You don't believe I killed the guy, do you?"

"Well, I know it's your gun, and your fingerprints are all over it. Just yours. Not Nambag's, not Fredericks's."

"Of course...they both handled it with a handkerchief. They weren't just trying to keep their prints off, they were trying to keep mine on. Sutter said they had some plans for it."

"Going to set you up. Maybe kill somebody else with it, somebody they wanted to take out anyway, and make it look like you did it, panicked and disappeared. Two birds with one stone."

Like maybe Carly or Janet or Little Finn? Jake shuddered.

"Charlie figured he may as well use it to waste Fredericks. Why use his Magnum when the Walther couldn't be linked to him? I believe you, Jake. And, hey, most juries would probably trust a journalist over a professional hit man." Ollie paused as if in deep thought. "Now that I think about it, it might be a toss up."

"I'm looking forward to seeing that guy nailed in court," Jake said.

"Yeah, well, that remains to be seen. Chances are he had a rough upbringing, dysfunctional family, parents were alcoholics, Sutter was a codependent. Or maybe I didn't pause long enough on a comma while reading his Mirandas or something, and he walks. In any case, after a few years of pumping iron and watching crime movies in prison, he'll be back out to blow people away again. With some luck, maybe by the time he gets out he'll have arthritis of the trigger finger. Heck, by then you might be retired and moved somewhere, and he won't bother coming after you for revenge. Just send you a letter bomb or something. They learn all kinds of useful skills in the slammer."

"You're very comforting, Ollie."

"Just giving you a teensy bit of the police officer's perspective. It's so rare to have the teachable moment with a journalist. Seriously, I'm glad you didn't pull the trigger on Fredericks. A chest wound or something wouldn't be a problem in a self-defense argument, but the double head shot at close range is generally frowned upon. Could have been *bookoo* problems for you. Some journalist would have hung you out to dry. Doesn't matter if the guy you shot was Stalin's meaner brother, they'd crucify you anyway."

Jake heard the bitterness in Ollie's voice. The wound was still open.

"Okay, Ollie, you've heard my story. Now I want yours. How'd I end up here? Who found me out in the middle of nowhere?"

"An ambulance got you here. I found you."

"You? No. How?"

"I kept you alive till the EMTs took over. In fact, you owe me a shirt. I ripped it to shreds making bandages to stop the bleeding. You're lucky it was a clean shirt. Last week was wash week. You owe me dinner. You owe me a freezer full of Häagen-Dazs. In fact, you owe me a house in the suburbs with the mortgage paid off."

"I'll buy you a burger at Lou's and we'll call it even."

"Throw in onion rings and a shake and you got a deal."

"Since you apparently have no intention of ever answering my question, Ollie, I may as well just say thanks. I owe you."

"Hey, when other reporters were lynching me, you helped save my career and you saved my family from hell on earth, or at least you cut the hell short. Saving your life was probably the highlight of mine. Don't mention it. As for your question, how I found you, there's a simple answer."

"You want me to guess, is that it?"

"Okay, okay, keep your pants on...uh, keep your cute little smock on. The truth is, a week ago I put a bird dog on your car."

"A bird dog?"

"An electronic gadget that emits a silent pulse. It's on a set frequency. I've got the mother device. It gives a direction and an approximate distance based on the strength of the pulse. When I checked and found you were way out in the boondocks, I thought something was wrong. You've been Mr. Investigator, and I figured you weren't out fishing. Not for fish anyway. It was a hunch. I called and told

Rebecca I wouldn't be home for dinner, then I took off after the trace."

"You missed dinner for me, Ollie?"

"Yeah. The further we go, the more of a hero I come out, huh?"

"But how'd you find me in the woods?"

"Well, the bird dog got me to your car, and then I saw the Volvo. Of course, I didn't know whose it was. So, I pulled my peacemaker and went in the cabin. I saw some odds and ends, then came back out and studied the broken porch light. I poked around with a flashlight. Saw ground that looked like it had taken some bullets, several Magnum shells. Major bad omen. Tracks went some different directions, but I followed the only sets of tracks with three different footprints, which I assumed were you being followed by a couple of goons."

"You got that right."

"It wasn't easy tracking, especially in the underbrush, but between the three of you it was doable. I kept listening, but there was nothing. The bread crumbs led me to Fredericks, and I thought, this guy looks like a meteorite hit him. His back and neck weren't at the right angles. Man, you wasted him. I assume the beating was your work, right? Everything that preceded the bullets?"

Jake nodded.

"Not bad for a pantywaist reporter. Remind me not to get you aggravated. The man was probably relieved when the bullets came. Mercy killing, isn't that what we call it now? Anyway, the crime scene was a detective's paradise. The footprints, the gunshots, the flashlight, this crushed and executed guy in a business suit, carrying federal ID. I formed about a half dozen hypotheses, but I knew even if he got you, the other goon must still be out there somewhere. He wouldn't have left his car behind.

"I turn off my flashlight so I can't be used for target practice, and I just listen. After thirty seconds, I hear this sound. Like nothing I've ever heard before. It was eerie, like a deep voice whispering in the darkness, beckoning me over. Gives me the shivers just thinking about it. Everybody tells me it must have been you or Charlie moaning, but when I got to you twenty seconds later, you were both unconscious. And it wasn't like any moan I ever heard. Anyway, whatever it was, it saved your life. Charlie could have lasted the night, bless his heart, but you wouldn't have lasted another five minutes. That's what the doctors tell me. Did you hear how much blood they pumped into you?"

"No."

"Lots. I think it was four units, at least. Did you know you were in ICU till just a few hours ago? Yeah. They said you couldn't afford to lose any more blood. But I still don't know why you didn't. The blood had soaked through your bandages and it was seeping out like crazy. The doctor said if that cut hadn't had a lot of pressure applied against it, and some fresh bandages, it would have been your last hurrah. Even then, the ambulance wasn't a minute too soon. I had a portable phone on me so I didn't even have to get to the car radio. I called as soon as I slowed down the bleeding. I'm hoping a cellular phone company will feature me in a commercial or something."

Jake tried to recall what had happened in the darkness. All he could remember was the strange combination of regret for a life of missed opportunities, and peace and anticipation about a better life beyond. For a moment, he thought he could recall something else, someone else out there in the darkness. He must just be remembering Ollie hovering over him in his semiconscious state. Ollie grabbing hold of his arm and talking in a strange voice.

"I guess I should confess to you that it wasn't really kosher for me to put the bird dog on your car. You could probably sue me. I assume you won't, since it saved your life."

"I'll think about it. Maybe some time if you tell me your orangutan story, and it's good enough, I'll forget you invaded my privacy. But what made you decide to put the tracer on in the first place?"

"Call it a hunch, intuition, fate, I don't know. I just got suspicious that day in the park blocks when you lied to me about why you thought organized crime could be in on this. To tell you the truth, someone else at the department had suggested that, but I didn't tell you, partly because I couldn't, and even if I could have it just seemed too improbable. In any case I knew I hadn't mentioned it to you, and unless you were holding something back from me, why would you even think of it? When you lied to me I knew something was wrong. So I put the bird dog on your car myself, an hour after our stroll in the park."

"It was that obvious I was lying?"

"Let's just say you wouldn't be my first choice for an undercover agent. To tell you the truth, I was a little surprised. My experience with journalists is that they're darn good liars."

"Sorry to disappoint you," Jake said, slightly stung by his lack of cover up prowess.

"Don't be too sorry, Jake. If you'd been a better liar, you'd be dead. The only lying you'd be doing would be out in the woods next to a dead hit man, with another trying to crawl like a slug through a soaked forest with his hands and feet tied like a roped calf, eating moss and beetles for nourishment." Ollie enjoyed the imagery. "So maybe there is a payoff for telling the truth. Or for being a rotten liar."

"I'll keep that in mind."

"Jake, I've got something else to tell you."

"Yeah? Hot dogs two for a buck down on Sixth street?"

"No, it's serious. Real serious. As of this morning, I know who killed your friends."

"What?"

"We're still doing follow up, but we've got a confession."

"Tell me, Ollie, who?"

"Nobody you know. It wasn't your phony FBI agents, as you probably figured out by now. Early this morning we got a call from a psychiatrist. You do know him. A Dr. Scanlon."

"Scanlon. Yeah? Why'd he call you?"

"Because he's required by law to report knowledge of a felony committed by one of his patients. He wasn't absolutely sure, but the indications were very strong. Enough that I could order we bring in his patient for questioning. He denied everything, but he was awfully nervous and sometimes downright weird. There was enough doubt that I got an order to run his fingerprints and take a blood test.

"We did the blood test and ran a rush on it in the lab while I stalled the guy. I figured he'd bolt if we let him go. Three hours later we got the results. The genetic fingerprints, the DNA from the hair follicle we found under the Suburban? Perfect match with our suspect. Conclusive. One in ten billion."

"No kidding. Great work, Ollie."

"We had him nailed. But until they confess there's a lot of info we still don't have. And you know how I hate to be in the dark. So I got a little creative."

"Creative?"

"Yeah, I told him we knew everything, so he may as well admit it. I said we knew he was wearing blue sweat pants, carrying a hacksaw with a brand new red twenty-four-tooth Snap On hacksaw blade. I told him how he was lying under the Suburban, that he moved from one side to the other, and caught his beard when he brushed against the undercarriage. That he was nervous and shaky and made a lot of noise sawing the thing, and kept looking back and forth to see if anyone was watching. I even showed him my saw blade, you know the one I used when I timed the cut job? Still had it in my desk, hoping for a chance like that. You should have seen the look in his eyes when I showed him that blade. He knew for a fact we had a witness who saw the whole thing, and somehow we'd even found his blade. I never said that, mind you, but I think that may be what he concluded."

Jake looked at Ollie with feigned disapproval, unsuccessfully masking his admiration.

"Hey, it's not my fault if he jumped to conclusions. Anyway, suddenly he just gave up. The floodgates opened. He almost seemed relieved to talk about it, like he was in group therapy or something."

Jake tried to imagine Ollie as a therapist, but gave up quickly.

"Oh, and guess where the perp works?"

"Don't have a clue."

"Regent's."

"No kidding?"

"Yeah, he probably gets his whole wardrobe there, blue sweat pants and all, with an employee discount."

"So what exactly did he end up telling you?"

"Everything. An hour's worth. Just finished with him at noon. Here's the condensed version. His mother was in a coma over at Lifeline. The doctor, I forget his name, came and told him Mom had died. Well, apparently she really hadn't, at least not by the most popular definitions of death. I'm in homicide and I was naive enough to think death was death, but after a conversation with a doctor this morning, now I know better. Anyway, she wasn't a total flatline, but she was an organ donor, and they wanted to use her heart or kidney or something for some important guy waiting in the wings.

"Our buddy, the perp, was wiped out after hearing his mother had died. He took a walk in the hospital and happened to see Mom's doctor from a distance. He had a few things he wanted to ask, so he followed him. Well, apparently the doctor ended up slinking off to your friend's office, which of course is off the beaten path from the main hospital. It was night, so this guy had a pretty easy time tailing him.

"Something seemed suspicious to him. He's not the trusting sort anyway. So he eavesdropped at the door. He heard the good doctors discussing the fact that somebody was doing the transplant on the rich guy that very minute, loading in Mrs. Dalinger's heart, and that the rich guy's lawyer would be paying them off within a few days. Like $200,000 apiece, with maybe another $100,000 going to a middle man. And, between us, I don't think they were going to report it on their Form 1040."

Jake stared at the hallway beyond his open door.

"Sorry, Jake. I know he was your friend. I hate to be the one to tell you all this."

"Between Sutter and Marsdon and Finney's notes to Doc, this isn't all new. But I kept hoping there was some other explanation. What happened next?"

"Well, the perp waited around a corner till they both came out of the office, and when he saw your friend, he recognized him immediately from years ago."

"What do you mean?"

"You're not going to believe it."

"Try me."

"Four years ago this guy took in his wife or live-in girlfriend, or whoever, to get an abortion. Later she committed suicide, and the guy blamed the doctor that gave her the abortion. And guess who the doctor was? Your buddy. He'd seen him up close when he'd assaulted him at the clinic. Remember? This was our guy that Jeb gave me the police report on—marijuana tattoo on his right bicep and the whole nine yards.

"I haven't got him to admit it yet, but a hundred bucks says he's the same guy who came back that night and torched the clinic. Since he's up for murder, eventually he may not mind confessing to a little arson. Maybe I'll go pull the evidence in that case and figure out a way to convince him we had an eyewitness back then too."

Ollie rubbed his hands together. Jake sat quietly, not feeling the satisfaction he'd anticipated at the murderer getting nailed.

"Anyway, when our guy realized it was the same doctor, he flipped. He couldn't handle it. He felt like your friend had killed his kid, ruined his marriage, drove his wife to suicide, and now he'd topped it off by killing his mother. He felt like if justice had been done against him for killing the kid and his wife in the first place, he wouldn't still be around to kill his mom. Instead of jumping the doctors on the spot and getting hauled away, he decided to bide his time, make his plan.

"He became obsessed with justice. He started tailing your buddy, thought of different ways to kill him—guns and knives and poison and everything, but using a line of logic I'm not familiar with, instead of killing him outright, he decided to 'let fate decide his punishment.' That's when he cut the tie-rod ends."

"When?"

"Same day as the crash. Right where it was parked at the end of the driveway while you guys were inside watching the first quarter. He'd cased out the neighborhood a few Sundays and said no one ever walked around that time of day. If someone caught him under the car, he even had a contingency plan. Had a Frisbee with him and was going to say it landed under the Suburban and he was just getting it. He would have stuffed the hacksaw up under the car's undercarriage and no one would have suspected. But he didn't have to. Says he was in and out in ten minutes or less, just like I figured.

"This guy thought it might be a few days or even a week before the tie-rods broke. If no one was hurt, fine. He'd live with that. If someone in Doc's family died, then, in his weird kind of thinking, he would accept that as the judgment on Dr. Lowell, sort of a just retribution for Doc killing his child and wife and mother. The guy needs a shrink, that's for sure.

"Actually, he felt really sorry someone besides Doc got killed. He was surprised to see all three of you pile into Doc's car."

Jake gave a questioning look.

"Yeah, his car was parked down the street. He followed you to and from the pizza place just in case something happened. He saw the whole thing. In fact, he was so upset he pulled over to the first phone and called an ambulance. The guy may be a fruitcake, but I have to tell you, I feel for him. He's pathetic, and he's been through hell. He flipped. You know me. I rarely have sympathy for the perp. This guy's just a real sad case."

"What's his name, Ollie?"

"No one you'd know."

"Humor me."

Ollie took out his pad. "Name is...Clay Dalinger."

"Tall dark-haired guy with a beard?"

"Yeah. How'd you know that?"

"I met him in Dr. Scanlon's office."

"No kidding. Small world."

"Yeah, small world."

Jake lay there thinking about lanky long-faced Clay in his old Levis, sitting in Scanlon's office. He pictured him wearing some blue sweats and probably those same old Reeboks, crawling under Doc's Suburban. Hadn't he even said he worked in a store? Jake marveled he'd been right there a few feet from the guy he was looking for, and the thought never dawned on him. He recalled that slow self-tortured voice. "I always remember the date," Clay had said. He thought of Clay's wife swallowing the bottle of pills. Above all, he remembered him say, "I lost Janet because of the abortion."

Clay had lost his Janet, whom he'd talked into an abortion. For that alone, Jake felt a strange link to this pitiful man, despite what he'd done to his friends. What was that Clay had said to Jake? "Tell the men they lie to you. They lie to your wife and you don't find out till it's too late." And that last inexplicable statement in that hollow tear-drained voice—"And they lie about your mother too."

"They lie about your mother too," Jake said aloud.

"What?" Ollie asked. He'd been quiet while Jake absorbed all that happened.

"Nothing, Ollie. Nothing. I'm really glad you found out. I'm just sorry it was Clay."

"Yeah. Poor guy seems pretty confused. But he's a goner. Even if some fancy lawyer talks him into unconfessing, we've got him cold with the DNA match. Regent's won't be holding his job."

A month ago Jake wanted to get his hands around this guy's throat. Now other images came to mind. The image of Hyuk, his Montagnard sidekick who lost sight of everything else in his thirst for vengeance. Both men had been robbed of three loved ones they should have been there to protect. Both felt there was one man to blame. Both risked everything to get revenge or enact justice or however it was they saw it. Clay, in his own pathetic way, succeeded. Jake still wondered if Hyuk had, remembering how he'd wished for his success at the time. Jake couldn't hate Clay, wrong as he'd been. It was hard to hate someone you understood.

"One thing still doesn't add up though." Ollie broke the silence.

"What's that?"

"The yellow note card that clued us in to everything in the first place."

"Did Clay send it?"

"Nope. Wasn't his fingerprint. And he says he doesn't know a thing about it. I told him somebody must have suspected him, probably a woman. He said no way. Then I showed him the yellow card. It really spooked him. Anyway, Jake, you and I've got more to talk about, and you need to rest. But you've got another visitor or two waiting and I promised I'd make way for them."

"If Charlie and his lawyer want to see me right now, I'm not in the mood."

Ollie chortled as he stepped out in the hallway and gestured. All of a sudden, Carly and Janet came bursting into the room. Carly got to Jake first, throwing her arms around him with reckless abandon, trying to hug him without squashing his bandaged left arm. His IV tubes were swinging in the wind.

"Oh, Daddy. I'm so glad you're okay." She was sobbing. Jake felt that if he died that moment he'd die happy just to have been called "Daddy" and be loved by his little girl.

Janet smiled, reaching out and squeezing his right hand with hers. Jake looked at her, still caring after all he'd done, and all he'd failed to do. He felt so different than the last time she'd visited him in a hospital.

Ollie watched from the doorway in silence. Tears came down three sets of cheeks huddled closely together on the bed. The nurse walked in the room past Ollie. Seeing the two women hovering over Jake she almost asked them to leave. But her eyes met Jake's, and instead she beckoned Ollie to step out with her, and gently shut the door.

Nearby, unheard by the momentarily deaf of the dark world, a strong other-worldly voice quoted an ancient prophet. "He will turn the hearts of the fathers to their children and the hearts of the children to their fathers."

* * *

Two weeks later Jake finally got his arm out of the sling and no longer needed to keep it wrapped. It was a relief just to take a shower with freedom and mobility. He found himself thanking God for little blessings that now seemed bigger than they'd ever been.

He sat down on a Friday to read the *One Minute Bible* Sue had given him. "The core of the Bible arranged in 365 daily readings," it said. He liked it. He could sit down with a cup of coffee, read for a minute, reread and underline. Then, like Clarence had showed him, he'd look up the surrounding context in his Bible.

"His" Bible was actually Finney's old one. Sue insisted he keep it. He'd sit back in his recliner and think about what he had read, then try to figure out how it could make his life different that day. Then he'd get down on his knees and pray for a few minutes. It seemed so odd at first. But it was growing on him.

Even some at the *Trib* most dismayed by his changed perspectives had to admit he seemed a more thoughtful person. Others came out of the woodwork, affirming him in unexpected ways. He was surprised at the people at the *Tribune* he never would have expected to have an interest in spiritual things.

Clarence was reading the *One Minute Bible* too, and they'd usually touch base some time during the day to talk about what they were reading. Clarence was calling Jake his "soul brother" and Jake liked the sound of it. He told him it was the first time he'd ever been interested in reading the Bible. Clarence said, "The sure way to get excited about a book is to get to know the author."

Sue had insisted Jake try out a dozen different music CDs she dropped by. Some just weren't his style, but others he enjoyed. When he asked Sue where he could get his own, she took him to an interesting place he'd never been—a Christian book store. He'd been back again and spent two hours looking over the books. He found himself listening to his new music as he shaved and dressed in the mornings, and again sometimes in the evenings, lights turned off and stereo turned up.

A few evenings a week Jake was home reading a bunch of Finney's books Sue had given him. He'd underline and scratch questions in the margins. It wasn't only interesting, it was surprisingly fun. He began to realize how much he'd neglected his intellect feeding on television, videos, newspapers, magazines, and trivial fiction. His mind had stagnated, become cluttered with trivia and politically correct buzzwords that substituted for thought. For the first time in years, maybe decades, his mind was being stretched. It felt good.

Jake found himself reading the newspaper less; it seemed to say the same things over and over. The same things would happen, just in different places with different names. But when he went to his Bible and the books he read in the evenings, there was always something new and surprising and challenging. They had a depth, a quality that could never be mined to exhaustion.

Jake wrote in his journal, *I feel like a sea captain learning for the first time to chart his course by the stars. Until now, I've tried to find my way by watching the clouds.*

But they came and went, changed direction on me, led me nowhere. It's good to finally have reference points that don't keep changing.

It was as if one foot was now in a different world, which made things a bit awkward in this one. But the awkwardness was more than compensated for by the peace and excitement. He'd begun to sense as never before the reality of two invisible realms, of the existence of good and evil that impregnated the earthly realm, showing up here and there in brave surrenders to conscience or cowardly violations of it. Some people at some moments seemed pregnant with heaven, others pregnant with hell. Such visitations in what used to be the moral bluriness of an ordinary day thrilled and alarmed him, leaving him at times greatly encouraged and at other times troubled and depressed.

As for his newfound joy of discovery, he hoped it would never end. His journal had always been self-talk, valuable but fatally limited to his self-understanding. Now it was more a daily letter to someone else, Someone beyond himself he could talk to and ask guidance from.

He'd written that morning, *I've kept going back to think about wonderful days with Finney in the past. Now I find myself thinking that perhaps the best days with him may still be in the future.*

Though he felt embarrassed to write it, even to someone who knew his every thought, he even dared to hope they'd one day explore heaven together as they'd explored the woods as boys. The little he'd heard about heaven so far sounded rather monotonous and boring compared to this world, but a man could hope for something more, couldn't he?

Finney. He knew how to live, and he knew how to die. Jake hadn't known how to do either. But he felt now he was taking his first toddler steps on the right road, headed the right direction. For some reason he thought of the reunion in Bangkok, sneaking up on Finney and asking, "What's up, bro?" Bro had a new and deeper meaning now. It sounded good.

"Maybe you're able to see me, Finn. I hope so. I think you'd get a kick out of all this."

I am getting a kick out of it, bro, said a voice from another world. *And so am I,* thought a towering figure standing guard next to Jake, but invisible to him. *And I too,* thought still Another who looked over them, taking delight in each, and in them all together.

Jake sat quietly at his desk. Unknown to him, Sandy watched him around the edge of her terminal, noticing his eyes land on a picture of Carly, a recent one with Jake standing next to her. She saw something different in his eyes now whenever they landed on the photo.

Sandy had been watching him carefully, sometimes disheartened, sometimes pleased, often amazed at the changes in her favorite columnist. More than once she'd stood up for him to colleagues engaged in newsroom chatter at his expense.

Sandy thought Jake might just be going through a phase, some overzealous religious response that would fade or taper off, as such things often did when reality set in and the world turned out to be no different than it had always been. Still, she would continue to watch him. She would see.

Jake's most recent in a series of controversies at the *Trib* was his column laying out the inside story of Clay Dalinger. He talked about the pain and rage men feel when their children are harmed by any violent act, including abortion. He wrote the column in direct response to the *Trib's* headline, "Anti-abortionist linked to murders of doctor and businessman." Jake said that was misleading, that he'd done thorough research (why hadn't anyone else?) and Clay Dalinger had never attended a single prolife rally or given a dime to a prolife cause. He wasn't even on anyone's mailing list. He wasn't an activist—he was just a man whose child had died.

Then he'd told the story of Hyuk. Jake hadn't defended Dalinger—the man had killed his two best friends. He simply pointed out how men can feel a burning compulsion to enact retribution against those who've violated loved ones they were meant to defend. Jake also related the irony of coming back from Vietnam twenty-five years ago and being called a "baby killer." And now, he said, those holding to the political ideals of the anti-war movement, including many journalists, were the very ones obscuring, denying, or defending the wholesale killing of babies in America.

"Perhaps it is time," Jake had said, "journalists actually take the moral high ground on this issue they've kidded themselves into believing they've occupied all along."

Jake's column pushed all the wrong buttons.

Some supported him, others disagreed but understood, still others issued a barrage of outrage and venom. They accused him of defending a murderer; they said he'd be responsible for any violent acts done by those reading his column. The abortion lobby and a coalition of feminist groups threatened to boycott the *Tribune* unless Jake was reprimanded and wrote a public apology in his column. Some of his fellow reporters called for his resignation. He'd been voted off the multicultural-ism committee, with only Clarence, Jess, and Misty voting to keep him on.

These were not easy days at work. It was a hurricane. But he felt as though he was in its eye, surrounded by wild, threatening winds, yet somehow centered and secure.

Jake was about to leave the *Trib* this Friday afternoon, ready for a most welcome weekend, when he was buzzed by Elaine at the front desk.

"Jake, there's a man here to see you. He says it's police business."

"Big guy, raspy voice, ketchup stains on his tie?"

"Yes, I think we're talking about the same fellow. Says his name is Elliot Ness."

"Tell him his badge means nothing in this building. I'll come down."

Ollie had taken some heat from his lieutenant for working too closely in the investigation with someone outside the precinct. So he told Jake they'd better not talk again until he and his partner wrapped some things up. Ollie had been tight-lipped since the day in the hospital, and to make it easier on him Jake hadn't made any contact. It had been a few weeks, and Jake missed the old redneck.

He put a few papers in his briefcase, packed in all the extra mail—"hate mail" and "love mail" and "not-too-sure-what-they-think-about-the-change-in-me mail," he now called it. With a springier step than usual, his mind on tonight's dinner at Janet and Carly's, he headed to the elevator.

He ducked down low on the first floor and sneaked over to the side of the reception counter where Ollie stood across from Elaine. He jumped up suddenly, punching Ollie in the stomach. Elaine let out a startled cry and Ollie rolled his eyes as if to say, "It takes more than that to scare me."

"Never sneak up on an armed man. You're lucky I have the steely nerves of Wyatt Earp, or you'd be looking down a gun barrel."

"I'll remember that. To what do I owe your visit to my turf, Marshal?"

"From what I've been hearing, thought this might be my last chance to visit you while you still worked here."

Elaine looked down uncomfortably. She'd told Jake how much she appreciated his recent columns. He felt a growing friendship with her, one he hoped he wouldn't be losing.

"No, I think I'll be around here for a long time, Ollie. I'm a newspaper man. I still love the place."

"One or two last turns in the case you should know about," Ollie said. "Let's take a walk."

February was taking its last strong stand before succumbing to the newness of March. Jake shivered and dug his hands deep in his coat

"What's up? Clay have an accomplice?"

"No. It's weirder."

"How so?" It was like old times, trying to get Ollie to spill it.

"Clay didn't murder Doc."

Jake stopped in his tracks and faced Ollie.

"What?"

"Oh, he tried to murder him. He cut the rods and put him in critical condition. But he didn't finish him off."

"What are you saying, Ollie?"

"You remember the doctor Clay said he followed to see your friend, you know, the one who was in on declaring his mother dead?"

"Yeah, I remember."

"Turned out to be Dr. Simpson."

"Simpson? You're kidding." Jake flashed back to their encounter in Doc's room, and two months later in the hallway outside ICU. "What about him?"

"Well, at first Clay didn't remember his name, but the next day we gave him a list of doctors and he picked him out. So, we started surveillance on Dr. Simpson. Figured he was probably the other doctor mentioned in the computer file note. Guess who we found out he had all kinds of connections with?"

Jake sighed. "Elvis? JFK?"

"Mary Ann, your buddy's secretary. Sums of money and important papers were exchanged. We ran background on Mary Ann, and it turns out she was a set up from day one. Doc's old secretary got a great job offer in another town, underwritten by money from the syndicate. She had no idea, of course. So Mary Ann applies and fills this sudden vacancy. Her real job was to make sure Dr. Lowell and Dr. Simpson and anyone else in the transplant business didn't pull any fast ones. Turns out she knew your phony FBI buddies. Works for the same organization, known for its retirement plans.

"We got our hands on some hot stuff, including a payoff Simpson took for bumping somebody else up the transplant list, just a few weeks after the deal with Clay's mother. Simpson and Mary Ann pulled it off themselves, even with your buddy gone. They came up with a plausible reason, no other doctors questioned Simpson's judgment, and he got his payoff."

Jake closed his eyes, waiting for his brain to catch up with Ollie's words.

"Mary Ann? And Simpson? Incredible."

"You haven't heard the most incredible part. See, Simpson didn't just bump a guy up the list. He provided the organ donor. Guess whose fresh heart was sold to our eager cash customer?"

A light turned on in Jake, but he didn't want to think it.

"Whose?"

"Your friend's. Dr. Lowell's."

Jake shook his head in amazement.

"See, once we got interested in Simpson, I started checking out nurses who worked with him. I have this way with the ladies, you know. Anyway, I hit the jackpot. Talked to a nurse named Robin Bender. Name sound familiar?"

"Not the last name, but I know Nurse Robin. Bumped into her twice at the hospital. Nervous type."

"Real nervous. She was super eager to talk, like she'd been waiting for somebody to ask her some questions. Felt guilty she hadn't said anything earlier. See, I'm there nosing around about Simpson related to the deal with Clay's mom. But now she's telling me this whole other story about how she was on duty the morning your friend died. She tells me one minute she's in there checking on your friend. She swears the tube was perfectly in place and he was totally unconscious from the drugs." Ollie made a dramatic pause.

"Less than five minutes later everybody was rushing to his room to revive him, but it was too late, he was already brain dead. Then she saw the air tube in your buddy's hand, and everyone said he must have pulled it. She said she couldn't believe that. No way. But the only one she saw go into the room between the time he was alive and dead was, guess who?"

"Simpson?"

"None other. Given all the other stuff we know about Simpson, it makes a powerful case. There's more, but let me fill you in on Nurse Robin."

"About what?"

"I feel like I should work up to it. I hate to just come right out and say it, you know..."

"Ollie!"

"Okay, okay. She's the one that sent you the yellow card."

"What?"

"Yep. Red fingernail polish and all."

"But...how did she know about Clay cutting the tie-rods?"

"That's just it. She didn't. Didn't even have a clue."

"I don't get it. Then why the note?"

"She wasn't talking about the car accident. She was talking about the accident with your friend's air hose. That's what she meant when she said, 'It wasn't an accident.'"

"You're kidding."

"The whole time we didn't get it. See, she was so uptight about this thing, she wasn't thinking about the car wreck, she was just thinking about the accident with her patient supposedly pulling out his air hose.

"But I still don't get the note."

"Robin was terrified to come forward. She just wanted someone to come ask her questions so it wouldn't seem like squealing. See, she didn't actually see it happen, but gut-level she felt sure something was wrong. She was afraid to go to anybody at the hospital, but she knew about you from your column. She figured when she sent you the note, you'd go to the police and then we'd come ask her questions. Well, nobody ever showed up till I came in three months later asking about Simpson."

"I never told you, Ollie, but I bumped into her just before Christmas. We came really close to talking, but I wrote her off as a basket case and got distracted. By Simpson in fact." Jake stopped to think.

"Ollie, what you're telling me is if we had really known what the note was talking about..."

"Then we would never have known Clay tried to kill Doc. We would have found out the nurse's suspicions about Simpson, but we wouldn't have had him. He would have denied it, and we'd have left it there. We wouldn't have all the other pieces to the puzzle. If we understood her note, we'd have never gotten either killer. Sometimes it pays off to not get it, huh?"

Almost seems providential.

They kept walking, Jake considering how incredibly close the truth came to being buried. Why wasn't her note more clear? He was just glad it wasn't. It had happened again. Things were so different than they appeared. What seemed to be true so often wasn't.

"I haven't finished on Simpson," Ollie said. "I took him in, showed him what we had, right down to the financial records and names and places and times he met with Mary Ann. Then I think maybe he misunderstood me to say we had a witness, a nurse who saw him pull Dr. Lowell's tube. After he sat there choking for a few minutes, I suggested he might get some leniency if he coughed up some names. Like every name he's known since kindergarten. I kept reminding him he didn't have to answer any questions without a lawyer, but he kept talking. What was I supposed to do, gag him? The mention of possible leniency made him real cooperative. Confessed to everything, including some things we didn't even suspect. Even admitted pulling your buddy's air tube, but then, he knew we already knew that, so we didn't act real surprised.

"Know what he said to me, Jake? This will really frost you. He said he was acting in your friend's best interests, death with dignity and all that. He said Doc probably wouldn't have recovered and with his neck injuries likely would have been handicapped anyway. He knew Doc would have wanted his organs to go to someone else. He said doctors have to make tough decisions all the time, and there were other people who needed the hospital bed, and Doc's heart could save someone else's life. I told him I was deeply moved by his compassion, that in my book he was sort of a cross between Florence Nightingale and Mother Teresa."

"What's next for Simpson?"

"We'll pit him and Mary Ann against each other, get him to incriminate her, then cut a deal with whichever can deliver some bigger fish to us, probably Mary Ann. Between her and your friend Charlie, we might reel in a marlin or two."

Jake walked quietly, gazing at the patches of sidewalk not covered by snow, studying the cracks he'd stared at so many times before. Just when he thought he'd finally come to terms with all that had happened, it kept getting bigger. Doc was taken out by two men. One was paying him back for killing his child, wife, and mother. The other was treating him exactly as Doc had treated Clay's mother, and rationalizing it just as he had. What was that Bible verse he'd read the other day? "Whatever a man plants, he also reaps."

Jake thought about Mary Ann. No wonder she could afford such nice clothes and jewelry! He shuddered at how close he'd come to getting in bed with her, literally and perhaps figuratively. Why had she tried to seduce him? His ego hadn't considered anything but the obvious, but now he realized she had an angle. Who knows what he might have told her that would help the wrong people, or how she might have steered him the wrong direction.

Thank you, Lord, for getting me away from Mary Ann that night. And thanks, Finney. For once, I listened.

"Something else I'm following up on now. You know the rash of murders that were holding us back from this case? Some of them were your usual street killings, but remember me telling you about this group of murders with no robberies or apparent motive?"

"Yeah?"

"Well, some of them may be related to this case."

"Really?"

"We suspected the murders weren't random, and we knew some of them were committed with the same gun. But we couldn't find any link between the victims, so there was no way to come up with suspects. But something Simpson said turned my wheels. So I followed a hunch and did some cross-checks. And guess what?"

"No clue."

"In the last four months, three people on the waiting list for vital organ transplants at Lifeline have been murdered. It appears while your friend and Simpson were tinkering with the list on the inside, someone else was adjusting it their own way. The doctors had no idea this was happening. I don't think so anyway. But someone had a plan. There's more than one way for a wealthy unprincipled person to move up the list. I don't know where this will lead us, but I can't believe it's a coincidence."

"Incredible."

"Which leads me to my last item. When I ran the cross-check and hit pay dirt, I thought of something else. So I pulled some strings and got hold of a different list, ran a different check. Three other victims—all yuppies—and no apparent motive for their murders. None of them were waiting for transplants, but they had one thing in common. You heard of Life-Givers, the organ repository in town that recruits organ donors through TV and newspaper ads and lectures?"

"I've seen their ads in the *Trib.*"

"Well, our three yuppies, with no other known connection between them, had all signed up with Life-Givers as organ donors within the last year. And they were killed in such a way that vital organs were still intact, with someone—we don't know who in any of the three cases—calling 911 immediately."

"You mean..."

"Why not? You need to get your vital organ sooner? There's at least three ways. Bribe some doctors and get your name bumped up the list. Decrease the number of recipients ahead of you. Increase the number of donors. It's supply and demand, right? We can't prove anything yet. But if I could get hold of Life-Giver's donor sign-up list, complete with home addresses, you can be sure someone else could too."

Jake looked at Ollie, making sure his revelations were finally over. They walked a ways further in the wet silence of the sidewalk.

"Amazing, isn't it? You've got good people donating organs and getting transplants, then greed gets its hand on it and turns it into a nightmare. I guess anything, no matter how good, can be corrupted." Jake mulled it over.

"You know, Ollie, I used to think Finney was overreacting to all the changes in this country. But now I think he was right about a lot of things. We say you can't go by the old standards of right and wrong any more, so we've left everyone to decide for themselves what's right and wrong. Well, it isn't working. It just isn't working."

Ollie shrugged. "You're telling me? Remember what I do for a living."

"Yeah. Right. You know, when organized crime first came into the picture I thought, these guys are dangerous because they break all the rules. But now I'm not so sure. Maybe the greatest danger isn't when the rules get broken. Maybe it's when the rules get changed. Once they're changed, you can follow the new rules and think you're doing the right thing. And all the time your new truth is just the old lies. You tell yourself it's okay because the standards have changed, but if the standards mean anything at all, they don't change. They can't. I mean, a yard is still thirty-six inches long, even if everybody says otherwise, right?"

"Sounds like you've been doing some heavy thinking, Socrates."

"Yeah, I guess so. I know we're all biased, and we're going to be driven by our biases. But we need to make sure our biases are based on truth. That's what I want to do, Ollie. With whatever time I have left in this world, I want to find the truth and then build my biases on truth instead of just whatever society happens to be saying. I've been thinking about something Jesus said—'the truth will set you free.' I want to pursue the truth no matter where it takes me. I don't care anymore whether something is liberal or conservative. I only care whether it's true or false."

He paused, then added, "If I'm going to be part of a conspiracy of shared values, I want to make sure they're the right values. I don't want to be caught short come deadline."

Ollie registered surprise and lack of comprehension, and he looked at Jake's eyes as if examining someone for a concussion.

After a few minutes more silence, Ollie said, "Jake, I'm going to have to tell Dr. Lowell's wife about this latest stuff. I hate to just call her. You want to go with me to her place?"

"Yeah, sure." Jake didn't want to go, but he knew he should. Betsy had been shocked and humiliated by all that had come out about Doc. He needed to be there for her with this latest shock, to help however he could. It was his responsibility. No matter how unpleasant, he wouldn't shirk it.

Jake stopped at a pay phone to call Janet and Carly, telling them something urgent had materialized and he couldn't come tonight. He said if it was okay he'd be there tomorrow, Saturday, and wanted to spend all afternoon with them. Janet was disappointed he couldn't come tonight but said she understood. Both she and Carly would look forward to tomorrow.

CHAPTER THIRTY-FIVE

J ake arrived at Janet and Carly's around noon, with nachos, salsa, a box of Lemon Zinger tea, pink carnations, and a Bogart movie. After the movie Jake helped Carly with her journalism project and listened to her first run of an upcoming speech. He was impressed. She had her father's skills in crafting sentences and her mother's warmth in relating to an audience.

The HIV hadn't produced any noticeable effects yet, and the doctor was optimistic that the baby, due in June, would remain unaffected. Carly was considering her options, whether to raise the child or give him up for adoption. She hadn't decided, but carrying this little person, being responsible not only for her welfare but for his, was maturing Carly, deepening her. In the face of all this teenage girl's challenges, the baby had become a comfort to her, a source of strength. So, too, had her father, who promised her he'd support and help whether she chose adoption or single parenting.

Janet baked her legendary cinnamon rolls. The warm, sweet, doughy smell permeated the apartment until Jake paced the kitchen floor in anticipation of his first bite. Gooey and mouthwatering, he'd forgotten how delicious they were. He savored them, putting down three of them with two large glasses of cold milk. He ate to the point of feeling delightfully sick, like he had as a little boy.

The three played 221b Baker Street in the late afternoon, and now, at half past five, sprawled out in the living room, talking and relaxing. The phone rang, and Carly answered.

"It's for me. I'll take it in my room."

She looked at her parents sitting on the couch next to each other and flashed them a deliberate approving smile.

Janet reached over to Jake, picking off a stray piece of cinnamon roll. Her hand touched his shoulder right where Mary Ann's had. Jake remembered the lure of the forbidden he'd felt then but found himself enjoying much more the warmth and familiarity he felt now.

Jake and Janet talked about Betsy. Janet had called her four hours earlier, right after Jake filled her in on last night. She'd called Sue too, and they already had plans to spend tomorrow afternoon at Betsy's. Sunday afternoons were especially tough, and though tomorrow would be fifteen weeks since the accident, for Betsy it promised to be one of the toughest yet.

Jake was surprised his concern for Betsy ran as deep as it did. He'd always left Janet to do the caring for the both of them, but now he thought about writing Betsy a note, taking her to lunch, and maybe spending some time with her kids. Especially Molly. Maybe he could take her and Carly out, do something special with them.

"You know, I keep thinking about Mayhew, using that Nazi gun to blow away Sutter," Jake said. "This whole crazy episode was like the Nazi doctors revisited. Choosing some people to live instead of others. Using human beings for their spare parts. Exploiting women and children, all in the name of medicine and social evolution. Getting power and money from the whole thing. Doc got what he gave. So did Sutter. Executed by a Nazi gun firing a Nazi bullet. Trigger pulled by a modern Nazi. I was reading the other day about doing to others what you'd want them to do to you. Well, Doc and Sutter ended up getting treated just like they treated others."

Jake looked at Janet.

"People don't really change, do they? Times don't change that much. What's right and what's wrong doesn't really change at all."

She gazed back attentively. He'd forgotten how easy she was to talk to. Jake took a deep breath.

"Janet, I'm going to ask you something, but I don't want you to think I've gone wacko or anything, okay?"

Janet nodded.

"I was thinking about doing something, and..." He took a second run at it. "Well, actually, tomorrow morning...I was thinking of going to Sue and Finney's church."

He watched her try to hide her surprise, and he quickly groped for a rational explanation.

"Little Finn's been asking me, and it's hard to say no to the guy. And, anyway, I guess I was wondering if...I was wondering if you'd be willing to come with me."

"Jake. I haven't been to church for twenty years, except for—"

"Weddings and funerals. Yeah, I know. Me too. I've decided I should though. But I'm a little...nervous, I guess. It sounds funny, but I feel like I need you to be there with me. I understand if you'd rather not. It's no problem, really."

"Oh, no, Jake, I'd love to. Really."

"I was at Mom's this morning," Jake said, piling up one surprise on another. "I spoke to the old folks about journalism. You know," Jake suddenly lit up, "there was a guy there, Jim, they call him 'Uncle Jim,' who used to write for the *Chicago Tribune*. He's in his nineties. He was a war correspondent in occupied Europe. He chased down news in London during the air raids. Are you ready for this? He interviewed Winston Churchill. Fascinating guy. I thought, what do I have to tell these people about the newspaper business? They should just listen to Uncle Jim! He edits this little newspaper just for the Vista Manor. It's great. Features different people there, like this guy who flew a World War I bomber. World War I. Can you imagine? And this woman, Pat, who taught in a one-room schoolhouse before the depression, and over half her graduates went on to college. Mom introduced me to both of them. Then Jim sat with Mom and me for a little tea time afterward. I think he's got a crush on her."

Janet raised her eyebrows and laughed. "Mom must have been in heaven being at the same table with her pride and joy *and* a potential suitor!"

"Well, she was a lot perkier than I've seen her in years, I'll tell you that. I admitted to her something I did when I was ten years old. Smoking out in the shed with Doc and Finney. You should have seen the look on her face. Anyway, I was going to tell you, I invited Mom to come with me to church tomorrow. So I could pick you up at 9:30, and we could go get her together. If that's okay, I mean."

Janet caught herself staring at Jake. "Of course that's okay. That's fine, Jake."

"Well, great."

Jake rubbed his hands on his pantlegs, relieved to have finally asked the question and pleased at Janet's answer.

"It's not exactly a wild and crazy date, a guy asking you to go to church with him and his mother, but..."

Janet laughed. She hadn't heard Jake say *date* for twenty years.

Jake paused, then said, "I've thought about this church thing, and it just seems right. It's something I've made up my mind to do."

Wait till I ask her to go with me for counseling with Dr. Scanlon. Then she'll know I've lost it.

"I'm glad, Jake. I've been feeling a need for something too. Life's been hard and...pretty cold. I worry about Carly all the time. I keep thinking there has to be something to help get me through it, something better than my way."

"I took Alan Weber to lunch a couple of days ago, you know, the pastor at Finney's church? It was really a great time. I can see why Finney liked him so much."

Janet tried to remember Jake ever saying something kind about a pastor. She couldn't.

"Alan invited me to some men's thing next Saturday, something called Promise Keepers. I don't exactly know what it is, but I said I'd go. It's funny. I actually want to go. Maybe I'll ask Clarence to come too."

Janet nodded, not knowing what to say. She just looked at Jake.

"Janet...do you think Carly would come with us? To church I mean?"

"I think so. If her dad asked her, I think she'd go just about anywhere."

"Okay, I'll ask her."

He started to get up, then turned back to Janet.

"How 'bout you and I go to Lou's for dinner?"

"That sounds great."

Janet smiled and with a mischievous look reached for her purse and pulled out a quarter.

"Call it. Loser pays." She flipped the coin in the air.

"Tails."

The quarter fell on the coffee table, bounced up and wobbled for one uncertain moment, then fell tails up.

Janet smiled. "You win. I pay."

"No." Jake's voice was firm. "I win, so it's my choice, and I choose to buy you dinner. I owe you a lot of dinners. It's been a long time, Janet."

Janet looked Jake in the eyes, and for the first time she could remember, he returned her look without hesitation, like a man no longer proud and no longer ashamed.

"Jake?"

"Yeah?"

"Lou's isn't that far. I feel like walking."

"It's over a mile. And it's cold." Jake looked out the window. "Still snowing out there."

"That's okay. We'll bundle up. It'll be fun."

Janet, despite the wrinkles, looked younger and more alive than Jake had seen her in years. He'd kept looking at her all day. It was as though he could see through her eyes into her soul.

"Yeah. Walking sounds good. It'll give you time to tell me any dreams you've had lately." Jake grinned.

"You're asking for trouble. You're just lucky I haven't been writing them all down, mister!"

"I'll be right with you. I need to talk to Carly about tomorrow."

Jake stood by Carly's open bedroom door as she was hanging up the phone. Janet was reaching in the closet for her coat, and had a clear view of Carly's room at the far end of the hall. Janet could see the big new maroon scrapbook Carly was using to collect Jake's newest columns. Jake was asking her something. Carly looked surprised, then nodded and reached out to hug him. The image of father and daughter hugging grew blurry in Janet's eyes.

A few minutes later, buried under thick coats, hoods up, Jake and Janet went down the apartment steps and out to the sidewalk. They walked the street alone. The fresh snow was undisturbed, every footprint on virgin ground, every step as if it were the first step there had ever been.

They'd walked but a short distance when the man reached out his hand and the woman took it, leaning against his side. The two coats seemed joined at the cuffs. They thought no one noticed. They were wrong.

Far away, in another place, hands applauded and mouths voiced approval that could be heard only by the most sensitive ears on earth, and even then only as whispers in the wind. One of the voices would have been familiar to the couple, had they been able to hear it.

And very near, from a second story apartment window, a seventeen-year-old girl with a silly smile and teary eyes, her hand just that moment sensing the movement of life within her, watched the couple as they walked around the corner.

Even after they disappeared, the girl continued to gaze at their footprints in the snow.

This is a work of fiction. While it contains many factual details which are the product of careful research, it intermingles these with fictitious settings and persons. The newspaper portrayed in the novel is a composite of various newspapers around the country. It is not a depiction of any single paper. While many of the things described at the newspaper have in fact happened, they have involved different people in different places, and have been adapted and interwoven. All of the book's characters are likewise fictitious.

As to those events and dialogues in the afterlife, it should go without saying that these are fiction! The information, direct and indirect, Scripture provides us about the world to come is substantial, with just enough detail to help us envision it, but not so much to make us think we can fully comprehend it. I believe God expects us to recognize the limits and flaws of our imaginations, but to utilize them nonetheless. To his followers Jesus says heaven, not earth, is our real home. That eternal home, which has always been a source of great encouragement and daily perspective to God's people, has in the modern western world become so eclipsed by the here and now that many believers virtually never give a thought to the realm where their true citizenship resides. But what could be more natural and healthy than to think about home and the relationships and sustaining values it represents? As C. S. Lewis said, "It is since Christians have largely ceased to think of the other world that they have become so ineffective in this one."

Secular bookstores are now burgeoning with accounts of afterdeath experiences and interactions with angelic beings, many of them unbiblical and misleading, some fatally so. If those who believe the Scriptures fail to reverently exercise our God-given imaginations where the Bible opens the door for us to do so, we will leave all portrayals of the eternal realm in the hands of those unconcerned with fidelity to God's Word. This, it seems to me, justifies the inherent risks in attempting to portray the other side of death in a way more consistent with biblical truth.

I have therefore taken biblically revealed truths and developed (hopefully not distorted) them in a speculative (hopefully not reckless) fashion. I have carefully studied the biblical accounts of the afterlife and sought only to include concepts and portrayals which conform to or at least do not violate any biblical teaching. While much herein is extrabiblical, I have sought never to be unbiblical, though people's different backgrounds and interpretations will naturally result in considerable disagreements.

While the experience that awaits us will inevitably prove many of my afterdeath depictions inaccurate in the details, and all of them woefully incomplete, I have sought to fuel and govern my imagination by the Scriptures. To the extent I have failed in this task, I ask the reader's—and more importantly, God's—understanding and forgiveness.

It is of paramount importance that the reader's mind and imagination be submitted to the Word of God as its sole and final authority. This novel lays no claim whatsoever to divine revelation. I have received no such revelation, and even if I claimed to have done so, the only proper response would be to skeptically scrutinize it in light of the Scriptures.

Not only do I not claim infallibility, I specifically and emphatically claim fallibility. Any readers who take issue with my portrayals should not be distracted from contemplating the realities of eternity but all the more encouraged to study the Scriptures to determine what is true (Acts 17:11).

The publisher and author would love to hear your comments about this book. *Please contact us at:* www.mpbooks.com

About the Author

Randy Alcorn is the founder and director of Eternal Perspective Ministries (EPM). Prior to this he served as a pastor for fourteen years. He has spoken around the world and has taught on the adjunct faculties of Multnomah Bible College and Western Seminary in Portland, Oregon.

Randy is the best-selling author of eighteen books (over one million in print), including the novels *Deadline, Dominion, Lord Foulgrin's Letters* and the 2002 Gold Medallion winner *Safely Home.* His ten nonfiction works include *Money, Posessions and Eternity, Prolife Answers to Prochoice Arguments, In Light of Eternity, The Treasure Principle, The Grace and Truth Paradox, The Purity Principle* and *The Law of Rewards.* His two latest books, *Why Pro Life?* and *Heaven: Resurrected Living on the New Earth,* will be out in the fall of 2004.

Randy has written for many magazines and produces the popular periodical *Eternal Perspectives.* He's been a guest on over 450 radio and television programs including Focus on the Family, the Bible Answer Man, Family Life Today and Truths that Transform.

The father of two married daughters, Randy lives in Gresham, Oregon, with his wife and best friend, Nanci. He enjoys hanging out with his family, biking, tennis, research and reading.

Feedback on books and inquiries regarding publications and other matters can be directed to Eternal Perspective Ministries (EPM), 2229 East Burnside #23, Gresham, OR 97030, 503-663-6481. EPM can also be reached at info@epm.org. For information on EPM or Randy Alcorn, and for resources on missions, persecuted church, prolife issues, and matters of eternal perspective, see www.epm.org.

The Next Page-Turner from Bestselling Author
RANDY ALCORN

DECEPTION

a novel

RANDY
ALCORN

Chapter one from Randy Alcorn's forthcoming novel,
Deception,
due in stores September 2006

*"My eyes have been trained to examine faces and not their trimmings.
It is the first quality of a criminal investigator that he should see
through a disguise."* –Sherlock Holmes, The Hound of the Baskervilles

The phone rang at 2:59 a.m. I know this because three enormous red digits
assaulted my eyes.

I knocked the phone off the cradle, then groped for it in the darkness. My
tongue was stuck.

"Hello?" The voice was deep and croaky. "Anyone there?"

It's not enough that I pick up the phone at 2:59 a.m.? I have to say something too?

"Chandler?"

I nodded my head, admitting it.

"Detective Ollie Chandler?"

"Yeah," I groaned.

"You didn't answer your cell phone," he said, sounding like a hacksaw cutting a rain gutter. "You awake?"

"No. But you may as well finish the job."

"In bed?"

"Nope. Mowin' the lawn. Who died?"

Welcome to my world.

I've been waiting all my life to get good news from a 3:00 a.m. phone call.
It's been a fifty-six-year wait; a wait of Red Sox and White Sox proportions.

Many people imagine middle-of-the-night phone calls mean someone's
been killed. I don't imagine it. That's just how it is.

Jake Woods tells me there's a God who's in charge of the universe. Tell the
truth, I'm not convinced. But if there is, I'd appreciate it if He would schedule
murders during day shift.

"The victim's Jimmy Ross," said the voice, which only then I realized
belonged to Sergeant Jim Seymour. Sarge worked day shift. I pictured him sitting home in his underwear. It was not a pretty picture.

"Drug dealer."

I didn't shed a tear. They say cops are cynical. Okay, to me drug dealers are
a waste of protoplasm. They should be shot, then injected, then put on the

electric chair on a low setting. Does that sound cynical?

"Officer Foley is the patrol," Sarge said. "2229 Northeast Burnside, apartment 34." I scratched it down in the dark. I hate subjecting my eyes to the daggers of first light, so I postpone it as long as I can.

The moment I put down the phone, I sensed a presence in the dark room. An intelligence was near me, watching, breathing. I knew it. My throat tightened and I reached my hand toward my Smith & Wesson 340 revolver on the night stand. I heard a groan. Then I saw the whites of two eyes, three feet away.

I stared at the intruder, seeing nothing but eyes. My hand rested uneasily on my revolver.

Suddenly the cloud of disorientation lifted. I recognized the sympathetic eyes of Mike Hammer, my bullmastiff, who spends his nights getting in and out of my bed, licking my toes to reassure me he's back.

I slowly drew my hand back from the gun, not wanting to send the wrong message to my bullie.

What was wrong with me? How could I forget Mike Hammer, my roommate? I shuddered, remembering the time five years ago that I drew the gun on Sharon when she came back to bed.

The problem with morning is that it comes before my first cup of coffee. I stumbled toward the kitchen, stubbing my toe on the exercise bike Sharon gave me. I've used it twice in four years. I keep it around to maintain the illusion that it's making me healthy. This helps me justify the next cheeseburger, which means it's worth every penny she paid.

As firemen keep their boots at bedside, I keep water in my top-of-the-line Mr. Coffee, poured to the seven-cup mark, with Starbucks French roast always waiting. I load the filter almost to the top, in a quest for maximum blackness. Whether it's 7:00 a.m. or 3:00 a.m., I can throw the switch and console myself that even if the world's going to hell in a handbasket, coffee's brewing…so there's hope.

I did what I always do: lean against the fridge and pull the pot off the burner every few ounces to get whatever's there—like a nomad gathering drinking water from leaves in the desert. I'd mainline it if I could. I was trying to remember whether I'd had three hours of sleep or two.

I put Mike Hammer—I call him Mulch for short—out the back door to do his business. Every morning he acts like it's his first time, and me letting him out is the privilege he's been waiting for all his life.

After two minutes outside, and six more ounces of coffee for me, Mulch blew open the door to get his biscuit. I walked from Mr. Coffee to the bathroom and put my face two inches from the shower head. I let it pummel me into a paradigm shift: that instead of dreaming I was awake, maybe I really was awake. Maybe this was the real world and I had a job to do.

Presumably I dressed, then poured the last of the coffee into my thirty-ounce mug. After taking a few more gulps, I said good-bye to two of my favorite people—Mulch and Mr. Coffee. Mulch licked my face. I wiped off Mulch slobber with a paper towel and tossed it at the sink, coming up short. I slowly shut the front door, watching Mulch tear apart the paper towel—his reward whenever I miss. I told him, "You're in charge while I'm gone, okay?" He loves it when I say that.

Legs heavy as sandbags, I negotiated the slick walkway like a polar bear on ice. I made it to my white Ford Taurus and dropped into the driver's seat.

I kicked aside a Big Gulp cup and a Burger King bag. The smell of fries tempted me, but knowing my habits (a good detective does), I realized the bag had to be empty. I must have been on a stakeout the night before. Or maybe a couple of nights before. Eventually, I'd remember.

You should not assume I was actually conscious while all this was going on. A detective establishes his routine so he can do it in his sleep. You wake up on the way, a little more each stoplight. By the time you really need consciousness, it's usually there. You just hope it doesn't arrive at the scene very long after you do.

It was dripping cold, so I drew the window half down to double-team with the coffee, fast-tracking my wake-up. Every few blocks I stuck my face out—I learned this from Mulch—gulping a quick fix of wet oxygen. Then I pulled in my frozen face and warmed it with the coffee. It's sort of a ritual, like those Scandahoovian men who go back and forth from ice baths to saunas.

The December Portland morning, almost uninhabited, smelled of frosty rain on asphalt. It reminded me of the five years I worked night shift on the beat. One year I never saw daylight between November and February. From what I heard, I didn't miss much.

When you're homicide, on the "up team"—on call for the next murder— getting yanked from the netherworld in the middle of the night comes with the territory. (It's the only thing easier now than it was when Sharon was alive; at least now I don't have to worry about her worrying about me.)

Occasionally other people don't understand that what I'm doing is more important than what they're doing. That morning, headed to the Jimmy Ross murder scene, I was driving on Burnside next to the light-rail tracks, where there's only one lane. The guy in front of me—in only the fourth car I'd seen— just sat there in his low-riding Acura Integra, figuring that since it was 3:23 a.m., he could roll down his window and talk to some moron standing on the curb, even after the light turned green.

I honked the horn. Nothing. My Taurus is a slick-top, unmarked, which is usually handy, but in this case not.

I honked again. Then I reached to my right and typed in the license number on my Mobile Data Computer. I honked the horn a third time.

The guy charged out of his car, yelling and swearing. When he got two feet from my window, I pulled out my Glock 19 and pointed it at his face.

"Get back in your car and move it out of my way. Now."

For a moment he froze, with the fixated expression of a man wetting his pants. He scuttled back to his car sideways, like a crab, and hopped in, banging his head on the door frame. He turned his key with a garbage-disposal grind, forgetting he'd left the car running. He screeched through the light that by now had turned red.

I flipped on my flashing red and blue grill-mounted strobe lights, giving myself a free pass through the intersection. He pulled over to the right. A name popped up on my computer screen. As I passed the guy, I lowered my passenger window and shouted, "Have a nice day, Nathan Roberts!"

Okay, maybe when he first approached my car I should have identified myself as a cop. But many people assume that if you are a cop, you won't shoot them. I did not want Nathan to labor under this assumption.

Having been a cop for thirty years, I find that you can get most of what you want with a kind word. But sometimes you can get more of what you want with a kind word and a gun.

"Foley?" I spoke into the car phone. "Chandler. Homicide. On my way. 2229 Burnside, right? Apartment complex?"

"Right. Greenbridge Arms. We're on third floor, four doors left off elevator. Room 34's sealed. My partner's notifying neighbors that we're here. A lot of them heard the shots. We've got one possible witness."

"Be there in five."

When I was a street cop, I always told people on my beat that I'd give them the benefit of the doubt. I'll look the other way if you jaywalk or tear the tag off your mattress. But if you mess with me, you'll regret it. I'd always say, "Messin' with me is like wearin' cheese underwear down rat alley."

When I'm on the up team, anybody who kills somebody does it on my watch. That means they're messin' with me. And wearing cheese underwear.

I pulled up to the Greenbridge Arms, studying the shadowy outline of the four-story brick building. I pulled up next to one of three patrol cars, in a no parking zone.

A van labeled KAGN was parked illegally—meaning it was doing one of the few things cops can do, but media aren't supposed to.

Four people approached me like autograph hounds. One was armed with notepad and pen, with a partner alongside carrying a professional still camera. The other team brandished video camera and microphone.

"Detective Chandler?"

They know me by name. With a few exceptions, I make it a point not to know theirs.

"What can you tell us, Detective?" The Oregon Tribune reporter had her notepad out, all ready to scribble.

"Nothing. If you check your notes, you'll see I just arrived."

"They're denying us entrance to the apartments."

"Good for them." This was standard procedure, but they can never get over how outrageous it is that they aren't allowed to trample over a crime scene.

"We've been told the victim's name is Jimmy Ross, in apartment 34. Is that correct?"

"There's a victim? Really? Is he hurt?" I knew they'd been eavesdropping on police radio. Apparently someone had slipped up and said the victim's name.

"Just confirm the identity. Is his name Jimmy Ross?"

"No comment."

"We called two of his neighbors and they said that it was Jimmy Ross. Could you confirm that it's Jimmy Ross?"

"If I knew his name, why would I tell you?"

"What's the harm? We heard it on the radio. We just want you to confirm it."

"Don't hold your breath."

"We're just doing our job."

"You're getting in the way of me doing my job. Monitor your own calls."

"The police don't own the air waves. Your job is to serve the public interest. That's what we're trying to do."

"Yeah. Right."

"The public deserves to know what's going on."

I turned away just as her cameraman took a photo. He grabbed the sleeve of my trench coat. I yanked it back from him.

I turned toward him, and his camera flash did that dagger thing in my eyes.

"Out of my face, bozo!"

That moment I saw the red light of a television news camera right behind him. In my mind's eye I saw the images of my anger management class from two years ago, which I swore I would never subject myself to again. Like a dog zapped by a shock collar, I restrained my bark.

I smiled and waved to the camera and said, "I want to thank you newspaper and TV folks for showing your support by coming to our little crime scene. God bless you, every one. I only wish I had time for tea and cookies. But we have a crime to solve, and people's lives to protect, so if it's not inconvenient for you, I'll be going up to the crime scene now. Enjoy."

The Tribune and TV reporters and their cameramen followed me to the front door of the apartments, where Officer Brandon Gentry opened the door for me. Gently, but firmly, he positioned himself in front of them, backed in and closed the door. He and I nodded at each other, two professionals trying to beat off the vultures. I wondered if he too had been to anger management class. I signed his log sheet and wrote down the time.

The TV photographer opened the front door and did a sweep with his video. As I stepped in the elevator, I said, "Officer Gentry, there's a van illegally parked out there. I think it has the letters KAGN on it. Would you be so kind as to write a parking violation?"

The door closed and I tried not to ponder how the media, especially the Tribune, had been my judge, jury, and nearly my executioner fifteen years before. I needed to switch gears to the job at hand. At least I was awake now.

The elevator was old, with a bad case of asthma. As I got out on the third floor, I popped a stick of Blackjack gum in my mouth.

I headed up the hall to the left and saw a cop, maybe twenty-five, poised like a jackal guarding the tomb of a pharaoh.

"Foley?"

He nodded, too eagerly. Academy written all over him, Officer Foley exuded a Secret Service alertness. I thought, If he lives long enough, eventually it'll give way to the fear of dying on duty and leaving behind young kids and the wife he'll promise to never forsake. Eagerness to jump into the middle of a dangerous situation is inversely proportionate to your age. Twenty years ago I was chasing armed fugitives down back alleys, by myself. Now my first thought is to call for SWAT teams, armored cars, helicopters, guided missiles, or stealth bombers, whatever's available.

As a Vietnam vet, to me having a guy watch my back means everything. Officer Foley was also protecting my crime scene from intruders. So he was my new best friend. We might never have a drink together, but we were closer already than I am to most of my neighbors and half my family.

Entering apartment 34, I stepped from hallway to crime scene. There he was, sprawled out in a classic death pose—Jimmy Ross, two shots to the head. Physical evidence all over the place, with a bonus: a sealed Ziploc bag of ecstasy, and a half-spilled bag of meth.

While I was taking a mental photograph of my first view of the scene, Foley's partner poked his head in. He introduced me to the apartment manager, who assured me Ross lived alone. No wife, live-in girlfriend, brother, cousin, friend, or boarder. Foley confirmed that the neighbors agreed, but said there was a lot of coming and going. The manager appeared shocked, as if he never suspected one of his renters was a drug dealer.

Since most murders are done by family, that's where you look first. Domestic arguments normally begin in the living room, where there are few available weapons. Then they migrate to the kitchen, where there are many available weapons, or the bedroom, where there's often a gun, which has a way of ending arguments. This argument, if there was one, had stayed right in the living room. There was no sign the killer had been anywhere else in the house—only between the door and the body. It didn't fit the domestic-murder profile. It had been an outsider.

Foley told me the paramedic who'd come twenty minutes ago had pronounced Jimmy Ross dead. I looked at what used to be him. Yeah. He was definitely dead.

The medical examiner, Carlton Bowers—who I'd seen at a dozen other homicides—showed up ten minutes after I did. Most MEs ask you to call them when you want the body removed, after the crime scene's been cleaned and detailed, and photographs have been taken. So unless time of death is a big unknown, the ME may not arrive until three or four hours later. But not Carlton Bowers. Every time I'd worked with him, he'd come immediately.

Bowers was a number two pencil, head as pink and bald as an eraser. He had a nicely fitted suit, but a poorly fitted face. His pointy chin wasn't a good match for his pale bloated cheeks. He looked like there'd been too much chlorine in his gene pool.

I gazed down at my Wal-Mart jacket, over my flannel shirt spotted with yesterday's Tabasco sauce. I considered my rumpled slacks, pockets likely containing Tuesday's Taco Bell receipt, and possibly a packet of hot sauce. Then I looked again at the ME's tailored suit.

"Tuxedo at the dry cleaner's?" I asked him.

His smile came quick and left quicker. I'd have preferred no smile at all. This guy wanted to be home watching Quincy reruns. I wanted to be home sleeping it off, or if not, seeing Jack Bauer interrogate an uncooperative terrorist.

"Blood spattered here," he pointed to the wall. "Isn't that interesting?"

I nodded, though it really wasn't. Furthermore, he was the ME, not one of the CSI techs, who report to me and quietly do their jobs collecting evidence, not interpreting it. The ME's specialty is the state of the body itself, cause of death and time of death.

"Probable cause of death was gunshots to the head," he said slowly, as if he had drawn on years of training to come up with this. Never mind that any kindergartner on Ritalin could have told me the same.

"Another splatter here. Don't you find that interesting?"

"Isn't that what you would expect with two head shots at close range?" I asked.

"Perhaps. Still, it's interesting, don't you think?"

"About as interesting as last month's cricket scores."

It was a full five minutes before he used the word interesting again.

Two CSI guys, one dressed in his forensic bunny suit, arrived. One vacuumed, while the other followed carefully behind him taking pictures. They collected blood samples, carpet fibers, and anything that might contain DNA fragments. I was making a sketch of the scene with my pencil on yellow pad, thinking that Picasso might have liked my sketches better than I like his. I supplemented my sketch with photos on my digital camera.

"Chandler?" The loud voice startled the ME. My partner, Manny Rodriquez, wiry and short and snippy, barged in the door.

"You look terrible," he said. "I mean, worse than usual."

Manny is grumpy at 10:00 a.m. At 3:40 a.m. the difference isn't noticeable.

"What have we got?" he asked.

"It's interesting," I said, eying the ME.

Manny and I spent ten minutes discussing the one thing that really was interesting—the small bloodstains by the door that weren't splattered from the victim. By then the ME declared Ross had probably died one to two hours ago. Good estimate, since the gunshot ninety minutes ago had woken up most of the apartment complex.

After CSI went over Ross's cell phone, I looked through all the names in its directory. I jotted down the numbers of the last five incoming and outgoing calls. I checked his messages, then had Manny listen to all four of them. He contacted two of the callers, on a middle-of-the-night fishing expedition. Meanwhile, I talked with the sort-of witness in apartment 36.

She'd been taking a walk at 2:30 a.m., up and down the hallway.

"Why?" I asked.

"Because I had rats in my legs." She gave a detailed description of a tall guy with lots of hair and red sweatpants who'd been in the hallway five minutes before she heard the shot. He'd scared her. She pretended not to look at him and walked back to her room.

Within twenty minutes, Manny and I determined it was a case of drug dealer blown away by a competitor, probably over a turf dispute. We found one of the bullets embedded in the floor, probably the second shot. Apparently the other bullet hadn't exited. Fingerprints with blood traces were on the doorknob and the table. I called headquarters to see if we could get the lab to do a rush on the three good fingerprints collected.

About the only things missing were the killer's name, Social Security number, Blockbuster card, and a confession written in lipstick on the bathroom mirror.

Murder is never convenient. But solving a murder is sometimes routine. This one had routine written all over it.

While Manny canvassed the apartments, knocking on doors, waking up the select few who hadn't heard the gunshot or had fallen back asleep, I went to the end of the hallway and stepped outside on an old fire escape. I opened my mouth wide, gulping air, tasting life, trying to wrest myself from the death grip squeezing the room of Jimmy Ross.

It seemed so easy. Fingerprints and DNA and a good description?

That's when I should have suspected something was wrong.

Napoleon said—I heard this on The History Channel—that in every campaign there's ten or fifteen minutes in which the battle will be won or lost. Sometimes it's that way in an investigation. Looking back at it, the ten or fifteen minutes in which I botched that investigation were right when everything was falling together so perfectly.

Things moved quickly. By 6:00 a.m. we found the other druggie, tall, big-haired Lincoln Caldwell, asleep in his room, red sweatpants hanging on his bedpost. His gun, in the top dresser drawer, had been recently fired. And—surprise—as I looked at the four rounds left in it, I didn't need ballistics to convince me the gun would prove a perfect match for the round that went through Ross. His cell phone confirmed he'd called Jimmy Ross six hours earlier.

He denied it, of course. They always do. We arrested him and took him to the precinct.

It was gratifying, but not. Sort of like a crossword puzzle champion looking at a puzzle with answers so obvious there's no point writing them down. I'm a Sherlock Holmes fan. I like to follow bread crumbs, not six baguettes leading me to someone standing twelve feet away who hands me a business card saying "Murderer."

Still, I couldn't argue with the bottom line. Two drug dealers for the price of one. One dead, the other off the streets for however long the court decides. Never long enough for me.

Sometimes the bad guys help out the good guys by doing what we can't—blowing each other away. Kill a killer and you may save a half-dozen lives. Kill a drug dealer and you may save a couple dozen. Okay, that's what cops say to each other off the record—and cop to cop is always off the record.

There weren't many details requiring attention in the Jimmy Ross case. Too bad, I thought, since often the devil's in the details.

I once cracked a case based on my discovery that one Monday morning a woman had ordered a grande white chocolate mocha. Remarkable for one reason: Every weekday for at least four years she had gone to the same coffee shop and ordered a regular skinny latte. Something had to account for her celebratory mood. Well, I was checking on her because her husband had died of "natural causes" on Saturday. The white chocolate mocha tipped me off that she might have contributed to those natural causes.

It took me a whole baseball season to prove it, but by the time the Yankees took the field for the first game of the World Series, I nailed her. No prize. No bonus. No street named after me. No letters of gratitude from husbands whose wives were on the verge of ordering their first white chocolate mochas. But that's okay. I don't do it for the thanks. I do it because it's my job, my one contribution to a world that is truly—and I mean big time—a mess.

I'm saying this because the Jimmy Ross murder didn't require turning over rocks to look for details. Everything that mattered fell into place. When they processed the fingerprints and the weapon and the blood DNA, it was a trifecta, a perfect triangle of independent evidence. Together they were irrefutable. The murder was open and shut. Lincoln Caldwell was our man.

I spent more time on the paperwork than the investigation. When two and two add up to four, you don't try to refigure it six different ways to see if it can come out three or five. You tie a bow around it, give it to the district attorney, and move on. You hoist a beer or two and watch a football game. Case closed.

I'm a pretty broadminded guy, but I have a low tolerance for murder. I take my murders personally. Whether or not they know it, killers dare me to take them down. Nine out of ten times that's exactly what I do. And when my mind wanders at a ball game, it lands back on the tenth.

You know that somebody's out there thinking they've gotten away with murder. And you just can't stand that. Your purpose in life is to show up on their doorstep some day and say, "Gotcha."

"You take this too personally," a police psychologist told me in the first of three mandatory sessions I did everything to avoid—short of bungee jumping off a bridge without the bungee cords. The last time I'd gotten in trouble, four months ago, my punishment—cruel and unusual—was seeing this shrink.

"That's the way I'm wired," I told him, using language I hoped would make the shrink see that I understood and respected his world, that we were fellow travelers on the road of life. Maybe, I hoped, as two self-actualized men, we could just pass on this counseling thing.

"Tell me what you're thinking," he said. "Whatever comes into your mind."

"Okay," I said, trying to appear cooperative so I could cut a deal to reduce my counseling sentence. "If someone gets away with shoplifting, I don't like it. But if they get away with murder, I can't stand it. I'll do anything to nail a killer. I admit, like my file says, not everything I've done is strictly legal. But when it comes to murder, I have no problem with doing what it takes to put the killer out of business. To me, there's only one thing as bad as murder: getting away with one."

This is about as deep as I went, because I could see by his nods and understanding looks and the notes he was feverishly writing that if I didn't shut up soon, I'd be spending a mandatory hour a week with him until I retired. I'd rather walk the Green Mile.

What I didn't tell him, but I'll tell you, is that of my 204 murder cases, I've solved 177. That's 87 percent. But who's counting? The rest, cold cases, still burn hot, deep in my gut. Every year or two, sometimes on my vacation, I solve one of those oldies, in my quest to raise my batting average to .900. Of course, if I ever make that, I'll want more.

If the shrink heard me say this, he'd think I was an obsessive-compulsive passive-aggressive dysfunctional codependent enabler…what we used to just call a jerk.

But what I really held back from telling him was that I once sent a man to jail for a double murder he didn't commit. Bradford Downs. I know his face well. Three witnesses, at least two of them completely credible, offered convincing testimony to back up some physical evidence. Naturally, he claimed he was innocent, but his criminal record made that hard to believe. After ten years of appeals he was executed by lethal injection. Turned out that two of the witnesses were the real killers. We'd never have known if the one who was dying hadn't confessed, and offered us proof…three years after an innocent man had been put to death.

See why I didn't tell this to Dr. Freud-face?

Maybe there is something as bad as murder and getting away with murder—being murdered for a murder you didn't commit. And because I put him away, that makes me an accessory to murder, doesn't it?

I don't need more reasons for sleepless nights. Bradford Downs wouldn't be my first choice for a face to fill the back of my eyelids every time the lights go out.

So why am I telling you what I wouldn't tell the shrink?

Because what I didn't realize that morning as I breathed fresh air on the fire escape outside Jimmy Ross's apartment—what I didn't realize until just a little while ago—was that nothing was as it appeared. That case was open and shut all right…it had been set up to open and shut on a conclusion that was dead wrong. I fell for it. And that makes me mad. It makes me even madder that it was only fate or circumstances or luck or providence—whichever you believe in doesn't matter to me—that made me realize it. Otherwise, I could have been seeing Lincoln Caldwell's face every night, alongside Bradford Downs.

There are five teams in Portland homicide, so my partner Manny and I get every fifth murder. It was our next murder, the one two weeks and three days later, that pulled the rug out from under me. Eventually it woke me up to a shocking truth that radically revised the story of Jimmy Ross and Lincoln Caldwell.

That next murder turned me, my job, and my friendships upside down. It shook all the change out of my pockets. It threatened to bring down an entire police department, end my career, and place me inside a white chalk outline with some other homicide detective trying to figure out who murdered me. (Even now, I'm not convinced it still won't.)

Not one of those 204 cases prepared me for that next murder, where someone sinister hid in the shadows of a violated house, gazing out at me through a broken window. It was the most radical and unconventional and baffling case I've ever worked.

If that's not enough, my investigation threatened to end the lives of some people I really cared about.

And, ultimately, that's exactly what it did.

RANDY ALCORN
FICTION

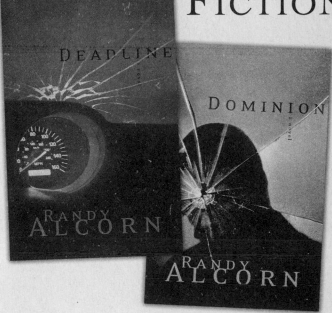

DEADLINE

When tragedy strikes those closest to him, award-winning journalist Jake Woods must draw upon all his resources to uncover the truth about their suspicious accident. Soon he finds himself swept up in a murder investigation that is both complex and dangerous. Unaware of the threat to his own life, Jake is drawn in deeper and deeper as he desperately searches for the answers to the immediate mystery at hand and—ultimately—the deeper meaning of his own existence.

DOMINION

When two senseless killings hit close to home, columnist Clarence Abernathy seeks revenge for the murders—and, ultimately, answers to his own struggles regarding race and faith. After being dragged into the world of inner-city gangs and racial conflict, Clarence is encouraged by fellow columnist Jake Woods (from the bestseller *Deadline*) to forge an unlikely partnership with a redneck homicide detective. Soon the two find themselves facing the powers of darkness that threaten the dominion of earth, while unseen eyes watch from above.

RANDY ALCORN
MORE GREAT FICTION

LORD FOULGRIN'S LETTERS

Foulgrin, a high-ranking demon, instructs his subordinate on how to deceive and destroy Jordan Fletcher and his family. It's like placing a bugging device in hell's war room, where we overhear our enemies assessing our weaknesses and strategizing attacks. *Lord Foulgrin's Letters* is a *Screwtape Letters* for our day, equally fascinating yet distinctly different—a dramatic story with earthly characters, setting, and plot. A creative, insightful, and biblical depiction of spiritual warfare, this book will guide readers to Christ-honoring counterstrategies for putting on the full armor of God and resisting the devil.

THE ISHBANE CONSPIRACY

Jillian is picture perfect on the outside, but terrified of getting hurt on the inside. Brittany is a tough girl who trusts almost no one. Ian is a successful athlete who dabbles in the occult. And Rob is a former gangbanger who struggles with guilt, pain, and a newfound faith in God. These four college students will face the ultimate battle between good and evil in a single year. As spiritual warfare rages around them, a dramatic demonic correspondence takes place. Readers can eavesdrop on the enemy, and learn to stave off their own defeat, by reading *The Ishbane Conspiracy*.

Non fiction titles from RANDY ALCORN

THE TREASURE PRINCIPLE:
Unlocking the Secret of Joyful Giving
Bestselling author Randy Alcorn uncovers the revolutionary key to spiritual transformation: joyful giving! Jesus gave his followers this life-changing formula that guarantees not only kingdom impact, but immediate pleasure and eternal rewards.

THE PURITY PRINCIPLE:
God's Safeguards for Life's Dangerous Trails
God has placed warning signs and guardrails to keep us from plunging off the cliff. Find straight talk about sexual purity in Randy Alcorn's one-stop handbook for you, your family, and your church.

THE GRACE AND TRUTH PARADOX:
Responding with Christlike Balance
Living like Christ is a lot to ask! Discover Randy Alcorn's two-point checklist of Christlikeness—and begin to measure everything by the simple test of grace and truth.

PROLIFE ANSWERS TO PROCHOICE ARGUMENTS
This revised and updated guide offers timely information and inspiration from a "sanctity of life" perspective. Real answers to real questions appear in logical and concise form. More than 85,000 copies sold!

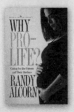

WHY PRO-LIFE?
Caring for the Unborn and Their Mothers
Bumpersticker slogans prevail, but you want the facts. Pro-choicers, pro-lifers, and fence-straddlers alike will appreciate the answers given here in a concise, straightforward, and nonabrasive manner.